"To discuss the work of Mervyn Peake presents a special difficulty; the reviewer is faced by the incredible diversity of his wide-ranging talents. Illustrator, painter, poet, novelist and playwright, he represents a creative phenomenon, a man with an intense and individual inner vision. . . .

"While in the army he began work on *Titus Groan*, the first book of the monumental 'Gormenghast' Trilogy. The first two volumes are set in an enormous crumbling castle, in which rituals are compulsively carried out by grotesque characters, grotesque in the way that Dickens' characters are grotesque, in a way that has meaning and purpose. In the trilogy there are dozens of major characters, each one finely drawn, all with the solidity of real people. In them will be found reality, human frailty, death and sexual love . . . there is strength and vitality going through everything he creates: although Peake feels the pulse of tragedy, he can observe without being dragged into a morass of confusion—his own personal vitality resists the impulse. And Peake's vision becomes, as a result, vast in scope.

"Here are some of the richest, most controlled novels of the language, a treasure-house of experience. Everyone with some feeling for language, some imagination, should be drawn irresistibly into their pages, and should remember the books for the rest of their lives."

New World

THE GORMENGHAST TRILOGY
by Mervyn Peake

TITUS GROAN

GORMENGHAST

TITUS ALONE

Published by Ballantine Books

GORMENGHAST

BY
MERVYN PEAKE

Illustrated by the Author

A Del Rey Book

BALLANTINE BOOKS • NEW YORK

A Del Rey Book
Published by Ballantine Books

Library of Congress Catalog Card Number: 67-26053

ISBN 0-345-27699-X

Ballantine Books Illustrated, Revised Edition:
First Printing: October 1968
Eighth Printing: February 1978

Cover art by Bob Pepper

for
MAEVE

Part Two

THE
GORMENGHAST
TRILOGY

Chapter One

Titus is seven. His confines, Gormenghast. Suckled on shadows; weaned, as it were, on webs of ritual: for his ears, echoes, for his eyes, a labyrinth of stone: and yet within his body something other—other than this umbrageous legacy. For first and ever foremost he is *child*.

A ritual, more compelling than ever man devised, is fighting anchored darkness. A ritual of the blood; of the jumping blood. These quicks of sentience owe nothing to his forbears, but to those feckless hosts, a trillion deep, of the globe's childhood.

The gift of the bright blood. Of blood that laughs when the tenets mutter "Weep." Of blood that mourns when the sere laws croak "Rejoice!" O little revolution in great shades!

* * *

Titus the Seventy-Seventh. Heir to a crumbling summit: to a sea of nettles: to an empire of red rust: to rituals' footprints ankle-deep in stone.

Gormenghast.

Withdrawn and ruinous it broods in umbra: the immemorial masonry: the towers, the tracts. Is all corroding? No. Through an avenue of spires a zephyr floats; a bird whistles; a freshet bears away from a choked river. Deep in a fist of stone a doll's hand wriggles, warm rebellious on the frozen palm. A shadow shifts its length. A spider stirs. . . .

And darkness winds between the characters.

II

Who are the characters? And what has he learned of them and of his home since that far day when he was born to the Countess of Groan in a room alive with birds?

He has learned an alphabet of arch and aisle: the language of dim stairs and moth-hung rafters. Great halls are his dim playgrounds: his fields are quadrangles: his trees are pillars.

And he has learned that there are always eyes. Eyes that watch. Feet that follow, and hands to hold him when he struggles, to lift him when he falls. Upon his feet again he stares unsmiling. Tall figures bow. Some in jewelry; some in rags.

The characters.

The quick and the dead. The shapes, the voices that throng his mind, for there are days when the living have no substance and the dead are active.

Who are these dead—these victims of violence who no longer influence the tenor of Gormenghast save by a deathless repercussion? For ripples are still widening in dark rings and a movement runs over the gooseflesh waters though the drowned stones lie still. The characters who are but names to Titus, though one of them his father, and all of them alive when he was born. Who are they? For the child will hear of them.

III

Let them appear for a quick, earthless moment, as ghosts, separate, dissimilar, and complete. They are even now moving, as before death, on their own ground. Is Time's cold scroll recoiling on itself until the dead years speak, or is it in the throb of *now* that the specters wake and wander through the walls?

There was a Library and it is ashes. Let its long length assemble. Than its stone walls its paper walls are thicker; armored with learning, with philosophy, with poetry that drifts or dances, clamped though it is in midnight. Shielded with flax and calfskin and a cold weight of ink, there broods the ghost of Sepulchrave, the melancholy Earl, Seventy-Sixth Lord of half-light.

It is five years ago. Witless of how his death by owls approaches he mourns through each languid gesture, each fine-boned feature, as though his body were glass and at its center his inverted heart like a pendent tear.

His every breath a kind of ebb that leaves him further from himself, he floats rather than steers to the island of the mad—beyond all trade routes, in a doldrum sea, its high crags burning.

* * *

Of how he died Titus has no idea. For as yet he has not so much as seen, let alone spoken to, the Long Man of the Woods, Flay, who was his father's servant and the only witness of Sepulchrave's death, when climbing demented into the Tower of Flints, the Earl gave himself up to the hunger of the owls.

Flay, the cadaverous and taciturn, his knee joints reporting his progress at every spiderlike step, he alone among these marshaled ghosts is still alive, though banished from the castle. But so inextricably has Flay been woven into the skein of the castle's central life, that if ever a man was destined to fill in the gap of his own absence with his own ghost it is he.

For excommunication is a kind of death, and it is a different man who moves in the woods from the Earl's first servant of seven years ago. Simultaneously, then, as ragged and bearded he lays his rabbit snares in a gully of ferns, his ghost is sitting in the high corridor, beardless, and long ago, outside his master's door. How can he know that it will not be long before he adds, by his own hand, a name to the roll of the murdered? All that he knows is that his life is in immediate peril: that he is crying with every nerve in his long, tense, awkward body for an end to this insufferable rivalry, hatred, and apprehension. And he knows that this cannot be unless either he or the gross and pendulous horror in question be destroyed.

*   *   *

And so it happened. The pendulous horror, the Chef of Gormenghast, floating like a moon-bathed sea-cow, a long sword bristling like a mast from his huge breast, had been struck down but an hour before the death of the Earl. And here he comes again in a province he has made peculiarly his own in soft and ruthless ways. Of all ponderous volumes, surely the most illusory, if there's no weight or substance in a ghost, is Abiatha Swelter, who wades in a sluglike illness of fat through the humid ground mists of the Great Kitchen. From hazy progs and flesh-pots half afloat, from bowls as big as baths, there rises and drifts like a miasmic tide the all but palpable odor of the day's belly-timber. Sailing, his canvas stretched and spread, through the hot mists, the ghost of Swelter is still further rarefied by the veiling fumes; he has become the ghost of a ghost, only his swedelike head retaining the solidity of nature. The arrogance of this fat head exudes itself like an evil sweat.

*   *   *

Vicious and vain as it is, the enormous ghost retreats a step to make way for the phantom Sourdust on a tour of inspection. Master of Ritual, perhaps the most indispensable figure of all, cornerstone and guardian of the Groan Law, his weak and horny hands are working at the knots of his tangled beard. As he shambles forward, the red rags of his office fall about his bleak old body in dirty festoons. He is in the worst of health, even for a ghost, coughing incessantly in a dry, horrible manner, the black-and-white strands of his beard jerking to and fro. Theoretically he is rejoicing that in Titus an heir has been born to the House, but his responsibilities have become too heavy to allow him any lightness of heart, even supposing he could ever have lured into that stuttering organ so trivial a sensation. Shuffling from ceremony to ceremony, his sere head raised against its natural desire to drop forward on his chest and covered with as many pits and fissures as a cracked cheese, he personifies the ancientry of his high office.

It was for his real body to die in the same fated Library which now, in specter form, is housing the wraith of Sepulchrave. As the old Master of Ritual moves away and fades through the feverish air of Swelter's kitchen, he cannot foresee or remember (for who can tell in which direction the minds of phantoms move?) that filled to his wrinkled mouth with acrid smoke he shall die, or has already died, by fire and suffocation, the great flames licking at his wrinkled hide with red and golden tongues.

He cannot know that Steerpike burned him up: that his Lordship's sisters, Cora and Clarice, lit the fuse, and that from that hour on, his overlord, the sacrosanct Earl, should find the road to lunacy so clear before him.

* * *

And lastly, Keda, Titus's foster-mother, moving quietly along a dappled corridor of light and pearl-gray shadow. That she should be a ghost seems natural, for even when alive there was something intangible, distant, and occult about her. To have died leaping into a great well of twilight air was pitiless enough, but less horrible than the last moments of the Earl, the Chef, and the decrepit Master of Ritual—and a swifter ending to life's gall than the banishment of the Long Man of the Woods.

As in those days, before she fled from the castle to her death, she is caring for Titus as though all the mothers who have ever lived advise her through her blood. Dark, almost lambent like a topaz, she is still young, her sole disfigurement the universal bane of the Outer Dwellers, the premature erosion of an exceptional beauty—a deterioration that follows with merciless speed upon an adolescence almost spectral. She alone among these fate-struck figures is of that poverty-stricken and intolerable realm of the ostracized, whose drear cantonment, like a growth of mud and limpets, clamps itself to Gormenghast's Outer Wall.

*   *   *

The sun's rays, searing a skein of cloud, burn with unhampered radiance through a hundred windows of the Southern Walls. It is a light too violent for ghosts, and Keda, Sourdust, Flay, Swelter, and Sepulchrave dissolve in sunbeams.

*   *   *

These, then, in thumbnail, are the Lost Characters. The initial few, who, dying, deserted the hub of the castle's life before Titus was three. The future hung on their activities. Titus himself is meaningless without them, for in his infancy he fed on footsteps, on the patterns that figures made against high ceilings, their hazy outlines, their slow or rapid movements, their varying odors and voices.

Nothing that stirs but has its repercussions, and it may well be that Titus will hear the echoes, when a man, of what was whispered then. For it was no static assembly of personalities into which Titus was launched —no mere pattern, but an arabesque in motion whose thoughts were actions, or if not, hung like bats from an attic rafter or veered between towers on leaflike wings.

Chapter Two

❋❋❋❋❋❋❋❋❋❋

WHAT of the living?

His mother, half asleep and half aware: with the awareness of anger, the detachment of trance. She saw him seven times in seven years. Then she forgot the halls that harbored him. But now she watches him from hidden windows. Her love for him is as heavy and as formless as loam. A furlong of white cats trails after her. A bullfinch has a nest in her red hair. She is the Countess Gertrude of huge clay.

* * *

Less formidable, yet sullen as her mother and as incalculable, is Titus's sister. Sensitive as was her father without his intellect, Fuchsia tosses her black flag of hair, bites at her childish underlip, scowls, laughs, broods, is tender, is intemperate, suspicious, and credulous all in a day. Her crimson dress inflames gray corridors, or flaring in a sunshaft through high branches makes of the deep green shadows a greenness darker yet, and a darkness greener.

* * *

Who else is there of the direct Bloodline? Only the vacant aunts, Cora and Clarice, the identical twins and sisters of Sepulchrave. So limp of brain that for them to conceive an idea is to risk a hemorrhage. So limp of body that their purple dresses appear no more indicative of housing nerves and sinews than when they hang suspended from their hooks.

Of the others? The lesser breed? In order of social precedence, possibly the Prunesquallors first, that is, the Doctor and his closely swathed and bone-protruding sister. The Doctor with his hyena laugh, his bizarre and elegant body, his celluloid face.

His main defects? The unsufferable pitch of his voice; his maddening laughter and his affected gestures. His cardinal virtue? An undamaged brain.

His sister Irma. Vain as a child; thin as a stork's leg, and, in her black glasses, as blind as an owl in daylight. She misses her footing on the social ladder at least three times a week, only to start climbing again, wriggling her pelvis the while. She clasps her dead, white hands beneath her chin in the high hope of hiding the flatness of her chest.

Who next? Socially, there is no one else. That is to say no one who, during the first few years of Titus's life, plays any part that bears upon the child's future: unless it be the Poet, a wedge-headed and uncomfortable figure little known to the hierophants of Gormenghast, though reputed to be the only man capable of holding the Earl's attention in conversation. An all-but-forgotten figure in his room above a precipice of stone. No one reads his poems, but he holds a remote status—a gentleman, as it were, by rumor.

Blue blood aside, however, and a shoal of names floats forward. The linchpin son of the dead Sourdust, by name Barquentine, Master of Ritual, is a stunted and cantankerous pedant of seventy, who stepped into his father's shoes (or, to be exact, into his *shoe,* for this Barquentine is a one-legged thing who smites his way through ill-lit corridors on a grim and echoing crutch).

Flay, who has already appeared as his own ghost, is very much alive in Gormenghast Forest. Taciturn and cadaverous, he is no less than Barquentine a traditionalist

of the old school. But, unlike Barquentine, his angers when the Law is flouted are uprisings of a hot loyalty that blinds him, and not the merciless and stony intolerance of the cripple.

*   *   *

To speak of Mrs. Slagg at this late juncture seems unfair. That Titus himself, heir to Gormenghast, is her charge, as was Fuchsia in *her* childhood, is surely enough to place her at the head of any register. But she is so minute, so frightened, so old, so querulous, she neither could, nor would, head any procession, even on paper. Her peevish cry goes out: "Oh, my weak heart! how *could* they?" and she hurries to Fuchsia either to smack the abstracted girl in order to ease herself, or to bury the wrinkled prune of her face in Fuchsia's side. Alone in her small room again, she lies upon her bed and bites her minute knuckles.

There is nothing frightened or querulous about young Steerpike. If ever he had harbored a conscience in his tough narrow breast he has by now dug out and flung away the awkward thing—flung it so far away that were he ever to need it again he could never find it.

The day of Titus's birth had seen the commencement of his climb across the roofs of Gormenghast and the end of his servitude in Swelter's kitchen—that steaming province which was both too unpleasant and too small to allow for his flexuous talents and expanding ambition.

High-shouldered to a degree little short of malformation, slender and adroit of limb and frame, his eyes close-set and the color of dried blood, he is still climbing, not now across the back of Gormenghast but up the spiral staircase of its soul, bound for some pinnacle of the itching fancy—some wild, invulnerable eyrie best known to himself, where he cán watch the world spread out below him, and shake exultantly his clotted wings.

*   *   *

Rottcodd is fast asleep in his hammock at the far end of the Hall of the Bright Carvings, that long attic room that houses the finest examples of the Mud Dwellers' art. It is five years since he watched from the attic window the procession far below him wind back from Gormenghast Lake, where Titus had come into his Earldom, but nothing has happened to him during the long years apart from the annual arrival of fresh works to be added to the colored carvings in the long room.

His small cannonball of a head is asleep on his arm and the hammock is swaying gently to the drone of a vinegar-fly.

Chapter Three

About the rough margins of the castle life—margins irregular as the coastline of a squall-rent island—there were characters that stood or moved gradually to the central hub. They were wading out of the tides of limitless negation—the timeless, opaque waters. Yet what are these that set foot on the cold beach? Surely so portentous an expanse should unburden itself of gods at least; scaled kings, or creatures whose outstretched wings might darken two horizons. Or dappled Satan with his brow of brass.

But no. There were no scales or wings at all.

It was too dark to see them where they waded; although a blotch of shadow, too big for a single figure, augured the approach of that hoary band of Professors, through whose hands for a while Titus will have to wriggle.

But there was no veil of half-light over the high-shouldered young man who was entering a small room rather like a cell that opened from a passageway of stones as dry and gray and rough as an elephant's hide. As he turned at the doorway to glance back along the corridor, the cold light shone on the high white lump of his brow.

As soon as he entered he closed the door behind him and slid the bolt. Surrounded by the whiteness of the walls he appeared, as he moved across the room, weirdly detached from the small world surrounding him. It was more like the shadow of a young man, a shadow with high shoulders, that moved across whiteness, than an actual body moving in space.

In the center of the room was a simple stone table. Upon it, and grouped roughly at its center, were a whorl-necked decanter of wine, a few sheafs of paper, a pen, a few books, a moth pinned to a cork, and half an apple.

As he moved past the table he removed the apple, took a bite, and replaced it without slackening his pace, and then suddenly looked for all the world as though his legs were shrinking from the ground up, but the floor of the room sloped curiously and he was on his way down a decline in the floor that sank to a curtain-hung opening in the wall.

He was through this in a moment, and the darkness that lay beyond took him, as it were, to herself, muffling the edges of his sharp body.

He had entered a disused chimney at the ground level. It was very dark, and this darkness was not so much mitigated as intensified by a series of little shining mirrors that held the terminal reflections of what was going on in those rooms which, one above the other, flanked the high chimneylike funnel that rose from where the young man stood in the darkness to where the high air meandered over the weather-broken roofs, which, rough and cracked as stale bread, blushed horribly in the prying rays of sundown.

Over the course of the last year, he had managed to gain entrance to these particular rooms and halls, one above the other, which flanked the chimney, and had drilled holes through the stonework, wood, and plaster

—no easy work when the knees and back are strained against the opposite walls of a lightless funnel—so that the light pierced through to him in his funnel'd darkness from apertures no wider than coins. These drilling operations had, of course, to be carried out at carefully chosen times, so that no suspicion should be aroused. Moreover, the holes had as nearly as possible to be drilled at selected points, so as to coincide with whatever natural advantages the rooms might hold.

Not only had he carefully selected the rooms which he felt it would be worth his while watching from time to time for the mere amusement of eavesdropping for its own sake—but also for the furtherance of his own designs.

His methods of disguising the holes, which might so easily have been detected if badly positioned, were varied and ingenious, as for example in the chamber of the ancient Barquentine, Master of Ritual. This room, filthy as a fox's earth, had upon its right-hand wall a blistered portrait in oils of a rider on a piebald horse, and the young man had not only cut a couple of holes in the canvas immediately beneath the frame where its shadow lay like a long black ruler, but he had cut away the rider's buttons, the pupils of his eyes as well as those of the horse's. These circular openings at their various heights and latitudes afforded him alternative views of the room according to where Barquentine chose to propel his miserable body on that dreaded crutch of his. The horse's eye, the most frequently used of the apertures, offered a magnificent view of a mattress on the floor on which Barquentine spent most of his leisure moments, knotting and reknotting his beard, or sending up clouds of dust every time he raised and let fall his only leg, a withered one at that, in bouts of irritation. In the chimney itself, and immediately behind the holes, a complicated series of wires and mirrors reflected the occupants of the de-privatized rooms and sent them down the black funnel, mirror glancing to mirror, and carrying the secrets of each action that fell within their deadly orbit—passing them from one to another, until at the base a constellation of glass provided the young man with constant entertainment and information.

In the darkness he would turn his eyes, for instance, from Craggmire, the Acrobat, who crossing his apartment upon his hands might frequently be seen tossing from the sole of one foot to the sole of the other a small pig in a green nightdress—would turn his eyes from this diversion to the next mirror, which might disclose the Poet, tearing at a loaf of bread with his small mouth, his long wedge of a head tilted at an angle, and flushed with the exertion, for he could not use both hands—one being engaged in writing; while his eyes (so completely out of focus that they looked as though they'd never get in again) were more spirit than anything corporeal.

But from the young man's point of view there were bigger fish than these—which were, with the exception of Barquentine, no more than the shrimps of Gormenghast—and he turned to mirrors more deadly, more thrilling: mirrors that reflected the daughter of the Groans herself—the strange raven-haired Fuchsia—and her mother, the Countess, her shoulders thronged with birds.

Chapter Four

I

ONE summer morning of bland air, the huge, corroding bell-like heart of Gormenghast was half asleep and there appeared to be no reverberation from its muffled thudding. In a hall of plaster walls the silence yawned.

Nailed above a doorway of this hall a helmet or casque, red with rust, gave forth into the stillness a sandy and fluttering sound, and a moment later the beak

of a jackdaw was thrust through an eye-slit and withdrawn. The plaster walls arose on every side into a dusky
and apparently ceilingless gloom, lit only by a high,
solitary window. The warm light that found its way
through the web-choked glass of this window gave hint
of galleries yet further above but no suggestion of doors
beyond, nor any indication of how these galleries could
be reached. From this high window a few rays of sunlight, like copper wires, were strung steeply and diago-
nally across the hall, each one terminating in its amber
pool of dust on the floor boards. A spider lowered itself,
fathom by fathom, on a perilous length of thread and
was suddenly transfixed in the path of a sunbeam and, for
an instant, was a thing of radiant gold.

There was no sound, and then—as though timed to
break the tension, the high window was swung open and
the sunbeams were blotted out, for a hand was thrust
through and a bell was shaken. Almost at once there
was a sound of footsteps, and a moment later a dozen
doors were opening and shutting, and the hall was
thronged with the criss-crossing of figures.

The bell ceased clanging. The hand was withdrawn
and the figures were gone. There was no sign that any
living thing had ever moved or breathed between the
plaster walls, or that the many doors had ever opened,
save that a small whitish flower lay in the dust beneath
the rusting helmet, and that a door was swinging gently
to and fro.

II

As it swung, broken glimpses were obtained of a
whitewashed corridor that wound in so slow and ample
a curve that by the time the right-hand wall had disappeared from view, the roof of the passageway appeared
no more than the height of an ankle from the ground.

This long, narrowing, ash-white perspective, curving
with the effortless ease of a gull in air, was suddenly the
setting for action. For something, hardly distinguishable

as a horse and rider until it had cantered a full third of the long curve to the deserted hall, was rapidly approaching. The sharp clacking of hoofs was all at once immediately behind the swinging door, which was pushed wide by the nose of a small gray pony.

Titus sat astride.

He was dressed in the coarse, loosely fitting garments that were worn by the castle children. For the first nine years of his life the heir to the Earldom was made to mix with, and attempt to understand the ways of, the lower orders. On his fifteenth birthday such friendships as he had struck would have to cease. His demeanor would have to change and a more austere and selective relationship with the personnel of the castle would take its place. But it was a tradition that in the early years, the child of the Family must, for certain hours, at least, of every day, be as the less exalted children, feed with them, sleep in their dormitories, attend with them the classes of the Professors, and join in the various time-honored games and observances like any other minor. Yet for all that, Titus was conscious of always being watched: of a discrepancy in the attitude of the officials and even at times of the boys. He was too young to understand the implications of his status, but old enough to sense his uniqueness.

Once a week, before the morning classes, he was allowed to ride his gray horse for an hour beneath the high Southern Wall, where the early sun would send his fantastic shadow careering along the tall stones at his side. And when he waved his arm, his shadow-self on a shadow-horse would wave its huge shadow-arm as they galloped together.

But today, instead of trotting away to his beloved Southern Wall he had, in a moment of devilment, turned his horse through a moss-black arch and into the castle itself. In the still silence his heart beat rapidly as he clattered along stone corridors he had never seen before.

He knew that it would not be worth his while to take French leave of the morning classes, for he had been

locked up more than once during the long summer evenings for such acts of disobedience. But he tasted the
sharp fruits of the quick bridle-wrench which had freed
him from the hostler. It was only for a few minutes that
he was alone, but when he came to a halt in the high
plaster-walled hall, with the rusting helmet above him,
and far above the helmet the dim mysterious balconies,
he had already dulled his sudden itch for rebellion.

Small though he looked on the gray, there was something commanding in the confident air with which he
sat the saddle—something impressive in his childish
frame, as though there were a kind of weight there, or
strength—a compound of spirit and matter; something
solid that underlay the whims, terrors, tears and laughter, and vitality of his seven years.

By no means good-looking, he had, nevertheless, this
presence. Like his mother, there was a certain *scale*
about him, as though his height and breadth bore no
relation to the logic of feet and inches.

The hostler entered the hall, slow, shuffling, hissing
gently, a perpetual habit of his whether grooming a
horse or not, and the gray pony was at once led away in
the direction of the schoolrooms to the west.

Titus watched the back of the hostler's head as he was
led along but said nothing. It was as though what had
just occurred were something they had rehearsed many
times before, and there was no need for comment. The
child had known this man and his hissing, which were
as inseparable as a rough sea from the sound that it
makes, for little more than a year, when the gray was
given him at a ceremony known as "The Pony Giving," a
ceremony that took place without fail on the third Friday
after the sixth birthday of any son of the Line who was
also, by reason of his father's death, an earl in his mi-
nority. But for all this length of time—and fifteen
months was a considerable span for a child who could
only remember with any distinctness his last four years
—the hostler and Titus had exchanged not more than a
dozen sentences. It was not that they disliked one another, the hostler merely preferring to give the boy

pieces of stolen seedcake to making any effort at conversation, and Titus quite content to have it so, for the hostler was to him simply the shuffling figure who took care of his pony, and it was enough to know his mannerisms, the way his feet shuffled, the white scar above his eye, and to hear him hissing.

Within an hour the morning classes were under way. At an ink-stained desk, with his chin cupped in his hands, Titus was contemplating, as in a dream, the chalk marks on the blackboard. They represented a problem in short division, but might as well have been some hieroglyphic message from a moon-struck prophet to his lost tribe a thousand years ago. His mind, and the minds of his small companions in that leather-walled schoolroom, was far away, but in a world not of prophets, but of swapped marbles, birds' eggs, wooden daggers, secrets and catapults, midnight feasts, heroes, deadly rivalries, and desperate friendships.

Chapter Five

FUCHSIA was leaning on her window sill and staring out over the rough roofs below her. Her crimson dress burned with the peculiar red more often found in paintings than in Nature. The window frame, surrounding not only her but the impalpable dusk behind her, enclosed a masterpiece. Her stillness accentuated the hallucinatory effect, but even if she were to have moved, it would have seemed that a picture had come to life rather than a movement had taken place in Nature. But the pattern did not alter. The inky black of her hair fell motionless and gave infinite subtlety to the porous shadowland beyond her, showing it for what it was, not so much a darkness in itself as something starved for sunbeams. Her face, throat, and arms were warm and tawny, yet seemed pale against her red dress. She stared down, out of this picture, at the world below her—at the North Cloisters, at Barquentine, heaving his miserable and vicious body forward on his crutch, and cursing the flies that followed him as he passed across a gap between two roofs and disappeared from sight.

Then she moved, suddenly turning about at a sound behind her, and found Mrs. Slagg looking up at her. In her hands the midget held a tray weighted with a tumbler of milk and a bunch of grapes.

She was peeved and irritable, for she had spent the last hour searching for Titus, who had outgrown the fussings of her love. "Where is he? Oh, where *is* he?" she whimpered, her face puckered up with anxiety and her weak legs, like twigs, that were forever tottering from one duty to another, aching. "Where is his wickedness, that naughty Earl of mine? God help my poor weak heart! Where can he be?"

Her peevish voice raised thin echoes far above her as though, in hall after hall, she had awakened nests of fledglings from their sleep.

"Oh, it's you," said Fuchsia, throwing a lock of hair from her face with a quick jerk of her hand. "I didn't know who it was."

"Of course it's me! Who else could it be, you *stupid?* Who else ever comes in your room? You ought to know that by *now,* oughtn't you? Oughtn't you?"

"I didn't see you," said Fuchsia.

"But I saw *you*—leaning out of the window like a great heavy thing—and never listening though I called you and called you and called you to open the door. Oh, my weak heart! It's always the same—call, call, call, with no one to answer. Why do I trouble to live?" She peered at Fuchsia. "Why should I live for *you?* Perhaps I'll die tonight," she added maliciously, squinting at Fuchsia again. "Why don't you take your milk?"

"Put it on the chair," said Fuchsia. "I'll have it later— and the grapes. Thank you. Good-by."

At Fuchsia's peremptory dismissal, which had not been

meant unkindly, abrupt as it had sounded, Mrs. Slagg's eyes filled with tears. But ancient, tiny, and hurt though she was, her anger rose again like a miniature tempest, and instead of her usual peevish cry of "Oh, my weak heart! how *could* you?" she caught hold of Fuchsia's hand and tried to bend back the girl's fingers and, failing, was about to try and bite her Ladyship's arm when she found herself being carried to the bed. Denied of her little revenge, she closed her eyes for a few moments, her chicken bosom rising and falling with fantastic rapidity. When she opened her eyes, the first thing she saw was Fuchsia's hand spread out before her and, rising on one elbow, she smacked at it again and again until exhausted, when she buried her wrinkled face in Fuchsia's side.

"I'm sorry," said the girl. "I didn't mean 'Good-by' in that way. I only meant that I wanted to be left alone."

"Why?" (Mrs. Slagg's voice was hardly audible, so closely was her face pressed into Fuchsia's dress.) "Why? why? why? Anyone would think I got in your way. Anyone would think I didn't know you inside out. Haven't I taught you everything since you were a baby? Didn't I rock you to sleep, you beastly thing? Didn't I?" She raised her old tearful face to Fuchsia. "Didn't I?"

"You did," said Fuchsia.

"Well, then!" said Nannie Slagg. *"Well*, then!" And she crawled off the bed and made her descent to the ground.

"Get off the counterpane at *once,* you *thing,* and don't stare at me! Perhaps I'll come and see you tonight. Perhaps. I don't know. Perhaps I don't want to." She made for the door, reached for the handle, and was within a few moments alone once more in her small room, where with her red-rimmed eyes wide open, she lay upon her bed like a discarded doll.

Fuchsia, with the room to herself, sat down in front of a mirror that had smallpox so badly at its center that in order to see herself properly she was forced to peer into a comparatively unblemished corner. Her comb, with a number of its teeth missing, was eventually found in a drawer below the mirror when, just as she was about to start combing her hair—a performance she had but lately taken to—the room darkened, for half the light from her window was suddenly obscured by the miraculous appearance of the young man with high shoulders.

Before Fuchsia had a moment to ponder how any human being could appear on her window sill a hundred feet above the ground—let alone recognize the silhouette—she snatched a hairbrush from the table before her and brandished it behind her head in readiness for she knew not what. At a moment when others might have screamed or shrunk away, she had showed fight—with what at that startling moment might have been a bat-winged monster for all she knew. But in the instant before she flung the brush she recognized Steerpike.

He knocked with his knuckle on the lintel of the window.

"Good afternoon, madam," he said. "May I present my card?" And he handed Fuchsia a slip of paper bearing the words:

His Infernal Slyness, the Arch-Fluke Steerpike.

But before Fuchsia had read it she had begun to laugh in her short, breathless way at the mock-solemn tone of his "Good afternoon, madam." It had been so perfectly ponderous.

But until she motioned him to descend to the floor of the room—and she had no alternative—he did not move an inch in that direction, but stood, with his hands clasped and his head cocked on one side. At her gesture he suddenly came to life again, as though a trigger had been touched, and within a moment had unknotted a rope from his belt and flung the loose end out of the window, where it dangled. Fuchsia, leaning out of the window, gazed upward and saw the rest of the rope ascending the seven remaining storeys to a ragged roof, where presumably it was attached to some turret or chimney.

"All ready for my return," said Steerpike. "Nothing like rope, madam. Better than a horse. Climbs down a wall whenever you ask it, and never needs feeding."

"You can leave off 'madaming' me," said Fuchsia, somewhat loudly, and to Steerpike's surprise. "You know my name."

Steerpike, rapidly swallowing, digesting, and purging his irritation, for he never wasted his time by mouthing his setbacks, seated himself on a chair in the reverse direction and placed his chin on the chair back.

"I will never forget," he said, "to always call you by your proper name, and in a very proper tone of voice, Lady Fuchsia."

Fuchsia smiled vaguely, but she was thinking of something else.

"You are certainly one for climbing," she said at last. "You climbed to my attic—do you remember?"

Steerpike nodded.

"And you climbed up the Library wall when it was burning. It seems very long ago."

"And the time, if I may say so, Lady Fuchsia, when I climbed through the thunderstorm and over the rocks with you in my arms."

It was as though all the air had been suddenly drawn from the room, so deathly silent and thin had the atmosphere become. Steerpike thought he could detect the faintest tinge of color on Fuchsia's cheekbones.

At last he said: "One day, Lady Fuchsia, will you explore with me the roofs of this great house of yours? I would like to show you what I have found, away to the south, your Ladyship, where the granite domes are elbow-deep in moss."

"Yes," she replied, "yes . . ." His sharp, pallid face repelled her, but she was attracted by his vitality and air of secrecy.

She was about to ask him to leave, but he was on his feet before she could speak and had jumped through the window without touching its frame, and was swinging to and fro on the jerking rope before he started swarming it, hand over hand, on his long, upward climb to the ragged roof above.

When Fuchsia turned from the window she found upon her rough dressing table a single rosebud.

As he climbed Steerpike remembered how the day of Titus's birth seven years previously had seen the commencement of his climb across the roofs of Gormenghast and the end of his servitude in Swelter's kitchen. The muscular effort required accentuated the hunching of his shoulders. But he was preternaturally nimble and reveled no less in physical than in mental tenacity and daring. His penetrating close-set eyes were fixed upon that point to which his rope was knotted as though it were the zenith of his fancy.

The sky had darkened, and with the rising of a swift wind came the driven rain. It hissed and spouted in the masonry. It found a hundred natural conduits where it slid. Air-shafts, flues, and blowholes coughed with echoes, and huge flumes muttered. Lakes formed among the roofs, where they reflected the sky as though they had been there forever like waters in the mountains.

With the rope neatly coiled about his waist, Steerpike ran like a shadow across an acre of sloping slates. His collar was turned up. His white face was beaded with the rain.

High, sinister walls, like the walls of wharves, or dungeons for the damned, lifted into the watery air or swept in prodigious arcs of ruthless stone. Lost in the flying clouds the craggy summits of Gormenghast were wild with straining hair—the hanks of the drenched rockweed. Buttresses and outcrops of unrecognizable masonry loomed over Steerpike's head like the hulks of moldering ships, or stranded monsters whose streaming mouths and brows were the sardonic work of a thousand tempests. Roof after roof of every gradient rose or slid away before his eyes: terrace after terrace shone dimly before him through the rain, their long-forgotten flagstones dancing and hissing with the downpour.

A world of shapes fled past him, for he was as fleet as

a cat and he ran without pause, turning now this way, now that, and only slackening his pace when some more than normally hazardous catwalk compelled. From time to time as he ran he leaped into the air as though from excess of vitality. Suddenly, as he rounded a chimney-stack, black with dripping ivy, he dropped to walking pace and then, ducking his head beneath an arch, he fell to his knees and hauled up, with a grating of hinges, a long-forgotten skylight. In a moment he was through and had dropped into a small empty room twelve feet beneath. It was very dark. Steerpike uncoiled himself of the rope and looped it over a nail in the wall. Then he glanced around the dark room. The walls were covered with glass-fronted showcases, filled with every kind of moth. Long, thin pins impaled these insects to the cork lining of each box, but careful as the original collector must have been in his handling and mounting of the delicate things, yet time had told, and there was not a case without its damaged moth, and the floors of most of the little boxes smoldered with fallen wings.

Steerpike turned to the door, listening a moment, and then opened it. He had before him a dusty landing, and immediately on his left a ladder leading down to yet another empty room, as forlorn as the one he had just left. There was nothing in it except a great pyramidal stack of nibbled books, its dark interstices alive with the nests of mice. There was no door to this room, but a length of sacking hung limply over a fissure in the wall, which was broad enough for Steerpike to negotiate, moving sideways. Again there were stairs, and again there was a room, but longer this time, a kind of gallery. At its far end stood a stuffed stag, its shoulders white with dust.

As he crossed the room he saw through the corner of his eye, and framed by a glassless window, the sinister outline of Gormenghast Mountain, its high crags gleaming against a flying sky. The rain streamed through the window and splashed on the boards, so that little beads of dust ran to and fro on the floor like globules of mercury.

Reaching the double door, he ran his hands through his dripping hair and turned down the collar of his coat; and then, passing through and veering to the left, followed a corridor for some way before he reached a stairhead.

No sooner had he peered over the banisters than he started back, for the Countess of Groan was passing through the lamplit room below. She seemed to be wading in white froth, and the hollow rooms behind Steerpike reverberated with a dull throbbing, a multitudinous sound, the echo of the genuine ululation which he could not hear, the droning of the cats. They passed from the hall below like the ebbing of a white tide through the mouth of a cave, at its center, a rock that moved with them, crowned with red seaweed.

The echoes died. The silence was like a stretched sheet. Steerpike descended rapidly to the room below and made for the east.

The Countess walked with her head bowed a little and her arms akimbo. There was a frown on her brow. She was not satisfied that the immemorial sense of duty and observance was universally held sacrosanct in the wide network of the castle. Heavy and abstracted as she seemed, yet she was as quick as a snake to detect danger, and though she could not put a finger, as it were, on the exact area of her doubt, she was nevertheless suspicious, wary, and revengeful of she knew not exactly what.

She was turning over all the fragments of knowledge which might relate to the mysterious burning of her late husband's Library, to his disappearance, and to the disappearance of his Chef. She was using, almost for the first time, a naturally powerful brain—a brain that had been purred to sleep for so long by her white cats that it was difficult at first for her to awaken it.

She was on her way to the Doctor's house. She had not visited him for several years, and on the last occasion it was only to have him attend to the broken wing of a

wild swan. He had always irritated her, but against her own inclination she had always felt a certain peculiar confidence in him.

As she descended a long flight of stone stairs, the undulating tide at her feet had become a cascade in slow motion. At the foot of the stairs she stopped.

"Keep . . . close . . . keep . . . close . . . together," she said aloud, using her words like steppingstones—a noticeable gap between each, which in spite of the depth and huskiness of her voice had something childlike in its effect.

The cats were gone. She stood on solid earth again. The rain thrummed outside a leaded window. She walked slowly to the door that opened upon a line of cloisters. Through the arches she saw the Doctor's house on the far side of a quadrangle. Walking out into the rain as though it were not there, she moved through the downpour with a monumental and unhurried measure, her big head lifted.

Chapter Six

❈❈❈❈❈❈❈❈❈

I

PRUNESQUALLOR was in his study. He called it his "study." To his sister, Irma, it was a room in which her brother barricaded himself whenever she wished to talk to him about anything important. Once within and the door locked, the chain up and the windows bolted, there was very little she could do save beat upon the door.

This evening Irma had been more tiresome than ever. What was it, she had inquired, over and over again, which prevented her from meeting someone who could appreciate and admire her? She did not want him, this hypothetical admirer, necessarily to dedicate his *whole* life to her, for a man must have his work—(as long as it didn't take too long)—mustn't he? But if he were wealthy and *wished* to dedicate his life to her—well, she wouldn't make promises, but would give the proposal a fair hearing. She had her long, unblemished neck. Her bosom was flat, it was true, and so were her feet, but after all a woman can't have everything. "I *move* well, don't I, Alfred?" she had cried in a sudden passion. "I say, I *move* well?"

Her brother, whose long pink face had been propped on his long white hand, raised his eyes from the table-cloth on which he had been drawing the skeleton of an ostrich. His mouth opened automatically into something that had more of a yawn than a smile about it, but a great many teeth were flashed. His smooth jaws came together again, and as he looked at his sister he pondered for the thousandth time upon the maddening coincidence of being saddled with such a sister. It being the thousandth time, he was well practiced, and his ponder lasted no more than a couple of rueful seconds. But in those seconds he saw again the stark idiocy of her thin, lipless mouth, the twitching fatuity of the skin under her eyes, the roaring repression that could do no more than bleat through her voice; the smooth, blank forehead (from which the coarse, luxuriant masses of her iron-gray hair were strained back over her cranium, to meet in the compact huddle of a bun as hard as a boulder)—that forehead which was like the smoothly plastered front of an empty house, deserted save by the ghost of a bird-like tenant which hopped about in the dust and preened its feathers in front of tarnished mirrors.

"Lord! Lord!" he thought. "Why, out of all the globe's creatures, should I, innocent of murder, be punished in this way?"

He grinned again. This time there was nothing of the yawn left in the process. His jaws opened out like a croc-odile's. How could any human head contain such terri-ble and dazzling teeth? It was a brand-new graveyard.

But oh! how anonymous it was. Not a headstone chiseled
with the owner's name. Had they died in battle, these
nameless, dateless, dental dead, those memorials, when
the jaws opened, gleamed in the sunlight, and when the
jaws met again rubbed shoulders in the night, scraping
an ever closer acquaintance as the years rolled by?
Prunesquallor had smiled. For he had found relief in the
notion that there were several worse things imaginable
than being saddled with his sister metaphorically, and
one of them was that he should have been saddled with
her in all its literal horror. For his imagination had
caught a startlingly vivid glimpse of her upon his back,
her flat feet in the stirrups, her heels digging into his
flanks as, careering round the table on all fours with
the bit in his mouth and with his haunches being cross-
hatched with the flicks of her whip, he galloped his miserable life away.

"When I ask you a question, Alfred—I say when I
ask you a question, Alfred, I like to think that you can
be civil enough, even if you *are* my brother, to answer
me instead of smirking to yourself."

Now if there was one thing that the Doctor could
never do it was to smirk. His face was the wrong shape.
His muscles moved in another way altogether.

"Sister mine," he said, "since thus you are, forgive,
if you can, your brother. He waits breathlessly your answer to his question. It is this, my turtledove. *What did
you say to him?* For he has forgotten so utterly that
were his death dependent on it, he would be forced to
live—with you, his fruit-drop, with you alone."

Irma never listened beyond the first five words of her
brother's somewhat involved periods, and so a great
many insults passed over her head. Insults, not vicious
in themselves, they provided the Doctor with a form of
verbal self-amusement without which he would have to
remain locked in his study the entire time. And, in any
case, it wasn't a study, for although its walls were
lined with books, it held nothing else beyond a very comfortable armchair and a very beautiful carpet. There was

no writing desk. No paper or ink. Not even a waste-paper basket.

"What was it you asked me, flesh of my flesh? I will do what I can for you."

"I have been saying, Alfred, that I am not without charm. Nor without grace, or intellect. Why is it I am never approached? Why do I never have advances made to me?"

"Are you speaking financially?" asked the Doctor.

"I am speaking spiritually, Alfred, and you know it. What have others got that I haven't?"

"Or conversely," said Prunesquallor, "what haven't they got that you already have?"

"I don't follow you, Alfred. I said I don't follow you."

"That's just what you do do," said her brother, reaching out his arms and fluttering his fingers. "And I wish you'd stop it."

"But my deportment, Alfred. Haven't you noticed it? What's wrong with your sex—can't they see I *move* well?"

"Perhaps we're too spiritual," said Dr. Prunesquallor.

"But my carriage! Alfred, my carriage!"

"Too powerful, sweet white-of-egg, far too powerful; you lurch from side to side of life's drear highway: those hips of yours rotating as you go. Oh, no, my dear one, your carriage scares them off, that's what it does. You terrify them, Irma."

This was too much for her.

"You've never *believed* in me!" she cried, rising from the table, and a dreadful blush suffusing her perfect skin. "But I can tell you"—her voice rose to a shrill scream— *"that I'm a lady!* What do you think I want with *men?* The beasts! I hate them. Blind, stupid, clumsy, horrible, heavy, vulgar things they are. And you're *one* of them!" she screamed, pointing at her brother, who, with his eyebrows raised a little, was continuing with his drawing of the ostrich from where he had left off. "And *you* are one of them! Do you hear me, Alfred, one of *them!*"

The pitch of her voice had brought a servant to the door. Unwisely, he had opened it, ostensibly to ask whether she had rung for him, but in reality to see what was going on.

Irma's throat was quivering like a bowstring.

"What have ladies to do with men?" she screamed; and then, catching sight of the face of the servant at the door, she plucked a knife from the table and flung it at the face. But her aim was not all it might have been, possibly because she was so involved in being a lady, and the knife impaled itself on the ceiling immediately above her own head, where it gave a perfect imitation of the shuddering of her throat.

The Doctor, adding with deliberation the last vertebra to the tail of the skeleton ostrich, turned his face firstly to the door, where the servant, his mouth hanging open, was gazing spellbound at the shuddering knife.

"Would you be so kind as to remove your redundant carcass from the door of this room, my man," he said, in his high, abstracted voice, "and keep it in the kitchen, where it is paid to do this and that among the saucepans, I believe . . . would you? No one rang for you. Your mistress's voice, though high, is nothing like the ringing of a bell . . . nothing at all."

The face withdrew.

"And what's more," came a desperate cry from immediately below the knife, "he never comes to see me any more! Never! Never!"

The Doctor rose from the table. He knew she was referring to Steerpike, but for whom she would probably never have experienced the recrudescence of this thwarted passion which had grown upon her since the youth had first dispatched his flattering arrows at her all too sensitive heart.

Her brother wiped his mouth with a napkin, brushed a crumb from his trousers, and straightened his long, narrow back.

"I'll sing you a little song," he said. "I made it up in the bath last night, ha! ha! ha! ha!—a whimsy little jangle, I tell myself—whimsy little jangle."

He began to move around the table, his elegant white hands folded about one another. "It went like this, I

fancy. . . ." But as he knew she would probably be deaf
to what he recited, he took her glass from beside her
plate and said, "A little wine is just what you need,
Irma dear, before you go to bed—for you are going
straight away, aren't you, my spasmic one, to Dreamland—ha, ha, ha!—where you can be a lady all night
long."

With the speed of a professional conjuror he whipped
a small packet from his pocket and, extracting a tablet,
dropped it into Irma's glass. He decanted a little wine
into the glass and handed it to her with the exaggerated
graciousness which seldom left him. "And I will take
some myself," he said, "and we will drink to each
other."

Irma had collapsed into a chair, and her long marmoreal face was buried in her hands. Her black glasses,
which she wore to protect her eyes from the light, were
at a rakish slant across her cheek.

"Come, come, I am forgetting my promise!" cried the
Doctor, standing before her, very tall, slender, and upright, with that celluloid head of his, all sentience and
nervous intelligence, tilted to one side like a bird's.

"First a quaff of this delicious wine from a vineyard
beneath a brooding hill—I can see it so clearly—and you,
O Irma, can *you* see it, too? The peasants toiling and
sweating in the sun—and why? Because they have no
option, Irma. They are desperately poor, and their bowed
necks are wry. And the husbandmen, like every good husband, tending his love—stroking the vines with his horny
hand, whispering to them, coaxing them. 'Oh little grapes,'
he whispers, 'give up your wine. Irma is waiting.' And
here it is; here it is, ha, ha, ha, ha! Delicious and cold
and white, in a cut-glass goblet. Toss back your coif
and quaff, my querulous queen!"

Irma roused herself a little. She had not heard a word.
She had been in her own private hell of humiliation. Her
eyes turned to the knife in the ceiling. The thin line of
her mouth twitched, but she took the glass from her
brother's outstretched hand.

Her brother clinked his glass against hers, and duplicating the movement of his arm, she raised her own automatically and drank.

"And now for the little jingle which I threw off in that nonchalant way of mine. How did it go? How did it go?"

Prunesquallor knew that by the third verse the strong, tasteless soporific which had dissolved in her wine would begin to take effect. He sat on the floor at her knees and, quelling a revulsion, he patted her hand.

"Queen bee," he said, "look at me, if you can. Through your midnight spectacles. It shouldn't be too dreadful—for one who had fed on horrors. Now, listen . . ." Irma's eyes were already beginning to close.

"It goes like this, I think. I called it *The Osseous 'Orse.*"

> *Come, flick the ulna juggler-wise*
> *And twang the tibia for me!*
> *O Osseous 'orse, the future lies*
> *Like serum on the sea.*

> *Green fields and buttercups no more*
> *Regale you with delight, no, no!*
> *The tonic tempests leap and pour*
> *Through your white pelvis ever so.*

"Are you enjoying it, Irma?" She nodded sleepily.

> *Come, clap your scapulae and twitch*
> *The pale pagoda of your spine,*
> *Removed from life's eternal itch*
> *What need for iodine?*

> *The Osseous 'orse sat up at once*
> *And clanged his ribs in Biblic pride.*

> *I fear I looked at him askance*
> *Though he had naught to hide. . . .*

> *No hide at all . . . just . . .*

At this point the Doctor, having forgotten what came next, turned his eyes once more to his sister Irma; she was fast asleep. The Doctor rang the bell.

"Your mistress's maid; a stretcher; and a couple of men to handle it." (A face had appeared in the doorway.) *"And* be rapid." The face withdrew.

When Irma had been put to bed and her lamp had been turned low and silence swam through the house, the Doctor unlocked the door of his study, entered, and sank back in his armchair. His friable-looking elbows rested upon the padded arms. His fingers were twined together into a delicate bunch, and on this bunch he supported his long and sunken jaw. After a few moments he removed his glasses and laid them on the arm of his chair. Then, with his fingers clasped together once again beneath his chin, he shut his eyes and sighed gently.

Chapter Seven

BUT he was not destined to more than a few moments of relaxation for feet were soon to be heard outside his window. Only two of them, it was true, but there was something in the weight and deliberation of the tread that reminded him of an army moving in perfect unison, a dread and measured sound. The rain had quieted and the sound of each foot as it struck the ground was alarmingly clear.

Prunesquallor could recognize that portentous gait among a million. But in the silence of the evening his mind flew to the phantom army it awakened in his leapfrogging brain. What was there in the clockwork stepping of an upright host to contract the throat and bring, as does the thought of a sliced lemon, that sharp astringent to throat and jaw? Why do the tears begin to gather? And the heart to thud?

He had no time to ponder the matter now, so at one and the same time he tossed a mop of gray thatch from his brow and an army-on-the-march from his mind.

Reaching the door before his bell could clang the servants into redundance, he opened it, and to the massive figure who was about to whack the door with her fist—"I welcome your Ladyship," he said. His body inclined a little from the hips and his teeth flashed, while he wondered what, in the name of all that was heterodox, the Countess thought she was doing in visiting her physician at this time of night. She visited nobody by day *or* night. That was one of the things about her. Nevertheless, here she was.

"Hold your horses." Her voice was heavy, but not loud.

One of Dr. Prunesquallor's eyebrows shot to the top of his forehead. It was a peculiar remark to be greeted with. It might have been supposed that he was about to embrace her. The very notion appalled him.

But when she said, "You can come in now," not only did his other eyebrow fly up his forehead, but it set its counterpart a-tremble with the speed of its uprush.

To be told he could "come in now" when he was already inside was weird enough; but the idea of being given permission to enter his own house by a guest was grotesque.

The slow, heavy, quiet authority in the voice made the situation even more embarrassing. She had entered his hall. "I wish to see you," she said, but her eyes were on the door which Prunesquallor was closing. When it had barely six inches to go before the night was locked out and the latch had clicked—"Hold!" she said, in a rather deeper tone. "Hold hard!" And then, with her big lips pursed like a child's, she gave breath to a long whistle of peculiar sweetness. A tender and forlorn note to escape from so ponderous a being.

The Doctor, as he turned to her, was a picture of per-

plexed inquiry, though his teeth were still shining gaily.
But as he turned something caught the corner of his
eye. Something white. Something that moved.

Between the space left by the all-but-closed door, and
very close to the ground, Dr. Prunesquallor saw a face
as round as a hunter's moon, as soft as fur. And this was
no wonder, for it was a face of fur, peculiarly blanched
in the dim light of the hall. No sooner had the Doctor
reacted to this face than another took its place, and
close upon it, silent as death, came a third, a fourth, a
fifth. . . . In single file there slid into the hall, so close
upon each other's tails that they might have been a continuous entity, her Ladyship's white clowder.

Prunesquallor, feeling a little dizzy, watched the undulating stream flow past his feet as he stood with his hand
on the doorknob. Would they never end? He had
watched them for over two minutes. He turned to the
Countess. She stood in coiling froth like a lighthouse. By
the dim glow of the hall lamp her red hair threw out
a sullen light.

Prunesquallor was perfectly happy again. For what
had irked him was not the cats, but the obscure com-
mands of the Countess. Their meaning was now self-
evident. And yet, how peculiar to have enjoined a swarm
of cats to hold their horses!

The very thought of it got hold of his eyebrows again,
which had lowered themselves reluctantly while he waited for his chance to close the door and they had leaped
up his forehead as though a pistol had been cracked and
a prize awaited the fastest.

"We're . . . all . . . here," said the Countess. Prunesquallor turned to the door and saw that the stream had,
indeed, run dry. He shut the door.

"Well, well, well, well!" he trilled, standing on his
toes and fluttering his hands, as though he were about
to take off like a fairy. "How *delightful!* how very, very
delightful that you should call, your Ladyship. God bless
my ascetic soul! if you haven't whipped the old hermit
out of his introspection. Ha, ha, ha, ha, ha! And here,
as you put it, you all are. There's no doubt about that, is

there? What a party we will have! *Mew*-sical chairs and
all! ha ha ha ha ha ha ha ha."

The almost unbearable pitch of his laughter created
an absolute stillness in the hall. The cats, sitting bolt
upright, had their round eyes fixed on him.

"But I keep you waiting!" he cried. "Waiting in my
outer rooms! And you are a mere valetudinarian, my
dear Ladyship, or some prolific mendicant whose be-
witched offspring she hopes I can return to human
shape? Of course you are not, by all that's evident, so
why should you be left in this cold—this damp—this obnoxious hell of a hall, with the rain pouring off you in
positive waterfalls . . . and so . . . and so, *if* you'll allow
me to lead on"—he waved a long, thin, delicate arm
with a white hand on the end of it, which fluttered like
a silk flag—"I'll throw a few doors open, light a lamp
or two, flick away a few crumbs in readiness for . . .
What wine shall it be?"

He began to tread his way to the sitting room with a
curious flicking movement of the feet.

The Countess followed him. The servants had cleared
the table of the supper dishes and the room had been
left with so serene a composure about it that it was
hard to believe that it was but a short while ago in this
same room that Irma had disgraced herself.

Prunesquallor flung wide the door of the sitting room
for the Countess to pass through. He flung it with a
spectacular abandon: it seemed to imply that if the
door broke, or the hinges snapped, or a picture was
jerked off the wall, what of it? This was his house; he
could do what he liked with it. If he chose to jeopardize his belongings, that was his affair. This was an occasion when such meager considerations would only enter the minds of the vulgar.

The Countess advanced down the center of the room
and then stopped. She stared about her abstractedly—
at the long lemon-yellow curtain, the carved furniture,
the deep green rug, the silver, the ceramics, the pale gray-
and-white stripes of the wallpaper. Perhaps her mind reverted to her own candle-smelling, bird-filled, half-lit

chaos of a bedroom, but there was no expression on her face.

"Are . . . all . . . your . . . rooms . . . like . . . this . . .?" she muttered. She had just seated herself in a chair.

"Well, let me see," said Prunesquallor. "No, not exactly, your Ladyship . . . not *exactly*."

"I . . . suppose . . . they're . . . spotless. Is . . . that it . . . eh?"

"I believe they are; yes, yes, I quite believe they are. Not that I see more than five or six of them during the course of a year; but what with the servants flitting here and there with dusters and brooms, and clanking their buckets and wringing things out—and what with my sister Irma flitting after them to see that the right things are wrung and the wrung things are right, I have no doubt that we are all but sterilized to extinction: no tartar on the banisters: not a microbe left to live its life in peace."

"I see," said the Countess. It was extraordinary how damning those two words sounded. "But I have come to talk to you."

For a moment she stared about her ruminatively. The cats, with not a whisker moving, were everywhere in the room. The mantelpiece was heraldic with them. The table was a solid block of whiteness. The couch was a snowdrift. The carpet was sewn with eyes.

Her Ladyship's head, which always seemed far bigger than any human head had a right to be, was turned away from the Doctor and down a little, so that her powerful throat was tautened: yet ample along the near side. Her profile was nearly hidden by her cheek. Her hair was built up, for the most part, into a series of red nests and for the rest smoldered as it fell in snakelike coils to her shoulders, where it all but hissed.

The Doctor twirled about on his narrow feet and flung open a silkwood cabinet door with a grandiose flourish, bringing his long white hands together beneath his chin and tossing a mop of gray hair from his forehead. He flashed his brilliant teeth at the Countess (who was still presenting him with her shoulder and about an eighth of her face), and then with eyebrows raised—"Your Ladyship," he said, "that you should decide to visit me, and to discuss some subject with me, is an honor. But first, *what* will you drink?"

The Doctor in flinging open the door of his cabinet had revealed as rare and delicately chosen a group of wines as he had ever selected from his cellar.

The Countess moved her great head through the air.

"A jug of goat's milk, Prunesquallor, if you please," she said.

What there was in the Doctor that loved beauty, selectivity, delicacy, and excellence—and there was a good deal in him that responded to these abstractions—shrank up like the horn of a snail and all but died. But his hand, which was poised in the air and was halfway to the trapped sunlight of a long-lost vineyard, merely fluttered to and fro as though it were conducting some gnomic orchestra, while he turned about, apparently in full control of himself. He bowed, and his teeth flashed. Then he rang the bell, and when a face appeared at the door—"Have we a goat?" he said. "Come, come, my man—yes or no. Have we, or haven't we, a goat?"

The man was positive that they had no such thing.

"Then you will find one, if you please. You will find one immediately. It is wanted. That will do."

The Countess had seated herself. Her feet were planted apart and her heavy freckled arms were along the sides of her chair. In the silence that followed even Prunesquallor could think of nothing to say. The stillness was eventually broken by the voice of the Countess.

"Why do you have knives sticking in your ceiling?"

The Doctor recrossed his legs and followed her impassive gaze, which was fixed on the long bread-knife that suddenly appeared to fill the room. A knife in the fender, on a pillow, or under a chair is one thing, but a knife surrounded by the blank white wasteland of a ceiling has no shred of covering—is as naked and blatant as a pig in a cathedral.

But any subject was fruitful to the Doctor. It was

only a lack of material, a rare enough contingency in him, that he found appalling.

"That knife, your Ladyship," he said, giving the implement a glance of the deepest respect, "bread knife though it be, has a history. A history, madam! It has indeed."

He turned his eyes to his guest. She waited impassively.

"Humble, unromantic, ill-proportioned, crude as it looks, yet it means much to me. Indeed, madam, it is so, and I am no sentimentalist. And *why?* you will be asking yourself. Why? Let me tell you all."

He clasped his hands together and raised his narrow and elegant shoulders.

"It was with that knife, your Ladyship, that I performed my first successful operation. I was among mountains. Huge tufted things. Full of character; but no charm. I was alone with my faithful mule. We were lost. A meteor flew overhead. What use was that to us? No use at all. It merely irritated us. For a moment it showed a track through the fever-dripping ferns. It was obviously the wrong one. It would only have taken us back to a morass we had just spent half a day struggling out of. What a sentence! What a vile sentence, your Ladyship, ha, ha, ha, ha, ha! Where was I? Ah, yes! Plunged in darkness. Miles from anywhere. What happened next? The strangest thing. Prodding my mule forward with my walking cane—I was riding the brute at the time—it suddenly gave a cry like a child and began to collapse under me. As it subsided it turned its huge hairy head and what little light there was showed me its eyes were positively imploring me to free it from some agony or other. Now agony is an agonizing thing to happen to anyone, your Ladyship, but to locate the seat of the agony in a mule in the darkness of a mountainous and fever-dripping night is—er . . . not easy (Lytotis), ha, ha, ha! But *do* something I must. It was already upon its side in the darkness—the great thing. I had leaped from its collapsing spine and at once my faculties began to do their damnedest. The brute's eyes, still fixed on mine, were

like lamps that were running out of oil. I put a couple of
questions to myself—pertinent ones, I felt at the time—
and still do; and the first was: IS the agony spiritual
or physical? If the former, the darkness wouldn't matter, but the treatment would be tricky. If the latter, the
darkness would be hell; but the problem was in my
province—or very nearly. I plumped for the latter, and
more by good fortune or that curious sixth sense one
has when alone with a mule, among tufted mountains, I
found almost at once it to have been a happy guess: for
directly I had decided to work on a carnal basis I got
hold of the mule's head, heaved it up, and swiveled it
to such an angle that by the glow of its eyes I was able
to illumine—faintly, of course, but to illumine, none the
less—with a dull glow, the *rest* of its body. At once I
was rewarded. It was a pure case of 'foreign body.'
Coiled—I couldn't tell you how many times—around
the beast's hind leg, was a python! Even at that ghastly
and critical moment I could see what a beautiful thing
it was. Far more beautiful than my old brute of a mule.
But did it enter my head that I should transfer my allegiance to the reptile? No. After all, there is such a thing
as loyalty as well as beauty. Besides, I hate walking, and
the python would have taken some riding, your Ladyship:
the very saddling would tax a man's patience. And besides . . ."

The Doctor glanced at his guest and immediately
wished he hadn't. Taking out his silk handkerchief, he
wiped his brow. Then he flashed his teeth, and with
somewhat less ebullience in his voice, "It was then that
I thought of my bread-knife," he added.

For a moment there was silence. And then, as the
Doctor filled his lungs and was ready to continue—"How
old are you?" said the Countess. But before Dr. Prunesquallor could readjust himself there was a knock at
the door and the servant entered with a goat.

"Wrong sex, you idiot!" As the Countess spoke she
rose heavily from her chair and, approaching the goat,
she fondled its head with her big hands. It strained toward her on the rope leash and licked her arm.

"You amaze me," said the Doctor to the servant. "No wonder you cook badly. Away, my man, away! Unearth yet another, and get the gender right, for the love of mammals! Sometimes one wonders what kind of a world one is living in—by all things fundamental, one really does."

The servant disappeared.

"Prunesquallor," said the Countess, who had moved to the window and was staring out across the quadrangle.

"Madam?" queried the Doctor.

"I am not easy in my heart, Prunesquallor."

"Your heart, Madam?"

"My heart and my mind."

She returned to her chair, where she seated herself again and laid her arms along the padded sides as before.

"In what way, your Ladyship?" Prunesquallor's voice had lost its facetious vapidity.

"There is mischief in the castle," she replied. "Where it is I do not know. But there is mischief." She stared at the Doctor.

"Mischief?" he said at last. "Some influence, do you mean—some bad influence, Madam?"

"I do not know for sure. But something has changed. My bones know it. There is someone."

"Someone?"

"An enemy. Whether ghost or human I do not know. But an enemy. Do you understand?"

"I understand," said the Doctor. Every vestige of his waggery had disappeared. He leaned forward. "It is not a ghost," he said. "Ghosts have no itch for rebellion."

"Rebellion!" said the Countess loudly. "By whom?"

"I do not know. But what else can it be you sense, as you say, in your bones, Madam?"

"Who would *dare* to rebel?" she whispered, as though to herself. "Who would dare? . . ." And then, after a pause: "Have you *your* suspicions?"

"I have no proof. But I will watch for you. For, by the

holy angels, since you have brought the matter up there is evil abroad and no mistake."

"Worse," she replied, "worse than that. There is perfidy."

She drew a deep breath and then, very slowly: ". . . and I will crush its life out! I will break it! Not only for Titus's sake and for his dead father's, but more—for Gormenghast."

"You speak of your late husband, Madam, the revered Lord Sepulchrave. Where are his remains, Madam, if he is truly dead?"

"And more than that, man, more than that! What of the fire that warped his brilliant brain? What of that fire in which, but for that youth Steerpike . . ." She lapsed into a thick silence.

"And what of the suicide of his sisters; and the disappearance of the Chef on the same night as his Lordship your husband—and all within a year, or little more: and since then a hundred irregularities and strange affairs? What lies at the back of all this? By all that's visionary, madam, your heart has reason to be uneasy."

"And there is Titus," said the Countess.

"There is Titus," the Doctor repeated as quick as an echo.

"How old is he now?"

"He is nearly eight." Prunesquallor raised his eyebrows. "Have you not seen him?"

"From my window," said the Countess, "when he rides along the South Wall."

"You should be with him, your Ladyship, now and then," said the Doctor. "By all that's maternal, you really should see more of your son."

The Countess stared at the Doctor, but what she might have replied was stunned forever by a rap at the door and the reappearance of the servant with a nanny goat.

"Let her go!" said the Countess.

The little white goat ran to her as though she were a magnet. She turned to Prunesquallor. "Have you a jug?"

The Doctor turned his head to the door. "Fetch a jug," he said to the disappearing face.

"Prunesquallor," she said, as she knelt down, a prodigious bulk in the lamplight, and stroked the sleek ears of the goat, "I will not ask you on whom your suspicions lie. No. Not yet. But I expect you to watch, Prunesquallor —to watch everything, as I do. You must be all aware, Prunesquallor, every moment of the day. I expect to be informed of heterodoxy, wherever it may be found. I have a kind of faith in you, man. A kind of faith in you. I don't know why. . . ." she added.

"Madam," said Prunesquallor, "I will be on tiptoe."

The servant came in with a jug, and retired.

The elegant curtains fluttered a little in the night air. The light of the lamp was golden in the room, glimmering on the porcelain bowls, on the squat cut-glass vases and the tall cloisonné ware: on the vellum backs of books and the glazed drawings that hung upon the walls. But its light was reflected most vividly from the countless small white faces of the motionless cats. Their whiteness blanched the room and chilled the mellow light. It was a scene that Prunesquallor never forgot. The Countess on her knees by the dying fire: the goat standing quietly while she milked it with an authority in the deft movement of her fingers that affected him strangely. Was this heavy, brusque, uncompromising Countess, whose maternal instincts were so shockingly absent: who had not spoken to Titus for a year: who was held in awe, and even in fear, by the populace: who was more a legend than a woman—was this indeed *she,* with the half-smile of extraordinary tenderness on her wide lips?

And then he remembered her voice again, when she had whispered: "Who would dare to rebel? Who would *dare?*" and then the full, ruthless organ-chord of her throat: "And I will crush its life out! I will break it! Not only for Titus's sake . . ."

Chapter Eight

✼✼✼✼✼✼✼✼✼✼✼

CORA and Clarice, although they did not know it, were imprisoned in their apartments. Steerpike had nailed and bolted from the outside every means of exit. They had been incarcerated for two years, their tongues having loosened to the brink of Steerpike's undoing. Cunning and patient as he was with them, the young man could find no other foolproof way of ensuring their permanent silence on the subject of the Library fire. No other way—but one. They believed that they alone among the inhabitants of the castle were free of a hideous disease of Steerpike's invention, and which he referred to as "Weasel plague."

The twins were like water. He could turn on or off at will the taps of their terror. They were pathetically grateful that through his superior wisdom they were able to remain in relative health. If a flat refusal to die in the face of a hundred reasons why they should could be called health. They were obsessed by the fear of coming into contact with the carriers. He brought them daily news of the dead and dying.

Their quarters were no longer those spacious apartments where Steerpike had first paid them his respects seven years ago. Far from them having a Room of Roots and a great tree leaning over space hundreds of feet above the earth, they were now on the ground level in an obscure precinct of the castle, a dead end, a promontory of dank stone, removed from even the less frequented routes. Not only was there no way through it, but it was shunned also for reason of its evil reputation. Unhealthy with noxious moisture, its very breath was double pneumonia.

47

Ironically enough, it was in such a place as this that the aunts rejoiced in the erroneous belief that they alone could escape the virulent and ghastly disease that was in their imaginations prostrating Gormenghast. They had by now become so self-centered under Steerpike's guidance as to be looking forward to the day when they, as sole survivors, would be able (after due precautions) to pace forth and be at last, after all these long years of frustration, the unopposed claimants to the Groan Crown, that massive and lofty symbol of sovereignty, with its central sapphire the size of a hen's egg.

It was one of their hottest topics: whether the Crown should be sawed in half and the sapphire split, so that they could always be wearing at least part of it, or whether it should be left intact and they should wear it on alternate days.

Hot and contested though this subject was, it stirred no visible animation. Not even their lips were seen to move, for they had acquired the habit of keeping them slightly parted and projecting their toneless voices without a tremor of the mouth. But for most of the time their long, solitary days were passed in silence. Steerpike's spasmodic appearances—and they had become less and less frequent—were, apart from their wild, bizarre and paranoiac glimpses of a future of thrones and crowns, their sole excitement.

How was it that their Ladyships Cora and Clarice could be hidden away in this manner and the iniquity condoned?

It was not condoned; for two years previously they had been as far as Gormenghast was concerned buried with a wealth of symbolism in the tombs of the Groans, a couple of wax replicas having been modeled by Steerpike for the dread occasion. A week before these effigies were lowered into the sarcophagus, a letter, as from the twins, but in reality forged by the youth, had been discovered in their apartments. It divulged the dreadful information that the sisters of the Seventy-Sixth Earl, who had himself disappeared from the castle without a

trace, bent upon their self-destruction, had stolen by
night from the castle grounds to make an end of themselves among the ravines of Gormenghast Mountain.

Search parties, organized by Steerpike, had found no
trace.

On the night previous to the discovery of the note,
Steerpike had conveyed the twins to the rooms which
they now occupied upon some pretext connected with
an inspection of a couple of scepters he had found and
regilded.

All this seemed a long time ago. Titus had been a
mere infant. Flay but lately banished. Sepulchrave and
Swelter had melted into air. Like teeth missing from
the jaw of Gormenghast, the disappearance of the
twins, added to those others, gave to the castle for a
time an unfamiliar visage and an aching bone. To some
extent the wounds had healed and the change of face
had been accepted. Titus was, after all, alive and well—
and the continuation of the Family assured.

The twins were sitting in their room, after a day of
more than usual silence. A lamp, set on an iron table (it
burned all day), gave them sufficient light to do their
embroidery; but for some while neither of them applied
herself to her work.

"What a long time life takes!" said Clarice at last.
"Sometimes I think it's hardly worthy encroaching on."

"I don't know anything about *encroaching,*" replied
Cora; "but since you have spoken I might as well tell
you that you've forgotten something, as usual."

"What have I forgotten?"

"You've forgotten that I did it yesterday and it is
your turn today—thus."

"My turn to what?"

"To *comfort* me," said Cora, looking hard at a leg of
the iron table. "You can go on doing it until half-past
seven, and then it will be your turn to be depressed."

"Very well," said Clarice; and she began at once to
stroke her sister's arm.

"No, no, no!" said Cora, "don't be so obvious. Do

things without any mention—like getting tea, for instance, and laying it quietly before me."

"All right," answered Clarice, rather sullenly. "But you've spoiled it now—haven't you?—telling me what to do. It won't be so thoughtful of me, will it? But perhaps I could get coffee instead."

"Never mind all that," Cora replied. "You talk too much. I don't want to suddenly find it's your turn."

"What! For *my* depression?"

"Yes, yes," her sister said irritably; and she scratched the back of her round head. "Not that I think you deserve one."

Their conversation was disturbed, for a curtain parted behind them and Steerpike approached, a sword-stick in his hand.

The twins rose together and faced him, their shoulders touching.

"How are my lovebirds?" he said. He lifted his slender stick and, with ghastly impudence, tickled their Ladyships' ribs with its narrow ferruled end. No expression appeared on their faces, but they went through the slow, wriggling motions of Eastern dancers. A clock chimed from above the mantelpiece, and as it ceased the monotonous sound of the rain appeared to redouble its volume. The light had become very bad.

"You haven't been here for a long while," said Cora.

"How true," said Steerpike.

"Had you forgotten us?"

"Not a bit of it," he said, "not a bit of it."

"What happened, then?" asked Clarice.

"Sit down!" said Steerpike harshly. "And listen to me." He stared them out of countenance until their heads dropped, abashed, and they found themselves staring at their own clavicles. "Do you think it is easy for me to keep the plague from your door and to be at your beck and call at the same time? Do you?"

They shook their heads slowly like pendulums.

"Then have the grace not to interrogate me!" he cried in mock anger. "How dare you snap at the hand that feeds you! How dare you!"

The twins, acting together, rose from their chairs and started moving across the room. They paused a moment and turned their eyes to Steerpike in order to make sure that they were doing what was expected of them. Yes. The stern finger of the young man was pointing to the heavy damp carpet that covered the floor of the room.

Steerpike derived as much pleasure in watching these anile and pitiful creatures, dressed in their purple finery, as they crawled beneath the carpet as he got from anything. He had led them gradually, and by easy and cunning steps, from humiliation to humiliation, until the distorted satisfaction he experienced in this way had become little short of a necessity to him. Were it not that he found this grotesque pleasure in the exercise of his power over them, it is to be doubted whether he would have gone to all the trouble which was involved in keeping them alive.

As he stared at the twin hummocks under the carpet he did not realize that something very peculiar and unprecedented was happening. Cora, in her warrenlike seclusion, crouched in the ignominious darkness, had conceived an idea. Where it came from she did not trouble to inquire of herself, nor *why* it should have come, for Steerpike, their benefactor, was a kind of god to her, as he was to Clarice. But the idea had suddenly flowered in her brain unbidden. It was that she would very much like to kill him. Directly she had conceived the idea she felt frightened, and her fear was hardly lessened by a flat voice in the darkness saying with empty deliberation: "So . . . would . . . I. We could do it together, couldn't we? We could do it together."

Chapter Nine

✼✻✼✻✼✻✼✻✼✻✼✻

THERE was an all-but-forgotten landing high in the southern wing, a landing taken over for many a decade by succeeding generations of dove-gray mice, peculiarly small creatures, little larger than the joint of a finger and indigenous to this southern wing, for they were never seen elsewhere.

In years gone by this unfrequented stretch of floor, walled off on one side with high banisters, must have been of lively interest to some person or persons; for though the colors had to a large extent faded, yet the walls and floor boards must once have been a deep and glowing crimson, and the three walls the most brilliant of yellows. The banisters were alternately apple-green and azure, the frames of the doorless doorways being also this last color. The corridors that led away in dwindling perspective continued the crimson of the floor and the yellow of the walls, but were cast in a deep shade.

The balcony banisters were on the southern side, and, in the sloping roof above them, a window let in the light and, sometimes, the sun itself, whose beams made of this silent, forgotten landing a cosmos, a firmament of moving motes, brilliantly illumined, an astral and at the same time a solar province; for the sun would come through with its long rays and the rays would be dancing with stars. Where the sunbeams struck, the floor would flower like a rose, a wall break out in crocus-light, and the banisters would flame like rings of colored snakes.

But even on the most cloudless of summer days, with the sunlight striking through, the colors had in their brilliance the pigment of decay. It was a red that had lost its flame that smoldered from the floor boards.

And across this old circus-ground of bygone colors the families of the gray mice moved.

When Titus first came upon the colored banisters of the staircase it was at a point two floors below the yellow-walled balcony. He had been exploring on that lower floor, and finding himself lost he had taken fright, for room after room was cavernous with shadow or vacant and afloat with sunlight that lit the dust on the wide floors—somehow more frightening to the child in its golden dereliction than the deepest shadows. Had he not clenched his hands he would have screamed, for the very lack of ghosts in the deserted halls and chambers was in itself unnerving; for there was a sense that something had either just left each corridor, or each hall as he came upon it, or else that the stages were set and ready for its appearance.

It was with his imagination dilated and his heart hammering aloud that Titus, suddenly turning a corner, came upon a section of the staircase two floors below the haunt of the gray mice.

Directly Titus saw the stairway he ran to it, as though every banister were a friend. Even in the access of his relief, and even while the hollow echo of his footsteps was in his ears, his eyes widened at the apple-green—the azure—of the banisters, each one a tall plinth of defiance. Only the rail which these bright things supported was hueless, being of a smooth, hand-worn ivory whiteness. Titus gripped the banisters and then peered through them and downward. There seemed little life in the fathoms beneath him. A bird flew slowly past a far landing; a section of plaster fell from a shadowy wall three floors below the bird, but that was all.

Titus glanced above him and saw how close he stood to the head of the stairway. Anxious as he was to escape from the atmosphere of these upper regions, yet he could not resist running to the top of the stairs, where he could see the colors burning. The small gray mice squeaked and scampered away down the passageways or into their holes. A few remained against the walls

and watched Titus for a short while before returning
to their sleeping or nibbling.

The atmosphere was indescribably golden and friendly
to the boy: so friendly that his proximity to the hollow
room below him did little to disturb his delight. He sat
down, his back against a yellow wall, and watched the
white motes maneuvering in the long sunbeams.

"This is *mine! mine!*" he said aloud. "I found it."

Chapter Ten

THROUGH the vile subterranean light that filled the Professors' Common-Room three figures appeared to float
as the brown billows shifted. Tobacco smoke had made
of the place a kind of umber tomb. These three were
the vanguard of a daily foregathering, as sacrosanct and
inevitable as the elm-top meeting place of rooks in
March. But how much less healthy! A foregathering of
the Professors, for it was eleven o'clock and the short
recreation had begun.

Their pupils—the sparrows, as it were—of Gormenghast were racing to the vast red-sandstone yard—a
yard surrounded on all sides by high ivy-covered walls
of the same stone. Innumerable knife blades had snapped
upon its harsh surface, for there must surely be a thousand spidery initials scored into the stone! A hundred
painfully incised valedictions and observations whose
significance had long since lost its edges. Deeper incisions
into the red-stone had mapped out patterns for some
game or other of local invention. Many a boy had sobbed
against these walls; many a knuckle been bruised as a
head flicked sideways from the blow. Many a child had
fought his way back into the open yard with bloody
mouth, and a thousand swaying pyramids of boys had

tottered and collapsed as the topmost clung to the ivy.

The yard was approached by a tunnel which commenced immediately beneath the long South Classroom, where steps led down through a trap door. The tunnel, old and thick with ferns, was at this moment echoing barbarically to the catcalls of a horde of boys as they made pell-mell for the red-stone yard, their immemorial playground.

But in the Professors' Common-Room the three gentlemen were finding relaxation through an abatement rather than an increase of energy.

To enter the room from the Professors' corridor was to suffer an extraordinary change of atmosphere, no less sudden than if a swimmer in clear white water were suddenly to find himself struggling to keep afloat in a bay of soup. Not only was the air fuscous with a mixture of smells, including stale tobacco, dry chalk, rotten wood, ink, alcohol, and, above all, imperfectly cured leather, but the general color of the room was a transcription of the smells, for the walls were of horsehide, the dreariest of browns, relieved only by the scattered and dully twinkling heads of drawing-pins.

On the right of the door hung the black gowns of office in various stages of decomposition.

Of the three Professors, the first to have reached the room that morning in order to establish himself securely in the only armchair (it was his habit to leave the class he was teaching—or pretending to teach—at least twenty minutes before its official conclusion, in order to be certain that the chair was free) was Opus Fluke. He lay rather than sat in what was known among the staff as "Fluke's Cradle." Indeed he had worn that piece of furniture—or symbol of bone laziness—into such a shape as made the descent of any other body than his own into that crater of undulating horsehair a hazardous enterprise.

Those daily indulgences before the midmorning break and their renewal before the dinner bell were much prized by Mr. Opus Fluke, who during these periods augmented the pall of tobacco smoke already obscur-

ing the ceiling of the Common-Room with enough of his
own exhaling to argue not only that the floor boards
were alight, but also that the core of the conflagration
was Mr. Fluke himself, lying, as he was, at an angle of
five degrees with the floor, in a position that might, in
any case, argue asphyxiation. But there was nothing on
fire except the tobacco in his pipe and as he lay supine,
the white wreaths billowing from his wide, muscular, and
lipless mouth (rather like the mouth of a huge and
friendly lizard), he evinced so brutal a disregard for his
own and other people's windpipes as made one wonder
how this man could share the selfsame world with hya-
cinths and damsels.

His head was well back. His long, bulging chin pointed
to the ceiling like a loaf of bread. His eyes followed
lugubriously the wavering ascent of a fresh smoke ring
until it was absorbed into the upper billows. There was
a kind of ripeness in his indolence, in his dreadful equa-
bility.

Of Opus Fluke's two companions in the Common-
Room the younger, Perch-Prism, was squatting jauntily
on the edge of a long ink-stained table. This ancient
span of furniture was littered with textbooks, blue pen-
cils, pipes filled to various depths with white ash and
dottle, pieces of chalk, a sock, several bottles of ink, a
bamboo walking cane, a pool of white glue; a chart of
the solar system, burned away over a large portion of
its surface through some past accident with a bottle of
acid; a stuffed cormorant with tin tacks through its feet,
which had no effect in keeping the bird upright; a faded
globe, with the words *"Cane Slypate Thursday"* scrawled
in yellow chalk across it from just below the equator to
well into the Arctic Circle; any number of lists, notices,
instructions; a novel called *The Amazing Adventures of
Cupid Catt;* and at least a dozen high, ragged pagodas
of buff-colored copybooks.

Perch-Prism had cleared a small space at the far end
of this table, and there he squatted, his arms folded. He
was a smallish, plumpish man, with self-assertion redolent in every movement he made, every word he ut-

tered. His nose was piglike, his eyes button-black and horribly alert, with enough rings about them to lasso and strangle at birth any idea that he was under fifty. But his nose, which appeared to be no more than a few hours of age, did a great deal in its own porcine way to offset the effect of the rings around the eyes, and to give Perch-Prism, on the balance, an air of youth.

Opus Fluke in his favorite chair: Perch-Prism perched on the table's edge: but the third of these gentlemen in the Common-Room, in contrast to his colleagues, appeared to have something to do. Gazing into a small shaving-mirror on the mantelpiece, with his head on one side to catch what light could force its way through the smoke, Bellgrove was examining his teeth.

He was a fine-looking man in his way. Big of head, his brow and the bridge of his nose descended in a single line of undeniable nobility. His jaw was as long as his brow and nose together and lay exactly parallel in profile to those features. With his leonine shock of snow-white hair there was something of the major prophet about him. But his eyes were disappointing. They made no effort to bear out the promise of the other features, which would have formed the ideal setting for the kind of eye that flashes with visionary fire. Mr. Bellgrove's eyes didn't flash at all. They were rather small, a dreary gray-green in color, and were quite expressionless. Having seen them it was difficult not to bear a grudge against his splendid profile as something fraudulent. His teeth were both carious and uneven and were his worst feature.

With great rapidity Perch-Prism stretched out his arms and legs simultaneously and then withdrew them. At the same time he closed his bright black eyes and yawned as widely as his small, rather prim mouth could manage. Then he clapped his hands beside him on the table, as much as to say: "One can't sit here dreaming all day!" Puckering his brow, he took out a small, elegant, and well-kept pipe (he had long since discovered it as his only defense against the smoke of others) and filled it with quick, deft fingers.

He half-closed his eyes as he lit up, his piglike nose catching the flare of the light on its underside. With his black and cerebral eyes hidden for a moment behind his eyelids, he was less like a man than a ravaged suckling.

He drew quickly three or four times at his pipe. Then, after removing it from his neat little mouth—*"Must* you?" he said, his eyebrows raised.

Opus Fluke, lying along his chair like a stretcher case, moved nothing except his lazy eyes, which he turned slowly until they were semifocusing bemusedly upon Perch-Prism's interrogatory face. But he saw that Perch-Prism had evidently addressed himself to someone else, and Mr. Fluke, rolling his eyes languidly back, was able to obtain an indistinct view of Bellgrove behind him. That august gentleman, who had been examining his teeth with such minute care, frowned magnificently and turned his head.

"Must I *what?* Explain yourself, dear boy. If there's anything I abominate it's sentences of two words. You talk like a fall of crockery, dear boy."

"You're a damned old pedant, Bellgrove, and much overdue for burial," said Perch-Prism, "and as quick off the mark as a pregnant turtle. For pity's sake stop playing with your teeth!"

Opus Fluke in his battered chair dropped his eyes and, by parting his long leather-lipped mouth in a slight upward curve, might have been supposed to be registering a certain sardonic amusement had not a formidable volume of smoke arisen from his lungs and lifted itself out of his mouth and into the air in the shape of a snow-white elm.

Bellgrove turned his back to the mirror and lost sight of himself and his troublesome teeth.

"Perch-Prism," he said, "you're an insufferable upstart. What the hell have my teeth got to do with you? Be good enough to leave them to me, sir."

"Gladly," said Perch-Prism.

"I happen to be in pain, my dear fellow." There was something weaker in Bellgrove's tone.

"You're a hoarder," said Perch-Prism. "You cling to bygone things. They don't suit you, anyway. Get them extracted."

Bellgrove rose into the ponderous prophet category once more. "Never!" he cried, but ruined the majesty of his utterance by clasping at his jaw and moaning pathetically.

"I've no sympathy at all," said Perch-Prism, swinging his legs. "You're a stupid old man, and if you were in my class I would cane you twice a day until you had conquered (one) your crass neglect, (two) your morbid grasp upon putrefaction. I have no sympathy with you."

This time as Opus Fluke threw out his acrid cloud there was an unmistakable grin.

"Poor old bloody Bellgrove," he said. "Poor old Fangs!" And then he began to laugh in a peculiar way of his own which was both violent and soundless. His heavy reclining body, draped in its black gown, heaved to and fro. His knees drew themselves up to his chin. His arms dangled over the sides of the chair and were helpless. His head rolled from side to side. It was as though he were in the last stages of strychnine poisoning. But no sound came, nor did his mouth open. Gradually the spasm grew weaker, and when the natural sand color of his face had returned (for his corked-up laughter had turned it dark red) he began his smoking again in earnest.

Bellgrove took a dignified and ponderous step into the center of the room.

"So I am 'Bloody Bellgrove' to you, am I, Mr. Fluke? That is what you think of me, is it? That is how your crude thoughts run. Aha! . . . aha! . . ." (His attempt to sound as though he were musing philosophically upon Fluke's character was a pathetic failure. He shook his venerable head.) "What a coarse type you are, my friend. You are like an animal—or even a vegetable. Perhaps you have forgotten that as long as fifteen years ago I was considered for Headship. Yes, Mr. Fluke, 'considered.' It was then, I believe, that the tragic mistake was made of your appointment to the staff. H'm . . . Since then· you have been a disgrace, sir—a disgrace for fifteen years—a disgrace to our calling. As for me, unworthy as I am, yet I would have you know that I have more experience behind me than I would care to mention. You're a slacker, sir, a damned slacker! And by your lack of respect for an old scholar you only . . ."

But a fresh twinge of pain caused Bellgrove to grab at his jaw.

"Oh, my *teeth!*" he moaned.

During this harangue Mr. Opus Fluke's mind had wandered. Had he been asked he would have been unable to repeat a single word of what had been addressed to him.

But Perch-Prism's voice cut a path through the thick of his reverie.

"My dear Fluke," it said, "did you, or didn't you, on one of those rare occasions when you saw fit to put in an appearance in a classroom—on this occasion with the Gamma Fifth, I believe—refer to me as a 'bladder-headed cock'? It has come to my hearing that you referred to me as exactly that. Do tell me: it sounds so like you."

Opus Fluke stroked his long, bulging chin with his hand.

"Probably," he said at last, "but I wouldn't know. I never listen." The extraordinary paroxysm began again —the heaving, rolling, helpless, noiseless body-laughter.

"A convenient memory," said Perch-Prism, with a trace of irritability in his clipped, incisive voice. "But what's that?"

He had heard something in the corridor outside. It was like the high, thin, mewing note of a gull. Opus Fluke raised himself on one elbow. The high-pitched noise grew louder. All at once the door was flung open from without and there before them, framed in the doorway, was the Headmaster.

Chapter Eleven

IF ever there was a primogenital figurehead or cipher, that archetype had been resurrected in the shape of Deadyawn. He was pure symbol. By comparison, even Mr. Fluke was a busy man. It was thought that he had genius, if only because he had been able to delegate his duties in so intricate a way that there was never any need for him to do anything at all. His signature, which was necessary from time to time at the end of long notices which no one read, was always faked, and even the ingenious system of delegation whereon his greatness rested was itself worked out by another.

Entering the room immediately behind the Head a tiny freckled man was seen to be propelling Deadyawn forward in a high rickety chair, with wheels attached to its legs. This piece of furniture, which had rather the proportions of an infant's high chair, and was similarly fitted with a tray above which Deadyawn's head could partially be seen, gave fair warning to the scholars and staff of its approach, being in sore need of lubrication. Its wheels screamed.

Deadyawn and the freckled man formed a compelling contrast. There was no reason why they should *both* be human beings. There seemed no common denominator. It was true that they had two legs each, two eyes each, one mouth apiece, and so on, but this did not seem to argue any similarity of *kind,* or if it did only in the way that giraffes and stoats are classified for convenience' sake under the commodious head of "fauna."

Wrapped up like an untidy parcel in a gun-gray gown emblazoned with the signs of the Zodiac in two shades of green, none of which signs could be seen very clearly for reason of the folds and creases, save for Cancer the crab on his left shoulder, was Deadyawn himself, and all but asleep. His feet were tucked beneath him. In his lap was a hot-water bottle.

His face wore the resigned expression of one who knew that the only difference between one day and the next lies in the pages of a calendar.

His hands rested limply on the tray in front of him at the height of his chin. As he entered the room he opened one eye and gazed absently into the smoke. He did not hurry his vision and was quite content when, after several minutes, he made out the three indistinct shapes below him. Those three shapes—Opus Fluke, Perch-Prism, and Bellgrove—were standing in a line, Opus Fluke having fought himself free of his cradle as though struggling against suction. The three gazed up at Deadyawn in his chair.

His face was as soft and round as a dumpling. There seemed to be no structure in it: no indication of a skull beneath the skin.

This unpleasant effect might have argued an equally unpleasant temperament. Luckily this was not so. But it exemplified a parallel bonelessness of outlook. There was no fiber to be found in him, and yet no weakness as such; only a negation of character. For his flaccidity was not a positive thing, unless jellyfish are consciously indolent.

This extreme air of abstraction, of empty and bland removedness, was almost terrifying. It was that kind of unconcern that humbled the ardent, the passionate of nature, and made them wonder why they were expending so much energy of body and spirit when every day but led them to the worms. Deadyawn, by temperament or lack of it, achieved unwittingly what wise men crave: equipoise. In his case an equipoise between two poles which did not exist: but nevertheless there he was, balanced on an imaginary fulcrum.

The freckled man had rolled the high chair to the center of the room. His skin stretched so tightly over his small bony and rather insectlike face that the freckles were twice the size they would normally have been. He was minute, and as he peered perkily from behind the legs of the high chair, his carrot-colored hair shone with hair oil. It was brushed flat across the top of his little bony insect-head. On all sides the walls of horsehide rose into the smoke and smelled perceptibly. A few drawing-pins glimmered against the murky brown leather.

Deadyawn dropped one of his arms over the side of the high chair and wriggled a languid forefinger. "The Fly" (as the freckled midget was called) pulled a piece of paper out of his pocket, but instead of passing it up to the Headmaster he climbed, with extraordinary agility, up a dozen rungs of the chair and cried into Deadyawn's ear: "Not yet! Not yet! Only three of them here!"

"What's that?" said Deadyawn, in a voice of emptiness.

"Only three of them here!"

"Which ones?" said Deadyawn, after a long silence.

"Bellgrove, Perch-Prism, and Fluke," said The Fly in his penetrating, flylike voice. He winked at the three gentlemen through the smoke.

"Won't *they* do?" murmured Deadyawn, his eyes shut. "They're on my staff, aren't . . . they . . .?"

"Very much so," said The Fly, "very much so. But your Edict, sir, is addressed to the whole staff."

"I've forgotten what it's all about. Remind . . . me. . . ."

"It's all written down," said The Fly. "I have it here, sir. All you have to do is to read it, sir." And again the small redheaded man honored the three masters with a particularly intimate wink. There was something lewd in the way the wax-colored petal of his eyelid dropped suggestively over his bright eye and lifted itself again without a flutter.

"You can give it to Bellgrove. He will read it when the time comes," said Deadyawn, lifting his hanging hand onto the tray before him and languidly stroking the hot-water bottle. ". . . Find out what's keeping them."

The Fly pattered down the rungs of the chair and emerged from its shadow. He crossed the room with quick, impudent steps, his head and rump well back. But before he reached the door it had opened and two

Professors had entered—one of them, Flannelcat, with his arms full of exercise books and his mouth full of seedcake, and his companion, Shred, with nothing in his arms, but with his head full of theories about everyone's subconscious except his own. He had a friend, by name Shrivell, due to arrive at any moment, who, in contrast to Shred, was stiff with theories about his own subconscious and no one else's.

Flannelcat took his work seriously and was always worried. He had a poor time from the boys and a poor time from his colleagues. A high proportion of the work he did was never noticed, but do it he must. He had a sense of duty that was rapidly turning him into a sick man. The pitiful expression of reproach which never left his face testified to his zeal. He was always too late to find a vacant chair in the Common-Room, and always too early to find his class assembled. He was continually finding the arms of his gown tied into knots when he was in a hurry, and that pieces of soap were substituted for his cheese at the masters' table. He had no idea who did these things, nor any idea how they could be circumvented. Today, as he entered the Common-Room, with his arms full of books and the seedcake in his mouth, he was in as much of a fluster as usual. His state of mind was not improved by finding the Headmaster looming above him like Jove among the clouds. In his confusion the seedcake got into his windpipe, the concertina of schoolbooks in his arms began to slip and, with a loud crash, cascaded to the floor. In the silence that followed there was a moan of pain, but it was only Bellgrove with his hands at his jaw. His noble head was rolling from side to side.

Shred ambled forward from the door and, after bowing slightly in Deadyawn's direction, he buttonholed Bellgrove.

"In pain, my dear Bellgrove? In pain?" he inquired, but in a hard, irritating, inquisitive voice—with as much sympathy in it as might be found in a vampire's breast.

Bellgrove bridled up his lordly head, but did not deign to reply.

"Let us take it that you *are* in pain," continued Shred.

"Let us work on that hypothesis as a basis: that Bell-grove, a man of somewhere between sixty and eighty, is in pain. Or rather, that he *thinks* he is. One must be exact. As a man of science, I insist on exactitude. Well, then, what next? Why, to take into account that Bell-grove, supposedly in pain, also thinks that the pain has something to do with his teeth. This is absurd, of course, but must, I say, be taken into account. For what reason? Because they are symbolic. Everything is symbolic. There is no such thing as a 'thing' per se. It is only a symbol of something else that is itself, and so on. To my way of thinking his teeth, though apparently rotten, are merely the symbol of a diseased mind."

Bellgrove snarled.

"And why is the mind diseased?" He took hold of Bellgrove's gown just below that gentleman's left shoulder and, with his face raised, scrutinized the big head above him.

"Your mouth is twitching," he said. "Interesting . . . very . . . interesting. You probably do not know it, but there was bad blood in your mother. Very bad blood. Or alternatively, you dream of stoats. But no matter, no matter. To return. Where were we? Yes, yes, your teeth —the symbols, we have said, haven't we?—of a diseased mind. Now what *kind* of disease? That is the point. What *kind* of disease of the mind would affect your teeth like this? Open your mouth, sir. . . ."

But Bellgrove, a fresh twinge undermining his scant reserves of patience and decorum, lifted his huge boot the size of a tray and brought it down with a blind relish upon Mr. Shred's feet. It covered them both and must have been excruciatingly painful, for Mr. Shred's brow colored and contracted; but he made no sound save to remark, "Interesting, very interesting . . . probably your mother."

Opus Fluke's body-laughter did everything except break him in half or find vent in a sound.

By now several other Professors had infiltrated through the smoke from the direction of the door. There was Shrivell, Shred's friend, or follower, for he held all

Shred's opinions in the reverse direction. But for sheer discipleship Mr. Shrivell was a rebel compared to the three gentlemen who, moving in a solid huddle, their three mortarboards forming between them a practically unbroken surface, had seated themselves in a far corner, like conspirators. They owed allegiance, those three, to no member of the staff, or to any such abstraction as the "staff" itself, but to an ancient savant, a bearded figure of no specific occupation, but whose view of Death, Eternity, Pain (and its nonexistence), Truth, or, indeed, anything of a philosophic nature, was like fire in their ears.

In holding the views of their Master on such enormous themes they had developed a fear of their colleagues and a prickliness of disposition which, as Perch-Prism had cruelly pointed out to them more than once, was inconsistent with their theory of nonexistence. "Why are you so prickly," he used to say, "when there ain't no pain or prickles?" At which the three, Spiregrain, Splint, and Throd, would all at once become a single black tent as they shot into conference with the speed of suction. How they longed at times for their bearded Leader to be with them! He knew all the answers to impertinent questions.

They were unhappy men, these three. Not with native melancholy, but in views of their theories. And there they sat: the smoke wreaths coiling round them, their eyes moving suspiciously from one face to another of their heretic brethren, in jealous fear of a challenge to their faith.

Who else had entered? Only Cutflower, the dandy; Crust, the sponger; and the choleric Mulefire.

Meanwhile The Fly had been standing in the corridor with his knuckles between his teeth, and had been emitting the shrillest of whistles. Whether they caused the sudden appearance of the few stragglers at the end of the corridor or whether these characters were in any case on their way to the Common-Room, there was no doubt that The Fly's shrill music added speed to their steps.

Hammelcat

Crust

Smoke hung above them as they approached the door, for they had no desire to enter Fluke's fug, as they called it, with virgin lungs.

"The 'Yawner's' here," said The Fly as the Professors came abreast, their gowns fluttering. A dozen eyebrows were raised. It was seldom that they saw the Headmaster.

When the door was closed upon the last of them the Leather Room was, indeed, no place for anyone with asthma. No flowers could flourish there unless, indeed, some gaunt and horny thing—some cactus long inured to dust and thirst. No singing birds could thrive—no, not the raven, even; for smoke would fill their thin, sweet wind-pipes. It knew nothing, this atmosphere, of fragrant pastures—of dawn among the dew-bright hazel woods—or rivulets or starlight. It was a leather cave of sepia fog.

The Fly, his sharp insect face hardly visible through the smoke, swarmed up the high chair, hand over hand, and found Deadyawn asleep and his water bottle stone cold. He prodded the Headmaster in the ribs with his little bony thumb just where Taurus and Scorpio were overlapping. Deadyawn's head had sunk even lower during his sleep and was barely above the tray. His feet were still tucked under him. He was like some creature that had lost its shell, for his face was disgustingly naked. Naked not only physically, but naked in its vacancy.

At The Fly's prod he did not wake with a start, as is the normal thing: that would have been tantamount to a kind of interest in life. He merely opened one eye. Moving it from The Fly's face, he let it wander over the miscellany of gownsmen below him.

He closed his eye again. "What . . . are . . . all . . . these . . . people . . . for?" His voice floated out of his soft head like a paper streamer. "And why am I?" he added.

"It's all very necessary," answered The Fly. "Shall I remind you, sir, yet again of Barquentine's Notice?"

"Why not?" said Deadyawn. "But not too loudly."

"Or shall Bellgrove read it out, sir?"

"Why not?" said the Headmaster. "But get my bottle filled first."

The Fly climbed down the chair rungs with the cold bottle and threaded his perky way through the group of masters to the door. Before he reached it he had, aided by the poor visibility in the room, but mainly by the exceptional agility of his small thin fingers, relieved Flannelcat of an old gold watch and chain, Mr. Shred of several coins, and Cutflower of an embroidered handkerchief.

When he returned with the hot-water bottle, Deadyawn was asleep again, but The Fly handed Bellgrove a roll of paper before he climbed up the wheeled chair to waken the Headmaster.

"Read it," said The Fly. "It's from Barquentine."

"Why *me?*" said Bellgrove, his hand at his jaw. "Damn Barquentine with his notices! Damn him, I say!"

He untied the roll of paper and took a few heavy paces to the window, where he held it up to what light there was.

The Professors were by then sitting on the floor, in groups or singly, like Flannelcat among the cold ashes under the mantelpiece. But for a lack of wigwams, squaws, feathers, and tomahawks there might have been a tribe encamped beneath the hanging smoke.

"Come along, Bellgrove! Come along, man!" said Perch-Prism. "Get those teeth of yours into it."

"For a classical scholar," said the irritating Shred, "for a classical scholar, I have always felt that Bellgrove must be handicapped, grievously handicapped, firstly by the difficulty he finds in understanding sentences of more than seven words, and secondly by the stultifying effect on his mind of a frustrated-power complex."

A snarl was heard through the smoke.

"Is *that* what it is? Is *that* what it is? La!"

This was Cutflower's voice. It came from the near end of the long table on which he sat, dangling his thin, elegant legs. There was so high a polish upon his narrow, pointed shoes that the highlights of the toecaps were visible through the smoke, like torches through a fog. No other sign of feet had been seen in the room for half an hour.

"Bellgrove," he continued, taking up where Perch-Prism had left off, "stab away, man! Stab away! Give us the gist of it, la! Give us the gist of it. Can't he *read,* la, the old fraud?"

"Is that you, Cutflower?" said another voice. "I've been looking for you all morning. Bless my heart! what a fine polish on your shoes, Cutflower! I wondered what the devil those lights were! But seriously, I'm very embarrassed, Cutflower. Indeed I am. It's my wife in exile, you know—ragingly ill. But what can I do, spendthrift that I am, with my bar of chocolate once a week? You see how it is, my dear chap; it's the. end: or almost: unless . . . I half-wondered—er—*could* you . . .? Something until Tuesday . . . Confidential, you know, ha . . . ha . . . ha . . . ! How one hates asking . . . squalor, and so on. . . . But seriously, Cutflower (what a dazzling pair of hoofs, old man!), but seriously, if you could manage . . ."

"Silence!" shouted The Fly, interrupting Crust, who had not realized he had been sitting so close to a colleague until he heard Cutflower's affected accents beside him. Everyone knew that Crust had no wife in exile, ill or otherwise. They also knew that his endless requests were not so much because he was poverty-stricken but were made in the desire to cut a dashing figure. To have a wife in exile who was dying in unthinkable pain appeared to Crust to give him a kind of romantic status. It was not sympathy he wanted but envy. Without an exiled and guttering mate what was he? Just Crust. That was all. Crust to his colleagues and Crust to himself. Something of five letters that walked on two legs.

But Cutflower, taking advantage of the smoke, had slipped from the table. He took a few dainty steps to his left and tripped over Mulefire's outstretched leg.

"May Satan thrash you purple!" roared an ugly voice from the floor. "Curse your stinking feet, whoever you bloody are!"

"Poor old Mulefire! Poor old hog!" It was yet another voice, a more familiar one; and then there was the sense of something rocking uncontrollably, but there was no accompanying sound.

Flannelcat was biting at his underlip. He was overdue for his class. They were all overdue. But none save Flannelcat was perturbed on that score. Flannel knew that by now the classroom ceiling would be blue with ink: that the small bow-legged boy, Smattering, would be rolling beneath his desk in a convulsion of excited ribaldry: that catapults would be twanging freely from every wooden ambush, and stink-bombs making of his room a nauseous hell. He knew all this and he could do nothing. The rest of the staff knew all this also, but had no desire to do anything.

A voice out of the pall cried, "Silence, gentlemen, for Mr. Bellgrove!" and another, "Oh, hell, my teeth! my teeth!" and another, "If only he didn't dream of stoats!" and another: "Where's my gold watch gone to?" and then The Fly again: "Silence, gentlemen! Silence for Bellgrove! Are you ready, sir?" The Fly peered into Deadyawn's vacant face.

In reply Deadyawn answered: "Why . . . not?" with a peculiarly long interval between the "Why" and the "not."

Bellgrove read:

Edict 15975773615443296217707193

To Deadyawn, Headmaster, and to the Gentlemen of the Professorial Staff: to all Ushers, Curators, and others in authority—

This———day of the ——th month in the eighth year of the Seventy-Seventh Earl, to wit: Titus, Lord of Gormenghast—Notice and warning is given in regard to their attitude, treatment, and methods of behavior and approach in respect of the aforementioned Earl, who now at the threshold of the age of reason, may impress Headmaster, Gentlemen of the Professorial staff, Ushers, Curators, and the like, with the implications of his lineage to the extent of diverting these persons from their duty in regard to the immemorial law which governs the attitude which Deadyawn, etc., are strictly bound to show, inasmuch that they treat the Seventy-Seventh Earl in every

*particular and on every occasion as they would treat
any other minor in their hands without let or favor: that
a sense of the customs, traditions, and observances—and
above all, a sense of the duties attached to every branch
of the castle's life—be instilled and an indelible sense of
the responsibilities which will become his when he attains
his majority, at which time, with his formative years
spent among the riffraff of the castle's youth, it is to
be supposed that the Seventy-Seventh Earl will not only
have developed an adroitness of mind, a knowledge of
human nature, a certain stamina, but in addition a degree
of learning dependent upon the exertions which you,
Sir, Headmaster, and you, Sirs, Gentlemen of the Professorial staff, bring to bear, which is your bounden duty,
to say nothing of the privilege and honor which it represents.*

*All this, Sirs, is, or should be, common knowledge to
you, but the Seventy-Seventh Earl now being in his eighth
year, I have seen fit to reawaken you to your responsibilities, in my capacity as Master of Ritual, etc., in which
capacity I have the authority to make appearances at
any moment in any classroom I choose in order to acquaint
myself with the way in which your various knowledge is
inculcated, and with particular regard to its effect upon
the progress of the young Earl.*

*Deadyawn, Sir, I would have you impress your staff
with the magnitude of their office, and in particular . . .*

But Bellgrove, his jaw suddenly hammering away as
upon a white-hot anvil, flung the parchment from him
and sank to his knees with a howl of pain which awoke
Deadyawn to such a degree that he opened *both* his eyes.

"What was that?" said Deadyawn to The Fly.

"Bellgrove in pain," said the midget. "Shall I finish the
notice?"

"Why not?" said Deadyawn.

The paper was passed up to The Fly by Flannelcat,
who had scrambled nervously out of the ashes, and was
already imagining Barquentine in his classroom and the
dirty liquid eyes of that one-legged creature fixed upon

the ink that was even now trickling down the leather walls.

The Fly plucked the paper from Flannelcat's hand and continued, after a preparatory whistle effected through a collusion of the knuckles, lips, and windpipe. So shrill was the sound of it that the recumbent staff were jolted upright on their haunches as one man. The Fly read quickly, one word running into the next, and finished Barquentine's edict almost at a single breath.

. . . would have you impress your Staff with the magnitude of their office, and in particular those members who confuse the ritual of their calling with mere habit, making of themselves obnoxious limpets upon the living rock; or, like vile bindweed round a breathing stem, stifle the castle's breath.

Signed (as for) Burquentine, Master of Ritual, Keeper of the Observances, and Hereditary Overlord of 'the Manuscripts by

Steerpike (Amanuensis).

Someone had lit a lantern. It did very little, as it stood on the table, but illumine with a dusky glow the breast of the stuffed cormorant. There was something disgraceful about its necessity at noon in summertime.

"If ever there was an obnoxious limpet swaddled in bindweed you are that limpet, my friend," said Perch-Prism to Bellgrove. "Do you realize that the whole thing was addressed to you? You've gone too far for an old man. Far too far. What will you do when they remove you, friend? Where will you go? Have you anyone that loves you?"

"Oh, rotten hell!" shouted Bellgrove, in so loud and uncontrolled a voice that even Deadyawn smiled. It was perhaps the faintest, wannest smile that ever agitated for a moment the lower half of a human face. The eyes took no part in it. They were as vacant as saucers of milk; but one end of the mouth lifted as might the cold lip of a trout.

"Mr. . . . Fly . . . ," said the Headmaster in a voice as far away as the ghost of his vanished smile. "Mr. . . . Fly . . . you . . . virus, where . . . are . . . you?"

"Sir?" said The Fly.

"Was . . . that . . . Bellgrove?"

"It was, sir," said The Fly.

"And . . . how . . . is . . . he . . . these . . . days?"

"He is in pain," said The Fly.

"Deep . . . pain . . . ?"

"Shall I inquire, sir?" said The Fly.

"Why . . . not . . . ?"

"Bellgrove!" shouted The Fly.

"What is it, damn you?" said Bellgrove.

"The Head is inquiring about your health."

"About mine?" said Bellgrove.

"About *yours*," said The Fly.

"Sir?" queried Bellgrove, peering in the direction of the voice.

"Come . . . nearer . . . ," said Deadyawn. "I . . . can't . . . see . . . you, . . . my . . . poor . . . friend."

"Nor I you, sir."

"Put . . . out . . . your . . . hand, . . . Bellgrove. Can . . . you . . . feel . . . anything?"

"Is this your foot, sir?"

"It . . . is . . . indeed, . . . my . . . poor . . . friend."

"Quite so, sir," said Bellgrove.

"Now . . . tell . . . me, . . . Bellgrove, . . . tell . . . me . . ."

"Yes, sir?"

"Are . . . you . . . unwell, . . . my . . . poor . . . friend?"

"Localized pain, sir."

"Would . . . it . . . be . . . the . . . mandibles . . . ?"

"That is so, sir."

"As . . . in . . . the . . . old . . . days . . . when . . . you . . . were . . . ambitious. . . . When . . . you . . . had . . . ideals, . . . Bellgrove. . . . We . . . all . . . had . . . hopes . . . of . . . you, . . . I . . . seem . . . to . . . remember." (There was a horrible sound of laughter like porridge.)

"Indeed, sir."

"Does . . . anyone . . . still . . . believe . . . in . . . you, . . . my . . . poor, . . . poor . . . friend?"

There was no answer.

"Come, . . . come. It is not for you to resent your destiny. To . . . cavil . . . at . . . the . . . sere . . . and . . . yellow . . . leaf. Oh . . . no, . . . my . . . poor . . . Bellgrove, . . . you . . . have . . . ripened. Perhaps . . . you . . . have . . . overripened. Who . . . knows? We . . . all . . . go . . . bad . . . in . . . time. Do . . . you . . . look . . . about . . . the . . . same, . . . my . . . friend?"

"I don't know," said Bellgrove.

"I . . . am . . . tired," said Deadyawn. "What . . . am . . . I . . . doing . . . here? Where's . . . that . . . virus . . . Mr . . . Fly?"

"Sir!" came the musket shot.

"Get . . . me . . . out . . . of . . . this. Wheel . . . me . . . out . . . of . . . it . . . into stillness, . . . Mr. . . . Fly. . . . Wheel . . . me . . . into . . . the . . . soft . . . darkness. . . ." (His voice lifted into a ghastly treble, which though it was still empty and flat had in it the seeds of life. "Wheel . . . me . . ." (it cried) "into . . . the . . . golden . . . void."

"Right away, sir," said The Fly.

All at once it seemed as though the Professors' Common-Room was full of ravenous sea gulls, but the screaming came from the unoiled wheels of the high chair, which were slowly turning. The door handle was located by Flannelcat after a few moments' fumbling and the door was pushed wide. A glow of light could be seen in the passage outside. Against this light the smoke wreaths coiled, and a little later the high, fantastic silhouette of Deadyawn, like a sack at the apex of the rickety high chair, made its creaking departure from the room like some high, black form of scaffolding with a life of its own.

The scream of the wheels grew fainter and fainter.

It was some while before the silence was broken. None present had heard that high note in the Headmaster's voice before. It had chilled them. Nor had they ever heard him at such length, or in so mystical a vein. It was horrible to think that there was more to him than the nullity which they had so long accepted. However, a voice did at last break the pensive silence.

"A very dry 'do' indeed," said Crust.

"Some kind of light, for grief's sake!" shouted Perch-Prism.

"What *can* the time be?" whimpered Flannelcat.

Someone had started a fire in the grate, using for tinder a number of Flannelcat's copybooks, which he had been unable to collect from the floor. The globe of the world was put on top, which, being of some light wood, gave within a few minutes an excellent light, great continents peeling off and oceans bubbling. The memorandum that Slypate was to be caned, which had been chalked across the colored face, was purged away and with it the boy's punishment, for Mulefire never remembered and Slypate never reminded him.

"My, my!" said Cutflower. "If the Head's subconscious ain't self-conscious call me purblind, la! . . . Call me purblind! What goings-on, la!"

"What is the time, gentlemen? What can it be, if you please?" said Flannelcat, groping for his exercise books on the floor. The scene had unnerved him, and what books he had recovered from the floor kept falling out of his arms.

Mr. Shrivell pulled one of them out of the fire and, holding it by a flameless corner, waved it for a moment before the clock.

"Forty minutes to go," he said. "Hardly worth it . . . or is it? Personally, I think I'll just . . ."

"So will I, la!" cried Cutflower. "If my class isn't either on fire by now or flooded out, call me witless, la!"

The same idea must have been at the back of most of their minds, for there was a general movement toward the door, only Opus Fluke remaining in his decrepit armchair, his loaflike chin directed at the ceiling, his eyes closed, and his leathery mouth describing a line as fatuous as it was indolent. A few moments later the husky, whispering sound of a score of flying gowns as they whisked along the walls of corridors presaged the turning of a score of door handles and the entry into their respective classrooms of the Professors of Gormenghast.

Chapter Twelve

A ROOF of cloud stretching to every horizon held the air motionless beneath it, as though the earth and sky, pressing toward one another, had squeezed away its breath. Below the cruddled underside of the unbroken cloud-roof the air, through some peculiar trick of light, which had something of an underwater feeling about it, reflected enough of itself from the gaunt back of Gormenghast to make the herons restive as they stood and shivered on a long-abandoned pavement half in and half out of the clouds.

The stone stairway which led up to this pavement was lost beneath a hundred seasons of obliterating ivy, creepers, and strangling weeds. No one alive had ever struck their heels into the great cushions of black moss that pranked the pavement or wandered along its turreted verge, where the herons were and the jackdaws fought, and the sun's rays, and the rain, the frost, the snow, and the winds took their despoiling turns.

There had once been a great casement facing upon this terrace. It was gone. Neither broken glass nor iron nor rotten wood was anywhere to be seen. Beneath the moss and ground creepers it may be that there were other and deeper layers, rotten with antiquity; but where the long window had stood the hollow darkness of a hall remained. It opened its unprotected mouth midway along the pavement's inner verge. On either side of this cavernous opening, widely separated, were the

raw holes in the stonework that were once the supporting windows. The hall itself was solemn with herons. It
was there they bred and tended their young. Preponderate-
ly a heronry, yet there were recesses and niches in
which by sacredness of custom the egrets and bitterns
congregated.

This hall, where once the lovers of a bygone time
paced and paused and turned one about another in forgotten measures to the sound of forgotten music, this
hall was carpeted with lime-white sticks. Sometimes the
setting sun as it neared the horizon slanted its rays into
the hall, and as they skimmed the rough nests the
white network of the branches flared on the floor like
leprous corals, and here and there (if it were spring) a
pale blue-green egg shone like a precious stone; or a nest
of young, craning their long necks toward the window,
their thin bodies covered with powder-down, seemed
stage-lit in the beams of the westering sun.

The late sunbeams shifted across the ragged floor and
picked out the long, lustrous feathers that hung from the
throat of a heron that stood by a rotten mantelpiece;
and then a whiteness once more as the forehead of an
adjacent bird flamed in the shadows . . . and then, as
the light traversed the hall, an alcove was suddenly dancing with the varied bars and blotches and the reddish-yel-
low of the bitterns.

As dusk fell, the greenish light intensified in the masonry. Far away, over the roofs, over the Outer Wall of
Gormenghast, over the marshes, the wasteland, the river,
and the foothills with their woods and spinneys, and
over the distant hazes of indeterminate terrain, the
claw-shaped head of Gormenghast Mountain shone like
a jade carving. In the green air the herons awoke from
their trances and from within the hall there came the
peculiar chattering and clanking sound of the young
as they saw the darkness deepening and knew that it
would soon be time for their parents to go hunting.

Crowded as they had been in their heronry with its
domed roof—once golden and green with a painting,
but now a dark, disintegrating surface where flakes of

paint hung like the wings of moths—yet each bird appeared as a solitary figure as it stepped from the hall to the terrace: each heron, each bittern, a recluse, pacing solemnly forward on its thin, stiltlike legs.

Of a sudden, the dusk knocking as it were a certain hollow note to which their sweet ribs echoed, they were in air—a group of herons, their necks arched back, their ample and rounded wings rising and falling in leisurely flight: and then another and another: and then a night-heron with a ghastly and hair-raising croak, more terrible than the unearthly booming note of a pair of bitterns who, soaring and spiraling upward and through the clouds to great heights above Gormenghast, boomed like bulls as they ascended. The pavement stretched away in greenish darkness. The windows gaped, but nothing moved that was not feathered. And nothing had moved there, save the winds, the hailstones, the clouds, the rain water, and the birds for a hundred years.

Under the high green claw-head of Gormenghast Mountain the wide stretches of marshland had suddenly become stretches of tension, of watchfulness.

Each in its own hereditary tract of water the birds stood motionless, with glistening eyes and heads drawn back for the fatal stroke of the daggerlike beak. Suddenly and all in a breath, a beak was plunged and withdrawn from the dark water, and at its lethal point there struggled a fish. In another moment the heron was mounted aloft in august and solemn flight.

From time to time during the long night these birds returned, sometimes with frogs or water mice in their beaks or newts or lily buds.

But now the terrace was empty. On the marshlands every heron was in its place, immobile, ready to plunge its knife. In the hall the nestlings were, for the moment, strangely still.

The dead quality of the air between the clouds and the earth was strangely portentous. The green, penumbral light played over all things. It had crept into the open mouth of the hall where the silence was.

It was then that a child appeared. Whether a boy or a

girl or an elf there was not time to tell. But the delicate proportions were a child's and the vitality was a child's alone. For one short moment it had stood on a turret at the far end of the terrace and then it was gone, leaving only the impression of something overcharged with life—of something slight as a hazel switch. It had hopped (for the movement was more a hop than a leap or a step) from the turret into the darkness beyond and was gone almost as soon as it had appeared, but at the same moment that the phantom child appeared, a zephyr had broken through the wall of moribund air and run like a gay and tameless thing over the gaunt, harsh spine of Gormenghast's body. It played with sere flags, dodged through arches, spiraled with impish whistles up hollow towers and chimneys, until, diving down a saw-toothed fissure in a pentagonal roof, it found itself surrounded by stern portraits—a hundred sepia faces cracked with spiders' webs; found itself being drawn toward a grid in the stone floor and, giving way to itself, to the law of gravity, and to the blue thrill of a down-draft, it sang its way past seven storeys and was, all at once, in a hall of dove-gray light and was clasping Titus in a noose of air.

Chapter Thirteen

❋❋❋❋❋❋❋❋❋❋❋

THE old, old man in whose metaphysical net the three disciples, Spiregrain, Throd, and Splint, were so irrevocably tangled, leaned forward in space as though weighing on the phantom handle of an invisible stick. It was a wonder he did not fall on his face.

"Always drafty in this reach of the corridor," he said, his white hair hanging forward over his shoulders. He struck his thighs with his hands before replacing them at a point in space where a stick would have been. "Breaks

a man up—wrecks him—makes a shadow of him—
throws him to the wolves and screws his coffin down."

Reaching down with his long arms, he drew his thick
socks over the ends of his trousers and then stamped
his feet, straightened his back, doubled it forward again,
and then threw a look of antagonism along the corridor.

"A dirty, drafty reach. No reason for it. Scuppers a
man," he said. "And yet"—he shook his white locks—"it
isn't true, you know. I don't believe in drafts. I don't believe I'm cold. I don't believe in anything! ha, ha, ha, ha,
ha! I can't agree with you, for instance."

His companion, a younger man, with long, hollow
cheeks, cocked his head as though it were the breech of
a gun. Then he raised his eyebrow as much as to say,
"Carry on . . . ," but the old man remained silent. Then
the young man raised his voice as though he were raising
the dead, for it was a singularly flat and colorless affair.

"How do you mean, sir, that you can't agree?"

"I just can't," said the old man, bending forward, his
hands gripped before him, "that's all."

The young man righted his head and dropped his eyebrow.

"But I haven't *said* anything yet: we've only just met,
you know."

"You may be right," replied the old man, stroking his
beard. "You may very well be right; I can't say."

"But I tell you I haven't *spoken!*" The colorless voice
was raised, and the young man's eyes made a tremendous
effort to flash; but either the tinder was wet or the
updraft insufficient, for they remained peculiarly spark-
less.

"I haven't *spoken,*" he repeated.

"Oh, *that!*" said the old man. "I don't need to depend
on that." He gave a low, horribly knowledgeable laugh.
"I can't agree, that's all. With your face, for instance.
It's wrong—like everything else. Life is so simple when
you see it that way—ha, ha, ha, ha!" The low, in-
testinal enjoyment which he got out of his attitude to
life was frightful to the young man, who, ignoring his own

nature, his melancholy, ineffectual face, his white voice, his lightless eyes, became angry.

"And *I* don't agree with *you!*" he shouted. "I don't agree with the way you bend your ghastly old knacker's-yard of a body at such an absurd angle. I don't agree with the way your white beard hangs from your chin like dirty seaweed. . . . I don't agree with your broken teeth. . . . I . . ."

The old man was delighted; his stomach laughter crackled on and on. "But nor do *I,* young man," he wheezed. "Nor do I. I don't agree with it, either. You see, I don't even agree that I'm here; and even if I did I wouldn't agree that I ought to be. The whole thing is ridiculously simple."

"You're being cynical!" cried the young man; "so you are!"

"Oh, no," said the old man with short legs. "I don't believe in being anything. If only people would stop trying to *be* things! What *can* they be, after all, beyond what they already are—or would be if I believed that they were anything?"

"Vile! Vile! VILE!" shouted the young man with hollow cheeks. His thwarted passions had found vent after thirty years of indecision. "Surely we have long enough in the grave, you old beast, in which to be *nothing*—in which to be cold and finished with! Must life be like that, too? No, no! let us burn!" he cried. "Let us burn our blood away in life's high bonfire!"

But the old philosopher replied: "The grave, young man, is not what you imagine. You insult the dead, young man. With every reckless word, you smirch a tomb, deface a sepulcher, disturb with clumsy boots the humble death-mound. For death is life. It is only living that is lifeless. Have you not seen them coming over the hills at dusk, the angels of eternity? Have you not?"

"No," said the young man, "I haven't!"

The bearded figure leaned even farther forward and fixed the young man with his gaze.

"What! you have never seen the angels of eternity, with their wings as big as blankets?"

"No," said the young man. "And I don't want to."

"To the ignorant nothing is profound," said the bearded ancient. "You called me a cynic. How can I be? I am nothing. The greater contains the less. But this I will tell you: though the castle is a barren image—though green trees, bursting with life, are in reality bursting for lack of it—when the April lamb is realized to be nothing more nor less than a lamb in April—when these things are known and accepted, then, oh, it is then"—he was stroking his beard very fast by this time—"that you are on the borderland of Death's amazing kingdom, where everything moves twice as fast, and the colors are twice as bright, and love is twice as gorgeous, and sin is twice as spicy. Who but the doubly purblind can fail to see that it is only on the Other Side that one can begin to Agree? But here, here"—he motioned with his hands as though to dismiss the terrestrial world—"what is there to agree *with?* There is no sensation here, no sensation at all."

"There is joy and pain," said the young man.

"No, no, no. Pure illusion," said the ancient. "But in Death's amazing kingdom Joy is unconfined. It will be nothing to dance for a month on end in the celestial pastures . . . nothing at all. Or to sing as one flies astride a burning eagle . . . to sing out of the gladness of one's breast."

"And what of pain?" said the youth.

"We have invented the idea of pain in order to indulge ourselves in self-pity," was the reply. "But Real Pain, as we have it on the Other Side, that *will* be worth having. It will be an experience to burn one's finger in the Kingdom."

"What if *I* set fire to your white beard, you old fraud!" shouted the young man, who had stubbed his toes during the day and knew the validity of the earthly discomforts.

"What if you did, my child?"

"It would sting your jaw, and you know it!" cried the youth.

The supercilious smile which played across the lips of the theorist was unbearable, and his companion had no strength to stop himself as he stretched out his arm for the nearest candle and lit the beard that hung there like a challenge. It flared up quickly and gave to the horrified and astonished expression of the old man an unreal and theatrical quality which belied the very real pain, terrestrial though it was, which he felt, first of all, against his jaw, and then along the sides of his head.

A shrill and terrible scream from his old throat, and the corridor was at once filled with figures, as though they had been awaiting their entrance cues. Coats were thrown over his head and shoulders and the flames stifled, but not before the excited youth with the hollow cheeks had made his escape, never to be heard of again.

Spiregrain, Throd, and Splint

The old man was carried to his room, a small dark-red box of a place, with no carpet on the floor, but a picture over the mantelpiece of a fairy sitting in a buttercup against a very blue sky. After three days he recovered consciousness only to die of shock a moment later when he remembered what had happened.

Among those present at the deathbed in the small red room were the three friends of the old fire-blackened pedagogue.

They stood in a line, stooping a little, for the room was very low. They were standing unnecessarily close to one another for, with the slightest movement of their heads, their old black leather mortarboards struck against one another and were tilted indecorously.

And yet it was a moving moment. They could feel the exodus of a great source of inspiration. Their master lay dying below them. Disciples to the end, they believed in the absence of physical emotion so implicitly, that when the master died what could they do but weep that the origin of their faith was gone forever from them?

Under their black leather mortarboards their heads dislodged the innocent air, remorselessly as though their brows, noses, and jaws, like the features of a figurehead, were cleaving paths for them through viewless water. Only in their hanging gowns, their flat leather mortarboards, and the tassels that hung like the grizzly spilths that swing from turkeys' beaks, had they anything in common.

Flanking the deathbed was a low table. On it stood a small prism and a brandy bottle which held a lighted candle. This was the only illumination in the room, yet the red walls burned with a somber effulgence. The three heads of the Professors, which were roughly at the same height from the ground, were so different as to make one wonder whether they were of the same genus. In running the eye from one face to the next, a similar sensation was experienced as when the hand is run from glass to sandpaper, from sandpaper to porridge. The sandpaper face was neither more nor less interesting than the glass one, but the eyes were forced to move slowly over a surface so roughened with undergrowth, so dangerous with its potholes and bony outcrops, its silted gullies and thorny wastes, that it was a wonder that any eye ever reached the other side.

Conversely, with the glassy face, it was all that an eye could do to keep from sliding off it.

As for the third visage, it was neither maddeningly slippery, nor rough with broken ravines and clinging groundweed. To traverse it with a sweep of the eye was as impossible as to move gradually across the glazed face.

It was a case of slow wading. The face was wet. It was always wet. It was a face seen under water. And so for an eye to take an innocent run across these *three,* there lay ahead this strange ordeal, by rock and undergrowth, by slippery ice and by a patient paddling.

Behind them on the red wall their shadows lay, about half as big again as the Professors themselves.

The glassy one (Professor Spiregrain) bent his head over the body of his dead master. His face seemed to be lit from within by a murky light. There was nothing spiritual about its lambency. The hard glass nose was long and exceptionally sharp. To have said he was well shaved would give no idea of a surface that no hair could penetrate, any more than a glacier could sprout grass.

Following his example, Professor Throd lowered *his* head likewise: its features were blurred into the main mass of the head. Eyes, nose, and mouth were mere irregularities beneath the moisture.

As for the third Professor, Splint, when he, following the example of his colleagues, bent his head over the candlelit corpse, it was as though a rocky and barbarous landscape had suddenly changed its angle in space. Had a cloud of snakes and parrots been flung out thereby on to the candle-bright sheets of the deathbed, it would have seemed natural enough.

It was not long before Spiregrain, Throd, and the jungle-headed Mr. Splint became tired of bending mutely over their master, who was, in any case, no pleasant sight even for the most zealous of disciples, and they straightened themselves.

The small red room had become oppressive. The candle was getting very low in the brandy bottle. The fairy in the buttercup over the mantelpiece smirked in the flickering light, and it was time to go.

There was nothing they could do. Their master was dead.

Said Throd of the wet face: "It is a grief's gravy, Spiregrain."

Said Spiregrain of the slippery head: "You are too crude, my friend. Have you no poetry in you? It is death's icicle impales him now."

"Nonsense," whispered Splint, in a fierce, surly voice. He was really very gentle, in spite of his tropical face—but he became angry when he felt his more brilliant colleagues were simply indulging themselves. "Nonsense. Neither icicle nor gravy it was. Straightforward fire, it was. Cruel enough, in all faith. But"—and his eyes became wild with a kind of sudden excitement more in keeping with his visage than they had been for years—"but look you! He's the one who wouldn't believe in pain, you know—he didn't *acknowledge* fire. And now he's dead I'll tell you something. . . . (He is dead, isn't he?)"

Splint turned his eyes quickly to the stiff figure below him. It would be a dreadful thing if the old man were listening all the time. The other two bent over also. There could be no doubt about it, although the candlelight flickering over the fire-bitten face gave an uncanny semblance of movement to the features. Professor Splint pulled a sheet over the corpse's head before he turned to his companions.

"What is it?" said Spiregrain. "Be quick!" His glass nose sliced the gloomy air as he turned his head quickly to the rugged Splint.

"It's *this,* Spiregrain. It's *this,*" said Splint, his eyes still on fire. He scratched at his jaw with a gravelly sound and took a step back from the bed. Then he held up his arms. "Listen, my friends. When I fell down those nine steps three weeks ago, and pretended that I felt no pain, I confess to you now that I was in agony. And now! And now that *he* is dead I glory in my confession, for I am afraid of him no more; and I tell you—I tell you both, openly and with pride, that I will have nothing to hide. I will cry out to all Gormenghast, 'I am in agony!'—and when my eyes fill with tears, they will be tears of joy and relief and not of pain. Oh, brothers! Colleagues! Do you not understand?"

Mr. Splint took a step forward in his excitement, dropping his hands, which he had kept raised all this time (and at once they were gripped on either side). Oh, what friendship, what an access of honest friendship, rushed like electricity through their six hands.

There was no need to talk. They had turned their

backs on their faith. Professor Splint had spoken for the three of them. Their cowardice (for they had never dared to express a doubt when the old man was alive) was something that bound them together now more tightly than a common valor could ever have done.

"'Grief's gravy' was an overstatement," said Throd. "I only said it because, after all, he *is* dead, and we *did* admire him in a way—and I like saying the right thing at the right time. I always have. But it was excessive."

"So was 'death's icicle,' I suppose," said Spiregrain, rather loftily; "but it was a neat phrase."

"Not when he was *burned* to death," said Throd, who saw no reason why Spiregrain should not recant as fully as himself.

"Nevertheless," said Splint, who found himself the center of the stage, which was usually monopolized by Spiregrain, "we are free. Our ideals are gone. We believe in pain. In life. In all those things which he told us didn't exist."

Spiregrain, with the guttering candle reflected on his glassy nose, drew himself up and, in a haughty tone, inquired of the others whether they didn't think it would be more tactful to discuss their dismissal of their dead master's Beliefs somewhat farther from his relics. Though he was doubtless out of earshot he certainly didn't look it.

They left at once, and directly the door had shut behind them the candle flame, after a short, abortive leap into the red air, groveled for a moment in its cup of liquid wax and expired. The little red box of a room had become, according to one's fancy, either a little black box or a tract of dread, imponderable space.

Once away from the death chamber a peculiar lightness sang in their bones.

"You were right, Splint, my dear fellow—quite right. We are free, and no mistake." Spiregrain's voice, thin, sharp, academic, had a buoyancy in it that caused his two confederates to turn to him.

"I knew you had a heart under it all," wheezed Throd. "I feel the same."

"No more Angels to look forward to!" yelled Splint, in a great voice.

"No more longing for Life's End," boomed Throd.

"Come, friends," screamed the glass-faced Spiregrain, forgetting his dignity, "let us begin to live again!" And catching hold of their shoulders, he walked them rapidly along the corridor, his head held high, his mortarboard at a rakish angle. Their three gowns streamed behind them, the tassels of their headgear also, as they increased their pace. Turning this way and that, almost skimming the ground as they went, they threaded the arteries of cold stone until, suddenly, bursting out into the sunshine on the southern side of Gormenghast, they found ahead of them the wide sun-washed spaces, the tall trees fringing the foothills, and the mountain itself shining against the deep blue sky. For a moment the memory of the picture in their late master's room flashed through their minds.

"Oh, lush!" they cried. "Oh, lush it is, forever!" And, breaking into a run and then a gallop, the three enfranchised Professors, hand in hand, their black gowns floating on the air, bounded across the golden landscape, their shadows leaping beside them.

Chapter Fourteen

❋❋❋❋❋❋❋❋❋❋

IT was in Bellgrove's class, one later afternoon, that Titus first thought consciously about the idea of color: of things having colors: of everything having its own *particular* color, and of the way in which every particular color kept changing according to where it was, what the light was like, and what it was next to.

Bellgrove was half asleep, and so were most of the boys. The room was hot and full of golden motes. A great clock ticked away monotonously. A bluebottle buzzed slowly over the surfaces of the hot window panes or from time to time zithered its languid way from desk to desk. Every time it passed certain desks, small inky hands would grab at it, or rulers would smack out through the tired air. Sometimes it would perch, for a moment, on an inkpot or on the back of a boy's collar and scythe its front legs together, and then its back legs, rubbing them, scything them, honing them, or as though it were a lady dressing for a ball drawing on a pair of long, invisible gloves.

Oh, bluebottle, you would fare ill at a ball! There would be none who could dance better than you; but you would be shunned: you would be too original: you would be before your time. They would not know your steps, the other ladies. None would throw out that indigo light from brow or flank—but, bluebottle, they wouldn't *want* to. There lies the agony. Their buzz of converse is not yours, bluebottle. You know no scandal, no small talk, no flattery, no jargon: you would be hopeless, for all that you can pull the long gloves on. After all, your splendor is a kind of horror-splendor. Keep to your inkpots and the hot glass panes of schoolrooms and buzz your way through the long summer terms. Let the great clock-ticks play counterpoint. Let the swish of a birch, the detonation of a paper pellet, the whispered conspiracy be your everlasting pards.

Down generations of boys, buzz, bluebottle, buzz in the summer prisons—for the boys are bored. Tick, clock, tick! Young Scarabee's on edge to fight the "Slogger" —young Dogseye hankers for his silkworms' weaving— Jupiter Minor knows a plover's nest. Tick, clock, tick!

Sixty seconds in a minute; sixty minutes in an hour; sixty times sixty.

Multiply the sixes and add how many noughts? Two, I suppose. Six sixes are thirty-six. Thirty-six and two noughts is 3,600. Three thousand and six hundred seconds in an hour. Quarter of an hour is left before the silkworms—before the "Slogger"—before the plover's nest. Buzz, fly, buzz! Tick, clock, tick! Divide 3,600 by four and then subtract a bit because of the time taken to work it all out.

$$4\overline{)3,600}$$
$$\underline{900}$$

Nine hundred seconds! Oh, marvelous! Marvelous! Seconds are so small. One—two—three—four—seconds are so huge.

The inky fingers scrubble through the forelock—the blackboard is a gray smear. The last three lessons can be seen faintly one behind the other—like aerial perspective. A fog of forgotten figures—forgotten maps—forgotten languages.

But while Bellgrove was sleeping—while Dogseye was carving—while the clock ticked—while the fly buzzed—while the room swam in a honey-colored milky way of motes—young Titus (inky as the rest, sleepy as the rest, leaning his head against the warm wall, for his desk was flush with the leather) had begun to follow a train of thought, at first lazily, abstractedly, without undue interest—for it was the first train of thought that he had ever troubled to follow very far. How lazily the images separated themselves from one another or adhered for a moment to the tissue of his mind!

Titus became dreamily interested, not in their sequence but in the fact that thoughts and pictures could follow one upon the other so effortlessly. And it had been the color of the ink, the peculiar dark and musty blue of the ink in its sunken bowl in the corner of his desk, which had induced his eyes to wander over the few objects grouped below him. The ink was blue, dark, musty, dirtyish, deep as cruel water at night: what were the other colors? Titus was surprised at the richness, the variety.

He had only seen his thumbmarked books as things to read or to avoid reading: as things that got lost: things full of figures or maps. Now he saw them as colored rectangles of pale, washed-out blue or laurel green, with the small windows cut out of them where, on the naked whiteness of the first page, he had scripted his name.

The lid of the desk itself was sepia, with golden browns and even yellows where the surface had been cut or broken. His pen, with its end chewed into a subdividing tail of wet fronds, shimmered like a fish, the indigo ink creeping up the handle from the nib, the green paint that was once so pristine blurred with the blue of the ink at the pen's belly, and then the whitish mutilated tail.

He even saw his own hand as a colored thing before he realized it was part of him; the ocher color of his wrist, the black of his sleeve; and then . . . and then he saw the marble, the glass marble beside the inkpot, with its swirling spirals of rainbow colors twisted within the clear, cold white glass: it was wealth. Titus fingered it and counted the colored threads that spiraled within— red, yellow, green, violet, blue . . . and their white and crystal world, so perfect, all about them, clear and cold and smooth, heavy and slippery. How it could clink and crack like a gunshot when it struck another! When it skidded the floor and struck! Crack like a gunshot on the round and brilliant forehead of its foe! Oh, beautiful marbles! Oh, blood-alleys! Oh, clouded ones, a-swim in blood and milk! Oh, crystal worlds, that make the pockets jangle—that make the pockets heavy!

How pleasant it was to hold that cold and glittering grape on a hot summer afternoon, with the Professor asleep at his high carved desk! How lovely it was to feel the cold slipping thing in the hot palm of his sticky hand! Titus clenched it and then held it against the light. As he rolled it between his thumb and forefinger the colored threads began to circle each other: to spiral themselves around and around and in and out in endless convolutions. Red: yellow: green: violet: blue . . . Red—yellow— green—red . . . yellow . . . red . . . *red*. Alone in his

mind the red became a thought—a color-thought—and
Titus slipped away into an earlier afternoon. The ceiling, the walls, the floor of his thought were red: he was
enveloped in it; but soon the walls contracted and all
the surfaces dwindled together and came at last to a
focus; the blur, the abstraction had gone, and in its place
was a small drop of blood, warm and wet. The light
caught it as it shone. It was on his knuckle, for he had
fought a boy in this same classroom a year ago—in that
earlier afternoon. A melancholy anger crept over Titus
at this memory. This image that shone out so redly,
this small brilliant drop of blood—and other sensations
—flitted across this underlying anger and brought on a
sense of exhilaration, of self-confidence, and fear also
at having spilled this red liquid—this stream of legendary
yet so real crimson. And the bead of blood lost focus, became blurred, and then, changing its hazy contour, became a heart . . . a heart. Titus put his hands against
his small chest. At first he could feel nothing, but moving
his fingertips he felt the double-thud, and the drumming
rushed in from another region of his memory: the sound
of the river on a night when he had been alone by the
high bullrushes and had seen between their inky, rope-
thick columns a sky like a battle.

And the battle-clouds changed their shapes momently,
now crawling across the firmament of his imagination like
redskins, now whipping like red fish over the mountains, their heads like the heads of the ancient carp in
Gormenghast Moat, but their bodies trailing behind in
festoons like rags or autumn foliage. And the sky,
through which these creatures swam, endlessly, in multitudes, became the ocean and the mountains below them
were underwater corals, and the red sun became the
eye of a subaqueous god, glowering across the sea bed.
But the great eye lost its menace, for it became no bigger than the marble in Titus's hand: for, wading toward
him hip-deep through the waters, dilating as they neared
until they pressed out and broke the frame of fancy, was
a posse of pirates.

They were as tall as towers, their great brows beetling over their sunken eyes, like shelves of overhanging rocks. In their ears were hoops of red gold, and in their mouths scythe-edged cutlasses a-drip. Out of the red darkness they emerged, their eyes half closed against the sun, the water at their waists circling and bubbling with the hot light reflected from their bodies, their dimensions blotting out all else: and still they came on, until their wire-glinting breasts and rocky heads filled out the boy's brain. And still they came on, until there was only room enough for the smoldering head of the central buccaneer, a great salt-water lord, every inch of whose face was scabbed and scarred like a boy's knee, whose teeth were carved into the shapes of skulls, whose throat was circled by the tattooing of a scaled snake. And as the head enlarged, an eye became visible in the darkness of its sockets, and in a moment nothing else but this wild and sinister organ could be seen. For a short while it stayed there, motionless. There was nothing else in the great world but this—globe. It *was* the world, and suddenly like the world it rolled. And as it rolled it grew yet again, until there was nothing but the pupil, filling the consciousness; and in that midnight pupil Titus saw the reflection of himself peering forward. And someone approached him out of the darkness of the pirate's pupil, and a rust-red pinpoint of light above the figure's brow became the coiled locks of his mother's wealth of hair. But before she could reach him her face and body had faded and in the place of the hair was Fuchsia's ruby; and the ruby danced about in the darkness, as though it were being jerked on the end of a string. And then it, also, was gone and the marble shone in his hand with all its spiraled colors—yellow, green, violet, blue, red . . . yellow . . . green . . . violet . . . blue . . . yellow . . . green . . . violet . . . yellow . . . green . . . yellow . . . *yellow.*

And Titus saw quite clearly not only the great sunflower with its tired, prickly neck which he had seen Fuchsia carrying about for the last two days, but a hand holding it, a hand that was not Fuchsia's. It held the heavy plant aloft between the thumb and forefinger as though it were the most delicate thing in the world. Every finger of the hand was aflame with gold rings, so that it looked like a gauntlet of flaming metal—an armored thing.

And then, all at once, blotting it out, a swarm of leaves was swirling through him, a host of yellow leaves, coiling, diving, rising, as they swept forward across a treeless desert, while overhead, like a bonfire in the sky, the sun shone down on the rushing leaves. It was a yellow world: a restless, yellow world: and Titus was beginning to drift into a yet deeper maw of the color when Bellgrove wakened with a jerk, gathered his gown about him like God gathering a whirlwind, and brought his hand down with a dull, impotent thud on the lid of his desk. His absurdly noble head raised itself. His proud and vacant gaze settled at last on young Dogseye.

"Would it be too much to ask you," he said at last, with a yawn which exposed his curious teeth, "whether a young man—a not very studious young man, by name Dogseye—lies behind that mask of dirt and ink? Whether there is a human body within that sordid bunch of rags, and whether that body is Dogseye's, also?" He yawned again. One of his eyes was on the clock; the other remained bemusedly on the young pupil. "I will put it more simply: is that really *you,* Dogseye? Are you sitting in the second row from the front? Are you occupying the third desk from the left? And were you—if, indeed, it is you, behind that dark-blue muzzle—were you carving something indescribably fascinating on the lid of your desk? Did I wake to catch you at it, young man?"

Dogseye, a nondescript little figure, wriggled.

"Answer me, Dogseye. Were you carving away when you thought your old master was asleep?"

"Yes, sir," said Dogseye, surprisingly loudly; so loudly that he startled himself and glanced about him as though for the voice.

"What were you carving, my boy?"

"My name, sir."

"What, the whole thing, my boy?"

"I'd only done the first three letters, sir."

Bellgrove rose swathed. He moved, a benign, august figure, down the dusty aisle between the desks until he reached Dogseye.

"You haven't finished the G," he said in a faraway, lugubrious voice. "Finish the G and leave it at that. And leave the EYE for other things"—an inane smirk began to flit across the lower part of his face—"such as your grammar book," he said brightly, his voice horribly out of character. He began to laugh in such a way as might develop into something beyond control, but he was brought up short with a twinge of pain and he clutched at his jaw, where his teeth cried out for extraction.

After a few moments, "Get up," he said. Seating himself at Dogseye's desk, he picked up the penknife before him and worked away at the G of DOG until a bell rang and the room was transformed into a stampeding torrent of boys making for the classroom door as though they expected to find upon the other side the embodiment of their separate dreams—the talons of adventure, the antlers of romance.

Irma Wants a Party

"Very well, then, and so you *shall!*" cried Alfred Prunesquallor. "So you shall, indeed."

There was a wild and happy desperation in his voice. Happy, in that a decision had been made at all, however unwisely. Desperate, because life with Irma was a desperate affair in any case; but especially in regard to this passion of hers to have a party.

"Alfred! Alfred! Are you serious? Will you pull your weight, Alfred? I say, will you pull your weight?"

"What weight I have I'll pull to pieces for you, Irma."

"You are resolved, Alfred—I say, you are *resolved?*" she asked breathlessly.

"It is you who are resolved, sweet Perturbation.

It is I who have submitted. But there it is. I am weak. I am ductile. You *will* have your way—a way, I fear, that is fraught with the possibility of monstrous repercussions—but your own, Irma, your own. And a party we will throw. Ha, ha, ha, ha, ha, ha, ha!"

There was something that did not altogether ring true in his shrill laughter. Was there a touch of bitterness in it somewhere?

"After all," he continued, perching himself on the back of a chair (and with his feet on the seat and his chin on his knees he looked remarkably like a grasshopper). "After all, you have waited a long time. A long time. But, as you know, I would never advise such a thing. You're not the type to give a party. You're not even the type to go to a party. You have nothing of the flippancy about you that makes a party *go,* sister mine; but you are determined."

"Unutterably," said Irma.

"And have you confidence in your brother as a host?"

"Oh, Alfred, I *could* have!" she whispered grimly. "I *would* have, if you wouldn't try to make everything sound clever. I get so tired of the way you say things. And I don't really like the things you say."

"Irma," said her brother, "nor do I. They always sound stale by the time I hear them. The brain and the tongue are so far apart."

"That's the sort of nonsense I *loathe!*" cried Irma, suddenly becoming passionate. "Are we going to talk about the party, or are we going to listen to your silly *soufflés?* Answer me, Alfred. Answer me at once."

"I will talk like bread and water. What shall I say?"

He descended from the chair back and sat on the seat. Then he leaned forward a little and, with his hands folded between his knees, he gazed expectantly at Irma through the magnifying lenses of his spectacles. Staring back at him through the darkened glass of her own lenses, the enlargement of his eyes was hardly noticeable.

Irma felt that for the moment she had a certain moral ascendancy over her brother. The air of submission which he had about him gave her strength to divulge to him the real reason for her hankering for this party she had in mind . . . for she needed his help.

"Did you know, Alfred," she said, "that I am thinking of getting married?"

"Irma!" cried her brother. "You aren't!"

"Oh, yes, I am," muttered Irma. "Oh, yes, I am."

Prunesquallor was about to inquire who the lucky man was when a peculiar twinge of sympathy for her, poor white thing that she was, sitting so upright in the chair before him, caught at his heart. He knew how few her chances of meeting men had been in the past: he knew that she knew nothing of love's gambits save what she had read in books. He knew that she would lose her head. He also knew that she had no one in view. So he said: "We will find *just* the man for you. You deserve a thoroughbred: something that can cock his ears and whisk his tail. By all that's unimpeachable, you do indeed. Why—"

The Doctor stopped himself: he had been about to take verbal flight when he remembered his promise: so he leaned forward again to hear what his sister had to say.

"I don't know about cocking his ears and frisking his tail," said Irma, with the suggestion of a twitch at one corner of her thin mouth; "but I would like you to know, Alfred—I said I would like you to know, that I am glad you understand the position. I am being wasted, Alfred. You realize that, don't you—don't you?"

"I do, indeed."

"My skin is the whitest in Gormenghast."

"And your feet are the flattest," thought her brother: but he said: "Yes, yes, but what we must *do,* sweet huntress (O virgin through wild sex's thickets prowling)"—he could not resist this image of his sister—"what we must *do* is to decide whom to ask. To the Party, I mean. That is fundamental."

"Yes, yes!" said Irma.

"And when we will ask them."

"That's easier," said Irma.

"And at what time of the day."

"The evening, of course," said Irma.

"And what they shall wear."

"Oh, their evening clothes, obviously," said Irma.

"It depends on whom we ask, don't you think? What ladies, my dear, have dresses as resplendent as yours, for instance? There's a certain cruelty about evening dress."

"Oh, that is of no avail."

"Do you mean 'of no account'?"

"Yes, yes," said Irma.

"But how embarrassing! Won't they feel it keenly, my dear—or will you put on rags, in an overflow of love and sympathy?"

"There will be no women."

"No women!" cried her brother, genuinely startled.

"I must be alone," his sister murmured, pushing her black glasses farther up the bridge of her long, pointed nose, ". . . with *them*—the males."

"But what of the entertainment for your guests?"

"I shall be there," said Irma.

"Yes, yes; and no doubt you will prove ravishing and ubiquitous; but, my love, my love, think again."

"Alfred," said Irma, standing up and lowering one of her iliac crests and raising its counterpart so high that her pelvis looked thoroughly dangerous—"Alfred," she said, "how can you be so perverse? What use could women be? You haven't forgotten what we have in mind, have you? Have you?"

Her brother was beginning to admire her. Had she

all this long while been hiding beneath her neuroticism, her vanity, her childishness, an iron will?

He rose and, cupping his hands over her hips, corrected their angle with the quick jerk of a bonesetter. Then, sitting back in his chair and fastidiously crossing his long, elegant, cranelike legs while going through the movements of washing his hands: "Irma, my revelation, tell me but this"—he raised his eyes quizzically—"who are these males—these stags—these rams—these tomcats—these cocks, stoats, and ganders that you have in mind? And on what scale is this carousal to be?"

"You know very well, Alfred, that we have no choice. Among the gentry, who are there? I ask you, Alfred, who are there?"

"Who, indeed?" mused the Doctor, who could think of no one. The idea of a party in his house was so novel that the effort of trying to people it was beyond him. It was as though he were trying to assemble a cast for an unwritten drama.

"As for the size of the party, Alfred—are you listening?—I have in mind a gathering of some forty men."

"No! No!" shouted her brother, clutching at the arms of his chair. "Not in *this* room, surely? It would be worse than the white cats. It would be a dog fight."

Was that a blush that stole across his sister's face?

"Alfred," she said after a while, "it is my last chance. In a year my glamor may be tarnished. Is it a time to think of your own personal comfort?"

"Listen to me." Prunesquallor spoke very slowly. His high voice was strangely meditative. "I will be as concise as I can. Only you must listen, Irma."

She nodded.

"You will have more success if your party is not too large. At a large party the hostess has to flutter from guest to guest and can never enjoy a protracted conversation with anyone. What is more, the guests continually flutter toward the hostess in a manner calculated to show her how much they are enjoying themselves.

"But at a smaller party where everyone can easily be seen the introductions and general posturing can be speedily completed. You will then have time to size up the persons present and decide on those worth giving your attention to."

"I see," said Irma. "I am going to have lanterns hanging in the garden, too, so that I can lure those whom I think fit out into the apple orchard."

"Good heavens!" said Prunesquallor, half to himself. "Well, I hope it won't be raining."

"It won't," said Irma.

He had never known her like this. There was something frightening in seeing a second side of a sister whom he had always assumed had only one.

"Well, some of them must be left out, then."

"But who *are* they? Who *are* they?" he cried. "I can't bear this frightful tension. What are these males that you seem to think of en bloc? This doglike horde who at, as it were, a whistle will be ready to stream across the quadrangle and through the hall, through this door, and to take up a score of masculine postures? In the name of fundamental mercy, Irma, tell me who they are."

"The Professors."

As Irma uttered the words her hands grappled with one another behind her back. Her flat bosom heaved. Her sharp nose twitched and a terrible smile came over her face.

"They are gentlemen!" she cried in a loud voice. "Gentlemen! And worthy of my love."

"What! All forty of them?" Her brother was on his feet again. He was shocked.

But at the same time he could see the logic of Irma's choice. Who else was there for a party with this hidden end in view? As for their being "gentlemen"—perhaps they were. But only just. If their blood was bluish, so for the most part were their jaws and fingernails. If their backgrounds bore scrutiny, the same could hardly be said for their fore-grounds.

"What a vista opens out before us! How old are you, Irma?"

"You know very well, Alfred."

"Not without thinking," said the Doctor. "But leave it. It's what you look like that matters. God knows you're clean! It's a good start. I am trying to put myself in your place. It takes an effort—ha, ha!—I can't do it."

"Alfred."

"My love?"

"How many do you think would be ideal?"

"If we chose well, Irma, I should say a dozen."

"No, no, Alfred, it's a party! It's a *party!* Things *happen* at parties—not at friends' gatherings. I've read about it. Twenty, at least, to make the atmosphere pregnant."

"Very well, my dear. Very *well*. Not that we will include a mildewed and wheezy beast with broken antlers because he comes twentieth on the list when the other nineteen are stags, are virile and eligible. But come, let us go into this matter more closely. Let us say, for sake of argument, that we have whittled the probable down to fifteen. Now, of this fifteen, Irma, my sweet co-strategist, surely we could not hope for more than six as possible husbands for you.—No, no, do not wince; let us be honest, though it is brutal work. The whole thing is very subtle, for the six you might prefer are not necessarily the six that would care to share the rest of their lives with *you;* oh, no. It might be another six altogether whom you don't care about one little bit. And over and above these interchangeables we must have the float-ing background of those whom I have no doubt you would spurn with your elegantly cloven hoofs were they to make the least advance. You would bridle up, Irma: I'm sure you would. But nevertheless they are needful, these untouchables, for we must have a

hinterland. They are the ones who will make the
party florid, the atmosphere potential."

"Do you think we could call it a soiree, Alfred?"

"There is no law against it that I know of," answered Prunesquallor, a little irritably perhaps, for
she had obviously not been listening. "But the Professors, as I remember them, are hardly the types I
would associate with the term. Who, by the way,
do comprise the Staff these latter days? It is a long
time since I last saw the flapping of a gown."

"I know that you are cynical, Alfred, BUT I would
have you know that they are my choice. I have always wished for a man of learning to be my own. I
would understand him. I would administer to him. I
would protect him and darn his socks."

"And a more dexterous darner never protected the
tendo Achilles with a double skein!"

"Alfred!"

"Forgive me, my own. By all that's unforeseeable
I am getting to like the idea. For my part, Irma,
I will see to the wines and liqueurs, the barrels and
the punch-bowl. For your part the eatables, the invitations, the schooling of the staff—our staff, not the
luminaries'. And now, my dear, *when?* This is the
question—*when?*"

"My gown of a thousand frills with its corsage
of hand-painted parrots will be ready within ten days,
and . . ."

"Parrots!" cried the Doctor in consternation.

"Why not?" said Irma, sharply.

"But," wavered her brother, "how many of them?"

"What on earth does it matter to you, Alfred?
They are brightly colored birds."

"But will they chime in with the frills, my sweet
one? I would have thought—if you must have hand-
painted creatures on your corsage, as you call it
—that something calculated to turn the thoughts of
the Professors to your femininity, your desirability,
something less aggressive than parrots might be wise.
. . . Mind you, Irma, I'm only . . ."

"Alfred!" Her voice jerked him back to his chair.

"My province, I *think*," she said, with heavy sarcasm. "I imagine when it comes to parrots you can leave them to me."

"I will," said her brother.

"Will ten days give us time, Alfred?" she said, as she rose from her chair and approached her brother, smoothing back her iron-gray hair with her long, pale fingers. Her tone had softened. To the Doctor's horror she sat on the arm of his chair.

Then, with a sudden kittenish abandon, she flung back her head so that her overlong yet pearl-white neck was tautened in a backward curve and her chignon tapped her between her shoulder blades in so peremptory a way as to make her cough. But directly she had ascertained that it was not her brother being willful, the ecstatic and kittenish expression came back to her powdered face, and she clapped her hands together at her breast.

Prunesquallor, staring up, horrified at yet another facet of her character coming to light, noticed that one of her molars needed filling, but decided it was not the moment to mention it.

"Oh, Alfred! Alfred!" she cried. "I *am* a woman, aren't I?" The hands were shaking with excitement as they gripped one another. "I'll *show* them I am!" she screamed, her voice losing all control. And then, calming herself with a visible effort, she turned to her brother and, smiling at him with a coyness that was worse than any scream—"I'll send their cards to them tomorrow, Alfred," she whispered.

Chapter Fifteen

✻✻✻✻✻✻✻✻✻✻✻✻

THREE shafts of the rising sun, splintering through the murk, appeared to set fire to the earth where they struck it. The bright impact of the nearest beam exposed a tangle of branches which clawed in a craze of radiance, microscopically perfect and adrift in darkness.

The second of these floodlit islands appeared to float immediately *above* the first, for the sky and the earth were a single curtain of darkness. In reality it was as far away again, but hanging as it did gave no sense of distance.

At its northern extremity there grew from the wasp-gold earth certain forms like eruptions of masonry rather than spires and buttresses of natural rock. The sunshaft had uncovered a mere finger of some habitation which, widening as it entered the surrounding darkness to the north, became a fist of stones, which, in its turn, heaving through wrist and forearm to an elbow like a smashed honeycomb, climbed through darkness to a gaunt, time-eaten shoulder only to expand again and again into a mountainous body of timeless towers.

But of all this nothing was visible but the bright and splintered tip of a stone finger.

The third "island" was the shape of a heart. A coruscating heart of tares on fire.

To the dark edge of this third light a horse was moving. It appeared no bigger than a fly. Astride its back was Titus.

As he entered the curtain of darkness which divided him from his citylike home, he frowned. One of his hands gripped the mane of his mount. His heart beat loudly in the absolute hush. But the horse moved without hesitation, and he was quieted by the regular movement beneath him.

All at once a new "island" of light, undulating as it ran from the east, enlarging its mercurial margins all the while as though to push away the darkness, created in the gloom a fantastic kaleidoscope of fleeting rocks and trees and valleys and ridges—the fluctuating "coastline" flaring in sharp and minute tracery. This flow of radiance was followed by another and another. Great saffron gaps had appeared in the sky—and then, from skyline to skyline, the world was naked light.

Titus shouted. The horse shook its head; and then, over the land of his ancestors, he galloped for home.

But in the excitement of the gallop Titus turned his head from the castle towers, which lifted themselves momently higher above the horizon, turned it to where, away in the cold haze of the dawn, Gormenghast Mountain with its clawlike peak threw out its challenge across the thrilling air. *"Do you dare?"* it seemed to cry. *"Do you dare?"*

Titus leaned back in the stirrups and tugged his horse to a standstill, for a rare confusion of voices and images had made a cockpit of his panting body. Forests as wet and green as romance itself heaved their thorned branches through him as he sat there shuddering, half turned on the saddle. Swathes of wet foliage shuffled beneath his ribs. In his mouth he tasted the bitterness of leaves. The smell of the forest earth, black with rotted ferns and pungent with fermentation, burned for a moment in his nostrils.

His eyes had traveled down from the high, bare summit of Gormenghast Mountain to the shadowy woods, and then again had turned to the sky. He stared at the sun as it climbed. He felt the day beginning. He turned his horse about. His back was toward Gormenghast.

The mountain's head shone in a great vacancy of light. It held within its ugly contour either everything or nothing at all. It awakened the imagination by its peculiar emptiness.

And from it came the voice again.

"Do you dare? Do you dare?"

And a host of voices joined. Voices from the sun-blotched glades. From the marshes and the gravel beds. From the birds of the green river reaches. From where the squirrels are and the foxes move and the woodpeckers thicken the drowsy stillness of the day with their far Arcadian tapping: from where the rotten hollow of some tree, mellow with richness, glows as though lit from within by the sweet and secret cache of the wild bees.

Titus had risen an hour before the bell. He had hurried into his clothes without a sound, and had then tiptoed through silent halls to a southern gateway; and then, running across a walled-in courtyard, had arrived at the castle stables. The morning was black and murky, but he was restless for a world without walls. He had paused at Fuchsia's door on his way and had tapped at it.

"Who's there?" Her voice had sounded strangely husky from the other side.

"It's me," said Titus.

"What do you want?"

"Nothing," said Titus. "I'm going for a ride."

"It's beastly weather," said Fuchsia. "Good-by."

"Good-by," said Titus; and had resumed his tiptoeing along the corridor when he heard the sound of a handle being rattled. He turned and saw, not only Fuchsia disappearing back into her bedroom, but at the same moment something which was traveling very fast through the air and at his head. To protect his face he threw up his arm and, more by accident than adroitness, found he had caught in his hand a large and sticky slice of cake.

Titus knew that he was not allowed out of the castle before breakfast. He knew that it was doubly disobedient to venture beyond the Outer Wall. As the only survivor of a famous Line he had to take more than ordinary care of himself. It was for him to give particulars of when and where he was going, so that should he be late in returning it would be known at once. But, dark as was the day, it had no power to suppress the craving which had been mounting for weeks—the craving to ride and ride when the rest of the world lay in bed: to drink the spring air in giant gulps as his horse galloped beneath him over the April fields, beyond the Outer Dwellings. To pretend, as he galloped, that he was free.

Free . . . !

What could such a conception mean to Titus, who hardly knew what it was to move from one part of his home to another without being watched, guided, or followed, and who had never known the matchless privacy of the obscure? To be without a famous name? To have no lineage? To be something of no interest to the veiled eye of the grown-up world? To be a creature that grew, as a redskin creeps: through childhood and youth, from one year to the next, as though from thicket to thicket, from ambush to ambush, peering from Youth's treetop vantages?

Because of the wild vista that surrounded Gormenghast and spread to every horizon as though the castle were an island of maroons set in desolate water beyond all trade routes: because of this sense of space, how could Titus know that the vague, unfocused dissatisfaction which he had begun to feel from time to time was the fretting of something caged?

He knew no other world. Here all about him the raw material burned: the properties and settings of romance. Romance that is passionate, obscure, and sexless: that is dangerous and arrogant.

The future lay before him with its endless ritual and pedantry, but something beat in his throat and he rebelled.

To be a Truant! A Truant! It was like being a Conqueror—or a Demon.

And so he had saddled his small gray horse and ridden out into the dark April morning. No sooner had he passed through one of the arches in the Outer Wall and cantered in the direction of Gormenghast Forest than he became suddenly, hopelessly lost. All in a moment the clouds seemed to have cut out all possible light from the sky, and he had found himself among branches which switched back and struck him in the darkness. At another time, his horse had found itself up to the knees in a cold and sucking mire. It had shuddered beneath him as it backed with difficulty to find firmer purchase for its hoofs. As the sun had climbed, Titus was able to make out where he was. And then, suddenly, the long sunshafts had broken through the gloom and he had seen away in the distance—far further than he would ever have guessed possible—the shining stone of one of the castle's western capes.

And then the flooding of the sun, until not a rag was left in the sky, and the thrill of fear became the thrill of anticipation—of adventure.

Titus knew that already he would be missed. Breakfast would be over; but long before breakfast an alarm must have been raised in the dormitory. Titus could see the raised eyebrow of his Professor in the schoolroom as he eyed the empty desk, and could hear the chatter and speculation of the pupils. And then he felt something more thrilling than the warm kiss of the sun on the back of his neck: it was a reedy flight of cold April air across his face—something perilous and horribly exciting— something very shrill, that whistled through his qualmy stomach and down his thighs. It was as though it were the herald of adventure that whistled to him to turn his horse's head, while the soft gold sunlight murmured the same message in a drowsier voice.

For a moment so huge a sense of himself swam inside Titus as to make the figures in the castle like puppets in his imagination. He would pull them up in one hand and drop them into the moat when he returned—*if* he returned. He would not be their slave any more! Who was he to be told to go to school: to attend this and to attend that? He was not only the Seventy-Seventh Earl of Gormenghast, he was Titus Groan in his own right.

"All right, then!" he shouted to himself. "I'll show them!" And, digging his heels into his horse's flanks, he headed for the mountain.

But the cold drift of spring air across his face was not only a prelude to Titus's truancy. It foretold yet another alternation in the weather, as rapid and as unexpected as the coming of the sun. For although there were no clouds in the upper air, yet the sun seemed now to have a haze upon it and the warmth on his neck was weaker.

It was not until he had covered over three miles of his rebellious expedition and was in the hazel woods that led to the foothills of Gormenghast Mountain that he positively noticed a mistiness in the atmosphere. From then onward a whiteness seemed to grow above him, to arise out of the earth and gather together on every side. The sun ceased to be more than a pale disk, and then was gone altogether.

There was no turning back now: Titus knew that he would be lost immediately if he turned his horse about. As it was, he could see nothing but a lambent glow, gradually growing dimmer—a glow immediately before and above him. It was the upper half of Gormenghast Mountain shining through the thickening mists.

To climb out of the white vapor was his only hope and, jogging the horse into a dangerous trot, for visibility was but a yard or two, he made (with the pale shimmer above him for a guide) for the high slopes; and at last he found the air begin to thin. When the sun shone down again unhindered and the highest wisps of the mist were coiling some distance below, Titus realized in full what it was to be alone. The solitude was of a kind he had never experienced before. The silence of a motionless altitude with a world of fantastic vapor spread below.

Away to the west the roofscape of his heavy home floated, as lightly as though every stone were a petal. Strung across the capstone jaws of its great head a hundred windows, the size of teeth, reflected the dawn. There was less the nature of glass about them than of bone, or of the stones which locked them in. In contrast to the torpor of these glazes, punctuating the remote masonry with so cold a catenation, acres of ivy spread themselves like dark water over the roofs and appeared restless, the millions of heart-shaped eyelids winking wetly.

The mountain's head shone above him. Was there no

living thing on those stark slopes but the truant child? It seemed that the heart of the world had ceased to beat.

The ivy leaves fluttered a little and a flag here and there stirred against its pole, but there was no vitality in these movements, no purpose, any more than the long hair of some corpse, tossing this way and that in a wind, can deny the death of the body it flatters.

Not a head appeared at any of those topmost, teethlike windows that ran along the castle's brow. Had anyone stood there he might have seen the sun hanging a hand's breadth above the margins of the ground mist.

From horizon to horizon it spread, this mist, supporting the massives of the mountains on its foaming back, like a floating load of ugly crags and shale. It laid its fumes along the flanks of the mountain. It laid them along the walls of the castle, fold upon baleful fold, a great tide. Soundless, motionless, beneath some exorcism more potent than the moons, it had no power to ebb.

Not a breath from the mountain. Not a sigh from the swathed castle, nor from the hollow hush of the mists. Was there no pulse beneath the vapor? Not a heart beating? For surely the weakest heart would reverberate in such white silence and thud its double drum-note in far gullies.

The sunlight gave no stain to the chalky pall. It was a white sun, as though reflecting the mists below it—brittle as a disk of glass.

Was it that Nature was restless and experimenting with her various elements? For no sooner had the white mist settled itself as though forever, lying heavily in the ravine like a river of cold smoke—lying over the flats like a quilt, feeling into every rabbit burrow with its cold fingers—than a chill and scouring wind shipped out of the north, and sweeping the land bare again, dropped as suddenly as it had risen, as though it had been sent specifically to clear the mist away. And the sun was a globe of gold again. The wind was gone and the mists were gone and the clouds were gone and the day was warm and young, and Titus was on the slopes of Gormenghast Mountain.

Chapter Sixteen

✳︎✳︎✳︎✳︎✳︎✳︎✳︎✳︎✳︎✳︎✳︎✳︎✳︎

FAR below Titus, like a gathering of people, stood a dozen spinneys. Between them the rough land glittered here and there where threads of water reflected the sky.

Out of this confusion of glinting water, brambles, and squat thorn bushes, the clumps of trees arose with a peculiar authority.

To Titus they seemed curiously alive, these copses. For each copse appeared singularly *unlike* any other one, though they were about equal in size and were exclusively a blend of ash and sycamore.

But it was plain to see that whereas the nearest of these groups to Titus was in an irritable state, not one of the trees having anything to do with his neighbor, their heads turned away from one another, their shoulders shrugged, yet not a hundred feet away another spinney was in a condition of suspended excitement, as with the heads of its trees bowed together above some green and susurrous secret. Only one of the trees had raised its head a little. It was tilted on one side as though loath to miss any of the fluttering conversation at his shoulder. Titus shifted his gaze and noticed a copse where, drawn back, and turned away a little on their hips, twelve trees looked sideways at one who stood aloof. Its back was to them. There could be no doubt that, with its gaze directed from them, it despised the group behind it.

There were the trees that huddled together as though they were cold or in fear. There were trees that gesticulated. There were those that seemed to support one of their number who appeared wounded. There were the arrogant groups, and the mournful, with their heads

115

bowed: the exultant copses and those where every tree appeared to be asleep.

The landscape was alive, but so was Titus. They were only trees, after all: branches, roots, and leaves. This was his day; there was no time to waste.

He had given the slip to that gray line of towers. Here about him were the rocks and ferns of the mountain, with the morning sunbeams dancing over them in hazes of ground-light.

A dragonfly hovered above a rock face at his elbow, and at the same moment he became aware of a great shouting of birds from beyond the copses.

To the north of the copses lay the shining flats, but it was from farther to the west, and closer to the foot of the mountain where he stood, that the voices of the birds floated, so thinly and clearly; it was there that the wide forests lay basking. Fold after green fold, clump after clump of foliage undulating to the notched skyline.

His yearnings became focused. His truancy no longer nagged him. His curiosity burned.

What brooded within those high and leafy walls? Those green and sunny walls? What of the inner shadows? What of the acorn'd terraces, and the hollow aisles of leaves? His truant conscience lay stunned beneath the hammers of his excitement.

He wanted to gallop, but the slopes of shale and loose stone were too dangerous. But as he picked his way to lower levels the ground became correspondingly easier, and he was able to move more rapidly over considerable stretches.

The green wall of the forest rose higher into the sunny sky as he neared, until he had to raise his head to see the highest branches.

Gormenghast was hidden behind a rise in the ground to the west. To the east and behind him the slopes of the mountain climbed in ugly shelves. He drew in the reins and slid from the horse's back.

The ground about him was of silky and rather ashen grass, which shone with a peculiar white light. Rough rocks lay scattered about, in the shadow of whose hot brows and thrust-out jaws a variety of ferns grew luxuriously.

Lizards ran across the hot upper surfaces, and with Titus's first step toward the forest wall a snake slid down a rock face like a stream of water and whipped across his path with a rattling of its loosely jointed tail.

What was this shock of love? A rattlesnake; a dell of silky grass; some great rocks with lizards and ferns; and the green forest wall. Why should these add up to so thrilling, so breathtaking a total?

He knotted the reins loosely about the pony's neck and gave it a long push in the direction of Gormenghast. "Go home," he said. The pony turned her head to him at once and then, tossing it to and fro, began to move away. In a few moments she had disappeared over the rise in the ground, and Titus was truly alone.

Chapter Seventeen

THE morning classes had begun. In the schoolrooms a hundred things were happening at the same time. But beyond their doors there was drama of another kind: a drama of scholastic silence, for in the deserted halls and corridors that divided the classes it surged like a palpable thing and lapped against the very doors of the classrooms.

In an hour's time the usher would rattle the brass bell in the Central Hall and the silence would be shaken to bits as, erupting from their various prisons, a world of boys poured through the halls like locusts.

In the classrooms of Gormenghast, as in the Master's Common-Room, the walls were of horsehide. But this was the only thing they had in common, for the

moods of the various rooms and their shapes could
not be more various.

Fluke's room, for instance, was long, narrow, and badly lit from a small top window at the far end. Opus Fluke
lay in an armchair, draped with a red rug. He was in
almost total shadow. Although he could hardly make
out the boys in front of him, he was in a better position
than they were, for they could not see him at all. He
had no desk in front of him, but sat there, as it were,
in the open darkness. One or two textbooks were littered about the floor beneath his chair for the sake of
form. The dust lay over them so thickly that they were
like gray swellings. Mr. Fluke had not yet discovered
that they had been nailed into the floor boards for over
a year.

Perch-Prism's room was deadly square and far too well
lit to please the neophytes. Only the leather walls were
musty and ancient, and even they were scrubbed and
oiled from time to time. The desks, the benches, and the
floor boards were scoured with soda and boiling water
every morning, so that apart from the walls there was a
naked whiteness about the room which made it quite the
most unpopular. Cribbing was almost impossible in that
cruel light.

Flannelcat's room was a short tunnel with a semicircular glass window which filled in the whole of the near
end. In contrast to Fluke, sitting in the shadows, Mr.
Flannelcat perched aloft at a very high desk presented a
different picture. As the only light in the room poured
in from behind him, Mr. Flannelcat might as well, in the
eyes of his pupils, have been cut out of black paper.
There he sat against the bright semicircular window at
the end of the tunnel, his silhouetted gestures jerking to
and fro against the light. Through the window could be
seen the top of Gormenghast Mountain, and this morning, floating lazily over its shining head, were three small
clouds like dandelion seeds.

But of the numerous classrooms of Gormenghast, each
one with its unique character, there was, that morning,
one in particular. It lay upon one of the upper floors,

a great, dreamy hull of a place with far more desks than were ever used and far more space than was ever (academically) needed. Great strips of its horsehide hung away from the walls.

The window of the classroom faced to the south, so that the floor which had never been stained was bleached, and the ink that had been spilled, term after term, had faded to so beautiful and wan a blue that the floor boards had an almost faery coloring. Certainly there was nothing else particularly faery about the place.

What, for instance, was that sacklike monster, that snoring hummock, that dead weight of disjointed horror? Vile and brutish it looked as it lay curled like a black dog on the Professor's desk; but what was it? One would say it was dead, for it was as heavy as death and as motionless; but there was a sound of stifled snoring coming from it, with an occasional whistle as of wind through jagged glass.

Whatever it was it held no terror, nor even interest for the score or so of boys who, in that dreaming and time-less hall in the almost forgotten regions of the Upper School, appeared to have something very different to think about. The sunbeams poured through the high window. The room was in a haze of motes. But there was nothing dreamy about the pupils.

What was happening? There was hardly any noise, but the tension in the air had a loudness of its own.

For there was in progress a game of high and dangerous hazards. It was peculiar to this classroom. The air was breathless. Those not taking part in the peculiar battle squatted on desks or cupboards. A fresh phase was about to begin. Their ingenuous faces were turned to the window. Seasoned creatures they looked, these wiry children of chance. The veterans moved into position.

Everything was ready. The two loose floor boards had been taken up and the first of them was propped against the window sill so that it slanted across and to-ward the floor of the classroom at a shallow angle. Its secret underside had been scraped and waxed with candle stubs for as long as could be remembered, and it was that underside which was facing the ceiling. The second of the long floor boards, equally polished, was placed end to end with the first, so that a stretch of narrow and slippery wood extended some thirty feet across the schoolroom from the window to the opposite wall.

The team which was standing close by the open window was the first to make a move, and one of its number—a black-haired boy with a birthmark on his forehead —jumped onto the window sill, apparently without giving a thought to the hundred-foot drop on the other side.

At this movement, members of the enemy team who were crouching behind a row of desks at the back of the schoolroom, marshaled their paper pellets, as hard as walnuts, which they proposed to let loose from small naked catapults, worn to a silky finish by ceaseless handling. There had been a time when clay—and even glass marbles—had been used; but after the third death and a deal of confusion in the hiding of the bodies, it was decided to be content with paper bullets. Those were by no means gentle substitutes, the paper having been chewed, kneaded, mixed with white gum, and then compressed between the hinges of desks. Traveling as they did with deadly speed, they struck like the lash of a whip.

But what were they to fire at? Their enemies stood by the window and were obviously not expecting anything to fly in their direction. The firing party were not even looking at them—they stared fixedly ahead, but at the same time were beginning to close their left eyes and stretch their strands of grim elastic. And then, suddenly, the significance of the game unfolded itself in a sharp and rhythmic whirl. Too rapid, too vital, too dangerous for any dance or ballet. Yet as traditional and as filled with subtleties. What was happening?

The black-haired boy with the birthmark had flexed his knees, hollowed his back, clapped his inky hands, and leaped from the window sill out into the morning sunlight, where the branches of a giant plane tree were like latticework against the sun. For a moment he was a creature of the air, his head thrown back, his teeth bared, his fingers outstretched, his eyes fixed upon a white branch of the tree. A hundred feet below him the dusty quadrangle shone in the morning sun. From the schoolroom it looked as though the boy were gone forever. But his pards by the window had flattened themselves against the flanking wall, and their enemies, crouched behind the desks, had their eyes fixed on the slippery floor board that ran across the classroom like a strip of ice.

The boy in midair had clawed at the branch, had gripped its end, and was swinging out on a long and breathtaking curve through the foliaged air. At the extremity and height of this outward-going arc, he wriggled himself in a peculiar manner which gave an added downlash to the branch and swung him high on the upswing of his return journey—high into the air and out of the leaves, so that for a moment he was well above the level of the window from which he had leaped. And it was now that his nerves must be like iron—now, with but a fraction of time to spare before his volition failed him, that he let go the branch. He was in midair again. He was falling —falling at speed, and at such an angle as to both clear the lintel of the window and the sill below it—and to land on his small tense buttocks—to land like a bolt from heaven on the slanting floor boards; and a fraction of a second later to thump into the leather wall at the far end of the schoolroom, having whirled down the boards with the speed of a slung stone.

But he had not reached the wall unscathed for all the suddenness of his reappearance and velocity of flight. His ear buzzed like a nest of wasps. A withering crossfire from the six catapults had resulted in one superlative hit, three blows on the body and two misses. But there had been no cessation in the game, for even as he crashed into the dented leather wall another of his team was already in midair, his hands stretched for the branch and his eyes bright with excitement, while the firing party, no less on the move, were recharging their weapons with fresh ammunition and were beginning to close their left eyes again and stretch the elastic.

By the time the birthmark boy had trotted back to
the window, with his ear on fire, another apparition had
fallen from the sunny sky, had whizzed down the sloping board and skidded across the schoolroom to crash
into the wall where the leather was grimed and torn with
years of collision. There was a schoolroom silence over
everything—a silence filled with the pale sunshine. The
floor was patterned with the golden shadow of the desks,
of the benches, of the enormous broken blackboard. It
was the stillness of a summer term—self-absorbed, unhurried, dreamlike, punctuated by the quick, inky hand-
clap of each boy as he leaped into space, the whizz of
the pellets through the air, the caught breath of the victim, the thud of a body as it collided with the leather
wall, and then the scuffling sound of catapults being re-
charged; and then again the clap of the boy at the window, and the far rustle of leaves as he swung through a
green arc above the quadrangle. The teams changed. The
swingers took out their catapults. The firing party moved
to the window. It had a rhythm of its own, this hazardous, barbaric, yet ceremonial game—a ritual as unquestioned and sacrosanct as anything could be in the soul
of a boy.

Devilry and stoicism bound them together. Their secrets were blacker, deeper, more terrible or more hilarious
through mutual knowledge of the throat-contracting thrill
of a lightning skid across a mellow schoolroom: through
mutual knowledge of the long, leaf-shrouded flights
through space: of their knowledge of the sound as the
stinging bullet spins past the head or the pain as it strikes.

But what of all this? This rhythm of stung boys? Or
boys as filled with life as fish or birds? Only that it was
taking place that morning.

What of the ghastly black huddle on the Professor's
desk? The sunlight streaming through the leaves of the
plane tree had begun to dapple it with shimmering lozenges of light. It snored—a disgraceful sound to hear during the first lesson of a summer morning.

But the moments of its indulgence were numbered, for
there was, all of a sudden, a cry from near the ceiling

and above the schoolroom door. It was the voice of an urchin, a freckled wisp of a thing, who was perched on a high cupboard. The glass of the fanlight above the door was at his shoulder. It was dark with grime, but a small circle the size of a coin was kept transparent and through this spy-hole he could command a view of the corridor outside. He could thus give warning not only to the whole class but to the Professor at the first sign of danger.

It was rarely that either Barquentine or Deadyawn made a tour of the schoolrooms, but it was as well to have the freckled urchin stationed on the cupboard from first thing in the morning onward, for there was nothing more irritating than for the class to be disturbed.

That morning, lying there like a toy on the cupboard top, he had become so intrigued by the changing fortunes of the game below him that it had been over a minute since he had last put his eye to the spy-hole. When he did so it was to see, not twenty feet from the door, a solid phalanx of Professors, like a black tide, with Deadyawn himself at the fore, out-topping the others, in his high chair on wheels.

Deadyawn, who headed the phalanx, was head and shoulders above the rest of the staff, although he was by no means sitting up straight in his high, narrow chair. With its small wheels squeaking at the feet of the four legs, it rocked to and fro as it was propelled rapidly forward by the usher, who was as yet invisible to the wisp at the spy-hole, being hidden by the high, ugly piece of furniture—ugly beyond belief—with its disproportionate feeding tray at the height of Deadyawn's heart and the raw little shelf for his feet.

What was visible of Deadyawn's face above the tray appeared to be awake—a sure sign that something of particular urgency was in the air.

Behind him the rustling darkness was solid with the Professors. What had happened to their various classes, and what on earth they could want on this lazy floor of the castle at any time, let alone at the beginning of the day, was unguessable. But here, nevertheless, they

were, their gowns whisking and whispering along the walls
on either side. There was an intentness in their gait, a
kind of mass seriousness, quite frightening.

The midget boy on the cupboard-top cried his warning with a shriller note in his voice than his schoolfel-
lows had ever heard before.

"The 'Yawner'!" he screamed. "Quick! Quick! Quick!
The Yawner'n all of 'em! Let me down! Let me down!"

The rhythm of the hazardous game was broken. Not a
single pellet whizzed past the head of the last boy to
burst out of the sunlight and crash into the leather wall.
In a moment the room was suspiciously quiet. Four rows
of boys sat half turned at their desks, their heads cocked
to one side, as they listened to the squeaking of Deadyawn's chair on its small wheels as it rolled toward them
through the silence.

The wisp had been caught, having dropped from what
must have seemed to him a great height into the arms
of a big straw-headed youth.

The two floor boards had been grabbed and shot back
into their long, narrow cavities immediately below the
Professor's desk. But a mistake had been made, and
when it was noticed it was too late for anything to be done
about it. One of the boards in the whirl of the moment
had been put back *upside down*.

On the desk itself the heavy black doglike weight was
still snoring. Even the shrill cry of the lookout had done
no more than send a twitch through the jointed huddle.

Any boy in the first row, had he thought it possible
to reach the Professor's desk and get back to his own
place before the entry of Deadyawn and the staff, would
have thrown the folds of Bellgrove's gown off Bellgrove's
sleeping head, where it lay sunk between his arms on the
desk top, and would have shaken Bellgrove into some sort
of awareness; for the black and shapeless thing was indeed the old master himself, lost beneath the awning
of his gown. For his pupils had draped it over his reverend head, as they always did when he fell asleep.

But there was no time. The squeaking of the wheels
had stopped. There was a great trampling and scuffling

of feet as the Professors closed their ranks behind their chief. The door handle was beginning to turn.

As the door opened, thirty or so boys, doubled over their desks, could be seen scribbling furiously, their brows knit in concentration.

There was for the moment an unholy silence.

And then the voice of the usher, Mr. Fly, cried out from behind Deadyawn's chair: "The Headmaster!" And the classroom scrambled to its feet. All except Bellgrove.

The wheels began to squeak again as the high chair was steered up one of the ink-stained aisles between the rows of desks.

By this time the mortarboards had followed the Head-master into the room, and under these mortarboards the faces of Opus Fluke, Spiregrain, Perch-Prism, Throd, Flannelcat, Shred and Shrivell, Cutflower, and the rest were easily recognizable. Deadyawn, who was on a tour of the classrooms, had, after inspecting each in turn, sent the boys to their red-stone yard and kept their mas-ters with him—so that he now had practically the whole staff at his heels. The boys would shortly be spread out in great fans and sent off on a day-long hunt for Titus. For it was his disappearance which was causing this un-precedented activity.

How merciful a thing is man's ignorance of his imme-diate future! What a ghastly, paralyzing thing it would have been if all those present could have known what was about to happen within a matter of seconds! For noth-ing short of preknowledge could have stopped the occur-rence, so suddenly it sprang upon them.

The scholars were still standing, and Mr. Fly, the usher, who had reached the end of the passage between the desks, was about to turn the high chair to the left and to run it up under Bellgrove's desk where Deadyawn could speak to his oldest Professor, when the calamity occurred, and even the dreadful fact of Titus's disappearance was forgotten. For The Fly had slipped! His feet had fled from under his perky body. His cocky little walk was sud-denly a splayed confusion of legs. They shot to and fro like a frog's. But for all their lashing they could get no grip on the slippery floor, for he had trodden on that deadly board which had been returned—upside down—to its place below Bellgrove's desk.

The Fly had no time to let go his grip of the high chair. It swayed above him like a tower—and then while the long line of the staff peered over one another's shoulders and the boys stood at their desks transfixed, something more appalling than they had ever contemplated took place before them.

For as The Fly came down in a crash on the boards, the wheels of the high chair whirled like tops and gave their final screech, and the rickety piece of furniture leaped like a mad thing and from its summit something was hurled high into the air! It was Deadyawn!

He descended from somewhere near the ceiling like a visitor from another planet, or from the cosmic realms of Outer Space, as with all the signs of the Zodiac fluttering about him he plunged earthward.

Had he but had a long brass trumpet at his lips and the power of arching his back and curling upward as he neared the floor boards, and of swooping across the room over the heads of the scholars in a riot of draperies, to float away and out through the leaves of the plane tree and over the back of Gormenghast, to disappear forever from the rational world—then, if only he had had the power to do this, that dreadful sound would have been avoided: that most dreadful and sickening sound which not a single boy or Professor who heard it that morning was ever able to forget. It darkened the heart and brain. It darkened the very sunlight itself in that summer classroom.

But it was not enough that their hearing was appalled by the sound of a skull being crushed like an egg—for, as though everything were working together to produce the maximum horror, Fate had it that the Headmaster, in descending absolutely vertically, struck the floor with the top of his cranium, and remained upside down, in a horrible state of balance, having stiffened with a form of premature *rigor mortis*.

The soft, imponderable, flaccid Deadyawn, that arch-symbol of delegated duties, of negation and apathy, appeared now that he was upside down to have more life in him than he had ever had before. His limbs, stiffened in the death-spasm, were positively muscular. His crushed skull appeared to balance a body that had suddenly perceived its reason for living.

The first movement, after the gasp of horror that ran across the sunny schoolroom, came from among the debris of what was once the high chair.

The usher emerged, his red hair ruffled, quick eyes bulging, teeth chattering with terror. At the sight of his master upside down he made for the window, all trace of cockiness gone from his carriage, his sense of propriety so outraged that there was nothing he wanted so much as to make a quick end to himself. Climbing on the window sill, The Fly swung his legs over and then dropped to the quadrangle a hundred feet below.

Perch-Prism stepped forward from the ranks of the Professors.

"All boys will make their way immediately to the redstone yard," he said in a crisp, high staccato. "All boys will wait there quietly until they are given instructions. Parsley!"

A youth, with his jaw hanging wide and his eyes glazed, started as though he had been struck. He wrenched his eyes from the inverted Deadyawn, but could not find his voice.

"Parsley," said Perch-Prism again, "you will lead the class out—and, Chives, you will take up the rear. Hurry now! Hurry! Turn your heads to the door, there. You! Yes, you, Sage Minor! And you there, Mint or whatever your name is—wake your ideas up. Hustle! Hustle! Hustle!"

Stupefied, the scholars began to file out of the door, their heads still turned over their shoulders at their late Headmaster.

Three or four other Professors had to some extent recovered from the first horrible shock and were helping Perch-Prism to hustle the remnants of the class from the room.

At last the place was clear of boys. The sunlight played across the empty desks: it lit up the faces of the Professors, but seemed to leave their gowns and mortarboards as black as though they alone were in shadow. It lit the soles of Deadyawn's boots as they pointed stiffly to the ceiling.

Perch-Prism, glancing at the Professors, saw that it was up to him to make the next move. His beady black eyes shone. What he had of a jaw he thrust forward. His round, babyish, piglike face was set for action.

He opened his prim, rather savage little mouth and was about to call for help in righting the corpse, when a muffled voice came from an unexpected quarter. It sounded both near and far. It was difficult to make out a word, but for a moment or two the voice became less blurred. "No, I don't think so, l'l man," it said, "for 't's love long lost, my queen, while Bellgrove guards you . . ." (the drowsy voice continued in its sleep) . . . "when lion . . . sprowl I'll tear their manes . . . awf . . . yoo. When serpents hiss at you I'll tread on dem . . . probably . . . and scatter birds of prey to left an' right."

A long whistle from under the draperies and then, all of a sudden, with a shudder, the invertebrate mass began to uncoil itself as Bellgrove's shrouded head raised itself slowly from his arms. Before he freed himself of the last layer of gown he sat back in his tutorial chair, and while he worked with his hands to free his head, his voice came out of the cloth darkness: "Name an isthmus!" it boomed. "Tinepott? . . . Quagfire? . . . Sparrowmarsh? . . . Hagg? . . . Dankle? . . . What! Can no one tell his old master the name of an isthmus?"

With a wrench he unraveled his head of the last vestment of gown, and there was his long, weak, noble face as naked and venerable as any deep-sea monster's.

It was a few moments before his pale-blue eyes had accustomed themselves to the light. He lifted his sculptured brow and blinked. "Name an isthmus," he repeated, but in a less interested voice, for he was beginning to be conscious of the silence in the room.

"Name . . . an . . . isthmus!"

His eyes had accustomed themselves sufficiently for him to see, immediately ahead of him, the body of the Headmaster balanced upon his head.

In the peculiar silence his attention was so riveted upon the apparition in front of him that he hardly realized the absence of his class.

He got to his feet and bit at his knuckle, his head thrust forward. He withdrew his head and shook himself like a great dog; and then he leaned forward and stared once more. He had prayed that he was still asleep. But no, this was no dream. He had no idea that the Headmaster was dead, and so, with a great effort (thinking that a fundamental change had taken in Deadyawn's psyche, and that he was showing Bellgrove this balancing feat in an access of self-revelation), he (Bellgrove) began to clap his big, finely constructed hands together in a succession of deferential thuds, and to wear upon his face an expression of someone both intrigued and surprised, his shoulders drawn back, his head at a slant, his eyebrows raised, and the big forefinger of his right hand at his lips. The line of his mouth rose at either end, but his upward curve might as well have been downward for all the power it had to disguise his consternation.

The heavy thuds of his hand-clapping sounded solitary. They echoed fully about the room. He turned his eyes to his class as though for support or explanation. He found neither. Only the infinite emptiness of deserted desks, with the broad, hazy shafts of the sun slanting across them.

He put his hand to his head and sat down suddenly.

"Bellgrove!" A crisp, sharp voice from behind him caused him to swing around. There, in a double line, silent as Deadyawn or the empty desks, stood the Professors of Gormenghast, like a male chorus or a travesty of Judgment Day.

Bellgrove stumbled to his feet and passed his hand across his brow.

"Life itself is an isthmus," said a voice beside him.

Bellgrove turned his head. His mouth was ajar. His carious teeth were bared in a nervous smile.

"What's that?" he said, catching hold of the speaker's gown near the shoulder and pulling it forward.

"Get a grip on yourself," said the voice, and it was Shred's. "This is a new gown. Thank you. Life is an isthmus, I said."

"Why?" said Bellgrove, but with one eye still on Deadyawn. He was not really listening.

"You ask me *why!*" said Shred. "Only think! Our Headmaster there," he said (bowing slightly to the corpse), "is even now in the second continent. Death's continent. But long before he was even . . ."

Mr. Shred was interrupted by Perch-Prism. "Mr. Fluke," he shouted, "will you give me a hand?" But for all their efforts they could do little with Deadyawn except reverse him. To seat him in Bellgrove's chair, prior to his removal to the Professors' Mortuary, was in a way accomplished, though it was more a case of leaning the Headmaster *against* the chair than seating him *in* it, for he was as stiff as a starfish.

But his gown was draped carefully about him. His face was covered with the blackboard duster, and when at last his mortarboard had been found under the debris of the high chair, it was placed with due decorum on his head.

"Gentlemen," said Perch-Prism, when they had returned to the Common-Room after a junior member had been dispatched to the Doctor's, the Undertaker's, and to the red-stone yard to inform the scholars that the rest of the day was to be spent in an organized search for their schoolfellow Titus. "Gentlemen," said Perch-Prism, "two things are paramount. One, that the search for the young Earl shall be pushed forward immediately in spite of interruption; and two, the appointment of the new Headmaster must be immediately made, to avoid anarchy. In my opinion," said Perch-Prism, his hands grasping the shoulder-tags of his gown while he rocked to and fro on his heels, "in my opinion the choice should fall, as usual, upon the senior member of the staff, *whatever his qualifications*."

There was immediate agreement about this. As one man they saw an even lazier future open out its indolent vistas before them. Bellgrove alone was irritated. For mixed with his pride was resentment at Perch-Prism's handling of the subject. As probable Headmaster he should already have been taking the initiative.

"What d'you mean by 'whatever his qualifications'—damn you, 'Prism?" he snarled.

A terrible convulsion in the center of the room, where Mr. Opus Fluke lay sprawled over one of the desks, revealed how that gentleman was fighting for breath.

He was yelling with laughter, yelling like a hundred hounds; but he could make no sound. He shook and rocked, the tears pouring down his crude, male face, his chin like a long loaf shuddering as it pointed to the ceiling.

Bellgrove, turning from Perch-Prism, surveyed Mr. Fluke. His noble head had colored, but suddenly the blood was driven from it. For a flashing moment Bellgrove saw his destiny. Was he, or was he not, to be a leader of men? Was this, or was this not, one of those crucial moments when authority must be exercised—or withheld forever? Here they were, in full conclave. Here was he—Bellgrove—within his feet of clay, standing in all his weakness before his colleagues. But there was something in him which was not consistent with the proud cast of his face.

At that moment he knew himself to be of finer marl. He had known what ambition was. True, it was long ago and he was no longer worried by such ideas, but he had known of it.

Quite deliberately, realizing that if he did not act at once he would never act again, he lifted a large stone bottle of red ink from the table at his side and, on reaching Mr. Fluke and finding his head thrown back, his eyes closed, and his strong jaws wide open in a paroxysm of seismic laughter, Mr. Bellgrove poured the entire contents down the funnel of Fluke's throat in one movement of the wrist. Turning to the staff, "Perch-Prism," he said, in a voice of such patriarchal authority as startled the Professors almost as much as the ink-pouring, "you will set about organizing the search for his Lordship. Take the staff with you to the red-stone yard. Flannelcat, you will get Mr. Fluke removed to the sickroom. Fetch the Doctor for him. Report progress this evening. I shall be found in the Headmaster's study. Good morning, Gentlemen."

As he swept out of the room with a bellying sweep of his gown and a toss of his silver hair, his old heart was beating madly. Oh, the joy of giving orders! Oh, the joy of it! Once he had closed the door behind him, he ran, with high monstrous bounds, to the Headmaster's study and collapsed into the Headmaster's chair—*his* chair from now onward. He hugged his knees against his chin, flopped over on his side, and wept with the first real sense of happiness he had known for many years.

Chapter Eighteen

LIKE rooks hovering in a black cloud over their nests, a posse of Professors, in a whirl of gowns and a shuffling roofage of mortarboards, flapped and sidled their individual ways toward, and eventually *through,* a narrow opening in a flank of the Masters' Hall.

This opening was less like a doorway than a fissure, though the remains of a lintel were visible and a few boards swung aimlessly near the head of the opening to show that there had once been a door. Faintly discernible on these upper boards were these words: *To the Professorial Quarters: Strictly Private*—and above them some irreverent hand had sketched the lively outline of a stoat in gown and mortarboard. Whether or not the

Professors had ever noticed this drawing, it is certain that it held no interest for them today. It was enough for them to work their way through the fissure in the wall where the darkness engulfed them, one by one.

Doorless as the opening was, yet there was no question about the Professors' Quarters being strictly private. What lay beyond that cleft in the heavy wall had been a secret for many generations, a secret known only to the succeeding staffs—those hoary and impossible bands with whom, by ancient tradition, there was no interference. There had once been talk of *progress* by a young member of a bygone staff, but he had been instantly banished.

It was for the Professors to suffer no change. To eye the scaling paint, the rusting pen-nib, the sculptured desk lid, with understanding and approval.

They had by now, one and all, negotiated the narrow opening. Not a soul was left in the Masters' Hall. It was as though no one had been there. A wasp zoomed across the empty floor boards with a roar; and then the silence filled the hall once again, as though with a substance.

Where were the Professors now? What were they doing? They were halfway along the third curve of a domed passageway which ended in a descending flight of steps at the base of which stood an enormous turnstile.

As the Professors moved like a black, hydra-headed dragon with a hundred flapping wings, it might have been noticed that for all the sinister quality of the monster's upper half, yet in its numerous legs there was a certain gaiety. The little legs of blackness almost twinkled, almost hopped. The great legs let fall their echoing feet in a jocular and carefree fashion as though they were smacking a friend on the back.

And yet it was not wholly gay, this great composite dragon. For there were two of its feet which moved less happily than the others. They belonged to Bellgrove.

Delighted as he was to be the Headmaster, yet the alteration which this was making in his way of life was beginning to gall him. And yet was there not something about him more imposing than before? Had he taken some kind of grip on himself? His face was stern and melancholy. He led his staff like a prophet to their quarters. *Their* quarters, for they were no longer *his*. With his accession to Headmasterdom he had forfeited his room above the Professors' Quadrangle which he had occupied for three-quarters of his life. Alone among the Professors it was for him to turn back after he had escorted his staff a certain distance of the way, and to return alone to the Headmaster's bedroom above the Masters' Hall.

It had been a difficult time for him since he had first put on the Zodiac gown of high office. Was he winning or losing his fight for authority? He longed for respect, but he loved indolence also. Time would tell whether the nobility of his august head could become the symbol of his leadership. To tread the corridors of Gormenghast the acknowledged master of Staff and pupil alike! He must be wise, stern, yet generous. He must be revered. That was it . . . *revered*. But did this mean that he would be involved in extra work . . . ? Surely, at his age . . . ?

The excitement in the multiform legs of the dragon had only begun to operate since the Professors had left the Masters' Hall behind them, and with the Hall their duties also. For their day in the classrooms of Gormenghast was over, and if there was one thing above others that the Professors looked forward to, it was this thrill, this five o'clock thrill of returning to their quarters.

They breathed in the secret air of their demesne. Over their faces a series of private smiles began to play. They were nearing a world they understood—not with their brains, but with the dumb, happy, ancestral understanding of their marrow bones.

The long evening was ahead. Not one ink-faced boy would they see for fifteen hours.

Taking deep breaths into its many lungs, the hydra-headed dragon approached the stone flight of steps. In its wake, along the domed ceiling of the long corridor, an impalpable serpent of exhaled pipe-smoke hovered and coiled.

An almost imperceptible widening of the corridor was now apparent. The Professors became less cramped in their movements as the dragon began to come to bits. The widening of the corridor had become something quite unique, for a great vista of wooden floor boards was spread before them until the walls (now about forty feet apart) turned abruptly away on either side to flank the wide wooden terrace which overlooked the flight of stairs. Although this flight was exceptionally broad and the Professors as they descended had plenty of space in which to indulge themselves (if the whim should take them) in a general loosening of their deportment, a more vigorous smacking or a fiercer twinkling of their feet—yet at the base of the stairs there was, once again, a bottleneck; for although there was plenty of room on each side of the ancient turnstile for them to stream past and into the great crumbling chamber beyond, yet the custom was that the turnstile should be the only means of access to the chamber.

Above the stone flight the sloping roof was in so advanced a state of disintegration that a great deal of light found its way through the holes in the roof, to lie in golden pools all over the great flight of stairs, with their low treads and wide terracelike shelves of shallow stone.

As with their difficult egress from the Masters' Hall, the Professors were now being held up at the Great Turnstile.

But here it was a more leisurely affair. There was neither the scuffling nor the agitation. They were in their own realms again. Their apartments that surrounded the small quadrangle would be waiting for them. What did it matter if they waited a little longer than they could have wished? The long, bland, archaic, nostalgic, almond-smelling evening lay ahead of them, and then the long, sequestered night before the clanging bell aroused them, and a day of ink- and thumb-marks, cribbing and broken spectacles, flies and figures, coastlines, prepositions, isthmuses and essays, paper darts, test tubes, catapults, chemicals and prisms, dates, battles and tame white mice, and its hundred half-formed, ingenious, and quizzical faces, with their chapped red ears that never listened, renewed itself.

Deliberately, almost *augustly,* the gowned and mortar-boarded figures followed one another through the great red turnstile and filed into the chamber beyond.

But for the most part, the Professors stood in groups, or were seated on the lower steps of the stone flights, where they waited to take their turn at the " 'stile." They were in no hurry. Here and there a savant could be seen lying stretched at full length along one of the steps or shelves of the stone stairs. Here and there a group would be squatting like aboriginals upon their haunches, their gowns gathered about them. Some were in shadow, and very dark they looked—like bandits in a bad light; some were silhouetted against the hazy, golden swathes of the sunshafts; and some stood transfixed in the last rays as they streamed through the honeycombed roof.

A small muscular gentleman with a spade-shaped beard was balancing himself upside down and was working his way down the wide steps on his hands. His head was, for the most part, hidden because his gown fell over and obliterated it, so that, apart from balancing, he had to feel for the edge of each step with his hidden hands. But occasionally his head would appear out of the folds of his gown and the beard could be seen for a quick moment, its harsh black spade a few inches from the ground.

Of the few who watched him bemusedly there were none who had not seen it all a hundred times before. A long-limbed figure, with his knees drawn up to his blue jaw, which they supported, stared abstractedly at a group which stood out in silhouette against a swarm of golden motes. Had he been a little closer and a little less abstracted he might have heard some very peculiar ejaculations.

But he could see quite clearly that at the center of this distant group a short, precise figure was handing out to his colleagues what looked like small, stiff pieces of paper.

And so it was. The sprightly Perch-Prism was dispens-

ing the invitation cards which he had received that same
afternoon by special messenger:

IRMA and ALFRED PRUNESQUALLOR
hope to have the
pleasure of ....'s company
on
.... (etc.)

One by one the invited parties were handed their invitations, and there was not a single Professor who could
withhold either a gasp or grunt of surprise or a twitch of
the eyebrow.

Some were so stupefied that they were forced to sit
down on the steps for a short while until their pulse rate
slackened.

Shred and Shrivell tapped their teeth with the gilded
edges of their cards, and were already making guesses
at the psychological implications.

Fluke, his wide lipless mouth disgorging endless formations of dense and cumulous smoke, was gradually
allowing a giant grin to spread itself across his gaunt
face.

Flannelcat was embarrassingly excited, and was already trying to rub a thumb-mark from the corner of his
card, which he had every intention of framing.

Bellgrove had his great prophet's jaw hanging wide.

There were sixteen invitations altogether. The entire
staff of the Leather Room had been invited.

They had arrived, these invitation cards, at a time
when Perch-Prism had been the only master present in
the Common-Room, and he had taken over the responsibility of delivering them personally to the others.

Suddenly Opus Fluke's long leather mouth opened like
a horse's, and a howl of insensitive laughter reverberated
through the sun-blotched place.

A score of mortarboards swiveled.

"Really!" said the sharp, precise voice of Perch-
Prism. "Really, my dear Fluke! What a way to receive
an invitation from a lady! Come, come."

But Fluke could hear nothing. The idea of being invited to a party by Irma Prunesquallor had somehow broken through to the most sensitized area of his diaphragm, and he yelled and yelled again until he was breathless. As he panted hoarsely to a standstill, he did not even look about him: he was still in his own world of amusement; but he *did* hold the invitation card up before his wet and pebbly eyes once more, only to open his wide mouth again in a fresh spasm; but there was no laughter left in him.

Perch-Prism's pug-baby features expressed a certain condescension, as though he *understood* how Mr. Fluke felt, but was nevertheless surprised and mildly irritated by the coarseness in his colleague's make-up.

It was Perch-Prism's saving grace that in spite of his old-maidishness, his clipped and irritatingly academic delivery, and his general aura of omniscience, yet he had a strongly developed sense of the ridiculous and was often forced to laugh when his brain and pride wished otherwise.

"And the Headmaster," he said, turning to the noble figure at his side, whose jaw still hung open like the mouth of a sepulcher. "What does *he* think, I wonder? What does our Headmaster think about it all?"

Bellgrove came to with a start. He looked about him with the melancholy grandeur of a sick lion. Then he found his mouth was open, so he closed it gradually, for he would not have them think that he would hurry himself for anyone.

He turned his vacant lion's eye to Perch-Prism, who stood there perkily looking up at him and tapping his shiny invitation card against his polished thumbnail.

"My dear Perch-Prism," said Bellgrove, "why on earth should you be interested in my reaction to what is, after all, not a very extraordinary thing in my life? It is possible, you know," he continued laboriously, "it is just possible that when I was a younger man I received more invitations to various kinds of functions than you have ever received, or can ever hope to receive, during the course of your life."

"But *exactly!*" said Perch-Prism. "And that is why we want his opinion. That is why our Headmaster alone can help us. What could be more enlightening than to have it straight from the horse's mouth?"

For neatness' sake he could not help wishing that he were addressing Opus Fluke, for Bellgrove's mouth, though hardly hyper-human, was nothing like a horse's.

"Prism," he said, "compared with me you are a young man. But you are not so young as to be ignorant of the elements of decent conduct. Be good enough in your puff-adder attitude to life to find room for one delicacy at least; and that is to address me, if you must, in a manner less calculated to offend. I will *not* be talked *across*. My staff must realize this from the outset. I will *not* be the third person singular. I am old, I admit it. But I am nevertheless here. *Here,*" he roared; "and standing on the selfsame pavement with you, Master Prism; and I *exist,* by hell! in my full conversational and vocative rights."

He coughed and shook his leonine head. "Change your idiom, my young friend, or change your tense, and lend me a handkerchief to put over my head—these sun-beams are giving me a headache."

Perch-Prism produced a blue silk handkerchief at once and draped it over the peeved and noble head.

"Poor old 'prickles' Bellgrove, poor old fangs," he mused, whispering the words into the old man's ears as he tied the corners of the blue handkerchief into little knots, where it hung over the elder's head. "It'll be just the thing for him, so it will—a *wild* party at the Doctor's, ha, ha, ha, ha, ha!"

Bellgrove opened his rather weak mouth and grinned. He could never keep his sham dignity up for long; but then he remembered his position again and in a voice of sepulchral authority—"Watch your step, sir," he said. "You have twisted my tail for long enough."

"What a peculiar business this Prunesquallor affair *is,* my dear Flannelcat," said Mr. Crust. "I rather doubt whether I can afford to go. I wonder whether you could possibly—er—lend me . . ."

But Flannelcat interrupted. "They've asked me, too," he said, his invitation card shaking in his hand. "It is a long time since . . ."

"It is a long time since our evenings were disturbed from the Outside like this," interrupted Perch-Prism. "You gentlemen will have to brush yourselves up a bit. How long is it since you have seen a lady, Mr. Fluke?"

"Not half long enough," said Opus Fluke, drawing noisily at his pipe. "Never cared for hens. Irritated me. May be wrong—quite possible—that's another point. But for me—no. Spoiled the day completely."

"But you will accept, of course, won't you, my dear fellow?" said Perch-Prism, inclining his shiny round head to one side.

Opus Fluke yawned and then stretched himself before he replied.

"When is it, friend?" he asked (as though it made any difference to him when his every evening was an identical yawn).

"Next Friday evening, at seven o'clock—R.S.V.P. it is," panted Flannelcat.

"If dear old bloody Bellgrove goes," said Mr. Fluke, after a long pause, "I couldn't stay away—not if I were paid. It'll be as good as a play to watch him."

Bellgrove bared his irregular teeth in a leonine snarl and then he took out a small notebook, with his eyes on Mr. Fluke, and made a note. Approaching his taunter, "Red Ink," he whispered, and then began to laugh uncontrollably. Mr. Fluke was stupefied.

"Well . . . well . . . well . . . ," he said at last.

"It is far from 'well,' Mr. Fluke," said Bellgrove, recovering his composure; "and it will not be well until you learn to speak to your Headmaster like a gentleman."

Said Shrivell to Shred: "As for Irma Prunesquallor, it's a plain case of mirror-madness, brought on by enlargement of the terror-duct—but not altogether."

Said Shred to Shrivell: "I disagree. It is the Doctor's shadow cast upon the shorn and naked soul of his sister, which shadow she takes to be destiny—and *here* I agree with you that the terror-duct comes into play, for the length of her neck and the general frustration have driven her subconscious into a general craving for males —a substitute, of course, for golliwoggs."

Said Shrivell to Shred: "Perhaps we are both right in our different ways." He beamed at his friend. "Let us leave it at that, shall we? We will know more when we see her."

"Oh, shut up! you bloody old woman," said Mule-fire, with a deadly scowl.

"Oh, come, come, la!" said Cutflower. "Let us be terribly gay, la! My, my! If it isn't getting chilly, la—call me feverish."

It was true, for looking up they found they were plunged in deep shade, the sun-blotch having moved on; and they saw also, as they raised their heads, that they were the last of the Professors to be left on the stone steps.

Motioning the others to follow, Bellgrove led them through the red turnstile; a moment or two after, they had all passed through its creaking arms and into the dark and crumbling hall beyond; he turned and climbed the staircase alone and eventually found himself in the Masters' Hall once more.

But the Staff, after passing through the crumbling chamber, Indian-filed its way along a peculiarly high and narrow passage; and at last, after descending yet another flight of stairs—this time of ancient walnut—they passed through a doorway on the far side of which lay their quadrangle.

It was here, in the communal privacy of their quarters, that the excitement which they had felt mounting within them once they had passed out of the Masters' Hall lessened; but another kind of excitement quickened. On reaching their quadrangle they had digested the fact that they were free for another evening. The sense of escape had gone, but an even lighter sensation freed their hearts and feet. Their bowels felt like water. Great lumps arose in their throats. There were tears in the corners of their eyes.

All about their quadrangle the pillars of the cloisters

glowed (although they were in shadow) with the dark rose-gold of the brick. Above the arches of the cloisters a terrace of rose-colored brickwork circumscribed the quadrangle at about twenty feet above the ground; and punctuating the wall at the rear of this high terrace were the doors of the Professors' apartments. On each door, according to custom, the owner's name was added to the long list of former occupants. These names were carefully printed on the black wood of each door, their vertical columns of small and exact lettering all but filling the available space. The rooms themselves were small and uniform in shape, but were as various in character as their occupants.

The first thing that the Professors did on returning to their quarters was to go to their several rooms and change their black gowns of office for the dark-red variety issued for their evening hours.

Their mortarboards were hung up behind their doors or sent skimming across their rooms to some convenient ledge or corner. The dog's-eared condition of most of their boards was due to this skimming. When thrown in the right way, out of doors and against a slight breeze, they could be made to climb into the air, the black cup uppermost, the tassels floating below like the black tails of donkeys. When thirty at a time soared at the sun above. the quadrangle, then was a schoolboy's nightmare made palpable.

Once in their wine-red gowns it was the usual custom to step out of their rooms onto the terrace of rose-red brick, where, leaning on its balustrade, the Professors would spend one of the pleasantest hours of the day, conversing or ruminating until the sound of the supper gong called them to the refectory.

To the old quadman, sweeping the leaves from the mellow brickwork of the quadrangle floor, it was a sight that never failed to please as, surrounded on every side by the glowing cloisters and above them by the long wine-red line of the Professors as they leaned with their elbows on the terrace wall, he shepherded the fluttering leaves together with his ragged broom.

On this particular night, although not a single mortarboard was sent skimming, the staff became very flighty indeed toward the end of their evening meal in the Long Hall, when innumerable suggestions were propounded as to the inner reason for the Prunesquallors' invitations. The most fantastic of all was put forward by Cutflower, to wit that Irma, in need of a husband, was turning to them as a possible source. At this suggestion the crude Opus Fluke, in an excess of ribald mirth, crashed his great, raw ham of a hand down on the long table so heavily as to cause a *corps de ballet* of knives, forks, and spoons to sail into the air and for a pair of table legs to do the splits; so that the nine Professors at his table found the remains of their supper lying at every angle below the level of their knees. Those who were holding their glasses in their hands were happy enough; but for those whose wine was spilled among the debris, a moment or two of reflection was occasioned before they could regain the spirit of the evening.

The idea that any one of them should get married seemed to them ludicrously funny. It was not that they felt themselves unworthy, far from it. It was that such a thing belonged to another world.

"But yes, but yes, indeed, Cutflower, you are right," said Shrivell at the first opportunity of making himself heard. "Shred and I were saying much the same thing."

"Quite so," said Shred.

"In my case," said Shrivell, "sublimation is simple enough, for what with the crags and eagles that find their way into every confounded dream I have—and I dream every night, not to speak of my automatic writing, which puts my absurd love for Nature in its place—for in reading what I have written, as it were in a trance, I can see how foolish it is to give a thought to natural phenomena, which are, after all, nothing but an accretion of accidents . . . er . . . where was I?"

"It doesn't matter," said Perch-Prism. "The point is that we have been invited: that we shall be guests, and that above all we shall do the right thing. Good grief!"

he said, looking at the faces of the staff. "I wish I were going alone."

A bell rang.

The Professors rose at once to their feet. A moment of traditional observance had arrived. Turning the long tables upside down—and there were twelve of them—they seated themselves, one behind another, within the upturned table tops as though they were boats and were about to oar their way into some fabulous ocean.

For a moment there was a pause, and then the bell rang again. Before its echo had died in the long refectory, the twelve crews of the motionless flotilla had raised their voices in an obscure chant of former days when, presumably, it had held some kind of significance. Tonight it was bayed forth into the half-light with a slow, knocking rhythm, but there was no disguising the boredom in their voices. They had intoned those lines, night after night, for as long as they had been Professors, and it might well have been taken for a dirge, so empty were their voices:

> *Hold fast*
> *To the Law*
> *Of the last*
> *Cold tome,*
> *Where the earth*
> *Of the truth*
> *Lies thick*
> *On the page,*
> *And the loam*
> *Of faith*
> *In the ink*
> *Long fled*
> *From the drone*
> *Of the nib*
> *Flows on*
> *Through the breath*
> *Of the bone*
> *Reborn*
> *In a dawn*

Of doom
Where blooms
The rose
For the winds
The Child
For the tomb
The thrush.
For the hush
Of song,
The corn
For the scythe
And the thorn
In wait
For the heart
Till the last
Of the first
Depart,
And the least
Of the past
Is dust
And the dust
Is lost.
Hold fast!

Chapter Nineteen

THE margin of the forest under whose high branches Titus was standing was an interwoven screen of foliage, more like a green wall constructed for some histrionic purpose than a natural growth. Was it to hide away some drama that it arose there, so sheer and so thick? Or was it the backcloth of some immortal mime? Which was the stage and which the audience? There was not a sound.

Titus, wrenching two boughs apart, thrust himself forward and wriggled into the green darkness; thrust again, prizing his feet against a great lateral root. The leaves and the moss were cold with the dew. Working forward on his elbows, he found his way almost completely barred by a tough network of boughs; but the edge of his eagerness to break his way through was whetted, for a branch had swung back and switched him across his cheek, and in the pain of the moment he fought the muscled branches, until the upper part of his body had forced a gap which he kept from reclosing with his aching shoulders. His arms were forward of his body and he was able to free his face of the leaves and, as he panted to regain his breath, to see ahead of him, spreading into the clear distances, the forest floor like a sea of golden moss. From its heaving expanses arose, as through the chimera of a daydream, a phantasmic gathering of ancient oaks. Like dappled gods they stood, each in his own preserve, the wide glades of moss flowing between them in swathes of gold and green and away into the clear, dwindling distances.

When his breath came more easily, Titus realized the silence of the picture that hung there before him. Like a canvas of gold with its hundreds of majestic oaks, their winding branches dividing and subdividing into gilded fingertips—the solid acorns and the deep clusters of the legendary leaves.

His heart beat loudly as the warm breath of the silence flowed about him and drew him in.

In his last wrench and thrust to escape from the marginal boughs, his coat was torn off bodily by a thorn-tree with a hand of hideous fingers. He left it there, hanging from the branch, the long thorns of the tree impaling it like the fingernails of a ghoul.

Once the noise of his fight with the branches had subsided and the warm everlasting silence had come down again, he stepped forward upon the moss. It was resilient and springy, its golden surface exquisitely compact. He moved again with a higher tread and found that on landing it was the easiest thing in the world to float off into the next movement. The ground was made for running on, for every step lifted the body into the next. Titus leaped to his right and began to lope off down the dark-green verge of the forest in giant bounds. The exhilaration of these "flights" through the air were for some while all-absorbing, but as their novelty staled so there came a mounting terror, for the thick screen of the forest's verge on his right appeared endless, stretching away, as it did, to the limit of his vision; and the motionless, soundless glow of the oaks and the great spaces of moss on his left seemed never to change, though tree after tree swam by him as he fled.

Not a bird called. Not a squirrel moved among the branches. Not a leaf fell. Even his feet when they struck the moss were soundless; only a faint sigh passed his ears as he floated, reminding him that there was such a thing as sound.

And now, what he had loved he loathed. He loathed this deathly, terrible silence. He loathed the gold light among the trees, the endless vistas of the moss—even the gliding flight from footmark to footmark. For it was as though he were being drawn toward some dangerous place or person, and had no power to hold himself back. The midair thrill was now the thrill of Fear.

He had been afraid of leaving the dark margin on his right, for it was his only hold upon his location; but now he felt it as part of some devilish plan, and that to cling to its tangled skirt would be to deliver himself to some ambushed horror; and so he turned suddenly to his left and, although the vistas of oakland were now a sickening and phantom land, he bounded into its gold heart with all the speed he could.

Fear grew upon him as he careered. He had become more an antelope than a boy, but for all his speed he must have been a novice in the art of travel—through moss-leaping—for suddenly, while he was in midair, his arms held out on either side for balance, he caught sight, for the merest fraction of an instant, of a living creature.

Like himself, it was in midair, but there was no other resemblance. Titus was heavily if sparsely built.

This creature was exquisitely slender. It floated through the golden air like a feather, the slender arms along the sides of the gracile body, the head turned slightly away and inclined a little as though on a pillow of air.

Titus was by now convinced that he was asleep: that he was running through the deep of a dream: that his fear was nightmare: that what he had just seen was no more than an apparition, and that though it haunted him he knew the hopeless absurdity of following so fleeting a wisp of the night.

Had he thought himself awake he must surely have pursued, however faint his hope of overtaking the slender creature. For the conscious mind can be set aside and subdued by the emotions, but in a dream world all is logic. And so, in fear of the gold oak woods of his dream, he continued in his loping, effortless, soundless, dreamlike bounds, deeper and deeper into the forest and over the elastic velvet of the moss.

For all his conviction that he was asleep, and in spite of the resilience and apparent ease of his flight-running, he had become very tired. The gilded and encrusted trunks of the great oak trees swam by him one after another. The emptiness seemed even more complete and terrible since that will-o'-the-wisp had floated across his path.

All of a sudden he became sharply aware of his fatigue and of hunger, and at the same time a weakening of his conviction that he was dreaming. "If I am dreaming," he thought, "then why should I need to spring from the ground? Why shouldn't I just be carried along?" And to test his idea he made no further effort, merely keeping his balance in the air each time his drop to earth lifted him again into those long and fantastic cruises; but the impetus weakened with every dwindling flight and the volitant boy came gradually to a standstill.

With the rhythm of his progress broken, his belief that he was in a state of dream was finally dispelled. For his hunger had become insistent.

He looked about him. The same scene enclosed him with its mellow cyclorama—its hateful dream of gold.

But for all this horror (it had laid hold of him again now that he no longer believed himself asleep), his fear was in some way lessened by a peculiar thrill which seemed to grow in intensity rather than quieten until it had become a trembling globe of ice under his ribs. Something for which he had unconsciously pined had shown either itself or its emblem in the gold oak woods. Realizing that he had been wide awake ever since he had crept (how long ago!) to the stables of Gormenghast, he knew that slender specter—that reedlike, featherlike thing with its head turned halfway as it rose in slanting volitation across a glade as wide as a lawn—was true, was here in the oak forest with him at that very moment: was perhaps watching him.

It was not only the uncanniness of such a phasma which haunted him now. It was his craving to see again that essence so far removed from what was Gormenghast.

And yet, what had he seen? Nothing that he could describe. It had been so rapid—that flight across his vision: gone, as it were, before his eyes were ready. The head turned away . . . turned away. What was it that cried to him? What was it that this shred, this floating shred of life, expressed? For in the air with which it had moved through space was a quality for which Titus unknowingly hungered. On the long glissade of the wasp-gold flight, like a figment from a rarer and more curious climate than Titus had ever breathed, it had expressed as it rose across the glade the quintessence of detachment: the sense of something intrinsically tameless, and of a distilled and thin-air beauty.

All this in a flash. All this, a confusion in Titus's heart and brain.

What he had felt when he had halted his horse that same morning and heard the voices of the mountain and the woods crying, "Do you dare!" was redoubled within him. He had seen something which lived a life of its own: which had no respect for the ancient lords of

Gormenghast, for ritual among the footworn flagstones:
for the sacredness of the immemorial House. Something
that would no more think of bowing to the Seventy-
Seventh Earl than would a bird, or the branch of a
tree.

He beat his fist into the palm of his other hand. He
was frightened. He was excited. His teeth chattered. The
glimpse of a world, of an unformulated world, where
human life could be lived by other rules than those of
Gormenghast, had shaken him; but for all the newness,
all the vague hugeness of the mutinous sensations that
were thronging in him, yet under the pain of his hunger,
even they began to give way to the consuming need for
food.

Was there a slightly different feeling about the light
as it slanted through the oak leaves and lay along the
glades? Was there a less deathly stillness in the air?
For a moment Titus thought he heard a sigh among the
leaves above him. Was there a quickening in the torpor
of the midday stillness?

There was no way for Titus to know which way to
turn. He only knew that he could not return in the
direction from which he had come. And so he began
to walk as quickly, yet as lightly, as he could (to avoid
the nightmare sensation that those loping and unbridled
flights through the air had bred in him) in the direction
in which the mysterious and floating creature had disappeared.

It was not long before the peerless lawns of moss that
stretched between the oaks became pranked by
clumps of ferns which, ignoring the sun's rays, appeared
silhouetted, so dark was the viridian of their hanging
fronds, so luminous their golden background. The relief
to the boy's spirit was instantaneous, and when the
sumptuous floor gave place to coarse grasses and the
rank profusion of flowering weeds, and when, most re-
freshing of all to Titus's eyes, the oaks no longer cast
their ancestral spell across the vistas, but were challenged by a variety of trees and shrubs, until the last of
those gnarled monarchs had withdrawn and Titus found

himself in a fresher atmosphere, then, at last, he was clear of the nightmare and, with his hunger for redundant proof, was once again in the clear, sharp, actual world that he knew. The ground began to drop away before him at a lively gradient. As on the far side of the oak forest, here also were scattered rocks and groups of ferns; and then all of a sudden Titus gave a shout of happiness to see a living thing after the emptiness and nervelessness of the golden glades—a dog fox that, disturbed by his footsteps, had waked out of its midday sleep in a quiet nest of ferns, had got to its feet with extraordinary self-possession and trotted away at an even pace across the slant of the falling ground.

At the base of the slope a hazel wood began. Here and there a silver birch lifted its feathery head above the thicker foliage; or a dark-green ilex seemed like a green shadow in the sunlight. Titus began to hear the voices of birds. How could he quiet his hunger? It was too early in the year for wild fruit or berries. He was utterly lost, and the exhilaration he had felt at escaping from the oak woods was beginning to dwindle and to turn into depression when, after threading his way for little more than a quarter of a mile through the hazel trees, he heard the sound of water; faint but distinct, away to the west. At once he began to run in the direction of the cool sound, but was forced to relapse into a walking pace, for his legs were heavy and tired, and the ground was uneven and patched with ground ivies. But as the sound of the water grew momently louder, so the ilex trees began to grow more thickly among the hazels, so that there was a rich, dark, blackish greenness about the shadows of the trees both overhead and at Titus's feet. The water now sounded loud in his ears, but so dense had the trees become that it was with a sudden shock that the dazzling breadth of a fast, foam-streaked river appeared before him, and at that very instant, from out of the shadows of the wood on the opposite bank, there stepped a figure.

He was a gaunt and marcid creature, very tall and thin; his high, scrawny shoulders twisted forward, his

cadaverous head lowered, with the thinly bearded jaw
protruding as though in defiance. He was clothed in what
had once been a suit of black material, but was now
so bleached by sun and soaked in a hundred dews that
it had become a threadbare blotchwork of olive-and-
gray rags indistinguishable among the leaves of the forest.

As this gaunt figure stepped down to the water's edge
a sound of clicking that Titus could in no way account
for floated over the bright waters. It appeared to break
out at his every step like a distant musket shot or
the breaking of a dry twig, and to cease whenever he
stopped moving. But Titus soon forgot about this peculiar noise, for the man on the opposite bank had
reached the river and waded out to where a flat, sun-
baked rock the size of a table basked in the midstream.

As he extracted from among his rags a length of line
and a hook, and as he began to fix the bait, he glanced
about him, comparatively carelessly at first and then
with a dawning apprehension, until finally he dropped
his line upon the rock beside him and, sweeping the
opposite shore with his eyes, he focused them upon
Titus.

Partially shielded behind a heavy branch of leaves,
Titus, who had made no sound, was horrified at being
so suddenly discovered, and the blood rushed into his
face. But he could not take his eyes from those of the
emaciated man. He was now crouching on the rock. His
small eyes, which had burned beneath his rocklike
brows, now glittered with a peculiar light and all at once
his hoarse voice sounded across the river: "My lord!" It
was a sharp, rough cry, with a catch in the throat as
though the voice had not been sounded for a long while.

Titus, whose instincts had been torn between flying
from those hot, wild eyes and his excitement at finding
another human being, however emaciated and uncouth,
stepped forward into the sunlight at the river's edge.
He was frightened and his heart beat loudly, but he was
famished also and deadly weary.

"Who are you?" he cried. The figure stood up on the

hot rock. His head was thrust forward toward Titus; his tall body trembled.

"Flay," he said at last, his voice hardly audible.

"Flay!" cried Titus. "I've heard of you."

"Aye," said Flay, his hands gripped together, "likely enough, my lord."

"They told me you were dead, Mr. Flay."

"No doubt of it." (He looked about him again, taking his eyes from Titus for the first time.) "Alone?" His interrogation sounded hoarsely across the water.

"Yes," said Titus. "Are you ill?"

Titus had never seen so gaunt a man before.

"Ill, Lordship? No, boy, no . . . but banished."

"Banished!" cried Titus.

"Banished, boy. When you were only a . . . when your father . . . my lord . . ." He ended suddenly. "Your sister Fuchsia?"

"She's all right."

"Ah!" said the thin man. "No doubt of it." There was a note almost of happiness in his voice, but then, with a new note: "You're done, my lord, 'n windless. What brought you?"

"I escaped, Mr. Flay—ran away. I'm hungry, Mr. Flay."

"Escaped!" whispered the long man to himself with horror; but he gathered and pocketed his hook and line and withheld a hundred burning questions.

"Water's too deep—too fast here. Made crossing— boulders—half-mile upstream—not far, Lordship, not far. Follow your edge with me, follow your river edge, boy—we'll have a rabbit" (he seemed to be talking to himself as he waded back to the bank on his side of the river); "rabbit and pigeon and a long cabin-sleep. . . . Blown he is . . . son of Lord Sepulchrave . . . ready to drop. . . . Tell him anywhere . . . eyes like her Ladyship's. . . . Escaped from the castle! . . . No . . . no . . . mustn't do that. . . . No, no . . . must send him back, Seventy-Seventh Earl. . . . Had him in my pocket . . . size of a monkey . . . long ago. . . ."

And so Flay rambled on as he strode along the bank,

with Titus following him on the opposite shore, until after what seemed an endless journey by the water's edge they came to the crossing of boulders. The river ran shallowly at this point, but it had been no easy work for Flay to shift and set the heavy boulders in place. For five years they had stood firm in the rushing water. Flay had made a perfect ford, and Titus crossed at once to him. For a moment or two they stood awkwardly staring at each other; and then, all of a sudden, the cumulative effects of the physical excitement, the shocks and privations of the day told upon Titus and he collapsed at the knees. The gaunt man caught him up in an instant and, putting the boy carefully over his shoulder, set off through the trees. For all his apparent emaciation there was no question as to Mr. Flay's stamina. The river was soon left far behind. His long, sinewy arms held Titus firmly in place across his shoulder; his lank legs covered the ground with a long, thin, muscular stride and, save for the clicking of his knee joints, with peculiar silence. He had learned during his exile among the woods and rocks the value of silence, and it was second nature for him to pick his way over the ground like a man born to the woods.

The pace and certainty of his progress testified to his intimate knowledge of every twist and turn of the terrain.

Now he was waist-deep in a valley of bracken. Now he was climbing a slope of reddish sandstone; now he was skirting a rock face whose crown overhung its base and whose extensive surface was knuckly with the clay nests of innumerable martins; now he had below him a drop into a sunless valley, and now the walnut-covered slopes from where, each evening, with hideous regularity a horde of owls set sail on bloody missions.

When Flay, topping the brow of a sandy hill, stood for a moment breathing heavily and staring down into the little valley, Titus, who had insisted upon walking by himself for some while past—for even Flay had not been able to sustain his weight during the uphill climbs—

stopped also, and with his hands on his knees, his tired legs rigid, he leaned forward in a position of rest.

The little valley, or dell, beneath them was shut in by tree-covered slopes, save to the south where walls of rock overgrown with lichen and mosses shone brightly in the rays of the declining sun.

At the far end of this gray-green wall were three deep holes in the rock—two of them several feet above the ground and one at the level of the valley's sandy floor.

Along the valley ran a small stream, broadening out into an extensive pool of clear water in the center, for at the far end of the lake where it had narrowed to a tongue was a rough dam. Long evenings had been spent in its making, simple as it was. Flay had hauled a couple of the heaviest logs he could manage and laid them close to one another across the stream. Titus could see them plainly from where he stood, and the thin stream of the overflow at the dam's center. The sound of this overflow trilled and splashed in the silence of the evening light, and the little valley was filled with its glasslike voice.

They descended to the patchwork valley of grass and sand and skirted the stream until they reached the dam and the broad expanse of the trapped water. Not a breath of air disturbed the tender blue of its glasslike surface in which the hillside trees were minutely reflected. Rows of stakes had been driven into and against the inner sides of the logs to form a crib. This space had been filled with mud and stones until a wall had risen and the lake had formed, and a new sound had come to the valley—the tinkling sound of the glittering overflow.

A few moments later they were at the mouth of the lowest of the three openings into the rock. It was but a cleft, about the width of an ordinary door, but it widened into a cave, a spacious and fern-hung place. This inner cave was lit by the reflected light thrown from the sides of the wide natural chimneys whose vents were those mouthlike openings in the rock face a dozen feet above the entrance. Titus followed Flay through this fissurelike doorway, and when he had reached the cool and roughly circular floor of the inner cave he marveled at its lightness, although it was not possible for a single ray of the sun to pierce unhindered, for the wide rocky chimneys wound this way and that before they reached the sunlight. Yet the sunbeams reflected from the sides of the winding chimneys flooded the floor with cool light. It was a high-domed place, this cave, with several massive shelves of rock and a number of natural ledges and niches. On the left-hand side the most impressive of these natural outcrops stood out from the wall in the form of a five-sided table with a smooth shelving top.

These few things Titus was able to take in automatically, but he was too exhausted and sick with hunger to do more than nod his head and smile faintly at the long man, who had lowered his tilted head at Titus as though to see whether the boy was pleased. A moment later Titus was lying on a rough couch of deep dry ferns. He closed his eyes and, in spite of his hunger, fell asleep.

Chapter Twenty

❇❇❇❇❇❇❇❇❇❇❇❇

WHEN Titus awoke the walls of the cave were leaping to and fro in a red light, their outcrops and shelves of stone flinging out their disproportionate shadows and withdrawing them with a concertina motion. The ferns, like tongues of fire, burned as they hung from the darkness of the domed roof, and the stones of the crude oven in which an hour or more ago Flay had lit a great fire of wood and fir cones glowed like liquid gold.

Titus raised himself on his elbow and saw the scarecrow silhouette of the almost legendary Mr. Flay (for

Titus had heard many stories of his father's servant)
as he knelt against the glow, with his twelve-foot shadow
reaching along the gleaming floor and climbing the wall
of the cave.

"I am in the middle of an adventure," Titus repeated to himself, several times, as though the words themselves were significant.

His mind raced over the happenings of the day which
had just ended. He had no sense of confusion when he
woke. He recollected everything instantaneously. But his
recollections were interrupted by the sudden teasing excitement of the rich odor of something being roasted—
it may have been this that had awakened him. The
long man was twisting something round and round, slowly, on the flames. The ache of his hunger became unbearable, and Titus got to his feet, and as he did so
Mr. Flay said, "It's ready, Lordship—stay where you
are."

Breaking pieces from the flesh of the pheasant, and
pouring over them a rich gravy, he brought them over
to Titus on a wooden plate which he had made himself. It was the cross section of what had been a dead
tree, four inches thick, its center scooped into a shallow
basin. In his other hand, as he approached the boy, was
a mug of spring water.

Titus lay down again on the bracken bed, resting himself on one elbow. He was too ravenous to speak but
gave the straggling figure that towered over him a gesture of the hand—as though of recognition—and then,
without a moment wasted, he devoured the rich meal
like a young animal.

Flay had returned to the stone oven, where he busied
himself with various tasks, feeding himself intermittent-
ly as he proceeded. Then he sat down on a ledge of
rock near the fire, on which he fixed his eyes. Titus had
been too preoccupied to watch him, but now, with his
wooden plate scraped to the grain, he drank deeply of
the cold spring water and glanced over the lip of the
mug at the old exile, the man whom his mother had
banished—the faithful servant of his dead father.

"Mr. Flay," he said.

"Lordship?"

"How far away am I?"

"Twelve miles, Lordship."

"And it's very late. It's nighttime, isn't it?"

"Aye. Take you at dawn. Time for sleep. Time for sleep."

"It's like a dream, Mr. Flay. This cave. You. The fire. Is it true?"

"Aye."

"I like it," said Titus. "But I'm afraid, I think."

"Not proper, Lordship—you being here—in my south cave."

"Have you other caves?"

"Yes, two others—to the west."

"I will come and see them—if I can escape, one day, eh, Mr. Flay?"

"Not proper, Lordship."

"I don't care," said Titus. "What else have you got?"

"A shanty."

"Where?"

"Gormenghast Forest—river bank—salmon—sometimes."

Titus got up and walked to the fire, where he sat down, his legs crossed. The flames hit his young face.

"I'm a bit frightened, you know," he said. "It's my first night away from the castle. I suppose they are all looking for me . . . I expect."

"Ah . . ." said Flay. "Most likely."

"Do you ever get frightened, all on your own?"

"Not frightened, boy—exiled."

"What does it mean—*exiled?*"

Flay shifted himself on the ledge of rock, and shrugged his high, bony shoulders up to his ears; like a vulture. There was a kind of tickling in his throat. He turned his small, sunken eyes at last to the young Earl as he sat by the flames, his head raised, a puzzled frown on his brows. Then the tall man lowered himself to the floor, as though he were a kind of mechanism, his knee joints cracking like musket shots as he bent and then straightened his legs.

"Exiled?" he repeated at last, in a curiously low and husky voice. "Banished, it means. Forbidden, Lordship, forbidden service, sacred service. To have your heart dug out; to have it dug out with its long roots, Lordship —that's what exiled means. It means, this cave and emptiness while I am needed. *Needed,*" he repeated hotly. "What watchmen are there now?"

"Watchmen?"

"How do I know? How do I know?" he continued, ignoring Titus's query. Years of silence were finding vent. "How do I know what devilry goes on? Is all well, Lordship? Is the castle well?"

"I don't know," said Titus. "I suppose so."

"You wouldn't know, would you, boy," he muttered. "Not yet."

"Is it true that my mother sent you away?" asked Titus.

"Aye. The Countess of Groan. She exiled me. How is she, my Lordship?"

"I don't know," said Titus. "I don't see her very often."

"Ah . . ." said Flay. "A fine, proud woman, boy. She understands the evil and the glory. Follow her, my lord, and Gormenghast will be well; and you will do your ancient duty, as your father did."

"But I want to be free, Mr. Flay. I don't want any duties."

Mr. Flay jerked himself forward. His head was lowered. In the deep shadows of their sockets his eyes glowed. His hand that supported his weight shook on the ground below him.

"A *wicked* thing to say, my lord, a *wicked* thing," he said at last. "You are a Groan of the Blood—and the last of the Line. You must not fail the Stones. No, though the nettles hide them, and the blackweeds, my lord— you must not fail them."

Titus stared up at him, surprised at this outburst in

the taciturn man; but even as he stared his eyes began
to droop, for he was weary.

Flay rose to his feet, and as he did so a hare loped
through the entrance of the cave where it was lit up
against the intense darkness like a thing of gold. It
stopped for a moment, sitting bolt upright, and stared
at Titus, and then leaped upon a fern-hung shelf of moss
and lay as still as a carving, its long ears laid like
sheaths along its back.

Flay lifted Titus and laid him along the bracken-bed.
But something had happened, suddenly, in the boy's brain.
He sat bolt upright the moment after his head had
touched the floor, and his eyes had closed, as it
seemed in that quick moment, in a long sleep.

"Mr. Flay," he whispered with a passionate urgency.
"Oh, Mr. Flay."

The man of the woods knelt down at once.

"Lordship? What is it?"

"Am I dreaming?"

"No, boy."

"Have I slept?"

"Not yet."

"Then I saw it."

"Saw what, Lordship? Lie quiet now—lie quiet."

"That thing in the oak woods, that flying thing."

Mr. Flay's body tautened and there was an absolute
silence in the cave.

"What kind of a thing?" he muttered at last.

"A thing of the air, a flying thing . . . sort of . . .
delicate . . . but I couldn't see its face. . . . It floated,
you know, across the trees. Was it *real?* Have you *seen*
it, Mr. Flay? What was it, Mr. Flay? Tell me, please, because . . . because . . ."

But there was no need for an answer to the boy's
question, for he had fallen into a deep sleep. Mr. Flay
rose to his feet and, moving across the cave where the
light was dying as the fire smoldered into ashes, made
his way to the entrance of his cavern. Then he leaned
against the outer wall. There was no moon but a
sprinkling of stars was reflected dimly in the dammed-up

lake of water. Faint as an echo in the silence of the night came the bark of a fox from Gormenghast Forest.

Chapter Twenty-One

❋❋❋❋❋❋❋❋❋❋❋

I

TITUS was to be kept in the Lichen Fort for a week. It was a round, squat edifice, its rough square stones obliterated by the unbroken blanket of the parasitic lichen which gave it its name. This covering was so thick that a variety of birds were able to make their nests in the pale-green fur. The two chambers of this fort, one above the other, were kept comparatively clean by a caretaker who slept there and kept the key.

Titus had been held prisoner in this fort on two previous occasions for flagrant offenses against the hierarch —although he never knew exactly what he had done wrong. But this time it was for a longer period. He did not particularly mind. It was a relief to know what his punishment was, for when Flay had left him at the hem of the woods that showed them the castle but a couple of miles away, his anxiety had grown to such a pitch that he had visions of the most frightful punishments ahead. He had arrived in the early morning and found three fresh search parties marshaled in the red-stone yard and about to set out. Horses were drawn up at the stables and their riders were being given instructions. He had taken a deep breath and entered the yard, and staring straight ahead of him all the time, had marched across it, his heart beating wildly, his face perspiring, his shirt and trousers torn almost to shreds. At that moment he was glad he was heir to the mountainous bulks of masonry that rose above him, of the towers, and of the tracts he had crossed that morning in the low rays of the sun. He held his head up and clenched his hands, but when within a dozen yards of the cloisters he ran, the tears gathering in his eyes, until he came to Fuchsia's room, into which he rushed, his eyes burning, a disheveled urchin, and falling upon his startled sister, clung to her like a child.

She returned his embrace, and for the first time in her life, kissed him and held him passionately in her arms; loved him as she had never loved a soul, and was so filled with pride to have been the one to whom he had fled, that she lifted her young, strident voice and shouted in barbaric triumph, and then breaking away from him, jumped to her window and spat into the morning sun. "That's what I think of them, Titus," she shouted, and he ran after her, and spat himself, and then they both began to laugh until they were weak and fell upon the floor, where they fought in a dizzy ecstasy until, exhausted, they lay side by side, their hands joined, and sobbed with the love they had found in one another.

Hungry for affection, yet not knowing what it was that made them restless, not even knowing that they *were* restless, the truth had sprung upon them at the same instant with a shock which found no outlet for its expression save in this physical tumult. In a flash they had found faith in one another. They dared, simultaneously, to uncover their hearts. A truth had come, empiric, irrational, and appallingly exciting. The truth that she, this extraordinary girl, ridiculously immature for all her twenty years, yet rich as harvest, and he, a boy on the brink of wild discoveries, were bound by more than their blood, and the loneliness of their hereditary status, and the lack of a mother in any ordinary sense, yes, more than this—were bound all at once in the cocoon of a compassion and an integration one with another as deep, it seemed, as the line of their ancestors; as inchoate, imponderable, and uncharted as the realms that were their darkened legacy.

For Fuchsia to have, not just a brother, but a boy who had run to her in tears because *she, she* out of all Gormenghast, was the one he trusted—oh, that made up for everything. Let the world do what it might, she would dare death to protect him. She would tell lies for him! Giant lies! She would steal for him! She would kill for him! She rose to her knees and lifted her strong, rounded arms, and as she sent forth a loud, incoherent shout of defiance, the door opened, and Mrs. Slagg stood there. Her hand, which was still on the door handle above her head, trembled, as with amazement she stared at the kneeling girl and heard the unrestrained cry.

Behind her stood a man, with raised eyebrows, a lantern-jawed figure, in gray livery with a kind of seaweed belt which by some obscure edict of many a decade ago, it was his business, holding the position he did, to wear. A festoon of the golden weed trailed down his right leg to the region of his knee. The weather being dry, it crackled as he moved.

Titus was the first to see them and jumped to his feet. But it was Mrs. Slagg who spoke first.

"Look at your hands!" she panted. "Your legs, your face! Oh, my weak heart! Look at the grime, and the cuts and bruises, and, and, oh, my wicked, *wicked* Lordship, look at the rags of you! Oh, I could smack you I could when I think of all I've mended, and washed and ironed and bandaged. Oh yes, I could, I could smack you and hurt you, you cruel, dirty, Lordship-thing. How *could* you? How could you? And me with my heart almost stopped—but *you* wouldn't care, oh no, not though . . ."

Her pitiful tirade was broken into by the man with the lantern jaw.

"I have to take you to Barquentine," he said simply, to Titus. "Get washed, my lord, and don't be long."

"What does *he* want?" said Fuchsia in a low voice.

"I know nothing of that, your Ladyship," said lantern-jaw. "But for your brother's sake, get him clean, and help him with a good excuse. Perhaps he has one. I don't know. I know nothing." His seaweed rattled dryly as he turned away from the door with his tongue in his cheek and his eyes on the ceiling.

II

The week that followed was the longest Titus had ever
spent, in spite of Fuchsia's illicit visits to the Lichen Fort.
She had found an obscure and narrow window through
which she passed what cakes and fruit she could, to vary
the adequate but uninteresting diet which the warden,
luckily a deaf old man, prepared for his fledgling-prisoner.
Through this opening she was able to whisper to her brother.

Barquentine had lectured him at length: had stressed
the responsibility that would become his; but as Titus
held to the story that he had, from the outset, lost himself and could not find his way home, the only crime was
in having set out on the expedition in the first place. For
such a misdemeanor several heavy tomes were fetched
down from high shelves, the dust was blown and shaken
from their leaves, and eventually the appropriate verses
were found which gave precedent for the sentence of
seven days in the Lichen Fort.

During that week the wrinkled and altogether beastly
face of Barquentine, the Lord of the Documents, came
before him in the darkness of the night. No fewer than
four times he dreamed of the wet-eyed, harsh-mouthed
cripple, pursuing him with his greasy crutch; of how it
struck the flagstones like a hammer; and of the crimson
rags of his high office that streamed behind the pursuer,
as they hurried down unending corridors.

And when he awoke he remembered Steerpike, who had
stood behind Barquentine's chair, or climbed the ladder
to find the relevant tomes, and how the pale man, for so
he was to Titus, had *winked* at him.

Beyond his knowledge, beyond his power of reason, a
revulsion took hold of him and he recoiled from that wink
like flesh from the touch of a toad.

One afternoon of his imprisonment he was interrupted
at his hundredth attempt at impaling his jackknife in the
wooden door, at which he flung the weapon in what he

imagined was a method peculiar to brigands. He had
cried himself to a stop during the morning, for the sun
shone through the narrow window slits and he longed for
the wild woods that were so fresh in his mind and for
Mr. Flay and for Fuchsia.

He was interrupted by a low whistle at one of the narrow windows, and then as he reached it, heard Fuchsia's
husky whisper.

"Titus."

"Yes."

"It's me."

"Oh, good!"

"I can't stay."

"Can't you?"

"No."

"Not for a little, Fuchsia?"

"No. Got to take your place. Beastly tradition business. Dragging the moat for the Lost Pearls or something.
I should be there now."

"Oh!"

"But I'll come after dark."

"Oh, good!"

"Can't you see my hand? I'm reaching as far as I can."

Titus thrust his arm as far as he could through the
window slit of the five-foot wall, and could just touch
the tips of her fingers.

"I must go."

"Oh!"

"You'll soon be out, Titus."

The silence of the Lichen Fort was about them like
deep water, and their fingers touching might have been
the prows of foundered vessels which grazed one
another in the subaqueous depths, so huge and vivid and
yet unreal was the contact that they made with one
another.

"Fuchsia."

"Yes?"

"I have things to tell you."

"Have you?"

"Yes. Secrets."

"Secrets?"

"Yes, and adventure."

"I won't tell! I won't ever tell. Nothing you tell me I'll tell. When I come tonight, or if you like when you're free, tell me then. It won't be long."

Her fingertips left his. He was alone in space.

"Don't take your hand away," she said after a moment's pause. "Can you feel anything?"

He worked his fingers even farther into the darkness and touched a paper object which with difficulty he tipped over toward himself and then withdrew. It was a paper bag of barley sugar.

"Fuchsia," he whispered. But there was no reply. She had gone.

III

On the last day but one he had an official visitor. The caretaker of the Lichen Fort had unbolted the heavy door and the grotesquely broad, flat feet of the Headmaster, Bellgrove, complete in his Zodiac gown and dog-eared mortarboard, entered with a slow and ponderous tread. He took five or more paces across the weed-scattered earthen floor before he noticed the boy sitting at a table in a corner of the fort.

"Ah. There you are. There you are, indeed. How are you, my friend?"

"All right. Thank you, sir."

"H'm. Not much light in here, eh, young man? What have you been doing to pass the time away?"

Bellgrove approached the table behind which Titus was sitting. His noble, leonine head was weak with sympathy for the child, but he was doing his best to play the role of Headmaster. He had to inspire confidence. That was one of the things that Headmasters had to do. He must be Dignified and Strong. He must evoke Respect. What else had he to be? He couldn't remember.

"Give me your chair, young fellow," he said in a deep and solemn voice. "You can sit on the table, can't you?

Of course you can. I seem to remember being able to do things like that when I was a boy!"

Had he been at all amusing? He gave Titus a sidelong glance in the faint hope that he *had* been, but the boy's face showed no sign of a smile, as he placed the chair for his Headmaster and then sat with his knees crossed on the table. Yet his expression was anything but sullen.

Bellgrove, holding his gown at the height of his shoulders and at the same time both leaning backward from the hips and thrusting his head forward and downward so that the blunt end of his long chin rested in the capacious pit of his neck like an egg in an egg-cup, raised his eyes to the ceiling.

"As your Headmaster," he said, "I felt it my bounden duty, *in loco parentis,* to have a word with you, my boy."

"Yes, sir."

"And to see how you were getting along. H'm."

"Thank you, sir," said Titus.

"H'm," said Bellgrove. There were a few moments of rather awkward silence and then the Headmaster, finding that the attitude which he had struck was putting too great a strain upon those muscles employed for its maintenance, sat down upon the chair and began unconsciously to work his long, proud jawbone to and fro, as though to test it for the toothache that had been so strangely absent for over five hours. Perhaps it was the unwonted relief of this long spell of normal health that caused a sudden relaxing of Bellgrove's body and brain. Or perhaps it was Bellgrove's innate simplicity, which *sensed* that in this particular situation (where a boy and a Headmaster equally ill at ease with the Adult Mind, sat opposite one another in the stillness) there was a reality, a world apart, a secret place to which they alone had access. Whatever it was, a sudden relaxing of the tension he had felt made itself manifest in a long, wheezing, horse-like sigh, and he stared across at Titus contemplatively, without wondering in the least whether his relaxed, almost *slumped* position in the chair was the kind that Headmasters adopt. But when he spoke, he had, of course, to frame his sentences in that threadbare, empty way to

which he was now a slave. Whatever is felt in the heart or
the pit of the stomach, the old habits remain rooted.
Words and gestures obey their own dictatorial, unimag-
inative laws; the ghastly ritual, that denies the spirit.

"So your old Headmaster has come to see you, my
boy."

"Yes, sir," said Titus.

". . . Leaving his classes and his duties to cast his eye on
a rebellious pupil. A very naughty pupil. A terrible child
who, from what I can remember of his scholastic progress,
has little cause to absent himself from the seats of learning."

Bellgrove scratched his long chin ruminatively.

"As your Headmaster, Titus, I can only say that you
make things a little difficult. What am I to do with
you? H'm. What indeed? You have been punished. You
are *being* punished: so I am glad to say that there is no
need for us to trouble any more about *that* side of it;
but what am I to say to you *in loco parentis*? I am an
old man, you would say, wouldn't you, my small friend?
You would say I was an old man, wouldn't you?"

"I suppose so, sir."

"And as an old man, I *should* by now be very wise and
deep, shouldn't I, my boy? After all, I have long white
hair and a long black gown, and that's a good start, isn't
it?"

"I don't know, sir."

"Oh, well it *is*, my boy. You can take it from me. The
first thing you must procure if you are anxious to be wise
and sagacious is a long black gown, and long white hair,
and if possible a long jawbone, like your old Headmaster's."

Titus didn't think that the Professor was being very
funny, but he threw his head back and laughed very
loudly indeed, and thumped his hands on the side of the
table.

A flush of light illumined the old man's face. His anxiety fled from his eyes and hid itself where the deep
creases and pits that honeycomb the skin of ancient men
provided caves and gullies for its withdrawal.

It was so long since anyone had really laughed at anything he had said, and laughed honestly and spontaneously.
He turned his big lion head away from the boy so that he
could relax his old face in a wide and gentle smile. His
lips were drawn apart in the most tender of snarls, and it
was some while before he could turn his head about and
return his gaze to the boy.

But at once the habit returned, unconsciously, and his
decades of schoolmastering drew his hands behind his
back, beneath his gown, as though there were a magnet
in the small of his back: his long chin couched itself in
the pit of his neck; the irises of his eyes floated up to
the top of the whites, so that in his expression there was
something both of the drug addict and the caricature of a
sanctimonious bishop—a peculiar combination, and one
which generations of urchins had mimicked as the seasons
moved through Gormenghast, so that there was hardly a
spot in dormitory, corridor, classroom, hall, or yard where
at one time or another some child had not stood for a
moment with his inky hands behind his back, his chin
lowered, his eyes cast up to the sky, and, perhaps, an exercise book on top of his head by way of mortarboard.

Titus watched his Headmaster. He had no fear of him.
But he had no love for him either. That was the sad thing.
Bellgrove, eminently lovable, because of his individual
weakness, his incompetence, his failure as a man, a scholar, a leader, or even as a companion, was nevertheless
utterly alone. For the weak, above all, have their friends.
Yet his gentleness, his pretense at authority, his palpable
humanity were unable, for some reason or other, to function. He was demonstrably the type of venerable and
absent-minded professor about whom all the sharp-
beaked boys of the world should swarm like starlings in
wheeling murmurations—loving him all unconsciously,
while they twitted and cried their primordial jests, flung
their honey-centered, prickle-covered verbiage to and fro,
pulled at the long black thunder-colored gown, undid with
fingers as quick as adders' tongues the buttons of his
braces; pleaded to hear the ticking of his enormous watch
of brass and rust-red iron, with the verdigris like lichen

on the chain; fought between those legs like the trousered stilts of the father of all storks; while the great, corded, limpish hands of the fallen monarch flapped out from time to time, to clip the ears of some more than venturesome child, while far above, the long, pale lion's head turned its eyes to and fro in a slow, ceremonious rhythm, as though he were a lighthouse whose slowly swiveling beams were diffused and deadened in the sea-mists; and all the while, with the tassel of the mortarboard swinging high above them like the tail of a mule, with the trousers loosening at the venerable haunches, with the catcalls and the thousand quirks and oddities that grow like brilliant weeds from the no-man's-land of urchins' brains—all the while there would be this love like a subsoil, showing itself in the very fact that they trusted his lovable weakness, wished to be with him because he was like them irresponsible, magnificent with his locks of hair as white as the first page of a new copybook, and with his neglected teeth, his jaw of pain, his completeness, ripeness, false nobility, childish temper, and childish patience; in a word, that he *belonged* to them; to tease and adore, to hurt and to worship for his very weakness' sake. For what is more lovable than failure?

But no. None of this happened. None of it. Bellgrove was all this. There was no gap in the long tally of his spineless faults. He was constructed as though expressly for the starlings of Gormenghast. There he was, but no one approached him. His hair was white as snow, but it might as well have been gray or brown or have molted in the dank of faithless seasons. There seemed to be a blind spot in the mass-vision of the swarming youths.

They looked this great gift-lion in the mouth. It snarled in its weakness, for its teeth were aching. It trod the immemorial corridors. It dozed fitfully at its desk through the terms of sun and ice. And now, it was a Headmaster and lonelier than ever. But there was pride. The claws were blunt, but they were ready. But not so, now. For at the moment his vulnerable heart was swollen with love.

"My young friend," he said, his eyes still on the ceiling of the fort and his chin tucked into the pit of his

neck, "I propose to talk to you as man to man. Now the
thing *is* . . ." (he lingered over the last word) ". . . the
thing . . . *is* . . . what shall we talk *about?*" He lowered
his rather dull eyes and saw that Titus was frowning at
him thoughtfully.

"We *could*, you see, young man, talk of so many things,
could we not, as man to man. Or even as boy to boy. H'm.
Quite so. But what? This is the paramount consideration
—isn't it?"

"Yes, sir. I suppose so," said Titus.

"Now, if you are twelve, my boy, and I am eighty-six,
let us say, for I think that ought to cover me, then let us
take twelve from eighty-six and have the result. No, no.
I won't make *you* do it because that would be most unfair. Ah yes, indeed it would—for what's the good of
being a prisoner and then being made to do lessons too?
Eh? Eh? Might as well not be punished, eh? . . . Let me
see, where were we, where were we? Yes, yes, yes, twelve
from eighty-six, that's about seventy-four, isn't it? Well,
what is half seventy-four? I wonder . . . h'm, yes, twice
three are six, carry one, and twice seven are fourteen . . .
thirty-seven, I do believe. Thirty-seven. And what *is* thirty-
seven? Why, it's just exactly the halfway age between us.
So if I tried to be thirty-seven years young—and you
tried to be thirty-seven years old—but that would be
very difficult, wouldn't it? Because you've never been
thirty-seven, have you? But then, although your old
Headmaster has *been* thirty-seven, long ago, he can't remember a thing about it except that it was somewhere
about that time that he bought a bag of glass marbles.
Oh, yes, he did. And why? Because he became tired of
teaching grammar and spelling and arithmetic. Oh, yes,
and because he saw how much happier the people were
who played marbles than the people were who didn't.
That's a bad sentence, my boy. So I used to play in the
dark after the other young Professors were asleep. We had
one of the old Gormenghast tapestry-carpets in the room
and I used to light a candle and place my marbles on the
corners of patterns in the carpet, and in the middle of
crimson and yellow flowers. I can remember the carpet

perfectly, as though it were here in this old fort, and there, every night, by the glow of a candle, I would practice until I could flick a marble along the floor so that when it struck another it spun round and round but stayed exactly where it was, my boy, while the one it had struck shot off like a rocket to land at the other end of the room in the center of a crimson carpet flower (if I was successful), or if not, near enough to couch itself at the next flick. And the sounds of the glass marbles in the still of the night when they struck was like the sound of tiny crystal vases breaking on stone floors—but I am getting too poetic, my boy, aren't I? And boys don't like poetry, do they?"

Bellgrove took off his mortarboard, placed it on the floor, and wiped his brow with the biggest and grubbiest handkerchief Titus had ever seen come out of a grown-up's pocket.

"Ah me, my young friend, the sound of those marbles . . . the sound of those silly marbles. Forlorn, it is, my boy, to remember the little glass notes—forlorn as the tapping of a woodpecker in a summer forest."

"I've got some marbles, sir," said Titus, sliding off the table and diving his hand into his trouser pocket.

Bellgrove dropped his hands to his sides where they hung like dead weights. It was as though his joy at finding his little plan maturing so successfully was so all-absorbing that he had no faculties left over to control his limbs. His wide, uneven mouth was ajar with delight. He rose to his feet and, turning his back on Titus, made his way to the far end of the small fort. He was sure that his joy was written all over his face and that it was not for Headmasters to show that sort of thing to any but their wives, and he had no wife . . . no wife at all.

Titus watched him. What a funny way he put his big flat feet on the ground, as though he were smacking it slowly with the soles of his boots—not so much to hurt it, as to wake it up.

"My boy," said Bellgrove at last when he had returned to Titus, having fought the smile away from his face— "this is an extraordinary coincidence, you know. Not

only do you like marbles, but you have six in your pocket and not only do I like marbles, but I . . ." And he drew from the decaying darkness of a pocket like a raw-lipped gulch exactly six glass globes.

"Oh, sir!" said Titus. "I never thought *you'd* have marbles."

"My boy," said Bellgrove, "let it be a lesson to you. Now where shall we play? Eh? Eh? Good grief, my young friend, what a long way down it is to the floor and how my poor old muscles creak. . . ."

Bellgrove was lowering himself by degrees to the dusty ground.

"We must examine the terrain for irregularities, h'm, yes, that's what we must do, isn't it, my boy? Examine the terrain, like generals, eh? And find our battle ground."

"Yes, sir," said Titus, dropping to the knees and crawling alongside the old, pale lion. "But it looks flat enough to me, sir. I'll make one of the squares here, and—"

But at this moment the door of the fort opened again and Dr. Prunesquallor stepped out of the sunlight and into the gray gloom of the small fort.

"Well! well! well! well! well!" he trilled, peering into the shadows. "Well, well, well! What a dreadful place to jail an Earl in, by all that's merciless. And where is he, this fabulous little wrongdoer—this breaker of bounds, this flouter of unwritten laws, this thoroughly naughty boy? God bless my shocked spirit if I don't see two of them —and one much bigger than the other—or is there someone with you, Titus, and if so, who can it be, and what in the name of dust and ashes can you find so absorbing on the earth's bosom, that you must crawl about on it, belly to stubble, like beasts that stalk their prey?"

Bellgrove rose, creaking, to his knees and then, catching his feet in the swathes of his gown, tore a great rent in its threadbare material as he struggled into an upright position. He straightened his back and struck the attitude of a Headmaster, but his old face had colored.

"Hullo, Dr. Prune," said Titus. "We were just going to play marbles."

"Marbles! eh? By all that's erudite, and a very fine invention too, God bless my spherical soul," cried the physician. "But, if your accomplice isn't Professor Bellgrove, your Headmaster, then my eyes are behaving in a very peculiar manner."

"My dear Doctor," said Bellgrove, his hands clasping his gown near the shoulders, its torn portion trailing the floor at his feet like a fallen sail, "it is indeed I. My pupil, the young Earl, having misbehaved himself, I felt it my bounden duty, *in loco parentis*, to bring what wisdom I have at my command to bear upon his predicament. To help him, if I can, for, who knows, even the old may have experience; to succor him, for, who knows, even the old may have mercy in their bones; and to lead him back into the current of wise living—for, who knows, even the old may—"

"I don't like 'current of wise living,' Bellgrove—a beastly phrase for a Headmaster, if I may make so damnably bold," said Prunesquallor. "But I see what you mean. By all that smacks of insight, I most palpably do. But what a place for incarcerating a child! Let's have a look at you, Titus. How are you, my little bantam?"

"All right, thank you, sir," said Titus. "I'll be free tomorrow."

"Oh, God, it breaks my heart," cried Prunesquallor. " 'I'll be free tomorrow,' indeed! Come here, boy."

There was a catch in the Doctor's voice. Free tomorrow, he thought. Free tomorrow. Would the child ever be free tomorrow?

"So your Headmaster has come to see you and is going to play marbles with you," he said. "Do you know that you are greatly honored? Have you thanked him for coming to see you?"

"Not yet, sir," said Titus.

"Well, you must, you know, before he leaves you."

"He's a good boy," said Bellgrove. "A very good boy." After a pause he added, as though to get back to firm, authoritarian ground again, "and a very wicked one at that."

"But I'm delaying the game—by all that's thoughtless,

I am indeed!" cried the Doctor, giving Titus a pat on the back of the head.

"Why don't you play, too, Dr. Prune?" inquired Titus. "Then we could have 'threecorners.'"

"And how do you play 'threecorners'?" said Prune-squallor, hitching up his elegant trousers and squatting on the floor, his pink, ingenuous face directed at the tousle-haired child. "Do *you* know, my friend?" he inquired, turning to Bellgrove.

"Indeed, indeed," said Bellgrove, his face lighting up. "It is a noble game." He lowered himself to the ground again.

"By the way," said the Doctor, turning his head quickly to the Professor, "you're coming to our party, aren't you? You will be our chief guest, as you know, sir."

Bellgrove, with a great grinding and creaking of joints and fibers, got all the way to his feet again, stood for a moment magnificently and precariously upright, and bowed to the squatting Doctor, a lock of white hair falling across his blank blue eyes as he did so.

"Sir," he said, "I *am*, sir—and my staff with me. We are deeply honored." Then he sank to his knees again with extraordinary rapidity.

For the next hour, the old prison warden, peering through a keyhole the size of a tablespoon in the inner door, was astounded to see the three figures crawling to and fro across the floor of the prison fort, to hear the high trill of the Doctor develop and strengthen into the cry of a hyena, the deep and wavering voice of the Professor bell forth like an old and happy hound as his inhibitions waned, and the shrill cries of the child reverberate about the room, splintering like glass on the stone walls while the marbles crashed against one another, spun in their tracks, lodged shuddering in their squares, or skimmed the prison floor like shooting stars.

Chapter Twenty-Two

✷✷✷✷✷✷✷✷✷✷✷✷

THERE was no sound in all Gormenghast that could strike so chill against the heart as the sound of that small and greasy crutch on which Barquentine propelled his dwarfish body.

The harsh and rapid impact of its ironlike stub upon the hollow stones was, at each stroke, like a whip-crack, an oath, a slash across the face of mercy.

Not a hierophant but had heard at one time or another the sound of that sinister shaft mounting in loudness as the Master of Ritual thrust himself forward, his withered leg and his crutch between them negotiating the tortuous corridors of stone, at a pace that it was difficult to believe.

There were few who had not, on hearing the crack of that stub of a crutch on distant flagstones, altered their directions to avoid the small smoldering symbol of the Law, as, in its crimson rags, it stamped its brimstone path along the center of every corridor, altering its course for no man.

Something of the wasp, and something of the scraggy bird of prey, there was, about this Barquentine. There was something of the gale-twisted thorn tree also, and something of the gnome in his blistered face. The eyes, horribly liquid, shot their malice through veils of water. They seemed to be brimming, those eyes of his, as though old, cracked, sandy saucers were filled so full of topaz-colored tea as to be swollen at their centers.

Endless, interwoven, and numberless as were the halls and corridors of the castle, yet even in the remotest of these, in the obscure fastnesses, where, infinitely removed from the main arteries, the dank and moldering silence was broken only by the occasional fall of rotten wood or the hoot of an owl—even in such tracts as these a wanderer would be haunted and apprehensive for fear of those ubiquitous tappings—faint though they might be, as faint as the clicking of fingernails, but a sound for all its faintness that brought with it a sense of horror. There seemed no refuge from the sound. For the crutch, ancient, filthy, and hard as iron, was the man himself. There was no good blood, no good red blood in Barquentine any more than there was in his support, that ghastly fulcrum. It grew from him like a diseased and nerveless limb—an extra limb. When it struck the stones or the hollow floor boards below him it was more eloquent of spleen than any word, than any language.

The fanaticism of his loyalty to the House of Groan had far outstripped his interest or concern for the living —the members of the Line itself. The Countess, Fuchsia, and Titus were mere links to him in the blood-red, the imperial chain—nothing more. It was the chain that mattered, not the links. It was not the living metal, but the immeasurable iron with its patina of sacred rust. It was the Idea that obsessed him and not the embodiment. He moved in a hot sea of vindication, a lust of loyalty.

He had risen as usual this morning, at dawn. Through the window of his filthy room he had peered across the dark flats to Gormenghast Mountain, not because it shone in a haze of amber and seemed translucent but in order to get some indication of the kind of day to expect. The ritual of the hours ahead was to some extent modified by the weather. Not that a ceremony could be altered or canceled *because* of adverse weather, but by reason of the sacred Alternatives, equally valid, which had been prescribed by leaders of the faith in centuries gone by. If, for example, there was a thunderstorm in the afternoon and the moat was churned and spattered with the rain, then the ceremony needed qualifying in which Titus, wearing a necklace of plaited grass, was to stand upon the weedy verge and, with the reflection of a par-

ticular tower below him in the water, so sling a golden
coil that, skimming the surface and bounding into the
air as it struck the water, it sailed over the reflection
of a particular tower in one leap to sink in the watery
image of a yawning window, where, reflected, his
mother stood. There could be no movement and no sound
from Titus or the spectators until the last of the sparkling ripples had crept from the moat, and the subaqueous
head of the Countess no longer trembled against the
hollow darkness of the cavelike window, but was motionless in the moat, with birds of water on her shoulders
like chips of colored glass and all about her the infinite,
tower-filled depths.

All this would necessitate a windless day and a glass
surface to the moat, and in the Tomes of Ceremony there
would, were the day stormy, be an alternative rendering,
an equally honorable way of enriching the afternoon to
the glory of the House and the fulfillment of the partic-
ipants.

And so, it was Barquentine's habit to push open his
window at dawn and stare out across the roofs and the
marshes beyond, to where the mountain, blurred, or
edged like a knife, gave indication of the day ahead.

Leaning forward, thus, on his crutch, in the cold light
of yet another day, Barquentine scratched savagely at
his ribs, at his belly, under his arms, here, there, everywhere with his claw of a hand.

There was no need for him to dress. He slept in his
clothes on a lice-infested mattress. There was no bed;
just the crawling mattress on the carpetless floor boards
where cockroaches and beetles burrowed and insects of
all kinds lived, bred, and died, and where the midnight rat
sat upright in the silver dust and bared its long teeth to
the pale beams, when in its fullness the moon filled up
the midnight window like an abstract of itself in a picture
frame.

It was in such a hovel as this that the Master of Ritual had woken every morning for the last sixty years.
Swiveling about on his crutch, he stumped his way from
the window and was almost immediately at the rough

wall by the doorway. Turning his back to this irregular wall, he leaned against it and worked his ancient shoulder blades to and fro, disturbing in the process a colony of ants which (having just received news from its scouts that the rival colony near the ceiling was on the march and was even now constructing bridges across the plaster crack) was busily preparing its defenses.

Barquentine had no notion that in easing the itch between his blades he was incapacitating an army. He worked his back against the rough wall, to and fro, to and fro in a way quite horrible in so old and stunted a man. High above him the door rose, like the door of a barn.

Then, at last, he leaned forward on his crutch and hopped across the room to where a rusted iron ring protruded from the floor. It was like the mouth of a funnel, and indeed a metal pipe led down from this terminal opening to where, several storeys below, it ended in a similar metal ring, or mouthpiece, which protruded several inches from the ceiling of an eating room. Immediately *beneath* this termination and a score of feet below it, a hollow, disused cauldron awaited the heavy stone which morning after morning rumbled its way down the winding pipe to end its journey with a wild clang in the belly of the reverberating bowl, murmuring to itself in an undertone for minutes on end with the boulder in its maw.

Every evening it was taken up and placed outside Barquentine's door, this boulder, and every morning the old man lifted it up above the iron ring in the floor boards of his room, spat on it, and sent it hurtling down the crooked funnel, its hoarse clanging growing fainter and fainter as it approached the eating room. It was a warning to the servants that he was on his way down, that his breakfast and a number of other preliminaries were to be ready.

To the clank of the boulder a score of hearts made echo. On this particular morning as Barquentine spat upon the heavy stone, the size of a melon, and sent it netherward on its resounding journey past many a dark-

ened floor of bedded inmates (who, waking as it leaped
behind their couches in the hollow of the walls, cursed
him, the dawn, and this cock-crow of a boulder)—on
this particular morning there was more than the normal
light of lust for ritual in the wreckage of the ancient's
face—there was something more, as though his greed
for the observances to take place in the shadow of his
aegis were filling him with a passion hardly bearable in
so sere a frame.

There was one picture on the wall of his verminous
hovel; an engraving, yellow with age and smirched with
dust, for it had no glass across it, save the small icelike
splinter at one corner that was all that remained of
the original glazing. This engraving, a large and meticulous affair, was of the Tower of Flints. The artist must
have stood to the south of the tower as he worked or as
he studied the edifice, for beyond the irregularity of turrets and buttresses that backed it and spread almost to the
sky like a seascape of stormy roofage, could be seen the
lower slopes of Gormenghast Mountain, mottled with
clumps of shrub and conifer.

What Barquentine had not noticed was that the doorway of the Tower of Flints had been cut away. A small
area of paper, the size of a stamp, was missing. Behind this hole the wall had been laboriously pierced so
that a little tunnel of empty darkness ran laterally from
Barquentine's chamber to the hollow and capacious shaft
of a vertical chimney, whose extremity was blocked from
the light by a landslide of fallen slates long sealed and
cushioned with gold moss, and whose round base, like
the base of a well of black air, gave upon the small
cell-like room so favored by Steerpike that even at this
early and chilly hour he was sitting there, at the base of
the shaft. All about him were mirrors of his own construction, placed to a nicety, each at its peculiar angle,
while above him, punctuating the tubular darkness, a
constellation of mirrors twinkled with points of light one
above the other.

Every now and again Barquentine would be reflected
immediately behind the hollow mouthway of the engraved

Tower of Flints where an angled mirror in the shaft sent down his image to another and then another—mirror glancing to mirror—until Steerpike, reclining at the base of the chimney, with a magnifying glass in his hands, peered amusedly at the terminal reflection and saw in miniature the crimson rags of the dwarfish pedant as he raised the boulder in his hands and flung it through the ring.

If Barquentine rose early from his hideous couch, Steerpike in a secret room of his own choosing, a room as spotless and bright as a new pin, arose earlier. This was not a habit with him. He had no habits in that sort of way. He did what he wanted to do. He did what furthered his plans. If getting up at five in the morning would lead to something he coveted, then it was the most natural thing in the world for him to rise at that hour. If there was no necessity for action he would lie in bed all morning reading, practicing knots with the cord he kept by his bedside, making paper darts of complicated design which he would float across his bedroom, or polishing the steel of the razor-edged blade of his swordstick.

At the moment it was to his advantage to impress Barquentine with his efficiency, indispensability, and dispatch. Not that he had not already worked his way beneath the cantankerous crust of the old man's misanthropy. He was in fact the only living creature who had ever gained Barquentine's confidence and grudging approval.

Without fully realizing it, Barquentine, during his daily administrations, was pouring out a hoard of irreplaceable knowledge, pouring it into the predatory and capacious brain of a young man whose ambition it was, when he had gained sufficient knowledge of the observances, to take over the ceremonial side of the castle's life, and, in being the only authority on the minutiae of the Law (for Barquentine was to be liquidated), to alter to his own ends such tenets as held him back from ultimate power and to forge such fresh, though apparently archaic, documents as might best serve his evil purposes as the years went by.

Barquentine spoke little. In the pouring out of his knowledge there was no verbal expansiveness. It was largely through action and through access to the Documents that Steerpike learned his "trade." The old man had no idea that day after day the accumulating growth of Steerpike's cognizance and the approach of his own death moved toward one another through time, at the same pace. He had no wish to instruct the young man beyond the point of self-advantage. The pale creature was useful to him and that was all, and were he to have known how much had been divulged of Gormenghast's inner secrets through the seemingly casual exchanges and periodical researches in the Library, he would have done all in his power to eliminate from the castle's life this upstart, this dangerous, unprecedented upstart, whose pursuit of the doctrines was propelled by a greed for personal power as cold as it was tameless.

The time was almost ripe in Steerpike's judgment for the Master of Ritual to be dispatched. Apart from other motives the wiping out of so ugly a thing as Barquentine seemed to Steerpike, upon aesthetic considerations alone, an act long overdue. Why should such a bundle of hideousness be allowed to crutch its way about, year after year?

Steerpike admired beauty. It did not absorb him. It did not affect him. But he admired it. He was neat, adroit, slick as his own swordstick, sharp as its edge, polished as its blade. Dirt offended him. Untidiness offended him. Barquentine, old, filthy, his face cracked and pitted like stale bread, his beard tangled, dirty, and knotted, sickened the young man. It was time for the dirty core of ritual to be plucked out of the enormous moldering body of the castle's life and for him to take its place, and from that hidden center—who knew how far his tangent wits might lead him?

It was a wonder to Barquentine how Steerpike was able to meet him with such uncanny precision and punctuality sunrise after sunrise. It was not as though his lieutenant sat there waiting outside the master's door, or at some landing on the stairs by which Barquentine made his way to the small eating room. Oh, no. Steerpike, his straw-colored hair smoothed down across his high globular forehead, his pale face shining, his dark-red eyes disconcertingly alive beneath his sandy eyebrows, would walk rapidly out of the shadows and, coming to a smart halt at the old man's side, would incline himself at a slight angle from the hips.

There was no change this morning in the dumb show. Barquentine wondered, for the hundredth time, how Steerpike should coincide so exactly with his arrival at the top of the walnut stairs, and as usual drew his brows down over his eyes and peered suspiciously through the veils of unpleasant moisture that smoldered there, at the pale young man.

"Good morning to you, sir," said Steerpike.

Barquentine, whose head was on a level with the banisters, put out a tongue like the tongue of a boot and ran it along the wreckage of his dry and wrinkled lips. Then he took a grotesque hop forward on his withered leg and brought his crutch to his side with a sharp report.

Whether his face was made of age, as though *age* were a stuff, or whether age was the abstract of that face of his, that bearded fossil of a thing that smoldered and decayed upon his shoulders—there was no doubt that archaism was there, as though something had shifted from the past into the current moment where it burned darkly as though through blackened glass in defiance of its own anachronism and the callow present.

He turned this head of his to Steerpike.

"To hell-fire with your 'good morning,' you peeled switch," he said. "You shine like a bloody land-eel! What d'you do to yourself, eh? Every poxy sunrise of the year, eh, that you burst out of the decent darkness in that plucked way?"

"I suppose it's this habit of washing I seem to have, sir."

"*Washing,*" hissed Barquentine, as though he were mentioning something pestilent. "*Washing,* you wire-worm. What do you think you *are,* Mr. Steerpike? A lily?"

"I'd hardly say that, sir," said the young man.

"Nor would I," barked the old man. "Just skin and

bones and hair. That's all you bloody are and nothing more. Dull yourself down. Get the shine off you—and no more of this oiled-paper nonsense every dawn."

"Quite so, sir. I am too visible."

"Not when you're wanted!" snapped Barquentine, as he began to hobble downstairs. "You can be invisible enough when you want to be, eh? Hag's-hell, boy, you can be nowhere when it suits you, eh? By the guts of the great auk! I see through *you*—my pretty whelp! I see through *you!*"

"What, when I'm invisible, sir?" asked Steerpike, raising his eyebrows as he trod lightly behind the cripple, who was raising echoes on all sides with the stamping of his crutch on the wooden stairs.

"By the piss of Satan, pug, your sauce is dangerous!" shouted Barquentine hoarsely, turning precariously in his tracks, with his withered leg two steps above his crutch.

"Are the North Cloisters done?" He shot the question at Steerpike, in a changed tone of voice—a tone no less vicious and cantankerous, but pleasanter to the young man's ear, being less personally vituperative.

"They were completed last night, sir."

"Under your guidance, for what it's worth?"

"Under my guidance."

They were approaching the first landing of the walnut stairs. Steerpike, as he trod behind Barquentine, took a pair of dividers from his pocket, and using them as though they were tongs, lifted up a hank of the old man's hair from the back of his head, to reveal a neck as wry as a turtle's. Amused by his success at being able to raise so thick a bunch of dirty gray hair without the cripple's knowledge, he repeated the performance while the harsh voice continued and the crutch clack-clack-clacked down the long flight.

"I shall inspect them immediately after breakfast."

"Quite so," said Steerpike.

"Has it occurred to your suckling-brain that this day is hallowed by the very dirt of the castle? Eh? That it is only once a year, boy, once a year, that the Poet is honored? Eh? Why, the lice in my beard alone know, but there it is, by the black souls of the unbelievers, there it is, a Law of Laws, a Rite of the first water, *dear* child. The cloisters are ready, you say; by the sores on my withered leg, you'll pay for it if they're colored the wrong red. Eh? Was it the darkest red of all? Eh—the darkest of all the reds?"

"Quite the darkest," said Steerpike. "Any darker and it would have been black."

"By hell, it had better be," said Barquentine. "And the rostrum?" he continued after crossing the gnarled landing of black walnut with its handrail missing from the banisters and the banisters themselves leaning in all directions and capped with dust as palings are capped with snow in wintertime.

"And the rostrum?"

"It is set and garnished," said Steerpike. "The throne for the Countess has been cleaned and mended, and the high chairs for the gentry polished. The long forms are in place and fill the quadrangle."

"And the Poet," cried Barquentine. "Have you instructed him, as I ordered you? Does he know what is expected of him?"

"His rhetoric is ready, sir."

"Rhetoric? Cat's teeth! Poetry, you bastard, Poetry."

"It has been prepared, sir!" Steerpike had repocketed his dividers and was now holding a pair of scissors (he seemed to have endless things in his pockets without disturbing the hang of his clothes) and was clipping off strands of Barquentine's hair where it hung below his collar, and was whispering to himself in an absurd undertone, "Tinker, tailor, soldier, sailor" as the matted wisps fell upon the stairs.

They had reached another landing. Barquentine stopped for a moment to scratch himself. "He may have prepared his poem," he said, turning his time-wasted visage to the slender, high-shouldered young man, "but have you told him about the magpie? Eh?"

"I told him that he must rise to his feet and declaim within twelve seconds of the magpie's release from the wire cage. That while declaiming his left hand must be clasping the beaker of moat-water in which the Countess has previously placed the blue pebble from Gormenghast River."

"That is so, boy. And that he shall be wearing the Poet's Gown, that his feet shall be bare, did you tell him that?"

"I did," said Steerpike.

"And the yellow benches for the Professors. Were they found?"

"They were. In the South Stables. I have had them repainted."

"And the Seventy-Seventh Earl, Lord Titus, does the pup know that he is to stand when the rest are seated, and seat himself when the rest are standing? Does the child know that—eh—eh—he is a scatterbrained thing—have you instructed him, you skinned candle? By the gripes of my seventy years, your forehead shines like a bloody iceberg!"

"He has been instructed," said Steerpike.

Barquentine set out again on his descent to the eating room. Once the walnut stairs had been negotiated, the Master of Ritual stuttered his way down the level corridors like something possessed. As the dust rose from the floor at each bang of the crutch, Steerpike, following immediately behind his master, amused himself by the invention of a peculiar dance, a kind of counterpoint to Barquentine's jerking progress—a silent and elaborate improvisation, laced, as it were, with lewd and ingenious gestures.

Chapter Twenty-Three

THE long summer minutes dragged by for Titus as he sat at his desk in the schoolroom where Professor Cutflower (who had once made a point of being at least one mental hour ahead of his class in whatever subject he

happened to be teaching, but who had long since decided
to pursue knowledge on an equal footing with his
pupils) was, with the lid of his high desk raised to hide his
activity, taking a long pull at a villainous-looking bottle
with a blue label. The morning seemed endless. . . .

But for Barquentine, with a score of preparations still
to be completed, and with his rough tongue victimizing
the workmen in the South Quadrangle, the hours sped
by with the speed of minutes.

And so, after what seemed an infinity to Titus and a
whisk of time's skirt to Barquentine, the morning that
was both fleet and tardy, fructified and like a grape of
air, in whose lucent body the earth was for that moment
suspended—that phantom ripeness throbbed, that thing
called *noon*.

Before it had woken to die on the instant of its
waking, a score of bells and clocks had shouted, "Midday," and for a minute after its death, from near and
far, the clappers in their tents of rusted iron clanged
across Gormenghast. It was as though no mechanism on
earth could strike or chain that ghost of time. The clocks
and the bells stuttered, boomed, and rang. They trod with
their iron imprint. They beat with their ancient fists and
shouted with archaic voices—but the ghost was older.

Noon, ripe as thunder and silent as thought, had fled
unfingered.

When every echo had died from even those clocks in
the western outcrops, whose posthumous tolling was pro-
verbial, so that the phrase, "Late as a western chime,"
was common in the castle—when every echo had died,
Titus became aware of another sound.

After the languid threnody of the chimes, this fresh
sound, so close upon the soft heels of the pendulums, appeared hideously rapid, merciless and impatient.

It had the almost dreamlike insistence, for all its
actuality, of some hound with feet of stone or iron; or
some coursing beast, that, rattling its rapacious and un-
alterable way in the wake of its prey, was momently
closing the gap between evil and innocence.

Titus heard the sound, as though its cause were alongside. Yet the corridor down which he was moving was

empty, and the tapping of the crutch was in reality coming from the parallel passageway, and Barquentine, although only a few yards from him, was separated from the boy by a solid wall of stone.

As Titus came to a halt, his heart beating, his eyes narrowed and an expression of hatred came over his childish features—an expression hardly credible in so young a face. To him, Barquentine was the symbol of tyranny, of age, of all that held him back from summer days among the woods, from diving in the moat with his friends, from all he longed for.

As he stood shuddering with his hot uprising of fear and detestation, he listened intently. In which direction, behind that wall of stone, was the crutch traveling?

At either end of Barquentine's corridor subsidiary passages led into the corridor in which Titus now stood. It seemed to him that the Master of Ritual was moving rapidly in a parallel direction to his own. He turned and began to retrace his steps, but the corridor was suddenly darkened by a solid block of Professors who bore down upon him with a fluttering of Ethiop draperies and a fleet of mortarboards. His only hope was to run in the original direction and cross the communicating passage, and away, before Barquentine's possible arrival at that juncture.

He began to run. It was not because of any particular misdeed or rational fear that he ran. It was a compulsion, a necessity for withdrawal. A revolt against anything that was old. Anything that had power. A nebula of terror possessed him and he ran.

Along the right-hand side of the corridor a phalanx of dusty statues loomed in the dim light that gave them the color of ash. Set, for the most part, on massive plinths, they towered above Titus, their silent limbs sawing the dark air, or stabbing it bluntly with broken arms. The heads were almost invisible, matted as they were with cobwebs, and shrouded in perpetual twilight.

He had known these monuments since childhood. But he no more noticed them or remembered them than another child would notice the monotonous pattern of some nursery wallpaper.

But Titus was brought again to a standstill by the tiny yet unmistakable silhouette of the cripple as it rounded the far corner and proceeded toward him out of the distance.

Before Titus had realized what he was doing he had leaped sideways, quick as a squirrel, and was all at once in an almost complete darkness that brooded behind the ponderous and muscled carving of a figure without head or arms. The plinth on which this great trunk of stone stood balanced was itself above the level of his head.

Titus stood there trembling as the noise of many feet approached from the west, and a crutch from the east. He fought away the knowledge that he must have been seen by the Professors. He clung to the empty hope that they had all had their eyes cast to the ground and had never seen him running ahead of them, had never seen him dive behind the statue; and, more fervent still, the passionate hope that Barquentine had been too far away to notice any movement in the corridor. But even as he trembled he knew his hope was based on his fear and that it was madness for him to stay where he was.

The noise was all about him, the heavy feet, the whisking of the gowns, the clanging of the ironlike crutch on the slabs.

And then the voice of Barquentine brought everything to a standstill. "Hold!" it cried. "Hold there, Headmaster! By the pox, you have the whole spavined staff with you, hell crap me!"

"My very good colleagues are at my back," said the old and fruity voice of Bellgrove. And then he added, "My *very* good colleagues," as though to test his own courage in the face of the thing in red rags that glared up at him.

But Barquentine's mind was elsewhere. "Which *was* it?" he barked, taking a fresh hop in Bellgrove's direction. "Which *was* it, man?"

Bellgrove drew himself up and struck his favorite position as a Headmaster, but his old heart was beating painfully.

"I have no idea," he said. "No idea whatsoever, as to

what it can be to which you are referring." His words could not have sounded heavier or less honest. He must have felt this himself, for he added, "Not an inkling, I assure you."

"Not an inkling! Not an inkling!" Barquentine cried. "Black blood on your inklings!" With another hope and a grind of the crutch he brought himself immediately below the Headmaster.

"By the reek of your lights, there was a boy in this corridor. There was a boy just now. What? What? There was a slippery pup just now. Do you deny it?"

"I saw no child," said Bellgrove. "Slippery or otherwise." He lifted the ends of his mouth in a smirk, where they froze upon his own little joke.

Barquentine stared at him, and if Bellgrove's sight had been better, the malice in that stare might have unnerved the old Headmaster to the brink of his undoing. As it was, he clenched his hands under his gown, and with a picture of Titus in his mind—Titus whose eyes had shone at the sight of the marbles in the fort—he held onto the lies he was telling with the grip of a saint.

Barquentine turned to the staff who were clustered behind their Headmaster like a black chorus. His wet, ruthless eyes moved from face to face.

For a moment the idea crossed his brain that his sight had played him false. That he had seen a shadow. He turned his head and stared along the line of silent monuments.

Suddenly his spleen and frustration found vent and he thrashed out with his stick at the stone torso at his side. It was a wonder that his crutch was not broken.

"There was a whelp!" he screamed. "But enough of that! Time runs away. Is all prepared, what? What? Is all in readiness? You know your time of arrival? You know your orders. By hell, there must be no slips this afternoon."

"We have the details," said Bellgrove, in so quick and relieved a voice that it was no wonder that Barquentine darted at him suspiciously.

"And what's your bloody joy in *that?*" he hissed. "By hell, there's perfidy somewhere!"

"My joy," said Bellgrove, twice as slowly and ponderously, "springs from the knowledge, which my Staff must share with me, as men of culture, that a considerable poem is in store for them this afternoon."

Barquentine made a noise in his throat.

"And the boy, Titus," he snapped. "Does he know what is expected of *him?*"

"The Seventy-Seventh Earl will do his duty," said Bellgrove.

This last retort of the Headmaster's had not been heard by Titus, for the boy had found that behind him in the darkness where he had thought the wall of the corridor would support him as he leaned back in a sudden tiredness—there was no wall at all. In breathless silence he had got to his hands and knees and crawled into emptiness, through a narrow opening, and when he had come to a damp barrier of stones, had found that a tunnel led to his right, a tunnel that descended in a series of shallow stairs. He did not know that a few minutes later, Barquentine was to strike his way down the center of the corridor of statues, the staff dividing to let him pass, nor that after the staff had disappeared in their original direction, Bellgrove had returned alone, and had whispered thickly, "Come out, Titus, come out at once and report to your Headmaster," and receiving no response had himself worked his way behind the stone only to find himself baffled and defeated in the empty darkness.

Chapter Twenty-Four

❀❀❀❀❀❀❀❀❀❀❀❀

THE floor of the quadrangle was of a pale whitish-yellow brick, a pleasant, mellow color, soothing to the eye. The bricks had been laid so that their narrow surfaces faced upward, a device which must have called for twice as many as would otherwise have been necessary. But what gave the floor of the quadrangle its peculiar character was the herring-bone pattern which the artificers had followed many hundred years ago.

Blurred and worn as the yellow bricks had become, yet there was a vitality about the surface of the quadrangle, as though the notion of the man who had once, long ago, given orders that the bricks were to be laid in such and such a way, were still alive. The bricks had breath in them. To walk across this quadrangle was to walk across an idea.

The pillars of the cloisters had been painted, a dreadful idea, for the dove-gray stone of which they were constructed could not have harmonized more subtly with the pale-yellow brickwork from which they seemed to grow. They had, nevertheless, been painted a deep and most oppressive red.

It is true that on the following day an army of boys would be set to work in scraping the color off again, but on the day of the year when the quadrangle came into its own as the setting for the Poet's declamation, it seemed doubly outrageous to smother up the soft gray stone.

The Poet's Rostrum, set against the red pillars, glowed and darkened only to glow again in the afternoon sunlight. The branch of a tree fluttered across the face of the sun, so that the quadrangle which was filled with benches appeared on the move, for the flickering shadows of the leaves swam to and fro as the high branch swayed in the breeze.

The silent congregation, seated solemnly on their benches, stared over their shoulders at the gate through which the Poet would, at any moment, make his entrance. It was a year since anyone present had caught sight of that tall and awkward man, and then it had been at this same ceremony, which, on that previous occasion, had taken place in a thin and depressing drizzle.

The Countess was seated in advance of the front row. Fuchsia's chair was to her mother's left. Standing beside them, with the sweat of irritable anxiety pouring down his face, was Barquentine with his eyes fixed (as were the eyes of the Countess and Fuchsia) not upon the Poet's Gate, but upon a small door in the south wall of the quadrangle through which Titus, who was over twenty minutes late, should long ago have come running.

Behind them in a long row, as though their yellow bench were a perch for black turkeys, sat the Professors. Bellgrove, at their center, in his Zodiac gown, was also staring at the small door in the wall. He took out a big grubby handkerchief and mopped his brow. At that moment the door was pulled open and three boys ran through and came panting up to Barquentine.

"Well?" hissed the old man. "Well? Have you found him?"

"No, sir!" they panted. "We can't find him anywhere, sir."

Barquentine ground the foot of his crutch against the pale bricks as though to ease his anger. Suddenly Steerpike appeared at his side as though out of the mellow ground. He bowed to the Countess while a shadow undulated across the irregular terrain of the scores of heads that filled the quadrangle. The Countess made no response. Steerpike straightened himself.

"I can find no trace of the Seventy-Seventh Earl," he said, addressing Barquentine.

"Black blood!" The voice of the cripple forced its way between his teeth. "This is the fourth time that the . . ."

"That . . . the . . . *what?*" The Countess launched the three short words as though they were made of lead. They fell heavily through the afternoon air.

Barquentine gathered his red rags of office about his stunted body, and turned his irritable head to the Countess, who stared at him with ice in her eyes. The old man bowed, sucking at his teeth as he did so.

"My lady," he said, "this is the fourth time in six months that the Seventy-Seventh Earl has absented himself from a sacred . . ."

"By the least hair of the child's head," said the Countess, interrupting, in a voice of deadly deliberation—"if he should absent himself a hundred times an hour I will not have his misdemeanors bandied about in public. I will

not have you mouth and blurt his faults. You will keep
your observations in your own throat. My son is no
chattel that you can discuss, Barquentine, with your pale
lieutenant. Leave me. The occasion will proceed. Find
a substitute for the boy from the tyros' benches. You
may continue."

At that moment a murmur was heard from the
populace behind them, for the Poet, preceded by a
man in the skin of a horse, and with that animal's tail
trailing the bricks behind him as he paced slowly forward, was to be seen emerging from the Gate. The Poet
in his gown, with a beaker of moat-water in his left
hand and his manuscript in his right, followed the figure
in the horse's hide with long, awkward paces. His face
was like a wedge. His small eyes flickered restlessly.
He was pale with embarrassment and apprehension.

Steerpike found a boy of about Titus's age and height
and instructed him in his role, which was simple enough.
He was to stand when the rest were seated, and to sit
when the rest were standing, and that was all, as Seventy-Seventh Earl, by proxy, he had to remember.

When the Countess had placed the pebble from Gormenghast River in the beaker of moat-water, and when
the populace had seated themselves again and none save
the Poet and the substitute for Titus were left on their
feet, then an absolute hush descended over the quadrangle, and the Poet, holding his poem in his hand and raising his head, lifted his hollow voice. . . .

"To her Ladyship, Gertrude Countess of Groan, and to
her children, Titus the Seventy-Seventh Lord of the Tracts,
and Fuchsia, sole vessel of the Blood on the distaff side:
to all ladies and gentlemen present and to all hereditary
officials: to all of varying duties whose observance of the
tenets justifies their presence at this ceremony, I dedicate
this poem which as the Laws decree shall be addressed to
as many as are here present in all the variance of their
receptivity, status, and acumen, insomuch as poetry is a
ritual of the heart, the voice of faith, the core of Gormenghast, the moon when it is red, the trumpet of the
Groans."

The Poet paused to breathe. The words he had just

used were invariably declaimed before the poem, and there was nothing left for the Poet to do but to open the door of the wire cage, which Barquentine had passed up to him, and let loose the magpie as a symbol of something the significance of which had long been lost to the records.

The magpie, which was supposed to flap away into the afternoon sunlight, until it was a mere dot in the sky, did no such thing. It hopped from the cage and stood for a moment on the rim of the rostrum before flying with a loud rattle of its wings to the Countess, on whose shoulder it perched for the rest of the proceedings, pecking from time to time at its black wings.

The Poet, raising his manuscript before his eyes, took a deep and shuddering breath, opened his small mouth, took a step backward, and, losing his balance, all but fell down the steps that descended steeply from his narrow rostrum to the ground seven feet below. An uncontrollable shriek of laughter from the tyros' benches stabbed into the warm afternoon like a needle into a cushion.

The offending youth was led away by an official. The drowsy silence came down again, drowning the shadow-dappled quadrangle as though with an element.

The Poet moved forward on the rostrum, his skin prickly with shame. He raised his manuscript again to read; and as he read the shadows lengthened across the quadrangle. A cloud of starlings moved like migraine across the upper air. The small boys on the tyros' benches, imitating the Poet and nudging one another, fell, one by one, asleep. The Countess yawned. The summer afternoon melted into evening. Steerpike's eyes moved to and fro. Barquentine sucked his teeth irritably.

The voice of the Poet droned on and on. A star came out. And then another. The earth swam on through space. The Countess yawned again and turned her eyes to the south doorway.

Where was Titus?

Chapter Twenty-Five

THE glade had been in darkness since the dawn. A strand of almost horizontal light had slid at cockcrow through a multitude of trees and inflamed for a moment an obscure corner of the glade where a herd of giant ferns arched their spines (the long fronds falling like the manes of horses). They had shone with a cold, green angry radiance. They had been exposed. The long ray had withdrawn as though it had not found what it was looking for.

As the sun climbed, the glade appeared to darken rather than to absorb the strengthening light. The air was domed with foliage; layer after voluminous layer hanging in darkened swathes!

All day long the darkness sat there, muffling the boles of the trees—a terrible daytime dusk, as thick as night.

But all the while the uppermost branches of these same trees and the topmost layers of leaf shone in the cloudless sunlight.

When evening came and the sun was hanging over the western skyline the drowned glade began to lighten. The level beams streamed from the west; the glade shuddered, and then, silent and motionless as a picture of itself, it gave up all its secrets.

Of the trees that grew from this sunken circle of ground there was one which claimed immediate attention. Its girth was such that the trees that surrounded it, though tall and powerful, were made to look like saplings. It was the king. Yet it alone was dead.

And yet its very deadness had given it a life. A life that had no need for the April sap. Its towerlike bulk of a bole mounted into the arbored gloom, and as the light from the west struck it, it shone with the hard,

smooth quality of marble or ivory, for it was the color
of a tusk.

It rose out of a sward, sepia in color, a treacherous
basin. This sick and rotting ground was dappled with gold
where it was struck by the direct rays, the lozenges of
light elongating as the sun sank.

Sixty feet from the ground the trunk of the dead giant
was pocked with cavities. They were like entrances, it
seemed, or like the portholes of a ship, their raised rims
smooth as silk and hard as bone.

And it was here, in these mouths of the great tree,
sixty feet above the ground, where the girth of the bole
was still as ponderous as its sward-lapped base—it was
here that the life of the dead tree was centered.

There was no cavern of that high and silky cliff but
had its occupant. Save for the bees, whose porthole
dripped with sweetness, and the birds, there were few of
the denizens of this dead-tree settlement that could get
any kind of grip upon the surface of the bole. But there
were branches, which swept from the surrounding trees
to within leaping range for the wildcat, the flying squirrel, the opossum, and for that creature, not always to be
found in the moss-lined darkness of its ivory couch, who,
separated by a mere membrane of honey-soaked wood
from the multitudinous murmur of a hive, was asleep as
the evening light stole through the small round opening
so high above the ground. As the light quickened the
creature moved in its sleep. The eyes opened. They were
as clear and green as sea stones and were set in a face
that was colored and freckled like a robin's egg.

The creature slid from its retreat, and paused for a moment as it crouched at the lip of its dizzy cave, and
then, leaping outward into space, it swung itself from
branch to branch like something without weight or substance, while the foliage of the evening forest closed about
it, and the faraway sound of a bell rang faintly from the
distant castle.

Chapter Twenty-Six

※※※※※※※※※※※

LIKE a child lost in the chasmic mazes of a darkening forest, so was Titus lost in the uncharted wilderness of a region long forgotten. As a child might stare in wonder and apprehension along an avenue of dusk and silence, and then, turning his head along another, and another, each as empty and breathless, so Titus stared in apprehension and with a hammering heart along the rides and avenues of stone.

But here, unlike the child lost in the forest, Titus was surrounded by a fastness without sentience. There was no growth, and no movement. There was no sense here that a sluggish sap was sleeping somewhere; was waiting in the stony tracts for an adamantine April. There was no presence here that shared the moment with him, the exquisitely frightening, long-drawn, terror-edged moment of his apprehension. Would nothing stir? Was there no pulse in all these mocking tracts? Nothing that breathed? Nothing among the adumbrate vistas and perspectives of stone that struggled to survive? Empty, silent, forbidding as a lunar landscape, and as uncharted, a tract of Gormenghast lay all about him.

There was no sound, no call of a bird or screech of an insect to break the silence of the stone. No rivulet slid lisping across the flagstones of Great Halls.

He was quite lost. All the sounds of the castle's life—the clanging of bells; the footsteps striking on the hollow stones; the voices and the echoes of voices; all were gone.

Was this what it was to be an explorer? An adventurer? To gulp this sleeping silence? To be so unutterably alone with it, to wade in it, to find it rising like a tide from the floors, lowering itself from the moldering caverns of high domes, filling the corridors as though with something palpable?

208

To feel the lips go dry; the tongue like leather in the mouth; to feel the knees weaken.

To feel the heart struggling as though to be allowed its freedom, hammering at the walls of his small ribs, hammering for release.

Why had he scrambled through that midnight gap, where his hands had felt and found nothing and then nothing and then again nothing as he edged his way into the gloom? Why had he descended that flight of rusty iron to the deserted corridor and seen how it stretched into how strange a murk of weeds? Why had he not turned back, before it was too late? Turned back and climbed those iron stairs again and waited behind the giant torso for the last echo to disappear from the corridor of carvings? The Headmaster had been on his side—had told lies for him. Had he been ungrateful to steal away? And now he was lost forever; forever, and evermore.

Clenching his hands he cried aloud in the hollow wilderness for *help*. Immediately a score of voices answered him, from the four quarters. *"Help, help,"* they cried, again and again, a clamor of voices that were all his own; and the last faint echo of his cry, thin, wan, frightened, and infinitely far, languished and died; and the thick silence crowded back from every side; and he was drowned again.

There was nowhere to go and there was everywhere to go. His sense of direction, of where he had come from, had been wiped away by what seemed an age of vacillation.

The silence filled his ears until they ached. He tried to remember what he had read about explorers, but he could recall no story of heroes lost in such a tract as this.

He brought his clenched fist to his mouth and bit his knuckles. For a moment the pain seemed to help him. It gave him a sense of his own reality, and as the pain weakened he bit again; and, in the vain hope of gaining help from yet another scrutiny of the surrounding vistas and avenues of masonry, for he was at a juncture of many ways, he braced himself. His muscles tautened; his head was thrust forward; he peered along the dwindling perspectives. But nothing helped him. Nothing that he saw suggested a course of action, a clue for freedom. There was no way of light to indicate that there was any outer world. What luminosity there was was uniform, a kind of dusk that had nothing to do with daylight. A self-contained thing, bred in the halls and corridors, something that seeped forth from the walls and floors and ceilings.

Titus moved his dry tongue across his lips and sat down on the flagged floor, but a sense of terror jerked him to his feet again. It seemed that he had begun to be absorbed into the stone. He must be on his feet. He must keep moving. He tiptoed to a wall like the wall of a wharf. For a moment he leaned his small, sweating cheek against the mortarless stone. "I must think . . . think . . . think. . . ." He formed the words with his dry tongue. "Have lost my way. My way? What does that mean?" He began to whisper the words so that he could hear them, but not the castle. There was no echo to this little husky sound. "It means I don't know where to go. What do I know then? I know that there is a north, south, east, and west. But I don't know which is which. Aren't there any other directions?"

His heart gave a leap. "Yes!" he cried, and a hundred affirmatives shouted from throats of stone. He stiffened at the leaping cries, his eyes flickering to left and right, his head motionless. Surely so great a clamor must blast from their retreats the dire ghosts of the place. The center of his thin chest was sick and bruised with his heartbeats.

But nothing appeared and the silence thickened again. What was it he had discovered, that it should have caught him unawares? Another direction? Something that was neither north, south, east, nor west. What was it? It was skyward. It was roofward. It was the direction that led to the air.

It was a mere spark, this hope that had ignited. He mouthed his words again. "There must be stairways," he said. "And floor above floor, until I reach the roof. If I climb long enough I must reach the roof, and then I can see where I am."

The relief which he felt at having an idea to grip was convulsive, and the tears poured down his face. Then he began to walk, as steadily as he could, along the widest of the gray stone channels. For a considerable distance, it continued in a straight line and then began to take slow curves. The walls on either side were featureless, the ceiling also. Not so much as a cobweb gave interest to the barren surfaces. All at once, after a sharper curve than usual, the passage subdivided into five narrow fingers, and all the child's terrors returned. Was he to return to the hollow silences from which he had come? He could not turn back. He *could* not.

In desperation he leaned against the wall and closed his eyes, and it was then that he heard the first sound— that was not of his own making. The first sound since he had slid into the darkness behind the remote statue. He did not jerk at the shock of it but became rigid so that he was unobserved by the raven when it appeared from the darkness of one of the narrow passageways. It walked with a sedate and self-absorbed air to within a few feet of Titus, when it lowered its big head and let fall from its beak a silver bracelet. But only for a moment, for directly it had pecked at the feathers of its breast it lifted up the bracelet and continued for a few paces before hopping, rather clumsily, upon an outcrop of the wall and thence to a larger shelf. Very gradually Titus altered the direction of his head so that he could observe it, this *living* thing. But at the first movement of his head, tentative as it had been, the bird, with a loud and throaty cry and a rattle of black wings, was, all in a moment, in the air, and a fraction of a second later had disappeared down the dark and narrow corridor from which it had so recently paced forth.

Titus at once decided to follow it: not because he wished to see more of the raven, but because the bird was to him a sign of the outer world. There was more than a chance that in returning to this inhospitable corridor, the raven was returning, indirectly, to the open air, and the woods and the wide sky.

As Titus followed, the darkness grew more profound with every step, and he began to realize that he was moving under the earth, for the roots of trees grew through the roof and the loam of the walls, and the smell of decay was thick in the air.

Had his fear and horror of the silent halls from which

he had so recently escaped been less real he would even
now have turned about in the constricted space and made
his way back to the hollow nightmare from which he had
come. For there seemed no end to this black and stifling
tunnel.

At first he had been able to walk upright, but that
was long ago. He was now forced, for long periods at a
time, to crawl, the smell of the bad earth thick in his
face. But for equally long stretches of time the tunnel
would widen, and he was able to stumble forward, his
body comparatively upright, until the roof would lower
itself again and he would be filled with the fear of suffocation.

There was no light at all. He had all but lost hope that
he would ever come out of this horrible experience alive.
Had it not been that to keep moving was less frightening
than to remain crouched in the darkness Titus would have
been tempted to cease forcing his tired body onward hour
after hour, for he had little strength and spirit left.

But at long last, when he had no longer the vitality to
feel any excitement or relief, so sick he was with fear
and exhaustion, he saw ahead of him, as in a dream, a
dim, rough-margined opening of light, darkly fringed with
coarse weeds and grasses, and he knew, in a flat and
colorless way, that he would not die in the dark tunnel;
that the hollow walls were a nightmare of the past and
that the most he had to fear was the punishment he would
receive on returning to the castle.

When he had dragged himself from the tunnel's weedy
mouth and had climbed the bank in which the opening
gaped, he saw far away to the north and to the west the
tower'd outline of his ancient home.

Chapter Twenty-Seven

※※※※※※※※※※※※※

IF the success of a hostess is in any way dependent upon the lavishness of her preparation for the soiree she proposes; upon her outlook, on the almost insane attention which she gives to detail and upon a wealth of forethought; then, theoretically at least, Irma Prunesquallor could look ahead to something that would correspond to those glimpses that came to her in the darkness, when she lay half asleep and saw herself surrounded by a riotous throng of males battling for her hand, while she, the cynosure, swayed coquettishly upon her silk-swaddled pelvis.

If the microscopic overhaul to which she was subjecting her person, her skin, her hair, her dresses, and her jewelry gave ground for the belief that so much passionate industry must necessarily wake and rescue a kind of beauty from where it had for so long been immured in her; wake it by a kind of surprise attack; a bombardment of her tall, angular clay—then, there was no need for Irma to have any fears upon the score of her attraction. She would be ravishing. She would set a new kind of standard in magnetism. After all, she had worked for it.

Having tried on seventeen necklaces and decided upon no necklace at all, so that the full length of her white throat might dip, bridle, and sway like a swan's in an absolute freedom of movement, she crossed to the door of her dressing room and, hearing a footstep in the hall below, she could not resist crying out, "Alfred! Alfred! Only three days more, my dear. Only three days more! Alfred! Are you there?"

But there was no reply.

The step she had heard was Steerpike's, who, knowing that the Doctor was attending a case in the South Kitchen where a rotier had slipped on a piece of lard and splintered his shoulder blade, had taken the opportunity which he had for some time been waiting for, and climbed through the Doctor's dispensary window, filled a bottle with poison, and, having stowed it away in a deep pocket, decided to leave by the front door with an assortment of explanations in his hand from which to choose were he to be discovered in the hall. Why had there been no answer to his knocking? he would say. Why did they leave the front door open? Where was Dr. Prunesquallor? and so on.

But he met no one and took no notice of Irma's cry.

When he got back to his room he poured the poison into a beautiful little cut-glass vessel, placed it against the light of the window where it shone. Then he stood back from it with his head on one side, stepped forward again to move it a little to the left, in the interest of symmetry, and then, returning to the center of the room, ran his tongue along his thin lips as he peered with his eyebrows at the little flask of death. Suddenly he stretched his arms out on either side, the fingers splayed like star-fish as though he were waking them to a kind of hyper-sentience of tingling life.

Then, as though it were the most natural thing in the world, he lowered his hands to the ground, threw up his slender legs, and began to perambulate the room on the palms of his hands with the peculiarly stilted, rolling, and predatory gait of a starling.

Chapter Twenty-Eight

❋❋❋❋❋❋❋❋❋❋

IT was on the following afternoon that Mrs. Slagg died. She was found lying upon her bed, toward evening, like a little grubby doll. The black dress was awry as though she had struggled. Her hands were clasped at her shrunken breast. It was hard to imagine that the broken thing had once been new; that those withered, waxen cheeks had been fresh and tinted. That her eyes had long ago glinted with laughter. For she had been sprightly once. A vivacious, pert little creature. Bright as a bird.

And here she lay. It was as though the doll-sized body had been thrown aside as too old and decrepit to be of any further use.

Fuchsia, directly she had been told, rushed to the small room that she knew so well.

But the doll on the bed was no longer her nurse. It was not Nannie Slagg, that little motionless bundle. It was something else. Fuchsia closed her eyes and the poignantly familiar image of her old nurse, who had been the nearest thing to a mother that Fuchsia had ever known, swam through her mind in a gush of memory.

It was in her to turn again to the bed and to take the beloved relic in her arms in a passion of love, but she could not. She could not. And she did not cry. Something, for all the vividness of her memory, had gone dead in her. She stared again at the shell of all that had nursed her, adored her, smacked her, and maddened her.

In her ears, the peevish voice kept crying—"Oh, my weak heart, how *could* they? How *could* they? Anyone would think I didn't know my place."

Turning suddenly from the bed Fuchsia saw for the first time that she had not been alone in the room. Dr. Prunesquallor was standing by the door. Involuntarily she turned to him, raising her eyes to his odd yet strangely compassionate features.

He took a step toward her. "Fuchsia, my dearest child," he said. "Let us go together."

"Oh, Doctor," she said, "I don't feel anything. Am I wicked, Dr. Prune? I don't understand."

The door was suddenly filled by the figure of the Countess who, although she stared at her daughter and at the Doctor, did not appear to realize who they were, for no expression appeared on her big pale face. She was carrying over her arm a shawl of rare lace. She moved forward, treading heavily on the bare boards. When she reached the bed she gazed for a moment as though transfixed at the pathetic sight below her, and then, spreading the beautiful black shawl over the body, she turned and left the room.

Prunesquallor, taking Fuchsia's hand, led her through the door, which he closed behind them.

"Fuchsia dear," he said as they began to move together down the corridor, "have you heard anything of Titus?"

She stopped dead and let go the Doctor's hand. "No," she said, "and if nobody finds him I will kill myself."

"Tut, tut, tut, my little threatener," said Prunesquallor. "What a tedious thing to say. And you such an original girl. As though Titus won't reappear like a jack-in-the-box, by all that's typical so he will!"

"He must! He must!" cried Fuchsia, and then she began to weep uncontrollably while the Doctor held her against his side and dabbed her flushed cheeks with his immaculate handkerchief.

Chapter Twenty-Nine

NANNIE Slagg's funeral was so simple as to appear almost offhand; but this seemingly casual dispatch of the old lady's relics bore no relation to the inherent pathos of the occasion. The gathering at the graveside was out of all proportion to the number of friends on whom, in her lifetime, she would ever have dared to count. For she had become, in her old age, a kind of legend. No one had troubled to see her. She had been deserted in her declining years. But it had been tacitly assumed that she would live forever. That she would no more pass out of the castle's life than that the Tower of Flints would pass from Gormenghast to leave a gap in the skyline, a gap never again to be filled.

And so, at her funeral, the majority of the mourners were gathered there, to pay their respects to the memory not so much of Mrs. Slagg, as to the legend which the tiny creature had, all unwittingly, allowed to grow about her.

It had been impossible for the two bearers to carry the small coffin across their shoulders, for this necessitated so close a formation one behind the other, that they could not walk without tripping one another up. The little box was eventually carried in one hand by the leading mute, while his colleague, with a finger placed on the lid, to prevent it from swaying, walked to one side and a little to the rear.

The bearer, as he strode along, might have been carrying a bird cage as he paced his way to the Retainers' Graveyard. From time to time the man would turn his eyes with a childish, puzzled expression to the box he carried, as though to reassure himself that he was doing what was expected of him. He could not help feeling that something was missing.

The mourners, led by Barquentine, came behind, followed by the Countess, at some distance. She made no effort to keep pace with the rapid, jerking progress of the cripple. She moved ponderously, her eyes on the ground. Fuchsia and Titus followed, Titus having been released from Lichen Fort for the funeral.

With the nightmare memory of his recent adventure filling his mind he moved in a trance, waking from time to time to wonder at this new manifestation of life's incalculable strangeness—the little box ahead of him, the sunshine playing over the head of Gormenghast Mountain, where it rose, with unbelievable solidity, ahead, like a challenge, on the skyline.

It crowned a region that had become a part of his imaginative being, a region where an exile moved like a stick-insect, through a wilderness of trees, and where, phantom or human, he knew not which, something else was, at this moment, floating again, as he had seen it float before, like a leaf, in the shape of a girl. A girl. Suddenly he broke from his trance at Fuchsia's side.

The word and the idea had fused into something fire-like. Suddenly the slight and floating enigma of the glade had taken on a sex, had become particularized, had waked in him a sensation of excitement that was new to him. Wide awake, all at once, he was at the same time plunged even deeper into a cloudland of symbols to which he had no key. And she was there—there, ahead of him. He could see, far away, the very forest roof that rustled above her.

The figures that moved ahead of him, Barquentine, his mother, and the men with the little box, were less real than the startling confusion of his heart.

He had come to a halt in a valley filled with mounds. Fuchsia was holding his hand. The crowd was all about him. A figure in a hood was scattering red dust into a little trench. A voice was intoning. The words meant nothing to him. He was adrift.

That same evening, Titus lay wide-eyed in the darkness and stared with unseeing eyes at the enormous shadows of two boys as they fought a mock battle of grotesque dimensions upon an oblong of light cast upon the dormitory wall. And while he gazed abstractedly at the cut and thrust of the shadow-monsters, his sister Fuchsia was crossing to the Doctor's house.

"Can I talk to you, Doctor?" she asked as he opened the door to her. "I know it isn't long since you had to bear with me, and—" But Prunesquallor, putting his finger to his lips, silenced her and then drew her back into a shadow of the hall, for Irma was opening the door of the sitting room.

"Alfred," came the cry. "What *is* it, Alfred? I said what *is* it?"

"The merest nothing, my love," trilled the Doctor. "I must get that hank of ivy torn up by its very roots in the morning."

"*What* ivy—I said *what* ivy, you irritating thing," she answered. "I sometimes wish that you could call a spade a spade, I really do."

"Have we one, sweet nicotine?"

"Have we what?"

"A spade, for the ivy, my love, the ivy that *will* keep tapping at our front door. By all that's symbolic, it *will* go on doing it!"

"Is that what it was?"

Irma relaxed. "I don't remember any ivy," she added. "But what *are* you cowering in that corner for? It's not like you, Alfred, to lurk about in the corner like that. Really, if I didn't know it was you, well really, I'd be quite . . ."

"But you're *not,* are you, my sweet nerve-ending? Of course you're not. So upstairs with you. By all that moves in rapid circles, I've had a seismic sister these last few days, haven't I?"

"Oh, Alfred. It *will* be worth it, won't it? There's so much to think of and I'm so excited. And so *soon* now. *Our* party! *Our* party!"

"And that's why you must go to bed and fill yourself right up with sleep. That is what my sister needs, isn't it? Of course it is. Sleep . . . Oh, the very treacle of it, Irma! So run away my dear. Away with you! Away with you! A-w-a-y!" He fluttered his hand like a silk handkerchief.

"Good night, Alfred."

"Good night, O thicker-than-water."

Irma disappeared into the upper darkness.

"And *now,*" said the Doctor, placing his immaculate hands on his brittle and elegant knees, and rising at the same time on his toes, so that Fuchsia had the strongest impression that he was about to fall forward on his speculative and smiling face—"and now, my Fuchsia, I think we've had enough of the hall, don't you?" And he led the girl into his study.

"Now if you'll draw the blinds and if I pull up that green armchair, we will be comfortable, affable, incredible, and almost insufferable in two shakes of a lamb's tail, won't we?" he said. "By all that's unanswerable, we will!"

Fuchsia, pulling at the curtain, felt something give way, and a loose sail of velvet hung across the glass.

"Oh, Dr. Prune, I'm sorry—I'm sorry," she said, almost in tears.

"Sorry! Sorry!" cried the Doctor. "How dare you pity me! How dare you humiliate me! You know very well that I can do that sort of thing better than you. I'm an old man; I admit it. Nearly fifty summers have seeped through me. But there's life in me yet. But *you* don't think so. No! By all that's cruel, you don't. But I'll show you. Watch me." And the Doctor, striding like a heron to a farther window, ripped the long curtain from its runner, and whirling it around himself stood swathed before her like a long green chrysalis, with the pale sharp eager features of his bright face emerging at the top like something from another life.

"There!" he said.

A year ago Fuchsia would have laughed until her sides were sore. Even at the moment it was wonderfully funny. But she couldn't laugh. She knew that he loved doing such a thing. She knew he loved to put her at her ease—and she *had* been put at her ease, for she no longer felt embarrassed—but she also knew that she should be laughing, and she couldn't *feel* the humor, she could only *know* it. For within the last year she had developed, not naturally, but on a zig-zag course. The emotions and the tags of half-knowledge which came to her fought and jostled, upsetting one another, so that what was natural to her appeared un-natural, and she lived from minute to minute, grappling with each like a lost explorer in a dream who is now in the arctic, now on the equator, now upon rapids, and now alone on endless tracts of sand.

"Oh, Doctor," she said, "thank you. That is very, very kind and funny."

She had turned her head away, but now she looked up and found he had already disengaged himself of the curtain and was pushing a chair toward her.

"What is worrying you, Fuchsia?" he said. They were both sitting down. The dark night stared in at them through the curtainless windows.

She leaned forward and as she did so she suddenly looked older. It was as though she had taken a grip on her mind—to have, in a way, grown up to the span of her nineteen years.

"Several important things, Dr. Prune," she said. "I want to ask you about them . . . if I may."

Prunesquallor looked up sharply. This was a new Fuchia. Her tone had been perfectly level. Perfectly adult.

"Of course you may, Fuchsia. What are they?"

"The first thing is, what happened to my father, Dr. Prune?"

The Doctor leaned back in his chair; as she stared at him he put his hand to his forehead.

"Fuchsia," he said, "whatever you ask I will try to answer. I won't evade your questions. And you must believe me. What happened to your father, I do not know. I only know that he was very ill—and you remember that as well as I do—just as you remember his disappearance. If anyone alive knows what happened to him, I do not know who that man might be unless it is either Flay or Swelter, who also disappeared at the same time."

"Mr. Flay is alive, Dr. Prune."

"No!" said the Doctor. "Why do you say that?"

"Titus has seen him, Doctor. More than once."

"Titus!"

"Yes, Doctor, in the woods. But it's a secret. You won't . . ."

"Is he well? Is he able to keep well? What did Titus say about him?"

"He lives in a cave and hunts for his food. He asked after me. He is very loyal."

"Poor old Flay!" said the Doctor. "Poor old faithful Flay. But you mustn't see him, Fuchsia. It would do nothing but harm. I cannot have you getting into trouble."

"But my father," cried Fuchsia. "You said he might know about my father! He may be alive, Dr. Prune. He may be *alive!*"

"No. No. I don't believe he is," said the Doctor. "I don't believe so, Fuchsia."

"But Doctor, Doctor! I must see Flay. He loved me. I want to take him something."

"No, Fuchsia. You mustn't go. Perhaps you will see him again—but you will become distressed—more distressed than you are now, if you start escaping from the castle. And Titus also. This is all very wrong. He is not old enough to be so wild and secret. God bless me— what else docs he say?"

"This is all in secret, Doctor."

"Yes—yes, Fuchsia. Of course it is."

"He has seen something."

"Seen something? What sort of thing?"

"A flying thing."

The Doctor froze into a carving of ice.

"A flying thing," repeated Fuchsia. "I don't know what he means." She leaned back in her chair and clasped her hands. "Before Nannie Slagg died," she said—her voice falling to a whisper—"she talked to me. It was only a few days before she died—and she didn't seem as nervy as usual, because she talked as she used to talk when she wasn't worried. She told me about when Titus was born, and when Keda came to nurse him, which I remember myself, and how when Keda went away again to the Outer Dwellings, one of the Carvers made love to her and she had a baby and how the baby wasn't really like other babies, because of Keda not being married, I mean, but different apart from that, and how there were various rumors about it. The Outer Dwellers wouldn't have it, she said, because it wasn't legitimate, and when Keda killed herself the baby was brought up differently as though it were her fault, and when she was a child she lived in a way that made them all hate her and never talked to the other children, but frightened them sometimes, and ran across the roofs and down the mud chimneys and began to spend all her time in the woods. And how the Mud Dwellers hated her and were frightened of her because she was so rapid and kept disappearing and bared her teeth. And Nannie Slagg told me that she left them altogether and they didn't know where she had gone for a long time, only sometimes they heard her laughing at them at night, and they called her the 'Thing,' and Nannie Slagg told me all this and said she is still alive and how she is Titus's foster-sister, and when Titus told me of the flying thing in the air I wondered, Dr. Prune, whether . . ."

Fuchsia lifted her eyes and found that the Doctor had risen from his chair and was staring through the window into the darkness where a shooting star was trailing down the sky.

"If Titus knew I had told you," she said in a loud voice, rising to her feet, "I would never be forgiven. But I am frightened for him. I don't want anything to happen

to him. He is always staring at nothing and doesn't hear
half I say. And I love him, Dr. Prune. That's what I
wanted to tell you."

"Fuchsia," said the Doctor. "It's very late. I will think
about all you have told me. A little at a time, you know.
If you tell me everything at once I'll lose my place, won't
I? But a little at a time. I know there are other things
you want to tell me, about this and that, and very important things too—but you must wait a day or two and
I will try and help you. Don't be frightened. I will do all
I can. What with Flay and Titus and the Thing I must
do some thinking, so run along to bed and come and see
me very soon again. Why, bless my wits if it isn't hours
after your bedtime. Away with you!"

"Good night, Doctor."

"Good night, my dear child."

Chapter Thirty

A few days later, when Steerpike saw Fuchsia emerge
from a door in the West Wing and make her way across
the stubble of what had once been a great lawn, he eased
himself out of the shadows of an arch where he had been
lurking for over an hour, and taking a round-about route
began to run, with his body half doubled, toward the object of Fuchsia's evening journey.

Across his back, as he ran, was slung a wreath of
roses from Pentecost's flower garden. Arriving, unseen,
at the servants' burial ground a minute or two before
Fuchsia, he had time to strike an attitude of grief as he
knelt on one knee, his right hand still on the wreath which
he was placing on the little weedy grave.

So Fuchsia came upon him.

"What are *you* doing here?" Her voice was hardly
audible. "*You* never loved her."

Fuchsia turned her eyes to the great wreath of red and yellow roses and then to the few wildflowers which were clasped in her hand.

Steerpike rose to his feet and bowed. The evening was green about them.

"I did not know her as you did, your Ladyship," he said. "But it struck me as so mean a grave for an old lady to be buried in. I was able to get these roses . . . and . . . well. . . ." (His simulation of embarrassment was exact.)

"But *your* wildflowers!" he said, removing the wreath from the head of the little mound and placing it at the dusty foot. "They are the ones that will please her spirit most—wherever she is."

"I don't know anything about that," said Fuchsia. She turned from him and flung her flowers away. "It's all nonsense anyway." She turned again and faced him. "But *you*," she blurted. "I didn't think *you* were sentimental."

Steerpike had never expected this. He had imagined that she would feel she had found an ally in the graveyard. But a new idea presented itself. Perhaps he had found an ally in *her*. How far was her phrase, "It's all nonsense anyway," indicative of her nature?

"I have my moods," he said, and with a single action plucked the great wreath of roses from the foot of the grave and hurled it from him. For a moment the rich roses glowed as they careered through the dark-green evening to disappear in the darkness of the surrounding mounds.

For a moment she stood motionless, the blood drained from her face, and then she sprang at the young man and buried the nails of her hands in his high cheekbones.

He made no move. Dropping her arms and backing away from him with slow, exhausted steps, she saw him standing perfectly quietly, his face absolutely white save for the bright blood on his cheeks that were red like a clown's.

Her heart beat as she saw him. Behind him the green porous evening was hung like a setting for his thin body, his whiteness, and the hectic wounds on his cheeks.

For a moment she forgot her sudden, inconsistent

hatred of his act; forgot his high shoulders; forgot her station as a daughter of the Line—forgot everything and saw only a human whom she had hurt, and a tide of remorse filled her, and half blind with confusion she stumbled toward him, her arms outstretched. Quick as an adder he was in her arms—but even at that moment they fell, tripping each other up on the rough ground—fell, their arms about one another. Steerpike could feel her heart pounding against his ribs, her cheek against his mouth, but he made no movement with his lips. His mind was racing ahead. For a few moments they lay. He waited for her limbs and body to relax, but she was taut as a bowstring in his arms. Not a move did he make, nor she, until lifting her head from his she saw, not the blood on his cheeks, but the dark-red color of his eyes, the high bulge of his shining forehead. It was unreal. It was a dream. There was a kind of horrible novelty about it. Her gush of tenderness had ended, and there she was in the arms of the high-shouldered man. She turned her head again and realized with a start of horror that they were using for their pillow the narrow grassy gravemound of her old nurse.

"Oh, horrible!" she screamed. "Horrible! Horrible!" And forcing him aside as she scrambled to her feet she bounded like a wild thing into the darkness.

Chapter Thirty-One

SITTING at her bedroom window, Irma Prunesquallor awaited the daybreak as though a clandestine meeting of the most hushed and secret kind had been agreed upon between herself and the first morning ray. And suddenly it came—the dawn—a flush of swallow light above a rim of masonry. The day had arrived. The day of the Party, or of what she now called her Soiree.

In spite of her brother's advice, she had passed a very poor night, her speculative excitement breaking through her sleep over and over again. At last she had lit the long green candles on the table by her bed, and frowning at each in turn had begun to polish yet again the ten long and perfect fingernails, her mouth pursed, her muscles tensed. Then she had slipped on her dressing gown and, drawing a chair to the window, had waited for the sunrise.

Below her window the quadrangle, as yet untouched by the pale light in the east, was spread like a lake of black water. There was no sound, no movement anywhere. Irma sat motionless, bolt upright, her hands clasped in her lap. Her eyes were fixed upon the sunrise. The candle flames in the room behind her stood balanced upon their wicks like yellow leaves upon tiny black stalks. Not a tremor disturbed their perfect lines—and then, suddenly, a cock crew—a barbarous, an imperious sound; primal and unashamed, it split the darkness, lifting Irma to her feet as it were on the updraft of its clarion. Her pulses raced. She sprang for the bathroom and within a few moments the hissing, steaming water had filled the bath and Irma, standing in an attitude of excruciating coyness, was tossing handfuls of emerald and lilac crystals into the sumptuous depths.

Alfred Prunesquallor, his head thrown back across his pillow, was only half asleep. His brows were drawn together and a strange frown gave to his face an unexpected quality. Had any of his acquaintances seen him lying there they would have wondered whether, after all, they had the slightest inkling as to his real nature. Was this the gay, irrepressible, and facetious physician?

He had passed a restless and unhappy night. Confused dreams had kept him turning on his bed, dreams that from time to time gathered themselves into vivid images of terrible clarity.

Struggling for breath and strength, he beat his way through the black moat-water to a drowning Fuchsia no bigger than a child's doll. But every time he reached her and stretched out his hand she sank beneath the surface, and there in her place were floating bottles half filled with colored poison. And then he would see her again, calling for help, tiny, dark, desperate, and he would flounder after her, his heart hammering, and he would waken.

At various moments through the night he could see Steerpike running through the air, his body bent forward, his feet a few inches above the ground but never touching it. And keeping pace with him and immediately below him as though it were his shadow, a swarm of rats with their fangs bared ran in a compact body like one thing, veering as he veered, pausing as he paused, most horrible and intent, filling the landscape of his midnight brain.

He saw the Countess on a great iron tray far out at sea. The moon shone down like a blue lamp, as she fished, with Flay as her frozen rod, attenuate and stiff beyond belief. Between the teeth of the petrified mouth he held a strand of the Countess's dark-red hair, which shone like a thread of fire in the blue light.

Effortlessly she held him aloft, her big hand gripping him about both ankles. His clothes were tight about him and he appeared mummified, the thin rigid length of him reaching up stiffly into the stars. With hideous regularity she would pluck at the line and swing aboard another and yet another of her white and sea-drowned cats, and place it tenderly upon the mounting heap of whiteness on the tray.

And then he saw Bellgrove galloping like a horse on all fours with Titus on his back. Through the ravine of terrible darkness and up the slopes of pine-covered mountains he galloped, his white mane blowing out behind his head while Titus, plucking arrow after arrow from an unfailing quiver, let fly at everything in view until, the image dwindling in the Doctor's brain, he lost them in the dire shade of the night.

And the dead, he saw. Mrs. Slagg clutching at her heart as she pattered along a tightrope, and the tears that coursed down her cheeks and fell to the earth far below, sounding like gunshots as they struck the ground.

And Swelter, for an instant, filled the darkness, so that even in his sleep, the Doctor retched to see so vile a volume forcing its boneless way, inch by inch, through a keyhole.

And Sepulchrave and Sourdust danced together upon a bed, leaping and turning in the air, their hands joined, and over their heads were great crude paper masks, so that over Sourdust's wizened shoulders the flapping face of a painted kitten put out its tongue at the cardboard sunflower through the great black center of which the eyes of the Seventy-Sixth Earl of Gormenghast glittered like broken glass.

Picture after moving picture all night long until, as dawn approached, the Doctor fell into a dreamless though shallow sleep through which he could hear the dreamland crowing of a cock and the water roaring into Irma's bath.

Chapter Thirty-Two

IN a score of schoolrooms all through the day innumerable urchins wondered what it was that made their masters even less interested than usual in their existence. Familiar as they were with being neglected over long periods and with the disinterest that descends on those who juggle through long decades with sow's ears, yet there was something very different about the kind of listlessness that made itself so evident at every master's desk.

Not a clock in all the various classrooms but had been stared at at least sixty times an hour: not by the bewildered boys, but by their masters.

The secret had been well kept. Not a child knew of the evening party, and when eventually, with the lessons over for the day, the Professors arrived back at their private quadrangle, there was a certain smug and furtive air about the way they moved.

There was no particular reason why the invitation to the Prunesquallors' should have been kept secret, but a tacit understanding between the masters had been rigidly honored. There was a sense, perhaps unformulated for the most part in their minds, that there was something rather ridiculous about their having *all* been invited. A sense that the whole thing was somewhat over-simplified. A trifle unselective. They saw nothing absurd in themselves, individually, and why should they? But a few of them, Perch-Prism in particular, could not visualize his colleagues en masse, himself among them, awaiting their entrance at the Prunesquallors' door, without a shudder. There is something about a swarm that is damaging to the pride of its individual members.

As was their habit, they leaned this evening over the balustrade of the veranda that surrounded the Masters' Quadrangle. Below them, the small, faraway figure of the quadman was sweeping the ground from end to end, leaving behind him the thin strokes of his broom in the fine dust.

They were all there, the evening light upon them; all except Bellgrove, who, leaning back in the Headmaster's chair in his room above the distant classrooms, was cogitating the extraordinary suggestions which had been made to him during the day. These suggestions, which had been put forward by Perch-Prism, Opus Fluke, Shred, Shrivell, and other members, were to the effect that they, for one reason or another and on one occasion or another, had heard from friends of friends or had half-heard through hollow panels, or in the darkness below stairs, at such times when Irma was talking to herself aloud (a habit which they assured Bellgrove she had no power to master), that she (Irma) had got the very devil of a passion for *him*, their reverend Headmaster—and that although it was not *their* affair, they felt he would not be offended to be faced with the reality of the situation—for what could be more obvious than that the party was merely a way for Irma to be near him? It was obvious, was it not, that she could never ask him alone. It would be too blatant, too indelicate, but there it was . . . there it was. They had frowned at him in sympathy and left.

Now Bellgrove was well used to having his leg pulled. He had had it pulled for as long as he had possessed one. He was thus, for all his weakness and vagueness, no simpleton when it came to banter and the kindred arts. He had listened to all they had said, and now as he sat alone he pondered the whole question for the twentieth time. And his conclusions and speculations came forth from him, heavily, like this.

1. The whole thing was poppycock.

2. The purpose of the fabrication was no more than that he should provide, unknowingly, an added zest to the party. These wags on his Staff looked forward no doubt to seeing him in constant flight with Irma on his tail.

3. As he had not questioned the story, they could have no idea that he had seen through it.

4. So far, very excellent.

5. How were the tables to be turned . . . ?

6. What was wrong with Irma Prunesquallor anyway?

A fine, upright woman with a long, sharp nose. But what about it? Noses had to be some shape or other. It had character. It wasn't negative. Nor was she. She had no bosom to speak of: that was true enough. But he was rather too old for bosoms anyway. And there was nothing to touch the cool of white pillows in summertime ("Bless my soul," he said aloud, "what *am* I thinking?"). . . .

As Headmaster he was far more alone than he had ever been before. Bad mixer as he was, he preferred to be "out of it" in a crowd than out of it altogether.

He disliked the sense of isolation when his staff departed every evening. He had pictured himself as a thwarted hermit—one who could find tranquillity alone with a profound volume on his knee, and a room about him spare, ascetic, the hard chair, the empty grate. But this was not so. He loathed it and bared his teeth at the mean furniture and the dirty muddle of his belongings. This was no way for a Headmaster's study to be! He thought of cushions and bedroom slippers. He thought

of socks of long ago with heels to their name. He even thought of flowers in a vase.

Then he thought of Irma again. Yes, there was no denying it, a fine young woman. Well set up. Vivacious. Rather silly, perhaps, but an old man couldn't expect all the qualities.

He rose to his feet and, plodding to a mirror, wiped the dust from its face with his elbow. Then he peered at himself. A slow, childish smile spread over his features as though he were pleased with what he saw. Then with his head on one side, he bared his teeth, and frowned, for they were terrible. "I must keep my mouth shut more than I usually do," he mused, and he began to practice talking with closed lips but could not make out what he was saying. The novelty of the whole situation and the fantastic project that was now consuming him set his old heart beating as he grasped for the first time its tremendous significance. Not less than the personal triumph with which it would fill him, and the innumerable practical advantages that would surely result from such a union, was the delight he was prematurely tasting of hoisting the Staff with its own petard. He began to see himself sailing past the miserable bachelors, Irma on his arm, an unquestioned patriarch, a symbol of success and married stability with something of the gay dog about him too—of the light beneath the bushel, the dark horse, the man with an ace up his sleeve. So they thought that they could fool him. That Irma was infatuated with him. He began to laugh in a sick and exaggerated way, but stopped suddenly. *Could* she be? No. They had made the whole thing up. But could she be, all the same? Coincidentally, as it were. No! No! No! Impossible. Why should she be? "God bless me!" he muttered. "I must be going mad!"

But the adventure was there. His secret plan was there. It was up to him. A sensation that he imagined was one of youth flooded him. He began to hop laboriously up and down on the floor as though over an invisible skipping rope. He made a jump for the table as though to land on the top, but failing to reach the necessary height, bruised his old leg below the knee.

"Bloody hell!" he muttered and sat down heavily in his chair again.

Chapter Thirty-Three

As the Professors were changing into their evening gowns, stabbing at startled hanks of hair with broken combs, maligning one another, finding in one another's rooms long-lost towels, studs, and even major garments that had disappeared in mysterious ways—while this was happening to the accompaniment of much swearing and muttering; and while the coarse jests rumbled along the veranda, and Flannelcat, half sick with excitement, was sitting on the floor of his room with his head between his knees as the heavy hand of Opus Fluke reached hairily through the doorway to steal a towel from a rack—while this and a hundred things were going on around the Masters' Quadrangle, Irma was perambulating the long white room which had been reopened for the occasion.

It had once been the original salon; a room which the Prunesquallors had never used, being too vast for their requirements. It had been locked up for years, but now, after many days of cleaning and repainting, dusting and polishing, it shone with a terrible newness. A group of skilled men had been kept busy, under Irma's watchful eye. She had a delicate taste, had Irma. She could not bear vulgar colors, or coarse furniture. What she lacked was the power to combine and make a harmony out of the various parts that, though exquisite in themselves, bore no relationship either in style, period, grain, color, or fabric to one another.

Each thing was seen on its own. The walls had to be a most tender shade of washed-out coral. And the carpet had to be the kind of green that is almost gray; the flowers were arranged bowl by bowl, vase by vase; and though each was lovely in itself, there was no general beauty in the room.

Unknown to her the bittiness that resulted gave to the salon a certain informality far from her intentions. This was to prove a lubricating thing, for the Professors might well have been frozen into a herd of lock-jawed specters had Irma made of the place the realm of chill perfection that was at the back of her mind. Peering at everything in turn she moved about this long room like something that had spent all its life in planning to counteract the sharpness of its nose, with such a flaunting splendor of silk and jewelry, powder and scent, as set the teeth on edge like colored icing.

About three-quarters of the way along the southern wall of the salon a very fine double window opened upon a walled-in garden where rockeries, crazy pavement, sundials, a small fountain (now playing after a two-day struggle with a gardener), trellis work, arbors, statuettes, and a fish pond made of the place something so terrifying to the sensitive eye of the Doctor, that he never crossed the garden with his eyes open. Much practice had given him confidence and he could move across it blindly at high speed. It was Irma's territory; a place of ferns and mosses and little flowers that opened at odd hours during the night. Little miniature grottoes had been made for them to twinkle in.

Only at the far end of the garden was there any sense of Nature, and even there it was made manifest by no more than a dozen fine trees whose limbs had grown in roughly the direction they had found most natural. But the grass about their stems was closely mowed, and under their boughs a rustic chair or two were artlessly positioned.

On this particular evening there was a hunter's moon. No wonder. Irma had seen to it.

When she reached the French windows she was delighted with the scene before her, the goblin-garden, silver and mysterious, the moonbeams glimmering on the

fountain, the sundial, the trellis work, and the moon itself
reflected in the fish pond. It was all a bit blurred to her,
and that was a pity, but she could not have it both ways.
Either she was to wear her dark glasses and look less attractive, or she must put up with finding everything
about her out of focus. It didn't matter much *how* out of
focus a garden by moonlight was—in fact in the adding
of this supercharge of mystery it became a kind of emotional haze, which was something which Irma, as a
spinster, could never have enough of—but how would
it be when she had to disengage one Professor from another? Would she be able to appreciate the subtlety of
their advances, if they made any; those little twitches
and twists of the lips, those narrowings and rollings of
the eye, those wrinklings of the speculative temple, that
shrugging of an eyebrow at play? Would all this be lost to
her?

When she had told her brother of her intention to
dispense with her glasses, he had advised her, in that
case, to leave them off an hour before the guests were
due. And he had been right. She was quite sure he had
been. For the pain in her forehead had gone and she
was moving faster on her swathed legs than she had
dared to do at first. But it was all a little confusing, and
though her heart beat at the sight of her moon-blur
of a garden, yet she clenched her hands at the same
time in a gay little temper that she should have been
born with bad eyes.

She rang a bell. A head appeared at the door.

"Is that Mollocks?"

"Yes, madam."

"Have you got your soft shoes on?"

"Yes, madam."

"You may enter."

Mollocks entered.

"Cast your eye around, Mollocks—I said cast your eye
around. No, no! Get the feather duster. No, no. Wait a
minute—I said wait a minute." (Mollocks had made no
move.) "I will ring." She rang. Another head appeared.
"Is that Canvas?"

"Yes, madam, it is Canvas."

" 'Yes, madam' is quite enough, Canvas. Quite enough. Your exact name is not so enormously important. Is it? Is it? To the larder with you and fetch a feather brush for Mollocks. Away with you. Where are you, Mollocks?"

"Beside you, madam."

"Ah yes. Ah yes. Have you shaved?"

"Definitely, madam."

"Quite so, Mollocks. It must be my eyes. You look so dark across the face. Now you are to leave no stone unturned—not one—do you understand me? Move from place to place all over this room, backwards and forwards restlessly—do you understand me, with Canvas at your side—*searching* for those specks of dust that have escaped me—did you say you had your soft shoes on?"

"Yes, madam."

"Good. Very good. Is that Canvas who has just come in? Is it? Good. Very good. He is to travel with you. Four eyes are better than two. But *you* can use the brush —*whoever* finds the specks. I don't want anything spoiled or knocked over and Canvas can be very clumsy, can't you, Canvas?"

The old man Canvas, who had been sent running about the house since dawn, and who did not feel that as an old retainer he was being appreciated, said that he didn't know about that. It was his only line of defense, a repetitive, stubborn attitude beyond which one could not go.

"Oh, yes you are," repeated Irma. "*Quite* clumsy. Run along now. You are *slow,* Canvas, *slow.*"

Again the old man said he didn't know about that, and having said so, turned in a puny fury of temper from his mistress and, tripping over his own feet as he turned, grabbed at a small table. A tall alabaster vase swayed on its narrow base like a pendulum while Mollocks and Canvas watched it, their mouths open, their limbs paralyzed.

But Irma had surged away from them and was practicing a certain slow and languid mode of progress

which she felt might be effective. Up and down a little
strip of the soft gray carpet she swayed, stopping every
now and again to raise a limp hand before her, presumably to be touched by the lips of one or other of the
Professors.

Her head would be tilted away at these moments of
formal intimacy, and there would be only a segment of
her sidelong glance as it grazed her cheekbones, to reward the imaginary gallant as he mouthed her knuckles.

Knowing Irma's vision to be faulty and that they could
not be seen with the length of the salon between them,
Canvas and Mollocks watched her from under their
gathered brows, marking time, like soldiers the while, to
simulate the sounds of activity.

They had not long, however, in which to watch their
mistress, for the door opened and the Doctor came in.
He was in full evening dress and looked more elegant
than ever. Across his immaculate breast was the pick of
the few decorations with which Gormenghast had honored him. The Crimson Order of the Vanquished
Plague, and the Thirty-Fifth Order of the Floating Rib
lay side by side upon his narrow, snow-white shirt, and
were suspended from wide ribbons. In his buttonhole
was an orchid.

"Oh, Alfred," cried Irma. "How do I seem to you? How
do I seem to you?"

The Doctor glanced over his shoulder and motioned
the retainers out of the room with a flick of his hand.

He had hidden himself away all afternoon and, sleeping dreamlessly, had to a great extent recovered from
the nightmares he had suffered. As he stood before his
sister he appeared as fresh as a daisy, if less pastoral.

"Now I tell you *what,*" he cried, moving around her,
his head cocked on one side. "I tell you *what,* Irma. You've
made something out of yourself, and if it ain't a work
of art, it's as near as makes no matter. By all that
emanates, you've brought it off. Great grief! I hardly
know you. Turn around, my dear, on one heel! La!
La! *Significant* form, that's what she is! And to think

the same blood batters in our veins! It's quite embarrassing."

"What do you mean, Alfred? I thought you were praising me." (There was a catch in her voice.)

"And so I was, and so I was!—But tell me, sister, what is it, apart from your luminous, unsheltered eyes—and your general dalliance—what is it that's altered you—that has, as it were . . . aha . . . aha . . . h'm . . . I've got it—Oh, dear me . . . quite so, by all that's pneumatic, how silly of me—you've got a bosom, my love, or haven't you?"

"Alfred! It is not for you to prove."

"God forbid, my love."

"But if you *must* know—"

"No, no, Irma, no, no! I am content to leave everything to your judgment."

"So you won't listen to me—" (Irma was almost in tears.)

"Oh, but I will. Tell me all."

"Alfred dear—you liked the look of me. You *said* you did."

"And I still do. Enormously. It was only that, well, I've known you a long time and—"

"I'm *told*," said Irma, breaking in breathlessly, "that busts are . . . well . . ."

". . . That busts are what you make them?" queried her brother, standing on his toes.

"Exactly! Exactly!" his sister shouted. "And I've *made* one, Alfred, and it gives me pride of bearing. It's a hot-water bottle, Alfred; an expensive one."

There was a long and deathly silence. When at last Prunesquallor had reassembled the fragments of his shattered poise he opened his eyes.

"When do you expect them, my love?"

"You know as well as I do. At nine o'clock, Alfred. Shall we call in the Chef?"

"What for?"

"For final instructions, of course."

"What, again?"

"One can't be too final, dear."

"Irma," said the Doctor, "perhaps you have stumbled on a truth of the first water. And talking of water—is the fountain playing?"

"Darling!" said Irma, fingering her brother's arm. "It's playing its heart out," and she gave him a pinch.

The Doctor felt the blushes spreading all over his body, in little rushes like red Indians leaping from ambush to ambush, now here, now there.

"And *now,* Alfred, since it's nearly nine o'clock, I am going to give you a surprise. You haven't seen *anything* yet. This sumptuous dress. Those jewels at my ears, these flashing stones about my white throat . . ." (her brother winced) ". . . and the fancy knot-work of my silvery coif—all this is but a setting, Alfred, a mere setting. Can you bear to wait, Alfred, or shall I tell you? Or still more better—oh, yes! Yes, still more better, dear, I'll show you NOW."

And away she went. The Doctor had no idea she could travel so fast. A swish of "Nightmare Blue" and she was gone, leaving behind her the faint smell of almond icing.

"I wonder if I'm getting old?" thought the Doctor, and he put his hand to his forehead and shut his eyes. When he opened them she was there again—but O creeping hell! What had she done?

What faced him was not merely the fantastically upholstered and bedizened image of his sister to whose temperament and posturing he had long been immune, but something else, which turned her from a vain, nervous, frustrated, outlandish, excitable, and prickly spinster, which was bearable enough, into an *exhibit*. The crude inner workings of her mind were thrust nakedly before him by reason of the long flower-trimmed veil that she now wore over her face. Only her eyes were to be seen, above the thick black netting, very weak, and rather small. She turned them to left and right to show her brother the principle of the thing. Her nose was hidden, and in itself that was excellent, but in no way could it offset the blatancy, the terrible soul-revealing blatancy of the underlying idea.

For the second time that evening Prunesquallor

blushed. He had never seen anything so openly, ridiculously, predatory in his life. Heaven knew she would say the wrong thing at the wrong time, but above all she must not be allowed to expose her intention in that palpable way.

But what he said was: "Aha! H'm. What a flair you have, Irma! What a consummate flair. Who else would have thought of it?"

"Oh, Alfred, I knew you'd love it." She swiveled her eyes again, but her attempt at roguery was heart-breaking.

"Now what *is* it I keep thinking of as I stand and admire you?" her brother trilled, tapping his forehead with his finger. "Tut . . . tut . . . tut, what *is* it . . . something I read in one of your journals, I do believe—ah yes, I've almost got it—there . . . it's slipped away again . . . how irritating . . . wait . . . wait . . . here it comes like a fish to the bait of my poor old memory . . . ah, I almost had it. . . . I've *got* it, oh, yes indeed. . . . But, oh, dear me, no . . . that wouldn't do at all . . . I mustn't tell you *that*. . . ."

"What *is* it, Alfred? What are you frowning about? How irritating you are, just when you were studying me —I said how irritating you are."

"You would be most unhappy if I told you, my dear. It affects you deeply."

"Affects me! How do you mean?"

"It was the merest snippet, Irma, which I happened to read. What has reminded me of it is that it was all about veils and the modern woman. Now I, as a man, have always responded to the mysterious and provocative wherever it may be found. And if these qualities are evoked by anything on earth they are evoked by a woman's veil. But oh, dear me, do you know what this creature in the Women's Column wrote?"

"What did she write?" said Irma.

"She wrote that 'Although there may be those who will continue to wear their veils, just as there are those who still crawl through the jungle on all fours because no one has ever told them that it is the custom these days to walk upright, yet she [the writer] would know

full well in what grade of society to place any woman
who was continuing to wear a veil, after the twenty-
second of the month. After all,' the writer continued,
'some things are done and some things are not done, and
as far as the sartorial aristocracy is concerned, veils
might as well never have been invented.'

"But what nonsense it all is," cried the Doctor. "As
though women are so weak that they have to follow
one another so closely as all that." And he gave a high-
pitched laugh as though to imply that a mere male could
see through all that kind of nonsense.

"Did you say the twenty-second of this month?" said
Irma, after a few moments of thick silence.

"That is so," said her brother.

"And today is the . . ."

"The thirtieth," said her brother, "but surely, surely,
you wouldn't . . ."

"Alfred," said Irma. "Be quiet, please. There are some
things which you do not understand and one of them is
a woman's mind." With a deft movement of her hand she
freed her face of the veil, and there was her nose again
as sharp as ever.

"I wondered if you'd do something for me, dear?"

"What is it, Irma, my love?"

"I wondered if you'd take—oh, no, I'll have to do it
myself—and you might be shocked—but perhaps if you
would shut your eyes, Alfred, I could . . ."

"What in the name of darkness are you driving at?"

"I wondered, dear, at first, whether you would take
my bust to the bedroom and fill it with hot water. It has
got very cold, Alfred, and I don't want to catch a chill
—or perhaps if you'd rather not do that for me, you
could bring the kettle downstairs to my little writing
room and I'll do it myself—will you, dear—will you?"

"Irma," said her brother, "I will not do it for you. I
have done and will continue to do a lot of things for
you, pleasant and unpleasant, but I will not start running
around, looking for water bottles to fill for my sister's
bosom. I will not even bring down the kettle for you.
Have you no kind of modesty, my love? I know you

are very excited, and really don't know what you are doing or saying, but I must have it quite clear from the start that as far as your rubber bust is concerned, I am unable to help you. If you catch a chill, then I will dose you—but until then, I would be grateful if you would leave the subject alone. But enough of that! Enough of that! The magic hour approaches. Come, come! my tiger lily!"

"Sometimes I despise you, Alfred," said Irma. "Who would have thought that *you* were such a prude?"

"Ah, no! My dear, you're far too hard on me. Have mercy. Do you think it is easy to bear your scorn when you are looking so radiant?"

"Am I, Alfred? Oh, am I? Am I?"

Chapter Thirty-Four

IT had been arranged that the staff should gather in the quadrangle outside the Doctor's house at a few minutes past nine and wait for Bellgrove, who, as Headmaster, had ignored the suggestion that he should be first on the spot and wait for *them*. Perch-Prism's argument that it was a good deal more ludicrous for a horde of men to hang about as though they were hatching some kind of conspiracy than it would be for Bellgrove, even though he *was* Headmaster, cut no ice with the old lion.

Bellgrove, in his present mood, was peculiarly dogged. He had glowered over his shoulder at them as though he were at bay. "Never let it be said in future years," he had ended, "that a Headmaster of Gormenghast had once to wait the pleasure of his staff's arrival—by night, in the South Quadrangle. Never let it be said that so responsible an office had sunk into such disrespect."

And so it was that a few minutes after nine a great blot formed in the darkness of the quadrangle as though a section of the dusk had coagulated. Bellgrove, who had been hiding behind a pillar of the cloisters, had decided to keep his staff waiting for at least five minutes. But he was unable to contain his impatience. Not three minutes had passed since their arrival before his excitement propelled him forward into the open gloom. When he was halfway across the quadrangle, and could hear the muttering of their voices quite plainly, the moon slid out from behind a cloud. In the cold light that now laid bare the rendezvous, the red gowns of the Professors burned darkly, the color of wine. Not so Bellgrove's. *His* ceremonial gown was of the finest white silk, embroidered across the back with a large *G*. It was a magnificent, voluminous affair, this gown, but the effect was a little startling by moonlight, and more than one of the waiting Professors gave a start to see what appeared to be a ghost bearing down upon them.

The Professors had forgotten the ceremonial robe of Headship. Deadyawn had never worn it. For the smaller-minded of the staff there was something irritating about this sartorial discrepancy of their gowns which gave the old man so unique an advantage, both decoratively and socially. They had all been secretly rather pleased to have the opportunity of wearing their red robes in public, although the public consisted solely of the Doctor and his sister (for they didn't count each other)—and now, Bellgrove, of all people, Bellgrove, their decrepit Head, had stolen with a single peal, as it were, the wealth of their red thunder.

He could feel their discontent, short-lived though it was, and the effect of this recognition was to excite him still further. He tossed his white mane of hair in the moonlight and gathered his arctic gown about him in a great sculptural swathe.

"Gentlemen," he said. "Silence if you please. I thank you."

He dropped his head so that with his face in deep shadow he could relax his features in a smile of delight at finding himself obeyed. When he raised his face it was as solemn and as noble as before.

"Are all who are here gathered present?"

"What the hell does that mean?" said a coarse voice, out of the red gloom of the gowns, and immediately on top of Mulefire's voice, the staccato of Cutflower's laughter broke out in little clanks of sound.

"Oh, la! la! la! If that isn't ripeness, la! Are all who are here gathered present? La! . . . What a tease the old man is, lord help my lungs!"

"Quite so! Quite so!" broke out a crisper voice. "What he was trying to ask, presumably" (it was Shrivell speaking), "was whether everyone here was really here, or whether it was only those who thought themselves here when they weren't really here at all who were here? You see it's quite simple, really, once you have mastered the syntax."

Somewhere close behind the Headmaster there was a sense of strangled body-laughter, a horrible inaudible affair, and then the sound of a deep bucketful of breath being drawn out of a well—and then Opus Fluke's midstomach voice. "Poor old Bellgrove," it said. "Poor old bloody Bellgrove!" and then the rumbling again, and a chorus of dark and stupid laughter.

Bellgrove was in no mood for this. His old face was flushed and his legs trembled. Fluke's voice had sounded very close. Just behind his left shoulder. Bellgrove took a step to the rear and then, turning suddenly with a whirl of his white gown, he swung his long arm and at once he was startled at what he at first imagined was a complete triumph. His gnarled old fist had struck a human jaw. A quick, wild, and bitter sense of mastery possessed him, and the intoxicating notion that he had been underrating himself for seventy-odd years and that all unwittingly he had discovered in himself the "man of action." But his exhilaration was short-lived for the figure who lay moaning at his feet was not Opus Fluke at all, but the weedy and dyspeptic Flannelcat, the only member of his staff who held him in any kind of respect.

But Bellgrove's prompt action had a sobering effect.

"Flannelcat!" he said. "Let that be a warning to them. Get up, my man. You have done nobly. Nobly." At that moment something whisked through the air and struck an obscure member of the Staff on the wrist. At his cry, for he was in real pain, Flannelcat was at once forgotten. A small round stone was found at the feet of the obscure member, and every head was turned at once to the dusky quadrangle, but nothing could be seen.

High up on a northern wall, where the windows appeared no larger than keyholes, Steerpike, sitting with his legs dangling over one of the window sills, raised his eyebrows at the sound of the cry so far below him, and piously closing his eyes he kissed his catapult.

"Whatever the hell that was, or wherever it came from, it does at least remind us that we are late, my friend," said Shrivell.

"True enough," muttered Shred, who almost always trod heavily on the tail of his friend's remarks. "True enough."

"Bellgrove," said Perch-Prism, "wake your ideas up, old friend, and lead the way in. I see that every light is blazing in the homestead of the Prunes. Lord, what a lot we are!" He moved his small piglike eyes across the faces of his colleagues. "What a hideous lot we are—but there it is—there it is."

"You're not much of a silk-purse yourself," said a voice.

"In we go, la! In we go!" cried Cutflower. "Terribly gay now! *Terribly* gay! We must *all* be terribly gay!"

Perch-Prism slid up under Bellgrove's shoulder. "My old friend," he said. "You haven't forgotten what I said about Irma, have you? It may be difficult for you. I have even more recent information. She's dead nuts on you, old man. Dead nuts. Watch your steps, chief. Watch 'em carefully."

"I—will—watch—my—steps, Perch-Prism, have no fear," said Bellgrove with a leer that his colleagues could in no way interpret.

Spiregrain, Throd, and Splint stood hand in hand. Their spiritual master was dead. They were enormously glad

of it. They winked at each other and dug one another in
the ribs and then joined hands again in the darkness.

A mass movement toward the gate of the Prunesquallors' began. Within this gate there was nothing that
could be called a front garden, merely an area of dark-
red gravel which had been raked by the gardener. The parallel lines formed by his rake were quite visible in the
moonlight. He might have saved himself the trouble, for
within a few moments the neat striated effect was a thing
of the past. Not a square red inch escaped the shuffling
and stamping of the Professors' feet. Hundreds of footprints of all shapes and sizes, crossing and recrossing,
toes and heels superimposed with such freaks of placing
that it seemed as though among the Professors there
were some who boasted feet as long as an arm, and
others who must have found it difficult to balance upon
shoes that a monkey might have found too tight.

After the bottleneck of the garden gate had been negotiated and the wine-red horde, with Bellgrove at its van,
like an oriflamme, were before the front door, the Headmaster turned with his hand hovering at the height of
the bell pull and raising his lionlike head, was about to
remind his staff that as the guests of Irma Prunesquallor
he hoped to find in their deportment and general behavior that sense of decorum which he had so far had no
reason to suppose they possessed or could even simulate,
when a butler, dressed up like a Christmas cracker, flung
the front door open with a flourish which was obviously
the result of many years' experience. The speed of the
door as it swung on its hinges was extraordinary, but
what was just as dramatic was the silence—a silence so
complete that Bellgrove, with his head turned toward his
staff and his hand still groping in the air for the bell
pull, could not grasp the reason for the peculiar behavior
of his colleagues. When a man is about to make a speech,
however modest, he is glad to have the attention of his
audience. To see on every face that stared in his direction an expression of intense interest, but an interest
that obviously had nothing to do with *him,* was more
than disturbing. What had happened to them? Why were

all those eyes so out of focus—or if they were *in* focus why should they skim his own as though there were something absorbing about the woodwork of the high green door behind him? And why was Throd standing on tiptoe in order to look *through* him?

Bellgrove was about to turn—not because he thought there could be anything to see but because he was experiencing that sensation that causes men to turn their heads on deserted roads in order to make sure they are alone. But before he could turn of his own free will he received two sharp yet deferential knuckle-taps on his left shoulder blade—and leaping about as though at the touch of a ghost he found himself face to face with the tall Christmas cracker of a butler.

"You will pardon me, sir, for making free with my knuckle, I am sure, sir," said the glittering figure in the hall. "But you are impatiently awaited, sir, and no wonder if I may say so."

"If you *insist*," said Bellgrove. "So be it."

His remark meant nothing at all but it was the only thing he could think of to say.

"And now, sir," continued the butler, lifting his voice into a higher register which gave quite a new expression to his face, "if you will be so gracious as to follow me, I will lead the way to madam."

He moved to one side and cried out into the darkness.

"Forward, gentlemen! if you please," and turning smartly on his heel he began to lead Bellgrove through the hall and down a number of short passageways until a wider space, at the foot of a flight of stairs, brought him and his followers to a halt.

"I have no doubt, sir," the butler said, inclining himself reverentially as he spoke—and to Bellgrove's way of thinking the man was speaking overmuch—"I have no doubt, sir, that you are familiar with the customary procedure."

"Of course, my man. Of course," said Bellgrove. "What is it?"

"Oh, sir!" said the butler. "You are very humorous,"

and he began to titter—an unpleasant sound to come from the top of a cracker.

"There are many procedures, my man. Which one were you referring to?"

"To the one, sir, that pertains to the order in which the guests are announced—by name, of course, as they file through the doorway of the salon. It is all very cut and dried, sir."

"What is the order, my dear fellow, if it is not the order of seniority?"

"And so it is, sir, in all respects, save that it is customary for the Headmaster, which would be you, sir, to bring up the rear."

"The rear?"

"Quite so, sir. As a kind of shepherd, I suppose, sir, driving his flock before him, as it were."

There was a short silence during which Bellgrove began to realize that being the last to present himself to his hostess, he would be the first to hold any kind of conversation with her.

"Very well," he said. "The tradition must, of course, remain inviolate. Ridiculous as it seems in the face of it, I shall, as you put it, bring up the rear. Meanwhile, it is getting late. There is no time to sort out the Staff into age groups, and so on. None of them are chickens. Come along now, gentlemen, come along; and if you will be so kind as to stop combing your hair before the door is opened, Cutflower, I would, as one who is responsible for his staff, be grateful. Thank you."

Just then, the door which faced the staircase opened and a long rectangle of gold light fell across a section of the embattled masters. Their gowns flamed. Their faces shone like specters. Turning almost simultaneously after a few minutes of dazzling blankness, they shuffled into the surrounding shadow. Around the corner of the open door through which the light was pouring, a large face peered out at them.

"Name?" it whispered thickly. An arm crept around the door and drew the nearest figure forward and into the light by a fistful of wine-red linen.

"Name?" it whispered again.

"The name of Cutflower, *la!*" hissed the gentleman. "But take your great joint of clod's fist off me, you stupid bastard." Cutflower, whose gusts of temper were rare and short-lived, was really angry at being pulled forward by his gown and in having it clenched so clumsily into a web of creases. "Let go!" he repeated hotly. "By hell, I'll have you whipped, la!"

The crude footman bent down and brought his lips to Cutflower's ear. "I . . . will . . . kill . . . you . . ." he whispered, but in such an abstracted way as to give Cutflower quite a turn. It was as though the fellow was passing on a scrap of inside information—casually (like a spy) but in confidence. Before Cutflower had recovered he found himself pushed forward, and he was suddenly alone in the long room. Alone, except for a line of servants along the right-hand wall, and away ahead of him, his host and hostess, very still, very upright in the glow of many candles.

Had Bellgrove worked out beforehand the order in which to have his staff announced, it is unlikely that he would have hit upon so happy an idea as that of choosing Cutflower from his pack, and leading off, as it were, with a card so lacking in the solid virtues.

But *chance* had seen to it that of all the gowns it was Cutflower's that should have been within range of the groping hand. And Cutflower, the volatile and fatuous Cutflower, as he stepped lightly like a wagtail across the gray-green roods of carpet was, in spite of the shocking start he had been given, injecting the air, the cold expectant air, with something no other member of the staff possessed in the same way—a warmth or a gaiety of a kind, but not a *human* gaiety; rather, it was glasslike; a sparkling, twinkling quality.

It was as though Cutflower were so glad to be alive that he had never lived. Every moment was vivid, a colored thing, a trill or a crackle of words in the air. Who could imagine, while Cutflower was around, that there were such vulgar monsters as death, birth, love, art, and pain around the corner? It was too embarrassing to contemplate. If Cutflower knew of them he kept it secret. Over their gapings and sepulchral deeps he skimmed now here, now there, in his private canoe, changing his course with a flick of his paddle when death's black whale, or the red squid of passion, lifted for the moment its body from the brine.

He was not more than a third of the way to his hosts, and the echo of the stentorian voice, which had flung his name across the room, was hardly dead, and yet (with his wagtail walk, his spruceness, his perky ductile features so ready to be amused and so ready to amuse as long as no one took life seriously) he had already broken the ice for the Prunesquallors. There was a certain charm in his fatuity, his perkiness. His toecaps shone like mirrors. His feet came down tap-tap-tap-tap in a way all their own.

The Professors, craning their necks as they watched his progress, breathed more freely. They knew now that they could never accomplish that long carpet-journey with anything like Cutflower's air, but he reminded them at every footstep, every inclination of the head, that the whole point of life was to be happy.

And oh, the charm of it! The artless charm of it! When Cutflower, with but a few feet to go, broke into a little dancing run, and putting forward both his hands cupped them over the limp white fingers which Irma had extended.

"Oh, la! la!" he cried, his voice running all the way back down the salon. "This *is*, my dear Miss Prunesquallor, this positively is." And turning to the Doctor, "Isn't it?" he added as he clasped the outstretched hand, squaring his shoulders and shaking his head happily as he did so.

"Well, I hope it will *become* so, my friend," cried Prunesquallor. "How good to see you! And bye the bye, Cutflower, you give me heart, you do . . . by all that revivifies I thank you from its bottom. Don't disappear now, for the whole evening, will you?"

Irma leaned across her brother and drew her lips apart in a dead, wide, and calculated smile.

It was meant to express many things, and among them the sense of how unconditionally she associated herself with her brother's sentiment. It also tried to imply that for all her qualities as a *femme fatale,* she was little more than a wide-eyed girl at heart and terribly vulnerable. But it was early in the evening and she knew she must make many mistakes before her smiles came out right.

Cutflower, whose eyes were still on the Doctor, was fortunate enough to be unaware of Irma's blandishment. He was about to say something, when the loud and common voice from the other end of the room brayed forth, "Professor Mulefire," and Cutflower turned his head gaily from his hosts and shielded his eyes in imitation of a lookout man scanning some distant horizon. With a quick, delighted smile and a twirl of his dapper body, he was away to the side tables, where with his elbows raised very high, he worked his ten fingers together into a knot, as he passed his eye along the wines and delicacies. Self-absorbed, he rocked to and fro on the sides of his shoes.

How different was Mulefire with his long, clumsy, irritable strides! And indeed how disparate were all who followed one another that evening, with only the color of their gowns in common.

Flannelcat, like a lost soul for whom the journey was a mile at least; the heavy, sloppy, untidy Fluke, who looked as though, for all his strength and for all the forward thrust of his loaflike jaw, might at any moment fold up at the knees and go to sleep on the carpet. Perch-Prism, horribly alert, his porcine features shining white in the glow of the candles, his button-black eyes darting to and fro as he moved crisply with short, aggressive steps.

With this shape and that shape, with this walk and that walk, they emerged from the hall to the tocsin-bray of their names, until Bellgrove found himself alone in the semidarkness.

As one after another of the Professorial guests had made their carpet-journey toward her, Irma had had a world of time in which to ruminate on the vulnerability of each to the charm she would so soon be unleashing. Some, of course, were quite impossible—but even as she dismissed them she began to brood with favor upon such phrases as "rough diamond," "heart of gold," "still waters."

While the sides of the room filled with those who had presented themselves and their conversation became louder and louder as their numbers increased, Irma, standing rigid by her brother, speculating upon the pros and cons of those she had received, was wakened out of a more than usually sanguine speculation by her brother's voice.

"And how is Irma, that sister of mine, that sweet throb? Is she cooing? Is she weary of the flesh—or isn't she? Great spearheads, Irma! How determined, how martial you look! Relax a little, melt within yourself. Think of milk and honey. Think of jellyfish."

"Be quiet," she hissed out of the corner of a smile she was concocting, a smile more ambitious than she had so far dared to invent. Every muscle in her face was pulling its weight. Not all of them knew in which direction to pull, but their common enthusiasm was formidable. It was as though all her previous contortions were mere rehearsals. Something in white was approaching.

The "something in white" was moving slowly but with more purpose than for over forty years. While he had waited, sitting quietly by himself on the lowest step of the Prunesquallors' staircase, Bellgrove had repeated to himself, his lips moving to the slow rhythm of his thoughts, those conclusions he had come to.

He had decided, intellectually, that Irma Prunesquallor, dwarfed by lack of outlet for her feminine instincts, could find fruition in a life devoted to *his* comforts. That not only he, but she, in years to come, would bless the day when he, Bellgrove, was man enough, was sapient enough, to lift her from stagnation and set her marching through matrimony toward that equipoise of spirit that only wives can know. There were a hundred rational reasons why she should leap at the chance in spite of his advanced years. But what weight had all these arguments for a fine and haughty lady, sensitive as a blood horse

and gowned like a queen, if at the same time there was
no love? And Bellgrove remembered as he had crossed
the quadrangle an hour ago how it was this point that
irked him. But now, it was not the rightness of his reason-
ing that set his old knees trembling, it was something
more. For, from a wise and practical project, the whole
conception had been shifted into another light. His ideas
had suddenly been overlaid with stars. What was precise
was now enormous, unsubstant, diaphanous, for he had
seen her. And tonight it was not merely the Doctor's sister that awaited him, but a daughter of Eve, a living
focus, a cosmos, a pulse of the great abstraction, Woman.
Was her name Irma? Her name was Irma. But what was
the name Irma but four absurd little letters in a certain
order? To hell with symbols, cried Bellgrove to himself.
She is there, by God, from head to foot and matchless!

It is true that he had only seen her from a distance
and it is possible that the distance lent an enchantment
self-engendered. No doubt, his sight was not as sharp as
it used to be—and the fact that he could not remember
having seen any other woman for many years gave Irma
a flying start.

But he had obtained a general picture, as he peered
through a narrow chasm of light that shone between
Throd's and Spiregrain's bodies.

And he had seen how proudly she held herself. Stiff as
a soldier, and yet how feminine! That is what he would
like to have about him in the evening. A stately type. He
could imagine her, sitting bolt upright, at his side, her face
twitching a little from gentle breeding, her snow-white
hands darning away at his socks while he pondered on
this and that, turning his eyes from time to time to see
whether it was really true, that she was really there, his
wife, his wife, on the chocolate-colored couch.

And then suddenly he had found himself alone. The
big face was peering at him from the floor. "Name?"
it whispered hoarsely, for its voice was almost gone.

"I'm the Headmaster, you idiot," barked Bellgrove. He
was in no mood for fools. Something was in his blood.
Whether it was love or not he must find out soon. There

was an impatient streak in him—and this was no moment in which to suffer the man gladly.

The creature with the big face, seeing that Bellgrove was the last to be announced, took a deep breath, and to get rid of his pent-up irritability (for he was an hour late for his appointment with a blacksmith's wife), gathered all the forces of his throat together and yelled—but his voice collapsed after the first syllable and only Bellgrove heard the guttering sound that was intended for "master."

But there was something rather fine, rather impressive in the abbreviation. Something less formal, it is true, but more penetrating in the first simple syllable.

"The Head——!"

The short hammer-blow of the monosyllable reverberated along the room like a challenge.

It struck like a drumstick on the membranes of Irma's ear and Bellgrove, peering forward as he took his first few paces into the room, had the impression of his hostess rearing herself up on her hips, tossing her head before it froze into a motionless carving.

His heart, that was already beating wildly, had leaped at the sight. Her attention was riveted upon him. Of that there was no doubt. Not only her attention, but the attention of all those present. He became aware of a lethal hush. Soft as the carpet was, his feet could be heard as they lowered themselves one after another into the gray-green of the pile.

For a moment, as he moved with that fantastic solemnity which the urchins of Gormenghast were so fond of mimicking, he gave his eyes the run of his staff. There they stood, three-deep, a solid wine-red phalanx that completely obscured the side tables. Yes, he could see Perch-Prism, his eyebrows raised, and Opus Fluke with his horse's mouth half open in a grin so inane that for a moment it was difficult for Bellgrove to regain that composure necessary to the advancement of his immediate interests. So they were waiting to see in what way he would try and evade the "predatory" Irma, were they? So they expected him to back away from her immediately after he had received his formal reception, did they? So they looked for an evening of hide-and-seek between their hostess and their Headmaster, the low curs! By the light of a militant heaven, he would show the dogs! He would show them. And, by the powers, he would surprise them too.

By now he was about halfway along the carpet, already trodden into a recognizable highway, the pile of the carpet throwing out a greener sheen than elsewhere, the pile pressed forward by a hundred feet.

Irma, her eyes weak with peering, could just see him. As he approached and the blurred edges of his swan-white gown, and the contours of his leonine head, grew sharper, she marveled at his godlike quality. She had received so many half-men that she had tired, not of numbers, but of waiting for the kind of male she could reverence. There had been the perky ones, and the stolid ones and the sharp ones and the blunt ones—all *males* she supposed, but although she had a few of them at the back of her mind for further consideration, yet she had been sadly disappointed. There had been that irritating bachelor quality about them, a kind of dead self-sufficiency, a terrible thing in a man, who is, as every woman knows, a mere tag-end of a thing before the distaff side has stitched him together.

But here was something different. Something *old* it is true, but something noble. She maneuvered with her mouth. It had had a good deal of practice by this time and the smile she prepared for Bellgrove reflected to a great extent what she had in mind for it. Above all, it was winsome, devastatingly winsome. For a pretty face to be winsome is normal enough and very winsome it can be, but it is a tepid thing, a negative thing compared with the winsomeness to which Irma could subject her features. With her it was as startling as any foreground symbol set against an incongruous background. Irma's weak and eager eyes, Irma's pinnacle of a nose, Irma's length of powdered face; these were the incongruous background on which the smile deployed its artful self. She played with it for a moment or two, as an angler with a fish, and then she let it set like concrete.

Her body had simultaneously rhythmed itself into a stance both statuesque and snakelike, her thorax, amplified with its hot-water-bottle bosom, positioned in air so far to the left of her pelvis as to have no visible means of support. Her snow-white hands were clasped at her throat where her jewelry sparkled.

Bellgrove was almost upon her. "This," he said to himself, breathing deeply, "is one of those moments in a man's life when valor is tested."

The years ahead hung on his every move. His Staff had shaken hands with her as though a woman was merely another kind of man. Fools! The seeds of Eve were in this radiant creature. The lullabies of half a million years throbbed in her throat. Had they no sense of wonder, no reverence, no pride? He, an old man (but a not unhandsome one), would show the dogs the way of it—and there she was, before him, the maddeningly feminine bouquet of her pineapple perfume swimming about his head. He inhaled. He trembled, and then, lionlike, he tossed his venerable mane from his eyes, and raising his shoulders as he took her hands in his, he bowed his head above their milky limpness and planted in the damp of her palms the first two kisses he had given for over fifty years.

To say that the frozen silence contracted itself into a yet tighter globe of ice would be to underrate the exquisite tension and to shroud it in words. The atmosphere had become a physical sensation. As when, before a masterpiece, the acid throat contracts, and words are millstones, so when the supernaturally outlandish happens and a masterpiece is launched through the medium of human gesture, then all human volition is withered at the source and the heart of action stops beating.

Such a moment was this. Irma, a stalagmite of crimson stone, knew, for all the riot of her veins, that a page had turned over. At chapter forty? Oh, no! At chapter one, for she had never lived before save in a pulseless preface.

How long did they remain thus? How many times had the earth moved around the sun? How many times had the great blue whales of the northern waters risen to spurt their fountains at the sky? How many reed-bucks had

fallen to the claws of how many leopards, while that
sublime unit of two-figure statuary remained motionless?
It is fruitless to ask. The clocks of the world stood still
or should have done.

But at last the arctic stillness broke. A Professor at
the side tables gave forth a sharp scream, whether of
laughter or nerves was never established.

The Doctor glanced across at the wine-red gowns, his
eyebrows raised, his teeth glinting. There were a few
beads of moisture on his forehead. He was going through
a lot.

Irma had not consciously heard the sharp cry of
laughter nor knew what had broken her from a trance,
but she found herself inclining her head graciously above
the white locks of the Headmaster's reverential poll.

This was *it*. Something within her was laughing wildly,
like cowbells.

It was a pity that the Headmaster could not appreciate
the amplitude of her graciousness as she hung above him
—but, there it was—she couldn't have it both ways—but
wait—what was this?

Oh, sweetest mercy! And the wild thorn-throbs of it!
What was he doing, the great, gentle, august, brilliant
lion? He was raising his eyes to hers with his lips still
pressed against her fingers. It was as though he had di-
vined her most secret thoughts.

She lowered her lids and found that his dead-pebble
eyes were upon hers. With their gaze directed upward and
through the white tangle of the eyebrows they appeared to
be caged.

She knew the moment to be enormous—enormous in
its implications—in its future—but she knew also as a
woman that she must draw her hands away. As the first
suspicions of a movement crept through her flaccid fin-
ers, Bellgrove lifted his head, withdrew his big hands
from hers, and at that moment Irma's bosom began to
slip. In the complex arrangement of strings, safety pins,
and tape which held the hot-water bottle in place, Time
had found a weakness.

But Irma, tingling with excitement, was in so elevated

a frame of body and mind that, beyond her capacity as it were, her brain was planning for her in advance, those things she should do, and say, in or out of any emergency. And this was one of those moments when the cells of Irma's brain marched in solid ranks to her rescue.

Her bosom was slipping. She clasped her hands together at her throat so that her forearms might keep the hot-water bottle in place, and then with every eye upon her she lifted her head high and began to pace toward the doorway at the far end of the salon. She had not even glanced at her brother, but with a quite overweening confidence had started away, the folds of her evening gown trailing behind her.

The bottle had become horribly cold across her chest. But she reveled in its cruel temperature. Why should she care about such little things? Something on an altogether vaster scale was bearing her on its flood.

The barb had struck. She was naked. She was proud. Had love's arrow not been metaphorical she would have held it high in the air for all to see. And all this she was making plain, by the very movement of her pacing body, and by the volcanic blush which had turned her marmoreal head into something that might have been found among the blood-red ruins of some remote civilization.

Her jewelry took on another tint. Her blush burned through it.

But her expression bore no relation to the blush. It was strangely articulate, and thus, frighteningly simple.

There was no need for words. Her face was saying, "I am in his power; he has awakened me; I, a mere woman, have been blasted into sentience. Whatever the future holds it will not be through me that love goes hungry. I am aware; not only that history is being made, but of my duty, even at this pinnacled moment; and so, I am leaving the room, to readjust myself—to compose myself, and to bring back into the salon the kind of woman that the Headmaster may admire—no quivering love-struck damsel, but a dame in all the high sensuousness of her sex, a dame, composed and glorious!"

Irma, directly she had reached the door and had swept out into the hall, flew, a silken spinster, up the flight of stairs to her room. Slamming the door behind her she gave vent to the primeval jungle in her veins and screamed like a macaw, and then, prancing forward toward the bed, tripped over a small embroidered footstool and fell spread-eagled across the carpet.

What did it matter? What did anything ridiculous or shaming matter so long as *he* was not there to see it?

Chapter Thirty-Five

THERE are times when the emotions are so clamorous and the rational working of the mind so perfunctory that there is no telling where the *actual* leaves off and the images of fantasy begin.

Irma, in her room, could picture Bellgrove at her side as though he were there, but she could also see clean through him, so that his body was pranked with the pattern of the wallpaper beyond. She could see a great host of Professors, thousands of them, and all the size of hat-pins. They stood upon her bed, a massed and solemn congregation, and bowed to her; but she also saw that her pillow slip needed changing. She looked out of the window, her eyes wide and unfocused. The moonlight lay in a haze upon the high foliage of an elm, and the elm became Mr. Bellgrove again with his distinguished and lordly mane. She saw a figure, no doubt some figment, as it slid over the wall of her grotto'd garden and ran like a shadow to beneath the window of the dispensary. Far away at the back of her mind, there was something that said, "You have seen that movement before; crouching, rapid movement"—yet she had, in her transport, no clue as to what was real and what was fantasy.

And so, when she saw a figure steal across the garden below her she had no conception that it was a real, breathing creature, far less that it was Steerpike. The young man who had forced open the window in the room below that in which Irma was standing moon-struck had, by the light of a candle, wasted no time in finding the drug for which he was looking. The bottles on the packed shelves shone blue and crimson and deadly green as the small flame moved. Within a few moments he had decanted a few thimblefuls of a sluggish liquid into the flask he carried, and returned the Doctor's bottle to the shelf. He corked his own container and within a moment was halfway out of the window.

Above the walls of the garden the upper massives of Gormenghast Castle shone in the baleful moonlight. As he paused for a moment before dropping from the window sill to the ground, he shuddered. The night was warm and there was no cause to shudder save that a twinge of joy, of dark joy, can shake the body, when a man is alone, under the moon, on a secret mission, with hunger in his heart and ice in his brain.

Chapter Thirty-Six

WHEN Irma returned to her guests she paused before she opened the doors of the salon, for a loud and confused noise came from within. It was of a kind that she had never heard before, so happy it was, so multitudinous, so abandoned—the sound of voices at play. She had, of course, in her small way, at gatherings, heard, from time to time, the play of many voices. But what she was hearing now was *not* the play of voices; it was voices at play;

and as such it was novel and peculiar to her ears, in
the way that shadows at play (as against the play of shadows) would have been to her eyes. She had, on rare
occasions, enjoyed the play of her brother's brain—but in
her salon there was something very different going on,
and from the few remarks that she could distinguish
through the panels of the door it was obvious that
there was no play of language, no play of thought, but
language playing on its own; enfranchised notions playing by themselves, the truants of the brain.

Gathering the long wreaths of her gown about her she
crouched for a moment with her eyes to the keyhole, but
could see no more than the smoky midnight of the
gowns.

What had happened, she wondered, while she had
been upstairs? When she had left, in the motionless silence, like a queen, the room had throbbed with her
single personality, the silence, the flattering and significant silence, had been her setting, as the great sky is
the setting for the white flight of a gull. But now, the
stretched drum-skin of the atmosphere had split—and
the Professors, exultant that this was so, had, each in
his own way, erected within himself the romantic image
of what he fondly imagined himself to be. For the long-
lost glories, that never in fact existed save in the wishfulness of their brains, were being remembered with a
reality as vivid, if not more so, as truth itself. False
memories flowered within them. The days of brilliance
when their lances shone, when they leaped into the gold
saddle quick as thought and galloped through the white
rays of the dawn; when they ran like stags, swam like
fish, and, laughing like thunder, woke the swaddled towers. Ah, Lord, the callow days; the cocky days, the
days of sinew and the madcap evenings—the darkness at
their elbows, coconspirator, muffling their fire-tipped fol-
lies.

That but few of the Professors had ever tasted the
heady mead of youth in no way dulled the contours of
their self-portraits which they were now painting of themselves. And it had all happened so rapidly, this resur-

gence; this hark-back. It was as though some bell had been struck, some mountain-bell to which their guts responded. They had for so long a time made their evening way to their sacred, musty, airless quadrangle, that to be for a whole evening in a new atmosphere was like sunrise. True, there was only Irma on the female side, but she was a symbol of all femininity, she was Eve, she was Medusa, she was terrible and she was peerless; she was hideous and she was the lily of the prairies; she was that alien thing from another world—that thing called Woman.

Directly she had left the room a thousand imaginary memories had beset them of women they had never known. Their tongues loosened, and their limbs also, and the Doctor found there was no need to launch the evening. For the flame was alight and the Professorial torpor had been burned away, and they were back, all at once, in a time when they were brilliant, omniscient, and devastating and as dazzlingly attractive as the Devil himself.

With their brains illumined by these spurious and flattering images, the swarming gownsmen trod on air, and bridled up their hot and monstrous heads, flashed their teeth, or if toothless, grinned darkly, their mouths slung across their faces like hammocks.

As Irma turned the handle, taking a deep breath which all but destroyed her bust, she straightened herself and stood for a moment motionless, yet vibrant. As she opened the door and the gay thunder of their voices doubled its volume—she raised an eyebrow. Why, she wondered, should such potent happiness coincide with her absence? It was almost as though she had been *forgotten,* or worse, that her departure from the room had been welcomed.

She opened the door a little wider and peered around the corner, but in doing so her powdered head created all unknowingly so graphic a representation of something detached that a Professor who happened to be staring in the direction of the door, let fall his lower jaw with a clank, and dropped the plate of delicacies to his feet.

"Ah, no, no!" he whispered, the colors draining from

his face. "Not *now,* dire Death, not *now* . . . I am not ready . . . I—"

"Ready for what, sweet trout?" said a voice beside him. "By hell, these peacock-hearts are excellent. A little pepper, please!"

Irma entered. The man who had dropped his jaw swallowed hard and a sick grin appeared on his face. He had cheated death.

As Irma took her first few paces into the room her fear that the gracious authority of her presence had been undermined during her short absence was dispelled, for a score of Professors, ceasing their chatter, and whipping their mortarboards from their heads, cupped them over their hearts.

Swaying slightly as she proceeded toward the center of the room, she, in her turn, bowed with a superb and icy grandeur now to left, now to right, as the dark festooning draperies of the Professional jungle opened, at her every step, its musty avenues.

Veering to the east and west in gradual curves, like a ship that has no precise idea as to which port it is making for, she found all about her, wherever she was, a hush, most gratifying. But the avenues closed behind her, and the conversation was resumed with an enthusiasm.

And then, all of a sudden, there was Bellgrove, not a dozen feet away. A long glass of wine was in his hand. He was in profile; and what a profile—"grandeur," she hissed excitedly! "That's what it is—grandeur." And it was then, at her third convulsive stride in the Headmaster's direction, that something happened which was not only embarrassing but heart-rending in its simplicity, for a hoarse cry, out-topping the general cacophony, silenced the room and brought Irma to a standstill.

It was not the kind of cry that one expects to hear at a party. It had passion in it—and urgency. The very tone and timbre were a smack in the face of propriety, and broke on the instant all those unwritten laws of social behavior that are the result—the fine flower—of centuries.

As every head was turned in the direction of the

sound a movement became apparent in the same quarter where, from a group of Professors, something appeared to be making its way toward its rigid hostess. Its face was flushed and its gestures were so convulsive that it was not easy to realize that it was Professor Throd.

On sighting Irma, he had deserted his companions Splint and Spiregrain, and on obtaining a better view of his hostess had suffered a sensation that was in every way too violent, too fundamental, too electric for his small brain and body. A million volts ran through him, a million volts of stark infatuation.

He had seen no woman for thirty-seven years. He gulped her through his eyes as at some green oasis the thirst-tormented nomad gulps the well-head. Unable to remember any female face, he took Irma's strange proportions and the cast of her features to be characteristic of femininity. And so, his conscious mind blotted out by the intensity of his reaction, he committed the unforgivable crime. He made his feelings public. He lost control. The blood rushed to his head; he cried out hoarsely, and then, little knowing what he was doing, he stumbled forward, elbowing his colleagues from his path, and fell upon his knees before the lady, and finally, as though in a paroxysm, he collapsed upon his face, his arms and legs spread-eagled like a starfish.

The temperature of the room dropped to zero, and then, as suddenly, it rose to an equatorial and burning heat. Five long seconds went by. It would not have been strange in that intense temperature to have found a python hanging from the ceiling—nor, when the icy spell returned again, at the lapse of the third second, to find the carpet white with arctic foxes.

Would no one make a move to crack the glass, the great transparent sheet that spread unbroken from corner to corner of the long room?

And then a stride took place, a stride that brought Bellgrove's gaunt body to within four feet of Irma. With his next step he had halved the distance between himself and her—and then, all at once, he was above her and had found himself gazing down into the eyes that pleaded. It was as though he had been injected with lion's blood. Power rushed into him as though from a tap.

"Most dear madam," he said, "have no fear, I pray you. That one of my staff should be lying below you is shameful, yes, shameful, madam, but lo! is it not a symbol of what we all feel? What shame there is lies in his weakness, madam, not in his passion. Some, dear lady, would have his name expunged from all registers—but no. But no. For he has *warmth,* madam; warmth above all! In this case it has led to something distasteful, dammit" (he relapsed into his common tongue), "and so, dear hostess, allow me, as Headmaster, to have him removed from your presence. Yet forgive him, I implore you, for he recognized quality when he saw it, and his only sin is that in recognizing it too violently he had not the strength to hold his passion captive."

Bellgrove paused and wiped his forearm across his wet forehead and tossed back his white mane. He had spoken with his eyes shut. A sense of dreamlike strength had filled him. He knew in the self-imposed darkness that Irma's eyes were upon him; he could feel the intensity of her close presence. He could hear the feet of his staff, as his words continued, shuffling away in tactful pairs, and he could even hear himself talking as though the voice were another's.

What a deep and resonant organ the man has, he thought to himself, pretending for the moment that it was not his own voice he was hearing, for there was something humble in his nature which, every once in a while, found outlet.

But such thoughts were no more than momentary. What was paramount in him was the realization that here he was again, within a few inches of the lady whom he now pretended to pursue with all the cunning of old age and all the steeple-swarming, torrent-leaping, barnstorming impetus of recaptured youth.

"By the Lord!" he cried, voicelessly, and to himself yet very loud it sounded, in his own brain. "By the Lord, if I don't show 'em how it's done! Two arms, two legs, two eyes, one mouth, ears, trunk and buttocks, belly and skeleton, lungs, tripes and backbone, feet, and hands, brains, eyes, and testicles. I've got 'em all—so help me, right side up."

His eyes had remained closed, but now he lifted the heavy lids and, peering between his pale eyelashes, he found in the eyes of his hostess so hot and wet a succubus of love as threatened to undermine her marble temple and send its structure toppling.

He glanced about him. His staff, tactful to the point of tactlessness, were gathered in groups and were talking together like those gentlemen of the stage who, in an effort to appear normal, yet with nothing to say, repeat in simulated languor or animation, "One . . . two . . . three . . . four," and so on. But in the case of the Professors they mouthed their fatuities with all the over-emphasis of unrehearsal. In a far corner of the room a scrum of gownsmen were becoming restive.

"Talk about a wax giraffe, or slice me edgeways!" muttered Mulefire between his teeth.

"Certainly not, you hulk of flesh unhallowed," said Perch-Prism. "I'm ashamed of you!"

"And so indeed, la! Am I a beet-root? What it is, la, to have known better days and better ways, heaven shrive me—am I a beet-root?" It was the gay Cutflower talking, but there was something ruffled about his tone.

"As Theoreticus says in his diatribe against the use of the vernacular," whispered Flannelcat, who had waited for a long while for the moment when by coincidence he would both have the courage to say something and have something to say.

"Well, what did the old bleeder say?" said Opus Fluke.

But no one was interested and Flannelcat knew that his opportunity was gone, for several voices broke in and cut across his nervous reply.

"Tell me, Cutflower, is the Head still staring at her and why can't you pass the wine, by the clay of which we're made, it's given me the thirst of cactus-land," said Perch-Prism, his flat nose turned to the ceiling. "But for my breeding I'd turn round and see for myself."

"Not a twitch," said Cutflower. "Statues, la! Most uncanny."

"Once upon a time," broke in the mournful voice of Flannelcat, "I used to collect butterflies. It was long ago —in a swallow country full of dry river beds. Well, one damp afternoon when . . ."

"Another time, Flannelcat," said Cutflower. "You may sit down."

Flannelcat, saddened, moved away from the group in search of a chair.

Meanwhile Bellgrove had been savoring love's rare *apéritif,* the ageless language of the eyes.

Pulling himself together with the air of one who is master of every situation, he swept his gown across one shoulder as though it were a toga and, stepping back, surveyed the spread-eagled figure at their feet.

In stepping back, however, he had all but trodden upon Dr. Prunesquallor's feet and would have done so but for the agile side-step of his host.

The Doctor had been out of the room for a few minutes and had only just been told of the immobile figure on the floor. He was about to have examined the body when Bellgrove had taken his backward step, and now he was delayed still further by the sound of Bellgrove's voice.

"My dearest lady," said the old lion-headed man, who had begun to repeat himself, "warmth is everything. Yet no . . . not everything . . . but a good deal. That you should be caused embarrassment by one of my staff, shall I say one of my colleagues, yea, for so he is, shall always be to me like coals of fire. And why? Because, dearest lady, it was for me to have groomed him, to have schooled him, in the niceties, or more simply, dammit, to have left him behind. And that is what I must do now. I must have him removed," and he lifted his voice.

"Gentlemen," he cried, "I should be glad if two of you would remove your colleague and return with him to his quarters. Perhaps Professors . . . Flannelcat—"

"But no! But no! I will not have it!"

It was Irma's voice. She took a step forward and

brought her hands up to her long chin where she inter-
locked her fingers.

"Mr. Headmaster," she whispered, "I have heard what
you have had to say. And it was splendid. I said splendid.
When you spoke of 'warmth,' I understood. I, a mere
woman, I said a *mere* woman." She glared about her,
darkly, nervously, as though she had gone too far.

"But when, Mr. Headmaster, I found you were, in
spite of your belief, determined to have this gentleman
removed"—she glanced down at the spread-eagled figure
at her feet—"then I knew it was for me, as your hostess,
to ask you, as my guest, to think again. I would not have
it said, sir, that one of your staff was shamed in my
salon—that he was taken away. Let him be put in a chair
in a dim corner. Let him be given wine and pastries,
whatever he chooses, and when he is well enough, let
him join his friends. He has honored me, I say he has
honored me. . . ."

It was then that she saw her brother. In a moment
she was at his side. "Oh, Alfred, I am right, aren't I?
Warmth is everything, isn't it?"

Prunesquallor gazed at his sister's twitching face. It
was naked with anxiety, naked with excitement and also,
to make her expression almost too subtle for credulity,
it was naked with the lucence of love's dawn. Pray God
it is not a false one, thought Prunesquallor. It would kill
her. For a moment, the conception of how much simpler life would be *without* her flashed through his
mind, but he pushed the ugly notion away and, rising
on his toes, he clasped his hands so firmly behind his
back that his narrow and immaculate chest came forward like a pigeon's.

"Whether warmth is everything or not, my very
dear sister, it is nevertheless a comforting and a cozy
thing to have about—although mark you, it can be very
stuffy, by all that's oxidized, so it can, but Irma, my
sweet one—let that be as it may—for as a physician
it has struck me that it is about time that something
were done for the warrior at your feet; we must see to
him, mustn't we, we must see to him, eh, Mr. Bell-

grove? By all that's sacred to my weird profession, we most certainly must . . ."

"But he's not to leave the room, Alfred—he's not to leave the room. He's our *guest,* Alfred, remember that."

Bellgrove broke in before the Doctor could reply.

"You have humbled me, lady," he said simply, and bowed his lion's head.

"And you," whispered Irma, a deep blush raddling her neck, "have elevated me."

"No, madam . . . ah no!" muttered Bellgrove. "You are overkind." And then, taking a plunge, "Who can hope to elevate a heart, madam, a heart that is already dancing in the Milky Way?"

"Why *milky?*" said Irma, who, with no desire to drop the level of conversation, had a habit of breaking out with forthright queries. However engulfed she might be in the major mysteries, yet her brain, detached as it were from the business of the soul, took little flights on its own, like a gnat, asked little questions, played little tricks, only to be jerked back into place and subdued for a while as the voices of her deeper self took over.

Luckily for Bellgrove there was no need for him to reply, for the Doctor had signaled a couple of gownsmen over and the seemingly prostrate suppliant was lifted from the carpet, and carried, like a wooden effigy, to a candlelit corner, where a comfortable chair with plump green cushions stood ready.

"Seat him in the chair, gentlemen, if you will be so good, and I will have a look at him."

The two gownsmen lowered the rigid body. It lay straight as a board, supported by no more than its head on the chair back, with its heels on the ground. Between these extremities were thrust the plump green cushions so that they might, as it were, prop the plank— to take the little man's weight, but no weight descended and the cushions remained as plump as ever.

There was something frightful about it all and this frightfulness was in no way mitigated by the radiant smile that was frozen on the face.

With a magnificent gesture, the Doctor stripped himself of his beautiful velvet jacket and flung it away as though he had no further use for it.

Then he began to roll up his silk sleeves like a conjurer.

Irma and Bellgrove were close behind him. By this time the reservoirs of tact on which the Professors had been drawing were well-nigh dry and a horde stood watching in absolute silence.

The Doctor was fully conscious of this, but by not so much as a flicker did he reveal his awareness, let alone his delight in being watched.

The incident had changed the whole mood of the party. The hilarity and sense of freedom that had been so spontaneous had received an all but mortal blow. For some while, although certain jests were made, and glasses were filled and emptied, there was a darkness on the spirit of the room, and the jests were forced and the wine was swallowed mechanically.

But now that the first red blush of communal shame had died out of the staff; now that the embarrassment was merely cerebral and now that there was something to absorb them (for there was no resisting such an occasion as was now presented by Prunesquallor as he stood upright in his silken shirtsleeves, as slender as a stork, his skin as pink as a girl's, his glasses gleaming in the light of the candle)—now that there was all this, their equipoise began to return and with it a sense of hope; hope that the evening had not been ruined, that it held in store, once the Doctor had dealt with their seemingly paralyzed colleague, a modicum at least of that rare abandon which had begun to set their tongues on fire, and their blood a-jigging—for it was once in a score of years, they told themselves, that they could break the endless rhythm of Gormenghast, the rhythm that steered their feet each evening westward—westward to their quadrangle.

They were absolutely silent as they watched the Doctor's every movement.

Prunesquallor spoke. It seemed that he was talking to

himself, although his voice, in reaching those gownsmen who were at the rear of the audience, was certainly
a little louder than one would have thought necessary.
He took a pace forward and at the same time raised
his hands before him to the height of his shoulders,
where he worked his fingers to and fro in the air with
the speed of a professional pianist.

Then he brought his hands together and began to
draw them to and fro one across the other, palm to
palm. His eyes were closed.

"Rarer than Bluggs Disease," he mused, "or the spiral
spine! No doubt of it . . . by all that's convulsive . . .
no doubt of it at all. There *was* a case, quite fascinating
—now where was it and when was it . . . very similar—
a man if I remember rightly, had seen a ghost . . . yes,
yes . . . and the shock had all but finished him. . . ."

Irma shifted her feet.

"Now *shock* is the operative word," went on the Doctor, rocking himself gently on his heels, his eyes still
closed. "And shock must be answered with shock. But
how, and where . . . how and where . . . let me see
. . . let me see. . . ."

Irma could wait no longer. "Alfred," she cried, *"do*
something! *Do* something!"

The Doctor did not seem to hear her, so deep was he
in his reverie.

"Now, perhaps, if one knew the nature of the shock,
its scale, the area of the brain that received it—the *kind*
of unpleasantness—"

"Unpleasantness!" came Irma's voice again. "Unpleasantness! How dare you, Alfred! You *know* that it was I
who turned his head, poor creature, that it was for me
he fell headlong, for me that he is rigid and dreadful."

"Aha!" cried the Doctor. It was obvious he had not
heard a word that his sister had said. "Aha!" If he had
appeared animated and vital before, he was trebly so
now. His every gesture was as rapid and fluid as mercury. He took a prancing step toward his patient.

"By all that's pragmatical, it's this or nothing." He
slid his hand into one of his waistcoat pockets and with-

drew a small silver hammer. This he swiveled between his thumb and index finger for a few moments, his eyebrows raised.

In the meanwhile Bellgrove had begun to grow impatient. The situation had taken a queer turn. It was not in circumstances like these that he had hoped to present himself to Irma nor was this the kind of atmosphere in which his tenderness could flourish. For one thing he was no longer the center of attraction. His immediate desire was to be alone with her. The very words "alone with her" made him blush. His hair shone more whitely than ever against his dark-red brow. He glanced at her and immediately knew what to do. It was crystal-clear that she was uncomfortable. The figure on the chair was not a pleasant sight for anyone, let alone a lady of distinction, a lady of delicate tastes.

He tossed the shaggy splendor of his mane. "Madam," he said. "This is no place for you." He drew himself up to his full height, forcing back his shoulders and drawing his long chin into his throat. "No place at all, madam," and then, apprehensive that Irma might interpret him wrongly and find in his remark some slight upon her party, he shot a glance at her through his eyelashes. But she had found nothing amiss. On the contrary, there was gratitude in her small weak eyes; gratitude in the gleaming incline of her bosom, and in the nervous clasping of her hands.

She no longer heard her brother's voice. She no longer felt the presence of the robed males. Someone had been thoughtful. Someone had realized that she was a woman, and that it was not proper for her to stand with the rest as though there were no difference between herself and her guests. And this someone, this noble and solicitous being, was no other than the Headmaster—oh, how splendid it was that there should still be a *gentleman* on the face of the earth: youth had fled from him, ah yes, but not romance.

"Mr. Headmaster," she said, pursing her lips and lifting her eyes to his craggy face with an archness hardly

credible, "it is for *you* to say. It is for me to hearken.
Speak on. I am listening. I said, I am listening."

Bellgrove turned his head away from her. The wide,
weak smile that had spread itself across his face was
not the kind of thing that he would wish Irma to see. A
year or so ago, he had once, with no warning, caught
sight of himself in a mirror when a smile (an antecedent
of the uncontrollable expression that was even now undermining the spurious grandeur of his face) had shocked
him. It was to his credit that he had recognized the danger of allowing such a thing to become public for he
was, not without cause, proud of his features. And so he
turned his face away. How could he help giving vent to
some kind of demonstration of his feelings? For at
Irma's words, "It is for you to say," the wide rich panorama of married life suddenly appeared before him,
stretched out, it seemed, from horizon to horizon with
its vistas of pale gold, its gentle meads. He saw himself as an immemorial oak, its branches spreading godlike, with Irma, a sapling poplar, whose leaves like heart-
throbs twinkled in his shade. He saw himself as the proud
eagle, landing with a sigh of his wings upon a solitary
crag. He saw Irma, waiting for him in the nest, but curiously enough, she was sitting there in a nightdress. And
then, suddenly, he saw himself as a very old man, with
a toothache, and his memory caught sight of an ancient
face in the mirrors of a thousand shaving rooms.

He crushed this most unwelcome glimpse beneath the
heel of his immediate sensations.

He turned back to Irma.

"I offer you my arm, dear madam—such as it is."

"I will accompany you, Mr. Headmaster."

Irma lowered her little eyelids and then flicked a sideways glance at Mr. Bellgrove, who, having crooked out
his elbow somewhat extravagantly, paused a moment before dropping it with a sense of defeat that was quite
intoxicating.

"By hell!" he murmured passionately to himself. "I
am not so old that I miss the subtleties."

"Forgive my precipitation, dear madam," he said, bowing his head. "But perhaps . . . perhaps you understand."

Clasping her hands together at her bosom, Irma turned from the throng, and swaying strangely, began to pace into the empty regions of the room. The carpet lit by a hundred candles had lost something of its glow. It was even brighter but it was not so warm, for the chilly rays of the moon were now streaming through the open windows.

Bellgrove glanced about him as he turned to follow her. No one appeared to be interested in their departure. Every eye was fixed upon the Doctor. For a moment, Bellgrove felt disappointed that he could not stay, for there was drama in the air. The Doctor was evidently making an exhaustive overhaul of the stiffened figure whose clothes were being removed, one by one; no easy work; for the joints were quite inflexible. Mollocks and Canvas, the Prunesquallors' servants, had, however, a pair of scissors each and, when necessary, were, under the Doctor's supervision, using them to free the patient.

The Doctor still had the little silver hammer in one hand. With the other he was running his pianist-fingers over the rigid gentleman as though he were a keyboard —his eyebrows raised, his head cocked on one side like a tuner.

Bellgrove could see at a glance that in following Irma he was about to miss the climax of a considerable drama, but turning on his heel and seeing her again, he knew that a drama even more considerable was his for the making.

With his beautiful white gown rippling behind him, he strode in her wake, and on the eleventh stride he came within the orbit of her perfume.

Without pausing in the swaying movement of her gait she turned her head on its swan-white neck. Her emerald earring flashed with light. Her long, sharp nose, immaculately powdered, would have put most suitors off, but to Bellgrove it had the proportions of a beak on the proud head of a bird, exquisitely dangerous and sharp. Something to admire rather than love. It was almost a weapon, but a weapon which he felt confident would never be used against him. However that might be, it was hers—and in that simple fact lay its justification.

As they approached the bay window that was open to the night, Bellgrove inclined his head to her.

"This," he said, "is our first walk together."

She stopped as they reached the open window. What he had said had obviously touched her.

"Mr. Bellgrove," she whispered, "you mustn't say things like that. We hardly know one another."

"Quite so, dear lady, quite so," said Bellgrove. He took out a large grayish handkerchief and blew his nose. This is going to be a long business, he thought—unless he were to take some kind of a short cut—some secret path through love's enchanted glades.

Before them, shining balefully in the moonlight, lay the walled-in garden. The upper foliage of the trees shone as white as foam. The underside was black as well water. The whole garden was a lithograph of richest blacks and staring whites. The fish pool with its surrounding carvings appeared to blaze with a kind of lunar vulgarity. A fountain shot its white jets at the night. Under the livid pergolas, under the stone arches, under the garden tubs, under the great rockery, under the fruit trees, under each moon-white thing the shadows lay as black sea-drenched seals. There were no grays at all. There was no transition. It was a picture, terrifyingly simple.

They stared at it together.

"You said just now, Miss Prunesquallor, that we hardly knew each other. And how true this is when we measure our mutual recognition by the hands of the clock. But can we, madam, *can* we measure our knowledge thus? Is there not something in both of us which contradicts so mean a measure? Or am I flattering myself? Am I laying myself open to your scorn? Am I baring my heart too soon?"

"Your *heart,* sir?"

"My heart."

Irma struggled with herself.

"What were you saying about it, Mr. Headmaster?"

Bellgrove could not quite remember, so he joined his

big hands together at the height of the organ in question, and waited a moment or two for inspiration. He seemed to have proceeded rather faster than he had meant and then it struck him that his silence, rather than weakening his position, was enhancing it. It seemed to give an added profundity to the proceedings and to himself. He would keep her waiting. Oh, the magic of it! The power of it! He could feel his throat contracting as though he were biting into a lemon.

This time as he angled his arm he knew she would take it. She did. Her fingers on his forearm set his old heart pounding and then, without a word, they stepped forward together into the moonlit garden.

It was not easy for Bellgrove to know in which direction to escort his hostess. Little did he know that it was he who was being steered. And this was natural, for Irma knew every inch of the hideous place.

For some while they stood by the fish pond in which the reflection of the moon shone with a fatuous vacancy. They stared at it. Then they looked up at the original. It was no more interesting than its watery ghost, but they both knew that to ignore the moon on such an evening would be an insensitive, almost a brutish thing to do.

That Irma knew of an arbor in the garden was not her fault. And it was not her fault that Bellgrove knew it not. Yet she blushed inwardly, as casually turning to left and right at the corners of paths, or under flower-loaded trellises, she guided the Headmaster circuitously yet firmly in its direction.

Bellgrove, who had in his mind's eye just such a place as he was now unwittingly approaching, had felt it better that they should perambulate together in silence, so that when he had a chance to sit and rest his feet, his deep voice, when he brought it forth again from the depths of his chest, should have its full value.

On rounding a great moon-capped lilac bush and coming suddenly upon the arbor, Irma started, and drew back. Bellgrove came to a halt beside her. Finding her face was turned away from him, he gazed absently at the hard boulderlike bun of iron-gray hair which, with not a hair out of place, shone in the moonlight. It was nothing, however, for a man to dwell upon, and turning from her to the arbor which had caused her trepidation, he straightened himself, and turning his right foot out at a rather more aggressive angle, he struck an attitude, which he knew nothing about, for it was the unconscious equivalent of what was going on in his mind.

He saw himself as the type of man who would never take advantage of a defenseless woman, greathearted, and understanding. Someone a damsel might trust in a lonely wood. But he also saw himself as a buck. His youth had been so long ago that he could remember nothing of it but he presumed, erroneously, that he had tasted the purple fruit, had broken hearts and hymens, had tossed flowers to ladies on balconies, had drunk champagne out of their shoes and generally been irresistible.

He allowed her fingers to fall from his arm. It was at moments like this that he must give her a sense of freedom only to draw her further into the rich purdah of his benevolence.

He held the tabs of his white gown near the shoulders.

"Can you not smell the lilac, madam," he said, "the moonlit lilac?"

Irma turned.

"I must be honest with you, mustn't I, Mr. Bellgrove?" she said. "If I said I could smell it, when I couldn't, I would be false to you, and false to myself. Let us not start *that* way. No, Mr. Bellgrove, I cannot smell it. I have a bit of a cold."

Bellgrove had the sense of having to start life all over again.

"You women are delicate creatures," he said after a long pause. "You must take care of yourselves."

"Why are you talking in the plural, Mr. Bellgrove?"

"My dear madam," he replied slowly, and then, after a pause, "my . . . dear . . . madam," he said again. As he heard his voice repeat the three words for the second time, it struck him that to leave them as they were—inconsistent, rudderless, without preface or parenthesis, was by far the best thing he could do. He lapsed into silence and the silence was thrilling—the silence which to break with an answer to her question would be to make a commonplace out of what was magic.

He would not answer her. He would play with her with his venerable brain. She must realize from the first that she could not always expect replies to her questions —that his thoughts might be elsewhere, in regions where it would be impossible for her to follow him—or that her questions were (for all his love for her and for him) not worth answering.

The night poured in upon them from every side—a million cubic miles of it. Oh, the glory of standing with one's love, naked, as it were, on a spinning marble, while the spheres ran flaming through the universe!

Involuntarily they moved together into the arbor and sat down on a bench which they found in the darkness. This darkness was intensely rich and velvety. It was as though they were in a cavern, save that the depths were dramatized by a number of small and brilliant pools of moonlight. Pranked for the most part to the rear of the arbor these livid pools were at first a little disturbing, for portions of themselves were lit up with blatant emphasis. This arbitrary illumination had to be accepted, however, for Bellgrove, raising his eyes to where the vents in the roof let through the moonlight, could think of no way by which he could seal them.

From Irma's point of view the dappled condition of the cavernous arbor was both calming and irritating at the same time.

Calming, in that to enter a cave of clotted midnight, with not so much as a flicker of light to gauge her distance from her partner, would have been terrifying even with her knowledge of, and confidence in, so reliable and courteous a gentleman as her escort. This dappled arbor was not so fell a place. The pranked lights, more livid, it is true, than gay, removed, nevertheless, that sense of terror only known to fugitives or those benighted in a shire of ghouls.

Strong as was her feeling of gratification that the dark was broken, yet a sense of irritation as strong as her relief fought in her flat bosom for sovereignty. This irritation, hardly understandable to anyone who has neither Irma's figure, nor a vivid picture of the arbor in mind, was caused by the maddening *way* in which the lozenges of radiance fell upon her body.

She had taken out a small mirror in the darkness, more from nervousness than anything else, and in holding it up, saw nothing in the dark air before her but a long sharp segment of light. The mirror itself was quite invisible, as was the hand and arm that held it, but the detached and luminous reflection of her nose hovered before her in the darkness. At first she did not know what it was. She moved her head a little and saw in front of her one of her small weak eyes glittering like quicksilver, a startling thing to observe under any conditions, but infinitely more so when the organ is one's own.

The rest of her was indistinguishable midnight save for a pair of large and spectral feet. She shuffled them, but this blotch of moonlight was the largest in the arbor and to evade it involved a muscular strain quite insufferable.

Bellgrove's entire head was luminous. He was, more than ever before, a major prophet. His white hair positively blossomed.

Irma, knowing that this wonderful and searching light which was transfiguring the head was something that must not be missed—something in fact that she should pore upon—made a great effort to forget herself as a true lover should—but something in her rebelled against so exclusive a concentration upon her admirer, for she knew that it was *she* who should be stared at; *she* who should be pored upon.

Had she spent the best part of a day in titivating herself in order that she might sit plunged in darkness, with nothing but her feet and her nose revealed?

It was insufferable. The visual relationship was wrong; quite, quite wrong.

Bellgrove had suffered a shock when for a moment he had seen ahead of him, in quick succession, a moonlit nose and then a moonlit eye. They were obviously Irma's. There was no other nose in all Gormenghast so knife-like—and no eye so weak and worried—except its colleague. To have seen these features ahead of him when the lady to whom they belonged sat shrouded yet most palpable upon his right hand, unnerved the old man, and it was some while after he had caught sight of the mirror glinting on its return to Irma's reticule that he realized what had happened.

The darkness was as deep and black as water.

"Mr. Bellgrove," said Irma, "can you hear me, Mr. Bellgrove?"

"Perfectly, my dear lady. Your voice is high and clear."

"I would have you sit upon my right, Mr. Headmaster —I would have you exchange places with me."

"Whatever you would have I am here to have it given," said Bellgrove. For a moment he winced as the grammatical chaos of his reply wounded what was left of the scholar in him.

"Shall we rise together, Mr. Headmaster?"

"Dear lady," he replied, "let that be so."

"I can hardly see you, Mr. Headmaster."

"Nevertheless, dear lady, I am at your side. Would my arm assist you at our interchange? It is an arm that, in earlier days—"

"I am quite able to get to my own feet, Mr. Bellgrove— *quite* able, thank you."

Bellgrove rose, but in rising his gown was caught in some rustic contortion of the garden seat, and he found himself squatting in midair. "Hell!" he muttered savagely, and jerking at his gown, tore it badly. A nasty whiff of temper ran through him. His face felt hot and prickly.

"What did you say?" said Irma. "I said, *what* did you say?"

For a moment Bellgrove, in the confusion of his irritation, had unknowingly projected himself back into the Master's Common-Room, or into a classroom, or into the life he had led for scores of years.

His old lips curled back from his neglected teeth, "Silence!" he said. "Am I your Headmaster for nothing!"

Directly he had spoken, and had taken in what he had said, his neck and forehead burned.

Irma, transfixed with excitement, could make no move.
Had Bellgrove possessed any kind of a telepathic instinct
he must have known that he had beside him a fruit
which, at a touch, might have fallen into his hands, so ripe
it was. He had no knowledge of this, but luckily for him,
his embarrassment precluded any power on his part to
utter a word. And the silence was on his side.

It was Irma who was the first to speak.

"You have mastered me," she said. Her words, simple
and sincere, were more proud than humble. They were
proud with surrender.

Bellgrove's brain was not quick—but it was by no
means moribund. His mood was now trembling at the opposite pole of his temperament.

This by no means helped to clarify his brain. But he
sensed the need for extreme caution. He sensed that his
position though delicate was lofty. To find that his act of
rudeness in demanding silence from his hostess had
raised him rather than lowered him in her eyes appealed
to something in him quite shameless—a kind of glee. Yet
this glee, though shameless, was yet innocent. It was
the glee of the child who had not been found out.

They were both standing. This time he did not offer
Irma his arm. He groped in the darkness and found hers.
He found it at the elbow. Elbows are not romantic, but
Bellgrove's hand shook as he held the joint, and the joint
shook in his grasp. For a moment they stood together.
Her pineapple perfume was thick and powerful.

"Be seated," he said. He spoke a little louder than before. He spoke as one in authority. He had no need to
look stern, magnetic, or masculine. The blessed darkness
precluded any exertion in that direction. He made faces
in the safety of the night. Putting out his tongue; blowing
out his cheeks—there was so much glee in him.

He took a deep breath. It steadied him.

"Are you seated, Miss Prunesquallor?"

"Oh, yes . . . oh, yes indeed," came the answering
whisper.

"In comfort, madam?"

"In comfort, Mr. Headmaster, and in peace."

"Peace, my dear lady? What kind of peace?"

"The peace, Mr. Headmaster, of one who has no fear. Of one who has faith in the strong arm of her loved one. The peace of heart and mind and spirit that belongs to those who have found what it is to offer themselves without reserve to something august and tender."

There was a break in Irma's voice, and then as though to prove what she had said, she cried out into the night, "Tender! That's what I said. Tender and Unattached!"

Bellgrove shifted himself; they were all but touching.

"Tell me, my dearest lady, is it of me that you speak? If it is not, then humble me—be merciless and break an old man's heart with one small syllable. If you say 'No,' then, without a word I will leave you and this pregnant arbor, walk out into the night, walk out of your life, and maybe, who knows, out of mine also."

Whether or not he was gulling himself it is certain that he was living the very essence of his words. Perhaps the very use of words themselves was as much a stimulus as Irma's presence and his own designs; but that is not to say that the total effect was not sincere. He was infatuated with all that pertained to love. He trod, breast-deep, through banks of thorn-crazed roses. He breathed the odors of a magic isle. His brain swam on a sea of spices. But he had his own thought too.

"It was of you I spoke," said Irma. "You, Mr. Bellgrove. Do not touch me. Do not tempt me. Do nothing to me. Just *be* there beside me. I would not have us desecrate this moment."

"By no means. By no means." Bellgrove's voice was deep and subterranean. He heard it with pleasure. But he was sensitive enough to know that for all its sepulchral beauty, the phrase he had just used was pathetically inept —and so he added, "By no means whatsoever," as though he were beginning a sentence.

"By no means whatsoever, ah, definitely not, for who can tell, when, unawares, love's dagger . . ." but he stopped. He was getting nowhere. He must start again.

He must say things that would drive his former remarks out of her mind. He must sweep her along.

"Dear one," he said, plunging into the rank and feverish margin of love's forest. *"Dear* one!"

"Mr. Bellgrove—oh, Mr. Bellgrove," came the hardly audible reply.

"It is the Headmaster of Gormenghast, your suitor, who is speaking to you, my dear. It is a man, mature and tender—yet a disciplinarian, feared by the wicked, who is sitting beside you in the darkness. I would have you concentrate upon this. When I say to you that I shall call you Irma, I am not asking for permission from my lovelight—I am telling her what I shall do."

"Say it, my male!" cried Irma, forgetting herself. Her strident voice, quite out of key with the secret and muted atmosphere of an arbor'd wooing, splintered the darkness.

Bellgrove shuddered. Her voice had been a shock to him. At a more appropriate moment he would teach her not to do things of that kind.

As he settled again against the rustic back of the seat he found that their shoulders were touching.

"I will say it. Indeed I will say it, my dear. Not as a crude statement with no beginning or ending. Not as a mere reiteration of the most lovely, the most provocative name in Gormenghast, but threaded into my sentences, an integral part of our conversation, Irma, for see, already it has left my tongue."

"I have no power, Mr. Bellgrove, to remove my shoulder from yours."

"And I have no inclination, my dove." He lifted his big hand and tapped her on the shoulder she had referred to.

They had been so long in darkness that he had forgotten that she was in evening dress. In touching her naked shoulder he received a sensation that set his heart careening. For a moment he was deeply afraid. What was this creature at his side? And he cried out to some unknown God for delivery from the Unknown, the Serpentine, from all that was shameless, from flesh and the devil.

The tremendous gulf between the sexes yawned—and an abyss, terrifying and thrilling, sheer and black as the

arbor in which they sat; a darkness wide, dangerous, imponderable, and littered with the wrecks of broken
bridges.

But his hand stayed where it was. The muscle of her
shoulder was tense as a bowstring, but the skin was like
satin. And then his terror fled. Something masterful and
even dashing began to possess him.

"Irma," he whispered huskily. "Is *this* a desecration?
Are we blotting the whitest of all love's copybooks? It is
for you to say. For myself I am walking among rainbows
—for myself I . . ." But he had to stop speaking for he
wished, more than anything else, to lie on his back and to
kick his old legs about and to crow like a barn-cock. As
he could not do this he had no option but to put his
tongue out in the darkness, to squint with his eyes, to
make extravagant grimaces of every kind. Excruciating
shivers swarmed his spine.

And Irma could not reply. She was weeping with joy.
Her only answer was to place her hand upon the Headmaster's. They drew together—involuntarily. For a while
there was that kind of silence all lovers know. The silence
that it is sin to break until of its own volition, the moment comes, and the arms relax and the cramped limbs
can stretch themselves again, and it is no longer an insensitive thing to inquire what the time might be or to speak
of other matters that have no place in Paradise.

At last Irma broke the hush.

"How happy I am," she said very quietly. "How very
happy, Bellgrove."

"Ah . . . my dear . . . ah," said the Headmaster very
slowly, very soothingly. "That is as it should be . . . that
is as it should be."

"My wildest, my very *wildest* dreams have become real,
have become something I can touch." (She pressed his
hand.) "My little fancies, my little visions—they are no
longer so, dear master, they are substance, they are you
. . . they are You."

Bellgrove was not sure that he liked being one of Irma's
"little fancies, little visions," but his sense of the inappro-
priate was swamped in his excitement.

"Irma!" He drew her to him. There was less give in her body than in a cake stand. But he could hear her quick excited breathing.

"You are not the only one whose dreams have become a reality, my dear. We are holding one another's dreams in our very arms."

"Do you mean it, Mr. Bellgrove?"

"Surely, ah, surely," he said.

Dark as it was Irma could picture him at her side, could see him in detail. She had an excellent memory. She was enjoying what she saw. Her mind's eye had suddenly become a most powerful organ. It was, in point of fact, stronger, clearer, and healthier than those real eyes of hers which gave her so much trouble.

And so, as she spoke to him she had no sense of communing with an invisible presence. The darkness was forgotten.

"Mr. Bellgrove?"

"My dear lady?"

"Somehow, I knew . . ."

"So did I . . . so did I."

"It is more than I dare dwell upon—this strange and beautiful fact—that words can be so unnecessary—that when I start a sentence, there is no *need* to finish it and all this, so very suddenly. I said, *so very* suddenly."

"What would be sudden to the young is leisurely to us. What would be foolhardy in them is child's-play itself, for you, my dear, and for me. We are mature, my dear. We are ripe. The golden glaze, that patina of time, these are upon us. Hence we are sure and have no callow qualms. Let us admit the length of our teeth, lady. Time, it is true, has flattened our feet, ah yes, but with what purpose? To steady us, to give us balance, to take us safely along the mountain tracks. God bless me . . . ah. God bless me. Do you think that I could have wooed and won you as a youth? Not in a hundred years! And why . . . ah . . . and why? Inexperience. That is the answer. But now, in half an hour or less, I have stormed you; stormed you. But am I breathless? No. I have brought my guns to bear upon you, and yet, my dear, have scores of roundshot left. . . . Ah, yes, Irma, my ripe one . . . and you can see it all? . . . You can see it all? . . . Dammit, we have equipoise and that is what it is."

Irma's mental sight was frighteningly clear. His voice had sharpened the edges of his image.

"But I'm not very old, Mr. Bellgrove, am I," said Irma, after a pause. To be sure she felt as young as a fledgling.

"What is age? What is time!" said Bellgrove—and then, answering himself in a darker voice, "They're *hell!*" he said. "I hate 'em."

"No, no. I won't have it," said Irma. "I won't, Mr. Bellgrove. Age and time are what you make them. Let us not speak of them again."

Bellgrove sat forward on his old buttocks. "Lady!" he said suddenly, "I have thought of something that I think you will agree is more than comic."

"Have you, Mr. Bellgrove?"

"Pertaining to what you said about Age and Time. Are you listening, my dear?"

"Yes, Mr. Bellgrove . . . eagerly . . . eagerly!"

"What I think would be rather droll would be to say, in a gathering, when the moment became opportune—perhaps during some conversation about clocks—one could work round to it—to say, quite airily, 'Time is what you make it.'"

He turned his head to her in the darkness. He waited.

There was no response from Irma. She was thinking feverishly. She began to panic. Her face was prickling with anxiety. She could make no sound. Then she had an idea. She pressed herself against him a little more closely.

"How delicious!" she said at last, but her voice was very strained.

The silence that followed was no more than a few seconds, but to Irma it was as long as that ghastly hush that awaits all sinners when, at the judgment seat, they await the Verdict. Her body trembled, for there was so much at stake. Had she said something so stupid that no Headmaster, worthy of his office, could ever consider accept-

ing her? Had she, unwittingly, lifted some hatchway of
her brain and revealed to this brilliant man how cold,
black, humorless, and sterile was the region that lay
within?

No. Ah no! For his voice, rolling from the gloom, had,
if possible, even more tenderness in it than she would
have dared to hope for in a man.

"You are cold, my love. You are chilly. The night is
not for delicate skins. By hell, it isn't. And I? And what
of me? Your suitor? Is he cold also, my dear? Your old
gallant? He is. He is indeed. And what is more he is becoming sick of darkness. Darkness that shrouds. That
clogs the living lineaments of beauty. That swathes you,
Irma. By hell it's maddening and pointless stuff"—Bellgrove began to rise—"it's damnable, I tell you, my own,
this arbor's damnable."

He felt the pressure of fingers on his forearm.

"Ah, no . . . no . . . I will not have you swear. I will
not have strong language in our arbor . . . our sacred
arbor."

For a moment Bellgrove was tempted to play the
gay dog. His moods flitted across the basic excitement
of the wooing. It was so delicious to be chided by a
woman. He wondered whether to shock her—to shock
her out of the surplus of his love—would be worth the
candle. To taste again the sweetness of being reprimanded,
the never-before-experienced gushes of sham remorse—
would this be worth the lowering of his moral status? No!
He would stick to his pinnacle.

"This arbor," he said, "is forever ours. It is the darkness it holds captive; this pitchy stuff that hides your
face from me—it is this darkness that I called damnable
—and damnable it is. It is your face, Irma, your proud
face that I am thirsting for. Can you not understand? By
the great moonlight! my love; by the tremendous moonlight! Is it not natural that a man should wish to brood
upon his darling's brow?"

The word "darling" affected Irma as might a bullet
wound. She clasped her hands at her breast and press-

ing them inward, the tepid water in her false bosom gurgled in the darkness.

For a moment Bellgrove, thinking she was laughing at what he had said, stiffened at her side. But the terrible blush of humiliation that was about to climb his neck was quenched by Irma's voice. The gurgle must have been a sign of love, of some strange and aqueous love that was beyond his sounding, for "Oh, master," she said, "take me to where the moon can show you me."

"Show-you-me?" For a short while Bellgrove was quite unable to decipher what sounded to him like a foreign language. But he did not stand still, as lesser men would have done while pondering, but answering the first part of her command, he escorted her from the arbor. Instantaneously, they were floodlit—and at the same instant Irma's syntax clarified in the Headmaster's mind.

They moved together, like specters, like mobile carvings casting their long inky shadows across the little paths, down the slopes of rockeries, up the sides of trellises.

At last they stopped for a little while where a stone cherub squatted upon the rim of a granite bird bath. To their left they could see the lighted windows of the long reception room. But they could not see that in the midst of a rapt audience the Doctor was raising his silver hammer as though to put all to the test. They could not know that by a supernatural effort of the will, and the marshaling of all his deductive faculties, and the freeing of an irrational flair, the Doctor had come to the kind of decision more usually associated with composers than with scientists—and was now on the brink of success or failure.

The "body" had, to aid the physician in his exhaustive search for the cause of the paralysis, been stripped of all clothing save the mortarboard.

What happened next was something which, however much the stories varied afterward—for it seemed that every Professor present was able to note some minor detail hidden from the rest—was yet consistent in the main. The speed at which it happened was phenomenal,

and it must be assumed that the microscopic elabora-
tions of the incident which were to be the main subject
of conversation for so long a while afterward were no
more or less than inventions which were supposed to re-
dound to the advantage of the teller, in some way or
other—possibly through the reflected glory which they
all felt at having been there at all. However this may be,
what was agreed upon by all was that the Doctor, his
shirt sleeves rolled well back, rose suddenly upon his
toes, and lifting his silver hammer into the air, where it
flashed with candlelight, let it fall, as it were with a kind
of controlled, yet effortless downstroke, upon the nether
regions of the spinal column. As the hammer struck, the
Doctor leaped back and stood with his arms spread out
to his sides, his fingers rigid as he saw before him the instantaneous convulsion of the patient. This gentleman
writhing like an expiring eel leaped suddenly high into
the air, and on landing upon his feet, was seen to streak
across the room and out of the bay windows and over
the moonlit lawn at a speed that challenged the credulity of all witnesses.

And those who, standing grouped about the Doctor,
had seen the transformation and the remarkable athlet-
icism that followed so swiftly upon it, were not the only
ones to be startled by the spectacle.

In the garden, among the livid blotches and the cold
wells of shadow a voice was saying, "It is not meet,
Irma my dearest, that on this night, this *first* night, we
should tire our hearts . . . no, no, it is not meet, sweet
bride."

"Bride?" cried Irma, flashing her teeth and tossing her
head. "Oh, Master, not *yet*—surely!"

Bellgrove frowned like God considering the state of the
world on the Third Day. A knowing smile played across
his old mouth but it appeared to have lost its way among
the wrinkles.

"Quite so, my delicious helm. Once more you keep me
on my course, and for that I revere you, Irma . . . not
bride, it is true, but—"

The old man had jerked like a recoiling firearm, and

Irma with him, for she was in his gown-swathed arms. Turning her startled eyes from his she followed his gaze, and on the instant clung to him in a desperate embrace, for all at once they saw before them, naked in the dazzling rays of the moon, a flying figure which, for all the shortness of the legs, was covering the ground with the speed of a hare. The tassel of the inky mortarboard, sole claim to decency, streamed away behind like a donkey's tail.

No sooner had Irma and the Headmaster caught sight of the apparition, than it had reached the high orchard wall of the garden. How it ever climbed the wall was never discovered. It simply went up it, its shadow swarming alongside, and the last that was ever seen of Mr. Throd, the onetime member of Mr. Bellgrove's staff, was a lunar flash of buttocks where the high wall propped the sky.

Chapter Thirty-Seven

THERE were at least three hours to be burned. It was unusual for Steerpike to have to think in such terms. There was always something afoot. There were always, in the wide and sinister pattern of his scheduled future, those irregular pieces to find and to fit into the great jigsaw puzzle of his predatory life, and of Gormenghast, on whose body he fed.

But on this particular day, when the clocks had all struck two, and the steel of his swordstick which he had been sharpening was as keen as a razor and as pointed as a needle, he wrinkled his high shining forehead as he returned the blade to the stick. At the end of the three hours that lay before him he had something very important to do.

It would be very simple and it would be absorbing, but it would be very important also; so important that for the first time in his life he was at a loss for a few moments as to how to fill in the hours that remained before the business that lay ahead, for he knew that he could not concentrate upon anything very serious. While he pondered, he moved to the window of his room and looked out across the vistas of roofs and broken towers.

It was a breathless day, a frail mist tempering the warmth. The few flags that could be seen above various turrets hung limply from their mastheads.

This prospect never failed to please the pale young man. His eye ran over it with shrewdness.

Then he turned from the scene, for he had had an idea. Pouncing upon the floor, his arms outstretched, he stood upside down upon the palms of his hands and began to perambulate the room, one eyebrow raised. His idea was to pay a quick call upon the twins. He had not visited them for some while. Away across the roofscape he had seen the outskirts of that deserted tract, in one of whose forgotten corridors an archway led to a gray world of empty rooms, in one of which their Ladyships Cora and Clarice sat immured. Their presence and the presence of their few belongings seemed to have no effect upon the sense of emptiness. Rather, their presence seemed to reinforce the vacancy of their solitude.

It would take him the best part of an hour's sharp walking to reach that forgotten region, but he was in a restless mood, and the idea appealed to him. Flexing his elbows—for he was still moving about the room on his hands—he pressed, of a sudden, away from the floor and, like an acrobat, was all at once on his feet again.

Within a few moments he was on his way, his room carefully locked behind him. He walked rapidly, his shoulders drawn up and forward a little in that characteristic way that gave to his every movement a quality both purposeful and devilish.

The short cuts he took through the labyrinthian network of the castle led him into strange quarters. There were times when walls would tower above him, sheer and windowless. At other times, naked acres, paved in brick or stone, would spread themselves out, wastelands vast and dusty where weeds of all kinds forced their way from between the interstices of the paving stones.

As he moved rapidly from domain to domain, from a world of sunless alleys to the panoramic ruins where the rats held undisputed tenure—from the ruins to that peculiar district where the passageways were all but blocked with undergrowth and the carved façades were cold with sea-green ivy—he exulted. He exulted in it all. In the fact that it was only he who had the initiative to explore these wildernesses. He exulted in his restlessness, in his intelligence, in his passion to hold within his own hands the reins, despotic or otherwise, of supreme authority.

Far above him and to the east the sunlight burned upon a long oval window of blue glass. It blazed like lazuli—like a gem hung aloft against the gray walls. Without changing the speed of his walk he drew from his pocket a small, smooth, beautifully made catapult, into the pouch of which he fitted a bullet, and then, as though with a single action, the elastic was stretched and released and Steerpike returned his catapult to his pocket.

He kept walking, but as he walked his face was turned up to those high gray walls where the blue window blazed.

He saw the small gap in the glass and the momentary impression of a blue powder falling before he heard the distant sound, as of a far gunshot.

A head had appeared at the gap in that splintered window away in the high east.

It was very pale. The body beneath it was swathed in sacking. On the shoulder sat perched a blood-red parrot —but Steerpike knew nothing of this and was entering another district and was for a long while in the shadows, moving beneath a continuous roofscape of lichened slates.

When at last he approached the archway which led to the twins' quarters, he paused and gazed back along the gray perspectives. The air was chill and unhealthy; a smell of rotten wood, of dank masonry filled his lungs. He moved in a climate as of decay—of a decay rank with its own evil authority, a richer, more inexorable quality than freshness; it smothered and drained all vibrancy, all hope.

Where another would have shuddered, the young man merely ran his tongue across his lips. "This is a *place*," he said to himself. "Without any doubt, this is *somewhere*."

But the hands of the clock kept moving and he had little time for speculation, and so he turned his back on the cold perspectives where the long walls bulged and sagged, where plaster hung and sweated with cold and inanimate fevers, with sicknesses of umber, and illnesses of olive.

When he reached the door behind which the twins were incarcerated he took a bunch of keys from his pocket and, selecting one, which he had cut himself, he turned the lock.

The door opened to his pressure with a stiff and grating sound.

Stiff as were the hinges, it had not taken Steerpike more than a second to throw it wide open. Had he been forced to fight against the swollen wood for an entrance, to struggle with the lock, or to put his shoulder to the damp paneling—or even had his rapid entrance been heralded by the sound of his footsteps—then the spectacle that awaited him, for all its strangeness, would not have had that uncanny and dreamlike horror that now lay hold of him.

He had made no sound. He had given no warning of his visit—but there before him stood the twins, hand in hand, their faces white as lard. They were positioned immediately before the door, at which they must have been staring. They were like figures of wax, or alabaster, or like motionless animals, upright upon their quarters, their gaze fixed, it would seem, upon the face of their master, their mouths half open as though awaiting some titbit—some familiar signal.

No expression at all came into their eyes, nor would there have been room for any, for they were separately filled, each one of them, with a foreign body, for in each of the four glazed pupils the image of the young man was exquisitely reflected. Let those who have tried to pass love letters through the eyes of needles or to have written poems on the heads of pins take heart. Crude and heavy-handed as they found themselves, yet they will never appreciate the extent of their clumsiness, for they will never know how Steerpike's head and shoulders leaned forward through circles the size of beads, whose very equidistance from one another (the twins were cheek to cheek) was as though to prove by ghastly repetition the nightmare of it all. Minute and exquisite in the micro-cosm of the pupils, these four worlds, identical and ter-rible, gleamed between the lids. It would seem they had been painted—these images of Steerpike—with a single hair or with the proboscis of a bee—for the very whites of his eyes were crystalline. And when Steerpike at the door drew back his head—drew it back on a sudden impulse, then the four heads, no bigger than seeds, were drawn back at that same instant, and the eight eyes narrowed as they stared back from the four microscopic mirrors —stared back at their origin, the youth, mountain-high in the doorway, the youth on whom their quick and pulse-less lives depended—the youth with his eyes narrowed, and whose least movement was theirs.

That the eyes of the twins should be ignorant of that which they reflected was natural enough, but it was not natural that in carrying the image of Steerpike to their identical brains, there should not be, by so much as the merest shade, a clue to the excitement in their breasts. For it seemed that they felt nothing, that they saw nothing, that they were dead, and stood upon their feet by some miracle.

Steerpike knew at once that yet another chapter was over in his relationship with Cora and Clarice. They had become clay in his hands, but they were clay no more, unless there is in clay not only something imponderable but something sinister also. Not only this, but something adamantine. From now on he knew that they were no longer ductile—they had changed into another medium—a sister medium—but a harsher one—they were stone.

All this could be seen at a glance. But now, suddenly,

there was something which escaped his vigilance. It was this. His reflections were no longer in their eyes. Their Ladyships had unwittingly expelled him. Something else had taken place—and as he was unaware that he had ever been reflected so he was equally unaware that he was no longer so, and that in the lenses of their eyes he had exchanged places with the head of an ax.

But what Steerpike *could* see was that they were no longer staring at him—that their gaze was fixed upon something above his head. They had not tilted their heads back, although it would have been the normal thing to do, for whatever they were looking at was all but out of their line of vision. Their upturned eyes shone white. Save for this movement of their eyeballs they had not so much as stirred.

Fighting down his fear that were he to move his eyes from them, even for a second, he would fall in a peculiar way into some trap, he swung himself about and in a moment had seen a great ax dangling a dozen feet above him, and the complex network of cords and strings which, like a spider's web in the darkness of the upper air, held in position the cold and grizzly weight of the steel head.

With a backward leap the young man was through the doorway. Without a pause he slammed the door and before he had turned the key in the lock he heard the thud as the head of the ax buried itself in that part of the floor where he had been standing.

Chapter Thirty-Eight

✹✹✹✹✹✹✹✹✹✹✹

STEERPIKE'S return to the castle's heart was rapid and purposeful. A pale sun like a ball of pollen was hung aloft an empty and faded sky, and as he sped below it his shadow sped with him, rippling over the cobbles of great squares, or cruising alongside, upright, where, at his elbow, the lit and attenuate walls threw back the pallid light. For all that within its boundaries, this shadow held nothing but the uniform blankness of its tone, yet it seemed every whit as predatory and meaningful as the body that cast it—the body, that with so many aids to expressiveness within the moving outline, from the pallor of the young man and the dark-red color of his eyes, to the indefinable expressions of lip and eye, was drawing nearer at every step to a tryst of his own making.

The sun was blocked away. For a few minutes the shadow disappeared like the evil dream of some sleeper who on waking finds the substance of his nightmare standing beside the bed—for *Steerpike* was there, turning the corners, threading the mazes, gliding down slopes of stone or flights of rotten wood. And yet it was strange that with all the vibrancy that lay packed within the margins of his frame, yet his shadow when it reappeared reaffirmed its self-sufficiency and richness as a scabbard for malignity. Why should this be—why with certain slender proportions and certain tricks of movement should a sense of darkness be evoked? Shadows more terrible and grotesque than Steerpike's gave no such feeling. They moved across their walls bloated or spidery with a comparative innocence. It was as though a shadow had a heart—a heart where blood was drawn from the margins of a world of less substance than air. A world of darkness whose very existence depended upon its enemy, the light.

And there it was; there it slid, this particular shadow—from wall to wall, from floor to floor, the shoulders a little high, but not unduly, the head cocked, not to one or other side, but forward. In an open space it paled as it moved over dried earth, for the sun weakened—and then it fainted away altogether as the fringe of a cloud half the size of the sky moved over the sun.

Almost at once the rain began to fall, and the air yet further darkened. Nor was this darkening enough, for beneath the expanse of the cloud that moved inexorably to the north, dragging behind it miles and miles of what looked like filthy linen, beneath *this* expanse, yet another, of similar hugeness, but swifter, began to overtake it from beneath, and when *this* lower continent of cloud began to pass over that part of the sky where the sun had lately been shining, then something very strange made itself felt at once.

A darkness almost unprecedented had closed down over Gormenghast. Steerpike glancing left and right could see the lights begin to burn in scores of windows. It was too dark to see what was happening above, but judging from a still deepening of the pall, yet further clouds, thick and rain-charged, must have slid across the sky to form the lowest of three viewless and enormous layers.

By now the rain was loud on the roofs, was flooding along the gutterings, gurgling in crannies, and brimming the thousand irregular cavities that the centuries had formed among the crumbling stones. The advance of these weltering clouds had been so rapid that Steerpike had not entirely escaped the downpour, but it was not for more than a few moments that the rain beat on his head and shoulders, for, running through the unnatural darkness to the nearest of the lighted windows, he found himself in a part of the castle that he remembered. From here he could make the rest of the journey under cover.

The premature darkness was peculiarly oppressive. As Steerpike made his way through the lighted corridors he noticed how at the main windows there were groups gathered, and how the faces that peered out into the false night wore expressions of perplexity and apprehension. It was a freak of nature, and no more, that the world had been swathed away from the westering sun as though with bandages, layer upon layer, until the air was stifled. Yet it seemed as though the sense of oppression which the darkness had ushered in had more than a material explanation.

As though to fight back against the circumscribing darkness the hierophants had lighted every available lantern, burner, candle, and lamp, and had even improvised an extraordinary variety of reflectors, of tin and glass, and even trays of gold and plates of burnished copper. Long before any message could have been couriered across the body of Gormenghast, there was not a limb, not a digit that had not responded to the universal sense of suffocation, not the merest finger joint of stone that had not set itself alight.

Countless candles dribbled with hot wax, and their flames, like little flags, fluttered in the uncharted currents of air. Thousands of lamps, naked, or shuttered behind colored glass, burned with their glows of purple, amber, grass-green, blue, blood-red, and even gray. The walls of Gormenghast were like the walls of paradise or the walls of an inferno. The colors were devilish or angelical according to the color of the mind that watched them. They swam, those walls, with the hues of hell, with the tints of Zion. The breasts of the plumaged seraphim; the scales of Satan.

And Steerpike, moving rapidly through these varying flushes, could hear the loudening of the rain. He had come to something very like an isthmus—a corridor with circular windows on either side that gave upon the outer darkness. This arcade, or coverway—this isthmus that joined together one great mass of sprawling masonry with another—was illumined along its considerable length at three more or less regular intervals by, firstly, a great age-green oil lamp with an enormous wick as wide as a sheep's tongue. The glass globe that fitted over it was appallingly ugly; a fluted thing, a piece missing from its lower lip. But its color was something apart—or rather the color of the glass when lit from behind, as it now was. To say it was indigo gives no idea of its depth and richness, nor of the underwater or cavernous *glow* that filled that part of the arcade with its aura.

In their different ways the other two lamps, with their globes of sullen crimson and iceberg green, made within the orbits of their influence arenas no less theatrical. The glazed and circular windows, dark as jet, were yet not featureless. Across the blind blackness of those flanking eyes the strands of rain which appeared not to move but to be stretched across the inky portholes like harp strings—these strands, these strings of water burned blue, beyond the glass, burned crimson, burned green, for the lamplight stained them. And in the stain was something serpentine—something poisonous, exotic, feverish, and merciless; the colors were the colors of the sea snake, and beyond the windows on either hand was the long-drawn hiss of the reptilian rain.

And while Steerpike sped along this covered way, the shadow that he cast changed color. Sometimes it was before him as though eager to arrive at some rendezvous before the body of its caster; and sometimes it followed him, sliding at his heels, dogging him, changing its dark color as it flowed.

With the isthmus behind him, and a continent of stone once more about him, a continent into whose fastnesses he moved the deeper with every step and with every breath he took, Steerpike banished from his mind every thought of the twins and of their behavior. His mind had been largely taken up with conjecture as to the cause of their insurrection, and with tentative plans for their disposal.

But there were matters more pressing and one matter in particular. With enviable ease he emptied his mind of their Ladyships and filled it with Barquentine.

His shadow moved upon his right hand. It was climbing a staircase. It crossed a landing. It descended three steps. It followed for a short while at its maker's heels and then overtook him. It was at his elbow when it suddenly deepened its tone and grew up the side of the wall until the shadow-head, twelve feet above the ground, pursued its lofty way, the profile undulating from time to time, when it was forced to float across the murky webs that choked the junction of wall and ceiling.

And then the giant shade began to shrivel, and as it descended it moved a little forward of its caster, until finally it was a thick and stunted thing—a malformation, intangible, terrible, that led the way toward those rooms where its immediate journey could, for a little while, be ended.

Chapter Thirty-Nine

BARQUENTINE, in his room, sat with his withered leg drawn up to his chin. His hair, dirty as a fly-blown web, hung about his face, dry and lifeless. His skin, equally filthy, with its silted fissures, its cheeselike cracks and discolorations, was dry also—an arid terrain, dead it seemed, and waterless as the moon, and yet, at its center those malignant lakes, his vile and brimming eyes.

Outside the broken window at the far end of the room lay stretched the stagnant waters of the moat.

He had been sitting there, his only leg drawn up to his face, his crutch leaning against the back of his chair, his hands clasped about his knee, a hank of his beard between his teeth—he had been sitting there, for over an hour. On the table before him at least a dozen books lay spread; books of ritual and precedence, books of cross reference, ciphers, and secret papers. But his eyes were not on them. No less ruthless for being out of focus and gleaming wetly in their dry sockets, they could not see that a shadow had entered the room—that intangible as air, yet graphic to a degree, it had reared itself against high tiers of books—books of all shapes and in every stage of dilapidation, that glimmered in the bad light save where this shadow lay athwart them, black as a shade from hell.

And while he sat there, what was he thinking of, this wrinkled and filthy dwarf?

He was thinking of how a change had come over the workings of Gormenghast—over the workings of its heart and the temper of its brain. Something so subtle that he could in no way fix upon it. Something that was not to be located in the normal way of his thinking yet some-

thing which, nevertheless, was filling his nostrils with its
odor. He knew it to be evil, and what was evil in the eyes
of Barquentine was anything that smelled of insurrection,
anything that challenged, or worked to undo, the ancient
procedures.

Gormenghast was not what it was. He knew it. There
was devilry somewhere among these cold stones. And
yet he could not put his finger upon the spot. He could not
say what it was that was now so different. It was not
that he was an old man. He was not sentimental about the
days of his youth. They had been dark and loveless. But he
had no pity for himself. He had only this blind, passionate,
and cruel love for the dead letter of the castle's law. He
loved it with a love as hot as his hate. For the members
of the Groan Line itself he had less regard than for the
meanest and drearest of the rituals that it was their destiny
to perform. Only insofar as they were symbols did he
bow his ragged head. He had no love for Titus—only
for his significance as the last of the links in the great
chain. There was something about the way the boy
moved—a restlessness, an independence—that galled him.
It was almost as though this heir to a world of towers had
learned of other climes, of warm, clandestine lands, and
that the febrile and erratic movements of the child's
limbs were the reflection of what lived and throve in his
imagination. It was as though his brain, in regions remote and seductive, was sending its unsettling messages to
the small bones, to the tissues of the boy, so that there
was, in his movements, something remote and ominous.

But Barquentine, knowing that the Seventy-Seventh
Earl had never moved as far as a day's journey from his
birthplace, spat, as it were, these reflections from his
puzzled brain. And yet the taste lingered. The taste of
something acid; something rebellious. The young Earl was
too much himself. It was as though the child imagined he
had a life of his own apart from the life of Gormenghast.

And he was not the only one. There was this Steerpike
youth. A quick, useful disciple no doubt, but a danger,
for that very reason. What was to be done about him? He
had learned too much. He had opened books that were

not for him to open and found his way about too rapidly. There was something about him that set him apart from the life of the place—something subtly foreign—something ulterior.

Barquentine shifted his body on the chair, growling with irritation, both at the twinge which the altering of his position gave to his withered leg, and at the frustration of being unable to do more than gnaw at the fringe of his suspicions. He longed, as Master of the Groan Law, to take action, to stamp out, if necessary, a score of malcontents, but there was nothing clear—no tangible target—nothing definable upon which he could direct his fire. He only knew that were he to discover that Steerpike had in the smallest degree abused the grudging trust he had placed in him, then, bringing all his authority to bear, he would have the pallid snipe from the Tower of Flints—he would strike with merciless venom of the fanatic for whom the world holds no gradations, only the blind extremes of black and white. To sin was to sin against Gormenghast. Evil and doubt were one. To doubt the sacred stones was to profane the godhead. And there was this evil somewhere—close but invisible. His senses caught a whiff of it—but as soon as he turned his brain, as it were, over the shoulder of his mind, it was gone and there was nothing palpable—nothing but the hierophants moving here and there, upon this business or that, and seemingly absorbed.

Was there no way for him either to snare this wandering evil and turn its face to the light or to quell his suspicions? For they were harmful, keeping him awake through the long night hours, nagging at him, as though the castle's illness were his own.

"By the blood of hell," he whispered, and his whisper was like grit, "I will search it out, though it hide like a bat in the vaults or a rat in the southern lofts."

He scratched himself disgustingly, rumps and crutch, and again he shifted himself on the high chair.

It was then that the shadow that lay across the bookshelves moved a little. The shoulders appeared to rise as the whole silhouette shifted itself farther from the door and the impalpable body of the thing rippled across a hundred leather spines.

Barquentine's eyes took focus for a moment or two as they strayed over the documents on the table before him, and, unsolicited at the moment, the recollection of having once been married returned to him. What had happened to his wife he could not remember. He assumed that she had died.

He had no recollection of her face, but could remember—and perhaps it was the sight of the papers before him that had brought back the unwelcome memory—how, as she wept, she would, hardly knowing that she was doing so, make paper boats, which, wet with her tears and grimed from her cracked hands, she sailed across the harbor of her lap or left stranded about the floor or on the rope matting of her bed, in throngs like fallen leaves, wet, grimy, and delicate, in scattered squadrons, a navy of grief and madness.

And then, with a start he remembered that she had borne him a son. Or was it she? It was over forty years since he had spoken to his child. He would be hard to find; but found he must be. All he remembered was that a birthmark took up most of the face and that the eyes were crossed.

With his mind cast back to earlier days, a number of pictures floated hesitantly before his eyes, and in all of them he saw himself as someone with his head perpetually raised—as someone on a level with men's knees—as a target for jibes and scorn. He could see in the mind's eye the growth of hatred; he could feel again his crutch being kicked from beneath him, and hear the urchins hooting in his wake, "Rotten leg! Rotten spine!" "Ya! Ya! Barquentine!"

All that was over. He was feared now. Feared and hated.

With his back to the door and to the bookshelves he could not see that the shadow had moved again. He lifted his head and spat.

Picking up a piece of paper he began to make a boat, but he did not know what he was doing.

"It has gone on long enough," he said to himself, "too long, by the blood of hags. He must go. He is finished. Dead. Over. Done with. I must be alone, or by the cock of the great Ape, I'll jeopardize the Inner Secrets. He'll have the keys off me with his bloody efficiency."

And while he muttered in his own throat the shadow of the youth of whom he was speaking slid inexorably over the spines, and came to a stop a dozen feet from Barquentine, but the body of Steerpike was at the same moment immediately behind the cripple's chair.

It had not been easy for the young man to decide in what way he would kill his master. He had many means at his disposal. His nocturnal visits to the Doctor's dispensary had furnished him with a sinister array of poisons. His swordstick was almost too obviously efficacious. His catapult was no toy, but something lethal as a gun and silent as a sword. He knew of ways to break the neck with the edge of the palm, and he knew how to send a penknife through the air with extraordinary precision. He had not for nothing spent an allotted number of minutes every morning and for several years in throwing his knife at the dummy in his bedroom.

But he was not interested merely in dispatching the old man.

He had to kill him in some way which left no trace: to dispose of the body and at the same time to mix pleasure and business in such a compound that neither was the weaker for the union. He had old scores to pay off. He had been spat upon and reviled by the withered cripple. To merely stop his life in the quickest way would be an empty climax—something to be ashamed of.

But what really happened and how Barquentine really died in Steerpike's presence bore no relation to the plan which the young man had made.

For, as he stood immediately behind his victim's chair, the old man leaned forward across his books and papers and pulled toward himself a rusty, three-armed candle-stick, and after a great deal of scrabbling about among his rags, eventually set a light to the wicks. This had the double effect of sending Steerpike's shadow sidling across the book-filled wall and sucking the strength out of it.

From where Steerpike stood he could see over Barquentine's shoulder the honey-colored flames of the three candles. They were the shapes of bamboo leaves, attenuate and slender, and they trembled against the darkness. Barquentine himself was silhouetted against the glow of the candlelight, and suddenly, as his body shifted, and Steerpike obtained an even clearer view of the candle flame, an idea occurred to the young man which made all his carefully prepared plans for the death and disposal of the ancient's body appear amateurish: amateurish through lack of that deceptive simplicity which is the hall-mark of all great art; amateurish, for all their ingenuity, and for the very reason of it.

But here—here before him, ready-made, was a candle-stick with three gold flames that licked at the sullen air. And, here within his reach, was the old man he wished to kill, but not too quickly; an old man whose rags and skin and beard were as dry and inflammable as the most exacting of fire raisers could wish. What would be easier than for a man as ancient as Barquentine to lean forward accidentally at his work and for his beard to catch light from the candles? What would be more diverting than to watch the irritable and filthy tyrant caught among flames, his rags blazing, his skin smoking, his beard leaping like a crimson fish? It would only remain, at a later date, for Steerpike to discover the charred corpse and arouse the castle.

The young man glanced about him. The door through which he had entered the room was closed. It was an hour when there was small chance of their being disturbed. The silence in the room was only intensified by the thin grating of Barquentine's breathing.

No sooner had Steerpike realized the advantages of setting fire to the ragged silhouette which squatted like a black gnome immediately before him, than he drew the blade from his swordstick and raised it so that the steel point hovered within an inch of Barquentine's neck, and immediately below his left ear.

Now that Steerpike was so close upon the heels of the gross and bloody deed, a kind of cold and poisonous rage filled him. Perhaps the dry root of some long-deadened conscience stirred for a moment in his breast. Perhaps, for that sharp second, he remembered in spite of himself that to kill a man involved a sense of guilt: and perhaps it was because of the momentary distraction of purpose that hatred swept his face, as though a frozen sea were whipped of a sudden into a living riot of tameless water. But the waves subsided as quickly as they had risen. Once again his face was white with a deadly equipoise. The point of his blade had trembled beneath the age-bitten ear. But now it was motionless.

It was then that there was a knock at the door. The old head twisted to the sound, but *away* from the blade, so that Steerpike and his weapon were still invisible.

"To black hell with you whoever you are! I will see no son of a bitch today!"

"Very well, sir," said a door-blocked voice, and then the faint sound of footsteps could be heard, and then silence again.

Barquentine turned his head back, and then scratched himself across the belly.

"Saucy bullprong," he muttered aloud. "I'll have his face off him. I'll have his white face off! I'll have the shine off it! By the gall of the great mule he's overshiny. 'Very well, sir,' he says, does he? What's well about it? What's *well* about it? The upstart piss-worm!"

Again Barquentine began to scratch, loins, buttocks, belly, and ribs.

"O sucking fire!" he cried. "It gripes my heart! No Earl but a brat. The Countess, cat-mad. And for me, no tyro but this upstart of a Steerpike bastard."

The young man, his swordstick beautifully poised, its cold tip sharp as a needle, pursed his thin lips and clicked his tongue. This time Barquentine turned his head over his left shoulder so that he received half an inch of steel beneath his ear. His body stiffened horribly while his throat swelled into the semblance of a scream, but no scream came. When Steerpike withdrew the blade, and while a trickle of dark blood made its way over the wrinkled terrain of his turtle-neck, the whole frame became all of a sudden convulsively active, each part of him seeming to contort itself without relation to what was happening to the rest of the body. It was a miracle that he remained balanced on the high chair. But these convulsions suddenly ended and Steerpike, standing back with his chin cupped in his hands, was chilled, in spite of the half-smile on his face, by the direst expression of mortal hatred that had ever turned an old man's face into a nest of snakes. The eyes grew, of a sudden, congested, their vile waters taking on, it seemed, the flush of a dangerous sunrise. The mouth and the lines about it appeared to seethe. The dirty brow and neck were wet with venom.

But there was a brain behind it all. A brain which, while Steerpike stood by and smiled, was in spite of the young man's initial advantage, a step ahead of the youth. For the one thing without which he would indeed have been helpless was still in his power to capture. Steerpike had made a mistake at the outset. And he was taken completely by surprise when Barquentine, thrusting himself off the high chair, fell to the floor in a heap. The old man landed upon the object which was his only hope. It had fallen to the ground when he had stiffened at the sword-prick—and now in a flash he had grasped his chair, through the bars of which he directed his red gaze upon the face of his armed and agile enemy.

But the spirit in the old tyrant was something so intense that Steerpike, in spite of his two legs, his youth, and his weapons, was taken aback by the realization that so much passion could be housed in so dry and stunted a thing. He was also taken aback at having been outwitted. It was true that even now the duel was ludicrously one-sided—an ancient cripple with a crutch —an athlete with a sword—but nevertheless, had his first action been to remove the crutch, he would now have the old man in as helpless a position as a tortoise upon its back.

For a few moments they faced one another, Barquentine expressing everything in his face, Steerpike nothing. Then the young man began to walk slowly backward to the door, his eyes all the while on his quarry. He was taking no chances. Barquentine had shown how quick he could be.

When he reached the door he opened it and took a rapid glance along the attenuate corridor. It was enough to show him that there was no one in the neighborhood. He closed the door behind him and then began to advance toward the chair through the bars of which the dwarf was peering.

As Steerpike advanced with his slender steel in his hand, his eyes were upon his prey but his thoughts were centered upon the candlestick.

His foe could have no idea of how he was within reach of what would burn him up. The three little flames trembled above the melting wax. He had brought them to life, those three dead lumps of tallow. And they were to turn upon him. But not yet.

Steerpike continued his lethal advance. What was there that the cripple could do? For the moment he was partially shielded by the back of the chair. And then, in a voice strangely at variance with the demoniac aspect of his face, for it was as cold as ice, he uttered the one word, "Traitor."

It was not merely his life he was fighting for. That single word, freezing the air, had revealed what Steerpike had forgotten: that in his adversary he was pitting himself against Gormenghast. Before him he had a living pulse of the immemorial castle.

But what of all this? It merely meant that Steerpike must be careful. That he must keep his distance until the moment in which to make his attack. He continued to advance and then, when another step would have taken him within range of Barquentine's crutch, he side-stepped to the right and, speeding to the far end of the table, placed his rapier before him across the littered books and, taking his knife from his pocket, opened it with a single action and then, as Barquentine turned about in his tracks in order to face his assailant, he sent the sharp thing whipping through the candlelight. As Steerpike had intended, it pinned the old man's right hand to the shaft of his crutch. In the moment of Barquentine's surprise and pain, Steerpike leaped onto the table and sprang along it. Immediately below him the dwarf plucked at the knife in his blind fury. As he did so, Steerpike, all in a breath, snatched up the candlestick, and lunging forward, swept the tiny flame across the upturned face. In a moment, the lifeless beard shone out in sizzling fire and it was but a moment before the rotten rags about the shoulders of the old man were ablaze also.

But again, and this time while in the throes of mortal agony, Barquentine's brain had risen instantaneously to the call which was made upon it. He had no moment to lose. The knife was still in his hand though the crutch had fallen away—but all that was forgotten, as with a superhuman effort, one-legged though he was, he flexed his knee and in a spring caught hold of some portion of Steerpike's clothing. No sooner had he made his first grip than, with his arms straining themselves to breaking point, and his old heart pounding, he made good his purchase and began to swarm the youth like an ape on fire. By now he had a grip on Steerpike's waist and the flames were beginning to catch the clothing of his young enemy. The searing pain across his face and chest but made him cling the tighter. That he must die, he knew. But the traitor must die with him, and in his agony there was something of joy; joy in the "rightness" of his revenge.

At the same time, Steerpike was fighting to free himself, clawing at the burning leech, striking upward with his knees, his face transparent with a deadly mixture of rage, astonishment, and desperation.

His clothes, less inflammable than Barquentine's threadbare sacking, were nevertheless alight by now, and across his cheek and throat a flame had scorched his skin to crimson. But the more he struggled to wrench himself away the fiercer seemed the arms that gripped his waist.

Had anyone opened the door they would have seen, at

that moment, a young man luminous against the darkness, his feet striking and trampling among the sacred books that littered the table, the body writhing and straining as though demented, and they would have seen that his vibrating hands were locked upon the turtle-throat of a dwarf on fire: and they would have seen the paroxysm that toppled the combatants off the table's edge so that they fell in a smoking heap to the floor.

Even now in his pain and danger there was room in him for the bitter shame of his failure. Steerpike the arch-contriver, the cold and perfect organizer, had bungled the affair. He had been out-generaled by a verminous septuagenarian. But his shame took the form of desperate anger. It whipped him to a fever pitch.

In a kind of spasm, quite diabolical in the access of its ferocity and purpose, he struggled to his knees, and then with a jerk, to his feet. He had let go the throat and he stood swaying a moment, his hands free at his sides, and the pain of his burns so intense that, although he did not know it, he was moaning like something lost. It had nothing to do with his merciless nature, this moaning. It was something quite physical. It was his body crying. His brain knew nothing about it.

The Master of Ritual clung, like a vampire, at his breast. The old arms were clasped about him. Mixed with the pain in the agonized face, there was an unholy glee. He was burning the traitor with his own flame. He was burning an unbeliever.

But the unbeliever was, for all the fiery hugging of his master, by no means ready for sacrifice, however right or deserving his death might be. He had paused only to regain strength. He had dropped his arms only through an abnormal degree of control. He knew that he could not free himself from the clutch of the fanatic. And so for a moment he stood there, upright, his coat half burned away, his head thrust back to keep as great a distance as he could between his face and the flames that rose from the blackening creature that clung like a growth. To be able to stand for a moment under so horrific a duress—to be able to stand, to take a deep breath, and to relax the muscles of his arms—demanded an almost inhuman control of the will and the passions.

The circumstances having gone so far beyond his control, there was no longer any question of choice. It was no longer a case of killing Barquentine. It was a case of saving himself. His plans had gone so wildly astray that there was no recovery. He was ablaze.

There was only one thing he could do. Saddled as he was, his limbs were disencumbered. He knew that he had only a few moments in which to act. His head swam and a darkness filled him, but he began to run, his burned hands spread out like starfish at his sides, to run in a dizzy curve of weakness to the far end of the room—to where the night was a square of darkness. For a moment they were there, against the starless sky, lit like demons with their own conflagration, and then, suddenly, they were gone. Steerpike had hurdled the window sill and had fallen with his virulent burden into the black waters of the moat below. There were no stars, but the moon like a nail-paring floated unsubstantially in the low north. It cast no light upon the earth.

Deep in the horrible waters of the moat the protagonists, their consciousness having left them, still moved together as one thing, like some foul subaqueous beast of allegory. Above them the surface water through which they had fallen was sizzling and steam drifted up invisible through the darkness.

When, after what he could only recall as his death, Steerpike, his head having at last risen above the surface, found that he was not alone but that something clung to him below the water, he vomited and of a sudden, howled. But the nightmare continued and there was no answer to his howl. He did not waken. And then the excruciating pains of his burns racked him, and he knew it was no dream.

And then he realized what he must do. He must keep that charred and hairless head which kept bobbing against his breast, he must keep it below the water. But it was not easy for him to fasten upon the wrinkled throat. The mud had been churned up about them, and the burden he carried was, like his own hands, coated with slime. The vile arms clung about him with the tenacity of tentacles. That he did not sink like a stone was a wonder; perhaps it was the thickness of the water, or the violent stamping of his feet in the stagnant depth which helped him to keep afloat for long enough.

But gradually, inexorably, he fought the old head backward, his fierce hands clenched on the gullet strings—he fought it downward, down into the black water, while bubbles rose and the thick and slapping sound of the agitated water filled up the hollow of the listening night.

There was no knowing how long the old man's face remained under water before Steerpike could feel any loosening of the grip at his waist. To the murderer the act of death was endless. But by degrees the lungs had filled with water and the heart had ceased to beat, and the Hereditary Keeper of the Groan Lore and Master of Ritual had slid away into the muddy depths of the ancient moat.

The moon was higher in the sky, was surrounded by a sprinkling of stars. It could not be said that they gave light to the walls and towers that flanked the moat, but a kind of dusk was inlaid upon the inky darkness, a dusk in the shape of walls and towers.

Exhausted and in terrible pain, Steerpike had yet to swim on through the scum and duckweed—to swim on until the slimy walls of the moat gave way on the northern side to a muddy bank. It seemed that the walls on his either side were endless. The foul water got into his throat. The vile weeds clung to his face. It was difficult to see more than a few yards ahead; but all at once he realized that the wall upon his right had given way to a steep and muddy bank.

The water had drawn away what clothes the fire had left. He was naked, covered with burns, half drowned, his body shaking with an icy cold, his brow burning with a feverish heat.

Crawling up the bank, not knowing what he was doing, save that he must find some place of neither fire nor water, he came at last to a patch of level mud where a few rank ferns and mudplants flourished, and there, as though (now that his affairs were concluded) he could afford to faint, he collapsed into darkness.

And there he lay motionless, very small and naked on the mud, like something lifeless that had been discarded, or like a fish thrown up by the sea over whose minute and stranded body the great cliffs tower, for the walls of Gormenghast rose high above the moat, soaring like cliffs themselves into the upper darkness.

Chapter Forty

WHILE the dust that lay upon the gaunt back of the castle became warm in the sun, and the birds grew drowsy in the shadows of the towers, and while there was little to hear but the droning of the bees as they hovered over the wastes of ivy—at the same time, in the green hush of noon, the spirit of Gormenghast Forest held its breath like a diver. There was no sound. Hour followed hour and all things were asleep or in a state of trance. The trunks of the great oaks were blotched with honey-colored shadows and the prodigious boughs were stretched like the arms of bygone kings and appeared to be heavy with the weight of their gold bangles, the bracelets of the sun. There seemed to be no end to the gold afternoon, and then something fell from a high branch, and the faint swish of the leaves through which it passed awoke the region. The stillness had been for the moment punctured, but the wound healed over almost at once.

What was it that had fallen through the silence? Even the tree cat would have hesitated to drop so far through the green gloom. But it was no cat, but something human that stood dappled with leaf-shaped shadows, a child, with its thick hair hacked off close to its head and the face freckled like a bird's egg. The body, slender, indeed thin, appeared, when the child began to move, to be without weight.

The features of her face were quite nondescript—in fact, empty. It was as though she wore a kind of mask, neither pleasant nor unpleasant—something that hid rather than revealed her mind. And yet, at the same time, although by feature there was nothing to remember, nothing distinctive, yet the whole head was so set upon the neck, the neck so perfectly adjusted upon the slender shoulders, and the movements of those three so expressive in their relationship, that it seemed that there was not only nothing lacking, but that for the face to have had a life of its own would have ruined the detached and unearthly quality she possessed.

She stood there for a moment, entirely alone in the dreaming oak woods, and began, with strangely rapid movements of her fingers, to pluck the feathers from a missel thrush which, during her long fall through the foliage, she had snatched from its branch and throttled in her small fierce hand.

Chapter Forty-One

SURROUNDING the Outer Wall of Gormenghast Castle the mud city of the Outer Dwellers lay sprawled in the sun, its thousands of hovels hummocking the earth like molehills. These Dwellers, or Bright Carvers as they were sometimes called, had rituals of their own as sacrosanct as those of the castle itself.

Bitter with poverty and prone to those diseases that thrive on squalor, they were yet a proud though bigoted people. Proud of their traditions, of their power of carving—proud of their very misery, it seemed. For one of their number to have left them and to have become wealthy and famous would have been to them a cause for shame and humiliation. But such a possibility was unthinkable. In their obscurity, their anonymity, lay their pride. All else was something lower—saving only the family of the Groans to whom they owed allegiance and under whose patronage they were allowed their hold upon the Outer Walls. When the great sacks of crusts were lowered by ropes from the summit of those walls, over a thousand at a time making their simultaneous descents, they were received (this time-honored gesture on the part of the castle) with a kind of derision. It was they, the Bright Carvers, who were honoring the castle; it was they who condescended to unhook the ropes every morning of the year, so that the empty sacks might be hoisted up again. And with every mouthful of these dry crusts (which with the jarl root of the neighboring forest composed the beginning and end of their diet) they knew themselves to be conferring an honor upon the castle bakeries.

It was perhaps the pride of the subjugated—a compensatory thing—but it was very real to them. Nor was it built on nothing, for in their carvings alone they showed a genius for color and for ornament that had no kind of counterpart in the life of the castle.

Taciturn and bitter as they were in their ancient antipathies, yet their hottest enmity was directed, not against any that lived *within* the Outer Walls, but against those of their own kind who in any way made light of their own customs. At the heart of their ragged and unconventional life there was an orthodoxy as hard as iron. Their conventions were ice-bound. To move among them for a day without forewarning of their innumerable conventions would be to invite disaster. Side by side with an outrageous lack of the normal physical decencies was an ingrained prudery, vicious and unswervingly cruel.

For a child to be illegitimate was for that child to be loathed, as though it were a diseased thing. Not only this. A bastard babe was *feared*. There was a strong belief that in some way a love-child was evil. The mother would invariably be ostracized but it was only the babe who was to be feared—it was, in fact, a witch in embryo.

But it was never killed. For to kill, it would be only to kill the body. Its ghost would haunt the killer.

In a lane of flies that wound beneath a curve of the Outer Wall, the dusk began to settle down like pollen. It thickened by degrees until the lane and the irregular roofs of reeds and mud were drowned in it.

Along the wall of the lane or alleyway a line of beggars squatted. It seemed that they were growing out of the dust they sat in. It covered their ankles and their haunches. It was like a dead, gray sea. It was as though the tide were in—a tide of soft dust. It was voluptuously fine and feathery.

And in this common dove-colored dust they sat, their backs to the clay walls of a sun-warmed hovel. They had these luxuries, the soft dust and the warm fly-filled air.

As they sat there silently, while the night descended, their eyes were fixed upon those few figures on the other side of the alley who, their carving over for the day, were gathering up their chisels, rasps, and mallets and returning with them to their various huts.

Until a year ago there had been no need for the Bright Carvers to return their sculpture to the safety of their homes. It had remained all night in the open. It was never touched. No, not the meanest vandal of them all would dare to touch or move by an inch the work of another.

But now there was a difference. The carvings were no longer safe. Something horrible had happened. And so the beggars by the wall continued to stare as the removal of the wood sculpture proceeded. It had been going on now for twelve months, evening after evening, but they were not yet used to it. They could not grasp it. All their lives they had known the moonlight on the deserted lanes and, flanking these lanes, the wooden carvings like sentinels at every door. But now, after dark, the heart had gone out of the streets—a vibrancy, a beauty had departed from the alleys.

And so 'they still watched, at dusk, with a kind of hapless wonder, the younger men as they struggled to return the often massive and weighty horses with their manes like clusters of frozen sea foam, or the dappled gods of Gormenghast Forest with their heads so strangely tilted. They watched all this and knew that a blight had come upon the one activity for which the Dwellers lived.

They said nothing, these beggars, but as they sat in the soft dust, there was, at back of each one's mind, the image of a child. Of an illegitimate child, a pariah, a thing of not yet twelve years old, but a raven, a snake, witch, all the same, a menace to them all and to their carvings.

It had happened first about a year ago; that first midnight attack, secret, silent, and of a maliciousness quite terrible.

A great piece of sculpture had been found at dawn, its face in the dust, its body scarred with long, jagged knife wounds, and a number of small carvings had been stolen. Since that first evil and silent assault a score of works had been defaced and a hundred carvings stolen, carvings no bigger than a hand, but of a rare craftsmanship, rhythm, and color. There was no doubt as to who it was. It was the Thing. Shunned as a bastard ever since the day of her mother's suicide, this child had been a thorn in the flesh of the Dwellers. Running wild, like an animal, and as untamable; a thief as though by nature, she was, even before she ran away, a legend, a thing of evil.

She was always alone. It seemed unthinkable that she could be companioned. There was no soft spot in her self-sufficiency. She stole for her food, moving shadow-like in the night, her face utterly expressionless, her limbs as light and rapid as a switch of hazel. Or she would disappear completely for months on end, but then suddenly return and, darting from roof to roof, blister the evening air with sharp cries of derision.

The Dwellers cursed the day when the Thing was born;

the Thing that could not speak but could run, it was
rumored, up the stem of a branchless tree; could float
for a score of yards at a time on the wings of a high
wind.

They cursed the mother that bore her—Keda, the dark
girl, who had been summoned to the castle and who had
fed the infant Titus from her breast. They cursed the
mother, they cursed the child—but they were afraid,
afraid of the supernatural, and were oppressed with a
sense of awe—that the tameless Thing should be the
foster-sister of the Earl, Lord Groan of Gormenghast,
Titus the Seventy-Seventh.

Chapter Forty-Two

WHEN Steerpike had come out of his faint and when his
consciousness of the horrors through which he had passed
returned to him, as they did in a flash of pain, for he
was raw with the searings of the fire, he got to his feet
like a cripple and staggered through the night until he
came at last to the Doctor's doorway. There, after beating at the door with his feverish forehead, for his hands
were scalded, he fainted again where he stood and knew
no more until three days later when he found himself
staring at the ceiling of a small room with green walls.

For a long while he could recall nothing, but bit by
bit the fragments of that violent evening pieced themselves together until he had the whole picture.

He turned his head with difficulty and saw that the
door was to his left. To his right was a fireplace, and
ahead of him and near the ceiling was a fair-sized window over which the blinds were partially drawn. By the
dusky look in the sky he guessed it to be either dawn or
evening. Part of a tower could be seen through a gap of

the curtains, but he could not recognize it. He had no idea in what part of the castle he was lying.

He dropped his eyes and noticed that he was bandaged from head to foot, and as though he needed this reminder, the pain of his burns became more acute. He shut his eyes and tried to breathe evenly.

Barquentine was dead. He had killed him. But now, at the moment when he, Steerpike, should have been indispensable, being the sole confidant of the old custodian of the Law, he was lying here inert, helpless, useless. This must be offset, this derangement of his plans, by quick and authoritative action. His body could do little but his brains were active and resourceful.

But there was a difference. His mind was as acute as ever, it is true, but, unknown to himself, there was something that had been added to his temperament, or perhaps it was that something had left him.

His poise had been so shattered that a change had come about—a change that he knew nothing of, for his logical mind was able to reassure him that whatever the magnitude of his blunder in Barquentine's room, yet the shame was his alone, the mortification was private—he had only lost face to himself, for no one had seen the old man's quickness.

To have been so burned was too high a price to pay for glory. But glory would assuredly be his. The graver his condition the rarer his bravery in attempting to save the old man's life from the flames. His prestige had suffered nothing, for Barquentine's mouth was filled with the mud of the moat and could bear no witness.

But there was a *change* all the same, and when he was woken an hour later by a sound in the room, and when on opening his eyes he saw a flame in the fireplace, he started upright with a cry, the sweat pouring down his face, and his bandaged hands trembled at his sides.

For a long while he lay shuddering. A sensation such as he had never experienced before, a kind of fear, was near him, if not on him. He fought it away with all his reserves of undoubted courage. At last he fell again into a fitful sleep, and when some while later he awoke he knew before he opened his eyes that he was not alone.

Dr. Prunesquallor was standing at the end of his bed. His back was to Steerpike, his head was tilted up, and he was staring through the window at the tower that was now mottled with sunlight and the shadows of flying clouds. The morning had come.

Steerpike opened his eyes and on seeing the Doctor, closed them again. In a moment or two he had decided what to do, and turning his head to and fro slowly on the pillow, as though in restless sleep—"I tried to save you," he whispered, "Oh Master, I tried to save you," and then he moaned.

Prunesquallor turned around on his heel. His bizarre and chiseled face was without that drollery of expression which was so typical of him. His lips were set.

"You tried to save *who?*" said Prunesquallor very sharply as though to elicit some involuntary reply from the sleeping figure.

But Steerpike made a confused sound in his throat, and then in a stronger voice, "I tried . . . I tried."

He turned again on the pillow and then, as though this had awakened him, he opened his eyes.

For a few moments he stared quite blankly and then— "Doctor," he said, "I couldn't hold him."

Prunesquallor made no immediate reply but took the swathed creature's pulse, listened to the heart, and then after a while, "You will tell me about it tomorrow," he said.

"Doctor," said Steerpike, "I would rather tell you now. I am weak and I can only whisper, but I know where Barquentine is. He lies dead in the mud outside the window of his room."

"And how did he get there, Master Steerpike?"

"I will tell you." Steerpike lifted his eyes, loathing the bland physician—loathing him with an irrational intensity. It was as though his power of hatred had drawn fresh fuel from the death of Barquentine. But his voice was meek enough.

"I will tell you, Doctor," he whispered. "I will tell you

all I know." His head fell back on the pillow and he closed his eyes.

"Yesterday, or last week, or a month ago, for I do not know how long I have been lying here insensible—I entered Barquentine's room about eight o'clock, which was my habit every evening. It was at that hour that he would give me my orders for the next day. He was sitting on his high chair and as I entered he was lighting a candlestick. I do not know why but he started at my entrance, as though I had surprised him, but when he turned his head back again, after cursing me—but he meant no harm to me for all his irritability—he misjudged his distance from the flame, his beard swept across it and a moment later was alight. I rushed to him but his hair and clothing had already caught. There were no rugs or curtains in the room with which to smother the fire. There was no water. But I beat the flames with my hands. But the fire grew fiercer and in his pain and panic he caught hold of me and I began to burn."

The pupils of the young man's dark eyes dilated as he recounted the partial fabrication, for Barquentine's grip upon him had been no dream, and his brow began to sweat again, and a terrible authenticity appeared to give weight to his words.

"I could not escape, Doctor; I was caught and held against his burning body. Every moment the fire grew fiercer—and my burns more terrible. There was only one thing I could do to get away. I knew I must reach the water that lay below his window. And so I ran. I ran with his arms gripping me. I ran to the window and jumped into the moat—and there in the cold black water, his hands at last gave way. I could not hold him up. It was all I could do to reach the side of the moat, and there, I think I fainted—and when I came round, I found I was naked and I came to your door. But the moat must be dragged and the old man must be found—in the name of decency he must be found and given a true burial. It is for me to carry on his work. I . . . I . . . cannot tell . . . you more. . . I am . . . not . . ."

He turned his head on the pillow, and in spite of his pains fell asleep. He had played his card and could afford to rest.

Chapter Forty-Three

"My dear," said Bellgrove, "it is surely not for your betrothed to be kept waiting *quite* so long even though he is only the Headmaster of Gormenghast. Why on earth must you always be so late? Good grief, Irma, it isn't as though I'm a green youth who finds it romantic to be drizzled on by the stinking sky. Where have you been, for pity's sake?"

"I am inclined not to *answer* you!" cried Irma. "The humiliation of it! Is it nothing to you that I should take a pride in my appearance—that I should make myself beautiful for you? You *man,* you. It breaks one's heart."

"I do not complain lightly, my love," replied Bellgrove. "As I say, I cannot stand bad weather like a younger man. This was your idea of a place of rendezvous. It could hardly have been worse chosen, with not so much as a shrub to squat under. Rheumatism is on its way. My feet are soaked. And why? Because my fiancée, Irma Prunesquallor, a lady of quite exceptional talents in other directions—they always *are* in *other* directions—who has the entire day in which to pluck at her eyebrows, harvest her sheaves of long gray hair, and so on, cannot organize herself—or else has grown shall we say *casual* in regard to her suitor? Shall we say *casual,* my dear?"

"Never!" cried Irma. "Oh, never! my dear one. It is only my longing that you should find me worthy that keeps me at my toilet. Oh, my dearest, you must forgive me. You must forgive me."

Bellgrove gathered his gown about him in great

swathes. He had been staring into the gloomy sky while
he spoke but now, at last, he turned his noble face to her.
The landscape all about them was hazy with rain. The
nearest tree was a gray blur two fields away.

"You ask me to forgive you," said Bellgrove. He closed
his eyes. "And so I do, and so I do. But remember,
Irma, that a punctual wife would please me. Perhaps
you could practice a little so that when the time comes
I will have nothing to complain of. And now, we will
forget about it, shall we?"

He turned his head from her, for he had not yet
learned to admonish her without grinning weakly with the
joy of it. And so, with his face averted, he bared his
rotten teeth at a distant hedgerow.

She took his arm and they began to walk.

"My dear one," she said.

"My love?" said Bellgrove.

"It is my turn to complain, is it not?"

"It is your turn, my love!" (He lifted his leonine head
and shook the rain happily from his mane.)

"You won't be cross, dear?"

He raised his eyebrows and closed his eyes.

"I will not be cross, Irma. What is it that you wish
to say?"

"It's your neck, dearest."

"My neck? What of it!"

"It is very dirty, dear one. It has been for weeks . . .
do you think . . ."

But Bellgrove had stiffened at her side. He bared his
teeth in a snarl of impotence.

"Oh, stinking hell," he muttered. "Oh, stinking, rotten
hell."

Chapter Forty-Four

❈❈❈❈❈❈❈❈❈❈❈❈

MR. FLAY had been sitting for over an hour at the entrance to his cave. The air was breathless and the three small clouds in the soft gray sky had been there all day.

His beard had grown very long and his hair that was once cropped close to the skull was now upon his shoulders. His skin had darkened with the sun and the last few years of hardship had brought new lines to his face.

He was by now a part of the woods, his eyesight sharp as a bird's, and his hearing as quick. His footsteps had become noiseless. The cracking of his knee joints had disappeared. Perhaps the heat of the summer had baked the trouble out of them, for his clothes being as ragged as foliage, his knees were for the most part bare to the sun.

He must surely have been made for the woods, so congruously had he become dissolved into a world of branches, ferns, and streams. And yet for all his mastery of the woods, for all that he had been absorbed into the wilderness of the endless trees, as though he were but another branch—for all this, his thoughts were never far from that gaunt pile of masonry, that ruinous and forbidding as it was, was nevertheless, the only home he had ever known.

But Flay, for all his longing to return to his birthplace, was no sentimentalist in exile. His thoughts when they turned to the castle were by no means in the nature of reveries. They were hard, uneasy, speculative thoughts which, far from returning to his early memories of the place, were concerned with the nature of things as they were. No less than Barquentine, he was a tra-

325

ditionalist to his marrow. He knew in his heart that things were going wrong.

What chance had he had of taking the pulse of the halls and towers? Apart from the marshlight of his intuition and the native gloom of his temperament, on what else was he basing his suspicions? Was it merely his ingrained pessimism and the fear which had understandably grown stronger since his banishment, that, with himself away, the castle was the weaker?

It was this, and very little more. And yet had his fears been mere speculations he would never have made, during the last twenty days, his three unlawful journeys. For he had moved through the midnight corridors of the place—and although as yet he had made no concrete discoveries, he had become aware almost at once of a change. Something had happened, or something was happening, which was evil and subversive.

He knew full well that the risks involved in his being found in the castle after his banishment were acute, and that his chances of discovering in the darkness of sleeping halls and corridors the cause of his apprehension were remote indeed. Yet he had dared to flaunt the letter of the Groan Law in order, in his solitary way, to find whether or not its spirit, as he feared, was sickening.

And now, as he sat half hidden among the ferns that grew at the door of his cave, turning over in his mind those incidents that had in one way or another, over the past years, caused his suspicions of foul play to fructify, he was suddenly aware that he was being watched.

He had heard no sound, but the extra sense he had developed in the woods gave warning. It was as though something had tapped him between his shoulder blades.

Instantly his eyes swept the scene before him and he saw them at once, standing motionlessly at the edge of a wood away to his right. He recognized them instantaneously, although the girl had grown almost out of recognition. Was it possible that they did not recognize him? There was no doubt that they were staring at him. He had forgotten how different he must look, especially to Fuchsia, with his long hair, his beard, and ragged clothes.

But now, as they began to run in his direction, he stood up and began to make his way toward them over the rocks.

It was Fuchsia who first recognized the gaunt exile. Just over twenty years old, she stood there before him, a swarthy, strangely melancholy girl, full of love and fear and courage and anger and tenderness. These things were so raw in her breast that it seemed unfair that anyone should be so hotly charged.

To Flay, she was a revelation. Whenever he had thought of her it had always been as a child, and here suddenly she stood before him, a woman, flushed, excited, her eyes upon his face, her hands upon her hips, as she regained her breath.

Mr. Flay lowered his head in deference to his visitor. "Ladyship," he said—but before Fuchsia could answer Titus came up, his hair in his eyes.

"I told you!" he panted. "I told you I'd find him! I told you he had a beard and there's the dam he made and there's his cave over there and that's where I slept and where we cooked and . . . ." he paused for breath, and then, "Hullo, Mr. Flay. You look wonderful and wild!"

"Ah!" said Flay. "Most likely, Lordship, ragged life and no doubt of it. More days than dinners, Lordship."

"Oh, Mr. Flay," said Fuchsia. "I am so happy to see you again—you were always so kind to me. Are you all right out here, all alone?"

"Of course he's all right!" said Titus. "He's a sort of savage. Aren't you, Mr. Flay?"

"Like enough, Lordship," said Flay.

"Oh, you were too small and you can't remember, Titus," said Fuchsia. "I remember it all. Mr. Flay was Father's first servant—above them all, weren't you, Mr. Flay—until he disappeared—"

"I know," said Titus. "I've heard it all in Bellgrove's class—they told me all about it."

"They don't know anything," said Flay. "They don't know anything, Ladyship." He had turned to Fuchsia and then, dropping his head forward again, "Humbly invite you to my cave," he said, "for rest, for shade, and fresh water."

Mr. Flay led the way to his cave, and when they had passed through the entrance and Fuchsia had been shown the double chimney and they had drunk deeply from the spring, for they were hot and thirsty, Titus lay down under the ferny wall of the inner cave and their ragged host sat a little way apart. His arms were folded about his shanks; his bearded chin was on his knees—while his gaze was fixed upon Fuchsia.

She, on her side, while noticing his childlike scrutiny, gave him no cause to feel embarrassed, for she smiled when their eyes met, but kept her gaze wandering about the walls and ceiling, or turning to Titus asked him whether he had noticed this or that on his last visit.

But a time came when a silence fell upon the cave. It was the kind of silence that becomes hard to break. But it was broken in the end, and, strangely enough, by Mr. Flay himself, the least forthcoming of the three.

"Ladyship . . . Lordship," he said.

"Yes, Mr. Flay?" said Fuchsia.

"Been away, banished, many years, Ladyship." He opened his hard-lipped mouth as though to continue, but had to close it again for the lack of a phrase. But after a while he commenced again. "Lost touch, Lady Fuchsia, but forgive me—must ask you questions."

"Of course, Mr. Flay, what sort of questions?"

"I know the sort," said Titus. "About what's happened since I was last here and what's been discovered, isn't it, Mr. Flay? And about Barquentine's being dead and—"

"Barquentine dead?" Flay's voice was sudden and hard.

"Oh, yes," said Titus. "He was burned to death, you know, wasn't he, Fuchsia?"

"Yes, Mr. Flay. Steerpike tried to save him."

"Steerpike?" muttered the long, ragged, motionless figure.

"Yes," said Fuchsia. "He is very ill. I've been to see him."

"You haven't!" said Titus.

"I certainly have and I shall go again. His burns are terrible."

"I don't want you to see him," said Titus.

"Why not?" The blood was beginning to mount to her cheeks.

"Because he's—"

But Fuchsia interrupted him.

"What . . . do . . . you . . . know . . . about . . . him?" she said very softly and slowly, but with a shake in her voice. "Is it a crime for him to be more brilliant than we could ever be? Is it his fault that he is disfigured?" And then in a rush, "Or that he's so brave?"

She turned her eyes to her brother and seeing there, in his features, something infinitely close to her, something that seemed to be a reflection of her own heart, or as though she were looking into her own eyes—"I'm sorry," she said, "but don't let's talk about him."

But this is just what Flay wanted to do. "Ladyship," he said, "Barquentine's son—does he understand—has he been trained—Warden of the Documents—Keeper of the Groan Law—is all well?"

"No one can find his son, or whether he ever had a son," said Fuchsia. "But all is well. For several years now Barquentine has been training Steerpike."

Flay rose suddenly to his feet as though some invisible cord had plucked at him from above, and as he rose he turned his head to hide his anger.

"No! No!" he cried to himself, but there was no sound. Then he spoke over his shoulder.

"But Steerpike is ill, Ladyship?"

Fuchsia stared up at him. Neither she nor Titus could understand why he had suddenly got to his feet.

"Yes," said Fuchsia. "He was burned when he tried to save Barquentine, who was on fire—and he's been in bed for months."

"How much longer, Ladyship?"

"The Doctor says he can get up in a week."

"But the Ritual! The instructions; who has given them? Who has directed the Procedure—day by day—interpreted the Documents—O God!" said Flay, suddenly unable to control himself any longer. "Who has made the symbols come to life? Who has turned the wheels of Gormenghast?"

"It is all right, Mr. Flay. It's all right. He does not spare himself. He was not trained for nothing. He is covered in bandages but he directs everything. And all from his sickbed. Every morning. Thirty or forty men are there at a time. He interviews them all. Hundreds of books are at his side—and the walls are covered with maps and diagrams. There is no one else who can do it. He is working all the time, while he lies there. He is working with his brain."

But Flay struck his hand against the wall of the cave as though to let out his anger.

"No! No!" he said. "He's no Master of Ritual, Ladyship, not for always. No love, Ladyship, no love for Gormenghast."

"I wish there wasn't any Master of Ritual," said Titus.

"Lordship," said Flay after a pause, "you are only a boy. No knowledge. But you will learn from Gormenghast. Sourdust and Barquentine, both burned up," he continued, hardly knowing that he spoke aloud. "Father and son . . . father and son."

"Maybe I'm only a boy," said Titus hotly, "but if you know how we've come here today, by the secret passage under the ground (which I found by myself, didn't I, Fuchsia?), then . . ." But Titus had to stop, for the sentence was too involved for him.

"But do you know," he continued, starting afresh. "We've been in the dark, with candles, sometimes crawling but mostly walking all the way from the castle, except for the last mile where the tunnel comes out, only you'd never know it, under a bank, like the mouth of a badger's set—not too far from here—on the other side of the wood where you first saw us, so it was difficult to find your cave, Mr. Flay, because last time I came was mostly on horseback and then through the oak woods —and, oh, Mr. Flay, was it a dream or did I really see a flying thing and did I tell you about it? I sometimes think it was a dream."

"So it was," said Flay. "Nightmare; and no doubt of it." He seemed to have no desire to talk to Titus about the "flying thing."

"Secret tunnel to the castle, Lordship?"

"Yes," said Titus, "secret and black and smelling of earth and sometimes there are beams of wood to keep the roof up and ants everywhere."

Flay turned his eyes to Fuchsia as though for confirmation.

"It's true," said Fuchsia.

"And close by, Ladyship?"

"Yes," said Fuchsia. "In the woods across the near valley. That's where the tunnel comes out."

Flay stared at them both in turn. The news of the underground passage seemed to have had a great effect on him, although they could not think why—for although to them it had been a very real and forbidding adventure, yet from bitter experience they knew that what was wonderful to them was usually of little interest to the adult world.

But Mr. Flay was hungry for every detail. Where did the passage start from within the castle? Had they been seen in the Corridor of Statues? Could they find their way back to this corridor when the tunnel opened out into that silent and lifeless world of halls and passageways? Could they take him to the bank in the wood where the tunnel ended?

Of course they could. At once—and thrilled that a grownup, for Fuchsia never thought of herself as one, could be as excited by their discovery as they were themselves—they were on their way to the wood.

Flay had almost at once seen more in their discovery than Fuchsia and Titus could have guessed. If it were so, that within a few minutes of his cave there was, as it were, for Flay, an open door that led into the heart of his ancient home, a road which he could tread, if he wished, when the broad daylight lay upon the woods and fields five feet above his head, then surely his power to root out whatever evil was lurking in Gormenghast, to trace it to its source, was enormously increased. For it

had been no easy thing to enter the castle unobserved
and to make, sometimes by moonlight, those long journeys above ground from his cave to the Outer Wall
and from them across the quadrangles and open spaces
to the inner buildings and the particular rooms and passageways he had in mind.

But if what they said was true, he would, at any
time of the day or night, be able to emerge from behind
that statue in the Corridor of Carvings, to find the gaunt
anatomy of the place laid bare about him.

Chapter Forty-Five

THE days flowed on, and the walls of Gormenghast grew
chill to the touch as the summer gave way to autumn,
and autumn to a winter both dark and icy. For long
periods of time the winds blew night and day, smashing
the glass of windows, dislodging masonry, whistling and
roaring between towers and chimneys and over the
castle's back.

And then, no less awesome, the wind would suddenly
drop and silence would grip the domain. A silence that
was unbreakable, for the bark of a dog, or the sudden
clang of a pail, or the far cry of a boy seemed only
real in that they accentuated the universal stillness
through which, for a moment, they rose, like the heads
of fish, from freezing water—only to sink again and to
leave no trace.

In January the snow came down in such a way that
those who watched it from behind countless windows
could no longer believe in the sharper shapes that lay
under the blurred pall, or the colors that were sunk in
the darkness of that whiteness. The air itself was smothered with flakes the size of a child's fist, and the terrain

bulged with the submerged features of a landscape half
remembered.

In the wide, white fields that surrounded the castle,
the birds lay dead or leaned sideways, stiffening for death.
Here and there was the movement of a bird limping, or
the last frantic fluttering of a small ice-gummed wing.

From the castle windows it seemed that the dazzling
snow had been scattered with small coals, or that the
fields had become smallpox'd with the winter-murder'd
hosts. There was no clear stretch of snow untriturated
by this widespread death; no drift without its graveyard.

Against the blind brilliance of their background, the
birds, whatever their natural plumage, appeared as black
as jet, and differed only in their silhouettes, whose meticulous contours might have been scored with a needle,
so exquisite was the drawing of their beaks, like thorns,
the hairs of their feathers, their delicate claws and heads.

It seemed that, upon the vast funeral linen of the snow-
scape, each bird of all these hosts had signed, with an
exquisite and tragic artistry, the proof of its own death,
had signed it in a language at once undecipherable and
eloquent—a hieroglyphic of fantastic beauty.

And the snow that had killed them, covered them; covered them with a touch that was the more terrible for its
very tenderness. But for all its layer on layer of blinding
powder, there were always birds upon the point of death
—always this scattered, jet-black multitude. And on every
side there were still those that limped, or stood shiver-
ing, or pushed their agonizing way, breast-deep, through
the voluminous and lethal pall, leaving behind them their
little trenches in the snow to show where they had been.

And yet, for all this mortality, the castle was full of
birds. The Countess, her heart heavy in the knowledge
of so much thirst and pain, had taken every opportunity
to encourage the wildfowl to enter. No sooner had the
ice formed in the hundreds of baths and basins set about
the castle than it was broken again. Meat, bread crumbs,
and grain were laid in trails to encourage the birds to
enter the warmer air within the castle. And yet, in spite
of these enticements (and, fearless with hunger, thou-

sands of birds, including owls, heron, and even birds of prey were to be found within the walls), the castle was yet surrounded with the dead and dying. The severity of tho weather had made of the castle a focal point. Not only had the bird-life of the immediate region been drawn to Gormenghast, but the forests and moors of far-distant places had become empty. The sheer numbers of these migratory birds, descending snow-blind, famished, and deadly weary upon the castle—descending hourly, out of the snow-thick sky—were sufficient for so great a death roll, even though Gormenghast was open sanctuary.

The Countess had proclaimed (to the great inconvenience of those concerned) the dining hall to be their hospital. There, huge, red-haired, and solitary, she moved among them, nursing them back to strength. Branches of trees were brought in and propped against the walls. The tables were turned upside down so that those birds that cared to, could perch upon the upturned legs. After some while the place was loud with bird-song, with the strident shouting of crows and jackdaws, and with a hundred various thin or mellow voices.

What birds could be saved from the snow were saved, but it lay too deep and soft for it to be possible for any rescuing beyond the reach of an outstretched hand from a low window.

For a month or more the castle was snowbound. A number of the doors that opened on the outside world had been broken by the piled-up weight. Of those that stood the strain, none were usable. Lights burned everywhere within the walls of Gormenghast, for every window was either boarded up or heavily coated.

What Mr. Flay would have done had the underground tunnel never been discovered, or had Titus never told him of it, it is hard to say. The drifts about his cave were of such dangerous and voluminous dimensions, that it is doubtful whether he could have escaped being drawn sooner or later out of his depth. Apart from this, his chances of surviving the cruel cold, and of keeping himself from starving, would have been slender, for all his knowledge.

But all these problems were solved by the existence of the tunnel. It was now a commonplace for him to make his way, a candle in his hand, along its earth-smelling length, with its miles of roots and its floor littered with the skulls and bones of small animals. For many parts of the tunnel had been the retreat of foxes, rodents, and vermin of all kinds. It had been used both as a refuge from such weather as they were now experiencing and from their foes. His candle, held at arm's length before him, would light up familiar root formations that told him of a spinney overhead, or would disclose the secret cities of the ants.

Free of snow and invaluable as it was as a means of gaining access to the castle, yet the darkness was foul with death and decay, and there was no cause for Flay to linger on those long and friendless journeys below ground.

On the first occasion that he had emerged at the castle end of the tunnel and had followed the passageway and had come upon the outskirts of that region of lifeless halls and corridors, and when he had moved further into the silence, as Titus had done, he had felt something of the awe that had so terrified the boy, and he had lifted his bony shoulders up to his ears and thrust his jaw forward as his eyes turned this way and that as though he were being threatened by some invisible foe.

But when after a dozen daylight journeys he had explored a section of the deserted tract to his satisfaction, he retained no vestige of the apprehension that first affected him.

On the contrary, he began to make the silent halls peculiarly his own, in the way that he had unconsciously identified himself with the mood of Gormenghast Forest.

It was not in his nature to proceed hot-foot upon his quest for the castle's evil. These things could not be hurried. He must establish his position as he went along.

And so (after he had found the few steps that led up to the rear of the monument in the Corridor of Carvings), he confined his midnight journeys, for the first few weeks, to discovering what changes had taken place since

he had last`been in Gormenghast, in the nocturnal habits
of the populace. His life in the woods had taught him
patience and had made even more remarkable that power,
which he had always had, of losing himself against his
background. Saving for broad daylight he had no need
to hide; he had only to stand still and he was absorbed
into a wall, into a shadow, or into rotten woodwork.
When he lowered his head, his hair and beard were but
another cobweb in the gloom, and his rags the sunless
hart's-tongue that flourished in the dank gray corridors.

It was a strange experience for him to watch, from
one point of vantage or another, the familiar faces he
had once known so well. Sometimes they would pass within a few feet of him, some a little older, some a little
younger, some a little different from what he remembered; others, who were youths or boys when he was
exiled, now hardly recognizable.

But for all his ability to conceal himself, he took no
risks, and it was a long time before he made his long
midnight journeys of reconnaissance and began to discover where almost everyone of interest to him was likely
to be found at various hours of the day or night.

His late master's room had never been opened since
his death. Flay had noticed this with grim approval. He
had gazed down at the floor outside Sepulchrave's door,
where, for over twenty years, he had stretched himself
for sleep. And he had looked along the corridor and the
dreadful night returned to his mind—the night when the
Earl had walked in his sleep, and had later given himself
up to the owls—and the night when he, Flay, had fought
the Chef of Gormenghast and put him to the sword.

And Flay was forced to turn himself into both a thief
and a hoarder. This gave him little pleasure, but was
necessary in order that he should keep alive at all. Within a short time he had discovered how to enter the Cat
Room through the door of a loft, and to arrive at the
kitchen by way of the Stone Lanes.

It had become an absurdity for him to make his return journey every morning along the tunnel and to spend
the day in his cave. There was little he could do at

the cave, surrounded as it was with the deep snow-drifts. He could neither hunt for food nor gather enough fuel with which to warm himself. But in the Lifeless Halls there was all that he needed.

He had come across a small room, voluptuously soft with dust; a small, square place with a carved mantel-piece and an open grate. There were several chairs, a bookcase, and a walnut table on which, beneath the dust, the silver, glass, and crockery were laid out for two.

It was here that Flay established himself. His larder consisted of little more than bread and meat, fresh supplies of which were always plentiful in the Great Kitchen.

He took no advantage of the ample opportunities he had to vary his diet. As for his drinking water, it was only necessary for him to make his way at any hour after midnight and dip his iron can into the rain water of a near-by cistern.

Judging by the distances he had to cover during his journeys to and fro among the empty halls, and judging in particular by the distance between the room with the fireplace and the opening in the Corridor of Carvings (the only entrance he had found to the world he had previously known), he knew that lighting fires in his room involved no risk. Had smoke, for sake of argument, been *seen* to rise into the air above a forgotten tract of the castle, and were it to have caused any interest, it would have been as easy for the hypothetical observer to have found the chimney and then to have found a way into the compartment, fathoms below, as for a frog to play the fiddle.

There, on the bitter winter evenings, Mr. Flay enjoyed a comfort he had never experienced before. Had his exile in the woods not inured him to loneliness, then he must surely have found these long days insupportable. But isolation was now a part of him.

The silence of the Lifeless Halls, like the silence of the snow-bound world outside, was limitless. It was a kind of death. The very extent of the hollow expanses, the uncharted labyrinth that made, as it were, the silence visible, was something to raise the hairs upon the neck of any

but those long used to loneliness. And Mr. Flay, in spite
of his numerous expeditions through this dead world,
this forgotten realm of Gormenghast, was nevertheless
unable to locate its boundaries. It is true that after a
long search, guided to some extent by Titus's instructions, he had found the steps that led up the Corridor of
Carvings, but save for this and the few locked doors
through which he had heard voices, he had found no
other frontier points between his world and theirs.

But in the small hours of one morning, as he returned
to his room after a raid upon the kitchen, something
happened which turned the rest of his winter into something less isolated but more terrible. He had left the
Corridor of Carvings a mile or more behind, and was deep
in his own realm, when he decided that instead of taking
his usual path along the usually narrow and extended
passageway to the east, he would explore an alternative
corridor which, he imagined, would in its own good time
lead to his own district.

As he proceeded he made, upon the wall, following
his usual custom, the rough marks with white chalk which
had more than once helped him to find his way back to
familiar ground.

After about an hour of twisting and turning, of crossing
the open junctions of radiating alleyways, of making a
hundred arbitrary choices between this entrance and that,
this winding descent and that cold incline to a wider passageway—he began to sweat with fear at the very thought
of having taken no precautions for his return journey.
He knew that he would never have found his way back
without the chalk marks. Suddenly he began to feel
hungry. At the same time, noticing that his candle was
burning low, he drew another from the half-dozen or more
that were always in his belt, and sitting down on the floor,
placed his freshly lit candle carefully on the ground before him, and opening a long, narrow-bladed knife, began
to cut himself a slice of bread.

To his right and left the darkness was as thick as ink.
He sat illumined within the aura of candle flame, his
face and rags and hands and hair dramatically lit. Be-

hind him on the wall his shadow hovered heavily. He had stretched out his legs before him and was about to sink his teeth for the second time into the bread when he heard the peal of laughter.

Had it not been for its terrible strength and for the fact that it came from *behind* him—from the other side of the wall against which he leaned—he would have had no option but to recognize it as a cry of madness in his own brain—something that he had heard with the ears of his mind.

But there was no question of this. It had nothing to do with him, or his imagination; he was not mad. But he knew that he was in the presence of madness. For the demoniacal cry or howl was something that brought Flay to his feet as though he were drawn upward on a fishhook —something that took him, without his knowing that he had moved, to the opposite side of the passage where, flattened against the wall as though at bay, and with his head lowered, he stared at the cold bricks against which he had been leaning, as though the wall itself were affected by the lunacy it was hiding and was watching him, its every brick deranged.

Mr. Flay could hear his sweat splashing on the stones at his feet. His mouth was leather-dry. His heart was thumping like a drum. And he had nothing to see. Only the candlelight shining steadily at the base of the opposite wall.

And then it came again, with a kind of double note— almost as though whatever throat it was that was giving vent to this ghastly laughter was curiously formed—as though it were able to throw out two voices at once.

There was no question of an echo for there was no repetition and no overlapping—but a kind of duplex horror.

This time, the high pealing note tailed off into a thin whine, but even in this ghostly termination there was the twofold quality, the terrible, petrifying sense of double madness.

For some while after silence had returned, Mr. Flay could not move. He had been struck. His sense of privacy had been shattered; his inability to rationalize and make sense out of the small hours was like an insult, an insult hurled against his narrow but proud mind. And his fear, his naked fear of something he could not see, but something which was within a few yards of him—it was this that froze his limbs.

But the silence continued and there was no repetition, and at last he picked the candle from the floor, and with more than one glance behind him, he moved rapidly back the way he had come, following the chalk marks until at last he arrived at the fateful parting of the ways. Thereafter he was on his own ground and he strode it without hesitation until he arrived at his room.

It was, of course, impossible to let the matter rest. The enigmatic horror of that laughter was with him all the time, and no sooner had the sun risen on the following day than the grim place drew him. It was not that he wished to indulge himself with the vile thrill of a repetition, but rather that the mystery should be brought forward into the rational daylight, and that whatever it was, beast or human, it must stand revealed, for his deepest interests were those of the one-time first servant of Gormenghast—of a loyalist who could not bear to think that in the ancient castle there were forces or elements at work, happenings that were apart from the ceremonial life, secrets and practices that, for all he knew, were deadly poison in the castle's body.

It was his intention to explore further along the terrifying passage, and if possible to double back down some parallel artery when opportunity offered, and so discover, if he could, some clue to what lay on the other side of the wall.

And this is what he did, but with no success. Day after day he threaded his way through the cold brick lanes, crossing and recrossing his own tracks, losing himself a score of times a day—returning over and over again to the original corridor for reference—unable to comprehend the tortuous character of the architecture. Every now and again, on returning to the place where he had heard the wild laughter, he listened, but there was never any sound but the beating of his own heart.

There seemed no other way for him but to come again to that dread place, not in the daylight, but at the selfsame time as before, when the small hours of the morning sucked the courage from heart and limb. If he should hear it again, that crazed laughter, and if it was repeated and repeated, then with that sound to guide him it was possible that he could run to earth, in the darkness, what had foiled him by day.

And so, fighting down his terror, he set out in the icy blackness of the early hours. He came eventually to the brick corridor; and when he was still some distance away he heard a sound of crying and shouting. And when he was nearer still, a loud calling to and fro, as if something were calling to itself, for it seemed to be the same voice that was answering.

But there was fear in the voice, or voices, and what struck Mr. Flay most, as he listened with his ear to the wall, was that the cries were weaker than before. Whatever it was that cried had lost a lot of strength. But it was in vain that he tried to trace the sounds to their source. His questings through those same mazes of masonry that he had searched by daylight were fruitless. Directly he had left the corridor, the silence came down like an impalpable weight and the sharpness of his hearing was of no avail.

Again and again he did all in his power to locate the suffering creature, for Flay had begun to realize that it was nearing the end of its strength. It was not so much terror that he now felt as a blind pity. A pity that drew him to the place night after night. It was as though he had this nameless tragedy upon his conscience; as though his being there to listen to the weakening voice was in some way helpful. He knew that this was not so, but he could not keep away.

The night came when for all his listening there was no sound, and from that time onward the silence remained unbroken.

He knew that in some way the end had come to some

demented thing. What it was that had laughed with that
double note, that had cried out and answered itself
with the same flat and terrible voice, he never knew. He
never knew that he was the last to hear the voices of
their Ladyships Cora and Clarice, nor that he had been
within a few feet of those apartments into which they had
once been lured. He never knew that behind the locked
doors of this place of incarceration the twins had languished, their brains losing what grip they had, their
madness mounting, until, when their provisions began to
fail them, and Steerpike no longer came, they knew that
Death was on his way.

When weakness overpowered them they lay down side
by side and, staring at the ceiling, they died at the same
moment, on the other side of the wall.

Chapter Forty-Six

WHILE Flay, in his wilderness of hollow halls, was brooding upon the shock he had sustained, and fretting at its
insoluble nature, Steerpike, now up and about once more,
was losing no time in establishing his position as Master
of Ritual. He was under no illusions as to what the reaction of the castle would be, when it became borne in
upon them that he was performing no stop-gap office.
To neither be old, nor to be the son of Barquentine, nor
one of the accepted school of hierophants, nor indeed
to have any claim upon the title, save that of being the
only disciple of the drowned cripple's, and of having the
brains to perform the onerous office, was anything but an
encouraging inception.

Nor was he, physically, any longer personable. His
hunched shoulders, his pallor, his dark-red eyes had never
encouraged intimacy, even supposing he had ever courted

it. But now, how much the more so was he likely to be shunned, even in a society that laid no claim to beauty?

The burns upon his face and neck and hands were there to stay. Only the worms could put an end to them. The effect of the face was of something skewbald; the taut crimson tissue, forming fiery patterns against the waxlike pallor of his skin. His hands were blood-red and silky; their creases and wrinkles like those on the hand of a monkey.

And yet he knew that although he created a natural revulsion among those about him, the reason for his disfigurement stood in his favor. It was he who had (as far as the castle knew) risked his life to save the hereditary Master. It was he who had suffered delirium and excruciating pain because he had had the courage to try and wrest from death's grip a keystone of the Gormenghast tradition. How, in that case, could his diabolical appearance be held against him?

And what is more he knew, however prejudiced his opponents might be, that in the end they had no option but to accept him, in spite of his burns, his background, and the unproven rumors which he knew were in constant circulation—to accept him, for the simple reason that there was no one else with the necessary knowledge at his fingertips. Barquentine had divulged his secrets to no one else. The very tomes of cross reference would have been beyond the powers of even the most intelligent of men to comprehend, unless, as a preliminary, he were schooled to the symbols involved. The principle upon which the arrangement of the Library was based was, in itself, something which had taken Steerpike a year to unravel, even with Barquentine's irritable guidance.

But cunningly and by slow degrees, as he went about his work, he evoked a grudging acceptance and even a kind of bitter admiration. By not so much as a hair's breadth did he deviate from those thousand letters of the Groan Law, that day by day in one form of ritual or another, were made manifest. With every evening he knew himself more deeply entrenched.

His miscalculation over Barquentine's murder had been

unforgivable and he did not forgive himself. It was not so much what had happened to his body that galled him, but that he should ever have blundered. His mind, al-always compassionless, was now an icicle—sharp, lucent, and frigid. From now onward he had no other purpose than to hold the castle ever more tightly in the scalded palm of his hand. He knew that his every step must be taken with the utmost precaution. That although, on the face of it, the life of Gormenghast was, in spite of its rigid tradition, a dark and shambling affair, yet there was always this consciousness beneath the surface; there were those that watched and there were those that listened. He knew that in order to fulfill his dreams he must devote, if necessary, the next ten years to the consolidation of his position, taking no risk, learning all the while, and building up a reputation not only as an authority on all that pertained to the traditions of the place, but as someone who, indefatigable in his zeal, was nevertheless difficult to approach. This would both leave what free time he had for his own purposes, and help to create for himself the legend of a saint, someone removed, someone beyond questioning, for whom, in his early days, the tests of fire and water had not been too terrible to endure when the soul of Gormenghast was in jeopardy.

The years lay spread before him. To the younger generation he would be a kind of god. But it was now in the diligence and exactness of his offices that he must carve for himself the throne that he would one day occupy.

For all the evil of his early years he knew that, though from time to time he had been suspected of insurrection and worse, yet now with his feet well set upon the gold road of advancement, he was (with the darkest of his deeds but a week or two behind him) as free as ever he had been from any question of being unmasked.

He was now close upon twenty-five years old. The fire that had mottled his face had taken no lasting toll of his strength. He was now as wiry and tireless as before the catastrophe. He whistled to himself, between his teeth, tunelessly as he stood at the window of his room and stared out across the snow.

It was midday. Against a dark sky, Gormenghast Mountain, for all its ruggedness, was swathed as white as wool. Steerpike stared through it. In a quarter of an hour he would be on his way to the stables, where the horses would be lined up for his inspection. It being the anniversary of the death of a nephew of the Fifty-Third Countess of Groan, in his day a daring horseman, he would see that the grooms were in mourning and that the traditional equine masks were being worn at the correct angle of dejection.

He held up his hands and placed them before him against the windowpane. Then he spread them out like starfish, and examined his nails. Between the scarlet fingers and all about them was the white of the distant snow. It was as though he had placed his hand upon white paper. Then he turned and crossed the room to where his cape was folded over the back of a chair. When he had left the room and had turned the key and was on his way down the stairway, his mind turned for a moment to the twins. It had been an untidy business in many ways, but perhaps it was as well that circumstances beyond his control had forced the solution. Even at the time of his burns, the restocking of their larder had been long overdue. By now they could no longer be alive.

He had gone through his papers, and had refreshed his memory as to exactly what provisions they were likely to have left on the day of his burning, and from his none too simple calculations, he had deduced that they must have died from starvation on about that day when, swathed like a ragged pipe in frosty weather, he first rose from his sickbed. In point of fact they had died two days later.

Chapter Forty-Seven

❄❄❄❄❄❄❄❄❄❄

I

As the days went by, Titus was becoming more and more difficult to control. In the long dormitories where after dark the boys of his own age would light their shielded candles, squat in groups, perform strange rites, or eat their pilfered cakes, Titus was no watcher of the scene. He was no mere watcher from the safety of his bed, when, in fierce and secret grapple, old scores were settled in deathly silence while, in his cubicle by the dormitory door, the formidable janitor slept like a crocodile upon his back. The erratic breathing of this man, his tossings and turnings, his very wheezings and mutterings were an open book to Titus and his confederates. They all conveyed a certain *depth* of sleep, which at its deepest was shallow enough. But it was silence that they feared, for silence meant that his eyes were open in the darkness.

As sacred as the fact that there had always been an Earl of Gormenghast and always would be, and that when the time came he would be virtually unapproachable, a man out of range both socially and for reason of his intrinsic *difference*—as sacred as all this, was the tradition that as a boy the Earl of Gormenghast must be in no way treated as something apart. It was the pride of the Groans that their childhood was no time of cotton-wool.

As for the boys themselves, they found little difficulty in putting this into practice. They knew that there was no difference between themselves and Titus. It was only later that they would think otherwise. And in any case what a child may become in his later years is of little

346

interest to his friends or his foes. It is the world of
here and now that matters most. And so Titus fought with
the rest in the breathless dormitory—and from time to
time was caught out of his bed and was caned by the
janitor.

He took the risk and he took the punishment. But he
hated it. He hated the ambiguity of it all. Was he a lord
or an urchin? He resented a world in which he was
neither one thing nor another. That his early trials
would fit him for his responsibilities in later life made no
appeal to him. He was not interested in his later life,
and he was not interested in having responsibilities.
Somehow or other the whole thing was unfair.

And so he said to himself: "All right! So I'm the same
as anyone else, am I? Then why do I have to report to
Steerpike every evening, in case I'm lost? Why do I have
to do extra things after classes—when none of the others
have to? Turning keys in rotten old locks. Pouring wine
all over turrets—walking here and there until I'm tired!
Why should I do all this extra if I'm not any different?
It's a rotten trick!"

The Professors found him difficult, wayward, and on
occasions, insolent. All except Bellgrove, for whom
Titus had a fondness and an inexplicable respect.

II

"Are you thinking of doing any work this afternoon,
or were you planning to spend it in chewing that end of
your pen, dear boy?" asked Bellgrove, leaning forward
over his desk and addressing Titus.

"Yes, sir!" said Titus with a jerk. He had been far
away, in a daydream.

"Do you mean, 'Yes, sir, I'm going to work' or 'Yes,
sir, I'm going to chew my pen,' dear boy?"

"Oh, *work*, sir."

Bellgrove flicked a lock of his mane back over his
shoulder with the end of his ruler.

"I am *so* pleased," he said. "You know, my young

friend, that one day when *I* was about your age, I was suddenly taken with the idea of concentrating upon the paper which my old schoolmaster had set me. I don't know what gave me the idea. I had never thought of doing such a thing before. I had *heard* of people who had tried it, you know—of paying attention, of putting their minds to the work in hand—but I had never thought of doing it *myself*. But—and here you must listen, my dear boy—what happened? I will tell you. I found that the paper which my dear master had set me was quite, quite simple. It was almost an insult. I concentrated more than ever. When I had finished I asked for more. And then more again. All my answers were quite perfect. And what happened? I became so fascinated at finding I was so clever, that I did too much and *became ill*. And so I warn you—and I warn the whole class. Take care of your health. Don't overdo it. Go slow—or you may have a breakdown just as I had, long ago, when I was young, dear boys, and ugly, just as you are, and just as dirty, too, and if you haven't got your work finished by four o'clock, Master Groan, my dear child, I shall be forced to keep you in until five."

"Yes, sir," said Titus, and at that moment he felt a dig in the back. Turning, he found that the boy behind him was passing him a note. He could not have chosen a much worse moment for it, but Bellgrove had closed his eyes in a resigned and lordly way. When Titus unfolded the scrap of paper, he found it was no message but a crude caricature of Bellgrove chasing Miss Irma Prune-squallor with a long lasso in his hand. It was very feebly drawn and not particularly funny, and Titus, who was in no mood for it, felt suddenly angry, and screwing it up, threw it back over his shoulder. This time Bellgrove's attention was caught by the pellet.

"What was that, dear boy?"

"Just a screwed-up bit of paper, sir."

"Bring it up here, to your old master. It will give him something to do," said Bellgrove. "He can work away at it with his old fingers, you know. After all, there is nothing much he can do until the class ends." And then, musing aloud, "Oh, babes and sucklings . . . babes and sucklings . . . how tired of you your old Headmaster gets."

The pellet was retrieved and passed to Titus, who got up from his desk. And then, suddenly, when he had approached to within a few feet of the Headmaster's desk, he put the screwed-up drawing into his mouth, and with a gulp, swallowed it.

"I've swallowed it, sir."

Bellgrove frowned, and an expression of pain flitted across his noble face.

"You will stand on your desk," he said. "I am ashamed of you, Titus Groan. You will have to be punished."

When Titus had been standing on his desk for a few minutes he received another tap upon the back. He had already been in trouble through the stupidity of the boy behind, and in a flash of anger, "Shut up!" he cried, and swinging around at the same instant found himself staring at Steerpike.

The young Master of Ritual had come silently through the door of the schoolroom. It was his duty to make a periodic round of the classes, and it was an understood thing that in this official capacity it was not for him to knock before he entered. Only a few boys had noticed Steerpike's arrival, but the whole class turned at the sound of Titus's voice.

Gradually it dawned upon the class that the reason for the stiff, frozen position that Titus was in, his head turned sharply over his shoulder, his body swiveled around on the narrow pivot of his hips, his hands clenched, his head lowered angrily—that the reason for his tenseness was that his "Shut up!" must have been addressed to none other than the man with the skewbald face, Steerpike himself.

Standing upon the lid of his desk, Titus was in the unusual position of looking down at the face of this authority, who had suddenly appeared as though out of the floor, like an apparition. The face looked up at him, a wry smile upon the lips, the eyebrows raised a little, and a certain expectancy in the features, as though denoting that although Steerpike realized that it was impossible for the boy to have guessed who it was that had tapped him on the back, and was therefore guiltless of insolence, yet, an apology was called for. It was unthinkable that the Master of Ritual should be spoken to in this way by anyone—let alone a small boy—whatever his lineage.

But no apology came. For Titus, directly he realized what had happened—that he had cried, *"Shut up!"* to the arch-symbol of all the authority and repression which he loathed—knew instinctively that this was a moment in which to dare the blackest hell.

To apologize would be to submit.

He knew in the darkness of his heart's blood that he must not climb down. In the face of peril, in the presence of officialdom, age-old and vile, with its scarlet hands, and its hunched shoulders, he must not climb down. He must cling to his dizzy crag until, trembling but triumphant in the enormous knowledge of his victory, he stood once more upon solid ground, secure in the knowledge that as a creature of different clay he had not sold his birthright out of terror.

But he could not move. His face had gone white as the paper on the desk. His brow was sticky with sweat and he was heavy with a ghastly tiredness. To cling to his crag was enough. He had not the courage to stare into the dark-red eyes that, with the lids narrowed across them, were fixed upon his face. He had not the courage to do this. He stared over the man's shoulder, and then he closed his eyes. To refuse to say he was sorry was all that his courage could stand.

And then, all at once he felt himself to be standing at a strange angle, and opening his eyes he saw the rows of desks begin to circle in formation through the air, and then a far voice shouted as though from miles away as he fell heavily to the floor in a dead faint.

Chapter Forty-Eight

✵✵✵✵✵✵✵✵✵✵✵

"I am having the most moving time, Alfred. I said I am having the most *moving* time—are you listening or not? Oh, it's *too* galling the way a woman can be courted so splendidly, so nobly by her lover, only to find that her own brother is about as interested as a fly upon the wall. Alfred, I said a fly upon a *wall!*"

"Flesh of my flesh," said the Doctor after a pause (he had been lost in rumination), "what is it that you want to know?"

"Know," answered Irma, with a superb scorn. "Why should I want to *know* anything?"

Her fingers smoothed the back of her iron-gray hair, and then of a sudden, pounced upon the bun at the nape of her neck, where they fiddled with an uncanny dexterity. It might have been supposed that her long nervous fingers had an eye apiece, so effortlessly did they flicker to and fro across the contours of the hirsute knob.

"I was not *asking* you a question, Alfred. I sometimes have thoughts of my own. I sometimes make *statements*. I know you think very little of my intellect. But not everyone is like you—I can assure you. You can have no idea, Alfred, of what is being done to me. I am being drawn out. I am finding treasures in myself. I am like a rich mine, Alfred. I know it, I know it. And I have brains I haven't even used yet."

"Conversation with you, Irma," said her brother, "is peculiarly difficult. You leave no loops, dear one, at the end of your sentences, nothing to help your loving brother, nothing for his ever-willing, ever-eager, ever-shining hook. I always have to start afresh, sweet trout.

I have to work my passage. But I will try again. Now, you were saying?"

"Oh, Alfred. Just for one moment, do something to please me. Talk *normally*. I am so tired of your way of saying things with all its figures of eight."

"Figures of *speech!* Speech! Speech!" cried the Doctor, rising to his feet and wringing his hands. "Why do you always say figures of *eight?* Oh, bless my soul, what is the matter with my nerves? Yes, of course I'll do something to please you. What shall it be?"

But Irma was in tears, her head buried in a soft gray cushion. At last she raised it, and taking off her dark glasses, "It's too *much,*" she sobbed. "When even one's brother snaps one up. I did trust *you!*" she shouted. "And now *you're* letting me down too. I only wanted your advice."

"Who has let you down?" said the Doctor sharply. "Not the Headmaster?"

Irma dabbed her eyes with an embroidered handkerchief the size of a playing card.

"It's because I told him his neck was dirty, the dear, sweet lord—"

"*Lord!*" cried Prunesquallor. "You don't call him *that,* do you?"

"Of course not, Alfred . . . only to myself . . . after all he is my lord, isn't he?"

"If you say so," said her brother, passing his hand across his brow. "I suppose he could be anything."

"Oh, he is. He is. He's anything—or rather, Alfred, he's everything."

"But you have shamed him, and he feels wounded—proud and wounded, is that it, Irma, my dear?"

"Yes, oh, yes. It is that exactly. But what can I *do?* What can I *do?*"

The Doctor placed the tips of his fingers together.

"You are experiencing already, my dear Irma," he said, "the stuff of marriage. But so is he. Be patient, sweet flower. Learn all you can. Use what tact God gave you, and remember your mistakes and what led up to them. Say nothing about his neck. You can only make things worse. His resentment will fade. His wound will heal in time. If you love him, then simply love him and never fuss about what's dead and gone. After all you love him in spite of all *your* faults, not *his*. Other people's faults can be fascinating. One's own are dreary. Be quiet for a bit. Don't talk too much. And can't you walk a little less like a buoy in a swell?"

Irma got up from her chair and moved to the door.

"Thank you, Alfred," she said, and disappeared.

Dr. Prunesquallor sank back on the couch by the window, and with an ease quite astonishing, dismissed his sister's problem from his mind and was once more in the cogitative reverie from which she had interrupted him.

He had been thinking of Steerpike's accession to the key position that he now occupied. He had also been reflecting upon the way he had behaved as a patient. His fortitude had been matchless and his will to live quite savage. But for the most part, the Doctor was turning over in his mind something that was quite different. It was a phrase which, at the height of Steerpike's delirium, had broken loose from the chaos of his ravings: *"And the twins will make it five,"* the young man had shouted. *"And the twins will make it five."*

Chapter Forty-Nine

I

ONE dark winter morning, Titus and his sister sat together on the wide window seat of one of Fuchsia's three rooms that overlooked the South Spinneys. Soon after Nannie Slagg had died Fuchsia had moved, not without much arguing and a sense of dire uprooting, to a more handsome district—and to a set of rooms which, in comparison with her old untidy bedroom of many memories, were full of light and space.

Outside the window the last of the snow lay in patches across the countryside. Fuchsia, with her chin on her hands and her elbows on the window sill, was watching the swaying motion of the thin stream of steel-gray water as it fell a hundred feet from the gutter of a nearby building—for a small, restless wind was blowing erratically and sometimes the stream of melted snow as it fell from the high gutter would descend in a straight and motionless line to a tank in the quadrangle below, and sometimes it would swing to the north and stay outstretched when a gust blew angrily, and sometimes the cascade would fan out in a spray of innumerable leaden drops and fall like rain. And then the wind would drop again and the steady tubular overflow would fall once more vertically, like a stretched cable, and the water would spurt and thud within the tank.

Titus, who had been turning over the pages of a book, got to his feet.

"I'm glad there's no school today, Few," he said—it was a name he had started giving her—"it would have been Perch-Prism with his foul chemistry and Cutflower this afternoon."

"What's the holiday *for?*" said Fuchsia, with her eyes still on the water which was now swaying to and fro across the tank.

"I'm not sure," said Titus. "Something to do with Mother, I think. Birthday or something."

"Oh," said Fuchsia, and then after a pause, "It's funny how one has to be told everything. I don't remember her having birthdays before. It's all so inhuman."

"I don't know what you mean," said Titus.

"No," said Fuchsia. "You wouldn't, I suppose. It's not your fault and you're lucky in a way. But I've read quite a lot and I know that most children see a good deal of their parents—more than we do anyway."

"Well, I don't remember Father at *all,*" said Titus.

"I do," said Fuchsia. "But he was difficult too. I hardly ever spoke to him. I think he wanted me to be a boy."

"Did he?"

"Yes."

"Oh . . . I wonder why."

"To be the next Earl, of course."

"Oh . . . but *I* am . . . so it's all right, I suppose."

"But he didn't know you were going to be born, when *I* was a child, did he? He couldn't have. I was about fourteen when you were born."

"Were you really?"

"Of course I was. And for all that time he wished I were you, I suppose."

"That's funny, isn't it?" said Titus.

"It wasn't funny at all—and it isn't funny now—is it? Not that it's your fault—"

At that moment there was a knock at the door and a messenger entered.

"What do you want?" said Fuchsia.

"I have a message, my lady."

"What is it?"

"Her Ladyship, the Countess, your mother, wishes Lord Titus to accompany me back to her room. She is going to take him for a walk."

Titus and Fuchsia stared at the messenger and then at one another. Several times they opened their mouths to speak but closed them again. Then Fuchsia turned her eyes back to the melting snow—and Titus walked out through the half-open door, the messenger following him closely.

II

The Countess was waiting for them on the landing. She gestured the messenger to be gone with a single, lazy movement of her head.

She gazed at Titus with a curious lack of expression. It was as though what she saw interested her, but in the way that a stone would interest a geologist, or a plant, a botanist. Her expression was neither kindly nor unkindly. It was simply absent. She appeared to be unconscious of having a face at all. Her features made no effort to communicate anything.

"I am taking them for a walk," she said in her heavy, abstracted, millstone voice.

"Yes, Mother," said Titus. He supposed she was talking of her cats.

A shadow settled for a moment on her broad brow. The word "Mother" had perplexed her. But the boy was quite right, of course.

Her massive bulk had always impressed Titus. The hanging draperies and scollop'd shadows, the swathes of musty darkness—all this he found most awesome.

He was fascinated by her but he had no point of contact. When she spoke it was in order to make a statement. She had no conversation.

She turned her head and, pursing her lips, she whistled with a peculiar ululation. Titus gazed up at the sartorial mass above him. Why had she wanted him to accompany her? he wondered. Did she want him to tell her anything? Had she anything to tell *him?* Was it just a whim?

But she had started to descend the stairs and Titus followed her.

From a hundred dim recesses, from favorite ledges, from shelves and draft-proof corners, from among the tattered entrails of old sofas, from the scarred plush of chairs, from under clock stands, from immemorial sun traps, and from nests of claw-torn paper—from the inside of lost hats, from among rafters, from rusty casques, and from drawers half open, the cats poured forth, converged, foamed, and with a rapid pattering of their milk-white feet filled up the corridors, and a few moments later had reached the landing and were on their way, in the wake of their great mistress, down the stairway they obscured.

When they were in the open and had passed through an archway in the Outer Wall and were able to see Gormenghast Mountain clear before them, with dark-gray snow on its cruel heights, the Countess waved her ponderous arm, as though she were scattering grain, and the cats on the instant, fanning out, sped in every direction, and leaped, twisting in the air, curvetting for the very joy of their only release from the castle since first the snow had come down. And though a number of them sported together, rolling over one another; or sitting up straight with their heads bridled back, tapped at each other, sparring like fighters, only to lose all interest of a sudden, their eyes unfocusing, their thoughts turning— yet for the main the white creatures behaved as though each one were utterly alone, utterly content to be alone, conscious only of its own behavior, its own leap into the air, its own agility, self-possessed, solitary, enviable, and legendary in a beauty both heraldic and fluent as water.

Titus walked by his mother's side. For all the interest in the scene before him he could not help turning his eyes to his mother's face. Its vague, almost masklike character was something which he was beginning to suspect of being no index to her state of mind. For more than once she had gripped his shoulder in her big hand and led him from the path and without a word she had shown him, all but shrouded by the ivy on a tree stem, a cushion of black star-moss. She had turned off a rough track, and then pointed down a small snow-filled gully to where a fox had rested. Every now and again she would pause and gaze at the ground, or into the branches of a tree, but Titus, stare as he would, could see nothing remarkable.

For all that the birds had died in their thousands, yet as Titus and his mother drew near to a strip of woodland where the snow had melted from the boughs, and small streams were running over the stones and snow-flattened grass, they could see that the trees were far from empty.

The Countess paused, and holding Titus by his elbow, they stood motionless. A bird whistled and then another, and then suddenly the small kingfisher, like a blue legend, streaked along a stream.

The cats were leagues away. They breathed the sharp

air into their lungs. They roamed to the four quarters. They powdered the horizons.

The Countess whistled with a shrill, sweet note, and first one bird and then another flew to her. She examined them, holding them cupped in her hands. They were very thin and weak. She whistled their various calls and they responded as they hopped about her or sat perched upon her shoulders, and then, all at once a fresh voice from the wood silenced the birds. At every whistle of the Countess, this new answer came, quick as an echo.

Its effect on the Countess seemed out of all reason.

She turned her head. She whistled again and her whistle was answered, quick as an echo. She gave the calls of a dozen birds and a dozen voices echoed her with an insolent precision. The birds about her feet and on her shoulders had stiffened.

Her hand was gripping Titus's shoulder like an iron clamp. It was all he could do not to cry out. He turned his head with difficulty and saw his mother's face—the face that had been as calm as the snow itself. It had darkened.

It was no bird that was answering her; that much she knew. Clever as it was, the mimicry could not deceive her. Nor did it seem that whatever gave vent to the varying calls was anxious to deceive. There had been something taunting about the rapidity with which each whistle of the Countess had been flung back from the wood.

What was it all about? Why was his arm being gripped? Titus, who had been fascinated by his mother's power over the birds, could not understand why the calls from the wood should have so angered her. For she trembled as she held him. It seemed as though she were holding him back from something, as though the wood were hiding something that might hurt him—or draw him away from her.

And then she lifted her face to the treetops, her eyes blazing.

"Beware!" she cried, and a strange voice answered her. *"Beware!"* it called, and the silence came down again.

From a dizzy perch in a tall pine, the Thing peered through the cold needles and watched the big woman and the boy as they returned to the distant castle.

Chapter Fifty

❦❦❦❦❦❦❦❦❦❦❦

I

IT was not until close upon the Day that Titus learned how something quite unusual was being prepared for his tenth birthday. He was by now so used to ceremonies of one kind or another that the idea of having to spend his birthday either performing or watching others perform some time-hardened ritual made no appeal to his imagination. But Fuchsia had told him that there was something quite different about what happened when a child of the Line reached the age of ten. She knew, for it had happened to her, although in her case the festivities had been rather spoiled by the rain.

"I won't tell you, Titus," she had said. "It will spoil it if I do. Oh, it's so lovely."

"What kind of lovely?" said Titus, suspiciously.

"Wait and see," said Fuchsia. "You'll be glad I haven't told you when the time comes. If only things were always like that."

When the Day arrived Titus learned to his surprise that he was to be confined for the entire twelve hours in a great playroom quite unknown to him.

The Custodian of the Outer Keys, a surly old man with a cast of the left eye, had opened up the room as soon as dawn had broken over the towers. Apart from the occasion of Fuchsia's tenth birthday, the door had been locked since her father, Sepulchrave, was a child. But now, again, the key had turned with a grinding of rust and iron, and the hinges had creaked, and the great playroom opened up again its dusty glories.

This was a strange way to treat a boy on his tenth anniversary; to immure him for the entire day in a strange land, however full of marvels it might be. It was true that there were toys of weird and ingenious mechanism; ropes on which he could swing from wall to wall, and ladders leading to dizzy balconies—but what of all this, if the door was locked and the only window was high in the wall?

And yet, long as the day seemed, Titus was buoyed up by the knowledge that he was there not only because of some obsolete tradition but for the very good reason that he must not be allowed to see what was going on. Had he been abroad he could not fail to have gained some inkling, if not of what lay in store for him that evening, at least of the scale on which the preparations were being conducted.

And the activity of the castle was fantastic. For Titus to have seen a tenth of it must have taken the edge, not off his wonder or speculation, but off the shock of pleasure that he was finally to receive when evening came. For he had no idea what kind of activities were taking place. Fuchsia had refused to be drawn. She remembered her own pleasure too keenly to jeopardize a hundredth part of his.

And so he spent the day alone, and save for those times when his meals were brought in on the golden trays of the occasion, he saw no one until an hour before sunset. At that hour four men came in. One of them carried a box, which when it was opened revealed a few of the garments which Titus was invited to put on. Another carried a light basketwork palanquin, or mountain chair that rested on two long poles. Of the other two, one carried a long green scarf, and the other a few cakes and a glass of water on a tray.

They retired while Titus got into his ceremonial clothes. They were very simple. A small red velvet skullcap and a seamless robe of some gray material that reached to his ankles. A fine chain of gold links clasped the garment at his waist. These, with a pair of sandals, were all that had been brought, and while he strapped the sandals he called to the men to re-enter.

They came in at once and one of them approached Titus with the scarf in his hand.

"Your Lordship," he said.

"What's *that* for?" said Titus, eying the scarf.

"It's part of the ceremony, Lordship. You have to be blindfolded."

"No!" shouted Titus. "Why should I be?"

"It's nothing to do with me," said the man. "It's the Law."

"The Law! the Law! the Law! How I *hate* the Law," cried the boy. "Why does it want me blindfolded—after keeping me in prison all day? Where are you going to take me? What's it all about? Can't you talk? Can't you talk?"

"Nothing to do with me," said the man; it was his favorite phrase. "You see," he added, "if we don't blindfold you it won't be such a surprise when you get there and when we undo the scarf. And you see" (he continued as though he had suddenly become interested in what he was talking about), "you see—with your eyes blindfolded you won't have any idea of where you are going—and then, you know, the crowds are going to be deathly silent and—"

"Quiet!" said another voice—it was the man who had the mountain chair. "You have overreached yourself! Enough sir, for me to say," he continued, turning to the boy, "that it will be for your pleasure and your good."

"It had *better* be," said Titus, "after all *this!*"

His longing to get out of the playroom mitigated his distaste for the blindfolding, and after taking a drink of water and cramming a small cake in his mouth, he took a step forward.

"All right," he said, and standing before the scarf-man, he suffered himself to be bandaged. At the second turn of the scarf he was in total blackness. After the fourth he felt the cloth being knotted at the base of his head.

"We are going to lift you into the chair, your Lordship."

"All right," said Titus.

Almost immediately after he was seated in the basketwork chair he found himself rising from the ground, and then after a word from one of the men, he felt himself moving forward through black space and the slight swaying of the men beneath him. Without a word, or a pause, each man with an end of the long bamboo poles resting upon his shoulder, they began to move ever more rapidly.

Titus had had no sensation of their leaving the room, although he knew that by now they must have left it far behind. It was obvious that they were still within the walls of the castle, for he could both feel the frequent changes of direction which the tortuous corridors made necessary, and hear the hollow echoing of the bearers' feet—an echoing which seemed so loud to Titus in his blindness that he could not help feeling that the castle was empty. There was not a sound, not a whisper in the whole labyrinthine place to compete with the hollow footfalls of the men, with the sound of their breathing, or with the regular creaking of the bamboo poles.

It seemed that it would never end—this darkness, and these sounds—but suddenly a breath of fresh air against his face told him that he was in the open. At the same time he could feel that he was being borne down a flight of steps, and when they had reached the level ground he felt for the first time that airborne jogging, as the four men began to trot through an empty landscape.

And it was as utterly deserted as the castle. All the feverish activity of the day had been brought to a close. The gentry, the dignitaries, the officials, the workmen, the performers, the populace, man, woman, and child—there was not one who had not arrived at his appointed station.

And the bearers ran on over the darkening ground.

Above their heads and reaching down into the east was a great tongue of yellow light.

But with every movement that passed the luster faded and the moon began to slide up through the darkness of the west so that the light on Titus's upturned face grew sharper and colder.

And the bearers ran on, over the dark ground.

There were no echoes now. Only the isolated sounds of the night—the scurry of some small animal through the undergrowth, or the distant barking of a fox. From time to time Titus could feel the cool sweet gusts of a night breeze blowing across his forehead, lifting the strands of his hair.

"How much farther?" he called. It seemed that he had been floating in the basketwork chair forever.

"How much farther? How much farther?" he called again, but there was no reply.

It was impossible to carry so rare a burden as the Seventy-Seventh Earl—to carry him shoulder-high along forest tracks, across precarious fords, and over stony slopes of mountains—and to have at the same time, while they kept running, any room in their minds for anything else besides. All their awareness was focused upon his safety and the measured smoothness of their rhythmic running. Had he called to them ten times as loudly they would not have heard him.

But Titus was near to the end of his blind journey. He did not know it but the four bearers who had, for the last mile or more, been loping through pine woods, had come suddenly upon an open shoulder of land. The ground swept downward and away before them in swathes of moon-chilled ferns and at the base of this slope lay what seemed like a natural amphitheater, for the land rose on all sides. The floor of this gigantic basin appeared at first sight to be entirely forested, and yet the eyes of the bearers had already caught sight of innumerable and microscopic points of light no bigger than pinpricks, that flashed, now here, now there among the branches of the distant trees. And they saw more than this. They saw that in the air above the basin'd forest there was a change of hue. In the darkness that brooded over the branches there was a subtle warmth, a kind of smoldering dusk that in contrast to the cold moon, or to the glints of light among the trees, was almost rose-ate.

But Titus knew nothing of this swarthy light. Nor that he was being taken down a steep track through the ferns to a district where the great chestnuts, far from forming a solid forest, as it falsely appeared from the surrounding slopes, were marshaled a furlong deep about the margin of a wide expanse of water. The points of light that had caught the bearers' attention were all that they had been able to see of the moonlit lake when for a moment they had paused on a high open shoulder.

But what of the glow? It was not long before Titus knew all about it. He was by now among the deep moon-dappled chestnut groves. His exhausted bearers, the sweat pouring down their bodies and running into their eyes, were turning into a ride of ancient trees that led to the center of the southern bank.

Had his vision been free he would have seen upon his left, and tethered to the low branches of the nearby trees, a hundred or more horses. Their harnessings, bridles, halters, and saddles were slung across the higher branches. Here and there the moonlight penetrating the upper foliage set a stirrup dazzling in the gloom or gloated upon the leather of long traces. And then, a little farther along the track where the trees were not so numerous, there stood ranged in lines, as though for inspection, a great variety of carriages, carts, and traps. Here where there was less covering, the moonlight shone almost unimpeded, and was by now so high and was casting so strong a light that the varying colors of the carriages could be distinguished one from another. The wheels of each were decorated with foliage of young trees whose branches were threaded through the spokes, and with sunflowers also; in the long horse-drawn cavalcade which a few hours previously had made its overland journey to the chestnut woods there had not been one wheel out of the many hundreds that, in turning,

had not set the foliage revolving and the heads of sunflowers circling in the dusk.

All this had been lost to the boy—all this and many
another flight of fancy which from hour to hour during
the day had been set in motion or enacted according to
old customs whose origin or significance was long forgotten.

But the bearers were for the first time slackening their
pace. Once again he leaned forward, his hands grasping
the basketwork rim of his chair. "Where are we?" he
shouted. "How much longer will it be? Can't you answer me?"

The silence about him was like something that
hummed against his eardrums. This was another kind of
silence. This was not the silence of nothing happening—of emptiness, or negation—but was a positive thing
—a silence that knew of itself—that was charged, conscious, and wide awake.

And now the bearers stopped altogether, and almost at
once, across the stillness, Titus heard the sound of approaching footsteps, and then: "My lord Titus," said
a voice, "I am here to bid you welcome and to offer
you on behalf of your mother, your sister, and all who
are here gathered, our felicitations on your tenth birthday.

"It is our desire that what has been prepared for your
amusement will give you pleasure; and that you will
find the tedium of the long and solitary day that now lies
at your back has been worth the suffering; in short, my
lord Titus, your mother the Countess Gertrude of Gormenghast, Lady Fuchsia, and every one of your subjects
are hoping that what is left of your birthday will be
very happy."

"Thank you," said Titus. "I would like to get down."

"At once, your Lordship," said the same voice.

"And I'd like this scarf off my eyes."

"In one moment. Your sister is on her way to you.
She will remove it when she has taken you to the south
platform."

"Fuchsia!" his voice was sharp and strained. "Fuchsia! Where are you?"

"I'm coming," she shouted. "Hold his arm, you man, there! How do you think he can stand in the dark like that—give him to me, give him to me. Oh, Titus," she panted, holding her blind brother tightly in her arms. "It won't be long now—and oh, it's wonderful! Wonderful! As wonderful as it was when it was all for me, years ago, and it's a better night than I had, and absolutely calm with a great white moon on top."

She led him along as she talked, and all at once the marginal trees were behind them and Fuchsia knew that every step they took and every movement they made were watched by a multitude.

As Titus stumbled at her side he tried to imagine in what kind of place he could be. He could form no picture from Fuchsia's disjointed comments. He was to be taken to a platform of some kind, that there was a moon, and that the whole castle seemed resolved to make amends for the long prefatory day he had spent alone were all that he could gather.

"Twelve steps up," said Fuchsia, and he felt her placing his foot upon the first of the rough treads. They climbed together, hand in hand, and when they reached the platform she guided him to where a large horsehair chair bloated with moonlight, an ugly thing if ever there was one—a heavy beast with a purple skin that had tired out the two cart horses by the time they had covered half the journey.

"Sit down," said Fuchsia, and he sat down gingerly in the darkness, upon the edge of the ugly couch.

Fuchsia stood back from him. Then she raised both her arms above her head. In reply to her signal a voice called out of the darkness, "It is time! Let the scarf be unwound from his eyes!"

And another voice—quick as an echo—"It is time! Let his birthday begin!"

And another—"For his Lordship is ten."

Titus felt Fuchsia's fingers undoing the knot and then the freeing of the cloth about his eyes. For a moment he remained with his lids closed, and then he slowly opened them, and as he did so he rose involuntarily to his feet with a gasp of wonder.

Before him, as he stood, one hand at his mouth, his eyes round as coins, there was stretched, as it were, across the area of his vision, a canvas—a canvas hushed and unearthly. A canvas of great depth; of width that spread from east to west and of a height that wandered way above the moon. It was painted with fire and moon-light—upon a dark, impalpable surface. The lunar rhythms rose and moved through darkness. A counter-point of bonfires burned like anchors—anchors that held the sliding woods in check.

And the glaze! The earthless glaze of that midnight lake! And the multitude across the water, motionless in the shadow of the sculptured chestnut trees. And the bonfires burning!

And then a voice out of the paint cried, "Fire!" and a cannon roared, recoiled, and smoked upon the bank. "Fire!" cried the voice again, and then again, until the gun had bellowed ten times over.

It was the sign, and suddenly the picture, as though at the stroke of a warlock's wand, came suddenly to life. The canvas shuddered. Fragments detached themselves and fragments came together. From the height to the depths it was that that Titus saw.

Firstly the moon, by now immediately overhead; a thing as big as a dinner plate and as white, save where the shadows of its mountains lay. The moon whose luster was over everything like a veil of snow.

And all about the moon, the midnight sky. It came down, this sky, like a curtain, expansive as Nemesis, and under the sky the hilltops in a haze of ferns that, over-lapping one another with their fronds, descended the hill, fold after fold, until the chestnut forest, luxuriant in its foliage, its upper canopies shining, stretched, on Titus's eye level, in a great curve. And under these trees, along the water's edge, as thick upon the ground as nettles in a wasteland, was the life of the distant castle, the teem-ing populace. A hundred at a time would be contained in

the cast shadow of a single tree; a hundred more be lit
in a lozenge of moonlight. And then the swarms of faces,
thick as bees, illumined and flushed in the red light of
the lakeside bonfires. Now that the gun had fired its
salute, this long strip of the canvas had begun to seethe.
Across the lake it was too far for Titus to be able to make
out any single creature, but movements ran through these
crowds as a ripple of wind over a field of tares. But this
was not all. For these ripples, these trembling blotches of
shadow and moonlight, these movements on the shore,
were being simultaneously repeated in the lakes. Not the
least motion of a head beneath the trees but its ghost
had moved beneath it in the water. Not the flicker of a
fire was lost in the reflecting water.

And it was this nocturnal glass in whose depths shone
the moon-bathed foliage of the chestnut trees that held
the eye the longest. For it was nothingness, a sheet of
death; and it was everything. Nothing it held was its own
although the least leaf was reflected with microscopic
accuracy—and, as though to light these aqueous forms
with a luminary of their own, a phantom moon lay on the
water, as big as a plate and as white, save where the
shadow of its mountains lay.

II

And yet this visual richness gave less a sense of satisfaction than of expectancy. This was a setting if ever
there was one—but a setting for *what?* The stage was
set, the audience was gathered—what next? Titus turned
his eyes for the first time to where his sister had been
standing, but she was no longer there. He was alone on
the platform with the horsehair chair.

And then he saw her seated on a log with her mother
beside her. From their feet the land dipped gradually to
the water and on this decline was gathered what was
pleased to think itself the upper stratum of Gormenghast
society. To right and left the ground swarmed with
officials of every kind—and over Titus, and over them
all were the spreading terraces of the trees.

Finding himself alone, Titus sat down on the purple chair and then, to make himself more comfortable, curled his feet under him, and rested his arm on the bolsterlike arm. He lifted his eyes to the lake with its upside-down picture of all that was spread above it.

Fuchsia trembled as she sat beside her mother. She remembered how the chestnut woods had held back their secret until this moment, years ago, and how they would now throw out their startling characters. She turned her head to see whether she could catch her brother's eye, but he was staring straight ahead, and as she watched him his hand went to his mouth again and she saw him sit forward on the couch as rigidly as though he had been turned to stone.

For immediately ahead of him, across the unblemished lake, figures as tall as the chestnut trees themselves were straddling out of the shadows, and to the verge of the opposite bank, where they stood, unbelievably. Before them, their liquescent stage lay spread. The reflections of their fantastically elongated bodies were already deep in the lake.

There were four of them, and they came out one after another from various parts of the forest. They appeared to take no notice of one another, although they turned their heads to right and left. The movements of their bodies appeared stiff and exaggerated, but extraordinarily eloquent.

From the high masks that topped them to the grass on which they balanced could not have measured less than thirty feet.

They were beings of another realm and the crowds that stared up at them from below had not only been shriveled up into midgets, but were also made to appear gray and prosaic. For these four giants were in every way most beautiful and extraordinary. The woods behind them seemed darker than ever now, for these lofty specters were tinted under the moon's rays with colors as sharp and barbaric as the plumage of tropical birds.

From one to another, Titus turned his gaze, unable

to resist the movements of his eyes, although he longed to dwell on each one separately.

Upon their lofty shoulders they carried their heads like kings—abstracted and inscrutable. Their dignity was something that infused their slightest movement. In the stiff and measured raising of an arm the very humus appeared to be drawn out of the soil below. The tilting of their faces to the sky made the sky naked—made the moon guilty.

The group had stalked out of that part of the forest that faced Titus across the lake. Their four heads were very different. That of the most northerly was crowned with a high conical hat like a dunce's, under which a great white head resembling a lion's turned slowly to left and right, upon the shoulders that supported it. The eyes, perfectly circular, were painted the purest emerald green and when the head was raised they shone to the moon.

But its mane was its glory. From close above the eyes, and from the sides and back of the head, it billowed forth luxuriantly and fell as far as the waist in undulations of imperial purple. From the waist downward—a twenty-foot drop to the feet of the stilts—a prodigious skirt descended like a cascade, weighted down by its own length of material. It was quite black, as were those of the other three. This mutual darkness of the lower two-thirds of their bodies gave an illusory effect to their upper parts. The skirts could be seen, and their reflections could be seen, but with nothing like the same clarity. It was, at times, almost as though their colored "heights" were floating. The arms emerged from halfway down the mane. In either hand the Lion held a dagger.

Next to this figure with its purple mane stood one as far removed as the Lion from the natural, but more sinister in that the wolfish character of the head was not redeemed by either a noble cast of feature, or lightened by the charadelike nature of the long white dunce's hat.

This vulpine monster was undeniably wicked—but so decoratively wicked! The head was crimson, and the cocked and pointed ears were deepest azure. This azure was repeated in the circles that were scattered over the gray hide of the upper body. In either hand was an enormous cardboard bottle of poison. As with the Lion the black skirt fell like a wall of darkness.

Even now as they stood in what might be thought of as the "wings," for they had not set foot in the watery stage, their every movement was something awesome. For the Wolf to lift its poison bottle was for a shudder to run through the swarming populace; for the Lion to shake its mane was for the lake to be circled with goose-flesh.

Next to the Wolf, and separated by half an acre of upturned heads, was the Horse—a horse unlike any other travesty of that noble animal that had ever been concocted—and yet it was more a horse than anything else. It was monstrous, in its own way, with an expression of such fatuous melancholy that Titus could neither laugh nor cry, for neither expression was true to what he felt.

Upon its head, this giantess wore an enormous basket-work hat whose brim cast a circular shadow upon the moonlit water far beneath. Long powder-blue ribbons fell ludicrously from the crown of the hat and clustered about the hairy shoulder ten feet below. All about the lower part of the crown the hat was decorated with grass and livid lilies.

From beneath all this resplendence the loose-lipped head of the Horse protruded with baleful idiocy. Like the Lion, its long maudlin head was white, but red circles were painted on either side between the eyes and the curve of the jaws. The neck was long and absurdly supple, with a stubby fringe of orange hair along the spine.

It was clothed in an apple-green smock from under which the long skirt descended, hiding the tall and perilous stilts that protruded for no more than six inches beneath the black hem. In one hand the Horse carried a parasol and in the other a book of poems. From time to time the Horse would slowly turn its head and incline it, with a sort of sad and smirking deference, to the Lamb upon its left.

This Lamb, a little less in height than its companions, for all its towering stature, was a mass of pale golden curls. Its expression was one of unspeakable sanctity. However it moved its head—whatever the angle, whether it scanned the heavens in search of some beatific vision, or lowered its face as though to muse upon its own unspotted breast—there was no escape from its purity. Between its ears, and set upon the golden curls, was a silver crown. The swathes of a gray shawl were drawn demurely over the shoulders, across the golden breast, and fell in sculpturesque folds of some length, so that there was less to be seen of the inevitable skirt. It carried nothing in its hands, for they were clasped upon its heart.

These four, with their heads as big as doors, yet appearing almost small in proportion to the awe-inspiring loftiness of the bodies, these four had not stood at the margin of the reflecting lake for more than a minute before, with startling unanimity of purpose, they set forth upon the waters.

Titus, crying with excitement, gripped the rotten upholstery of the chair on either side, his fingers working their way into the ancient horsehair.

The four ahead of him appeared to be moving upon the surface across the lake. Their strange, spidery strides took them far from the shore, but the hems of their skirts were still dry! Titus could in no way understand it, until suddenly he realized that in spite of the clear reflections that seemed to plunge into fathomless water, the great lake was in reality but a few inches deep. It was a film.

For a moment he was disappointed. There is danger in deep water, and danger is more real than beauty in a boy's mind. But this disappointment was immediately forgotten, for there could have been nothing of all this had the lake not been the merest glaze of water.

The masque of the four upon the lake was designed, many hundreds of years ago, for this setting among the nocturnal chestnuts. The gestures of the Lion, grandiloquent, absurd yet impressive—the shaking of its purple mane, from which tremendous operation the other three

invariably drew back—the terrible, sidelong progress of
the Wolf with the poison bottle as he maneuvered himself ever nearer the golden Lamb, and the outlandish
gait of the Horse with its garnished hat, as it straddled
from one end of the lake to the other, reading from its
book of poems, while with its parasol it beat time in
the upper air to the rhythm of the verses—all this was
a formula as ancient as the walls of the castle itself.

And all the while this masked drama, played upon
stilts as tall as trees and upon a lake that reflected not
only the progress of the performers, but the moon over
whose liquid image the monstrous Horse would invariably stumble as though it had been tripped—all the
while the silence continued unbroken. For although a
strong strain of the ridiculous ran through everything,
this was not the dominant impression. When the Horse-
creature tripped or waved its parasol; when the Wolf
was thwarted and its lower jaw fell open like a draw-
bridge; when the Lamb cast its eyes to the moon, only
to be distracted in the throes of its sanctity by the
whisking of the Lion's mane—when these things happened there was no laughter but only a kind of relief,
for the grandeur of the spectacle, and the godlike
rhythms of each sequence, were of such a nature that
there were few present who were not affected as by some
painful memory of childhood.

At last, the time-hallowed ritual drew to its end, and
the lofty creatures stepped from the shallow lake, and
turning before they disappeared into the deep woods,
bowed across the shallows to Titus, as might the gods of
Poetry and Battle bow to one another, as equals across
enchanted water.

The Four, as they departed, took the silence with them.
The rest of the night was by way of being a release
from perfection, and was given over to every kind of
scattered activity.

Between the bonfires that surrounded the lake and
warmed the air above the chestnut forest, fresh fires
were being lit, and under the lakeward boughs, hampers
and baskets of provisions were being unpacked.

The Countess of Groan, who had remained throughout the masque as immovable as the log on which she
sat, now turned her head over her shoulder.

But Titus was no longer on the platform, nor was
Fuchsia at her side.

She rose from the log, the traditional place of honor,
and moved abstractedly down to the lake's edge between lines of functionaries, who on seeing her rise knew
that they were now free for the rest of the night to dis-
port themselves as they wished.

Against the shimmering lake her massive form loomed
darkly save for the moonlight on her shoulders and her
dark-red hair.

She gazed about her but seemed to be unaware of
the crowds that thronged the water's edge.

A giant picnic was piecing itself together as the fish
and fruit and loaves and pies were laid out beneath the
trees, and it was not long before the lake was surrounded by an unbroken feast.

And while all these preparations were going on, shrill
packs of urchins raced through the chestnut woods,
swarmed among the branches, or streaming out of the
trees, pranced or cartwheeled to the center of the lake,
their reflections flying beneath them, and the film of
water spouting from their feet. And when a pack would
meet its rival pack, then hand to hand, a hundred watery
combats would churn the shallows, as scattered over
the aqueous arena the children grappled, the moonlight
sliding on their slippery limbs.

And Titus, watching, longed with his whole being
to be anonymous—to be lost within the core of such a
breed—to be able to live and run and fight and laugh
and if need be, cry, on his own. For to be one of those
wild children would have been to be *alone* among
companions. As the Earl of Gormenghast he could never
be alone. He could only be lonely. Even to lose himself
was to be lost with that other child, that symbol, that
phantom, the Seventy-Seventh Earl of Gormenghast who
hovered at his elbow.

Fuchsia had signaled him to jump from the platform,

and together they had raced into the chestnut woods immediately behind, and for a moment or two, in the darkness, they had held each other in the deep shadows of the trees and had heard one another's hearts beating.

"It was wicked of me," said Fuchsia at last, "and dangerous. We are supposed to have our midnight supper at the long table, with Mother. And we must go back soon."

"You can if you like," said Titus, who was trembling with a deep hatred of his status. "But I'm leaving."

"Leaving?"

"Leaving forever," said Titus. "Forever and ever. I am going into the wild, like . . . Flay . . . and like that . . ."

But he could think of no way to describe that wisp of a creature who had floated through a forest of gold oaks.

"You can't do that," said Fuchsia. "You would die and I wouldn't let you."

"You couldn't stop me," cried Titus. "Nobody could stop me." And he began to tear off the long gray tunic, as though it were in his path.

But Fuchsia, her lips trembling, held his arms to his sides.

"No! No!" she whispered passionately. "Not now, Titus. You can't. . . ."

But with a jerk he freed himself, but immediately tripped in the darkness and fell upon his face. When he raised himself, and saw his sister above him, he pulled her down, so that she knelt at his side. In the distance they could hear the cries of the children by the lake, and then, suddenly, the harsh ringing of a bell.

"That is for supper," whispered Fuchsia, at last, for she had waited in vain for Titus to speak, "and after supper we will go along the shore together and see the cannon."

Titus was crying. The long day he had spent alone, the lateness of the hour, the excitement, the sense of his essential isolation—all these things had worked together to weaken him. But he nodded. Whether Fuchsia saw his silent answer to her question or not, she made no further remark, but lifting him from the ground, she dried his eyes with the loose sleeve of her dress.

Together they picked their way to the edge of the wood, and there were the bonfires again and the crowds and the lake with the chestnut trees beyond, and there was the platform where he had sat alone, and there was their mother at the long table with her elbows on the moonlit linen, and her chin in her hands, while before her, and seemingly unnoticed, for her gaze was fixed upon the distant hills, the customary banquet lay spread in all its splendor, a rich and crowded masterpiece, the gold plate of the Groans burning with a slow and mellow fire and the crimson goblets smoldering at the moon.

Chapter Fifty-One

❀❀❀❀❀❀❀❀❀❀❀

I

AND all the while the progress of the seasons, those great tides, enveloped and stained with their passing colors, chilled or warmed with their varying exhalations, the tracts of Gormenghast. And so, as Fuchsia wanders across her room in search of a lost book, the South Spinneys below her window are misty with a green hesitation, and a few days later the sharp green fires have broken out along the iron boughs.

II

Opus Fluke and Flannelcat are leaning over the veranda railing above the Professors' Quadrangle. The old Quadman is sweeping the dust thirty feet below them. It is thick and white with heat, for the spring has long since passed.

"Hot work for an old fellow!" shouts Fluke to the old man. The ancient lifts his head and wipes his brow. "Ah!" he calls up in a voice that could not have been used for weeks. "Ah, sir, it's a dry do." Fluke retires and in a few minutes has returned with a bottle which he has stolen from Mulefire's apartment. This he lowers on a length of string to the old man, far below in the dust.

III

In his study, and locked away from the world, Prune-squallor, lying rather than sitting in his elegant armchair, reads, with his crossed feet resting just below the mantelpiece.

The small fire in the grate lights up his keen, absurdly refined, and for all its weirdness of proportion, delicate face. The magnifying lenses of his spectacles, which can give so grotesque an effect to his eyes, gleam in the firelight.

It is no book of medicine that he is so absorbed in. On his knee there is an old exercise book filled with verses. The handwriting is erratic but legible. Sometimes the poems are in a heavy, ponderous, and childish hand—sometimes in a quick, excited calligraphy, full of crossings-out and misspellings.

That Fuchsia should have ever asked him to read them is the most thrilling thing that he has ever experienced. He loves the girl as though she were his own daughter. But he has never sought her out. Little by little, as the times have gone by, she has taken him into her confidence.

But as he reads, and while the autumn wind whistles in the branches of the garden trees, his brow contracts and he returns his gaze to the four curious lines which Fuchsia had crossed out with a thick pencil:

How white and scarlet is that face!
Who knows, in some unusual place
The colored heroes are alight
With faces made of red and white.

IV

It is a cold and dreary winter. Once again Flay, who is
now as much at home in the Silent Halls as he has been
in the forests, sits at the table in his secret room. His
hands are deep in his ragged pockets. Before him is
spread a great sail of paper that not only covers the table,
but descends in awkward folds and creases to the floor
on every side. A portion near its center is covered with
markings, laboriously scripted words, short arrows, dot-
ted lines, and incomprehensible devices. It is a map; a
map which Mr. Flay has been working upon for over a
year. It is a map of the district that surrounds him—the
empty world, whose anatomy, little by little, he is piecing
together, extending, correcting, classifying. He is, it
seems, in a city that has been forsaken, and he is making
it his own; naming its streets and alleys, its avenues of
granite, its winding flights and blackened terraces—exploring even further its hollow hinterlands, while over
all, like a lowering sky, as continuous and as widespread,
are the endless ceilings and the unbroken roof.

He is no master of calligraphy. A pen sits awkwardly
in his hand. But, both while engaged upon his expeditions and when adding with painful slowness to his map,
during the long days, his life in the pathless woods is
standing him in good stead.

With no stars to help him, his sense of orientation
has become uncanny.

Tonight he will keep watch upon Steerpike's door as
has become his custom in the small hours, and if the
opportunity arises, he will follow him upon whatever
business he is bent. Until then he has seven hours in
which to push forward with this task of reconnaissance,
which has now become a passion.

He takes his hands out of his pockets and with a scarred and bony forefinger he traces for himself the path he proposes to follow. It takes a northward course, sweeping in a number of arcs before it zigzags through a veritable cross-hatching of narrow alleys to reappear as a twelve-foot corridor with a worn pavement on its either side. This corridor heads undeviatingly to the north and fades out in a series of small, hesitant dots on that part of Mr. Flay's paper that has all but overlapped the table. It has reached the margin of his knowledge to the north.

He pulls the chart toward him and the loose paper on the far side of the table slides upward from the floor, and then, in creeping forward to beneath his outstretched head, it opens out its wastes of untrodden whiteness with an arctic yawn.

V

And the days move on and the names of the months change and the four seasons bury one another and it is spring again and yet again, and the small streams that run over the rough sides of Gormenghast Mountain are big with rain while the days lengthen and summer sprawls across the countryside, sprawls in all the swathes of its green, with its gold and sticky head, with its slumber and the drone of doves and with its butterflies and its lizards and its sunflowers, over and over again, its doves, its butterflies, its lizards, its sunflowers, each one an echo-child, while the fruit ripens and the grotesque boles of the ancient apple trees are dappled in the low rays of the sun and the air smells of such rotten sweetness as brings a hunger to the breast, and makes of the heart a sea-bed, and a tear, the fruit of salt and water, ripens, fed by a summer sorrow—ripens and falls . . . falls gradually along the cheekbones, wanders over the wastelands listlessly, the loveliest emblem of the heart's condition.

And the days move on and the names of the months change and the four seasons bury one another and the field-mice draw upon their granaries. The air is murky and the sun is like a raw wound in the grimy flesh of a beggar, and the rags of the clouds are clotted. The sky has been stabbed and has been left to die above the world, filthy, vast, and bloody. And then the great winds come and the sky is blown naked, and a wild bird screams across the glittering land. And the Countess stands at the window of her room with the white cats at her feet and stares at the frozen landscape spread below her, and a year later she is standing there again but the cats are abroad in the valleys and a raven sits upon her heavy shoulder.

And every day the myriad happenings. A loosened stone falls from a high tower. A fly drops lifeless from a broken pane. A sparrow twitters in a cave of ivy.

The days wear out the months and the months wear out the years, and a flux of moments, like an unquiet tide, eats at the black coast of futurity.

And Titus Groan is wading through his boyhood.

Chapter Fifty-Two

A kind of lull had settled upon the castle. It was not that events were lacking but that even those of major importance had about them a sense of unreality. It was as though some strange wheel of destiny had brought to the earth its preordained lacuna.

Bellgrove was now a husband. Irma had not wasted a moment before she began to raise those formidable earthworks that can so isolate the marital unit from the universe.

She always knew what was best for Bellgrove. She always knew what he most needed. She knew how the Headmaster of Gormenghast should behave and she knew how his inferiors should behave in his presence. The Staff were terrified of her. There was no difference between them and their pupils where Irma was concerned. It was a case of whispering behind the hand; tiptoeing past the door of Bellgrove's apartment; looking to the condition of their fingernails; and worst of all, attending their classes at the scheduled time.

She had changed almost out of recognition. Marriage had given her vanity both drive and direction. It had not taken her long to discover the inherent weakness of her husband. She loved him no less for this, but her love became militant. He was her child. Noble, but ah, no longer wise. It was she who was wise and in her loving wisdom it was for her to guide him.

From Bellgrove's point of view it was a sad story. Having had her in the palm of his hand—it was now a bitter business, this reversal. He had been unable to keep it up. Little by little, his lack of will, his native feebleness, became apparent. She had found him, one day, practicing a series of noble expressions before the mirror. She had seen him shake his beautiful white locks, and she heard him chiding her for some imaginary misdemeanor. "No, Irma," he was saying, "I will not have it. I would be gratified if you would remember your station." And then he had smirked, as though ashamed, and on looking into the mirror again, had seen her standing behind him.

But he knew himself to be her superior. He knew that there was in him a kind of golden fund, a reserve of strength, but at the same time he knew that this strength was of no avail, for he had never drawn upon it. He did not know how to. He didn't even know exactly what kind of strength it was. But it was there, and it was real to him in the way that an ultimate innocence, like a nest egg, awaits its moment in the breasts of sinners.

And yet for all his subjugation it was a relief to be able to be weak again. Gradually he gave himself up to it, bearing in mind, all the time, his own secret superiority—as a man—and as a broken reed. Better, he argued, to have been a thing of mystery and music and to have been broken, than to have never been a reed but to have been composed of some prosaic if quite unbreakable material with about as much mystery or music in its bloodstream as there is love in a condor's eye.

All these thoughts, of course, he kept strictly to himself. To Irma's mind he was her lord upon a leash. To the Staff he was simply on a leash. In his own mind, leash or not, a philosophy was growing. The philosophy of invisible revolution.

He peered at her, not unlovingly, through his white eyelashes. He was glad she was there, mending his ceremonial gown. It was better than being baited by the Staff as in the old days. After all, she couldn't tell what he was thinking. He watched her pointed nose. How had he ever admired it?

But, oh, the glee of thinking to himself. Of dreaming of impossible escapes, or of reversing the *status quo,* so that once again she would be in his power, as on that magical evening in the dappled arbor. But then—the strain of it, the strain of it. There was no joy in will power.

He settled back in his chair and reveled in his weakness, his old mouth twisting a little at one corner, his eyes half-closing as he relaxed the leonine features of his magnificent old head.

The sense of unreality which had spread through the castle like some strange malaise had muffled Bellgrove's marriage so that although there was no lack of incident, and no question as to its importance, a sharpness, an awareness was missing and nobody really believed in what was happening. It was as though the castle were recovering from an illness, or was about to have one. It was either lost in a blur of unfocused memory or in the unreality of a disquietening premonition. The immediacy of the castle's life was missing. There were no sharp edges. No crisp sounds. A veil was over all things, a veil that no one could tear away.

How long it lasted was impossible to say, for although there was this general oppression that weighed on every action, all but annihilating its reality of significance, making, for instance, of Bellgrove's marriage a ceremony of dream, yet the sense of unreality in each individual was different; different in intensity, in quality, and in duration, according to the temperaments of all who were submerged.

There were some who hardly realized that there was a difference. Thick, bullet-headed men with mouths like horses were scarcely aware. They felt that nothing mattered quite as much as it used to do, but that was all.

Others were drowned in it, and walked like ghosts. Their own voices, when they spoke, appeared to be coming to them from far away.

It was the influence of Gormenghast, for what else could it have been? It was as though the labyrinthian place had woken from its sleep of stone and iron and in drawing breath had left a vacuum, and it was in this vacuum that its puppets moved.

And then came a time when, on a late spring evening, the castle exhaled and the distances came forward in a rush, and the faraway voices grew sharp and close, and the hands became aware of what they were grasping, and Gormenghast became stone again and returned to its sleep.

But before the weight of emptiness had lifted, a number of things had happened which, although when seen in retrospect appeared vague and shadowy, had nevertheless taken place. However nebulous they had appeared at the time, their repercussions were concrete enough.

Titus was no longer a child, and the end of his school days was in sight. He had, as the years went by, become more solitary. To all save Fuchsia, the Doctor, Flay, and Bellgrove he presented a sullen front. Beneath this dour and unpleasing armor his passionate longing to be free of his hereditary responsibilities smoldered rebelliously.

His hatred was not for Gormenghast, for its very dust was in his bloodstream, and he knew no other place, but for the ill fate that had chosen him to be the one upon whose restless shoulders there would rest, in the future, the heavy onus of an ancient trust.

He hated the lack of choice: the assumption on the part of those around him that there were no two ways of thinking: that his desire for a future of his own making was due to ignorance or to a willful betrayal of his birthright.

But more than all this he hated the confusion in his own heart. For he was proud. He was irrationally proud. He had lost the unself-consciousness of childhood where he was a boy among boys; he was now Lord Titus and conscious of the fact. And while he ached for the anonymity of freedom, he moved erect with a solitary pride of bearing, sullen and commanding.

And it was this contradiction within himself that was as much as anything else the cause of his blunt and uncompromising manners. With the youths of his own age he had become more and more unpopular, his schoolmates seeing no cause for the violence of his outbursts. He had ripped the lid off his desk for less than nothing. He could be dangerous, and as time went on his isolation grew more complete. The boy who had been ready for any act of mischief, for any midnight venture, in the long dormitories, was now another being!

The tangle of his thoughts and emotions—the confused groping for an outlet for his wayward spirit, his callow lust for revolt, left no room in him for those things that would once have quickened his pulse. He had found that to be alone was more intoxicating. He had changed.

And yet, in spite of the long years that had passed since he, Dr. Prunesquallor, and Professor Bellgrove had played marbles in the small fort, he was still able to delight in the most childish of amusements. He would be sitting by the moat, and launching by the hour small wooden boats of his own making. But more abstractedly than in the old days, as though for all his apparent concentration, as he carved with his penknife the taper-ing bows or the blunt stern of some monarch of the waves, his mind was really far away.

Yet he carved away at these small craft and he named them as he launched them upon their perilous missions to the isles of blood and spices. And he would visit the Doctor and watch him making those peculiar draw-ings which Irma had never cared for, those drawings of small spidery men, a hundred on a page, engaged now in battle, now in conclave, now in scenes of hunting, now in worship before some spidery god. And for the hour he would be very happy. And he would visit Fuch-sia and they would talk and talk until their throats were sore . . . would talk about all there was in Gormenghast, for they knew no other place—but neither to his sister nor to Bellgrove, who would sometimes, when Irma was engaged elsewhere, shamble down to the moat's edge to launch a ship or two—neither to him, nor to the Doctor, did Titus ever unburden himself of his secret fear, the fear that his life would become no more than a round of preordained ritual. For there was no one, not even Fuchsia, however much she might sympathize, who could help him now. There was no one who would dare to encourage him in his longing to free himself of his yoke to escape and to discover what lay beyond the margins of his realm.

Chapter Fifty-Three

THE unearthly lull that had descended upon Gormen-ghast had not failed to affect so imaginative and highly strung a nature as Fuchsia's. Steerpike, although sensi-tive to atmosphere in a high degree, was less submerged, and moved as it were with his crafty head protruding above the weird water. He could see Fuchsia, as she walked in a transparent world, far below the surface. Acutely aware of this trancelike omnipresence, Steerpike, following the course of his nature, was at once concerned with how best he could use this drug to further his own ends, and it was not long before he had come to a decision.

He must woo the daughter of the House. He must woo her with all the guile and artistry in his power. He must break down her reserve with an approach both simple and candid, with an assumed gentleness, and a concentration upon those things which he could pretend they had in common: and with a charming yet manly deference to her rank. At the same time he would both give the impression of those fires within him that were undoubtedly there, if for the wrong reason, and by devious means so engineer their assignations and coincidental meetings that she would often come upon him in hazardous situations, for he knew already how much she admired his bravery.

But at the same time he must keep his face hidden as much as possible. He had no illusions about its power to horrify. That she was impregnated with the heavy yet faraway atmosphere of the place was no reason for him to assume that she was impervious to the fearfulness of his ruined face. They would meet after dark, when with no visual distraction she could gradually realize that only in him could she find that complete companionship, that harmony of mind and spirit—that sense of confidence, of which she had been so starved. But she was starved for more than this. He knew her life had been loveless—and he knew of the warmth and vibrancy of her nature. But he had always waited. And now the time had come.

He laid his plans. He made his first advances in the dusky evenings. As Master of Ceremonies, it was not difficult for him to know what parts of the castle would be clear of possible intruders at varying times of the late evening.

Fuchsia, deeply affected by the unearthly atmosphere

that had made of her ancient home a place that she could hardly believe in, was led by subtle degrees, through a period of weeks, to a state of mind where she felt it a natural thing to have her advice solicited, as to this point or that, and for Steerpike to tell her of what had happened to him during the day. His voice was quiet and even. His vocabulary, rich and flexible. She was attracted by his grip upon whatever subject they conversed about—it was so far beyond her own powers. Her admiration for his vitality of mind developed, in its turn, into an excited interest in the whole being, this Steerpike, this nimble, fearless confidant of their nocturnal meetings. He was unlike anyone else. He was wide awake and alive to his fingertips. Her old revulsion at the memory of his burned face and red hands became buried under the ever-growing structure of this propinquity.

That she, the daughter of the Line, should see so much of an officer of the castle, for unofficial reasons, was, she knew, a crime against her station. But she had been so long a time alone. To be able to feel that she could interest anyone to the extent of their wanting to see her night after night was something so new to her that it was but a short way to the outskirts of that treacherous land whose paths she would so soon be treading.

But she did not look ahead. Unlike this new companion, this man of the dusk, whose every sentence, every thought, every action was ulterior, she lived in the moment of excitement, savoring the taste of an experience that was enough in itself. She had no instinct of self-preservation. She had no apprehension. For Steerpike had moved toward her with a gradual and circuitous cunning until the evening came when their hands met involuntarily in the darkness, and neither hand was withdrawn, and from that moment it seemed to Steerpike that his road to power was clear before him.

And for a long time everything continued to develop in the way he had foreseen, the intimacy of their secret meetings leading them ever more deeply into, as Fuchsia thought, each other's confidence.

But, with the evil knowledge of the power that was now his, Steerpike, indulging himself in the anticipation of final conquest, made no rash attempt to seduce Fuchsia. He knew that with Fuchsia no longer a virgin, he would have her, if for no other reason than that of simple blackmail, in the palm of his hand. But he was not ready yet. There was a lot to be considered.

As for Fuchsia, it was all so new and tremendous to her that her emotions had enough on which to feed. She was happier than she had ever been in her life.

Chapter Fifty-Four

❋❋❋❋❋❋❋❋❋❋❋

THE disappearance of the Earl, Sepulchrave, Titus's father and of his sisters, the twins, and their terrible and secret ends; the death of Sourdust by burning, and of his son Barquentine by fire and water; what of all this mystery and violence in the eyes of the castle? They had spread themselves, these horrors, over a period of twelve or more years, and although the minds, active in their different ways, of the Countess, the Doctor, and Flay had, from their different angles, made periodic efforts to discover in the tragedies some common ground, yet no proof of foul play had yet been found which could support their suspicions.

Flay alone knew the grizzly truth about the secret death of his master, Lord Sepulchrave, and of his enemy the gross Swelter whom he had killed. This knowledge he had never divulged.

But his own banishment had been the result of Steerpike's gesture of disloyalty to his mad master, when the skewbald man was a youth of seventeen or eighteen years, and this disloyalty had remained rooted in Flay's mind. But of the incarceration and death of the twins he knew nothing, although, witless of its origins and significance, he had heard their terrible laughter as they died in the hollow halls.

He had strained his brain and memory, as had the Doctor and the Countess, to draw some significant conclusion from the common deaths by fire of the father and son—Sourdust and Barquentine—and from the fact that Steerpike had been the hero of both occasions. Try as they would they were unable to rationalize their suspicions.

And yet there were, over the course of the years, small concrete, although disconnected, reasons for apprehension. As yet they fitted into no pattern, but they were there, and they were not forgotten.

The Doctor had always been anxious to discover Steerpike's reason for leaving his service and establishing himself as confidant and retainer of the vacant twins. His was no mind to find pleasure in such surroundings. His only reason must have been for social advancement or for some darker motive. The identical twins had disappeared. Their note, which Steerpike had found on their table, had told of their intention to kill themselves. Prunesquallor had got hold of this note and compared its calligraphy with a letter Irma had once received from them. He compared them in mirrors—he devoted an entire evening to their scrutiny. It seemed that they were by the same hand, the formation of letters big and round and uncertain as a child's.

But the Doctor had known these retarded women for many years and he did not believe, for all the oddness of their thwarted natures, that they would ever take their own lives.

Nor did the Countess believe that they were capable of making an end to themselves. Their puerile ambition and vanity—and their only too obvious longing to assume, one day, the roles in which they were always seeing themselves, the roles of ladies, great and splendid, bedecked with jewels—precluded any such idea as suicide. But there was no proof either way.

The Doctor had told the Countess of Steerpike's delirious cry, "And the twins will make it five!" She had stared out of the window of her room.

"Five what?" she had said.

"Exactly," said the Doctor. "Five what?"

"Five enigmas," she answered heavily, without a change of expression.

"And what are they, your Ladyship? Do you mean five . . .?"

She interrupted him heavily. "The Earl, my husband," she said, "vanished: one. His sisters, vanished: two. Swelter, vanished: three. Sourdust and Barquentine, burned: five."

"But the deaths of Sourdust and Barquentine were hardly enigmatic."

"One wouldn't be. Two would," said the Countess. "And the youth at them both."

"The youth?" queried the Doctor.

"Steerpike," said the Countess.

"Ah," said the Doctor, "we have the same fears."

"We have," said the Countess. "I am waiting."

The Doctor thought of Fuchsia's poem:

> *How white and scarlet is that face!*
> *Who knows, in some unusual place*
> *The colored heroes are alight*
> *With faces made of red and white.*

"But your Ladyship," he said—she was still staring through the window. "The words, 'And the twins will make it five,' suggest to me that their Ladyships Cora and Clarice would make two of the group he had in his delirious mind. He was making a list of individuals, in his fever, I will stake my brightest penny."

"And so . . ."

"And so, your Ladyship, the deaths and disappearances would be six, not five."

"Who knows?" said the Countess. "It is too early. Give him rope. We have no proof. But by the black taproot of the very castle, if my fear is founded, the towers themselves will sicken at his death: the oldest stones will spew."

Her heavy face flushed. She lowered her hand into a wide pocket, and drawing forth some grain she extended her arm. A small mottled bird appeared out of nowhere and, running along her outstretched arm, perched with its claws about her index finger and with a sideways movement began to peck from her palm.

Chapter Fifty-Five

"But he can't help giving you your ritual for each day, can he?" said Fuchsia. "And instructing you. It's not his fault, it's the Law. Father had to do it when he was alive —and *his* father had to—and they've all had to. It isn't possible for him to do any different. He *has* to tell you what's in the books, however trying it is for you."

"I hate him," said Titus.

"Why? Why?" cried Fuchsia. "What's the good of hating him because he's doing what he has to do? You don't expect that he can make an exception, do you, after thousands of years? I suppose you'd rather have Barquentine. Can't you see how bigoted you are? I think he does his work wonderfully."

"I hate him!" said Titus.

"You're becoming a bore!" said Fuchsia, with heat. "Can't you say anything except 'I hate him'? What's wrong with him? Do you hold his appearance against him? Do you? If so, you're mean and damnable."

She shook her thick black hair away from her eyes. Her chin trembled.

"Oh, God! God! Do you think I want to quarrel with you, Titus, my darling? You know how I love you. But you're unfair. *Unfair.* You know nothing about him."

"I hate him," said Titus. "I hate the cheap and stinking guts of him."

Chapter Fifty-Six

As the months passed the tension increased. Titus and Steerpike were at daggers drawn, although Steerpike, the soul of bland discretion, showed nothing of his feelings, and gave no sign to Titus or the outside world of his loathing of this forward boy—the boy who unconsciously stood between him and the zenith of his ambition.

Titus, who ever since that day when, little more than a child, he had defied Steerpike in the classroom silence, and had fallen fainting from his desk, had held on grimly to the dangerous ascendancy he had gained by that curious and childish victory.

Every day the details of his after-school duties were read to Titus in the Library, Steerpike flicking through the pages of cross reference, and explaining the obscurer passages with clarity and precision. Up till now the Master of Ceremonies had kept rigidly to the letter of the Law. But now, in the all but invulnerable position of being the only one who had access to the tomes of reference and procedure, he was making a list of duties which he would insert among the ancient papers. He had been able to unearth some of the original paper, and it was only for him to forge the copper-plate writing and the archaic spelling, and invent a series of duties for Titus which would be both galling and, on occasion, sufficiently hazardous for there to be always the outside chance of the young Earl coming to grief. There were, for instance, stairways that were no longer safe—there were the rotten beams and crumbling masonry. Beyond this there would always be the possibility of deliberately weakening and undermining certain catwalks that stretched along the upper walls of the castle, or in some way or another of making sure that in the following out of the forged procedures, Titus would sooner or later fall *accidentally* to his death.

And with the death of Titus, and with Fuchsia in his power, the Countess alone would stand between him and a virtual dictatorship.

There would yet be enemies. There would be the Doctor, whose intelligence was rather more acute than Steerpike would have wished; and there was the Countess herself, the only character for whom he held a puzzled and grudging respect—not for her intelligence, but for the reason of the very fact that she baffled his analysis. What was she? What was she thinking and by what processes? His mind and hers had no point of contact. In her presence he was doubly careful. They were animals of different species. They watched one another with the mutual suspicion of those who have no common tongue.

As for Fuchsia, it was but a step toward mastery. He had surpassed himself. Her heart was now as tender as his overtures had been, with their delicate gradations, their subtle cadences, their superb restraint.

It was no longer a case of their meeting at dusk, now here, now there, at varying rendezvous. For some while, Steerpike had for his own delectation been furnishing yet another secret room for himself. He now had nine, scattered throughout the castle—only one of which, a large bedroom-study, was known to the castle. Of the rest five were in obscure quarters of Gormenghast, and three, though in the most populous areas, were as curiously hidden as a wren's nest in a bank of grass and weeds. Their doors, abutting on major arteries of the castle, were never seen to open. They were there for all to see, but no one saw them.

In one of these rooms which he had but recently appropriated, and which he only visited at night when thick silence lay along the corridor, he had got together a few pictures, some books, a cabinet of shallow drawers in which he kept his collection of stolen jewelry, old coins, a range of poisons, and various secret papers. A thick crimson carpet covered the floor. The small table and the two chairs were of elegant design and he had skillfully repaired the damage that long years had worked upon them. How different was this interior from the rough stone corridor without, with its stone pillars on either side of every door and the heavily protruding shelflike slabs of stone above!

It was to this room that Fuchsia made her nocturnal journeys, her heart beating, her pupils dilated in the darkness. And it was here that she was so courteously received. A shaded lamp threw out a soft golden glow. A book or two, carefully chosen, lay casually here and there. It was always irksome for Steerpike to make those last few changes in the disposition of the objects which were calculated to give an air of informality to the room. He detested untidiness as he detested love. But he knew that Fuchsia would be ill at ease with the kind of formal and perfect arrangement that gave him pleasure.

Even so, she seemed strangely incongruous in that tasteful and orderly trap. For Steerpike could not entirely destroy the reflection of his own coldness. She seemed too much alive—alive in so different a sense from the glittering and icy vitality of her companion—too much alive in the way that love like an earthquake or some natural and sinless force is incompatible with a neat and formal world. However quietly she sat back in her chair, her black hair about her shoulders, she was potentially disruptive.

But she admired what she saw. She admired all that she was not. It was all so different from Gormenghast. When she remembered her old untidy attic and the rooms she now occupied with the floor littered with poems, and the walls with drawings, she supposed that there must be something wrong with her.

When she remembered her mother, she felt, for the first time, embarrassed.

One night when she tapped upon the door with her

fingertips there was no reply. She tapped again, glancing apprehensively along the corridor on either side. The silence was absolute. She had never before had to wait for more than the fraction of a second. And then a voice said, "Be careful, my lady."

Fuchsia had started at the sound as at the touch of a red iron. The voice had come from nowhere. There was no sound of a step. In fear and trembling she lit the candle she carried in her hand—a rash and risky thing to do. But there was no one. And then, in the far distance, something began to approach her rapidly. Long before she could see Steerpike she knew it was he. It was but a few moments before his swift, narrow, high-shouldered form was upon her and had snatched the candle from her hand and crushed out the flame. In another moment his key had been turned in the lock and she had been hustled through the door. He locked it from the inside, in the darkness, but he had already whispered fiercely, "Fool." With that word the world turned over. Everything changed.

The delicate balance of their relationship was set in violent agitation—and a dead weight came down over Fuchsia's heart.

Had the crystalline and dazzling structure which Steerpike had gradually erected, adding ornament to ornament until, balanced before her in all its beauty, it had dazzled the girl—an outward sign of his regard for her —had the exquisite structure been less exquisite, less crystalline, less perfect, then its crash upon the cold stones far beneath would never have been so final. Its substance, brittle as glass, had been scattered in a thousand fragments.

The short, brutal word, and the push which he had given her, had turned her on the instant from a dark and eager girl into something more somber. She was shocked and resentful—but less resentful, for those first moments, than hurt. She had also become, without her knowing it, *Lady Fuchsia*. Her blood had risen in her— the blood of her Line. She had forgotten it when love was tender, but now in bitterness she was again the daughter of an Earl.

She had known, of course, that to light a candle outside the very door was against all their strictest rules of care and secrecy. But she had been frightened. Maddening as it would have been for their rendezvous to have been discovered, yet there had been no sin in it, save that of her conducting her affairs in secret, and of allowing herself to be the close friend of a commoner.

But his face had been ugly with anger. She had never known that he could so lose that perfect, that chiseled quietness of pose and feature. She had never known that his clear, neat, and persuasive voice could take on a tone so savage and cruel.

And to have been pushed! To have been thrust forward in the darkness. His hands, which once, like those of a musician, had been so thrilling in their delicate strength, had been rough as the claws of an animal. As surely as the change of his voice, as surely as the word *"fool,"* this shove in the darkness had woken her to a reality both bitter and galling.

But, as she trembled, there was, mixed with the mortification, the ghostly and exciting memory of that voice out of nowhere. It had evolved out of the darkness and at no more distance from her than a few feet, but there had been no one there. She had no more idea of how it had originated than of the intention or meaning of its warning. She only knew now that she would not seek assistance from Steerpike; she would not confide her fear of this inexplicable voice in someone who had degraded her. All the Lords of Gormenghast were at her shoulder.

She turned on her heel, in the darkened room, and before he had lit the lamp, "Let me out of here," she said. But almost immediately the familiar room was filled with the gold lamplight and she saw upon the table, sitting with its face cupped in its wrinkled hands, a monkey. It was dressed in a little costume of red and yellow diamonds. On its head was a small velvet hat, like a pirate's, with a violet feather curling from the crown.

Steerpike had covered his face with his hands, but he was watching Fuchsia through the slits between his fingers. He had lost command. The sight of a flame, where it had no cause to be, had struck at him like a lash. He had not been burned for nothing and fire was his only fear. Once again he had failed.

But he did not know how seriously. He watched her through his fingers.

She stared at the monkey with an expression quite indefinable. What surprise she felt was not in evidence. The turmoil and the shock of having been so roughly treated were still too strong in her for any other emotion to supplant them, however bizarre the stimulus might be. But when the vivid little animal rose to its feet and took off its hat, and when it replaced it after scratching its head and yawning, then, for an instant, something less sad suffused her face with a fleeting animation.

But it was impossible for her mood to be swung so rapidly from one extreme to another. A part of her mind was fascinated by the oddness of it all, but nothing touched her heart. It was a monkey dressed up and that was all. What would once have inflamed her with excitement, left her now, at this paralyzing moment, quite frozen.

Steerpike had gained a moment or two, but what could he do with them? She had commanded him to let her go from the room when the monkey had caught her eye.

Once again she turned her gaze to him. Her black eyes appeared quite dead, the luster drained away. Her lips were tightly closed.

She saw him with his hands across his face. And then she heard his voice.

"Fuchsia," he said, "allow me one moment, only one, in which to tell you of the danger from which we have just escaped. There was no time to be lost and though there could never be any excuse, and although I can never ask for forgiveness, yet you must allow me a short moment in which to explain my violence.

"Fuchsia! It was for you. My violence was for you. My roughness was the roughness of love. I had no time to do other than to save you. Have you not heard the footsteps? She has just gone by. One moment later and your light would have brought her to this door. And you know the punishment. Of course you do, the punishment, which by ancient law is meted out to those daughters of the Line who consort with the mere outsiders. It is too awful to think about. And that is why our plans have been so secret, our rules so rigorous. And you know this. And you have been meticulous. But tonight you misjudged the time, did you not? You were four minutes early. Oh, that was risky enough. But to add to such a peril the lighting of your candle. And then, as always happens, it was precisely when all this was happening that your mother should follow me."

"My mother?" Fuchsia's voice was a whisper.

"Your mother. I had led her away, for I knew that she was near. I doubled back. I crossed my tracks. I doubled back again and yet she was there, and moving slowly—I cannot understand it—but I came as I intended to this door with the length of the corridor between us— the length of the corridor and the odd twenty feet that would give me the chance of whipping into our room in time—but no, it wasn't this that I was going to do. No. For what would have been more likely than for you to have met her—and then . . ."

Steerpike dropped his hands from his face where they had been all this time. His voice had been running on with a certain charm, for he had managed to vary it with a kind of stutter—not so much nervous in effect as eager and candid.

"But what happened, Fuchsia? Well, you know that as well as I do. I turned the north corner with your mother the length of a corridor behind—and there you were, like a bonfire, the length of the corridor before me. Put yourself in my place. One cannot have all the noble emotions at the same time. One cannot mix up desperation with being a perfect gentleman. At least I can't. Perhaps I should have been given lessons. All I could do was to save the situation. To hide you. To save you. You were there too early; and Fuchsia, it made me angry. I have never been angry with you. And perhaps even now, it wasn't really *you* I was angry with, but fate, or destiny or whatever it is that might have upset our plans. And it was because our plans have always been so carefully prepared—so that there shall be no risk, and you shall come to no harm—that my rage boiled up. You were no longer Fuchsia to me, at that moment. You were this *thing* that I was to save. After I had got behind the door, then you would be Fuchsia again. Had I waited for a moment before stifling your light or getting you through the door, then our lives might indeed have been ruined. For I love you, Fuchsia. You are all I ever longed for. Can't you see that it was because of this that I had no time to be polite? It was a boiling moment. It was a maelstrom. I called you 'fool,' yes, 'fool,' out of my love for you—and then, . . . and then . . . here in this room again, it all seemed so unbelievable and it does so still, and I am half ashamed of the gift I had brought you and the writing I have done for you—oh, Fuchsia—I don't even know if I can show it to you now . . ." He turned abruptly with his hand clenched at his forehead, and then, as though to say he would not give way to his despair, "Come on then, Satan," he whispered. "Come on, my wicked boy!" And the monkey leaped onto Steerpike's shoulder.

"What writing?" said Fuchsia.

"I had written you a poem." He spoke very softly, in a way that had often proved successful, but he was a step too far in advance of his progress.

"But perhaps now," he said, "you will not wait to see it, Fuchsia."

"No," she said after a pause. "Not now."

Her inflection was so strange that it was impossible to tell whether she meant "not now" in the sense of its being no longer possible for her to do anything so intimate as to read a love poem; or not *now*, but some other time.

Steerpike could only cry, "I understand," and placed the monkey on the table where it walked rapidly to and fro, on all four legs, and then leaped onto one of his cabinets.

"And I will understand, if you have no wish for Satan."

"Satan?" Her voice was quite expressionless.

"Your monkey," he said. "Perhaps you would rather not be bothered. I thought he would please you. I made his clothes myself."

"I don't know! I don't know!" cried Fuchsia suddenly. "I don't *know*, I tell you, I don't *know!*"

"Shall I take you to your room?"

"I will go myself."

"As you please," said Steerpike. "But recall what I have said, I implore you. Try and understand; for I love you as the shadows love the castle."

She turned her eyes to him. For a moment a light came into them, but in the next moment they appeared empty once more; empty and blank.

"I will never understand," she said. "It is no good however much you talk. I may have been wrong. I don't know. At any rate everything is changed. I don't feel the same any more. I want to go now."

"Yes, of course. But will you grant me two small favors?"

"I suppose so," said Fuchsia. "What are they? I'm tired."

"The first one is to ask you from the bottom of my heart to try to understand the strain which was put upon me, and to ask you whether, even if it is for the last time, you will meet me, as we have done for so long, meet me that we can talk for a little while—not about us, not about our trouble, not about my faults, not about this terrible chasm between us, but about all the happy things. Will you meet me tomorrow night, on those conditions?"

"I don't *know!*" said Fuchsia. "I don't know! But I suppose so. O God, I suppose so."

"Thank you," said Steerpike. "Thank you, Fuchsia. And my other request is only this. To know whether, if you have no use for Satan, you will let me have him back—because he *is* yours . . . and . . ." Steerpike turned his head from her and moved away a few paces.

"You would like to know, wouldn't you, Satan, to whom

you belong . . . ," he cried in a voice that was intended to sound gallant.

Fuchsia turned on him suddenly. It seemed that she had now realized the natural edge of her own intellect. She stared at the skewbald man with the monkey on his shoulder and then her words cut into the pale man like knives. "Steerpike," she said, *I think you're going soft."*

From that moment Steerpike knew that when she came on the following night he would seduce her. With so dark a secret to keep hidden, the daughter of the Countess would indeed be at his mercy. He had waited long enough. Now, upon the heels of his mistake, was the only time for him to strike. He had felt the first intimation of something slipping away beneath his feet. If guile and coercion failed him, then there could be no two ways about it. This was no time for mercy—and though she proved a tigress he would have her—and blackmail would follow as smoothly as a thundercloud.

Chapter Fifty-Seven

I

WHEN Flay heard the door open quietly below him he held his breath. For a few moments no one appeared and then a shape still darker than the darkness stepped out into the corridor and began to walk rapidly away to the south. When he heard the door close again he lowered himself from the great stone shelf that stretched above Steerpike's doorway, and with his long, bony arms outstretched to their full extent he dropped the odd few inches to the ground.

His frustration at being unable to gain any clue as to what had been going on inside the room was only equalled by his horror at finding that it was Fuchsia who had been the clandestine visitor.

He had sensed her danger. He knew it in his bones. But he could not have persuaded her, suddenly, in the night, that she was in peril. He could not have told her what kind of peril. He did not know himself. But he had acted on the spur of the moment and in whispering to her out of the darkness he hoped that she might be put upon her guard, if only for reasons of supernatural fear.

He followed Fuchsia only so far as to be sure that she was safely upon her way to her own rooms. It was all he could do not to call after her, or overtake her, for he was deeply perplexed and frightened. His love for her was something quite alone in his sour life. Fond as he was of Titus, it was the memory of Fuchsia, more than of the boy, or of any other living soul, that gave to the flinty darkness of his mind those touches of warmth which, along with his worship of Gormenghast, that abstraction of outspread stone, were seemingly so foreign to his nature.

But he knew that he must not speak to her tonight. The distracted way in which she moved, sometimes running and sometimes walking, gave him sufficient evidence of her fatigue and, he feared, of her misery.

He did not know what Steerpike had done or said but he knew he had hurt her, and if it were not that he felt upon the brink of gaining some kind of damning evidence, then he would have returned to that room from which Fuchsia had emerged, and on the reappearance of Steerpike at the doorway, he would have plucked the skewbald face, barehanded, from the head.

II

As he returned in the direction of the fateful corridor, a heavy pain lay across his forehead and his thoughts pursued one another in a confusion of anger and speculation. He could not know that with every step he was traveling, not nearer to his room but farther from it— farther in time, farther in space—nor that the night's adventures, far from coming to a close, were about to begin in earnest.

By now the night was well advanced. He had returned with a slow and somewhat dragging pace, lingering here and there to lean his head against the cold walls while his headache hammered behind his eyes and across his angular brow. Once he sat down for an hour upon the lowest step of a flight of age-hollowed stairs, his long beard falling upon his knee, and taking the sharp curve of them and falling again in a straggle of stringlike hair to within a few inches of the floor.

Fuchsia and Steerpike? What could it mean? The blasphemy of it! The horror of it! He ground his teeth in the darkness.

The castle was as silent as some pole-axed monster. Inert, breathless, spread-eagled. It was a night that seemed to prove by the consolidation of its darkness and its silence the hopelessness of any further dawn. There was no such thing as dawn. It was an invention of the night's or of the old wives of the night—a fable, immemorially old —recounted century after century in the eternal darkness; retold and retold to the gnomic children in the tunnels and the caves of Gormenghast—a tale of another world where such things happened, where stones and bricks and ivy stems and iron could be seen as well as touched and smelled, could be lit and colored, and where at certain times a radiance shone like honey from the east and the blackness was scaled away, and this thing they called dawn arose above the woods as though the fable had materialized, the legend come to life.

It was a night with a bull's mouth. But the mouth was bound and gagged. It was a night with enormous eyes, but they were hooded.

The only sound that Flay could hear was the tapping of his heart.

III

It was later, and at an indeterminate hour of the same night, or inky morning, that Mr. Flay, long after passing the door in the passage, came to an involuntary halt as he was about to cross a small cloistered quadrangle.

There was no reason why he should have been startled by the single band of livid yellow in the sky. He must have known that the dawn could not have been much longer delayed. He was certainly not held by its beauty. He did not think in that way.

In the center of the quadrangle was a thorn tree, and his eyes turned to the pitchy silhouette of that part of it that cut across the yellow of the sunrise. His familiarity with the shape of the old tree caused him to stare more intently at the rough and branching stem. It seemed thicker than usual. He could only see with any clarity that portion of its bole that crossed the sunrise. It appeared to have shaped its outline. It was as though something were leaning against it and adding a little to its bulk. He crouched so that still more of the unfamiliar shape came into view, for the upper part was criss-crossed with branches. As his vision was lowered and he commanded a clearer view beneath the overhanging boughs his muscles became tense, for it seemed that against the livid strip of sky—which threw everything else both on the earth and in the air into yet richer blackness—it seemed that against this livid strip the unfamiliar outline on the left of the stem was narrowing to something the shape of a neck. He got silently to his knees and then, lowering his head and lifting his eyes, he obtained an uninterrupted view of Steerpike's profile. His body and the back of the head were glued together as though he and the tree had grown up as one thing from the ground.

And that was all there was. The universal darkness above and below. The horizontal stream of saffron yellow and, like a rough black bridge that joined the upper darkness to the lower, the silhouette of the ragged thorn stem, with the profile of a face among the stems.

What was he doing there in the darkness alone and motionless?

Flay raised himself and leaned against the nearest of the cloistered pillars. The cut-out face of his enemy was immediately obscured by branches. But what had caught his eye, the unfamiliar outline of the bole, he now recognized as being formed by an angle of the young man's elbow and the line of his hip and thigh.

Without wasting a moment in trying to rationalize his instinctive belief that some fresh act of evil was afoot, Mr. Flay prepared himself for, if necessary, a protracted vigil. There was nothing evil in leaning against a thorn tree as the first light broke in a yellow band—even though the leaning form was Steerpike's. There was no reason why he should not return at any moment to his room and sleep or indulge in some other equally innocent occupation.

He knew that he was caught up in one of those stretches of time when for anything to happen normally would be abnormal. The dawn was too tense and highly charged for any common happening to survive.

Steerpike, while he leaned there, rigid with the cold and flexible steel of his own conspirings, eyed the yellow light. He now knew that whatever steps were to be taken for his own advancement should be taken *now*. However much he may have wished to delay his designs there was no gainsaying the sense of urgency—the sense that time was not, for all the logic of his mind, upon his side.

It was true that there was still no evidence of his guilt. But there was something almost as bad. An indescribable sensation that his power was somehow crumbling away; that the earth was slippery beneath his feet; that in spite of his formidable position, there was that in Gormenghast that, with a puff, could blow him into darkness. However much he told himself that he had made no fundamental error—that the few slips he had made had been invariably in minor matters, maddening as they might be —yet this sensation remained. It had come upon him with the shutting of the door—when Fuchsia had left him and he was alone in his room. It was new to him. He had believed in nothing that could not be proven one way or another, in the cells of his agile brain. Apart from the inconvenience that his carelessness would, for a short time, cause him, what else was there for him to rack his brains about in regard to the incident of a few hours earlier?

What was there for Fuchsia to hold against him—or even to give as evidence, save that he, the Master of Ceremonies, had been rude to her?

And yet all this was beside the point of his apprehension. If it was Fuchsia's resentment that had uncovered, witlessly, the dark pit into which he was now staring, what then was this pit, wherefore was its depth, and why its darkness?

It was the first time that he had ever known that sleep, though he craved it, was beyond him. But his habit of making good use of every moment was deeply rooted —and especially when the time at his disposal was that in which the castle lay abed.

And Flay knew this. He knew that it was hardly a part of Steerpike's nature to lean against a tree for the sake of watching the sun rise. Nor was it characteristic of him to brood. He was no romantic. He lived too much upon the edge of instancy for introspection. No. It was for some other reason that he leaned there, biding his time—for what?

Flay knelt down again, and with his chin almost touching the ground and his small eyes swiveled upward, he stared once more at that sharp profile, its edges razor-keen against the yellow band. And then, while on his knees, two things occurred to him almost simultaneously. The first, that it was more than possible that Steerpike was waiting for sufficient light to enable him to make his way to unfamiliar ground. That he wished to go secretly and yet not lose his way, for even now the darkness was intense, the bar of light that lay like a livid ruler across the black east in no way lightening the earth or the sky about it. It kept its brilliance to itself; saffron inlaid on ebony. And this was Flay's guess: that the silhouette was waiting for the first diffusion of the light—that the line of the elbow and the hip would alter—that a profile would detach itself from a thorn tree and that a figure, lithe as a lynx, would steer into the gloom. But not alone. Flay would be following and it was when Flay, still upon his bony knees, his head near the ground, his beard spread, was turning this over in his mind that the need for some confederate, not for reason of companionship or safety, but in order to bear witness, occurred to him. Whatever he was to find, whatever lay ahead, however innocent or however bloody, it would be his word alone against the pale man's. It would be the word of an exile against that of the Master of Ritual. In being within the precincts of the castle at all, he was committing a grievous sin. He had been banished by the Countess and it would ill become him to point his finger at an officer unless his accusation was doubly backed with proof.

No sooner had this notion occurred to him than he was on his feet. He judged that he had, at the most, another quarter of an hour in which to wake—whom? He had no choice. Titus and Fuchsia alone knew of his return to the castle and that he lived in secret among the Hollow Halls.

It was of course grotesquely out of the question either that Fuchsia should be disturbed or allowed within Steerpike's range. As for Titus, he was now almost grown to his full height. But he was of an odd, highly strung nature—sullen and excitable by turns. Strong as need be for his years, he was more apt to have his energy sapped by the excess of his imagination than of his body. Flay did not understand him, but he trusted him, and he knew of how the boy's loathing of Steerpike had estranged him from Fuchsia. He had no doubt that Titus would join him, but he doubted for a moment his own courage to do so dangerous a thing as to draw the heir of Gormenghast within the circle of expected danger. Yet he knew that above all else it was his duty to unmask if possible his enemy, for upon so doing hung the safety of the young Earl and all he symbolized. And what is more, he swore by the iron of his long muscles, and by the strong teeth in his bony head, that whatever danger might menace his own person, no harm would come to the boy.

And so, without a moment to lose, he turned and re-entered the door in the cloisters and set off upon what in saner moments he would have considered an unthinkable mission. For what could be more iniquitous than to jeopardize the safety of his Lordship? But now he saw only that by awakening Titus and launching him at dawn upon so dark a game as that of shadowing a suspect, he was perhaps bringing closer the day when the heart of Gormenghast, purged and loyal, would beat again unthreatened.

With every moment the yellow band in the sky was brightening. He sped with the awkward speed of the predatory spider, his long legs eating up the corridors, four feet at a stride, and treading the stairways beneath them as though he were on stilts. But when he came to the dormitory he moved with the circumspection of a thief.

He opened the door by degrees. On his right was the janitor's cubicle. Directly he heard the sound of sandpaper scraping away behind the woodwork he recognized the breathing of the same old man who had held this watchdog office from the early days, and he knew that he was safe enough from that quarter.

But how to recognize the Earl? He had no light. Apart from the breathing of the janitor the dormitory was in absolute silence. There was no time for anything but to put his first notion into operation. There were two rows of beds that stretched away to the southwest. Why he turned to the right-hand wall he did not know, but he did so without hesitation. Feeling for the end-rail of the first bed, he leaned over. "Lordship!" he whispered. "Lordship!" There was no reply. He turned to the second bed and whispered again. He thought he heard a head turn upon a pillow, but that was all. He repeated this quick, harsh whisper at the foot of every bed. "Lordship! . . . Lordship!" But nothing happened and the time was slipping by. But at the fourteenth bed he repeated the whisper for a third time, for he could feel rather than hear a restlessness in the darkness below him. "Lordship!" he whispered again. "Lord Titus!"

Something sat up in the darkness and he could hear the catch in a boy's breathing.

"Have no fear," he whispered fiercely, and his hand shook on the bedrail. "Have no fear. Are you Titus, the Earl?"

Immediately there was a reply. "Mr. Flay? What are you doing here?"

"Have you a coat and stockings?"

"Yes."

"Put them on. Follow me. Explain later, Lordship."

Titus made no reply but slid over the side of his bed, and after fumbling for his shoes and garments, clasped them like a bundle in his arms. Together they tiptoed to the dormitory door and, once without, walked rapidly in the darkness, the bearded man with his hand upon the boy's elbow.

At the head of a staircase Titus got into his clothes, his heart beating loudly. Flay stood beside him and when he was ready they descended the stairs in silence.

As they drew nearer to the quadrangle Flay in short, broken phrases was able to give Titus a disjointed idea of why he had been woken and whisked out into the night. Much as Titus sympathized with Flay's suspicions and of his hatred of Steerpike, he was becoming afraid that Flay himself had gone mad. He could see that it was a very odd thing for Steerpike to spend the night leaning against a thorn tree, but equally there was nothing criminal in it. What, he wondered, in any event, was Flay doing to be there himself? And why should the long, ragged creature of the woods be so anxious to have him with him? There was no doubt about the excitement of it all and that to be sought out was deeply flattering, but Titus had but a vague idea as to what Flay meant by needing a *witness*. A witness to what, and to prove what? Deeply as Titus suspected Steerpike of being intrinsically foul, yet he had never suspected him of actually doing other than his duty in the castle. He had never hated him for any understandable reason. He had simply hated him for being alive at all.

But when they reached the cloisters and when he peered along Flay's outstretched arm as they lay upon the cold ground, and saw, all at once, after a long and abortive scrutiny of the thorn, the sharp profile, as angular as broken glass save for the doming forehead, then he knew that the gaunt man lying beside him was no more mad

than himself, and that for the first time in his life he was
tasting upon his tongue the acid of an intoxicating fear, of
a fearful elation.

He also knew that to leave Steerpike where he was
and to return to bed would be to deliberately turn away
from a climate of sharp and dangerous breath.

He put his lips to his companion's ear.

"It's Doctor's quadrangle," he whispered.

Flay made no reply for several moments, for the
remark made little sense to him.

"What of it?" he replied in an almost inaudible voice.

"Very close—on our side," whispered Titus, "just
across the quadrangle."

This time there was a longer silence. Flay could see
at once the advantage of yet another witness and also
of a double bodyguard for the boy. But what would the
Doctor think of his reappearance after all these years?
Would he countenance this clandestine return to the
castle—even in the knowledge that it was for the
castle's sake? Would he be prepared, in the future, to
deny all knowledge of his, Mr. Flay's return?

Again Titus whispered, "He is on our side."

It seemed to Mr. Flay that he was now so deeply involved that to argue each problem as it posed itself, to
study each move, would get him nowhere. Had he behaved in a rational way he would never have left the
woods, and he would not now be lying upon his stomach,
staring at a man leaning innocently against a tree. That
the figure's profile against the saffron dawn was sharp
and cruel was no proof of anything.

No. It was for him to obey the impulse of the moment
and to have the courage to risk the future. This was no
time for anything but action.

The dawn, although fiercer in the east, was yet withheld. There was no light in the air—only a strip of intense
color. But at any moment a diffusion of the sunrise
would begin and the sun would heave itself above the
broken towers.

There was no time to lose. In a matter of minutes the
quadrangle might become impossible to cross without

attracting Steerpike's attention, or Steerpike, judging himself to have sufficient light for whatever journey he wished to make, might slip away suddenly into the gloom and be irreparably lost among a thousand ways.

The Doctor's house was on the far side of the quadrangle. To get there would necessitate a detour around the margin of the quadrangle, for the thorn tree was at the center.

Obeying Flay's instructions Titus took off his shoes and, like Flay with his boots, tied the laces together and slung them around his neck. It was Flay's first idea that they should go together, but they had no sooner taken the first few silent paces than the sudden disappearance of Steerpike reminded Flay that it was only from the particular place where they had been lying that they could keep a check upon his movements. From the Doctor's side of the quadrangle there would be no way of knowing whether or not he was still beneath the tree.

It was a full minute before Flay knew what he ought to do; and then, it was only because one of his hands, thrust deep into a ragged pocket, came upon a piece of chalk that a solution occurred to him. For a piece of white chalk meant only one thing to him. It meant a *trail*. But who was to blaze it? There was only one answer, and for two reasons.

In the first place, if one of them were to remain where he was and keep Steerpike under observation, and in the event of Steerpike's moving away from the thorn tree, to follow him and leave chalk marks upon the ground or upon walls—then it were best for Flay to perform this none too simple function, not only because of his experience of stalking in the woods and of the danger of being discovered, but because secondly, in learning of what was afoot, the Doctor would more readily and speedily accompany the young Earl than Mr. Flay, the long-lost exile, with whom a certain amount of time-wasting explanation would be a preliminary necessity.

And so Flay explained to Titus what he must do. He must wake the Doctor, silently. How this was to be done he did not know. He must leave this to the boy's ingenuity. He must impress upon the Doctor that there was no time to be lost. It was not the moment in which to warn him that the whole venture was based upon guess-work—that in sober fact there was no cause to rouse the Doctor from his bed. That in the open air, there was not a leaf that was not whispering of treachery, not a stone but muttered its warning, was not the kind of argument to impress anyone waked of a sudden from their sleep. And yet he must impress the Doctor with a sense of urgency. They must return across the quadrangle to where they were now crouching, for only from this position could they tell whether Steerpike was still beneath the tree, unless, as might have happened, the sun had suddenly risen. Had it not done so, and if Steerpike was still there beneath the thorn, then they would find Mr. Flay where Titus had left him; but if Steerpike had gone, then Mr. Flay would also have disappeared and it was for them to move swiftly to the thorn tree, and if there was enough light, to follow the chalk trail which Flay would have begun to blaze. If, however, it was still too dark to see the marks, they were to follow them directly there was enough light. It was for them to move suffi-ciently rapidly to be able to overtake Mr. Flay, but ab-solute silence was the prime essential, for the gap between Flay and Steerpike might, for reasons of darkness, be of necessity perilously narrow.

Feeling his way from pillar to pillar, Titus began to make a circuit of the quadrangle. His stocking'd feet made no noise at all. Once a button on the sleeve of his coat clicked against an outcrop of masonry and sounded like the snapping of a twig, so that he stopped dead in his tracks and listened for a moment or two anxiously in silence, but that was all, and a little afterwards he was standing beneath the Doctor's wall.

Meanwhile Flay lay stretched out beneath the pillar on the far side of the square, his bearded chin propped by his bony hands.

Not for a moment did his eyes wander from the sil-houette of the head against the dawn. The yellow band had widened and still further intensified so that it was now not so much a thing that might be painted as a radiance beyond the reach of pigment.

As he watched he saw the first movement. The head raised itself and as the face stared up into the branches the mouth opened in a yawn. It was like the yawning of a lizard; the jaws sharp, soundless, merciless. It was as though all thought was over, and out of some reptilian existence the yawn grew and opened like a reflex. And it was so, for Steerpike, leaning there, had, instead of pitying himself and brooding upon his mistakes, been tabulating and regrouping in his scheduled brain every aspect of his position, of his plans, of his relationship not only with Fuchsia but with all with whom he had dealings, and making out of the maze of these relationships and projects a working pattern—something that was a masterpiece of cold-blooded systemization. But the plan of action, condensed and crystallized though it was, was nevertheless, for all its ingenuity, somehow less microscopically careful in its every particular than usual. He was prepared for the first time to take risks. The time had come for drawing together the hundred and one threads that had for so long been stretched from one end of the castle to another. This would need action. For the moment he could relax. This dawn would be his own. Tonight he must bewilder Fuchsia; dazzle her, awake her; and if all failed, seduce her so that, compromised in the highest degree, he would have her at his mercy. In her present mood she was too dangerous.

But today? He yawned again. His brainwork was done. His plans were complete. And yet there was one loose end. Not in the logic of his brain, but in spite of it—a loose end that he wished to tuck away. What his brain had proved his eyes were witless of. It was his eyes that needed confirmation.

He ran his tongue between his thin, dry lips. Then he turned his face to the east. It shone in the yellow light. It shone like a carbuncle, as, breaking suddenly out of the darkness, the first direct ray of the climbing sun broke upon his bulging brow. His dark-red eyes stared back into

the heart of the level ray. He cursed the sun and slid
out of the beam.

Chapter Fifty-Eight

IT was lucky for Titus that when the Doctor started
from his sleep he immediately recognized the boy's shape
against the windowpane.

Titus had climbed the thick creeper below the Doctor's
window and had with difficulty forced up the lower sash.
There had been no other way to enter. To knock or ring
would have been to have lost Steerpike.

Dr. Prunesquallor reached for the candle by his bed
but Titus bent forward in the darkness.

"No, Dr. Prune, don't light it . . . it's Titus . . . and
we want your help . . . terribly . . . sorry it's so early
. . . can you come? . . . Flay is with me. . . ."

"Flay?"

"Yes, he has come from exile—but out of concern for
Fuchsia, and me, and the Laws. . . . But quickly, Doctor,
are you coming? We are trailing Steerpike—he's just
outside."

In a moment the Doctor was in his elegant dressing
gown—had found and put on his spectacles, a pair of
socks, and his soft slippers.

"I am flattered," he said, in his quick, stilted, yet very
pleasant voice. "I am more than flattered—lead on, boy,
lead on."

They descended the dark stairs; on reaching the hall the
Doctor vanished but reappeared almost at once with two
pokers, one a long, top-heavy brass affair with a murderous club-end and the other a short, heavy iron thing
with a perfect grip.

The Doctor hid them behind his back. "Which hand?"

he said. Titus chose the left and received the iron. Even with so crude a weapon in his grip the boy's confidence rose at once. Not that his heart beat any the less rapidly or that he was any the less aware of danger, but the feeling of acute vulnerability had gone.

The Doctor asked no questions. He knew that this strange business would unfold its meaning as the minutes went by. Titus was in no state to give an explanation now. He had begun breathlessly to tell the Doctor of how Flay would leave a trail of chalk, but had ceased, for there was no time to act and to explain together. Before they opened the front door Dr. Prunesquallor drew the blind of the hall window. The quadrangle, though still extremely dark, was no longer a featureless and inky mass. The buildings on the far side loomed, and a blot of ebony blackness that appeared to float in the gun-gray air showed where the thorn tree grew.

Titus was at the Doctor's side and peered through the pane.

"Can you see him, Doctor?"

"Where ought he to be, my boy?"

"Under the thorn."

"Hard to say . . . hard to say . . ."

"Easy to tell from the other side, Doctor. Shall we go around by the cloisters? If he's gone there's no time to lose, is there?"

"I take it from you that there isn't, Titus, though what in the name of guilt we are doing only the screech-owl knows. However, away!"

He stood upon his toes in the hall, and lifting his arms, stretched them before him. Between his outstretched fingertips the brass poker was poised as though it were a mace, or some symbolic rod. His dressing gown was corded tightly at his slender waist. His delicate features were set in an extraordinary expression of speculative determination both impressive and bizarre.

He unlatched the door and the two of them set off down the garden path. The Doctor in his slippers, Titus in his socks, with his shoes slung loosely around his neck, they moved rapidly and silently along the skirting cloisters until Titus, gripping the Doctor's arm, brought his companion to a halt. There was the thorn, an inky etching against the rising sun, but the silhouette of Steerpike was missing. This was no surprise, for Flay had also vanished. Without loss of time they sped across the quadrangle, and in the early light were able at once to see the dim sign of a chalk mark on the ground at their feet. Titus went down on his knees to it at once. That it was a rough arrow pointing to the north was apparent enough, but there were some words scrawled below which were not so easy to decipher, but at last Titus was able to disentangle the roughened phrase, *"Every twenty paces."*

" 'Every twenty paces,' I think it is," Titus whispered.

Together they counted their steps as they moved gingerly to the north, the pokers in their hands, their eyes peering into the darkness ahead of them for the first sign of Flay or of danger.

Sure enough, at roughly the twentieth pace another arrow pointed them their way and showed Titus's interpretation of Flay's crude lettering to have been correct. They went forward now with more confidence. It seemed certain that they must come first upon Mr. Flay, and that so long as they made no sound they could do no harm by moving swiftly from one arrow to another. There were times when these arrows were of necessity closer together; when the paths divided, or there was any kind of choice of direction. At other times, when, with high flanking walls on either side, or a mile of doorless passageways ahead, and where there was no alternative direction to confuse his followers, Flay had not troubled to make his chalk marks for long stretches. There were times when the length of these stone arteries was such that, all unknowing, the Doctor and Titus had more than once set forth along a fresh corridor before Steerpike, at the other end, had made his exit. Flay alone could hazard the guess that before him and behind him his friends and his enemy were all at once beneath the same long ceiling.

Rapid as Titus had been in calling the Doctor, yet there was a great space between them and Mr. Flay, for no sooner had Titus left Flay's side than Steerpike had yawned and sped into the night.

As the light grew it became easier for the Doctor and Titus to accelerate their pace and to see what part of the castle they were moving through. The chalk arrows had become short, brusque marks upon the ground. Suddenly, as they turned a corner, they came upon the second of the bearded man's messages. It was scrawled at the foot of some stone stairs. *"Faster,"* it read. *"He is in a hurry. Catch me but silence."*

By now the light was strong enough for them both to know that they were lost. Neither of them could recognize the masonry that rose about them, the twisting passageways, the shallow flights of stairs, and the long, treadless inclines; they were speeding through a new world. A world unfamiliar in its detail—new to *them,* although unquestionably of the very stuff of their memories and recognizable in this general and almost abstract way. They had never been there before, yet it was not alien—it was all Gormenghast.

But this did not mean it was not dangerous. It was obvious that they were in a deserted province. Early as was the hour, yet that was not the reason for the silence. There was an abandoned, empty, voiceless, hollow atmosphere that had nothing to do with the dawn or with multitudes abed and asleep.

What beds there were would be broken and empty. What multitudes there were would be the multitudes of the ant and the weevil.

And now began a series of dusky journeys across open squares, with the sky reddening overhead. The Doctor, wildly incongruous in so grim a setting, moved with surprising speed, his brass poker held in both hands at the height of his breast, his head erect, the skirt of his dressing gown flaring behind him.

Titus beside him looked by contrast like a beggar. His socks had worn out, and although they gripped his ankles, the soles had gone, and his feet were cut and bruised. But this he hardly noticed. His hair was across his face. His jacket was bundled over his nightshirt. His trousers were half undone. His shoes jogged at his shoulders.

They had increased their speed, even to the point of running when it seemed safe to do so. But whenever they came to a corner they invariably stopped and peered cautiously about it before proceeding. The chalk marks never failed them, though from the way they had changed from thick white arrows to the merest flick of chalk on stone or boarding it was plain not only that the speed of Flay's progress had increased but that the stick of chalk itself was wearing out.

There was no longer any difficulty as far as visibility was concerned. They moved in the naked light. It was surely no longer possible for Mr. Flay to keep at close range with his quarry. And yet, with all their swiftness, they had not yet caught up with him. The Doctor's brow was glistening with perspiration. Both he and Titus were growing increasingly weary. The unfamiliar buildings came and went. One after another, square after square, hall after hall, corridor after corridor, winding and turning to and fro in a maze of dawn-lit stone.

And then, half in a state of disbelief—as though it were all in a dream—the Doctor, mechanically stopping at the corner of a high wall, moved his head so that he could command a view of the next expanse or artery that lay ahead. But instead of rounding the corner, his body recoiled a fraction and his arm moved backward.

When his hand had found Titus and had gripped his elbow he drew the boy to his side. Together they could see him—the gaunt and bearded figure. He was at the far end of a narrow lane, the floor of which was a foot deep in dust and plaster. He was in an almost identical position to their own, for he was also stationed at a corner, around which he was peering; and like themselves he had his eyes fixed upon some object of vivid and immediate interest, for even at so considerable a distance the Doctor could see how tense was his scarecrow body.

Had they been a few moments later they would have missed him, for even as they watched he slid around the base of the high, sharp corner and was lost to them. At once, Titus and the Doctor set off in hot pursuit until they came to that angle of stone which Flay had so recently vacated. Cautiously, they moved their heads until once again they were afforded yet another long perspective with its floor crisp and ashen with fallen plaster. And there at the end of the corridor was a replica of the picture they had been witnessing a minute earlier, with Flay at yet another angle of stone. It was as though they were reliving the incident, for, visually, it differed in no particular. But this time they did not wait for Mr. Flay to disappear. At a sign from the Doctor they began to run toward him. Evidently Steerpike was still in view, for Mr. Flay, motionless as a stick-insect, made no move until Titus and the Doctor were within a short way of him. Then suddenly at the sound of plaster breaking under Titus's feet, faint though it was, he turned his craggy face over his shoulder and saw them.

He touched his brow with his hand, and darted a questioning glance at the Doctor. Then he put his finger to his lips as he bared his irregular teeth. The Doctor inclined his body, so splendidly sheathed in its dressing gown, in the gaunt man's direction. Meanwhile Titus crept to the angle of the wall, and peering around the corner saw, at a distance of about sixty feet, something which set his heart pounding. It was the Master of Ritual, Steerpike; the man with the red-and-white face. It was his foe—long since defied in the summer schoolroom—the pale and agile officer of the realm—the one who had spoiled his happiness and weaned his sister from him.

There he sat upon the edge of some kind of low stone basin like a drinking trough that protruded from the wall at the side of the plaster-littered passage. Beyond him there was an arch, hung with torn sacking, which obscured whatever lay beyond.

As Titus watched, he saw the sitting figure draw up his knees so that his feet were beneath him on the rim of the trough. His head and shoulders were turned a little away so that it was not easy for Titus to tell what he had taken from his pocket. It seemed that Steerpike's hands were near his mouth and a little forward of it and then suddenly, as the first thin reedy note of a bamboo pipe shrilled along the resonant corridor, all became plain. For some little while, it was impossible to know how long, the three watchers listened to the solitary figure, to his nimble fingering of the stops, to the shrill and plaintive improvisations. Only the Doctor realized how well he played. Only the Doctor knew how quick and cold it was. How brilliant and empty.

"Is there nothing he can't do?" muttered Prunesquallor to himself. "By all that's versatile, he frightens me."

The music had come to an end, and Steerpike stretched out his arms and legs and then, slipping his recorder into a pocket, stood up. It was then that Titus gasped, and as he did so was plucked back from the corner by the two men behind him. For a few moments they hardly dared to draw breath. But no footsteps approached them from the adjacent corridor. What was it he had seen? Neither the Doctor nor Flay dared question him, but after a little while the latter, squinting round the corner, could see what it was that had startled the boy. He had himself been puzzled by Steerpike's monkey. For a long while he had been unable to tell what it was that sat hunched upon his quarry's shoulder, or bounded at his side. At other times it disappeared altogether. It had not added, for instance, to the silhouette beneath the thorn tree, and Flay could only think that it clung closely to his side and was lost for long periods at a time beneath the folds of his cape.

But now it bounded beside him, or stood on two legs, its long thin arms hanging loosely, its wrinkled hands trailing among the scraps of plaster.

And so there was a double need for silence. What Steerpike might miss, his monkey might easily hear.

But the discovery of what had startled Titus was of small importance compared with the fact that Flay was only just in time to see the man and his monkey pass through the hangings, and under the arch. A moment later and there would have been no knowing whether he had turned to the left or the right. As it was it was not easy to tell save by the indicative rippling of the ragged hangings.

What lay beyond? There was no reason to suppose that there would be any further repetition of this corner-to-corner trailing. Save for the fatigue of the journey and for their constant grip upon the silence, they had as yet encountered neither problem nor peril. But now, as they stared at the hangings that were yet moving a little in the still air, they knew that they were entering upon a new phase.

Titus gripped the short iron poker in his hand as though to squeeze the life out of it. The Doctor tossed his head, arched his nostrils, and tiptoed to the very point where Steerpike had disappeared. Flay, who insisted on leading, had already drawn back, by no more than half an inch, a fold of the drapery, and was peering to his left. What he saw brought the blood to his head and his hand trembled violently.

He found himself staring along a short passage to where the slanting section of yet another and broader corridor slanted darkly. This further corridor was faced with cold bricks; its floor also, and that was all; but it brought the sweat suddenly to his brow and to the palms of his hands. Yet why, for he was looking at no more than the sort of things he had seen a score of times already on this same morning? But there was this difference. He had seen those bricks before. He had come upon the outskirts of his own domain. Unwittingly, as he had moved through the uncharted hinterlands, he had come upon the outskirts of the Hollow Halls—the world he had made his own. He was no longer lost. Steerpike had led them by a trail of his own to a domain which Mr. Flay had thought to be impregnable.

What was he doing here? *Here,* where Mr. Flay had stood, his blood running cold, and had heard the grizzly laughter long ago? *Here,* where night after night and day after day he had sought the screaming nest to no avail? Here, where ever since those days the silence had come down like a dead weight—so that he had not dared to

return, for the stillness had become more terrible than the
demoniac laughter.

He alone knew of this. He passed the back of his hand
across his eyes.

Without waiting to make so much as a sign to the two
behind him he paced out grotesquely, on tiptoe, to the
juncture, and again to his left he saw the young man.
Had Steerpike turned to the right he might well have
proceeded toward those districts which Mr. Flay knew
so well. Turning to the left, however, took him into that
labyrinth in which he had so often lost himself in his
search for the haunted room.

Mr. Flay knew only too well that to keep Steerpike
in sight would be no easy task. There was the double
difficulty of their following him closely enough to keep
him in sight, and yet to remain inaudible and unseen
themselves.

Nothing would be more embarrassing than for them
to be discovered—for Steerpike was committing no crime
in moving rapidly through this deserted place. If there
were anything nefarious going on, it was upon their side,
in shadowing the Master of Ritual.

But there was no need for Flay to warn the Doctor
and the boy that the necessity for absolute silence was
even more acute. As they slid along the brickwork corridor they felt a closing in of the world.

And now began the threading of a maze so labyrinthine
as to suggest that the builders of these sunless walls had
been ordered to construct a maze for no other purpose
than to torture the mind and freeze the memory. It was
no wonder that Flay had never done more, in those past
days, than stumble blindly through so tortuous a region.
And yet, in spite of the confusion, and the necessity for
his concentrating upon keeping Steerpike in view, his instincts were working upon their own, and they told him
that they were returning by devious and contradictory
roads to the proximity of the cold brick corridor from
which they had started. Steerpike had slowed his pace.
His head hung forward on his chest, not dejectedly but
with an air of abstraction. His feet moved even slower,

until he was virtually loitering. When he came to flights of shallow stairs he descended with a kind of loose-jointed and collapsing motion of the legs—as though his body had forgotten its own existence. He wandered around corners with a dreamlike motion, his body at so strange an angle of relaxation as to be almost dangerous.

When at last he came to a certain door he straightened himself with a jerk—stretched out his fingers and became on the instant all awareness. He made a sound between his teeth and the monkey scrambled from the folds of his cape and sat upon his shoulder, the feather in its hat nodding to and fro. For a moment, as the monkey turned its head and its black eyes peered from that small and wrinkled face, peered back along the way it had come, the Doctor thought he had been seen. But he did not draw back his head or make any movement, and the creature with its naked face and its costume of colored diamonds scratched itself and turned away at last. Only then did the Doctor and his companions withdraw themselves even more deeply into the shadows.

Meanwhile Steerpike sorted out a key from a bunch in his pocket and, after pausing a moment or two, turned it with difficulty in the lock. But he did not touch the handle of the door. He turned his back upon it and gazed along the way he had come, tapping his teeth with his thumbnail.

It was obvious that for some reason best known to himself he was chary of walking in. The monkey on his shoulder shifted its position, and in doing so its long tail tapped lightly across Steerpike's face. But that was seemingly enough to irritate its master, for the little beast was flung to the floor, where it crouched and whimpered.

As Steerpike turned his eyes from his bruised plaything, his attention was caught by sprawling heaps of rubbish, stones, and broken timbers that lay a little way along the side passage. As he stared at them, his anger drained from his face, and his features became set again and the corner of his lips lifted into a dead line.

For a moment or two the three watchers feared that they had lost him, for he moved suddenly out of their

range of vision. It was fortunate for them that the monkey
remained where it was, outside the door, where it nursed
its bruised forearm. Had they followed Steerpike they
would at once have met him face to face, for he returned
within a minute with a long, broken pole.

And now began an operation that completely baffled
the hidden spectators. With extreme care Steerpike
turned the handle and released the latch. The door was
now free but was not yet opened by so much as a quarter of an inch. He stood back from it, and holding the
broken pole like a battering ram, pushed gently at the
black wooden panel of the mysterious door. It moved
upon its hinges with no great difficulty and Steerpike
was able to obtain a view of a section of the room beyond. For a little while he held the pole motionless as he
stared along its length and through the narrow opening.
It was obvious that what he saw concerned him deeply.
He rose upon his toes. He cocked his head to one side.
Then he withdrew the pole and laid it on the ground at
his feet. It was now, at this same moment, as he took a
scarf from his pocket and tied it about his face so that
only his eyes were visible, that the Doctor, Flay, and Titus became conscious of a sickly and musty odor. But the
strange performance that was going on before their eyes
so riveted their attention that at first they hardly noticed
it. Again Steerpike raised the pole and, pushing at the
panels with the utmost caution, was able momently to see
more and more of the room which he was evidently so
anxious to inspect. When the door was sufficiently ajar
to admit the entry of a man, he paused.

As he did so the monkey, whose feathered hat had
fallen in the dust, began to make its inquisitive way to
the open door. It was evident that its arm was hurting it.
Once or twice, in spite of its eagerness to explore the
room beyond the door, it glanced apprehensively over its
shoulder at Steerpike, baring its teeth in a nervous gri-
mace. But its resilient nature became dominant and, springing off its back legs, it clung to the door handle with its
nervous little hands. Again Steerpike pressed upon the
long pole, this time with more force, and as the door

swung ajar the monkey, swinging with it, let go and dropped upon the great moldering carpet that lay within. But it did not drop alone, for no sooner had its four feet touched the ground than with a sickening thud an ax-head fell from high above the door, severing the long tail of the monkey as it buried its murderous edge in the floor. The shrill and appallingly human scream of the little creature rang through the hollow district, echoing and re-echoing the agony of that moment, while, beside itself with pain, surprise, and rage, it tore about the huge room that lay spread before it, leaping from chair to chair, from window sill to mantelpiece, from cupboard to cupboard, scattering vases, lamps, and small objects of all kinds to left and right in its wild circuits.

Into this room, now spattered with the monkey's blood, Steerpike advanced at once. There was no longer any caution in his bearing. He gave the careering creature not so much as a single glance. Had he done so he might have noticed that on seeing him the monkey halted its flight and was crouched quivering upon the back of a chair. Its eyes were upon him and in them was a moist and lethal hatred, as though all the spleen and gall of the vile tropics were floating there beneath the small gray eyelids. Its pain and its humiliation were laid at the door of the man who had flung it from his shoulder. As it watched its master it bared its teeth and wrung its hands together. The blood dripped freely from the stump of its tail. What had happened to the monkey—what had caused its harrowing outcry—was, of course, unknown to Titus, the Doctor, and Mr. Flay. But the urgency of that human cry lifted them out of their hiding places, and brought them to the door. They saw at once that Steerpike had left this first room and had presumably descended the three or four steps that led to a second apartment. But the monkey caught sight of them at once and ran toward them. When it reached Titus it rose to its back legs and began a series of grimaces, which in any other circumstances would have been amusing enough, but were at that moment almost heartbreaking. But they had no time for it. Too much was at stake.

Their nerves were at full stretch. They were all but exhausted and above all they were still in the invidious position of following a man without any warrant or rational excuse. Nevertheless the last half-hour had intensified their suspicions to a high degree. They knew in their hearts that they had been right to follow him. They were now prepared for anything that might unfold.

Their apprehension had grown so dark, their speculation so fantastic, that when they crept to the second door and peered into the apartment below, and when they saw in the center of the great carpet that filled the room the two skeletons lying side by side in their fast-decaying dresses of imperial purple, their pulses beat no faster. Their emotions had been overstrained and had gone limp. But their brains raced.

The Doctor, who had been holding his silk handkerchief across his face, had known for some while that there was death in the air. He was also the first to know that they were looking at all that was left of Cora and Clarice Groan. Titus had no idea that he was staring at his aunts. He was simply looking at skeletons. He had never seen skeletons before.

It was a moment or two before Mr. Flay remembered the invariable purple of the twins. That there had been foul play was immediately apparent to them all.

The remoteness of these rooms from the castle; the double death; the windowless walls; the possession by Steerpike of a key and his familiarity with the corridors of approach—and more than all this, his present behavior. For as they watched him the young man, never doubting the security of his solitude, began to behave in a way which could only be interpreted by those who watched him as a form of madness, or if not madness, something so eccentric as to tread its arbitrary borderland.

Steerpike was aware, directly he had entered the terrible room, that he was behaving strangely. He could have stopped himself at any moment. But to have stopped himself would have been to have stopped a valve—to have bottled up something which would have clamored for release. For Steerpike was anything if inhibited. His control that had so seldom broken had never frustrated him. In one way that this new expression had need of an outlet he gave himself up to whatever his blood dictated. He was watching himself, but only so that he should miss nothing. He was the vehicle through which the gods were working. The dim primordial gods of power and blood.

There at his feet were the decomposing relics, the purple of their dresses hanging over the ribs in clotted folds, the skulls protruding horribly, their sockets staring at the ceiling. No less than had been their vanished faces, these skulls were identical save that across a single socket some spider, fastidious in his craftsmanship, had spun a delicate web. At its center struggled a fly, so that in a way a kind of animation had come to either Cora or Clarice.

In some kind of way the Doctor, though he could not understand, was able to gain an inkling as to what was happening in Steerpike's mind, as the skewbald homicide began to strut like a cockerel about the bodies of the women he had imprisoned, humiliated, and starved to death. The Doctor could see that Steerpike was by no means mad in any accepted sense, for every now and then he would repeat a number of high-stepping paces as though to perfect them. It was as though he were identifying himself with some archetypal warrior, or fiend. A fiend, which although it had no sense of humor, had a ghastly gaiety—a kind of lethal lightness that struck at the very heart of the humanities; struck at it, darted at it, played about it, jabbing here and there, as though with a blade of speargrass.

When Flay and the Doctor, in their different ways, saw what was happening in the room, they were both aware that Titus should not be with them. He was no child, but this was no scene for a boy. But there was nothing they could do. For them to separate would be criminally unwise. He could never in any event have found his way back alone. That as yet there had been no movement on their part to disturb the criminal was fortunate, but this deathly silence, in which the only sound was that of Steerpike's footsteps, could not last forever.

The Doctor was appalled, but at the same time, as a man of high intelligence and curiosity, he was fascinated by what he saw. Not so Flay. An eccentric himself, he despised and abhorred any form of eccentricity in others, and what he was now witnessing had the effect of all but blinding him with a kind of bourgeois rage. Only in one thing was he happy—that the upstart had unmasked himself and that from now onward the battle was joined in earnest.

His small eyes were fixed upon his enemy. His neck was thrust out like a turtle's. His long beard trembled as it hung forward on his chest. His forest knife shook in his hand.

It was not the only weapon that was shaking. The short, heavy poker in Titus's clenched fist was far from steady. The young Earl was quite frankly terrified by what he saw. An area of solid ground had given way beneath his feet and he had fallen into an underworld of which he had no conception. A place where a man can pace like a cock about the ribs and skulls of his victims. A place where the air was rank with their corruption.

The Doctor was gripping his arm to steady him, and the grip tightened suddenly. Steerpike had stopped for a moment to retie his shoelace. When this was completed he rose from his knee and stood on tiptoe where he remained poised, his head thrown back. Then he dropped his heels and flexed his knees and at the same time, turning his toes outward, he raised his arms to his sides, and with his elbows bent at right angles, he began to stamp, his fists clenched at the height of his shoulders. The sound of his feet was very loud and close.

He was in the posture of some earthish dancer, but he soon tired of this strange display—this throwback to some savage rite of the world's infancy. He had given himself up to it for those few moments, in the way that an artist can be the ignorant agent of something far greater and deeper than his conscious mind could ever understand. But as he strutted, his knees bent, his feet turned outward, his body and head erect, his elbows crooked, and his hands clenched, he had enjoyed the novelty of what he was doing. He was amused at this peculiar need of his body; that it wished to stamp, to strut, to rear on tiptoes, to sink upon the heels—and all because he was a murderer—all this intrigued him, titillating his brain, so that now, as he ceased to stamp, and sank into a dusty chair, the muscles of his throat went through the contractions that form laughter—but no sound came.

He shut his eyes, and in the darkness it seemed to him that he was in peril, and he opened them again with a start and sat forward in his chair, glancing about the room. This time as his gaze returned to the skeletons he was revolted. Not with what *he* had done to bring them to this state—but that they should pollute this room; that they should show him their ugly skulls and hollow bones.

He rose from his chair in anger. But he knew in his heart that he was not angry with them. He was enraged with himself. For what had seemed amusing a few moments ago was now almost a source of fear to him. In looking back and seeing himself strutting like a cock about their bodies, he realized that he had been close to lunacy. This was the first time that any such thought had entered his head, and to dismiss it he crowed like a cock. He was not afraid of strutting; he had known what he was doing; to prove it he would crow and crow again. Not that he wished to do so, but to prove that he could stop whenever he wanted, and start when he wished to, and be all the while in complete control of himself, for there was no madness in him.

What he did not realize was that the death of Barquentine, and the nightmare of the fire and the vile waters of the moat and the long fever that followed, had made a difference in him. Whatever he now believed about himself was based on the assumption that he was the same Steerpike as his former self of a few years earlier. But he was no longer that youth. The fire had burned a part of him away. Something of him was drowned forever in the waters of the moat. His daring was no longer a thing that fanned itself abroad; it had contracted into a fist of brimstone.

He was meaner, more irritable, more impatient for the ultimate power which could only be his through the elimination of all rivals; and if he had ever had any scruples, any love at all for even a monkey, a book, or a sword-hilt, all this, and even this, had been cauterized and drowned away.

As he had entered this second apartment, he had propped the broken pole against the wall on his left. He now felt himself gravitating toward it. He no longer stamped or strutted. He was himself again, or perhaps he had ceased to be himself. At any rate, the three watchers recognized again that familiar walk, with the shoulders hunched and the catlike footsteps. When he reached the pole he ran his hand along its side. The scarf was still about his face. His dark-red eyes were like small circular pits.

As his hand strayed over the surface of the pole, rather as a pianist will fondle a keyboard, his fingers came across a fissure in the wood, and as they played about it they found how easy it would be to tear from the beam a long and narrow splinter. Abstractedly, hardly knowing that he was doing it—a score of disquieting impressions had taken the place of the surety within him—he prized the splinter away, using, at the last, the whole strength of his arm as it arched, in its tension, from the pole. He did not look at it, and he was about to throw it away, for the tearing of it from the pole had been his only interest, when, his gaze having returned to the skeletons, he wandered toward them, and running the long, resilient splinter along their ribs as a child might run a stick along a railing, he heard the bone-notes of an instrument.

For a few minutes he spent his time in this way, creating by a series of taps and runs, a kind of percussive rhythm in key with his mood.

But he was tiring of the place. He had returned in order to satisfy his eyes that the twins were truly dead, and he had stayed longer than he had intended. Now he flung the splinter away and, kneeling, unclasped the strings of pearls that hung about the vertebrae. Rising, he dropped them into his pocket and made at once for the three steps that led to the upper room, and as he did so, Mr. Flay stepped out from his hiding place.

The effect upon Steerpike was electric. He bounded backward, with a leap like the leap of a dancer, his cloak swirling about him and his thin lips parted in a murderous snarl of amazement.

There was no longer any case of symbolism. The strutting and the stamping were nothing to the fierce reality of that leap which sent him, as though from a springboard, backward through the air.

Quick as a reflex, even at the height of his elevation, he felt for his knife. Before he landed he knew that he was unmasked. That from now onward, unless he slew the bearded figure on the instant, he would be on the run. In a flash he saw the life of a fugitive spread out before him.

It was only as he landed that he realized at whom he was looking. He had not seen Flay for many years and had supposed him dead. The beard had altered him. But now he knew him, and this knowledge did nothing to stay his hand. Of all men, Flay would have the least sympathy for a rebel.

He had found his knife, and balanced it upon the palm of his hand, and had drawn back his right arm when he saw the Doctor and Titus.

The boy was white. The poker shook in his hand but his teeth were gritted. A terrible sickness had hold of him. He was in a nightmare. The last sixty minutes had added more than an hour to his age.

The Doctor was pale also. His face had lost all trace of its habitual drollery. It was a face cut out of marble, strangely proportioned but refined and determined.

The sight of the three of them, blocking the stairs,

halted Steerpike's arm as he was about to launch the knife.

And then, in a peculiarly quiet voice, clear and precise, a voice that told nothing of the hammering heart— "You will drop your penknife to the ground. You will come forward with your arms raised. You are under arrest," said the Doctor.

But Steerpike hardly heard him. His future was ruptured. His years of self-advancement and intricate planning were as though they had never been. A red cloud filled his head. His body shuddered with a kind of lust. It was the lust for an unbridled evil. It was the glory of knowing himself to be pitted, openly, against the big battalions. Alone, loveless, vital, diabolic—a creature for whom compromise was no longer necessary, and intrigue was a dead letter. If it was no longer possible for him to wear, one day, the legitimate Crown of Gormenghast, there was still the dark and terrible domain—the subterranean labyrinth—the lairs and warrens where, monarch of darkness like Satan himself, he could wear undisputed a crown no less imperial. Poised like an acrobat and vividly aware of the slightest move that was made by the three figures before him, the Doctor's voice, for all his sensory acuteness, seemed to come from far away.

"I give you one last chance," said his ex-patron. "If you have not dropped your knife within five seconds from now, we will advance upon you!"

But it was not the knife that dropped. It was Flay. The loyal seneschal fell backward with a grinding cry and was half-caught in the arms of Titus and the Doctor, and in that instant, while the blade of Steerpike's knife still quivered in his heart, and while the four hands of Flay's friends were engaged with the weight of the long, ragged body, the young man, following the path of the flung knife, as though he were tied behind it, sped over their shoulders and was in the upper room before they could recover.

Now, with the fear of retributory death upon him, and the redoubled cunning that comes to the marked man,

Steerpike lost not a second in speeding from the room. But he did not pass through the door alone, for as he slammed it and turned the key in the lock he was bitten savagely in the back of the neck. With a scream he swiveled on his feet and clutched at nothing.

A panic possessed him and he ran as he had never run before, turning left and right like a wild creature as he made his way ever deeper into a nether empire.

Outside the door of what had been the twins' apartment, the monkey, squatting on a rafter, chattered and wrung his hands.

Chapter Fifty-Nine

❊❊❊❊❊❊❊❊❊❊

A FEW days after the murder of Mr. Flay and the subsequent smashing of the door and escape of the Doctor and Titus from those dread apartments, the relics of the twins were heaped into a single coffin and were buried, at the orders of the Countess, with all the rites and solemnities that were due to the sisters of an Earl.

Mr. Flay was buried on the same day in the graveyard of the Elect Retainers, a small space of nettle-covered ground. At evening the long shadow of the Tower of Flints lay across this simple boneyard with its conical heaps of stones to show where not more than a dozen servants of exceptional loyalty lay silently under the tall weeds.

Had Mr. Flay been able to foresee his funeral he would have appreciated the honor of joining so small and loyal a company of the dead. And if he had known that the Countess herself, in draperies as black and as intense as the plumage of her own ravens, was to be there at the graveside, then his wounds would indeed have been healed.

The Poet had taken over as Master of Ritual. He had no easy task. Night after night, his long, wedge-shaped head was bowed over the manuscripts.

When the Countess had been told by Prunesquallor of the finding of the twins, of the manner of Flay's death, and of Steerpike's escape, she had risen from the upright chair in which she had been sitting, and without any change of expression in her big face had lifted the chair from the floor and had methodically broken its curved legs off one by one, and had then, in what seemed to be a state of abstraction, tossed the chair legs one after another through the glass panes of the nearest window.

When she had done this she moved to the smashed window and stared through the jagged hole. There was a white mist in the air and the tops of the towers appeared to be floating.

From where the Doctor stood he saw, for the first time, a picture. He was not looking for one. What pictures he had ever painted had been very delicate and charming. But this was quite different. He saw something dynamic, something quite wonderful in the contrast of the sharp and angular edges of the broken glass, and the smooth and doming line of her Ladyship's shoulders that, in the immediate foreground, curved heavily across the jaggedness. And at the same time he saw the deep copper-beech color of her hair against the pearl-gray tower tops that floated in the distance. And the blackness of her dress, and the marble of her neck and the sheen of the glass, and the pollenlike softness of the sky and towers so jaggedly circumscribed. She was a monument against a broken window and beyond the broken window her realm, tremulous and impalpable in the white mist.

But Dr. Prunesquallor had only a few moments in which to regret that he had not learned to paint, for the monument turned about.

"Sit down," she said.

Prunesquallor looked about him. The confusion in the room made it difficult for him to see anything that could possibly be sat on, but he found himself a perch at last in the corner of a window sill that was scattered with bird seed.

She approached and stood above him. She did not look down, but gazed through a small casement above his head while she spoke. Finding that she never turned her eyes to him and that for him to look up when listening or speaking was neither noticed nor necessary, and what is more that it gave him a pain at the back of his neck, the Doctor gazed at the scallops of sartorial coverings immediately ahead of him and within a few inches of his nose, or simply shut his eyes as they conversed.

It was soon obvious to the Doctor that he was in conversation with someone whose thoughts were concentrated upon the capture of Steerpike not only to the exclusion of everything else, but with a menacing power and a ruthless simplicity.

Her heavy voice was slower than ever.

"All normal work shall be suspended. Man, woman, and child shall be given their orders-of-search. Every known spring and wellhead, every cistern, tank, and cachement shall have its sentry. No doubt the beast must drink."

The Doctor suggested a meeting of officers, the drawing up of a plan of campaign, the working out of a timetable or rota of sentries and search parties, and the formation of redoubtable bands drawn from the young blood of the castle's lower life, where there was no lack of spleen, and where the price which was to be set upon Steerpike's head would encourage their intrepidity.

They agreed that there was no time to waste, for with every hour that passed the fugitive would be withdrawing ever more deeply into some forgotten quarter, or constructing some ambuscade or hiding place, even at the heart of the castle's activities. There was no place on earth so terrible and so suited to a game of hide and seek as this gaunt warren.

Leaders were to be chosen. Weapons were to be

served out. The castle was to be placed upon a war footing. A curfew was to be imposed, and wherever he might be lurking, from vault to eyrie, the murderer was to have no respite from the sound of feet and the light of torches. Sooner or later he would make his first mistake. Sooner or later, in the corner of some eye, the tail of his shadow would be seen. Sooner or later, if there was no relaxation in the search, he would be found at some wellhead, drinking like an animal, or flying from some storehouse with his plunder.

The Countess was using her powerful brain as though for the first time. The Doctor had never known her like this. Had her cats entered the room or a bird descended flapping to her shoulder it is doubtful whether, at this moment, she would have noticed them. Her thoughts were so concentrated upon the seizure of Steerpike that she had not moved a muscle since she and the Doctor had started talking. Only her lips had moved. She had talked very slowly and quietly, but there was a thickness in her voice.

"I shall outwit him," she said. "The ceremonies shall continue."

"The Day of the Bright Carvings?" queried the Doctor. "Shall it proceed as usual?"

"As usual."

"And shall the Outer Dwellers be allowed within the gates?"

"Naturally," she said. "What could stop them?"

What could stop them? It was Gormenghast that spoke. A fiend might be wandering the castle with dripping hands, but the traditional ceremonies were at the back of it all, enormous, immemorial, sacrosanct. In a fortnight's time it was their day, the day of the Mud Dwellers, when all along the white-stone shelf at the foot of the long courtyard wall the colored carvings would be displayed; and at night, when the bonfires roared and all but the three chosen statues were turned to ash in their flames, Titus, standing on the balcony with the Outer Dwellers below him in the firelit darkness, would hold aloft in turn each masterpiece. And as each was raised above his head, a gong would clash. And after the echoes of the third reverberation had died away he would order them to be taken to the Hall of Bright Carvings where Rottcodd slept and the dust collected and the flies crawled over the tall slatted blinds.

Prunesquallor rose to his feet. "You are right," he said. "There must be no difference, your Ladyship, save for an eternal vigilance, and unflagging pursuit."

"There is never any difference," she replied. "There is never any difference." Then she turned her head for the first time and looked at the Doctor. "We will have him," she said. Her voice, as soft and heavy and thick as velvet, was in so grim and incongruous a contrast to the merciless pinhead of light that glittered in her narrowed eyes that the Doctor made for the door. He was in need of an atmosphere less charged. As he turned the door handle he caught sight of the smashed window, and saw through the jagged star-shaped opening the towers floating. The white mist seemed lovelier than ever, and the towers more fairylike.

Chapter Sixty

BELLGROVE and his wife sat opposite one another in their living room. Irma, very upright, as was her habit, her back as straight as a yard of pump water. There was something irritating in this unnecessary rigidity. It was, perhaps, ladylike, but it was certainly not feminine. It annoyed Bellgrove, for it made him feel that there was something wrong in the way that *he* had always used a chair. To his mind an armchair was something to curl up in, or to drape oneself across. It was a

thing for human delectation. It was not built to be
perched on.

And so he curled his old spine and draped his old
legs and lolled his old head, while his wife sat silently
and stared at him.

". . . And why on earth should you think that he
would dream of risking his life in order to attack *you?*"
the old man was saying. "You deceive yourself, Irma. Peculiar as he is, there is no reason why he should flatter
you to the extent of killing you. To climb in at your bedroom window would be highly hazardous. The entire
castle is on the watch for him. Do you really imagine
that it matters to him whether you are alive or dead,
any more than whether *I* am alive or dead, or that fly
up there on the ceiling is alive or dead? Good grief,
Irma, be reasonable if you can, if only for the sake of
the love that once I bore you."

"There is no need for you to speak like that," Irma
replied, in a voice as clipped as the sound of castanets.
"Our love has nothing to do with what we are talking
about. Nor is it anything to mock at. It has changed,
that is all. It is no longer green."

"And nor am I," murmured Bellgrove.

"What an obvious thing to say!" said Irma, with forced
brightness. "And how very trite—I said how very trite!"

"I heard you, my dear."

"And this is no time for shallow talk. I have come
to you as a wife should come to her husband. For guidance. Yes, for guidance. You are old, I know, but—"

"What the hell has my age got to do with it?" snarled
Bellgrove, lifting his magnificent head from a cushion.
The milk-white locks were clustered on his shoulders.
"You were never one to ask for advice. You mean
you're terrified."

"That is so," said Irma. She said it so simply and
so quietly that she did not recognize her own voice. She
had spoken involuntarily. Bellgrove turned his head
sharply in her direction. He could hardly believe that
it was she who had spoken. He rose from his chair and
crossed the ugly carpet to where she sat bolt upright.

He squatted on his heels before her. A sense of pity stirred in him. He took her long hands in his.

At first she tried to withdraw them, but he held them tightly. She had tried to say, "Don't be ridiculous," but no words came.

"Irma," he said at last, "let us try again. We have both changed—but that is perhaps as it should be. You have shown me sides of your nature which I never knew existed. Never. How could I ever have guessed, my dear, that you should for instance have thought that half my staff were in love with you—or that you could become so irritated with my innocent habit of falling asleep? We have our different spirits, our different needs, our different lives. We are fused, Irma, it is true; we are integrated—but not all that much. Relax your back, my dear. Relax your backbone. It makes it easier for me to talk. I've asked you so often—and in all humility— knowing as I do that your spine is your own."

"My dearest husband," said Irma, "you are talking overmuch. If you could leave a sentence alone, it would be so much stronger." She bowed her head to him. "But I will tell you something," she continued. "It makes me happy to see you there, crouched at my feet. It makes me feel young again—or it would do, it *would* do, if they could only lay their hands on him and end the suspense. It is too much—*too* much . . . night after night . . . night after night . . . Oh, can't you see how it racks a woman? Can't you? Can't you?"

"My brave one," said Bellgrove. "My lady love; pull yourself together. Sinister as the business is, there is no need for you to take the whole thing personally. You are nothing to him, Irma, as I have said before. You are not his foe, my dear, *are* you? Nor yet his accomplice? Or *are* you?"

"Don't be ridiculous."

"Quite so. I am being ridiculous. Your husband, the Headmaster of Gormenghast, is being ridiculous. And why? Because I have caught the germ. I have caught it from my wife."

"But in the darkness . . . in the darkness . . . I seem to *see* him."

"Quite so," said Bellgrove. "But if you *did* see him you would feel worse still. Except of course that we could claim a reward, you know!"

Bellgrove found that his legs were aching, so he rose to his feet.

"My advice, Irma, is to put a little more trust in your husband. He may not be perfect. There may be husbands with finer qualities. With nobler profiles for instance, eh? Or with hair like almond blossom. It is not for me to say. And of course there may be husbands who have become Headmasters, or whose intellect is wider, or whose youth was more dazzling in its gallantry. It is not for me to say. But such as I am I have become yours. And such as you are you have become mine. And such as we both are we have become one another's. And what does this lead to? It leads to this. That if all this is so, and yet you quake at every sound of the night, then I take it that your trust in me has waned since those early days when I had you at my feet. Oh, you have schemed . . . schemed . . . l"

"How *dare* you!" cried Irma. "How dare you!"

Bellgrove had forgotten himself. He had forgotten what his argument was intended to prove. A little whiff of temper springing from some unformulated thought had caught him unaware. He tried to recover.

"*Schemed,*" he continued, "for my happiness. And you have very largely succeeded. I like you sitting there, if you weren't so upright. Can't you melt, my dear one —just a little? One grows so very tired of straight lines. As for Steerpike, take my advice; make use of *me* when you are frightened. Run to *me*. Fly to *me*. Press yourself against my chest; run your fingers through my locks. Be comforted. If he ever *did* appear before me, you know very well how I would deal with him."

Irma looked at her venerable husband. "I certainly do *not,*" she said. "How would you?"

Bellgrove, who had even less idea than Irma, stroked

his long chin, and then a sickly smile appeared on his lips.

"What I would do," he said, "is something that no gentleman could possibly divulge. Faith: that is what you need. Faith in me, my dear."

"There would be nothing you could do," said Irma, ignoring her husband's suggestion that she should have faith in him. "Nothing at all. You are too old."

Bellgrove, who had been about to resume his seat, remained standing. His back was to his wife. A dull pain began to grow beneath his ribs. A sense of the black injustice of bodily decay came over him, but a rebellious voice cried in his heart *"I am young, I am young,"* while the carnal witness of his threescore years and ten sank suddenly at the knees.

In a moment Irma was at his side. "Oh, my dear one! What *is* it? What *is* it?"

She lifted his head and put a cushion beneath it. Bellgrove was fully conscious. The shock of finding himself suddenly on the floor had upset him for a moment or two and had taken his breath away, but that was all.

"My legs went," he said, looking up at the earnest face above him with its wonderfully sharp nose. "But I am all right again."

Directly he had made this remark he was sorry for it, for he could have done with an hour of nursing.

"Perhaps you had better get up in that case, my dear," said Irma. "The floor is no place for a Headmaster."

"Ah, but I feel very—"

"Now, now!" interrupted Irma. "Let me have no nonsense. I shall go and see whether the doors have been locked. When I return I expect to find you in your chair again." She left the room.

After kicking his heels irritably on the carpet, the Headmaster struggled to his feet, and when he was in his chair again he put out his tongue at the door through which Irma had passed, but immediately he had done so he blushed for shame and blew a kiss in the same direction from the wasted palm of his hand.

Chapter Sixty-One

※※※※※※※※※※※

THERE was a part of the Outer Wall which was so
deeply hidden with canopies of creeper that for over a
hundred years no eyes had seen the stones of the wall
itself but the eyes of insects, mice, and birds. These undulating acres of hanging foliage overlooked a certain
lane which lay so close to the Outer Wall of Gormenghast
that had the mice or the hidden birds been capable of
tossing a twig out of the leafy darkness, it would have
fallen into this lane that lay below.

It was a narrow way, in deep shadow for most of the
day. Only in the late evening, as the sun sank over Gormenghast Forest, a quiverful of honey-colored beams
would slant along the alley and there would be pools of
amber where all day long the chill, inhospitable shadows had brooded.

And when these amber pools appeared the curs of the
district would congregate out of nowhere and would
squat in the golden beams and lick their sores.

But it was not in order to watch those half-wild dogs
or to marvel at the sunbeams that the Thing had taken
to working her way through the dense growth of the wall-
draped creepers, threading the vertical foliage with the
noiseless ease of a snake until, twenty feet above the
ground, she moved outward from the wall to such
a position that she could look down upon certain sec-
tions of the lane. It was for a reason more covetous. It
was because the solitary Carver who shared this evening
hour with the dogs and the sunbeams never failed to be
at his accustomed place at sundown. It was then that he
worked upon the block of jarl wood. It was then that the
image grew under his chisel. It was then that the Thing

watched, with her eyes wide as a child's, the evolution of the wooden raven. And it was for this carving that she pined angrily, impatiently. It was so that she might snatch it from its maker, and then away, in a breath, to the hills, that she crouched there evening after evening, watching greedily from the loose ivy for the completion of so pretty a toy.

Chapter Sixty-Two

WHEN Fuchsia heard the news of Steerpike's treachery and when she realized how her first and only affair of the heart had been with a murderer, an expression of such sickness and horror darkened her face that her aspect was, from that moment, never wholly free of that corrosive stain.

For a long while she spoke to no one, keeping herself to her room, where, unable to cry, she became exhausted with the emotions that fought in her to find some natural outlet. At first there was only the sense of having been physically struck, and the pain of the wound. Her arms gave little jerks and tingled. A depression of utter blackness drowned her. She had no wish to live at all. Her breast pained her. It was as though a great fear filled the cage of her ribs, a globe of pain that grew and grew. For the first week after the crushing news she could not sleep. And then a kind of hardness entered her. Something she had never housed before. It came as a protection. She needed it. It helped her to grow bitter. She began to kill at birth all thoughts of love that were natural to her. She changed and she aged as she wandered to and fro across her solitary room. She began to see no reason why others, as well as Steerpike, should not be double-faced and merciless. She hated the world.

When Titus called to see her he was amazed at the change in her voice, and the sunken look of her eyes. He saw for the first time that she was a woman as well as being his sister.

On her side, she saw a change in him. His restlessness was as real as her disillusion. His longing for freedom as pressing as her longing for love.

But what could he do, and what could she do? The castle was round and about them, widespread and as unchartable as a dark day.

"Thank you for coming," she said, "but there's nothing we can talk about!"

Titus said nothing but leaned against a wall. She looked so much older. His heel began to work away at a piece of loose plaster above the skirting board until it came away.

"I can't believe he's dead," said the boy at last.

"Who?"

"Flay, of course. And all the things he did. What about his cave? Empty forever, I suppose. Would you like to—"

"No," said Fuchsia, anticipating his question. "Not now. Not any more. I don't want to go anywhere, really. Have you seen Dr. Prune?"

"Once or twice. He asked me to tell you that he'd like to see you, whenever you want. He's not very well."

"None of us are," said Fuchsia. "What are you going to do? You look quite different. Was it awful, seeing what happened? But don't tell me. I don't want to dwell on it!"

"There are sentries everywhere," said Titus.

"I know."

"And a curfew. I have to be in my room by eight o'clock. Who's the man outside the door here?"

"I don't know his name. He's there most of the day and all night. A man in the courtyard too, under the window."

Titus wandered to the window and looked down. "What good is he doing there?" And then, turning about, "They'll never catch *him*," he said. "He's too cunning, the bloody beast. Why can't they burn the whole place down, and him with it, and us with it, and the world with it, and finish the whole dirty business, and the rotten ritual and everything and give the green grass a chance?"

"Titus," she said, "come here." He approached her, his hands shaking.

"I love you, Titus, but I can't feel anything. I've gone dead. Even you are dead in me. I know I love you. You're the only one I love, but I can't feel anything and I don't want to. I've felt too much, I'm sick of feelings. . . . I'm frightened of them."

Titus took another step toward her. She gazed at him. A year ago they would have kissed. They had needed each other's love. Now, they needed it even more but something had gone wrong. A space had formed between them, and they had no bridge.

But he gripped her arm for a moment before walking quickly to the door and disappearing from her sight.

Chapter Sixty-Three

THE Day of the Bright Carvings was at hand. The Carvers had put the final touches to their creations. The expectancy in the castle was as acute as it was possible for it to be, when at the same time the larger and more horrible awareness that Steerpike might at any moment strike again took up the larger part of their minds. For the skewbald man had struck four times within the last eight days with accuracy, a small pebble being found, in every case, near the fractured heads of the newly slain, or lodged in the bone above the eyes. These killings, so wicked in their want of purpose, took place in such widely separated districts as to give no clue as to where the haunt of the homicide might be. His deadly catapult had spread a clammy terror through Gormenghast.

But in spite of this preponderant fear, the imminence
of the traditional Day of Carvings had brought a certain
excitement of a less terrible kind to the hearts of the
denizens. They turned with relief to this age-old ceremony as though to something on which they could re-
ly—something that had happened every year since they
could remember anything at all. They turned to tradition as a child turns to its mother.

The long courtyard where the ceremony was to be held
had been scrubbed and double-scrubbed. The clanking
of buckets, the swilling and hissing of water, the sound
of scouring had echoed along the attenuate yard, sunrise after sunrise, for a week past. The high Southern
Wall in particular was immaculate. The scaffolding to
which the scrubbers had clung like monkeys while they
ferreted among the rough stones, scraping at the interstices and sluicing every vestige of accumulated dust
from niche and crack, had been removed. It sailed away,
this wall, in a dwindling perspective of gleaming stone—
and five feet from the ground along its entire length the
Carvers' Shelf protruded. The solid shelf or buttress was
of so handsome a breadth that even the largest of the
colored carvings stood comfortably upon it. It had already been whitewashed in preparation for the great day,
as had also the wall above it, to the height of a dozen
feet. What plants and creepers had forced their way
through the stones during the past year were cut down,
as usual, flush with the stones.

It was into this courtyard so unnaturally lustrated that
the Carvers from the Outer Dwellings were to pour like a
dark and ragged tide, bearing their heavy wooden carvings in their arms or upon their shoulders—or when the
works were too weighty for a man to sustain he would
be aided by his family—the children running alongside,
barefooted, their black hair in their eyes, their shrill, excited voices jabbing the heavy air as though with stilettos.

For the air was full of an oppressive weight. What
breath there was moved hotly on its way as though it
were fanned by the moldering wings of huge and sickly
birds.

The Steerpike terror had been still further intensified by these stifling conditions, and the ceremony of the Bright Carvings was for this reason all the more eagerly anticipated, for it was a relief for the mind and spirit to be able to turn to something the only purpose of which was beauty.

But, for all the consummate craft and rhythmic loveliness of the carvings, there was no love lost between their jealous authors. The interfamily rivalries, the ancient wrongs, a hundred bitter quarrels, all were remembered at this annual ceremony. Old wounds were reopened or kept green. Beauty and bitterness existed side by side. Old clawlike hands, cracked with long years of thankless toil, would hold aloft a delicate bird of wood, its wings as thin as paper, spread for flight, its breast afire with a crimson stain.

On the penultimate evening all was ready. The Poet, now fully established as Master of Ritual, had made his final tour of inspection with the Countess. On the following morning the gates in the Outer Wall were opened and the Bright Carvers began the three-mile trail to the Carvers' Courtyard.

From then onward the day blossomed like a rose, with its hundred blooms and its thousand thorns. Gray Gormenghast became bloodshot, became glutted with gold, became chill with blues as various as the blue of the flowers, and the waters became stained with evergreen from the softest olive to veridian, became rich with all the ochres; flamed and smoldered, shuddered with the hues of earth and air.

And holding these solid figures in their arms were the dark and irritable mendicants. By afternoon the long stone shelf had been loaded with its colored forms, its birds, its beasts, its fantasies, its giant grasshoppers, its reptiles, and its rhythms of leaf and flower; its hundred heads that turned upon their necks, that dropped or were raised more proudly from the shoulders than any living head of flesh and blood.

There they stood in a long, burning line with their shadows behind them on the Southern Wall. From all these carvings three were to be chosen as the most original and perfect, and these three would be added to those that were displayed in the unfrequented Hall of the Bright Carvings. The rest were to be burned that same evening.

The judging was a long and scrupulous affair. The Carvers would eye the judges from a distance as they squatted about the courtyard in families, or leaned against the opposite wall. Hour after hour the fateful business proceeded—the only sound being the shouting and crying of the scores of urchins. At about six o'clock the long tables were carried out by the castle servants and placed end to end in three long lines. These tables were then loaded with loaves, and bowls of thick soup.

When dusk began to fall the judging was all but completed. The sky had become overcast and an unusual darkness brooded over the scene. The air had become intolerably close. The children had ceased to run about, although in other years they had sported tirelessly until midnight. But now they sat near their mothers in a formidable silence. To lift an arm was to become tired and to sweat profusely. Many faces were turned to the sky where a world of cloud was gathering together its gloomy continents, tier behind tier like the foliage of some fabulous cedar.

As a minor Titus was not directly involved in the actual choice of the "Three," but his technical approval had to be obtained when the decisions were finally made. He had wandered restlessly up and down the line of the exhibits, threading his way through the crowds, which parted deferentially at his approach. The weight of the iron chain about his neck and the stone that was strapped to his forehead became almost too much to bear. He had seen Fuchsia but had lost her again in the crowds.

"There's going to be an almighty storm, my boy," said a voice at his shoulder. "By all that's torrential, there most certainly is!"

It was Prunesquallor.

"Feels like it, Dr. Prune," said Titus.

"And looks like it, my young stalker of felons!"

Titus turned his gaze to the sky. It seemed to have

gone mad. It bulged and shifted itself as though it were
not moved by any breeze or current of the air, but only
through its own foul impulses.

It was a foul sky, and it was growing. It was accumulating filth from the hot slums of hell. Titus turned his
eyes from its indescribable menace and faced the Doctor
again. Prunesquallor's face was gleaming with sweat.
"Have you seen Fuchsia?" he said.

"I saw her," answered Titus. "But I lost her again. She
is somewhere here."

The Doctor lifted his head high and stared about him,
his Adam's apple very angular, his teeth flashing, but in
a smile that Titus could see was empty.

"I wish you would see her, Dr. Prune. She looks awful, suddenly."

"I will certainly see her, Titus, and as soon as I can."

At that moment a messenger approached. Titus was
wanted by the judges.

"Away with you," cried the Doctor in this new voice
that had lost its ring. "Away with you, young fellow!"

"Good-by, Doctor."

Chapter Sixty-Four

❦❦❦❦❦❦❦❦❦❦❦

THAT night, upon the balcony, his mother sat upon his
right hand like an enormous stranger, and the Poet upon
his left, an alien figure. Below him was a vast field of
upturned faces. Away ahead of him and far beyond the
reach of the great bonfire's radiance the mountain was
just visible against the dark sky.

The moment was approaching when he must call for
the three successful Carvers to come forward and for
him to draw up the carvings from below with a cord and
to place them in full sight of the crowd.

The flames of the bonfire around which the multitude was congregated streamed up into the sky. Its insatiable heat had already reduced a hundred dreams to ashes.

As he watched, a glorious tiger, its snarling head bent back along its spine, and its four feet close together beneath its belly, was flung through the air by one of the twelve hereditary "Vandals." The flames appeared to flick out their arms to receive it, and then they curled about it and began to eat.

His longing to escape came upon him with a sudden and elemental force. He hated this gross wastage that was going on below him. The heat of the evening made him sick. The nearness of his mother and of the abstracted Poet disquieted him. His eyes moved to Gormenghast Mountain. What lay beyond? Was there another land? Another world? Another kind of life?

If he should leave the castle! The very notion of it made him shake with a mixture of fear and excitement. His thought was so revolutionary that he glanced at his mother's back to see whether she had heard his mind at work.

If he should leave Gormenghast? He was unable to hazard a guess as to what such a thought implied. He knew of no other place. He had thought before, of Escape. Escape as an abstract idea. But he had never thought seriously of where he would escape to, or of how he would live in some place where he would be unknown.

And a seditious fear that he was in reality of no consequence came over him. That Gormenghast was of no consequence and that to be an Earl and the son of Sepulchrave, a direct descendant of the Bloodline—was something of only local interest. The idea was appalling.

He raised his head and gazed across the thousands of faces below him. He nodded his head in a kind of pompous approval as yet another carving was tossed into the great bonfire. He counted a score of towers to his left. "All mine," he said, but the words sounded emptily in his head, when suddenly something happened which blew his terror and his hope sky-high, which filled him with a joy too huge for him to contain, which took him and shook him out of his indecisions, and swept him into a land of hectic and cruel brilliance, of black glades, and of a magic insupportable.

For, as he was watching, something happened with great rapidity. A coal-black raven, its head cocked, its every feather exquisitely chiseled, its claws gripping a wrinkled branch, was about to be thrown into the flames when, as Titus watched, in a half-dream, a ripple in the silent, heat-heavy crowd showed where a single figure was threading its way with an unusual speed. The hereditary "Vandal" had hold of the wooden raven by its head and swung back his hand. The bonfire leaped and crackled and lit his face. The arm came forward; the fingers loosed their grip; that raven sailed up in the air, turning over and over, and began to fall toward the fire when, as unforeseen and rapid as the course of a dream, there leaped from the body of the fire-lit crowds something that, with a mixture of grace and savagery quite indescribable, snatched at the height of its leap the raven from the air, and holding it above its head continued without a pause or break in the superb rhythm of its flight, and apparently floating over an ivy-covered wall disappeared into the night. For more than a minute there was no movement at all. A dreadful embarrassment held the witnesses immobile as though with a vise. The individual shock that each sustained was heightened by the stunned condition of the mass. Something unthinkable had been done, something so flagrant that the anger that was so soon to show itself was for the moment held back as though by a wall of embarrassment.

Such violation of a hallowed ceremony was unprecedented.

The Countess was one of the first to stir. For the first time since Steerpike's escape she was moved by a tremendous anger that had no connection with the skewbald rebel. She rose to her feet and with her big hands gripping the balustrade stared into the night. The congested clouds hung with a terrible nearness and an in-

creasing weight. The air sweated. The crowds began
to mutter and to move like bees in a hive. Isolated cries
of rage from below the balcony sounded close, raw and
horrible.

What was the death of a few hierophants at Steerpike's hand compared with the stabbing of the castle's
very heart? The heart of Gormenghast was not its gar-
rison—its transient denizens—but that invisible thing
that had been wounded in their sight. As the cries rose
and the swollen clouds pressed down, Titus, the last to
move, turned his eyes to his mother's with a sidelong
sweep. Sick with excitement he rose gradually to his
feet.

He alone, of all who had been so fundamentally affected by the profane insult to tradition, was affected for
a reason of his own. The shock he had suffered was
unique. He had not been drawn into the maelstrom of
the general shock. He was alone in his unique excitement. At the first sight of that mercurial creature he
was transported in a flash to an earlier day, a day which
he had no longer believed in, and had relegated to the
world of dreams: to a day when among the spectral
oak woods he had seen, or had thought he had seen, an
air-borne figure with its small head turned away. It was
so long ago. It had become no more than a fume of
his mind—a vapor.

But it was she. There was no doubting that it had
all been true. He had seen her before, when lost among
the oak woods she had floated past like a leaf. And now
again! Taller, of course, as he was taller. But no less
fleet, no less uncanny.

He remembered how the momentary sight of her had
awakened in him an awareness of liberty. But now! How
much more so! The heat was terrible in the air, but his
spine was icy with excitement.

He looked about him again, with an air of cunning
quite out of character. Everything was as it was. His
mother was still beside him, her big hands on the balustrade. The bonfire roared and spat red embers into the
dark and stifling air. Someone in the crowd was shout-

ing, *"The Thing! The Thing!"* and another voice with dreadful regularity cried, "Stone her! Stone her!" But Titus heard nothing of this. Moving gradually backward step by step, he turned at last and in a few quick paces was in the room behind the balcony.

Then he began to run, his every step a crime. Through midnight corridors in any one of which the skewbald Steerpike might well have been lurking, he sped. His jaw ached with fear and excitement. His clothes stuck to his back and thighs. Turning and turning, sometimes losing himself, and sometimes colliding with the rough walls, he came at last to a flight of broad shallow steps that ran out into the open. A mile away to his right the light of the bonfire was reflected on the bulging clouds that hung above it like the ghostly bolsters of some beldam's bed.

Ahead of him, Gormenghast Mountain and the widespread slopes of Gormenghast Forest were hidden from his vision in the night, but he ran to them as a migratory bird flies blindly through the darkness to the country that it needs.

Chapter Sixty-Five

His sense of supreme disobedience, rather than retarding his progress through the night, gave it impetus. He could feel the angry breath of retribution on the nape of his neck as he stumbled on. There was yet time for him to return, but in spite of his hammering heart it never occurred to him to do so. He was propelled forward by his imagination having been stirred to its depths by the sight of her. He had not seen her face. He had not heard her speak. But that which over the years had become a fantasy, a fantasy of dreaming trees and moss, of golden acorns and a sprig in flight, was fantasy no longer. It was here. It was now. He was running through heat and darkness toward it; to the verity of it all.

But his body was profoundly tired. The sickening heat was something to be fought against, and at last, when within a mile of the foothills, he fell to his knees and then onto his side, where he lay soaked in perspiration, his flushed face in his arms.

But his mind did not rest. His mind was still running and stumbling alone. A thousand times as he lay with his eyes closed, he saw her take the ivy-covered wall with that maddening beauty of flight; effortless, and over-weeningly arrogant, her small bragging head turned away from him, and perched so exquisitely upon the neck— the whole thing floating in his mind with a kind of aerial ease.

A hundred times he saw her as he lay and a hundred times he turned restlessly from side to side, while the sprite flew on and on and its legs like water reeds appeared to trail in the body's wake rather than cause the earthless speed of it.

And then he heard the hoarse voice of a cannon and before the heavy, tumbling echoes that followed it had ended he was on his feet again and running dangerously through the darkness, to where the high masses of Gormenghast Mountain arose in the sightless night. It was the single explosion that was the traditional warning of danger. He knew it meant that his disappearance had not only been discovered, but that his defiance of Gormenghast had been suspected by his mother.

When the time came for the three chosen carvings to be drawn up to the balcony and to be flourished before the crowd, he was no longer there. On top of the sickening heat and the terror of the swollen sky; on top of the fear of the beast of Gormenghast and of his roving catapult —on top of the unprecedented snatching of a carving from the flames, and the sight of the Thing in their midst, there was now this unimaginable offense to the castle's honor, to gall not only the hierophants but the Carvers.

At first they had imagined that the young Earl had

fainted in the heat. This had occurred to the Poet, who
with the permission of the Countess disappeared into the
room at the rear of the balcony. But he found no sign
of the boy. As the minutes passed the anger grew, and
only the heaviness of the stifling night and the resulting
weariness of the crowds prevented the indiscriminate
violence that might easily have developed.

The acid of this dreadful night bit deep. Something
fundamental to the life of Gormenghast had been affected
and weakened.

At a time when a devil was loose and the whole energy
of the place was concentrated upon his capture, it was
stupefying to find that the castle had been stabbed to
the heart by the perfidy of its brightest symbol, the heir
himself to the sacred masonry, the Seventy-Seventh Earl.

This child of fate was climbing through the gloom;
stumbling among the roots of trees, forcing his way
through undergrowth, pressing fanatically onward.

How he would find her when the sun rose over the
mazes of the forest and played across the trackless expanses of Gormenghast Mountain he had no idea. He
simply believed that the power that drew him could not
fail to show itself.

But a time came when he was so benighted that further
progress was impossible. He was sufficiently far from
the castle, sufficiently lost, to evade immediate capture.
He knew that search parties were even now being organized and that the vanguard of those levies was probably
already on their way. He knew also that the sending
forth of a single searcher redounded in Steerpike's favor.
This would not be forgiven him.

Whether his absence would be associated with the
sudden appearance of the Thing, he could not tell. Perhaps the coincidence was all too apparent. What he did
know was that the sin to cap all sins would be for any
member of the castle, let alone its rightful sovereign, to
have the remotest association with an Outer Dweller—
for the Earl of Gormenghast to go in search of a
daughter of that squalid cantonment, and a bastard child
at that. He knew that from his mother downward to the

most obscure of her menials the conception of any such happening would be equally revolting. It would be worse than shameless treachery. It would be at the same time a *defilement* of the Bloodline.

He knew all this. But he could do nothing. He could only pretend, if ever he were caught, that the impending storm had affected his brain. But he could not alter anything. Something more fundamental than tradition had him in its grip. If he was caught, he was caught. If they imprisoned him, or held him up for public contumely, then that was what he deserved. If he was disinherited he had only himself to blame. He had slapped a god across its age-old face. It was so. . . . It was so. . . . But as the night-heat swaddled him in a near-sleep his thoughts were not of his mother's mortification, of the castle's peril, of his treachery, or of his sister's anxiety, but of a Thing of fierce and shameless insolence—of a rebel like himself who gloried in it: of a rebel like a lyric in green flight.

Chapter Sixty-Six

HE awoke to the first crash of thunder. There was a shadowy light in the dark air that could only have come from some remote and cloud-choked sunrise. And as the thunder spoke the first of the great rain came.

The danger of it was at once apparent. This was no ordinary downpour. Even the first streaks from the sky were things that lashed and kicked the dust out of the ground with a vicious deliberation.

The air was like the air in an oven. Titus had leaped to his feet as though he had been prodded with a stick. The sky seethed and rumbled. The clouds yawned like hippopotami; deep holes or funnels, opening and closing, mouthlike, now here, now there.

He began to run again, climbing all the while through a kind of half-light. The forms of trees and rocks, suddenly looming over him, forced him to turn to left and right in a sudden and jerky way, for it was not until he was upon them that they made themselves known.

His immediate object was to strike the fringe of the close-set trees of Gormenghast Forest, for only beneath their boughs could he hope to shield himself from the rain. It hissed in the loose foliage about him which was no kind of shelter, even for this first flurry of the storm.

For all its initial violence there was yet no sense of hurry about the rain. It gave the impression of an endless reserve of sky-wide energy.

And as he stumbled on through the rain that spilled itself from the canopies of leaf above, a streak of lightning, like an outrider, lit up the terrain so that for a moment the world was made of nothing but wet steel.

And in that moment his eyes fled over the glittering landscape, and before the enormous gloom had settled again he had seen a pair of solitary pines on a hill of boulders, and he at once recognized the place, for one of the pines had been broken by the wind and was caught in the upper arms of its brother.

He had never climbed these pines nor stood in their shade nor heard the rustle of their needles; but they were more than familiar to him, for years ago he had stared at them every time he had emerged from the long tunnel —the tunnel that led from the Hollow Halls to within a mile of Mr. Flay's cave.

When he saw the pines in the lightning-flash his heart leaped. But the darkness came down again and it was at once apparent how difficult it would be not only to arrive at the pines but to strike off from them, with confidence, toward the tunnel mouth. To arrive at the pines would yet not be to come to any place where he had stood before. In the moment that he had recognized those trees he had also realized that the rest of the dazzling panorama was unknown to him. He had taken some strange path in the darkness.

But though it might well be difficult, even with the increasing light, to know exactly in which direction to move, when at last he should come to the pines (for it would of course be impossible to see the caveward mouth of the tunnel), yet it was useless to dwell upon the difficulties, and Titus, altering his direction, struck out across the wilderness of coarse grasses that was already under water. The churned "lake" reached upward to his ankles. It spouted all about him. What had been fierce streaks of rain were now no longer streaks. Nor even ropes. Each one was like pump water or a tap turned to its full. And yet there was still the dreadful closeness in the air; although the tepid water, hammering him and streaming over his body, mitigated the heat.

Beyond the soaking grasslands, and the alder copses, beyond the stony and grassless foothills where the big ponds were forming; beyond the old silver mines and the gravel quarries; beyond all these in a district of harsher country than he had so far encountered, he came at last to a group of giant rocks.

By now the light had to some extent percolated through the clouds of black water and when he climbed upon the back of the largest of the rocks he was able to see the two pines, not away to his right, as he suspected they would be, but immediately ahead of him.

But there was no need for him to approach them further. He could not have found a better lookout station than the rock on which he stood. Nor was there any need for him to strain his eyes to find features in the landscape by which he could determine the position of the tunnel's mouth. For there to the east, not a mile away, was that high line of trees that overhung the shelving masses of green-gravel, which, overgrown with every kind of vegetable life, descended steplike to where among the valley rocks the small stream chattered, the stream which Flay had dammed, and which ran within a stone's throw of what had been the exile's cave.

With the dusky light of morning strengthening, the

rain, through which it had been difficult to recognize any object, so solidly had it descended, began to lessen. There was no question of the rain wishing to rest itself; far less that the sky was running out of water. No, it was only that the clouds withdrew their claws into the black pads of the storm as a wild beast might draw in its talons for no other reason than to savor the contraction.

But still the rain came down. A body of water had been held in check, but there was no stopping the overflow. Titus no longer felt the rain. It was as though he had always lived in water.

He sat down on the rock, and like a fly in amber, was a prisoner of the morning. All about him on the flat head of the rock the rebounding rain threw up its short, fierce fountains, and the hard slopes seethed with it. What was he doing here, soaked to the skin, far from his home? Why was he not frightened? Why was he not repentant and ashamed?

He sat there alone, his knees drawn up to his chin, his arms clasping his legs, how small a thing beneath those continents of gushing cloud.

He knew that it was no dream, but he had no power to override the dreamlike nature of it all. The reality was in himself—in his longing to experience the terror of what he already thought of as love.

He had heard of love: he had guessed at love: he had no knowledge of love but he knew all about it. What, if not love, was the cause of all this?

The head had been turned away. The limbs had floated. But it was not the beauty. It was the sin against the world of his father's. It was the arrogance! It was the wicked swagger of it all! It was the effrontery! It was that Gormenghast meant nothing to this elastic switch of a girl!

But it was not only that she was so much the outward expression of all he meant by the word "Freedom," or that the physical *she* and what she symbolized had become fused into one thing—it was not only this that intoxicated Titus—it was more than an abstract excitement that set his limbs trembling when he thought of her.

He lusted to touch those floating limbs. She was romance to him. She was freedom. But she was more than these. She was a thing that breathed the same air and trod the same ground, though she might have been a faun or a tigress or a moth or a fish or a hawk or a martin. Had she been any of these she would have been no more dissimilar from him than she was now. He trembled at the thought of this disparity. It was not closeness or a sameness, or any affinity or hope of it, that thrilled him. It was the difference, the *difference* that mattered; the *difference* that cried aloud.

And still the rain came down, rapid and warm from the hot air it passed through. Titus's eyes were on those trees that crowned the long hill in whose shadow was the cave. A few miles to the west, a huge blur showed where Gormenghast Mountain brooded. It was streaked with the vertical bars of the rain as though it were a beast in prison.

Titus got to his feet and made his way down the rock, and all at once he felt frightened. Too much had happened to him in too short a time. It was the thought of the cave, and thence the thought of Flay, and from the thought of Flay as he had first seen him in his cave there sprang the image of that faithful servant with a knife in his heart and the vile room where his aunts lay side by side. And so the face of Steerpike swam across the lines of the rain, the terrible pattern of red and white, like the mask of some horror-dance, expanding and contracting, the shoulders very spare, very high; and for a hundred paces Titus was all but sick as he ran, and more than once he turned his head over his shoulder, and peered into the rain on either hand.

It was a long journey to the cave. Even had there been no deluge he would have made for it. He thought of it as a center from which he could move in the wilderness and to which he could return.

But when he reached it he was hesitant to enter. The old stone mouth gaped emptily. It was no longer as he remembered it. It was a deserted place.

Above the cave the hill arose, tier upon streaming tier

of shelving rock, the broken ledges thick with ferns and shrubs, and even trees that leaned out fantastically into space.

Titus stared up to where the upper heights were lost in the clouds, but his eyes were almost at once drawn back to the cave mouth.

His head was a little lowered and thrust forward from his shoulders in a characteristic position that suggested that he was ready to butt whatever enemy might appear. His nondescript hair was black with the rain and clung across his face in streaks and rats' tails.

The melancholy look of the entrance had for a moment dulled his excitement at seeing the place again. He stood about a dozen feet away from the mouth, and could see through the streaks of the rain the dark, dry tunnel that led to the spacious interior.

As he stood there, hesitant, his head forward, his rain-heavy clothes clinging to his body like seaweed, it could be seen how much the last few months had changed him. His eyes were still as clear as spring water, with that glitter of willfulness, but a frown had made a permanent groove above them. A nest of faint and shallow lines had formed between his eyes. The boyish proportions of his face were clear evidence that he was no more than his seventeen years, but the somber expression which had become ever more typical of him was more to be expected in a person twice his age.

This *darkness* in his face was by no means the outcome of sad or tragic experience. He had had his times of loneliness, of fear, of frustration, and of late, of horror, but equally like any other child, he had had his carefree golden days, his laughter, and his excitements. He was no cowed and mournful child of misfortune. He was, if anything, too much alive. Too much aware. It was that that had forced him, in the end, to wear a mask. To scowl at his school friends, while at the same moment his heart would be beating wildly, and his imagination racing. To scowl because, by scowling, he was left alone. And when he was alone he was able to brood by the hour upon his lot, to whip himself into unhealthy and self-indulgent fits of rebellion against his heritage and against the ritual that so hampered him, and conversely he was able to sit undisturbed at his desk while his thoughts flickered to and fro across the realm of Gormenghast, marveling, as he did so, at all that it was, and how it was his mammoth legacy.

His physical vitality had begun to find its outlet through solitary exploration of the castle and the surrounding country, but it was the expeditions of his imagination, of his daydreams, that drew him farther and farther away from companionship.

He had been, virtually, an orphan. That his mother, deep in her heart, too deep for her own recognition, had a strange need for him, as a son of the Line, was of no value to him, for he knew nothing of it.

To be alone was nothing new to him. But to have defied his mother and his subjects as he had done this day was new, and this knowledge of his treachery made him feel, for the first time since he had escaped from the Carvers' Balcony, lonely in the extreme. Lonely, not for his home, but lonely in the knowledge of his inward isolation.

He took a step nearer the cave. The rain, surging over his head, had so glued down his hair that his skull showed its shape like a boulder. His slightly heavy cheekbones, his blunt nose, his wide mouth were by no means handsome in themselves, but, held in by the oval outline of the face, they formed a kind of simple harmony that was original and pleasant to the eye.

But his habit of drawing down his eyebrows and scowling to hide his feelings was making him look more than his seventeen years, and it appeared that a young man rather than a boy was approaching the cave. Directly he had decided to wait no longer, and had passed under the rough natural archway, he was startled at the freedom of his head and body from the battering of the rain. He had become so used to it that, standing there in the dry dust beneath the vaulting roof of the tunnel, he felt a sudden buoyancy as though a burden had been lifted.

And now another wave of fatigue heaved up in him, and he longed for nothing so much as sleep in a dry place. The air was warm in the cave, for the rain, heavy as it was, had done nothing to relieve the heat. He longed to lie down, in his new-found lightness of body, and with nothing pouring down upon him from above, to sleep forever.

Now that he was inside the cave, the melancholy atmosphere of desertion had lost its potency. Perhaps he was too tired, and his emotions too blunted, to be conscious any more of such subtleties.

When he came to the main, inner chamber with its ample space, its natural shelves, its luxuriating ferns, he could hardly keep his eyes open. He hardly noticed that a number of small woodland animals had taken shelter and were lying upon the stone shelves, or squatting on the ferny floor, watching him with bright eyes.

Automatically he tore off his clinging clothes and, stumbling to a dark corner of the cave, lay down beneath the arched arms of a great fern and fell, incontinently, fast asleep.

Chapter Sixty-Seven

As Titus slept the small animals were joined by a drenched fox and a few birds which perched on outcrops of rock near the doming roof. The boy was all but invisible where he lay beneath the overhang of the ferns. So deep was his sleep that the lightning that had begun to play across the sky and illumine the mouth of the cave had no effect upon him. The thunder, when it came, for all that it was louder than before, was equally powerless to wake him. But it was drawing closer all the while, and the last of the bull-throated peals caused him to turn over in his sleep.

By now it was afternoon but the air had darkened so that there was now less light than there was when Titus sat upon the lookout rock.

The roaring and hissing of the rain were mounting steadily in volume, and the noise of it upon the stones and the earth outside the mouth of the cave made all but the most violent of the thunder-peals inaudible. A hare with its ears laid along its back sat motionless with its eyes fixed upon the fox. The cave was filled with the noise of the elements, and yet there was a kind of silence there, a silence *within* the noise; the silence of stillness, for nothing moved.

When the next flash of lightning skinned the landscape, ripping its black hide off it so that there was no part of its anatomy that was not exposed to the floodlight, the reflections of that blinding illumination were fanned to and fro across the cavern walls so that the birds and beasts shone out like radiant carvings among the radiant ferns, and their shadows flew away across the walls and contracted again as though they were made of elastic: and Titus stirred beneath the archery of the giant hearts-tongue which shielded him from the momentary glare, so that he did not wake, and he could not see that at the mouth of the cave stood the Thing.

Chapter Sixty-Eight

❈❈❈❈❈❈❈❈❈❈❈

I

IT was hunger that finally woke him. For a while as he lay with his eyes still closed he imagined himself to be in his room at the castle. Even when he opened his eyes and found on his right-hand side the rough wall of a rock and on his left a curtain of thick ferns, he could not re-

member where he was. And then he became aware of a
roaring sound and all at once he remembered how he
had escaped from the castle and had made his way
through an eternity of rain until he had come to a cave—
to Flay's cave—to *this* cave in which he was now lying.

It was then that he heard something move. It was not
a loud sound and it was only audible above the thrum-
ming of the storm because of its nearness.

His first thought was that it was one of the animals,
perhaps a hare, and his hunger made him cautious as he
rose up on his elbow and parted the long tongue of the
ferns.

But what he saw was something that made him forget
his hunger as though it had never been: that made him
start backward against the rock and sent the blood rushing to his head. For it was she! But not as he remembered
her. It was she! But how different!

What had his memory done to her that he should now
be seeing a creature so radically at variance with the
image that had filled his mind?

There she sat, the Thing, balanced upon her heels,
unbelievably small, the light of a fresh fire flickering
over her as she swiveled a plucked bird on a spit above
the flames. All about her were scattered the feathers of
a magpie. Was this the lyric swallow? The flute-limbed
hurdler?

Was this small creature who was now squatting there
like a frog in the dust, and scratching her thigh with a
dirty hand the size of a beech leaf, was this what had
floated through his imagination in arrogant rhythms that
spanned the universe?

Yes, it was she. The vision had contracted to the
small and tangible proportions of the uncompromising
urchin—the rarefaction had become clay.

And then she turned her head and Titus saw a face
that shocked and thrilled him. All that was Gormenghast
within him shuddered: shuddered and bridled up in a
kind of anger. All that was rebellious in him cried with
joy: with the joy of witnessing the heart of defiance. The
confusion in his breast was absolute. His memory of her,

of a proud and gracile creature, was now destroyed. It was no longer true. It had become trite, shallow, and saccharine. Proud she was, and vibrant in all conscience. And graceful, perhaps in flight—but not now. There was nothing graceful in the way her body, uninhibited as an animal's, crouched over the flames. This was something new and earthy.

Titus, who had been in love with an arrogance and a swallowlike beauty of limb, so that he longed savagely and fearfully to clasp it, was now aware of how there were these new dimensions, this dark reality of slaughtered birds, of scattered feathers, of an animal's posture, and above all of an ignorant originality that was redolent in her every gesture.

Her head had turned. He had seen her face. He was staring at an *original*. It was not that the face had any unique peculiarity of proportion or feature, but that it was so blatant an index of all she was.

And yet it was not through any particular mobility of the features that it conveyed the independence of her life. The line of the mouth seldom altered, save when, in devouring the roasted bird, she bit with an undue ferocity. No: the face was more masklike than expressive. It symbolized her way of life, not her immediate thoughts. It was the color of a robin's egg, and as closely freckled. Her hair was black and thick but she had hacked it away, a little above her shoulders. Her rounded neck was set upright upon her shoulders, and was so flexible that the liquid ease with which she turned it was reminiscent of a serpent.

It was through such motions as this, and the movements of her small shoulders and in the quickness of her fingers, that she conveyed to Titus, more vividly than any expression of the features could ever do, the quality of her fanatical independence.

As he watched she tossed the bones of the magpie over her shoulder, and dipping her hand into the shadows at her side, drew up, out of the darkness that she cast, the little carving of the raven. Turning it round and round in her hand, she stared at it intently, but no vestige of an expression crossed her face. She placed it on the ground at her side, but the earth was uneven and it fell forward upon its face. Without a moment's hesitation she struck it with her clenched fist as a child might strike a toy in anger, and then, rising in a smooth and single action to her feet, she flicked it out of her way with her foot so that it lay upon its side against the wall.

Upon her feet she had become another thing. It was difficult to reconcile her with the creature who had squatted by the fire. She had become a sapling. Her face was turned to where the water streamed across the cave mouth. For a few moments she stared expressionlessly at the rain-filled opening, and then she moved toward it, but at her third step she stopped and as her body tautened, her head gyrated on her neck. Her shoulders had not moved, but as her head swiveled, her eyes sped around the walls of the cave. Something had disturbed her.

Her slender body was poised for instantaneous action. Again her eyes flew across the walls, piercing every shadow, and then for a moment they stayed their flight and Titus could see from his dark recess that she had seen his shirt where it lay, torn and sodden, on the floor of the cave.

She turned and with a tread both light and apprehensive approached the garment that lay in a pool of its own making. She sat down on her heels at its side, and again she was a frog, an almost repellent thing. Her eyes still moved about the cave, suspiciously. For a little while they lingered upon the giant ferns that, arching over Titus, hid him in their shadows.

Swiveling her head, she stared backward toward the mouth of the cave, but only for a second; for the next moment she had taken the shirt, and held it up before her. A stream of rain water slid from its folds to the floor; she crushed the cloth together and then began to wring it out with a surprising strength, and then, spreading it out upon the ground, she gazed at it, her expressionless head upon one side like a bird's.

Titus, half numbed by his cramped position, was forced to lie back and rest his arms and straighten his leg. When he rose again upon his elbow she was no longer by the shirt but was standing at the cave mouth. He knew that he could not stay where he was forever. Sooner or later he must make his presence known—and he was about to get to his feet whatever the consequences when a glare of lightning showed him the Thing silhouetted against the brilliance, her backbone arched a little, her head thrown back to catch the stream of translucent rain that golden as the lightning itself was falling directly into her upturned mouth. For that split second of time she was something cut out of black paper, her head meticulous in its contour, the mouth wide open as though to drink the sky.

And then the dark came down, and he saw her appear out of the gloom and grow more visible as she approached the embers of the fire. It was evident that the shirt fascinated her, for she paused when she reached it, and stared at it now from one angle, now from another. Finally she took it up and, pulling it over her head and thrusting her arms through the sleeves, she stood as though in a nightgown.

Titus, whose conception of the Thing had been flung from one side of his mind to the other, so that he hardly knew whether she was a frog, a snake, or a gazelle, was now powerless to assimilate the bizarre transfiguration that now stood within a few feet of him.

All he knew was that what he had so avidly sought was with him in the cave, had sheltered, like himself, from the storm, and was now standing like a child, staring down at his shirt that fell in wet folds almost to the ankles.

And he forgot the wilderness within her. He forgot her ignorance. He forgot the raw blood and the speed. He only saw the stillness. He only saw the deceptive grace of her head as it hung forward. And seeing only this, he pushed aside the ferns and rose to his feet.

II

The effect of his sudden appearance upon the Thing was so violent that Titus took a step backward. Encumbered as she was with her new garment, she leaped to the side of the cave where the floor was littered with loose stones, and all in a breath she had snatched at one and flung it with a vicious speed at Titus. He jerked his head to one side, but the rough stone scraped his cheekbone and stung him badly, the blood running down his neck.

The pain and surprise which lit his face were in contrast to her inscrutable features. But it was his body that was still, and hers that moved.

She had swarmed up the rock face on her side of the cave and was leaping from ledge to ledge in an attempt to circumscribe the rough circle of wall beneath the dome. Titus had been between her and the entrance tunnel, and she was even now springing to a position from which she could swing herself over his head and drop on the stormward side—and so away.

But Titus, just in time to realize what she was doing, retreated farther down the tunnel, so that he blocked the way for her escape. But he was still in a position to observe her. Thwarted in her plan, she sprang backward to one of the higher ledges that she had already used, and there, twelve feet above him, her head among the ferns that hung downward from the roof, she directed her gaze upon him, her freckled face expressionless, but her head moving continuously from side to side like an adder's.

The effect of the blow on his cheek was to wake Titus out of his adulation. His temper flared out, and his fear of her lessened, not because she was not dangerous, but because she had resorted to so ordinary a means of warfare as the flinging of a stone. That was something he could understand.

Had she been able to pluck out rocks from the fern-cloaked roof she would even now be doing so, and hurling them down upon him. But even as he stared up at her with angry amazement, he felt an irrational longing for her, for what was she doing but defying, through him, the very core of Gormenghast? And it was this solitary insurrection that had first affected him with wonder and excitement. And while the stinging of his cheekbone angered him so that he wished to shake her, strike her and subdue her, at the same time the ease with which she had flitted from ledge to perilous ledge, the long wet garment slapping on the rocks as she sped, had made him lust for her small breasts and her slender limbs. He yearned to crush and master them. And yet he was angry.

How it was that she had been able to move at all across the rock face with his shirt impeding the freedom of her legs, let alone travel so speedily, he could not tell. The long sleeves flapped about her hands, but somehow or other she had been able to flick out her fingers from the folds, time after time, to grasp the cavern outcrops.

Now, as she crouched in the upper shadows, the damp cloth clinging to her and taking the form of her narrow limbs as though it had been sculptured, Titus, watching from below, cried out suddenly in a voice that seemed not his own.

"I am your friend! Your friend! Can't you understand? I am Lord Titus! Can't you hear me?"

The face like a robin's egg stared down at him from among the ferns, but there was no reply, save what sounded like a distant hissing.

"Listen to me," he shouted again, more loudly than before, although his heart beat wildly and the words were difficult to form.

"I have followed you. Don't you see? Followed you . . . Oh, can't you understand! I've run away. . . ."

He took a step nearer the wall so that she was almost directly overhead.

"And I've found you! So speak to me, for God's sake, can't you? Can't you?"

He saw her mouth open above him, and at that moment she might have been a giant phantom, something too earthless to be held in by the worldly dimensions of this cave, something beyond measurement. And her open mouth gave him the answer to his question.

"So *speak,*" he shouted, "can't you?" And this is what she could not do, for the first sound which Titus heard her utter bore no relation to human speech. Nor did the tone of it convey that he was being answered even in a language of her own. It was a sound, quite solitary and detached. It had no concern with communication. It was inward and curiously pitched.

So divorced was it, this nameless utterance, from the recognized sounds of the human throat, that it left Titus in no doubt that she was incapable of civilized speech, and not only this, but that she had not understood a word he had said.

What could he do to show her he was not her enemy, that he had no wish to avenge himself for the blood on his cheek? The thought of his wound gave him an idea, and he immediately lowered himself to his knees, never taking his eyes off her, and felt about him for a stone, her eyes following his every movement with the concentration of a cat. He could see the tenseness of her body vibrating through the shirt. When his fingers closed upon a stone he rose to his feet, and stretched out his hand with the missile displayed upon his open palm. Surely she must realize that it was now in his power to fling the thing at her. For a moment or two he showed her the stone, and then tossed it backward over his shoulder, where it clanged on the solid rock of the wall behind him.

But no expression crossed the freckled face. She had seen everything, but as far as Titus could tell it had meant nothing to her. But as he stared up he became conscious that she was preparing to change her position, or to make some kind of attempt at escape. For the hundredth part of a second her eyes had flicked away as though to remind herself of the surrounding footholds and the dangerous ledges, and then again her eyes switched from his face, but this time it was to something that lay behind Titus on the other side of the cave. Quick as thought he turned his head and saw what he had forgotten all about, the two wide natural chimneys through the rock, that, twelve feet above the entrance of the cave, led to the outer air.

So that was what she would try and do. He knew that she could not reach these rounded vents from where she was, but that if she could circle the cave, she might spring from the opposite side into the upper chimney, and so out into the open, where, no doubt, she would be able to swarm across the moss-gray walls of streaming rain.

For the rain was still pounding. It was an inevitable background to all they did. They were no longer conscious of the steady roaring, of the shouts of the thunder, or of the intermittent lightning. It had become normality.

And then, from where she crouched, the Thing rose in the air, and was all at once upon a broader ledge six feet to her right. There seemed to have been no muscular effort. It was flight! But once there, she tore at Titus's shirt, hauling it over her head as though she were freeing herself of a sail, but somehow it had become entangled about her, during her leap; and blinded for a moment by its folds across her face, she had, in a momentary panic, shifted her foothold and, misjudging the area of the ledge, she had overbalanced in the darkness and, with a muffled cry, had toppled from the height.

Involuntarily, as she had leaped to the broader shelf of rock, Titus had moved after her, as though drawn by the magic of her mobility, so that as she overbalanced he was within a few feet of where she would have struck the floor. But before she had fallen more than her own length he was stationed beneath her, his knees flexed, his hands raised, his fingers spread, his head thrown back.

But what he caught was so unsubstantial that he fell with it to the floor from the very shock of its lightness. His legs weakened beneath him with surprise, as though they had been cheated of the weight, however slight, that they were prepared to sustain. He had caught at a feather and it had struck him down. But his arms closed about the sprite that struggled in the cold wet linen, and Titus gripped her with an angry strength, the full weight of his body lying across hers, for they had rolled over one another and he had forced her under.

He could not see her face; it was closely shrouded in the wet linen, but the shape of it was there as her head tossed to and fro; it was like the head of sea-blurred marble long drowned beneath innumerable tides, save where a ridge of cloth was stretched across the forehead and took the shape of the temples. Titus, his body and his imagination fused in a throbbing lust, gripping her even more savagely than before with his right arm, tore at the shirt with his left until her face was free.

And it was so small that he began to cry. It was a robin's egg, and his whole body weakened as the first wild virgin kiss that trembled on his lips for release died out. He laid his cheek along hers. She had ceased to move. His tears ran. He could feel her cheek grow wet with them. He raised his head. He had become far away and he knew that there would be no climax. He was sick with a kind of glory.

Her head was turned to one side upon the ground and her eyes were fixed upon something. Her body had become rigid. For a moment it had melted and was like a stream in his arms, but now it was frozen once more, like ice.

Slowly he turned his head, and there was Fuchsia, the rain water streaming from her to the ground, her drenched hair hanging snakelike over her face.

III

All of a sudden Titus knew that he was lying alone. The sleeve of the shirt was clenched in his hands but the Thing had gone.

He had forgotten there was any other world. A world in which he had a sister and a mother, in which he was an Earl. He had forgotten Gormenghast.

And then he heard the shrill scream of derision which he was never to forget. He leaped to his feet and ran dizzily to the door of the cave. There he saw her standing in the downpour, knee-deep in water, naked as the rain itself. The lightning was playing continuously now, lighting her as though she were a thing of fire herself, now flickering across her in a yellow half-light.

As he stared a kind of ecstasy filled him. He had no sense of losing her—but only the blind and vaunting pride that he had held her in his arms; that naked creature that was now crying again, derisively, in a language of her own.

It was finality. Titus knew in his bones that he could expect no more than this. His teeth had met in the dark core of life. He watched her almost with indifference—for it was all in the past—and even the present was nothing to the pride of his memory.

But when, out of the heart of the storm, that searing flash of flame broke loose, ripping a path across the dazzled floods, burned up the Thing as though she had been a dry leaf in its path, and when Titus knew that the world was without her forever, then something fled in him—something fled away—or was burned away even as she had been burned away. Something had died as though it had never been.

At seventeen he stepped into another country. It was his youth that had died away. His boyhood was something for remembrance only. He had become a man.

He turned and retraced his steps to where Fuchsia leaned against the wall. They could not speak.

How pitifully human she was. When he parted the long locks that straggled over her face and saw how defenseless she was, and when she pushed his hand away with the tired disillusion of a woman twice her age, then he realized his own strength.

At a time when he should have been broken by the scene he had just witnessed—by the death of his imagination—he found himself to be emptied of distress. He was himself. He was free for the first time. He had learned that there were other ways of life from the ways of his great home. He had completed an experience. He had emptied the bright goblet of romance: at a single gulp he had emptied it. The glass of it lay scattered on the floor. But with the beauty and the ugliness, the ice and the fire of it on his tongue and in his blood, he could begin again.

The Thing was dead . . . dead . . . lightning had killed her, but had Fuchsia not been there he would have shouted with happiness, for he had grown up.

IV

It was a long time before a word was exchanged. They sat exhausted side by side. Fuchsia had been persuaded to take off her long red dress, and Titus had wrung it out and it was now spread before the fire he had rekindled. He longed to leave the cave. It was now so much dead rock. It was over and done with. But Fuchsia, sick with exhaustion, was in no state to start the return journey for an hour or more.

While he moved about the cave, Titus caught sight of some dead birds on a ledge of rock, but his hunger had never returned.

Then he heard Fuchsia's voice, very low and heavy.

"I thought perhaps you'd be here. I am better now. We must go back. The flood is rising."

Titus walked quickly to the door of the cave. It was true. They were in danger. Far from lessening, the rain was heavier than ever, with formidable massings of cloud.

He returned quickly to her side.

"I told them you had lost your memory," she said. "I told them you had been like this before. You must say the same. We'll part near the castle. Come on."

She got to her feet and pulled her damp red dress over her head. Her heart was raw with disappointment. Her fear had been for Titus's safety and she had risked her neck for him, but her hopes had been that he would be proud of her. To struggle all that way, and to find him with—the Thing!

Clinging fiercely and painfully to her pride, she swore to herself that she would never ask him—would never speak of her. She had thought that there was no one so close to him as herself—or that if there was, he would tell her. She knew that she was only his sister, but she had had a blind faith that even though she had defied him over Steerpike, yet she was more necessary to him than Steerpike had ever been to her.

Titus was gazing at her as he tucked the torn and fateful shirt into his trousers.

"She is dead, Fuchsia."

She lifted her head.

"Who?" she murmured.

"The wild girl."

"The . . . wild . . . girl? So soon?"

"The lightning."

Fuchsia turned to the cave mouth and began to move toward the storm.

"Oh, God," she whispered as though to herself. "Is there nothing but death and beastliness?" And then, not turning as she spoke, but raising her voice, "Don't tell me, Titus. Don't tell me anything. I would rather know nothing. You live your life and I'll live mine."

Titus joined her at the mouth of the cave. It was a frightening sight that lay before them. The landscape was filling up with water. There was not a moment to lose.

"There's only one hope," said Titus.

"I know," said Fuchsia. "The tunnel."

They stepped forward together and received the weight of the cascading sky. Thereafter their journey was a nightmare of water. Time after time they saved one another in the treacherous flood as they waded toward the entrance of the long underground passage. A hundred incidents befell them. Their feet were caught in underwater creepers; they stumbled over submerged bushes; the limbs of trees fell headlong into the water at their sides, and all but struck or drowned them. At times they were forced to return and make long detours where the water was too deep, or too marshy. When they came to the high bank on the hill they were all but drowned. But the tunnel was there and although the water had begun to pour down its black throat, yet their relief at seeing it was such that they involuntarily clasped each other. For a fleeting moment the years rolled back and they were brother and sister again in a world of no heartburn.

They had forgotten that the tunnel was so long, so inky dark, so full of vegetable beastliness, of hampering roots and foul decay. As they neared the castle the water became deeper; for on every side of Gormenghast the landscape shelved gradually downward, the widespread mazes of rambling masonry lying at the center in a measureless basin.

When eventually they were able to stand upright and emerged from the tunnel, and began to wade along the corridors that led to the Hollow Halls, the water was up to their waists.

Their progress was maddeningly slow. Step by step they forced their way through the heavy element, the inky water curling at their waists. Sometimes they would climb steps and would be able to rest for a while, at the top of a flight, but they could not stay for long, for all the while the water was rising. It was a mercy that Titus had become familiar with the one route that took them by degrees to that point behind the giant carving where, so long ago, he had escaped from Barquentine to lose himself in those watery lanes that they were now so slowly wading through.

It came at last: the halt behind the statue. Titus was in front and he worked his way around the base of the carving and, cautiously leaning forward, peered to left and right along the dusky corridor. It was deserted, and no wonder. Here as elsewhere the water lay like a dark and slowly moving carpet. It was obvious that the flood had poured in on every side and that the ground level of Gormenghast had been evacuated. His dormitory was upon the floor above, and Fuchsia's room was likewise above flood level. Fuchsia was now beside him and they were about to step forward through the water and proceed along their separate paths to their rooms when they heard the sound of a splash, and Titus dragged his sister back. The sound was repeated and repeated again in a regular beat, and then as it grew louder, they saw a glimmer on the water as a soft red light began to approach from the west.

Holding their breaths, they waited, and a moment later they saw the flat nose of a punt or narrow raft slide into their line of vision. An oldish man sat upon a low seat at its center. He held in either hand a short pole, and these were dipped simultaneously on either side of his craft. They had not far to submerge before they struck the stone beneath and the punt was propelled forward in a smooth and unhurried manner. At the bows was a red lantern. Across the stern lay a firearm, its hammer cocked.

Both Fuchsia and Titus had seen the man before. He was one of the many watchmen or sentries who had been detailed to patrol these lower corridors. Evidently neither the storm nor Titus's disappearance had caused any relaxation in the daylong, nightlong search for the skew-bald beast.

Directly the light of his lantern and its red reflection had grown small in the distance, the brother and sister waded to the nearest of the great stairways.

As they climbed they became aware, even before they had reached the stairhead of the first of the spreading storeys, that a great change had come about. For looking up they saw, out-topping the stone banisters, high piles of books and furniture, of hangings and crockery, of crate on crate of smaller objects, of carpets and swords, so that the landing was like a great warehouse or emporium.

And lying across tables, or slouched over chairs, in every kind of attitude of fatigue, were numbers of exhausted men. There were few lanterns still alight, but no one seemed awake, and nothing moved.

Tiptoeing past the sleepers, and leaving trails of water behind them as they went, Titus and Fuchsia came at last to a junction of two corridors. There was no time for them to linger or to talk, but they stood still for a moment and looked at one another.

"This is where we part," said Fuchsia. "Don't forget what I told you. You lost your memory and found yourself in the woods. I never found you. We never saw each other."

"I won't forget," said Titus.

They turned from each other and, following their diverging paths, disappeared into the darkness.

Chapter Sixty-Nine

THERE was no one alive in Gormenghast who could remember a storm in any way comparable to this black and endless deluge that, flooding the surrounding country, and mounting with every passing minute, was already lapping at the landings of the first storey.

The thunder was continuous. The lightning went on and off as though a child were playing with a switch. On the vast expanse of water, the heavy branches of riven trees floated and tossed like monsters. The fish of Gormenghast River swam out in every direction, and could be seen steering through the castle's lowest windows.

Where high ground or an isolated rock or a watchtower broke the surface, these features were crowded with small animals of all kinds, that huddled together in heterogeneous masses, and took no notice of one another. By far the vastest of these natural sanctuaries was, of course, Gormenghast Mountain, which had become an island of dramatic beauty, the thick forest trees hanging out of the water at its base, its streaming skull flickering balefully with the reflection of the vibratory lightning.

By far the greatest proportion of the animals still alive was congregated upon its slopes, and the sky above it, violent and inhospitable as it was, was never free of birds that wheeled and cried.

The other great sanctuary was the castle itself, toward whose walls the tired foxes swam, the hares beside them, the rats in their wake, the badgers, martins, otters, and other woodland and river creatures.

From all the quarters of the compass they converged, their heads alone visible above the surface, their breath coming quick and fast, their shining eyes fixed on the castle walls.

This gaunt asylum, like the mountain that faced it across the rain-lashed lakes, that were so soon to form an inland sea, had become an island. Gormenghast was marooned.

As soon as it became evident to the inhabitants that it was no ordinary storm that had broken upon them and that the outer ramifications of the castle were already threatened and were liable to be isolated from the main mass, and that the outbuildings, in particular the stables and all structures of wood, were in peril of being washed away, instructions were given for the evacuation of the remote districts, for the immediate recall of the Bright Carvers, and for the driving of all livestock from the stables to within the walls. Bands of men and boys were dispatched for the bringing in and the salvaging of carts, plows, and all kinds of farm equipment. All this, along with the carriages and harnessings of the horses, was temporarily housed in the armory on the east side of one of the inner quadrangles. The cattle and the horses were herded into the great stone refectory, the beasts being segregated by means of improvised barriers made largely from the storm-snapped boughs of trees that were piling up continuously beneath the southern windows.

The Outer Dwellers, already smarting with the insult of the broken Ceremony, were in no mood to return to the castle, but when the rain began to loosen the very foundation of the encampments, they were forced to take advantage of the order they had received, and to make a sullen exodus from their ancient home.

The magnanimity that was shown them in their time of peril, far from being appreciated, still further embittered them. At a time when they had no other work than to withdraw themselves and to brood over the vile insult they had sustained at the hands of the House of Groan, they were forced to accept the hospitality of its figurehead. Carrying their infants and their few belongings over their shoulders, a horde of sodden malcontents drew in upon the castle, the dark water gurgling about their knees.

An extensive peninsula of the castle, a thing of rough unpointed masonry, a mile or more in length and several storeys high, had been given over to the Carvers. There they staked their claims upon the moldering floor boards, each family circumscribing its sites in thick lines drawn with lumps of chalky plaster.

In this congested atmosphere their bitterness flourished, and unable to vent their spleen on Gormenghast, the great abstract, they turned upon one another. Old scores were remembered and a kind of *badness* filled the long, sullen promontory. Floor above floor was rancor. Their homes of clay were gone. They had become something which they would never have admitted in the days when they had lived in open squalor *beyond* the castle walls —they had become a dependency.

From their windows they could see the dark rain pouring. With every day that passed the sky seemed thicker, and fouler in the sagging horror of its black and glutted belly. From the upper halls at the far and straggling limit of the promontory, the prisoners, for so they were in everything but name, were able to obtain a view of Gormenghast Mountain. With the first light of dawn, or by lightning flashes during the night, they noted how the flood had climbed its flanks. The horizontal branch of a far tree, or a peculiarity of some rock face near the water's edge, would be taken as a reference point, and it became their morbid interest to gauge how high and at what speed the flood was rising.

And then a kind of relief came to them—not from any outside source but through the foresight of an old Carver, and this relief to their frustration took the form of boat-building. It was not carving in the creative sense in which they excelled, but it was carving. Directly the idea was launched, it sent forth its ripples that spread from one end of the peninsula to the other.

That they had been unable to carve had been as galling as the insult they had swallowed. Their rasps and chisels, saws and mallets had been the first things that they had gathered together when all hope of remaining in their hovels had disappeared. But they had been unable to carry with them the heavy timber or the jarl roots which they had always used. Now, however, their former media would be useless. Something of a very different nature was needed for the construction of boats or rafts or dugouts, and it was not long before the redundant beams that spanned the ceilings, the panels from the inner walls, the doors themselves, and where possible the joists and floor boards, began to disappear. The competition among the families to build up within their chalk-marked sites a pile of board and timber was deadly and humorless, and was only to be compared with the subsequent rivalry to build not only the most navigable and watertight craft but the most original and beautiful.

They asked for no permission; they acted spontaneously, ripping away or prizing apart floor board and panel; they climbed for hours among filthy rafters and sawed through solid pine and timbers of black oak; they stole by night and they denied their thefts by day; they kept watch and set forth on expeditions; they argued over the safety of the floors; over which timbers were dangerous to move and which were ornamental. Great gaps appeared in the floors, through which the ragged children flung filth and dust upon the heads of the Carvers on the floor below. The lives of the Outer Dwellers had become almost normal again. Bitterness was their bread and rivalry their wine.

And the boats began to take shape, and hammering filled the air, as in the semidarkness, with the rain lashing through the windows and the thunder rolling, a thousand forms of craft grew into beauty.

Meanwhile in the main body of the castle there was little time for any other activity than that of moving upward, eternally upward, the multitudinous effects of Gormenghast.

The second floor was by now untenable. The flood, finding its own level within the honey-combed interiors, had become more than a threat to property. A growing number of the less agile or intelligent had already been trapped and drowned, doors being unopenable by reason of the weight of pressing water or directions being lost among the unfamiliar waterways.

There were few who were not engaged upon the back-breaking business of forcing a world of belongings up the scores of stairways.

The cattle so necessary to the survival of the marooned had changed their quarters time after time. Driving them up the broadest flights, it had been difficult to control their panic. The stout banisters had given way like match-sticks—iron railings had been bent by the pressing weight of the climbing herds; masonry had been loosened, a huge stone lion at the head of a stairway falling down the well of the stairs, four cows and a heifer following it to their deaths in the cold water below.

The horses were led up one by one, their hoofs pawing at the treads of the stairs, their nostrils distended, the whites of their eyes shining in the gloom.

A dozen men were kept busy all day shifting the loads of hay up to the upper halls. The carts and plows had had to be abandoned, as had a heavy and irreplaceable inventory of machines and bulk of every description.

On every floor an abandoned conglomeration was left behind, for the climbing water to despoil. The armory was a red pond of rust. A score of libraries were swamps of pulp. There were pictures floating down long corridors, or being lifted gradually from their hooks. The crevices in wood or brick and tiny caves between the stones of the innumerable walls had been swilled free of the complexity of insect life. Where generations of lizards had lived in secrecy there was only water now. Water that rose like terror, inch by clammy inch.

The kitchens had been moved to the highest of the suitable areas. The gathering together and transporting of the thousand and one things necessary to the feeding of the castle had been itself an epic undertaking, as also, in another way, had been the frantic packing and dragging from the Central Library of the traditional manuscripts, the sacred Laws of Ritual, and the thousands of ancient volumes of reference but for which the complex machinery of the castle's life could never be revived. These heavy crates of sacrosanct and yellowing papers were dragged at once to the high attics, and a couple of sentries were posted before them.

As every landing filled with salvage the exhausted men, their shirts stuck to their backs, their brows shining like candle-wax from the sweat that poured into their eyes, cursed the storm, cursed the water, cursed the day they were born. It seemed to have gone on forever, this shouldering of giant cases up tortuous stairs; of straining upon ropes, only to hear them snap and the burden crash headlong down the flights they had won so dearly; the aching of their bodies and thighs; this ghastly fatigue. There was no end to it; to the mechanics of gear and rigging; to a hundred extempore inventions; to the levering and the cranking; to the winding of home-made pulleys; to the gradual raising of stock and metal; of fuel, grist, and treasure; of vintage and hoards of miscellaneous lumber. From storehouse, depository, vault, and warehouse, from magazine, dump, and coffer, from granary and arsenal; from the splendid rooms of bygone days where the great "pieces" moldered; from the private rooms of countless officers; from the communal halls and the dormitories of the hierophants—from all these places everything went up, the furniture, the chattels, the works of vanity and the works of art; from the enormous tables of carved oak, to the least of silver bracelets.

But all this was not without organization. Behind it all there was a brain at work. A brain that had been drowsing since girlhood—that had been for so long a time unfocused that it had taken no less a thing than Steerpike's rebellion to make it yawn and stretch itself. It was now fully awake. It belonged to the Countess.

It was she who had given the first orders; who had called in the Bright Carvers; who had, with a great map of the central district of Gormenghast spread before her, remain seated at a table on one of the central landings, and, coordinating the multifarious activities of salvage and resettlement, had given her subjects no time to think of the peril they were in but only of their immediate duties.

From where she sat she could see the last of the removals from the landing below. The water had reached to about the fifth tread of this upper staircase. She stared down at the four men who were struggling with a long, blackish chest. As it moved water poured out of it. Step by step it was hoisted up the wide flight. The lapping water was choked with floating objects. Every floor had delivered to the flood its quota of things lost, forgotten, or worthless, the lower regions lifting their buoyant chattels inch by inch to loftier waterways where, joined by fresh flotillas, newly launched, the heterogeneous flotsam grew and grew.

For a few moments the Countess eyed the dark water in the well of the stairs before turning to a group of runners who were stationed before her.

As she turned to face them a fresh messenger arrived panting. He had been to check the rumors that had reached the central castle of how the Bright Carvers were engaged upon boat-building and had all but gutted the promontory.

"Well?" she said, staring at the runner.

"It is true, your Ladyship. They are building boats."

"Ah," said the Countess. "What else?"

"They ask for awnings, your Ladyship."

"Awnings. Why?"

"The lower storeys have been flooded out, as here. They have been forced to launch their boats, unfinished, through the windows. They have no protection from the rain. The upper storeys refuse them entry. They are already overcrowded."

"What kind of boats?"

"All shapes, your Ladyship. Excellently made."

She propped her chin on her big hand. "Report to the Master of the Rough Hangings. Have him send all the canvas that has been salvaged. Inform the Carvers their craft may be requisitioned in emergency. They must make all the vessels they can. Send me the Custodian of the River Boats. We have some craft of our own, have we not?"

"I believe so, your Ladyship. But not many."

"Next messenger!" said the Countess.

An old man came forward. "Well?" she said.

"I see no break in the storm," he said. "On the contrary—"

"Good," said the Countess.

At this remark every eye was turned to her. At first they did not trust their hearing. Turning to each other, the score or so of officials and messengers who surrounded her could see, however, that none of them had misheard. They were all equally perplexed. She had spoken softly, heavily, hardly above a whisper. "Good," she had said. It was as though they had overheard some private thought.

"Is the leader of the Heavy Rescue here?"

"Yes, your Ladyship." A tired and bearded figure came forward.

"Rest your men."

"Yes, your Ladyship. They need it."

"We all need it. What of it? The waters are rising. You have your list of priorities?"

"Yes."

"Have the leaders of every section made their working copies?"

"They have."

"In six hours' time the flood will be at our feet. In two hours' time all hands are to be awakened. There is no possibility of the night being spent on this level. The Chequered Stairway is the widest. You have my order of priority; livestock, carcasses, corn; and so on, have you not?"

"Certainly, your Ladyship."

"Are the cats comfortable?"

"They have the run of the twelve blue attics."

"Ah . . . and then . . . ," her voice trailed away.

"Your Ladyship?"

". . . And then, gentlemen, we shall begin. The mounting water draws us all together. Is that not so, gentlemen?"

They bowed their perplexed assent.

"With every hour less rooms are tenable. We are driven up, are we not, into a confine. Tell me, gentlemen, can traitors live in air and feed on it? Can they chew the cloud? Or swallow the thunder or fill their bellies with lightning?"

The gentlemen shook their heads and eyed one another.

"Or can they live beneath the surface of the water like the pike I see below me in the darkness? No. He is like us, gentlemen. Are the sentries posted as usual? Is the kitchen guarded?"

"It is, your Ladyship."

"Enough! We are squandering the time. Give orders that there are two hours' sleep. You will leave me."

She got to her feet as her audience retired to propagate her instructions and leaned over the heavy balustrade that surrounded the stairhead. The water had risen half the height of a tread since she had heard of the Carvers' boats. She leaned there, like something over lifesize, her heavy arms folded on the balustrade, a lock of her dark-red hair hanging over her wide, pale brow as she stared over and down to where the black water brooded in the well of the stairs.

Chapter Seventy

WHEN the Countess had heard of Titus's return to the castle, she had summoned him at once and had heard from him of how the heat had overpowered him, and of how he had lost his memory and, after he knew not how long a time, had found himself alone on the outskirts of Gormenghast Forest.

As Titus had recounted these falsehoods, she had stared at him but made no comment save, after a long pause, to ask him whether on his return he had seen Fuchsia.

"I say on your *return*" (she had added), "as on your *outward* journey you were in no state to recognize anyone. Is that so?"

"Yes, Mother."

"And did you see her, when you were returning, or after you returned?"

"No."

"I will have your story circulated throughout the castle. Within an hour the Carvers will be informed of your loss of memory. Your oblivion was ill-timed. You may go now."

Chapter Seventy-One

❈❈❈❈❈❈❈❈❈❈❈

FOR little short of a fortnight the rain continued unabated; so great a proportion of the castle was now under water that in spite of the rain it was necessary for encampments to be formed upon the suitable roofs, which were approached through attic hatchways. The congestion in the upper zones was appalling.

The first of the commandeered flotillas had been paddled across the deep water from the Carvers' promontory. On their return journey across the roofs and upper floors the Carvers were permitted to take with them what loose timber they could carry.

The Countess had a broad and handsome craft. It

was designed for oarsmen and had an ample space for
her at the stern to sit and steer with comfort.

The Carvers had been supplied with tar and great
drums of paint, and this solid boat was decorated with
devices of red, black, and gold. Its bows rose out of the
water with a slow and massive grace and terminated in a
carved head that resembled a bird of prey, its throat of
sculptured feathers and its bald forehead a dusky scarlet,
its eyes yellow and petaled like the heads of sunflowers,
its curved beak black and sinister. This idea of a figurehead had been almost universally adopted by the Carvers.
As much care had been lavished in this way as upon the
structure and the safety of the boats.

One day Titus was informed that a special craft had
been created for him, and that it awaited him in a southern corridor. He went at once and alone to where it lay
floating. At any other time Titus would have cried with
joy to receive the slim and silver creature of the waterways, so exquisitely balanced on the flood; to have been
allowed to step from the water-logged and immovable
table that was half afloat on the castle's ninth floor—to
step into this canoe, which, unlike any he had ever seen
in his picture books when a child, seemed eager to be
away, at the dip of a paddle.

As it was he loved it; but with heartache. It seemed to
remind him of all he vaguely longed for. It reminded him
of the day when he had hardly known himself to be an
Earl; when to have no father and no affection from his
mother had seemed normal enough; when he had seen
no violence; no death; no decay. Of days when there
had been no Steerpike at large like a foul shadow that
darkened everything and kept the nerves on edge; and
more than this; the slight canoe beneath him reminded
him of the days when he had known nothing of the terrible antithesis within him—the tearing in two directions
of his heart and head—the divided loyalties—the growing and feverish longing to escape from all that was meant
by Gormenghast, and the ineradicable, irrational pride in
his lineage, and the love, as deep as the hate, which he

felt, unwittingly, for the least of the cold stones of his loveless home.

What else was it that brought the tears to his eyes as he took the paddle that was handed down to him, and dipped its blue blade in the sullen water? It was his memory of something that had fled as surely as his boyhood had fled; something that was as swift and slight and tameless as he knew this craft would be. It was his memory of the Thing.

He dipped his blade. A craftsman's masterpiece, cock'd, as it were, her sweet and tapering head, whispered a curve of silver to the north, and slipping through a dusky gallery, leaped at the quickening of his paddle-stroke. Ahead of him, at the hinge of perspective, far away, a point of light, the water halfway up its distant frames, sped toward him, as, skimming the flood of a black corridor, he drew, with every stroke, the nearer to the cold and rain-churned sea.

And all the time his heart was crying, and the exhilaration and the beauty of it all were the agents of his pain. Swiftly as he sped he could not outstrip his body or his mind. The paddles dipped and the craft flew, but could not leave his haunted heart behind. It flew with him on the sepulchral water.

And then, as he neared the all but flood-filled window, he realized for the first time how dangerously close was its upper lintel to the surface. The light from without had strengthened considerably during the last hour and the reflection of the square of light had been so strong as to have given Titus the impression that the entire area of light, the reflections included, was an opening through which he could pass. But now he saw that he had only the top half of the bright square through which to skim. Flying toward it, he fell back suddenly, and lying with his head below the level of the sides and with his eyes shut he heard the faintest of gritty whispers as, shooting the window, the delicate prow of the vessel grated the lintel.

Suddenly the sky was wide above him. An inland sea was ahead of him. A steady rain was pouring down, but compared with the long deluge they had grown to accept as normal, it seemed that he was afloat in good weather. He allowed the canoe to slacken speed of its own and when it had come to a bobbing standstill he turned her about with a stroke, and there ahead of him the upper massives of his kingdom broke the surface. Great islands of sheer rock weather-pock'd with countless windows, like caves or the eyries of sea-eagles. Archipelagos of towers, gaunt-fisted things, with knuckled summits—and other towers so broken at their heads as to resemble pulpits, high and sinister; black rostrums for the tutelage of evil.

And then a qualm, empty, cold and ringing, as though he were himself a hollow bell, stirred in his bowels like a clapper. An exquisite sense of loneliness grew beneath his ribs, like a bubble of expanding glass.

The rain had ceased to fall. The agitated water had become silent, motionless. It had taken on a dark translucence. Afloat upon a yawning element he gazed down to where, far below him, trees grew, to where familiar roads wound in and out, to where the fish swam over walnut trees and, strangest of all, to the winding bed of Gormenghast River, so full of water that it had none of its own.

What had all this that filled his eyes with amazement and pleasure, what had it all to do with the despoiling flood, the wreck of treasures, the death of many, the haunt of Steerpike who, driven slowly upward, was hiding even now? Was this where Fuchsia lived? And the Doctor and the Countess, his own mother, who, it seemed, after trying to approach him, had drawn away again.

In a state of overwrought melancholy he began to slide forward over the still waters, dipping his paddle every now and again. A dull light from the sky played over the water that streamed in sheets from gutterless roofs.

As he neared the isles of Gormenghast, he saw, away to the north, the Carvers' navy like scattered jewels on the slate-gray flood. Immediately ahead of him, as he proceeded, was the wall through one of the windows of which he had so dangerously skimmed. What was left of the window and of those on either side was now submerged, and Titus knew that yet another floor of the central castle had by now been abandoned.

This wall, which formed the blunt nose of a long stone headland, had a counterpart a mile to the east. Between these two a vast and somber bay lay stretched, with not a break in its surface. As with its twin, this second headland had no windows open at flood level. The water had a good twelve feet to climb before the next tier of casements could be entered or affected. But turning his eyes to the base, or curve, of the great bay—to where (had it been in reality a bay) the sands might well have stretched, Titus could see that the far windows in that line of cliffs, no larger in his sight than grains of rice, were, unlike those of the headlands, far from regular.

Those walls, covered with ivy, were in many ways peculiar. Stone stairs climbed up and down their outer sides and led to openings. The windows, as he had already observed, appeared to be sprinkled over the green façades of the cliff with an indiscriminate and wayward profluence that gave no clue as to how the inner structures held together.

It was toward this base of the "bay" that Titus now began to paddle, the limpid flood as chill as death beneath him, with all its rain-drowned marvels.

Chapter Seventy-Two

❈❈❈❈❈❈❈❈❈❈

It seemed to Titus a deserted place, a fastness of no life—rank with ivy, dumb with its toothless mouths, blind with its lidless eyes.

He drew in to the base of the abandoned walls where a flight of steps rose slanting out of the depths of the water, and, climbing alongside the wet green wall of ivy, rose to a balcony forty feet above his head—a stone affair surrounded by an iron railing decoratively wrought but so corroded with rust, that it only waited the tap of a stick to send it crumbling to the water.

As Titus stepped from his craft onto the stone steps at water level, and kneeling, lifted it dripping from the water and laid it carefully along the length of a stone tread, for he had no painter, he became conscious of a distinct malevolence. It was as though the great walls were watching his every move.

He pushed his brown hair back from his forehead and lifted his head so that he faced the towering masonry. His eyebrows were drawn together, his eyes were narrowed, his trembling chin was thrust aggressively forward. There was no sound but the dripping of the rain from the acres of ivy.

Unpleasant as was this sense of being under observation, he fought back the panic that might so easily have developed and, more to prove to himself that he was not afraid of mere stone and ivy rather than because he really wished to mount the stairway and discover what lay within the melancholy walls, he began to climb the slippery steps that led to the balcony. And as he began his ascent, the face that had been watching him disappeared from a small window close to the summit of the lowering wall. But only for a moment, for it reappeared so suddenly again at another opening that it was difficult to believe that it could be the same face that now stared down to where the steps slid under the water and where Titus's canoe lay "beached." But there could be no doubt of it. No two faces could either be so identical of blemish, nor so cruelly similar. The dark-red eyes were fixed upon the little craft. They had watched its approach across the "bay." They noted how light, rapid, and maneuverable it was, how it had answered to the merest whim of its rider.

He turned his eyes from the craft to Titus, who by now, having climbed a dozen steps, was within a couple more of being immediately below the heavy block of stone which Steerpike had loosened, and which he had half a mind to send hurtling down upon the youth below.

But he knew that the death of the Earl, much as it would have gratified him, would not in fact materially advance his chance of escape. Had it been certain that the stone would strike his Lordship dead, he would have had no hesitation in satisfying what had now become a lust for killing. But were the stone to miss its prey and splinter on the steps far below, then not only would Titus have every right to imagine that he had been ambushed—and who would ambush the Earl save he himself?—but also a more immediate dislocation of his plans would result. For there was little doubt that Titus on recovering from his shock would not dare to continue with his upward climb, but would return immediately to his craft. And it was this boat that Steerpike was after. To be able to move at speed through the tortuous waterways of the castle would double his mobility.

Driven from haunt to haunt, from hiding place to hiding place, by the rising water, his operations conditioned always by the necessity of his being within striking range of the stores and larders, it had in the narrowing zone of maneuver become imperative for him to be able to travel with equal speed and silence over both land and water. For days he had starved when the mobile kitchens were so positioned in a curve of the spacious West Wing that it was impossible for him, guarded as they were, to plunder.

But they had moved, since then, at least three times, and now, with the possibility of the rain having stopped for good, it was his savage hope that they had found a fixity in that high subattic room above which in a barricaded and all but lightless loft he had established his headquarters. In the ceiling of this murky refuge a trap door opened upon a sloping roof of slates, where swathes of creeper bandaged it from sight. But it was the hatch in the floor below him which, when lifted with a tender and secret care more usually associated with the handling of sucklings, gave him access to the most pressing of his need: for below him lay the stores. In the small hours, when it became necessary, he would lower himself inch by noiseless inch on a long rope. The sack he brought down with him he would fill with the least perishable provisions. A dozen or more of the staff would be asleep on the floor, but the sentries were naturally posted on the *outer* side of the three doors and were no bother to him.

But this was not his only hide-out. He knew that sooner or later the floods would fall. The kitchens would again become nomadic. It was impossible to tell in which direction the life of the castle would sway as on its slow downward journey it trod upon the wet heels of the subsiding water.

The spreading roofs themselves furnished him with seven secret strongholds. The attics of the three dry floors below provided for at least four as safe, in their varying ways, as his garret above the kitchen. And now that the flood had stayed at the same level for three days, a few feet above the majority of the landings of the ninth floor, it had become possible for him to prepare in advance a number of aqueous asylums.

But how much simpler and safer it would be for him were he able to reconnoiter the high canals in such a craft as he now saw below him.

No. He could not afford to send the rough stone hurtling down. There was more than a chance of his failure to slay. The acute temptation to crush at a single blow that life out of the heir to Gormenghast—and leave nothing more than brick and stone behind—the intoxicating temptation to take the risk and to do this, was hard to resist.

But before all else came his own survival, and if by so much as an iota he deviated in any way from what he considered to be his final advantage then the end would surely come if not now, then very soon. For he knew he was walking on a razor's edge. He gloried in it. He had slid into the skin of a solitary Satan as though he had never enjoyed the flourish of language, the delights of civil power. It was war, now. Naked and bloody. The simplicity of the situation appealed to him. The world closed in upon him, its weapons drawn, eager for his death. And it was for him to outwit the world. It was the simplest and most fundamental of all games.

But his face was not the face of a thing at play. Or even of the Steerpike of a few years back—at play; or even of sin at play, for something new had happened to it. The terrible pattern that made of it a map, the white of the sea, the red, the continents and spattered islands, was hardly noticeable now. For it was the eyes that drew away the attention from all else.

For all the characteristic cunning and agility of his brain, he was no longer living in the same world that he had lived in before he murdered Flay. Something had altered. It was his mind. His brain was the same but his mind was different. He was no longer a criminal because he chose to be. He had no longer the choice. He lived now among the abstractions. His brain dealt with where he would hide and what he would do if certain contingencies arose, but his mind floated above all this in a red ether. And the reflection of his mind burned through his eyes, filling the pupils with a grizzly bloodlight.

As he stared down like a bird of prey from its window'd crag, his brain saw, far below him, a canoe. It saw Titus standing on the stone balcony. It saw him turn and after a moment's hesitation enter the rotting halls and disappear from view.

But his mind saw nothing of all this. His mind was engaged in a warfare of the gods. His mind paced outward over no-man's-land, over the fields of the slain, paced to the rhythm of the blood's red bugles. To be alone and evil! To be a god at bay. What was more absolute?

Three minutes had passed since the Earl had disappeared into the maw of the building below him. Steerpike had given him time to move well into the fastness before he took action. There had been the chance of a sudden reappearance of the youth, for the lower halls were dark and sinister. But he had not reappeared, and the time was now ripe for Steerpike to make his leap. The descent was of a sickening duration. The blood hammered in the murderer's head. His stomach turned over and for a while he lost consciousness. When his reflection, flying upward from the depths to meet him, was shattered at the surface,

and as the spume of water rose like a fountain, Steerpike's
body, far below the surface, continued its descent until, at
last, as his feet touched lightly upon the submerged head
of a weather-cock, he began to rise again to the surface.

The disturbed water had become quite smooth again.

Dazed with the effort of the long fall, sick with swallowed water and with painful lungs, yet it was only a moment or two before he had struck out for the stone stairway.

When he reached it and climbed the few steps to where
the canoe lay quietly upon her side, he wasted not a
moment in setting her upon the water. Boarding her
nimbly, he grasped the paddle that lay within and with
the first half-dozen strokes was speeding beneath the ivy-
covered walls toward one of the few windows which coin-
cided with the water level.

It was of course necessary for Steerpike to make immediately for cover. The great bay ahead was a death trap,
where, were a fish to raise its head above the surface, it
would be seen at once!

At any moment the young Earl might return. It was for
him to skid unseen through the first of the flood windows,
leaving no trace. As Steerpike sped rapidly over the
water he had, as far as possible, kept his head turned
back over his shoulders for the possible reappearance of
the Earl. Were he to be seen it would be necessary for
him to make his way at once to one of his hiding places.
There would be no possibility of his being overtaken, but
to be sighted would, for many reasons, be unfortunate.
He had no wish for the castle to know he could travel by
water—nor that he roamed so far afield as to these
frowning headlands; the sentries might well be reinforced,
the vigilance sharpened.

So far he had been fortunate. He had survived his fall.
His enemy had been out of earshot when he had splashed
into the water; he had sighted a window through which he
would pass with ease and behind the dark jaw of which
he could remain until darkness descended.

For a few minutes at a time, as he slipped along the
base of the dark walls, he was forced to turn his head,

to correct the course of the canoe, but for the most part his eyes were fixed upon the empty balcony to which at any moment his enemy might return.

It was when, with but three or four lengths of his canoe to go, before he turned her into the castle, that, concentrating upon a faultless entry, he was unable to see that Titus had stepped out upon the open balcony.

He could not see that on immediately discovering the disappearance of his boat, Titus had started forward and had then swept his eyes across the bay until they had come to rest upon the only moving object—the far canoe as it began its curve into the cliff. Without a thought Titus drew backward into the doorway around which he now peered, his body shaking with excitement. Even at that distance there was no mistaking the hunched shoulders of the marauder. It was well that he had stepped backward so quickly, for as the canoe took its curve and straightening out, slid rapidly at the castle, as though to crash its delicate prow against its flank, Steerpike, certain of a perfect entry, returned his attention to the distant balcony, and as he noted its emptiness he disappeared into the wall like a snake into a rock.

Chapter Seventy-Three

THE Doctor was exhausted; his eyes red with lack of sleep, his features wasted and drawn. His skill was in unending demand. The flood had gathered in its wake a hundred subsidiary disasters.

In a long attic room which became known as the hospital, the improvised beds were not only filled with cases of fracture and accident of every description, but with the victims of exhaustion, and of various sicknesses resulting from the dank and unhealthy conditions.

He was now upon his way to a typical accident. The news had been brought to him of yet another case of broken bones. A man had fallen, apparently while trying to carry a heavy crate up a slippery stairway, its treads swimming in rain water. On reaching the place the Doctor found that it was a clean break of the femur. The man was lifted onto the professional raft at the spacious center of which the Doctor could apply his splints or perform whatever temporary operation was necessary, while at the same time his orderly at the rear propelled them back in the direction of the hospital.

Dipping his long pole with excellent regularity, the orderly would send the raft sliding steadily along the corridors. On this particular occasion as the raft, when about halfway to its goal, crept gingerly through a wooden arch somewhat narrow and difficult of maneuver, and came out into what must have once been a ballroom—in one of its hexagonal corners the upper levels of an ornate platform emerged above the surface, suggesting that an orchestra once filled the place with music—as the raft edged itself out of the restricted passageway and floated forward into all this wealth of space, Dr. Prunesquallor sank back against the rolled-up mattress he kept toward the stern of the raft. At his feet lay the man he had been attending, his trouser torn open from heel to hip; his thigh in a splint. The white bandages, bound with a beautiful and firm deliberation, were reflected in the ballroom water.

The Doctor shut his eyes. He hardly knew what was happening about him. His head swam; but when he heard his raft being hailed by some kind of dugout that was being paddled in his direction from the far end of the ballroom, he raised an eyelid.

It was indeed a dugout that was drawing closer, a long, absurd affair, obviously made by the men who were now manning it, for the Carvers would never have allowed such an object to leave their workshops. At its stern, with his hand on the tiller, was Perch-Prism, who was obviously in command. His black-gowned crew, using their mortarboards as paddles, sat in varying degrees of dejection, one

behind the other. They disliked not being able to face
the way they were going, and resented Perch-Prism's
captaincy and consequent control over their watery
progress. However, Bellgrove had appointed Perch-Prism
to his post and given orders (which he had never dreamed
would be carried out) that his staff should help patrol
the waterways. Schooling, of course, had become impossible, and the pupils, now that the rain had stopped, spent
most of their time leaping and diving from the battlements, the turrets, the flying buttresses, the tops of towers,
from any and every vantage point, into the deep clear
water where they swam like a plague of frogs in and out
of windows and over the wide breast of the flood, their
shrill screams sounding from near and far.

And so the Staff were free of scholastic duties. They
had little to do but yearn for the old days, and to chaff
one another until the chaff became acrimonious and a
morose and tacit silence had fallen upon them and none
of them had anything original left to say about the flood.

Opus Fluke, the stern oar, brooded darkly over the armchair that the flood had swallowed—the armchair which
he had inhabited for over forty years—the filthy, moldering, hideous, and most necessary support of his existence,
the famous "Fluke's Cradle" of the Common-Room—it
had gone forever.

Behind him in the dugout sat Flannelcat, a poor
oarsman if ever there was one. For Flannelcat to be glum
and speechless was nothing new. If Fluke brooded on the
death of an armchair, Flannelcat brooded on the death
of all things and had done so for as long as anyone
could remember. He had always been ineffectual and a
misery to himself and others, and so, having plumbed
the depths for so long, this flood was a mere nothing to
him.

Mulefire, the most difficult of the crew for Perch-
Prism to control, sat like a hulk of stupid, bull-necked irritability, immediately behind the miserable Flannelcat,
who looked to be in perpetual danger of being bitten in
the back of the neck by Mulefire's tombstone teeth, and
of being lifted out of his seat and slung away across the

ballroom water. Behind Mulefire sat Cutflower; he was the last of them all to admit that silence was the best thing that could happen to them. Chatter was lifeblood—and it was a mere shadow of the one-time vapid but ebullient wag who sat now staring at Mulefire's heavily muscled back.

There were only two other members to this crew: Shred and Shrivell. No doubt the rest of the Staff had got hold of boats from somewhere, or, like these gentlemen, had constructed something themselves, or even ignored Bellgrove's ruling, and kept to the upper floors.

Shred and Shrivell, dipping their mortarboards in the glassy surface, were of course the nearest to the approaching raft. Shrivell, the bow oar, turning his aging face to see whom it was that Perch-Prism was hailing, upset for a few moments the balance of the dugout which listed dangerously to the port side.

"Now then! Now then!" shouted Perch-Prism from the stern. "Are you trying to capsize us, sir?"

"Nonsense," shouted Shrivell, coloring, for he hated being reprimanded over the seven heads of his colleagues. He knew that he had behaved in an utterly unworthy way, for a bow oar, but, "Nonsense," he shouted again.

"We will not discuss the matter now, sir, if you please!" said Perch-Prism, dropping the lids over his small black and eloquent eyes, and half-turning away his head so that the underside of his porcine nose caught what light there was reflected from the water.

"I would have thought it were enough that you had endangered your colleagues. But no. You wish to justify yourself, like all men of science. Tomorrow you and Cutflower will change places."

"Oh, Lord! La!" said Cutflower, testily. "I'm comfy where I am, la!"

Perch-Prism was about to let the ungracious Cutflower in on a secret or two on the nature of mutiny when the Doctor came alongside.

"Good morning, Doctor," said Perch-Prism.

The Doctor, starting out of an uneasy sleep, for even after he had heard Perch-Prism's shout across the water he had been unable to keep his eyes open, forced himself upright on the raft and turned his tired eyes upon the dugout.

"Did somebody say something?" cried he, with a valiant effort at jocularity, though his limbs felt like lead and there was a fire in the top of his head.

"Did I hear a voice across the brine? Well, well, it's you, Perch-Prism, by all that's irregular! How are you, admiral?"

But even as the Doctor was flashing one of his Smiles along the length of the dugout, like a dental broadside, he fell back upon the mattress, and the orderly with the long pole, taking no notice of Perch-Prism and the rest, gave a great shove against the ballroom floor and the raft swam forward and away from the Professors in the direction of the hospital, where, he hoped, he could persuade the Doctor to lie down for an hour or two irrespective of the maimed and distressed, the dead and the dying.

Chapter Seventy-Four

❈❈❈❈❈❈❈❈❈❈❈

IRMA had not spared herself over the furnishing of her home. A great deal of work, a great deal of thought—and, in her opinion, a great deal of taste—had been lavished upon it. The color scheme had been carefully considered. There was not a discordant note in the whole place. It was so tasteful, in fact, that Bellgrove never felt at home. It gave him a sense of inferiority, and he hated the powder-blue curtains and the dove-gray carpets, as though it were *their* fault that Irma had chosen them. But this meant little to her. She knew that he as a mere man would know nothing of "artistic" matters. She had expressed herself, as women will, in a smug broadside of pastel shades. Nothing clashed because nothing had the strength to clash; everything murmured of safety among the hues; all was refinement.

But the vandal water came and the work and the thought and the taste and the refinement, oh, where were they now? It was too much! It was too much! That all the love she had lavished was drowned beneath the mean, beastly, stupid, unnecessary rain, that this thing, this *thing*, this useless, brainless element called rain, should turn her artistry to filth and pulp!

"I hate Nature," she cried. "I hate it, the rotten beast!"

"Tut, tut," muttered Bellgrove as he lolled in a hammock and stared up at one of the beams in the roof. (They had been assigned a small loft, where they were able to be miserable in comparative comfort.) "You can't talk about Nature like that, my ignorant child. Good gracious, no! Dammit, I should think not."

"Nature," cried Irma scornfully. "Do you think *I'm* frightened of it! Let it do what it likes!"

"You're a piece of Nature yourself," said Bellgrove after a pause.

"Oh, don't be stupid, you . . . you . . ." Irma could not continue.

"All right, what *am* I then?" murmured Bellgrove. "Why don't you say what's in your empty little woman's mind? Why don't you call me an old man like you do when you're angry with something else? If you're not Nature, or a bit of it, what the hell are you?"

"I'm a *woman*," screamed his wife, her eyes filling with tears. "And my home is under . . . under . . . the *vile* . . . rain water. . . ."

With a great effort Mr. Bellgrove worked his emaciated legs over the side of the hammock and when they touched the floor, rose shakily to his feet and shambled uncertainly in his wife's direction. He was very conscious of doing a noble action. He had been very comfortable in the hammock; he knew that there was a very slender chance of his chivalry being appreciated, but that was life. One had to do certain things to keep up one's spiritual status, but apart from that, her terrible outburst had unnerved him. He had to do *something*. Why did she

have to make such an unpleasant noise about it all? Her
voice went through his head like a knife.

But oh, it had been pathetic too: railing against Nature.
How maddeningly ignorant she was. As though Nature
should have turned back when it reached as far as her
boudoir. As though a flood would whisper to itself,
"Sh . . . sh . . . sh . . . less noise . . . less . . . noise . . . this
is Irma's room . . . lavender and ivory you know . . .
lavender and ivory." Tut-tut-tut, what a wife to be saddled with in all conscience . . . and yet . . . and yet . . .
was it only pity that drew him to her? He did not know.

He sat down by her side beneath a small top window,
and he put his long, loose arm about her. She shuddered
a moment and then stiffened again. But she did not ask
him to remove his arm.

In the small loft with the great castle beneath them
like a gigantic body with its arteries filled with water, they
sat there side by side, and stared at where a piece of
plaster had fallen from the opposite wall, and had left
a small gray pattern the shape of a heart.

Chapter Seventy-Five

❄❄❄❄❄❄❄❄❄❄❄❄

IT was not that Fuchsia did not struggle against her mounting melancholia. But the black moods closing in on her
ever more frequently were becoming too much for her.

The emotional, loving, moody child had had small
chance of developing into a happy woman. Had she as a
girl been naturally joyous yet all that had befallen her
must surely have driven away the bright birds, one by
one, from her breast. As it was, made of a more somber
clay, capable of deep happiness, but more easily drawn
to the dark than the light, Fuchsia was even more open to

the cruel winds of circumstances which appeared to have singled her out for particular punishment.

Her need for love had never been fulfilled; her love for others had never been suspected, or wanted. Rich as a dusky orchard, she had never been discovered. Her green boughs had been spread, but no travelers came and rested in their shade nor tasted the sweet fruit.

With her mind forever turning to the past, Fuchsia could see nothing but the ill-starred progress of a girl who was, in spite of her title and all it implied, of little consequence in the eyes of the castle, a purposeless misfit of a child, hapless and solitary. Her deepest loves had been for her old nurse Nannie Slagg, for her brother, for the Doctor, and in a strange way for Flay. Nannie Slagg and Flay were both dead; Titus had changed. They loved one another still but a wall of cloud lay between them, something that neither had the power to dispel.

There was still Dr. Prune. But he had been so heavily overworked since the flood that she had not seen him. The desire to see the last of her true friends had weakened with every black depression. When she most needed the counsel and love of the Doctor, who would have left the world bleeding to help her, it was then that she froze within herself; and locking herself away, became ill with the failure of her life, the frustration of her womanhood; and tossing and turning in her improvised bedroom twelve feet above the flood, conceived, for the first time, the idea of suicide.

What was the darkest of the causes for so terrible a thought it is hard to know. Her lack of love, her lack of a father or a real mother? Her loneliness. The ghastly disillusion when Steerpike was unmasked, and the horror of her having been fondled by a homicide. The growing sense of her own inferiority in everything but rank. There were many causes, any one of which alone might have been sufficient to undermine the will of tougher natures than Fuchsia's.

When the first concept of oblivion flickered through her mind, she raised her head from her arms. She was shocked and she was frightened. But she was excited also.

She walked unsteadily to the window. Her thought had taken her into a realm of possibility so vast, awe-inspiring, final, and noiseless that her knees felt weak and she glanced over her shoulder, although she knew herself to be alone in her room with the door locked against the world.

When she reached the window she stared out across the water, but nothing that she saw affected her thought or made any kind of visual impression on her.

All she knew was that she felt weak, that she was not reading about all this in a tragic book but that it was true. It was true that she was standing at a window and that she had thought of killing herself. She clutched her hands together over her heart and a fleeting memory of how a young man had suddenly appeared at another window many years ago and had left a rose behind him on her table passed through her mind and was gone.

It was all true. It wasn't any story. But she could still pretend. She would pretend that she was the sort of person who would not only think of killing herself so that the pain in her heart should be gone forever, but also be the kind of person who would know how to do it, and be brave enough.

And as she pondered, she slid moment by moment even deeper into a world of make-believe, as though she were once more the imaginative girl of many years ago, aloft in her secret attic. She had become somebody else. She was someone who was young and beautiful and brave as a lioness. What would such a person do? Why, such a person would stand upon the window sill above this water. And . . . she . . . would. . . . And as the child in her was playing the oldest game in the world, her body, following the course of her imagination, had climbed to the sill of the window, where it stood with its back to the room.

For how long she would have stood there had she not been jerked back into a sudden consciousness of the world—by the sound of someone knocking upon the door of her room—it is impossible to know, but starting at the sound and finding herself dangerously balanced upon a narrow sill above the deep water, she trembled uncontrollably, and in trying to turn without sufficient thought or care, she slipped, and clutching at the face of the wall at her side found nothing to grasp, so that she fell, striking her dark head on the sill as she passed, and was already unconscious before the water received her, and drowned her at its ease.

Chapter Seventy-Six

Now that the flood had reached its height it was vital that not a moment should be lost in combing the regions in which Steerpike might be lurking—in surrounding them with cordons of picked men who, converging inward to the center of each chosen district, by land and water, should, theoretically, sooner or later, close upon the beast. And now above all was the time to throw in every man. The Countess had circled areas of the Gormenghast map with a thick blue pencil. Captains of Search had been given their instructions. Not a cranny was to be left unscoured—not a drain unprobed. It would be difficult enough, with the flood at its present level, to run to earth so sly a quarry, yet with every day that passed the chances of Steerpike's capture would recede even farther—would recede as the flood receded, for as one floor after another began to open up its labyrinthian ways, so the fugitive in the multiplying warrens would burrow ever deeper into darkness.

It would of course be slow and gradual, this going-down of the flood, but the Countess was fiercely conscious of how time was the salient factor: how never again would she have Steerpike within so close a net. Even for the flood to leave a single floor would be for a hundred vistas to spread out on every side with all their countless alleys of wet stone. There was no time to be lost.

As it was the theaters of maneuver—the three dry topmost floors and the wet "floor of boats" (where the colored craft of the Carvers sped to and fro, or lay careening beneath the great mantelpieces, or tied up to the banisters of forgotten stairways, cast their rich reflections in the dark water)—these theaters of maneuver, the three dry levels and the one wet, were not the only areas which had to be considered in the drawing up of the master plan. The Countess also had to remember the isolated outcrops of the castle. Luckily most of the widely scattered and virtually endless ramifications of the main structure of Gormenghast were under water, and consequently of no use to the fugitive. But there were a number of towers to which the young man might well have swum. And there was also Gormenghast Mountain.

As far as this latter was concerned, the Countess was not apprehensive of his having escaped there, not merely because she had checked the boats each evening, and was satisfied that there had been no thefts, but because a string of boats like colored beads was, at her orders, in perpetual rotation around the castle summits, and would have cut him off by day or night.

The core of her strategy hinged upon the fact that the young man must eat. As for drink, he had a wet world brimming at his mouth.

That he might already be dead from accident or from starvation was ruled out by the body that on this very day had been discovered floating face downward alongside an upturned coracle. The man had been no more than a few hours dead. A pebble was lodged in his forehead.

The headquarters of the Countess was now in a long, narrow room that lay immediately and somewhat centrally above the "floor of boats."

There she received all messages; gave all orders; prepared her plans; studied the various maps and gave instructions for new ones to be rapidly prepared of the unplotted districts, so that she should have as powerful a grasp upon the smallest details as she had upon the comprehensive sweep of her master plan.

Her preparations completed, she rose from the table at which she had been sitting, and pursing her lips at the goldfinch on her shoulder, she was about to move with that characteristically heavy and ruthless deliberation toward the door when a panting messenger ran up to her.

"Well?" she said. "What is it?"

"Lord Titus, my lady . . . he's . . ."

"He's what?" She turned her head sharply.

"He's here."

"Where?"

"Outside the door, your Ladyship. He says he has important news for you."

The Countess moved at once to the door and, opening it, found Titus sitting upon the floor, his head between his knees, his sodden clothes in rags, his legs and arms bruised and scratched, and his hair gray with grime.

He did not look up. He had not the strength. He had collapsed. In a confused way he knew where he was, for he had been straining his muscles with long and hazardous climbs, struggling shoulder deep through flooded passageways, crawling giddily over slanting roofs, intent upon one thing—to reach this door under which he had slumped. The door of his mother's room.

After a little time he opened his eyes. His mother was kneeling heavily at his side. What was she doing there? He shut his eyes again. Perhaps he was dreaming. Someone was saying in a faraway voice, "Where is that brandy?" and then, a little later, he felt himself being raised, the cold rim of a glass at his lips.

When he next opened his eyes he knew exactly where he was and why he was there.

"Mother!" he said.

"What is it?" Her voice was quite colorless.

"I've seen him."

"Who?"

"Steerpike."

The Countess stiffened at his side. It was as though

something more of ice than of flesh were kneeling beside him.

"No!" she said at last. "Why should I believe you?"

"It is true," said Titus.

She bent over him and, taking his shoulders in her powerful hands, forced them with a deceptive tenderness to and fro, as though to ease some turmoil in her heart. He could feel through the gentle grasp of her fingers the murderous strength of her arms.

At last she said, "Where? Where did you see him?"

"I could take you there . . . northward."

"How long ago?"

"Hours . . . hours . . . he went through a window . . . in my boat . . . he stole it."

"Did he see you?"

"No."

"Are you sure of that?"

"Yes."

"Northward you say. Beyond the Blackstone Quarter?"

"Far beyond. Nearer the Stone Dogshead and the Angel's Buttress."

"No!" cried the Countess in so loud and husky a voice that Titus drew back on his elbow. She turned to him.

"Then we have him." Her eyes were narrowed. "Did you not have to crawl across the Coupée—the high knife-edge? How else could you have returned?"

"I did," said Titus. "That is how I came."

"From the North Headstones?"

"Is that what it is called, Mother?"

"It is. You have been in the North Headstones beyond Gory and the Silver Mines. I know where you've been. You've been to the Twin Fingers where Little Sark begins and the Bluff narrows. Between the Twins would be water now. Am I right?"

"There's what looks like a bay," said Titus. "If that's what you mean."

"The district will be ringed at once! And on every level!"

She rose ponderously to her feet, and turning to one of the men—"Have the Search Captains called immediately.

Take up the boy. Couch him. Feed him. Give him dry clothes. Give him sleep. He will not have long to rest. All craft will patrol the Headstones night and day. All search parties will be mustered and concentrated to the south side of the Coupée neck. Send out all messengers. We start in one hour from now."

She turned to look down at Titus, who had risen to one knee. When he was on his feet he faced his mother.

She said to him, "Get some sleep. You have done well. Gormenghast will be avenged. The castle's heart is sound. You have surprised me."

"I did not do it for Gormenghast," said Titus.

"No?"

"No, Mother."

"Then for whom or for what?"

"It was an accident," said Titus, his heart hammering. "I happened to be there." He knew he should hold his tongue. He knew that he was talking a forbidden language. He trembled with the excitement of telling the dangerous truth. He could not stop. "I am glad it's through me he's been sighted," he said, "but it wasn't for the safety or the honor of Gormenghast that I've come to you. No, though because of me he'll be surrounded. I cannot think of my duty any more. Not in that way. I hate him for *other* reasons."

The silence was thick and terrible—and then at last her millstone words. *"What . . . reasons?"* There was something so cold and merciless in her voice that Titus blanched. He had spoken as he had never dared to speak before. He had stepped beyond the recognized border. He had breathed the air of an unmentionable world.

Again the cold, inhuman voice: *"What reasons?"*

He was altogether exhausted, but suddenly out of his physical weakness another wave of nervous moral strength floated up in him. He had not planned to come out into the open, or to give any hint to his mother of his secret rebellion, and he knew that he could never have voiced his thoughts had he *planned* to do so, but finding now that he had shown himself in the colors of a traitor, he flushed, and lifting his head he shouted: "I will tell you!"

His filthy hair fell over his eyes. His eyes blazed with an upsurge of defiance, as though a dozen pent-up years had at last found outlet. He had gone so far that there was no return. His mother stood before him like a monument. He saw her great outline through the blur of his weakness and his passion. She made no movement at all.

"I will tell you! My reasons were for this. Laugh if you like! He stole my boat! He hurt Fuchsia. He killed Flay. He frightened me. I do not care if it was rebellion against the Stones—most of all it was theft, cruelty, and murder. What do I care for the symbolism of it all? What do I care if the castle's heart is sound or not? I don't want to be sound anyway! Anybody can be sound if they're always doing what they're told. I want to live! Can't you see? Oh, can't you see? I want to be myself, and become what I make myself, a person, a real live person and not a symbol any more. That is my reason! He must be caught and slain. He killed Flay. He hurt my sister. He stole my boat. Isn't that enough? To hell with Gormenghast."

In the unbearable silence the Countess and those present could hear the sound of someone approaching rapidly.

But it was an eternity before the footsteps came to rest and a distraught figure stood before the Countess and waited with head bowed and trembling hands for permission to give his message. Dragging her gaze from the face of her son, she turned at last to the messenger.

"Well," she whispered, "what is it, man?"

He raised his head. For a few seconds he could not speak. His lips were apart but no sound came, and his jaws shook. In his eyes was such a light that caused Titus to move toward him with sudden fear.

"Not Fuchsia! Not Fuchsia!" he cried with a ghastly knowledge, even as he framed the words, that something had happened to her.

The man, still facing the Countess, said, "The Lady Fuchsia is drowned."

At these words something happened to Titus. Something quite unpredictable. He now knew what he must do. He knew what he was. He had no fear left. The death of his sister, like the last nail to be driven into his make-up, had completed him, as a structure is completed, and becomes ready for use while the sound of the last hammer-blow still echoes in the ears.

The death of the Thing had seen the last of his boy-hood.

When the lightning killed her he had become a man. The elasticity of childhood had gone. His brain and body had become wound up, like a spring. But the death of Fuchsia had touched the spring. He was now no longer just a man. He was that rarer thing, a man in motion. The wound-up spring of his being recoiled. He was on his way.

And the agent of his purpose was his anger. A blind white rage had transformed him. His egotistic outburst, dramatic enough, and dangerous enough on its own account, was nothing to the fierce loosening of his tongue, that like a vent for the uprush of his rage and grief, amazed his mother, the messenger, and the officers who had only known him as a reserved and moody figurehead.

Fuchsia dead! Fuchsia, his dark sister—his dear sister. "Oh, God in Heaven, *where?*" he cried. "Where was she found? Where is she now? Where? Where? I must go to her."

He turned to his mother. "It is the skewbald beast," he said. "He has killed her. He has killed your daughter. Who else would kill her? Or touch a hair of her head? Oh, braver than *you* ever knew, who never loved her. Oh, God, Mother, get your captains posted. Every weap-on'd man. My tiredness has gone. I will come at once. I know the window. It is not yet dark. We can surround him. But by boat, Mother. That is the quickest way. There is no need for the North Headstones. Send out the boats. Every one. I *saw* him, Mother, the killer of my sister."

He turned again to the bearer of the shattering news. "Where is she now?"

"A special room has been prepared by the Doctor near the hospital. He is with her."

And then the voice of the Countess, low and deep. She was speaking to the Head Officer present.

"The Carvers must be informed that they are needed, and every watertight boat finished or unfinished. All boats already in the castle to be drawn up alongside the West Wall. All weapons to be distributed at once," and then, to the messenger who had spoken of where Fuchsia lay, "Lead the way."

The Countess and Titus followed the man. No word was spoken until they were within a stone's throw of the hospital, when the Countess without turning to Titus said, "If it were not that you are ill—"

"I am not ill," said Titus, interrupting.

"Very well, then," said the Countess. "It is upon your head."

"I welcome it," said Titus.

While he could feel no fear, he was at the same time surprised at his own audacity. But it was so small an emotion compared with the hollow ache with which the knowledge of Fuchsia's death had filled him. To be brave among the living—what was that compared with the bonfire of his rage against Steerpike at whose door he laid the responsibility for Fuchsia's death? And the tides of the loneliness that had surged over him drowned him in seas that knew no fear of the living, even of a mother such as his own?

When the door was opened they saw the tall thin figure of Dr. Prunesquallor standing at an open window, his hands behind his back, very still and unnaturally upright. It was a small room with low rafters and bare boards on the floor, but it was meticulously clean. It was obvious that it had been freshly scrubbed and washed, boards, walls, and ceiling.

Against the wall to the left was a stretcher supported at either end upon wooden boxes. On the stretcher lay Fuchsia, a sheet drawn up to her shoulders, her eyes closed. It seemed hardly her.

The Doctor turned. He did not seem to recognize either Titus or the Countess. He stared through them, only touching Titus's arm in a gentle way as he passed, for he had no sooner seen the mother and the brother of his favorite child than he had begun to move to the door.

His cheeks were wet, and his glasses had become so blurred that he stumbled when he reached the door, and could not find the handle. Titus opened the door for him and for a moment caught a glimpse of his friend in the corridor outside as he removed his glasses and began to wipe them with his silk handkerchief, his head bowed, his weak eyes peering at the spectacles in his hand with that kind of concentration that is grief.

Left together in the room, the mother and son stood side by side in worlds of their own. Had they not both been moved it might well have been embarrassing. Neither knew nor cared what was going on in the breast of the other.

The face of the Countess showed nothing, but once she drew the corner of the sheet up a little farther over Fuchsia's shoulder, with an infinite gentleness, as though she feared her child might feel the cold and so must take the risk of waking her.

Chapter Seventy-Seven

KNOWING that he had several hours to wait before it would be dark enough for him to venture forth, Steerpike had dropped off to sleep in the canoe. As he slept the canoe began to bob gently on the inky water a few feet from where the flood swam through the window entrance. This entrance, seen from the inside of the "cavern," was like a square of light. But the breast of the great bay, which, from the dark interior of Steerpike's refuge, appeared luminous, was in reality, as the moments passed, drawing across its nakedness shawl after shawl of shadow.

When Steerpike had slid from the outer world, and through the brimming window, seven hours earlier, he had of course been able to see exactly what kind of a room he had entered. The light striking through the window had glanced upward off the water and lit the interior.

His first reaction had been one of intense irritation, for there were no corridors leading from the room and no stairways to the floor above. The doors had been closed when the flood had filled the room so that they were immovable with the weight of water. Had the inner doors been open he might have slid through their upper airways into ampler quarters. But no. The place was virtually a cave—a cave with a few moldering pictures hanging precariously a few inches above high-water mark.

As such he suspected it from the first. It was no more than a trap. But to paddle out of its mouth and across the open water seemed to him more dangerous than to remain where he was for the few hours that remained before darkness fell.

A breeze was stirring the surface of the wide freshwater bay, and blowing from the direction of the mountain, and a kind of gooseflesh covered the surface of the water. These ripples began to move into the cave, one after another, and the canoe rocked with a gentle side-to-side motion.

On either side of the bay the two identical headlands, with their long lines of windows, had become silhouetted against the dusk.

Between them the ruffled waters faced the sky with an unusual agitation—a shuffling backward and forward of the surface which, though by no means dangerous in itself either to the smallest craft or even to a swimmer, was nevertheless peculiar and menacing.

Within a minute the breathless quiet of the evening had become something very different. The hush of dusk, the trance of stone-gray light was broken. There was no break in the silence but the air, the water, the castle, and the darkness were in conclave.

A chill breath from the lungs of this conspiracy, stealing across the gooseflesh water, must have moved into the cavelike chamber where Steerpike slept, for he sat up suddenly in his canoe and, turning his face at once to the window, the small hairs rose along his spine and his mouth became the mouth of a wolf, for as the blood shone behind the lenses of his eyes, his thin and colorless lips parted in a snarl that extended like an open gash in a mask of wax.

As his brain raced, he plucked at the paddle and whisked the boat to within a few feet of the window, where, in absolute darkness himself, he could command a view of the bay.

What he had seen had been the reflections only of what he now stared at in their entirety—for from where the canoe had been stationed the upper section of the window had been hidden by a hanging sail of wallpaper. What he had seen had been the reflections of a string of lights. What he now saw were the lanterns, where they burned at the bows of a hundred boats. They were strung out in a half-circle that even as he watched was drawing in his direction, thick as fireflies.

But worse than all this was a kind of light upon the water immediately outside the window. Not a strong light, but more than he could account for by the last of the day. Nor was it natural in color. There was something of green in the faint haze from which he now turned his eyes again. For with every moment the boats were narrowing the distance between themselves and the castle walls.

Whether or not there were other interpretations of the spectacle before him, it was not for him at this critical moment to give them the shadow of a thought. It was for him to assume the bloodiest and the worst.

It was for him to suppose that they were not only ranged across the bay in search of *him*—that they knew he was in hiding somewhere close at hand between the

twin headlands—but more than this, that they knew the
very window through which he had passed. He must assume that he had been seen as he entered this trap and
that not only were his pursuers fanned out across the
water and eager for his blood, but the cold sheen upon
the water immediately ahead of him was cast from
lanterns or torches that were even now burning from
the window above his head.

Whether or not his only hope was to slip out of the
cave and, risking a fusillade from the window above,
make all speed across the waters of the bay before the
approaching boats not only closed their ranks as they
converged, but made the cave mouth livid with the concentration of their lights—whether he should do this,
and by so doing and gaining speed in the dusk, fly like a
swallow across the face of the bay and swerving to and
fro as only this canoe had power to do, hope to pierce
the lanterned ring, and so, running his boat alongside
one or other of the creepered headlands, climb the
coarse foliage of the walls—whether he should do this
or not, it was now, in any event, too late—for a brilliant
yellow light was shining outside the window and danced
on the choppy water.

A pair of heavy castle craft, somewhat the shape of
barges, creeping in along the lapping walls from either
side of Steerpike's window, were the cause of the yellow
light which the murderer had observed to his horror
as it danced upon the water, for these heavy boats
bristled with torches; sparks flew over the flood and
died hissing upon its surface. The scene about the opening of the cave had been transformed from one of dark
and anonymous withdrawal to a firelit stage of water,
upon which every eye was turned. The stone supports
of the window, weather-scarred and ancient as they
were, had become things of purest gold, and their reflections plunged into the black water as though to ignite
it. The stones that surrounded the windows were lit with
equal brilliance. Only the mouth of the room, with the
firelit water running through and into the swallowing
blackness of the throat beyond, broke the glow. For

there was something more than black about the intensity of that rough square of darkness.

It was not for these barges to do more than to remain with their square noses in line with the stone edges of the window. It was for them to make the place as bright as day. It was for the arc of lanterned boats to close in and to form the thickset audience, armed and impenetrable.

But those that manned the barges and held the torches aloft, and those that rowed or paddled the hundreds of boats that were now within a stone's throw of the cave, were not the only witnesses.

High above the entrances to Steerpike's retreat the scores of irregularly positioned windows were no longer gaping emptily as when Titus had stared up at them from the canoe and felt the chill of that forsaken place. They were no longer empty. At every window where the illuminated waves rose and fell to such an extent that the shadows of the men upon the barges leaped up and down the firelit walls, and the sound of splashing could be heard below them as combers of rain water ran and broke upon the castle walls.

The wind was making, and certain of the boats that formed the chain found it difficult to keep in position. Only the watchers from above were unaffected by the worsening weather. A formidable contingent had traveled by land. There were few who had been that way before and none who had traveled so far afield as the Coupée and the Headstones of Little Sark, within the last five years.

The Countess had journeyed by water but it had been necessary for Titus to travel overland at the head of the leading phalanx, for it was no easy itinerary with the dusk falling and the innumerable choices to be made at the junctures of passages and rooftops. With his return journey fresh in his mind he had no choice but to put his knowledge at the disposal of the many hundreds whose duty it would be to scour the Headstones. But he was in no condition to make that long journey again on the same day, without assistance. While the officials were casting about for some appropriate conveyance Titus remembered the chair on poles in which he had been carried, blindfolded, on his tenth birthday. A runner was dispatched for this, and some time later the "land army" moved to the north with Titus leaning back in his "mountain chair," a jug of water in the wooden well at his feet, a flask of brandy in his hand, and a loaf of bread and a bag of raisins on the seat beside him. At different times during the journey, when crossing from one roof to another or when climbing difficult stairways, he would descend from the chair and continue on foot—but for most of the way it was possible for him to lean back in the chair, his muscles relaxed, merely giving fierce instructions to the Captain of the Land Searchers when occasion arose. A dark anger was gaining strength in him.

What passed through his mind as he moved through the evening air? A hundred thoughts and shadows of a hundred more. But among all these were those giant themes that overshadowed all else and were continually shouldering themselves back into his consciousness, and making his heart at their every return break out afresh with painful hammering. Within so short a time—within the last few hours—he had thrice been through an emotional turmoil for which he was in no way prepared.

Out of nowhere, suddenly the first sight of the elusive Steerpike. Out of nowhere, suddenly, the news of Fuchsia's death. Out of nowhere, and suddenly the uprush of his rebellion—the danger of it, the shock of it for all about him, the excitement of it, and the thrill of finding himself free of duplicity—a traitor if they liked, but a man who had torn away the brambles from his clothes, the ivy from his limbs, the bindweed from his brain.

Yet had he? Was it possible at a single jerk to wrench himself free of his responsibility to the home of his fathers?

As his bearers threaded their way through the upper storeys he was sure that he was free. When Steerpike had been dragged like a water rat from his lair and slain—what then would there be for him to stay for in this only world he knew? Rather would he die upon its borders, wherever they might be, than rot among the rites. Fuchsia was dead. Everything was dead. The Thing was dead and the world had died. He had outgrown his kingdom.

But behind all this, behind his stumbling thoughts, was this growing anger, an anger such as he had never known before. On the face of it, it might seem that the rage that was eating him was absurd. And the rational part of Titus might have admitted that this was so. For his rage was not that Fuchsia had died and as he thought at Steerpike's hand, nor that he had been thwarted in his love for the Thing by the arbitrary lightning flash—it was not, in his conscious mind, either of these that caused him to tremble with the eagerness to close with the skewbald man, and, if he could, to kill him.

No, it was because Steerpike had stolen his canoe, his own canoe—so light, so slight: so fleet upon the flood.

What he did not guess was that the canoe was neither more nor less than the *Thing*. Deep in the chaos of his heart and his imagination, at the core of his dream world, it was so—the Canoe had become, perhaps had already been, when he had first sent her skimming beneath him into the freedom of an outer world, the very centers of Gormenghast Forest, the Thing herself.

But more than this. For another reason also. A reason of no symbolism: no darkened origin: a reason clear-cut and real as the dagger in his belt.

He saw in the canoe, now lost to the murderer, the perfect vehicle for sudden and silent attack—in other words for the avenging of his sister. He had lost his *weapon*.

Had Titus thought sufficiently he would have realized that Steerpike could not have killed her, for he could not possibly have been so far to the north as the Headstones so soon after Fuchsia's fall. But his brain was not working in that way. Steerpike had killed his sister. And Steerpike had stolen his canoe.

When at long last the rooftop army had reached the
ultimate battlements and saw below them the black waters of the "bay," lookouts were posted and given instructions to inform their captains directly the first
lights appeared around the nose of the South Headland.
Meanwhile the hordes which covered the nearby roofs
were gradually drawn down by skylights, vents, and
hatches until they were absorbed into a deserted and
melancholy wilderness of room upon room, hall upon
hall, a wilderness that had yawned emptily and for so
many years until Steerpike had begun his explorations.

The torches were lit. It seemed that the advantages of
being able to tell at once whether a room were empty
or not outweighed the warning that the light would give
the fugitive. Nevertheless the work was slow. At last
and about the time that the four possible floors had
been proved as empty as tongueless bells, a message
came down that lights had been seen across the bay.

At once every window of the West Walls became filled
with heads, and sure enough the necklace of colored
sparks which Steerpike had seen through the mouth of
his flood-room was strung across the darkness.

That no sign of Steerpike had been found in the scores
of upper rooms more than suggested that he was still
within his lair at water level. Titus had at once descended
to the lowest of the unflooded floors, and leaning through
a window, roughly at the center of the façade, he was
able, by reaching out dangerously, with his hand gripping an ivy branch, to recognize the very window through
which Steerpike had sped into the castle.

Now that the light had appeared on the bay there
was no time to lose, for it was possible that if Steerpike was below, and saw them, he would make a dash
for it. In the meantime Titus and the three captains who
were with him turned back through the room and, gaining the corridor behind, ran for a matter of sixty or
seventy feet before they turned again into one of the
west rooms and, on reaching its window and looking
down, found that they were almost immediately above
the flooded window.

There was no sign of him on the bay. As far as they could judge they gauged him to be directly below the room to their right, which they could see through a connecting door, a largish, squarish room covered with a layer of dust as soft as velvet.

"If he's below there and it is necessary, my lord, we could cut through to him from above." And the man began to make his way into the room in question.

"No! No!" whispered Titus fiercely. "He may hear your footsteps. Come back."

"The boats aren't near enough," said another man. "I doubt he can get farther into the castle. The water's only four foot from the window top. Sooner or later the doors will all be water-jammed. Quite right, my lord. We must be silent."

"Then *be* silent," said Titus, and in spite of his anger, the heady wine of autocracy tasted sweet upon his tongue —sweet and dangerous—for he was only now learning that he had power over others, not only through the influence of his birthright but through a native authority that was being wielded for the first time—and all this he knew to be dangerous, for as it grew, this bullying would taste ever sweeter and fiercer and the naked cry of freedom would become faint and the Thing who had taught him freedom would become no more than a memory.

It was while the boats approached and converged and before the castle barges had stationed themselves on either side of the window with their effulgence, and while there was a comparative darkness still brooding upon the water outside the mouth of his lair, that Steerpike decided that he would rather remain for the moment where he was and fight the whole world if necessary with the knowledge that he could not be attacked from the rear, than skim from his retreat only to find himself surrounded in the bay. It was no easy choice and it is possible that he had not truly made it, before the barge lights flared—but in all events he stayed where he was, and turning his canoe about he made another turn of his dark room. It was then that the sudden yellow light flared cruelly outside the window and stayed—as though a curtain had gone up and the drama had begun. Even as he started at the light, he knew that his enemies could not know for *certain* that he was in this watery room. They could not possibly know, for instance, that the inner doors of the room were shut and impassable. They could not be absolutely certain that, although he had been seen passing through the window, he had not passed out again. But how, if ever, to make use of their uncertainty, he had, for the moment, no idea.

There was nothing but the empty picture-hung walls and the water; nothing in the room to help him, and then, for the first time he thought of the ceiling. He looked up and saw that there was but a single layer of floor boards laid across the rotting joists. He cursed himself for his delay and immediately began to balance himself upright in his canoe beneath a crumbling patch in the ceiling. As he reached upward to obtain a grip upon the joists, preparatory to striking, he heard the terrifying sound of footsteps above him and the floor boards trembled within a few inches of his head.

In a moment he had dropped back into the canoe that was now rocking appreciably. The freshening wind was sending sheets of water scurrying through the window across the comparatively even surface of the imprisoned flood.

He was cut off from above and from every side. His eyes were constantly upon the brilliant yellow square of water immediately outside the window. All at once a wave rather heavier than its forerunners sent its spray leaping up to the height of the window top, and the wave itself smacked spitefully at the stone supports. The dark room had become full of the slapping sound of imprisoned water. Not loud but cold and cruel—and then all at once Steerpike heard another sound—the first of the returning rain. With the sound of its hissing a kind of hope came to him.

It was not that he had lost hope. He had had none. He had not thought in those terms. He had so concentrated upon what he should do, second by second, that he had not envisaged that there might be a moment when all was lost. He had, furthermore, an overweening pride that saw in this concentration of the castle's forces a tribute to himself. This was no part of the ritual of Gormenghast. This was something original.

The unwitting pageantry of the lantern-lit boats was unique. It had not been thought out or dictated. There had been no rehearsal. It was necessitated. It was necessitated by the fear of him. But mixed with his vanity and pride was a fear of his own. Not a fear of the men who were closing in upon him, but of fire. It was the sight of the torches that stretched his face into that vulpine snarl—that whetted his evil cunning. The memory of his near-death when he and Barquentine had been wrapped together in a single flame had so festered within him, had so affected his brain, that at the approach of a flame madness grew very near.

At any moment he would see, beyond the window, the gold of the rain-spattered waves broken by the bows of a boat—or perhaps of several boats without an inch between them. Or perhaps a voice would hail him and order him forth.

The lanterned craft were now close enough for their crews to be recognizable by the light of the multi-colored flames that burned across the rough water.

Again he heard the footsteps above and again he turned up his red eyes to the rotten planks. As he did so he kept his balance with difficulty, for the waves were now by no means easy to ride.

As his gaze returned from the ceiling he saw something for the first time. It was a ledge, fortuitously formed by the protruding lintel of the window.

At once he knew it as his immediate perch. He had hopes of a returning storm and of the scattering abroad of the flotilla that rose and fell in the mounting waves.

But if a storm were to develop then there would be even less time to spare before his enemies made their first move. Time was on no one's side, neither theirs nor his. They would be entering at any moment.

But it was no easy task, to reach this ledge above the

window, where the shadows were at their deepest. He
stood in the bows of the slight canoe so that its stern
rose high out of the water. One of his hands clasped a
joist of the low roof above his head and the other felt
along the lintel's upper edge in search of a grip. All
this time it was necessary for him to keep the canoe
flush against the wall, while the swell in the cave lifted
it up and down.

It was vital that the canoe was kept from dancing
forward on a wave so that its bows protruded across the
square of the window and into the line of vision of those
without. It was a hideous exertion, stretched as he was
at an angle, his hands upon the ledge and ceiling, his
feet together in the volatile prow of the canoe, the water
dashing to and fro, lifting and falling, the thin spray
everywhere.

Luckily for him he had obtained by now a firm grip
with his right hand, for his fingers had found a deep
crack in the uneven stone of the protruding lintel. It
was not the height of this shelf that made him wonder
whether he would ever reach it with the rest of his body,
for, standing as he was in the canoe, it was only a foot
above his head. It was the synchronization of the various things he had to do before he could find himself
crouched above the window, with the canoe beside
him, that was so desperately difficult.

But he was as tenacious as a ferret and slowly, by
infinitesimal degrees, he withdrew his right leg from the
canoe and prized his knee against the inside edge of
the stone upright. The canoe was still standing practically
on its head by reason of the pressure of his left foot in
the bows. So vertical had she become that he was able
with a kind of febrile genius of his own to let go of
the joist above his head and with this same left hand to
lift the canoe clean out of the water. He was now left
with both his arms engaged—one in holding him where he
was and the other in holding the canoe away from the
light. He was suffering with his right knee prized as it
was against the upright of the window. The other leg
dangled like a dead thing.

For a little while he remained as he was, the sweat pouring over his piebald face, his muscles shrieking for release from so ghastly a strain. For this period he had no doubt that there was no end to this save that of dropping like a dead fly from a wall—dropping into the water below, where, bobbing in the golden torchlight below the lintel, he would be picked up by the nearest of his enemies.

But at the height of his pain he began to pull at the entire weight of his body, to pull at it with his single hand whose crooked finger shook in the lintel crack. Inch by inch, moaning to himself as though he were a baby or a sick dog, he drew the dead weight of his body up until, twisting over a little on one side, he was able to bring his other leg into play. But he could find no kind of irregularity in the stone upright for the questing toe of his shoe.

He rolled his eye up in a frenzy of despair. Again he thought he was dropping into the water. But as his eye rolled it had, half-consciously, become aware of a great rusty nail leaning out horizontally from the shadowy joist. It shriveled and it swelled out, this nail, as he turned his eyes to it again with a blurred conception floating in his mind that he could not at once decipher. But what his thoughts could not define, his arm put into practice. He watched it raise itself, this left arm of his; he watched it lift the canoe gradually until the bows were above his head and then, as a man might hang his hat upon a peg, he hung his craft upon the rusty nail. Now that his left hand was free he was able to get a second purchase upon the lintel crack, and to draw himself upward with a comparative lack of pain until he was kneeling on all fours upon the twelve-inch protuberance of the heavy lintel.

Where there had been so emphatic a division between the black waves within the room and the yellow waves that tossed beyond the window, there was no longer so sharp a demarcation. The tongues of golden water slithered further into the room and the black tongues flickered out less freely into the outer radiance.

Steerpike was now lying along the shelf face downward a few feet above the water. He was lowering his head gradually over the window's upper and northerly corner. A few dead strands of creeper that struggled across the outside wall and blurred to some extent the stone angle provided him with a kind of screen through which it was his intention to gain some knowledge of his enemies' intentions.

Lowering his head inch by inch, he suddenly saw them. A solid wall of boats not twelve feet away surrounded the entrance. They rose and subsided on a dangerous swell. The rain flew down, thin but vicious, slanting across the wet and torchlit faces.

They were armed, not as he had imagined they would be with firearms, but with long knives, and at once he remembered the Death Law of the place which decreed that, where possible, all homicides should die in a way as closely resembling the death of their victims as possible. It was obvious that his slaughter of Flay had precipitated the choice of weapons.

The torchlight flamed on the slippery steel. The noses of the boats wedged themselves even closer about the window's mouth.

Steerpike raised himself and sat back on his haunches. The light in the cave had grown. It was like a gold twilight. He glanced at the hanging canoe. Then he began deliberately, but rapidly, to take from his various pockets those few objects that were always on his person.

The knife and the catapult he placed side by side, carefully and neatly as a housewife arranging a mantelpiece. Most of his ammunition he left in his pocket, but a dozen pebbles were formed up like soldiers in three straight rows.

Then he took a small mirror and comb, and by the dull golden light that had crept into the cave, he arranged his hair.

When this was completed to his satisfaction, he lowered his head again over the corner of the lintel and saw how the thick-set boats had made between them something like a solid wall that heaved as it hemmed him in beyond all possibility of escape. Over this solid mass, crowded with men, a smaller boat was being carried, and even as he watched, was set down upon the turbulent water on the near side, so that its bows were within a few feet of the window mouth.

And then he noticed with a start that the two castle barges were nosing their way closer to one another across the window so that his means of exit to the outside world had become a mere passageway.

With the closing in of the barges, a number of the torches that they carried were now able to send their glow directly through the window, so that Steerpike found the surface of the water in the room below him was dancing with such brilliance that were he not immediately above the window he would have been fully exposed to view.

But he also noticed that the surface brilliance had robbed the water of its translucency. There was no sense of the walls continuing down below the water level. It might well have been a solid floor of gold that heaved like an earthquake and reflected its effulgence across the walls and ceiling. He lifted his catapult from beside him and raising it to his mouth he pursed his thin, merciless lips and kissed it as a withered spinster might kiss a spaniel's nose. He slid a pebble into the soft leather of the pouch, and as he waited for the bows of a boat to appear below him, or for a voice to hail him, a great wave lifted through the window and, swirling around the room like a mad thing, poured out again, leaving a whirlpool at the center of the room. At the same moment he heard a clamor of voices without, and shouts of warning, for the backwash had swept over the sides of several of the rocking boats. And at the same moment, as his weapon lay in his hand and the threatening water swirled below him, another thing happened. Behind the sound of the water, behind the sound of the voices outside the window, there was another sound, a sound that made itself apparent, not through its volume or stridency but through its persistence. It was the sound of sawing. Someone in the room above had worked some sharp instrument through a rotten piece of the floor—quite silently, for Steerpike had heard nothing—and now the end of a saw protruded through the ceiling into Steerpike's room, and was working rapidly up and down.

Steerpike's attention had been so concentrated upon what was happening outside the window where the small exploratory boat had been set upon the water, a few feet away, that he had neither ears nor eyes for what was happening above him.

But in a lull of the waves and the shouting he had suddenly heard it, the deliberate triding of a saw, and looking up he could see the jag-edged thing, shining in the water-reflected light, as though it were of gold, while it plunged and withdrew, plunged and withdrew at the center of the ceiling.

Chapter Seventy-Eight

❈❈❈❈❈❈❈❈❈❈❈

I

TITUS, as the minutes had passed, had grown more and more restless. It was not that the preparation for the storming of the flooded room had not been proceeding swiftly and well, but that far from his anger fading, it was gaining more and more of a grip on him.

Two images kept floating before his eyes: one of a creature, slender and tameless; a creature who, defying him, defying Gormenghast, defying the tempest, was yet innocent as air or the lightning that killed her; and the other of a small empty room with his sister lying alone upon a stretcher, harrowingly human, her eyes closed. And nothing else mattered to him but that these two should be avenged—that he should strike.

And so he had not remained at the window overlooking

the bright and heaving water. He had left the room and descended an outer staircase, and had boarded one of the boats, for now that Steerpike's cave was so closely ringed there were scores of craft that bobbed uselessly to and fro on the waves. He ordered the oarsman to land him where the inner circle of boats was forming an unbroken arc around the window's mouth. He made his way over the heaving floor of boats until he was facing the window, and peering along the water's surface he could see the room, filled with its bright reflections, so clearly that a picture hanging on its far wall was perfectly visible.

But the Countess had taken the opposite course—and though they did not see each other they must have crossed in the amber light, for as Titus peered into the flooded room, his mother was climbing the outer staircase. She had also conceived the idea of cutting through the roof immediately above the window, for she could see that it would be difficult for anyone to enter Steerpike's trap without great danger to himself. It was true that the room looked empty, but it had been of course impossible for her to know what lay within the shadows of the *nearest* corners or against the near walls that flanked the window.

And it would be there that Steerpike would crouch, were he in the room at all.

And so she thought of the room above. When she reached it and saw that what she had planned was already being put into practice, she moved to the window and looked down. The rain which had stopped for a little had returned and a steady, slanting stream was pouring itself against the walls, so that, before she had been a minute at the window, she was soaked to the skin. After a little time she turned her head to the left and stared along the adjacent wall. It reached away in wet perspective. She turned her head upward, and the stone acres rose dripping into the night. But the great façade was anything but blank; for from every window there was a head thrust forth. And every head in the glow of the torchlight was of the color of the wall from which it protruded, so that it seemed that the watchers were of stone, like gargoyles, each face directed to the brilliant barge-light that weltered on the waves outside the cave.

But as the Countess continued to stare at "carvings" that studded the walls to the left, a kind of subtraction came into play. It was as though embarrassment spread itself across the stone surfaces. One by one the heads withdrew until there was nothing to the left of the Countess but the emptiness of the streaming walls.

And then she turned her head the other way, where, in reverse, the scores of heads protruded and shone with the torchlit rain—until, like their counterparts, they also one by one withdrew themselves.

The Countess turned her eyes again to the scene immediately below her and the numberless wet faces were drawn forth, at once, as though by suction, from the castle walls, or in the way that the heads of turtles issue from their shells.

The small craft which had been carried over the back of the boat-cordon was now within a foot of the window. A man sat within and wielded a powerful paddle. A black leather hat with a broad brim shielded his eyes from the rain. Between his teeth he gripped a long dirk.

It was no easy task for him, this approach through the window, between the flanking barges. The small skiff rolled dangerously, shipping the gold water over her side. The wind was now something that could be heard whining across the bay.

All at once Titus called out to the man to return.

"Let me go first," he cried. "Come back, you *man*. Let *me* have your dagger." The face of his sister swam across the window. The Thing danced on the bright water like a sprite and he bared his teeth.

"Let *me* kill him! Let *me* kill him!" he cried again, losing in that moment his last four years of growth, for he had become like a child, hysterical with the intensity of his imagination—and for a moment the boatman wavered, his head over his shoulder, but a voice from the wall above roared out.

"No! by the blood of love! Hold the boy down!"

Two men held Titus firmly, for he had made as though to plunge into the water.

"Quiet, my lord," said the voice of one of the men who held him. "He may not be there."

"Why not?" shouted Titus, struggling. "I saw him, didn't I? Let go of me! Do you know who I am? Let go of me!"

II

Steerpike was as motionless as the lintel on which he crouched. Only his eyes moved to and fro, to and fro, from the saw that cut its circular path through the boards above him to the radiant water below him, where at any moment the nose of the skiff might appear. He had heard the roar of the Countess's "No!" sounding from above, and knew that when the ceiling had been cut through she would be one of the first to peer down for him—and there was no doubt that they would have a perfect view of him where he crouched in the reflected light.

To split each forehead open as it appeared at the gap of the ceiling—to leave his pebbles, half protruding like the most eloquent of tombstones in the foreheads of his foes—this might very well be what he would do, but he knew that his enemies had yet no proof positive that he was there. Directly the work of his lethal catapult became evident it would only be a matter of time before his capture.

It was obvious that he could do nothing to stop the regular progress of the man with the saw. Three quarters of a circle had been completed in the rotten planks. Pieces of wood had fallen already into the swirling water.

All depended upon the appearance of the skiff. Within a minute there would be a great round eye in the woodwork above him. Even as he itched for the boat, its bows appeared, bucking like a horse, and then, suddenly, as it leaped forward again, there below him, close enough

to touch, was the broad-brimmed hat of the oarsman
with the dirk in his mouth.

III

The Countess, satisfied that there was no longer any
danger of Titus leaping into the water, returned to where
the man with the saw was resting his arm before the last
dozen plunges and withdrawals of the hot and grinding
blade.

"The first to put his face through the hole is likely to
receive a pebble in his head. You need have no doubt of
this, gentlemen." She spoke slowly. Her hands were on her
hips. Her head was held high. Her bosom heaved with a
slow sealike rhythm. She was consumed with the passion
of the chase, but her face showed nothing. She was intent
upon the death of a traitor.

But what of Titus? The upheaval of his emotions, the
bitterness of his tone; his lack of love for her—all this
was, whether she wished it or not, mixed up with the
cornering of Steerpike. It was no pure and naked con-
test between the House of Groan and a treacherous
rebel, for the Seventy-Seventh Earl was, by his own confession, something perilously near a traitor himself.

She returned to the window, and as she did so, Steerpike in the room below, changing his plan completely
with the dawn of a fresh idea, thrust his catapult back
into his pocket and, grasping his knife, got gradually and
noiselessly to his feet, where he poised himself, his
head and shoulders bent forward, by the proximity of
the roof.

The figure in the boat, who had volunteered for
this hazardous mission, far from being able to keep his
eyes skinned for the enemy, was unable to concentrate
upon anything else but the control of the skiff, which, with
the waves that were now breaking upon the outer wall
and sending their surges through the window, had made
the flood-room into a wall of tossing water.

Nevertheless, the time came, when with a deceptive lull

in the riot of trapped waves, the boatman swung his head over his shoulder, and was able for the first time to focus his eyes upon the window end of the room. At once he saw Steerpike, his face lit from below.

Directly the man saw him he let forth a gasp of excited terror. He was no chicken-heart, having volunteered to enter the cave alone, and he was now prepared to fight as he had never fought before, but there was something so terrible in the poised overhanging aspect of the young man that it turned his bowels to water. For the moment, the volunteer was out of range of anything but the thrown knife—and it was his intention to put his lips to the whistle which hung by a cord around his neck, and warn them of the discovery of Steerpike by the single blast which had been agreed upon, when he found himself being swung forward on the crest of a wave that had entered a moment before and was following the walls as though to swill the cave out. He strained at the paddle but there was no holding back the skiff, and within a matter of moments he found himself slithering along the western side and into the shadowy corner of the "seaward" wall.

As the boat, running forward and striking its nose upon the stones at Steerpike's side, was about to make for the window below him, Steerpike sprang outward, and to the left, and fell with a stunning force, for all his lightness, upon the volunteer. There was no time for any struggle, the knife running between the ribs and through the man's heart three times within as many seconds.

As Steerpike delivered the third of the lightning stabs, the sweat pouring off his face like wet blood in the reflected torchlight, he turned his small hot eyes to the ceiling and found that the saw was within an inch of completing the circle. In another moment he would be exposed to the view of the Countess and the searchers.

The corpse was beside him in the boat, which at the impact of his jumping body had shipped a bucket or two of water. Perhaps it was this that slowed her upon her swirling course. Whatever it was, Steerpike was able to jam his foot against a support of the adjacent window and, grasping the paddle, to force the boat against the weakening sweep of water, until the last of the whirl had poured itself to "sea" again through the window. In the few seconds of respite as he bobbed in the comparative darkness of the outer corner he plucked the broad-brimmed hat of leather from the corpse's head and thrust it on his own. Then he ripped the coat off the limp and heavy body and got into it at once. There was no time for more. A sound of hammering above told him that the circle of floor boards was being knocked through. He caught the corpse beneath its knees and under its arms and with a supreme effort toppled it over the side, where it sank beneath the restless surge.

It was now up to him to control the skiff, for he wanted not only to keep it from capsizing but to station it below the hole in the ceiling. As he plunged the heavy paddle into the water and forced the skiff to the center of the room, the circle of wood fell out of the ceiling and a new light from above made a great pool of radiance at the watery center of Steerpike's lair.

But Steerpike did not look up. He fought like a demon to keep his boat immediately below the lamplit circle—and then he began to call in a husky voice which, if it was nothing like his victim's, was certainly nothing like his own.

"My lady!" he called.

"What's that?" muttered the Countess in the room above.

A man edged his way toward the opening.

Again the voice from below. "Ahoy there! Is the Countess there?"

"It's the volunteer," cried the man who had gone so far as to peer over the rim of the circular hole. "It's the volunteer, lady! He's immediately below."

"What does he say?" cried the Countess in a hollow voice, for a black fear tugged at her heart. "What does he *say,* man! For the love of the stones!"

And then she took a step forward so that she could see the broad-brimmed hat and the heavy coat twelve feet below her. She was about to call down to the figure, although the volunteer made no move to raise his head, but it was his voice that broke the silence. For there *was* a kind of silence, although the rain hissed, and the wind blew, and the waves slapped against the walls. There was a tension which overrode the natural sounds. And a terror that the grizzly fowl had flown.

The voice came up from under the rim of the hat. "Tell her Ladyship there's nothing here! Only a room full of water. There's no way out but the window. The doors are water-jammed. Nothing but water, tell her. Nowhere to hide an eyelash! He's gone, if ever he was here, which I doubt."

The Countess went down on her knees as though she were going to pray. Her heart had gone dead in her. This was the moment, if ever there was one, for an enemy of Gormenghast to be caught and slain. Now, with the eyes of the world focused upon his capture and his punishment. And yet the man had cried, "Only a room full of water."

But something in her would not have it that so great a preparation, so formidable a massing of the castle's strength, should prove abortive—and more than this, there was something in her, at a deeper level, that refused to believe that the certainty, the quite irrational certainty that this was the day of vengeance, was but her wishfulness.

She lowered herself to her elbows and dropped her head below the level of the floor.

At the first glance it was desperately true. There was nowhere to hide. The walls were blank, save for a few moldering pictures. The floor was nothing but water. She turned to the man below.

It was true that it was difficult for him to contend with the restless swell of the waves in the cave, but at the same time it seemed odd that this volunteer made no effort to dart a single glance toward the roof, where he knew his audience lay and watched expectantly.

She had seen him step into his boat some time earlier and paddle his way between the barges. She had gazed down from the window, the rain striking her face, and had wondered what he would find. She had had no doubt that Steerpike would be waiting for him. It was this certainty which still lingered in spite of the emptiness below which prompted her to stare again at the man who had found nothing but water.

When it struck her that he was of slighter build than she had thought, her notion brought no suspicion in its trail. But her eyes, which had left the volunteer again and were following the curve of the wall, now came to rest on something which she had previously missed. The shadows were darker to the right of the single window and she had failed to detect that there was something hanging from the ceiling. At first she could make nothing of it, save that it appeared to be suspended from a joist and that it was about six feet in length, but gradually, as her eyes became used to the peculiar vibrations of the reflected light, and as now one part and now another of the object became illuminated by a glancing beam, so she became at last aware that she was looking at Titus's canoe, the canoe which Steerpike had stolen and in which he had entered this very room. Then where was he? The room was empty of life, empty of everything save the water, the canoe, and the volunteer. And there was no way to escape on foot and no reason why he should have wished to do so with so slight and safe a vessel at his command. Whatever the cause of Steerpike's disappearance, why should the canoe be hanging from the ceiling?

When she turned her eyes back to the broad-brimmed hat below her and noted the shoulders beneath it, and saw the nervous strength and agility with which the man handled the boat, she was affected by the first shadow of a suspicion that this volunteer below her had altered in some subtle and curious way from the solid boatman she had seen from the window. But her suspicion was so tenuous that she had no grasp upon its implications. Yet that a kind of disturbance, a kind of suspicion, had been aroused, however vague, was enough for her to draw a deep breath and then, in a voice of such power and volume that the figure below her started at the sound—"Volunteer!" she roared.

The man beneath her appeared to be in such trouble with his boat that it was impossible for him to keep her from shipping water and to look up at the Countess at the same time.

"My lady?" he cried up, wielding his paddle feverishly, as though to keep immediately below her. "Yes, my lady?"

"Are you blind?" came the voice from the ceiling. "Have your eyes rotted in your head?" What could she mean by that? Had she seen . . . ? "Why have you made no report on it?" boomed the voice. "Have you not seen it?"

"Very . . . difficult . . . keep afloat, my lady, let alone—"

"The *canoe*, man! Does it mean nothing to you that the traitor's boat is hanging from the ceiling? Let me see your—"

But at that moment a fresh surge swept through the window below and twisted Steerpike's boat about as though it had been a leaf, and as it rotated the wash and swell of the water turned it so far over upon its side that as it was carried away from the center of the flooded room, the Countess saw a flash of white and scarlet beneath the broad-brimmed hat; and at almost the same moment her eyes were attracted away from their prize, for an empty face appeared out of the waves immediately below her; for a moment it bobbed about like a loaf of bread and then it sank again.

The world had gone dead in her and then, with almost unbelievable rapidity, the two faces, appearing one after another, had transformed her gloom, her brooding spleen, her hungry malice, her disappointment into a sudden overriding vigor of brain and body. Her anger fell like a whiplash upon the waters below. She had seen, within a moment of each other, the skewbald traitor and the volunteer.

Why the boat was hanging from the ceiling and a score of other questions were no longer of the remotest interest. They were entirely academic. Nothing mattered at all save the death of the man in the broad-brimmed hat.

For a moment she thought that she would bluff him, for it was unlikely that he had seen the head appear out of the waves, or knew that she had glimpsed his mottled face. But this was no time for games of bluff and blarney—no time to spin it out. It was true that she might have given secret orders to the outer boats to enter the cave in force and to take him at a moment when he was diverted from his scrutiny of the window by some object being thrown into the water from above, but all such niceties were not relevant to her mood, which was for quick and final slaughter in the name of the Stones.

IV

Titus had ceased to struggle and was only waiting for the moment when the two louts, who (no doubt with the most loyal intentions) were saving him from himself, relaxed for a moment and gave him the opportunity to jerk himself clear of them.

They had him by his coat and collar, on either side. His hands, which were free, had crept gradually together across his chest and he had secretly undone all but one of the jacket buttons.

The scores of boatmen, dizzy with the rising and falling of the water, and drenched with the rain, and tired with the eternal rekindling of the torches, had been unable to understand what was happening within the flooded "cave," or in the room above it. They had heard voices and a few excited shouts but had no idea of the true situation.

But suddenly the Countess herself appeared at the window and her resonant voice bored its way through the wind and rain.

"All boatmen will attend! There will be no fumbling! The volunteer is dead. The traitor who is now wearing his hat and coat is immediately below the window, in the room you are surrounding."

She paused, and wiped the rain off her face with the flat of her hand, and then, her voice again, louder than ever—"The four central boats will be sculled by their stern oars. Three armed men will be on the bows of each boat. These boats will move forward when I lift my hand. He will be brought out dead. Draw your knives."

As these last words were thrust out into the storm the excitement was so great and there was such pressing forward of all the men and boats that it was with difficulty that the four central boats of the cordon freed themselves from one another and maneuvered into line.

It was then that Titus, noticing how his captors had loosened their grip upon him as they stared spellbound at the window of the fateful room, wrenched himself forward and slipped his arms suddenly out of the sleeves of his jacket, and dodging through a group of boatmen dived into the water, leaving his empty coat behind him, in their hands.

He had had no sleep for many hours. He had had little to eat. He was living upon the raw end of his nerves, as a fanatic will walk upon spikes. A fever had started. His eyes had become big and hot. His nondescript hair was plastered over his forehead like seaweed. His teeth chattered. He burned and froze alternately. He had no fear. It was not that he was brave. It was that fear had been left somewhere behind. It had been mislaid. And fear can be wise and intelligent. Titus had no wisdom at this moment and no sense of self-preservation. No sense of anything at all except a hunger for finality. All his heartache had been laid, unfairly for the most part, at Steerpike's door—as had been his sister's death and the death of his Passion, the mercurial sprite.

As he swam he gloried. The torchlit water closed over him, and broke away again in yellow flakes. He rose and subsided on the flood, his arms thrashing at the waves. All that the sky had emptied from its maw, the giant reservoirs, broke at his brow. He gloried.

His fever mounted. As he grew weaker he grew fiercer. Perhaps he was in a dream. Perhaps it was all a delusion—the heads at a thousand windows—the boats tossing like gold beetles at the foot of the midnight heights; the flooded window that yawned for blood and drama; the upper window where his mother loomed, her red hair smoldering, her face like marble.

Perhaps he was swimming to his death. It didn't matter. He knew that what he was doing was what he must do. He had no option. His whole life had been a time of waiting. For this. For this moment. For all it was and all it would mean.

Who was it that swam within him, whose limbs were his limbs and whose heart was his heart? Who was he— what was he, as he battled through bright waters? Was he the Earl of Gormenghast? The Seventy-Seventh Lord? The son of Sepulchrave? The son of Gertrude? The son of the Lady at the window? The brother of Fuchsia? Ah yes, he was that. He was the brother of the girl with the white sheet to her chin and her black hair spread across the snow-white pillow. He was this. But he was no brother of her *Ladyship*—but only of the drowned girl. And he was no one's figurehead. He was only himself. Someone who might have been a fish of the water, a star, or a leaf or a stone. He was Titus, perhaps, if words were needed— but he was no more than that—oh, no, not Gormenghast, not the Seventy-Seventh, not the House of Groan, but a heart in a body that swam through space and time.

The Countess had seen him from her window but there was nothing she could do. He was not making for the cave mouth, where the boats were already filling the narrow entrance, but to one of those outer stairways that rose out of the water at irregular intervals along the castle's face.

But she had not time to wait and follow his progress. Three swimmers were already in the water and giving chase. Now that she had seen the first of the boats entering the cave mouth she turned back from the window and returned to the center of the room where a group of officers was gathered about the huge spy-hole. As she approached them, a tall man who had been kneeling above the opening fell backward with a crimson chin. Four of his teeth had been broken off and these with a small pebble rattled together in his mouth, while his head shook with pain. The others drew away at once from the dangerous opening.

As they did so Titus entered the room, leaving a trail of water at every step. It was obvious that he was ill with fever and exhaustion, and ungovernable with the fire of it. His naturally pale skin was flushed. His peculiarities of body appeared to be strangely accentuated.

The sense of scale, which he had inherited from his mother—that effect of being larger than he really was, of being oversize—was now peculiarly in evidence. It was as though it were not just that Titus Groan had entered, but that his abstract, or prototype, had come through the door, and that the flood water that dripped from his clothes was somehow spilled in heroic measure.

The rather bluntish cast of his face was even blunter and plainer. The lower lip, trembling with excitement, hung open like a child's. But his pale eyes, so often sullen, in their withdrawal were now not only bright with the fever but with a lust of revenge—no lovely sight—and were icy at the same time with a determination to prove himself a man.

He had seen his private world break up. He had seen characters in action. It was now for him to take the limelight. Was he the Earl of Gormenghast? Was he the Seventy-Seventh? No, by the lightning that killed her! He was the First—a man upon a crag with the torchlight of the world upon him! He was all here—there was nothing missing, brains, heart, and sentience—and individual in his own right—a thing of legs and arms, of loins, head, eyes, and teeth.

He walked sightlessly to the window. He made no sign to his mother. He was her traitor. Let her watch him, then! Let her watch him, then!

He had known, ever since he slipped from his coat and dived into the water, the radiant purpose of the single mind. He had no room in his system for fear. He knew that it was only for him to fall upon this symbol of all things tyrannical—Steerpike the cold and cerebral beast—for him to be fulfilled. His medium was

a short and slippery knife. He had bound a rag about
its handle. He stood at the window, clasping the ledge
with both hands, and stared out at the fantastic torchlit scene. The rain had stopped, and the wind that had
been so boisterous had dropped with remarkable suddenness. In the high northeast the moon disengaged itself of a smothering cloud.

A kind of ashen light spread itself over Gormenghast,
and a silence came down over the bay which was only
broken by the slapping of the water against the walls,
for although the wind had ceased the flood had not subsided.

Titus could not have said why he was standing there.
Perhaps it was because he was as near as he could be
to the fugitive—the flood-entrance being denied him, and
the circular opening guarded. From where he was, free
of his captors, he could at least be close to the man
he wished to kill. And yet it was more than this. He
knew that his would be no spectator's role. He knew
somehow or other that the human hounds, armed as they
were, would be no match for so sly an animal as the
one they had at bay. He could not believe that mere
numbers could deal with so lithe and ingenious a fiend.

None of this had been consciously argued within his
head. He was in no state to rationalize anything. As he
had known it was for him to escape and to swim to
the steps, so he knew that it was for him to enter this
room and to stand at this window.

V

All at once there was a terrible cry from below, and
then another. Steerpike, who had had no alternative but
to bring his skiff to the back of the room as the first
of the four boats nosed her way through the window,
had stretched and loosened his deadly elastic, twice, in
quick succession. His next three deliveries were aimed
at the torches that were stuck in iron rings along the

sides of the first boat, and two of these were sent hurtling into the water, where they hissed and sank.

These three pebbles were the last of his ammunition, save for those which he had left behind him on the lintel above the window.

He had his knife, but he knew that he could only throw it once. His enemies were countless. It was better for him to keep it as a dagger than to throw it away, and to waste it upon the death of some cipher.

By now his enemies were very close—the length of an oar away. The nearest man was hanging lifeless over the side. The two cries that had been heard were from the men toward the stern, who had received a stone apiece in the ribs and the cheekbone. There had been no cry from the first man, who was hanging over the stern like a sack of flour and trailing a hairy hand in the water, as his journey from this world to the next had been so rapid as to allow him no time for remonstrance.

With no pebbles left Steerpike tossed his catapult away, and following it with his body was all at once deep in the water and swimming beneath the keels of the boats. He had dived steeply and was quite certain that he could not be seen from above, for he had noticed how although there were reflections upon the water there was no sign of anything tangible *beneath* the surface.

The only one in the first boat who was in a condition to shout, lost no time about informing the world. In a voice that sounded more relieved than anything else, although the man had tried to hide his emotions, "He's dived!" he shouted. "He's under the boats! Watch the window, there, third boat! Watch the window!"

Steerpike slithered rapidly through the inky darkness. He knew that he must get as far as he could before rising to the air for breath. But like Titus he was deadly tired.

When he reached the window, the air was half gone from his lungs. He could feel the stone support with his left hand. The keel of the third boat was just above his head and to the right. For a moment he rested and lifted his head to it, and then shoving himself away he passed through the lower half of the window, grazing its rough stone sill, and then turning sharply to his left slid along the wall. Six feet above the darkness in which he swam, the sheen of the surface water lapped the wall beneath the Countess's window.

He remembered, of course, that one of the two barges was immediately above him. He was swimming beneath a wooden monster, its catwalks bristling with torches—its blunt nose crowded with men.

What he did not know as he rose to draw breath, his lungs all but bursting, was whether between the side of the long barge and the wall that towered above it there would be room for his head to rise above the surface.

He had never seen these castle barges before and had no idea whether their sides rose vertically out of the water, or whether they swelled slightly outward. If the latter, there was a chance of his being able to be hidden by the convexity, which reaching out as far as the wall, would leave a long roofed-in ditch where for a little while at least he could breathe and be hidden.

As he rose he felt for the wall. His fingers were spread out and ready for the touch of the rough stones; and it was with a shock that they made contact, not with stone but with a matted, fibrous, tough subaqueous blanket of that luxuriant wall-ivy which covered so great an area of the castle's face. He had forgotten how, as he had skimmed to the fateful flood room in the stolen canoe, he had noticed this ivy with its long tentacles, and how the face of the castle had appeared not only mutilated and pocked with sockets where once the glass eyes glittered, but was covered with these climbing rashes of black growth.

As he clawed at the underwater branches he continued to rise, and all at once his head struck upon the hull of the barge where it bulged out to the wall.

It was then that he knew that he was nearer death than he had ever been. Nearer than when he was caught in the burning arms of the dead Barquentine. Nearer than when he had climbed to Fuchsia's secret attic. For he had no more breath than for a few excruciating seconds. His way was blocked above him. The side of the barge, in swelling outward, made contact with the wall below the surface and blocked his upward path. There was no pocket of air. It was solid water. But even as a great hammer of desperation beat at his temples he turned to the ivy. To drag himself up by its outer branches would simply take him to the long, narrow, water-filled roof. But how deep was it, this labyrinthine underwater shuffle of saturated midnight; of endless leaves, of hairy arms and fingers?

With what remained of his strength he fought it. He fought the ivy. He tore at the scales of its throat. He pulled himself *into* it. He tore at its ligaments, he broke its small waterlogged bones; he forced its ribs apart and as they strained to return to their ancient curves he fought his way through them. And as he grappled and pulled his way inward, something inside him and very far away was saying, "You have not reached the wall. . . . You have not reached the wall. . . ."

But neither had he reached the air—and then, at a moment when unable to hold his breath any longer, he took his first inevitable draft of water.

The world had gone black, but with a kind of reflex, his arms and legs fought onward for a few seconds longer, and then with his head thrown back he collapsed, his body supported by the network of the ivy boughs about him.

It was some while before he opened his eyes to find that only the mask of his face was above water. He was in a kind of vertical forest—an undergrowth that stood upon its end. He found that he was doing nothing to support himself. He was cradled. He was a fly in a drowned web. But the last spasms of his upward straining body had taken his face above the water.

Slowly he turned his eyes. He was but a few inches above the level of the barge's catwalk. He could see nothing of the barge itself, but through gaps in the ivy the torches shone like jewels, and so he lay in the arms of the giant creeper and heard a voice from above.

"All boats will stand out from the cave mouth. A line

will be formed across the bay immediately. Light every torch aboard, every lantern, every stick! Ropes will be passed beneath the keel of every boat! This man could hide in a rudder. By the powers, he has more life in him than the lot of you. . . ."

Her voice, in the complete silence that had followed the withdrawal of the squall, sounded like cannon fire.

"Great hell, he is no merman! He has no tail or fins! He must breathe! He must breathe!"

The boats moved out with much splashing of oars and paddles, and the two barges wallowing in the still water were shoved away from the wall. But while the various craft moved into the open bay and began to form a line sufficiently far out as to be beyond the range of any underwater swimmer, Titus, standing beside his mother at the window, hardly knowing that she was there or that the boats had moved, for all the commotion and from all the violence and volume of his mother's orders, had his eyes focused, fanatically, upon something almost immediately below him. What his eyes were fixed upon seemed innocent enough, and no one but Titus in his febrile state would have continued to scrutinize a small area of ivy a foot above the surface of the water. It was no different from any other section that might be chosen at random from the great blanket of leaves. But Titus, who, before his mother's arrival at the window beside him, had been rocking in a kind of dizzy sickness to and fro, had, as the accumulated effect of his rising fever and physical exhaustion began to reach a final stage, seen a movement that he could not understand—a movement that was not a part of his dizziness.

It was a sharp and emphatic commotion among the ivy leaves. The water and the boats and the world were swaying. Everything was swaying. But this disturbance of the ivy was not a part of this great drift of illness. It was not inside his head. It was taking place in the world below him—a world that had become silent and motionless as a sheet of glass.

His heartbeat quickened with a leaping guess.

And out of his guess, out of his weakness, a kind of

power climbed through him like sap. Not the power of Gormenghast, or the pride of lineage. These were but dead-sea fruit. But the power of the imagination's pride. He, Titus, the traitor, was about to prove his existence, spurred by his anger, spurred by the romanticism of his nature, which cried not now for paper boats, or marbles, or the monsters on their stilts, or the mountain cave, or the Thing afloat among the golden oaks, or anything but vengeance and sudden death and the knowledge that he was not watching any more, but living at the core of drama.

His mother stood at his shoulder. Behind her a group of officers obtained the best view that they could of the scene without. He must make no mistake. At a slip or a sign a dozen hands would grab him.

He slipped his knife into his belt, his hand shaking as though it were blue with cold. Then he rested his hands upon the window sill again, and as he did so he stole a glance over his shoulder. His mother stood with her arms folded. She stared at the scene before her with a merciless intensity. The men behind him were dangerously close but were gazing past him to where the boats were forming a single line.

And then, almost before he had decided to do so, he gathered his strength together and half-vaulting, half-tumbling himself over the sill, fell the first half-dozen feet through the loose outer fringes of the ivy, before he snatched at the stems and, checking the momentum of his descent, found that he was at last hanging from branches that had ceased to break.

He had noted that the small, suspicious area of ivy for which he was making was directly below the window from which he had vaulted (and which was now filled with startled faces), directly below, and at water level. He could hear his name being called and orders being shouted across the bay for a boat to be brought up immediately, but they were sounds from another world.

And yet, while this sense of being far removed from what he was doing held him suspended in a world of dreams, he was, at the same time, drawn down the ivy wall as though by a magnet. Within the blur of weakness and remoteness was a core of vivid impulse, an immediate purpose.

He hardly knew what his body was doing. His arms and legs and hands seemed to be making their own decisions. He followed them downward through the leaves.

But Steerpike, who had had to alter his position when an unbearable cramp had affected his left leg and shoulder, and who had hoped that a careful stretching of his limbs would in no way affect the stillness of the outermost leaves, had by now heard the noise of branches breaking above him, and knew that the results of his movement were dire indeed. After so desperately fought a battle for refuge from his pursuers, it was indeed a malicious fate that saw to it that he should so soon be discovered.

He had of course no idea that it was the young Earl who was descending upon him. His eyes were fixed upon the dark tangle of fibrous arms above his face. It was obvious that whosoever it was would not make his descent through the body of the ivy, close to the wall. To do this would be to move at a snail's pace, and to battle all the way with the heaviest branches. His pursuer would slide down the outer foliage and probably burrow wallward when a little above and out of reach of him.

And this is what Titus intended, for when he was about five feet above the water he came to a stop and waited a little to regain his breath.

The moon which was now high in the sky had, to some extent, made the torches redundant. The bosom of the bay was leprous. The ivy leaves reflected a glossy light. The faces at the windows were both blanched and wooden.

For a moment he wondered whether Steerpike had moved, had climbed from where a foot above the water he had seen the telltale ivy come to life and shiver, and whether he, Titus, was even now within a few inches of his foe, and in mortal peril. It seemed strange at that instant that no daggered hand arose out of the leaves and stabbed him where he hung. But nothing happened. The silence was accentuated rather than lessened by the sound of distant oars rising and falling in the bay.

Then, with his left hand gripping some interior stem, he forced away the swathes before his face and peered into the heart of the foliage where the branches shone like a network of white and twisted bones at the inrush of the moonbeams.

There was but one course for him. To burrow in as deeply as he could, and then to descend in the gloom until he found his foe. The moonlight was now so strong that a kind of deep twilight had taken the place of the rayless midnight among the leaves. Only at the deeply hidden face of the wall itself was the darkness complete. If Titus could reach as far inward as the wall and work his way down, it might be possible to see, before he reached the level of the flood, some shape that was not the shape of ivy branch or leaf—some curve, or angle, that loomed among the leaves—perhaps an elbow, or a knee, or the bulge of a forehead. . . .

VI

The murderer had not moved. Why *should* he move? There was little to choose between one cradle of ivy and another. What was there to be gained by any temporary evasion? Where could he escape to, anyway? The patch of ivy was a mere seventy feet in breadth. It was only a matter of time before his capture. But time when it is short is very sweet and very precious. He would stay where he was. He would indulge himself—would taste the peculiar quality of near-death on the tongue—would loll above the waters of Lethe.

It was not that he had lost his will to live. It was that his brain was so exact and cold a thing that when it told him that his life, for this reason, and for that reason, was within a few hours of its end, he had no faculties wherewith to combat its logic. Below him was the water in which he could not breathe. To the north was the water through which to swim was immediate capture. To move to his left or right would bring him to the margins of the ivy. To climb would bring him to the scores of windows in every one of which there was a face.

Whoever it was who was crawling toward him down the wall had presumably informed the world of his purpose, or had been given orders to come to grips. Someone had seen a movement in the ivy.

But it was strange that, as far as he could hear, there was only *one* boat approaching. The rise and fall of the two oars were distant but perfectly distinct; why was not the whole flotilla on its way toward him?

As he drew his knife to and fro across his forearm some dust fell through the twisted stems above him and then a branch broke with a crack that seemed within a yard of his head.

But it was not *immediately* above him, this noise. It appeared to come from deeper in the ivy, from somewhere between himself and the wall.

For him to move would be to make a sound. He was curled up like an emaciated child in a cot of twigs. But with his right hand gripping the dagger at his left shoulder, he was prepared at any instant to make an upward stab.

His small, close-set eyes smoldered with an unnatural concentration in the darkness, but it was not their natural color, extraordinary as that was, that showed in the gloom, but something more terrible. It was as though the red blood in his brain, or behind his eyes, was reflected in the lenses. His lips, thin as a prude's, had fused into a single bloodless thread.

And now he began to experience again, but with even greater intensity, those sensations that had affected him when, with the skeletons of the titled sisters at his feet, he had strutted about their relics as though in the grip of some primordial power.

This sensation was something so utterly alien to the frigid nature of his conscious brain that he had no means of understanding what was happening within him at this deeper level, far less of warding off the urge to *show himself*. For an arrogant wave had entered him and drowned his brain in black, fantastic water.

His passion to remain in secret had gone. What was left of vigor in his body craved to strut and posture.

He no longer wanted to kill his foe in darkness and in silence. His lust was to stand naked upon the moonlit stage, with his arms stretched high, and his fingers spread, and with the warm fresh blood that soaked them sliding down his wrists, spiraling his arms and steaming in the cold night air—to suddenly drop his hands like talons to his breast and tear it open to expose a heart like a black vegetable—and then, upon the crest of self-exposure, and the sweet glory of wickedness, to create some gesture of supreme defiance, lewd and rare; and then with the towers of Gormenghast about him, cheat the castle of its jealous right and die of his own evil in the moonbeams.

There was nothing left, no, of the brain that would have scorned all this. The brilliant Steerpike had become a cloud of crimson. He wallowed in the dawn of the globe.

Ignoring all precautions, he wrenched the boughs about him, and every window heard the sound, as they cracked in the silence with reports like gunfire. The lenses of his eyes were like red-hot pinheads.

He tore away the thick ivy stems, and cleared a cave, within the masses of the foliage, stamping and descending with his feet until they found purchase a foot beneath the water. His left hand gripped a solid arm of the parasite, as hairy as a dog's leg.

The knife was ready for the strike. He had thrown back his head. In the darkness of the leaves above him he heard a sound. It was a kind of cry or gasp—and then, a great bush of branches fell in a crackling heap—fell, as it were, down the black chimney which Steerpike's sudden violence had created—fell with gathering speed with Titus riding upon its back.

As Titus fell he saw the two red points of light below him. He saw them through the tangle of the broken ivy.

Fear had a few moments earlier suddenly come to him, for his brain had cleared—as in a hot sky of continuous cloud, an area no bigger than one's thumbnail will clear,

and show the sky. And with this momentary clearance
of his brain from the fumes of fever and fatigue, came
the fear of Steerpike and darkness and death.

But directly the branches broke below him as he hung
in the twisted night, and directly he fell, the fear left him
again. He said to himself, "I am falling. I am moving
very fast. I will soon be on top of him. Then I will kill
him if I can."

The knife in his hand was quite steady as he fell: and
when he crashed his way through the branches which
had come to a thick and watery halt at the congested
surface of the flood, he saw it shine in his hand like a
splinter of glass in a penetrating ray of the moon. But
only for the fraction of a fleeting instant did he see that
thin blade of steel for, as he had fallen, he had been
shoveled outward into the moonlight so that suddenly
another object as brilliant as the thin blade held his eyes,
a thing with eyes like beads of blood, and a forehead like
a ball of lard—a thing whose mouth, thin as a thread,
was opening and as it opened was curling up its corners
so that no other note could possibly have come from
such a cavity as the note that now rang across the flood-
bay, that climbed the ancient walls and turned the silent
audience to stone—a note from the first dawn, the high-
pitched, overweening cry of a fighting cock.

But even as this blast of arrogance vibrated through
the night, and the crowing echoes rang through the hollow rooms and wandered to and fro, and thinly died—
Titus struck.

He could see nothing of the body into which his small
knife plunged. Only the head, with its distended mouth
and its grizzly bloodlit eyes, was visible. But he struck
the darkness under the head, and his fist was suddenly
wet and warm.

What had happened to Steerpike that he should have
been the first to receive a blow—and a blow so mortal? He
had recognized the Earl, who like himself had been lit by
the moonbeams. That the Lord of Gormenghast should
have been delivered into his hands at this great moment
and be his for the killing had so appealed to his sense

of fitness that the urge to crow had become irresistible.
He had swung full circle. He had given himself up to
the crowding forces. He, the rationalist, the self-contained!

And so, in a paroxysm of self-indulgence—or perhaps in the grip of some elemental agency over which he
had no power—he had denied his brain, and he had lost
the one and only moment of time in which to strike before his enemy.

But at the rip of the knife in his chest all vision left
him. He was again Steerpike. He was Steerpike wounded,
and bleeding fast, but not yet dead. Snarling with pain, he
stabbed, but as he stabbed Titus fell in a faint and the
knife cut a path across the cheek—not deep but long
and bloody. The sharp pain of it cleared the boy's mind
for a fraction of time and he thrust again into the darkness below his face. The world began to spin and he
was spinning with it and he heard again, very far away,
the sound of crowing, and then opening his eyes he saw
his fist at his enemy's breast, for the lozenge of moonlight had spread across them both, and he knew that he
had no strength to withdraw the knife from between the
ribs of a body arched like a bow in the thick leaves. Then
Titus stared at the face, as a child who cannot tell the
time will stare at the face of a clock in wonder and perplexity, for it was nothing any more—it was just a thing,
narrow and pale, with an open mouth and small, lackluster eyes. They were turned up.

Steerpike was dead.

When Titus saw that this was indeed so, he collapsed
at the knees and then slumped forward out of the ivy
and fell face downward into the open water. At once a
cry broke out from a hundred watchers, and his mother,
framed by the window overhead, leaned forward and her
lips moved a little as she stared down at her son.

She and the watchers from the windows all about her
and above her had, of course, seen nothing but the commotion of the ivy leaves at the foot of the wall. Titus had
disappeared from the air and had burrowed into the thick
and glossy growth; its every heart-shaped leaf had glinted

in the moonlight. For long seconds at a time the agitation of the leaves had ceased. And then they had begun again, until suddenly they had seen a fresh disturbance and realized that there were two figures under the ivy.

And when Steerpike had thrown his secrecy away and when Titus had fallen through the chimney of leaves, and while they had exchanged blows, the sound of their struggle and the breaking of branches and the splash and gurgle of the water as their legs moved under the surface —all these noises had sounded across the bay with peculiar clarity. The flotillas, in the meantime, unheard by the protagonists, had once again advanced upon the castle and were now very close to the wall. The captains had expected fresh orders on arriving beneath the walls, but the Countess, immobile in the moonlight, filled up her window like a carving, her hand on the sill, her gaze directed downward, with motionless concentration. But it was the cry of the cock, triumphant, terrible, that broke the atrophy and when, a little later, Titus fell forward out of the ivy and the blood from his cheek darkened the water about his head, she sent forth a great cry, thinking him dead, and she beat her fist upon the stone sill.

A dozen boats lunged forward to lift his body from the flood, but the boat which had been the first to leave the flotilla some while earlier and whose oars both Titus and Steerpike had heard was in advance of the rest, and was soon alongside the body. Titus was lifted aboard, but directly he had been laid at the bottom of the boat, he startled the awe-struck audience by rising, as it seemed, from the dead, for he stood up, and pointing to that part of the wall from which he had fallen, he ordered the boatmen to pull in.

For a moment the men hesitated, glancing up at the Countess, but they received no help from her. A kind of beauty had taken possession of her big, blunt features. That look which she reserved, unknowingly, for a bird with a broken wing, or a thirsty animal, was now bent upon the scene below her. The ice had been melted out of her eyes.

She turned to those behind her in the room. "Go away," she said. "There are other rooms."

When she turned back she saw that her son was standing in the bows, and that he was looking up at her. One side of his face was wet with blood. His eyes shone strangely. It seemed that he wished to be sure that she was there above him and was able to see exactly what was happening. For as the body of Steerpike was hauled aboard by the boatmen, he glanced at it and then at her again before a black faint overtook him and his mother's face whirled in an arc, and he fell forward into the boat as though in a trench of darkness.

Chapter Seventy-Nine

THERE was no more rain. The washed air was indescribably sweet. A kind of natural peace, almost a thing of the mind, a kind of reverie, descended upon Gormenghast—descended, it seemed, with the sunbeams by day, and the moonbeams after dark.

By infinitesimal degrees, moment by golden moment, hour by hour, day by day, and month by month, the great flood waters fell. The extensive roofscapes, the slates and stony uplands, the long and slanting sky-fields and the sloping altitudes, dried out in the sun. It shone every day, turning the waters, that were once so gray and grim, into a smooth and slumbering expanse over whose blue depths the white clouds floated idly.

But *within* the castle, as the flood subsided and the water drained away from the upper levels, it could be seen how great was the destruction that the flood had caused. Beyond the windows the water lay innocently, basking, as though butter would not melt in its soft blue mouth, but at the same time the filthy slime lay a foot

deep across great tracts of storeys newly drained. Foul
rivulets of water oozed out of windows. From the floors
lately submerged the tops of objects began to appear, and
all was covered with gray slime. It began to be apparent
that the shoveling away of the accumulated sediment,
the swilling and scouring of the castle, when at long
last, if ever, it stood on dry land again, would stretch
away into the future.

The feverish months of hauling up the stairways of
Gormenghast all that was now congesting the upper storeys
would be nothing to this regenerative labor that lay before the hierophants.

The fact that at some remote date the castle was likely
to be cleaner than it had been for a millennium held
little attraction for those who had never thought of the
place in terms of cleanliness—had never imagined it could
be anything but what it was.

That the flood had once threatened their very existence
was forgotten. It was the labor that lay ahead that was
appalling. And yet, the calm that had settled over Gormenghast had soothed away the rawness. Time lay ahead
—soft and immeasurable. The work would be endless but
it would not be frantic. The flood was descending. It
had caused havoc, ruin, death, but it was descending.
It was leaving behind it rooms full of mud and a
thousand miscellaneous objects, sogged and broken; but
it was descending.

Steerpike was dead. The fear of his whistling pebbles
was no more. The multitudes moved without fear across
the flat roofs. The kitchen boys and the urchins of the
castle dived from the windows and sported across the
water, climbing the outcrops as they appeared above the
surface, a hundred battling at a time to gain some island
tower—new-risen from the blue.

Titus had become a legend; a living symbol of revenge.
The long scar across his face was the envy of the castle's
youth, the pride of his mother—and his own secret
glory.

The Doctor had kept him in his bed for a month. His
fever had mounted dangerously. For a week of high

delirium the Doctor fought for his life and hardly left his bedside. His mother sat in a corner of the room, motionless as a mountain. When at last he became conscious of what was happening around him and his forehead was cool again his mother withdrew. She had no idea what to say to him.

The descent of the waters continued at its own unhurried pace. The rooftops had become the castle's habitat. The long, flat summit of the western massives had now, after three centuries of neglect, become a favorite promenade. There, the crowds would wander after sundown when their work was over, or lean upon the turrets to watch the sun sink over the flood. The roofs had come into their own. There, throughout the day, the traditional life of the place was, as far as possible, continued. The great Tomes of Procedure had been saved from the wreckage, and the Poet, now Master of Ceremonies, was ceaselessly at work. Extensive areas had been covered with shanties and huts of every description. The various strata of Gormenghast had been gradually drawn to such quarters as best suited their rank and occupation.

More and more of Gormenghast Mountain became visible. The high and jagged cone grew bigger every day. At sunrise with the thin beams slanting across it and lighting the trees and rocks and ferns, it was an island mad with birdsong. Noon brought the silence: the sun slid gently over the blue sky and was reflected in the water.

It was as though all that had happened over the last decade, all the violence, the intrigue, the passion, the love, the hate, and the fear, had need of rest and that now, with Steerpike dead, the castle was able at last to close its eyes for a while and enjoy the listlessness of convalescence.

Chapter Eighty

✻✻✻✻✻✻✻✻✻✻✻✻

DAY after day, night after night, this strange tranquillity swam through the realm. But it was the spirit that rested; not the body. There was no end to the coming and going, to the sheer manual labor, and to all the innumerable activities that hinged upon the reconditioning of the castle.

The tops of trees had begun to appear with all but their strongest branches broken. Fresh shapes of masonry lifted their heads above the surface. Expeditions were made to Gormenghast Mountain, from whose slopes the castle could be seen to be recovering its familiar shape.

There, on the rocky slopes, not more than three hundred feet from the clawlike summit, Fuchsia had been buried on the day following Steerpike's death.

She had been rowed by six men across the motionless flood in the most magnificent of the Carvers' boats, a massive construction, with a sculptured prow.

The traditional catacomb of the Groan family, with its effigies of local stone, had been fathoms under water, and there had been no alternative but to bury the daughter of the Line, with all pomp, in the only earth available.

The Doctor, who had not dared to leave the young Earl in his illness, had been unable to attend the ceremony.

The grave had been hacked out of the stony earth upon a sloping site, chosen by the Countess. She had battled her way to and fro across the dangerous ground in search of a place worthy to be her daughter's resting place.

From this location the castle could be seen heaving across the skyline like the sheer sea-wall of a continent; a seaboard nibbled with countless coves and bitten deep with shadowy embayments. A continent, off whose shores the crowding islands lay; islands of every shape that towers can be; and archipelagos; and isthmuses and bluffs; and stark peninsulas of wandering stone—an inexhaustible panorama whose every detail was mirrored in the breathless flood below.

By the time that Titus had to a great extent recovered not only from the horror of the night, but from the effects of the nervous exhaustion that followed, a year had passed, and Gormenghast was once again visible from top to bottom.

But it was dank and foul. It was no place to live in. After dark there was illness in every breath. Animals had been drowned in its corridors; a thousand things had decayed. The place was noxious. Only by day the swarms of the workmen, toiling indefatigably, kept the place inhabited.

The roofs had by now been deserted, and a gigantic encampment was spread abroad across the grounds and escarpments that surrounded the castle; a kind of shanty town had arisen, where huts, cabins, shacks, and improvised constructions of great ingenuity made from mud, branches, strips of canvas, and all kinds of odd pieces of iron and stone from the castle shouldered one another in a fantastic conglomeration.

And there, while the work proceeded, ever toward one end, that part of Gormenghast that was made of flesh and blood lived cheek by jowl.

The weather was almost monotonously beautiful. The winter was mild. A little rain came every few weeks; in the spring corn was grown on the higher and less waterlogged slopes. Above the encircling encampments the great masonry wasted.

But while the "drying out" of its myriad compartments and interstices proceeded and while this sense of peace lay over the scene, Titus, in contradiction to the prevailing atmosphere, grew, as his recovery became more complete, more and more restless.

What did he want with all this softness of gold light? This sense of peace? Why was he waking every day to the monotony of the eternal encampment; the eternal castle and the eternal ritual?

For the Poet was taking his work to heart. His high order of intelligence, which had up till now been concentrated upon the creation of dazzling, if incomprehensible, structures of verbiage, was now able to deploy itself in a way which, if almost as incomprehensible, was at the same time of more value to the castle. The Poetry of Ritual had gripped him and his long wedge-shaped face was never without a speculative twist of the muscles—as though he were forever turning over some fresh and absorbing variant of the problem of Ceremony and the human element.

This was as it should be. The Master of Ritual was, after all, the keystone of the castle's life. But as the months passed Titus realized that he must choose between being a symbol, forever toeing the immemorial line, or turning traitor in his mother's eyes and in the eyes of the castle. His days were full of meaningless ceremonies whose sacredness appeared to be in inverse ratio to their comprehensibility or usefulness.

And all the time he was the apple of the castle's eye. He could do no wrong—and there was honey to be tasted on the tongue, when the hierophants drew back from the rocky paths to let him pass and the children screamed his name excitedly from their shacks, or stared in big-eyed wonder at the avenger.

Steerpike had become an almost legendary monster— but here, alive and breathing, was the young Earl who had fought him in the ivy. Here was the dragon-slayer.

But even this became monotonous. The honey tasted sickly in his mouth. His mother had nothing to say to him. She had become even more withdrawn. Her pride in the courage he had shown had emptied her of words. She had reverted to the heavy and formidable figure, with her white cats forever within range of her whistle and the wild birds upon her massive shoulders.

She had risen to an occasion. The uprooting of Steerpike and the salvaging of the flooded castle.

Now she drew back into herself.

Her brain began to go to sleep again. She had lost interest in it and things that it could do. It had been brought forth like a machine from the darkness and set in motion —and it had proved itself to be measured and powerful, like the progress of an army on the march. But it now chose to halt. It chose to sleep again. Her white cats and her wild birds had taken the place of the abstract values. She no longer reasoned. She no longer believed that Titus had meant what he had said. She connected it with his delirium. It was impossible to believe that he could have known that his words were heresy. He had craved for a kind of freedom disconnected from the life of his ancient home—his heritage—his birthright. What could that mean? She relapsed into a state of self-imposed darkness, lit only by green eyes and the bright backs of birds.

But Titus could no longer bear to think of the life that lay ahead of him with its dead repetitions, its moribund ceremonies. With every day that passed he grew more restless. He was like something caged. Some animal that longs to test itself; to try its own strength.

For Titus had discovered himself. The Thing, when she had died in the storm, had killed his boyhood. The death of Flay had seasoned him. The drowning of Fuchsia had left a crater beneath his ribs. His victory over Steerpike had given him a kind of touchstone to his own courage.

The world that he pictured beyond the secret skyline— the world of nowhere and everywhere—was necessarily based upon Gormenghast. But he knew there would be a difference; and that there could be no other place exactly like his home. It was this difference that he longed for. There would be other rivers; and other mountains; other forests and other skies.

He was hungry for all this. He was hungry to test himself. To travel, not as an Earl, but as a stranger with no more shelter than his naked name.

And he would be free. Free of his loyalties. Free of his home. Free of the maddening forms and ceremonies. Free to become something more than the last of a great Line.

His longing to escape had been fanned by his passion for
the Thing. Without her he would never have dared to do
more than dream of insurrection. She had shown him by
her independence how it was only fear that held people
together. The fear of being alone and the fear of being
different. Her unearthly arrogance and self-sufficiency
had exploded at the very center of his conventions. From
the moment when he knew for certain that she was
no figment of his fancy, but a creature of Gormenghast
Forest, he had been haunted. He was still haunted.
Haunted by the thought of this other kind of world which
was able to exist without Gormenghast.

One evening, in the late spring, he climbed the slopes of
Gormenghast Mountain and stood by his sister's grave.
But he did not remain there for long, gazing down at the
small silent mound. He could only think what all men
would have thought: that it was pitiful that one so vivid
and full of love and breath should be rotting in darkness.
To brood upon it would only be to call up horrors.

A light wind was blowing and the green hair of the
grass was combed out all one way from the brow of the
mound. A faint coral-colored light filled the evening, and,
like the rocks and the ferns about his feet, his face was
lit with it.

His somewhat lank, pale brown hair was blown across
his eyes which, when he lifted them from the mound and
fixed them upon the towered massings of the castle, began
to glitter with a strange excitement.

Fuchsia had left. She had finished with Gormenghast.
She was in some other climate. The Thing was dead. She
also had taught him, by the least twist of her body in midair, that the castle was not all. Had he not been shown
how wide was life? He was ready.

He stood there quite silently, but his fists were clenched
and he pressed them against one another, knuckle to
knuckle, as though to fight down the excitement that was
accumulating in his breast.

His broad, rather pallid face was not that of any
romantic youth. It was, in a way, very ordinary. He
had no perfect feature. Everything seemed a little too big

and subtly uneven. His lower lip was thrust a fraction forward of the upper and they were parted so that his teeth were just visible. His pale eyes, a stone-ish blue with a hint of dim and sullen purple, were alone peculiar and even striking in their present animation.

His loose-limbed body, rather heavy, but strong and agile, was bent a little forward at the shoulders, with a kind of shrug. As a storm gathers its clouds together, so in his chest he felt a *gathering* as his thoughts fell into place and led one way, and his pulse-beat, as though underlining his will to rebel, throbbed at his wrists.

And all the while the sweet air swam about him, innocent, delicate, and a single cloud, like a slender hand, floated over the castle as though to bless the towers. A rabbit emerged from the shadows of a fern and sat quite still upon a rock. Some insects sang thinly in the air, and suddenly close at hand a cricket scraped away on a single bowstring.

It seemed a strangely gentle atmosphere to surround the turmoil in Titus's heart and mind.

He knew now that to postpone his act of treachery would make it no easier. What was he waiting for? No time would ever come when an atmosphere of sympathy, welling as it were out of the castle, would help him on his way, would say, "Now is the Time to go." Not a stone of the castle would own him from the moment he turned his back.

He descended the slopes, threading the trees of the foothills, and came at last to the marshland paths, and then after crossing the escarpment, approached the gate in the Outer Wall.

It was when he saw the great walls looming above him that he began to run.

He ran as though to obey an order. And this was so, though he knew nothing of it. He ran in the acknowledgment of a law as old as the laws of his home. The law of flesh and blood. The law of longing. The law of change. The law of youth. The law that separates the generations, that draws the child from his mother, the boy from his father, the youth from both.

And it was the law of quest. The law that few obey for lack of valor. The craving of the young for the unknown and all that lies beyond the tenuous skyline.

He ran, in the simple faith that in his disobedience was his inmost proof. He was no callow novice; no flighty child of some romance of sugar. He had no sweet tooth. He had killed and had felt the wide world rustle open from the ribs and the touch of death had set his hair on end.

He ran because his decision had been made. It had been made for him by the convergence of half-forgotten motives, of desires and reasons, of varied yet congruous impulses. And the convergence of all these to a focus point of *action*.

It was this that made him run as though to keep pace with his brain and his excitement.

He knew that he could not now turn back save in the very teeth of his integrity. His breath came quick and fast, and all at once he was among the shacks.

The sun was now upon the rim of the skyline. The rose-red light had deepened. The great encampment wore a strange beauty. A populace meandered through the wandering lanes and turned at his approach and made a path for him. The ragged children cried out his name, and ran to tell their mothers that they had seen the scar. Titus, drawn back suddenly into the world of reality, came to a halt. For some time he remained with his hands on his knees and his head dropped forward, and then when he had regained his breath and had wiped the sweat from his brow, he walked rapidly to that part of the cantonment where a stockade had been built to surround the long shanty where the Countess lived.

Before he entered the stockade through the clumsy iron gate he motioned to some passing youths.

"You will find the Master of the Stables," he said, in his mother's peremptory manner. "He should be with the horses in the West Enclosure. Tell him to saddle the mare. He will know her. The gray mare with a white foot. He will bring her to the Tower of Flints. I will be there shortly."

The youths touched their brows and disappeared into the gathering dusk. The moon was beginning to float up and from behind a broken tower.

As Titus was about to push open the iron gate he paused, turned on his heel, and set off into the heart of a town of looted floor boards. But he had no need to advance as far as the Professors' quarters nor to turn east to where the Doctor's hospital lifted its raw woodwork to the rising moon. For there ahead of him, and walking in his direction along the footworn track, were the Headmaster, his wife, and his brother-in-law, the Doctor.

They did not see him until he was close upon them. He knew they would wish to talk to him, but he knew he would not be able to make conversation, or even listen to them. He was out of key with normality. And so, before they knew what had happened, he reached out and simultaneously gripped the Doctor and the old Professor by their hands, and then releasing them he bowed a little awkwardly to Irma, before he turned on his heel and, to their amazement, began to walk rapidly away until he was lost to their sight in the thick of the dusk.

When he reached the stockade he made no pause but entered and told the man who stood outside the door of the long shanty to announce him.

He saw her at once as he entered. She was sitting at a table, a candle before her, and was gazing expressionlessly at a picture book.

"Mother."

She looked up slowly.

"Well?" she said.

"I am going."

She said nothing.

"Good-by."

She got heavily to her feet and, raising the candle and bringing it toward him, she held it close to his face and fixed her eyes on his—and then, lifting her other hand, she traced the line of his scar very gently with her forefinger.

"Going where?" she said at last.

"I am leaving," said Titus. "I am leaving Gormenghast.

I cannot explain. I do not want to talk. I came to tell you and that is all. Good-by, Mother."

He turned and walked quickly to the door. He longed with his whole soul to be able to pass through and into the night without another word being spoken. He knew she was unable to grasp so terrible a confession of perfidy. But out of the silence that hung at his shoulder blades, he heard her voice. It was not loud. It was not too hurried.

"There is nowhere else," it said. "You will only tread a circle, Titus Groan. There's not a road, not a track, but it will lead you home. For everything comes to Gormenghast."

He shut the door. The moonlight flowed across the cold encampment. It shone on the roofs of the castle and lit the high claw of the mountain.

When he came to the Tower of Flints his mare was waiting. He mounted, shook the reins, and moved away at once through the inky shadows that lay beneath the walls.

After a long while he came out into the brilliant light of the hunter's moon, and some time later he realized that unless he turned about in his saddle there was no cause for him to see his home again. At his back the castle climbed into the night. Before him there was spread a great terrain.

He brushed a few strands of hair away from his eyes, and jogged the gray mare to a trot and then into a canter, and finally with a moonlit wilderness before him, to a gallop.

And so, exulting, as the moonlit rocks fled by him, exulting as the tears streamed over his face—with his eyes fixed excitedly upon the blurred horizon—and the battering of the hoofbeats loud in his ears—Titus rode out of his world.